P. R. Frost's
Tess Noncoiré Chronicles:

**HOUNDING THE MOON
MOON IN THE MIRROR
FAERY MOON
FOREST MOON RISING**

P. R. FROST

THE
TESS NONCOIRÉ
CHRONICLES
VOLUME ONE

HOUNDING
THE MOON

MOON IN
THE MIRROR

DAW BOOKS, INC.
DONALD A. WOLLHEIM, FOUNDER
375 Hudson Street, New York, NY 10014
ELIZABETH R. WOLLHEIM
SHEILA E. GILBERT
PUBLISHERS
www.dawbooks.com

First Printing, October 2014
1 2 3 4 5 6 7 8 9

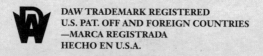

Author's Note

Writing a series of four books is sort of like inviting the cast of characters to move in with you, along with all of their baggage (and their music). Tess and Scrap took over my life as well as my office. Donovan brought along his gargoyles. And Gollum wouldn't let me forget the filk—the folk music of science fiction and fantasy. The songs I have quoted and built stories around still rise to the surface of my listening queue. But I'm cautious about delving into the grunge Celtic rock I foresee the children from *Forest Moon Rising* playing as part of their anger management. I've tackled worse chores in the name of getting the story right.

For all the good, the bad, and the distasteful these people forced upon me, I found I liked them, and continue to like them. I want them to succeed and find happiness, I want to continue the friendship. Many of their sorrows and joys echo people and places in my life. My music and landscapes colored theirs. If Scrap resembles a psycho-Siamese kitten in places, there are reasons for that.

I've missed these people and look forward to inviting them back into my life with the two omnibus editions of the books. I thank the editors and production crews of DAW Books for giving Tess and her companions new life.

Thank you to my readers as well. Without you I'd only be writing for myself, and that isn't nearly as much fun as sharing my madhouse.

P. R. Frost
Welches, Oregon
Summer 2014

HOUNDING
THE MOON

To my agent
Carol McCleary of the Wilshire Literary Agency,
and to my editor
Sheila Gilbert of DAW Books,
both of whom I cherish.

Acknowledgments

Many thanks to Maya Kaathryn Bohnhoff and Jeff Bohnhoff for their awesome music and hilarious filk. They have inspired many wonderful images.

My thanks also to Lea Day, Deborah Dixon, Bob Brown, and Maya Bonhoff for their patient reading and wonderful suggestions as well as pointing out my flaws to make this a better book. Appreciation also to the joysofresearch@yahoogroups.com and SF-FFWs@yahoogroups.com for keeping me going when I stalled. Any errors are mine, not theirs.

Prologue

"WHAT YOUS THINK yous doin' here, imp?" the head Kajiri Sasquatch demanded. Three of his comrades bore down on me with fangs bared and paws clenched to hammer me back into my own dimension. Two brown and one red. All of them ugly as a twenty-year drought and twice as mean.

"Just passing through," I quipped, keeping my eyes on those sledgehammer fists.

I edged around the chat room, keeping my back to the barriers and the myriad doors that opened up from here. Each door led to another dimension. All of them warmer and more comfortable than my own. But I had other reasons for trying to escape my home. First I had to get by the Sasquatch.

You'd think I could pick a better day when something smaller and less excitable than a Sasquatch had guard duty. And Kajiri are the worst of any species: half-breeds out to prove themselves better than both species that spawned them.

The lead guard had more smarts than his three cohorts combined. He (very obviously and blatantly male) turned his big black body to keep me in sight. He couldn't swivel his neck, so he had to move his entire skeleton. His buddies, one of them female with pendulous breasts covered in matted red fur, took a few minutes to figure out that I had moved.

I fluttered my little wings as if I expected them to support me in flight. Fat chance of that. My wings are as stunted as the rest of me. My bat-wing ears might do a better job, come to think of it.

Big Black lunged for me. I hopped to the left. He sprawled on the stone floor with a roar.

The three dimwits finally turned in the right direction. I

feinted into a fairyland filled with inviting floral perfumes and pretty little beings who giggled a lot.

Big Red reached for me with a fist the size of a turkey platter. She was faster than I expected. My tail crimped in her grip.

"Yeaow! That hurts, lady," I protested, trying to yank my appendage free.

"No imps in fairyland," Big Black said.

Red hauled me out of the fairyland doorway and flung me against the portal back to impland. The freezing temperature of home nearly burned my belly and my nose when I thumped against the doorway. Mum had firmly closed it against me.

Blood oozed out of my nose and from scrapes on my tail. I groaned. If my wings had been big enough to support me, I could have eased my landing. Not a proper imp at all. Not even any warts to make me cute.

"Need some help opening the door, imp?" Big Black lumbered over.

"Jus aw 'ittle," I said, trying to breathe through my mouth and talk at the same time.

"You talk funny for an imp," Big Red said, arms akimbo.

"Ya' boke my nothse."

"Well, that's what you get for trying to sneak out of your home dimension, imp. No trespassing. That's what we're here for, to keep unauthorized personnel from moving between dimensions." Big Black pronounced each word carefully as if he'd memorized his mission statement.

"I can see that."

"When we've served enough guard time, we'll get twenty hours' home time in the dimension of our choice."

And if you believe that, I've got some sunshine in the rain clouds of Oregonia I can sell you. Duping demons to doing guard duty is the primary entertainment of the powers that be in most dimensions. Fulfilling the promised free time never happens. Can't have demons roaming freely. Have to keep them in their ghettos so they don't contaminate the rest of the universe.

No being in their right mind would let a bloodthirsty demon run free. We keep them in the worst corners of the bleakest dimension for a reason. Like maybe they'll die off.

Big Black bent down to pull aside the leather flap that marked the portal to impland.

I darted between his legs and slid through the nearest doorway, right into Earth, the land of humans. This time I kept my tail tucked between my legs so Red couldn't grab it.

I just hoped they wouldn't track the trail of blood I left behind. Or, worse, let Mum know where I'd gone.

My day had begun just as weird as it ended.

"Out!" Mum had screamed at me for the umpteenth time that day. That week. That decade. "Look at you. Fully two hundred years old and no bigger than a twenty-year-old. You're just a scrap of an imp and will never amount to anything."

Hence my name. Scrap. She'd named me something else at birth, but no one remembered what it was. Likely she'd recycled the name to one of my one hundred two siblings. Most of them still lived, much to my torment and dismay.

Her tirade went on for a few hours as she swatted me with her broom. She only uses her broom to discipline her multitude of offspring, never to clean anything. Not my mum. She's a proper imp who likes living in a refuse heap.

I hopped ahead of her from couch to corner to dining table. But finally she managed to herd me out the door. All the while my siblings laughed hilariously at me.

Of course, if I'd had enough of a wingspan to properly fly, I might have eluded her. But then, if I had a proper wingspan, she wouldn't be kicking me out of the old garbage dump—I mean homestead. The fact that it was a dimensional garbage dump piled high with the detritus of a dozen different realms doesn't mean I need to insult Mum's cozy home.

I kind of liked growing up playing amid broken refrigerators, some skeletons dragons had discarded, and a few hidden demon artifacts. I spent many happy hours every day arranging them in some kind of order. Only my sibs took equal delight in messing things up again.

Most imps can't abide tidiness.

"We only have respectable imps in my family. All a proper size, of course! Fit warrior companions by their first century," dear old Mum called after me. Her angry skin, nicely blotched with warts, shifted from normal gray green to an ominous vermilion. In a minute she'd transform into something ugly.

Uh-oh, I was in real trouble now. I tried to hide by going transparent. But I can't do that in my own dimension, and Mum can always find one of her one hundred three offspring, no matter what color or shape they are. Just so long as they live, she can find them.

So that left me out in the cold and having to make my own way across the dimensions. When I say cold, I mean cold. When-hell-freezes-over cold. Nothing-ever-decays-here-so-let's-dump-anything-that-might-prove-useful-later cold. Hence impland is also the garbage dump of the universe.

We got stuck there because the same internal combustion engine that allows us to change color at will also generates heat.

We can generate enough body heat to cultivate vast quantities of mold in our otherwise cold and damp home. Mum cultivates it. I eat it, cleaning her walls on a regular basis. Mold is quite a delicacy. My family eats it because they have to. Fuel for their bodies, you know. Not a lot of energy left over to go out across the dimensions and find ourselves a warrior to meld with. So a lot of us get kind of trapped there.

Not me. Free from Mum's tyranny so I didn't have to obey the rule that says you have to be at least four feet tall and have a wingspan twice as wide before you can survive a portal transfer, I took off for parts unknown.

That's when I first saw Tess. Teresa Noncoiré to those who haven't met her. She's absolutely gorgeous, and strong, and intelligent, and all the things a heroine is supposed to be.

But that's now. And she still doesn't know this about herself.

She was dissolving into a puddle of tears, forty pounds overweight, and wearing her emotions on her sleeve the first time I saw her. In the Pacific Northwest where they grow great mold.

And I couldn't do anything to help her. She hadn't been infected with the imp virus yet. I wasn't big enough to transmit the disease to her.

But I knew in that first moment, as she walked away from her husband's wake, held in a rustic bar in a timber town on a mountain, that I loved her. I knew in that instant that she was going to make a formidable Warrior of the Celestial Blade. She was going to kick some demon ass and knock the uppity Sisterhoods on their ignoble butts.

But that's a long story. Let's cut to the chase. She managed to stumble into the infection, survived it, and emerged . . . well, she and I both emerged.

Outcasts.

Not exactly ready to confront anything the dimensions could throw at us. But we were stuck together like glue.

That's when life started to get interesting.

Chapter 1

Bats do not tangle in people's hair; if they can locate a mosquito to eat in a dark night, they can certainly avoid human heads.

"I MISS YOU SO MUCH, Dilly, my teeth ache," I cried. "I miss you so much I can't believe in anything but my memories of you."

I traced the letters on the tombstone.

DILLWYN BAILEY COOPER
REST IN PEACE
BELOVED SON AND FRIEND

And the dates of his life, cut short two years ago.

He had been so much more than just a friend to me. I choked back a sob. Dill's parents, two more D. B. Coopers, hadn't allowed me to put the precious word "Husband" on the grave marker. We hadn't been married long enough for that, they said.

When I had control of my voice again, I said aloud, "Dill, I'm sorry I couldn't visit you sooner. I got sort of lost. You are probably the only person I know who would believe my tale. It's more unbelievable than the stuff I write. I got very sick. Then a Sisterhood adopted me and nursed me back to health—not a convent as we know it, more a sorority of warriors. We battle . . .

"Come to think of it, maybe you wouldn't believe my

story." The fantasy fiction in my novels was more believable.

Out of the corner of my eye I spotted movement. An adolescent girl with the dark hair and copper skin of a Native American stooped to pick some flowers on the verge of the cemetery. Queen Anne's lace, chicory, and dandelion blooms filled her hands. One by one she scattered them around the graves.

I smiled at the image of innocence. My grief had no place in her young life. I should have outgrown it by now. But then I *had* gotten sidetracked and never found an opportunity to visit Dill's grave until now. I was still having trouble letting go of the man I loved so intensely.

The girl looked up and smiled back. Then she ambled over and offered me one of the white filigree blooms. "Here. You didn't bring any flowers. You look like you need one."

"Thank you," I choked out. After a moment, when I'd regained control over my voice, I added, "Do you have someone special here?" I couldn't say the word "dead," or "buried." That would make the wound of Dillwyn's absence from my life too raw. Again.

"Not here. Back home on the Colville reservation." She turned and looked wistfully to the north. "I can't give them flowers, so I spread them here, on graves that look lonely."

A moment of comfortable silence passed between us.

"Thank you again for the flower. I'm Tess." I held out my hand to the girl.

She shook my hand with all of the solemnity of an almost adult. "Cynthia. Cynthia Stalking Moon."

"Hey, Cindy!" a boy called from the nearby skate park. "Come show us that twisty thing you do."

"Gotta go." Cynthia waved and ran off to join her friends. She scattered her flowers randomly as she ran.

Nice kid, Scrap said. He reclined against Dill's headstone, a translucent pudgy shape without much definition. Except for his stinking cigar, a black cherry cheroot. He remained his usual tranquil gray.

My imp companion didn't truly live in this dimension. I sometimes wondered if I did. His ubiquitous cigar appeared all too real and noxious. But then tobacco comes from here and now.

Other than Scrap, I had this Alder Hill, Oregon, pioneer cemetery to myself once more. The traffic roaring up Highway 26 toward Mount Hood gave me the sense of privacy and isolation I craved while I mourned Dill.

I heard an indelicate snort from Scrap near my left shoulder, but I ignored it. Scrap liked to perch there. He was so insubstantial I couldn't feel his weight. But I always "sensed" him there.

"Even your weird sense of humor, Dill, can't explain Scrap." I laid the long-stemmed flower at the base of the tombstone. "He's an imp from another dimension. A scrap of an imp. Not fully grown and not fully functional yet. We're supposed to grow together as we work our way up through the ranks of the Sisterhood of the Celestial Blade Warriors. You'd like Scrap. The two of you could trade sarcastic and irreverent comments on life and compete for the most outrageous puns."

Dill had embodied everything I enjoyed in life. He was my hero, cut down in the prime of his life. He had saved my life at the cost of his own.

I chuckled through another closing of my throat. "I told your favorite joke at your funeral, Dill. Your folks disapproved, of course. Afterward, they went back to the house for a formal reception."

I looked up toward the white house with gray stone facing and gray trim that squatted on the hill above the cemetery. No signs of life there. Dill's parents were probably at work in the family furniture store in Gresham, the closest city to Alder Hill.

I continued to tell Dill about his final send-off. "Your friends and I, the ones who truly knew you, retired to a bar after the service. We all lifted a glass in your honor and then we sang all of your favorite filk songs, you know, the parodies full of puns, and recounted every hideous joke you ever told, over and over. We laughed until we cried. That's the only kind of tears you approved of. We left your wake with many fond memories of you. Just the way you wanted us to."

D. R. Frost

Would I ever be happy again without Dillwyn Bailey Cooper?

One lonely tear dripped down my cheek. I swallowed and swallowed again, trying to force the useless emotion back into its dungeon behind my heart.

"Jokes won't dull the pain and loneliness, Dill."

A whiff of cigar smoke and an itching tingle along my spine jolted me back into reality. Scrap.

Can the waterworks, Tess, dahling. We have work to do.

"Scrap, you know you are not supposed to smoke those foul things where someone might smell them," I snapped at my companion. Bad enough that the gaseous emissions from his lactose intolerance brought dogs sniffing at my heels from miles around. I didn't need the reek of tobacco clinging to my clothes and hair as well.

The imp pulled my hair and jumped off my shoulder. His chubby body with bandy legs, pot belly, vestigial wings, bat-wing ears, (ugh, I hate bats, but that's the only description that fits his huge, jagged ears), and snub nose became almost visible to my sharpened eyesight. His spike tail beat an arrhythmical tattoo against Dill's tombstone. Pale pink replaced his gray skin. He wasn't totally pissed at me.

Trouble is brewing, babe, Scrap informed me in an accent that was part flamboyant interior decorator, part leering cabbie, and all obnoxious sarcasm.

"What kind of trouble? I don't have a lot of time," I replied, checking my watch. "I need most of an hour just to drive the twenty-five miles between here and the city." With air-conditioning in the rental car, thank God . . . or Goddess . . . whoever might be listening.

If anyone listened at all to my prayers.

They hadn't when Dill died.

Later. Scrap jumped back up onto my shoulder.

I heaved myself off the ground, scanning the vicinity for what had alarmed Scrap. All I could hear over the roar of traffic was Cynthia and her friends with their boards at the skate park behind the cemetery.

We've got trouble. Now. Scrap started to turn vermilion. Waves of heat radiated out from him.

I began to sweat through my goose bumps.

This had never happened to us before. I'd almost begun

to believe the lost year of my life was just that, lost in a fever dream.

"What and where?" I asked in alarm. The base of my spine tingled in warning. Just like Sister Serena said it would.

The noise from the skate park grew a little louder. The thumps and bangs became shrill with fear. I jogged across the cemetery, zigzagging around tombstones.

Right direction, dahling. Wrong speed. Scrap puffed on his cigar like an old steam engine.

I lengthened my stride to a ground-covering lope, hurdling tombstones and other obstacles. Scrap had to tangle his claws in my frizzy hair to stay on board.

He grumbled something that I couldn't quite understand.

The normal squeals of adolescents burning off energy turned to terrified screams.

"Hang on, Scrap." I ran full out, defying three cars to hit me as I crossed the back street at a gallop.

No one seemed to notice the frightened commotion close by.

I skidded onto the green space between a ski rental shop, closed for the season, and an abandoned church, painted white with a steeple and a red front door. Dill had attended Sunday School there as a child. The park sloped steeply downward to a creek. A half-pipe wooden ramp took advantage of the landscape. But no kids flew down the polished wood and up the other side on their boards. They were all huddled beneath the support struts.

Not quite all. Two boys lay sprawled facedown upon the grass. Their arms and legs were twisted at unnatural, broken angles. Blood pooled from mouths and gaping wounds in backs and throats. A third boy tried to crawl toward the protective illusion of the shade beneath the ramp. He collapsed at every third movement. His left arm was a mangled mass of raw meat, torn tendons, and protruding bone.

So much blood! I gagged. The smell brought back memories of the night Dill died. I wanted to run away from here. As far and fast as I could. With or without Scrap.

Cynthia stood in the middle of the carnage. Her screams split the air like nails on a chalkboard. A huge, ugly dog, with jaws big enough to engulf the girl's head, enclosed the fleshy part of her upper arm and tugged.

I could not abandon Cynthia or her friends.

She'd given me a flower because I was as lonely as Dill's grave.

My heart beat double time and my focus narrowed to the dog. The rest of the world seemed to still around me. My assignment, my quest, justified this fight.

No time to call for help. I yanked my cell phone out of my belt pouch and tossed it toward the huddled kids.

"Call 911," I shouted. Then I snapped my fingers. "Scrap, I need a weapon."

Instantly he jumped into my extended palm, elongated, thinned, became more solid. Between one eye blink and the next I grasped a . . .

"A soup ladle!" I screamed. "How am I supposed to fight off that dog with a *soup ladle?*"

I threw away the useless tool and grabbed an abandoned skateboard. With all of the strength in my upper arms I swung at the dog's flank.

I smacked his brindled, fur-covered body with a satisfying whomp and crack of the skateboard.

Dog yelped and released my thoughtful friend.

He turned on me with bared yellow fangs as long as my fingers. His massive head was nearly level with my shoulder. He growled and drooled long ropes of greenish slime.

"At least I got your attention," I said to Dog, gulping back my fear. I had trained for situations like this. But facing the real thing was different in the field than on the training ground.

Sorry. Scrap's face appeared in the metal bowl of the ladle, cigar still clamped in his wide mouth. He stretched again, darkened, became heavier and sharper.

I grabbed the fireplace poker he had become. "Better," I sighed.

The dog, bigger than a wolfhound, meaner than a pit bull, and uglier than a mastiff, bunched his powerful haunches for a lunge.

I met him with a sharp thwap across the nose. I heard something crunch.

He kept on coming.

I let my momentum carry me full circle and out of his direct path as I shifted my grip on the poker.

The dog twisted in midair and landed beside me, grabbing my forearm.

An uppercut to his snout from my poker. Then I brought the weapon down hard on the dog's spine. He yelped and released me.

We stared at each other for several long moments; judging, assessing.

Scrap hissed at the dog from the crosspiece at the tip of the poker.

I blinked.

Scrap blinked.

The dog ran off, downhill into the tangled undergrowth. I heard him splash into the creek.

Then I heard the sirens. One of the kids must have gotten through to 911.

I sank to the ground and stared dumbly at four puncture wounds on my forearm. Top and bottom. Blood and green slime oozed out of them.

I retched. Long painful spasms tried to turn my stomach inside out.

My head threatened to disconnect from my neck. Darkness encroached on my vision.

"I thought you were only a legend. But you are real," a gentle masculine voice with a slight British accent whispered in my ear. His finger traced the crescent scar on my face that ran from left temple to jaw. A scar that Scrap had promised me was not visible in this dimension to anyone other than the Sisterhood of the Celestial Blade Warriors.

<hr/>

Crap!

Who was this guy? He really wasn't supposed to see the scar unless he'd had a touch of the imp flu.

Wish I knew how to research him.

I'm too tired. Transformation takes energy. A quick trip back to my own dimension would restore me. If I survived the trip through the portal. The Sasquatch that guard the portals around here are pretty mean. They make Mum look nice.

Maybe a good shot of mold. I wonder if Tess' coffee cup in the car has had time to decay yet.

But Tess is going to need help to see this situation through.

What to do? What to do?

Maybe a cigar will help.

Chapter 2

ADRENALINE SHOT THROUGH ME. I bounced to my feet, away from the stranger's touch and his all-too-keen gaze. A glance told me that he was gangly, skinny, very blond. He peered at me curiously. His glasses slid down his nose.

I could not allow this stranger to penetrate my secrets. Every nerve ending in my body came alive in warning.

Then I was off, keeping my back to him.

I had to check on Cynthia. I had to stay away from this stranger.

A paramedic sprayed something on Cynthia's upper arm. I did not see any blood.

Between us and the skateboard ramp, two more paramedics worked on the boy with the mangled arm. The scent of blood and vomit and fear drove me away from the primary victims, toward Cynthia.

Two uniformed policemen stood with notebooks open, trying to make sense of what the kids under the ramp said. Their voices still shrilled with hysteria. One of them ran over to return my phone rather than have to relate what happened.

Two more cops thrashed through the blackberries toward the creek with weapons drawn. I knew the dog was long gone. The itching tingle at the base of my spine had vanished.

But the stranger hovered. I could *feel* him staring at me. I almost heard his questions. Questions I dared not answer.

Another contingent of uniforms directed traffic around the park entrance. They did their best to keep curiosity seekers at bay.

I knelt beside Cynthia, murmuring soothing phrases that meant nothing. I wrapped an arm about her thin shoulders, clinging to her for my own comfort as well as hers. I had no idea what had become of Scrap. He probably had his own recovery ritual after transforming. He'd never had to become a weapon for me before.

"I don't understand it." The paramedic shook his head. "The dog's teeth didn't penetrate the skin." He rubbed a damp pad over the girl's arm, cleaning off some of the green drool. His fingers quested from the edge of her red-and-white-striped tank top to her wrist.

I spotted two red dimples that might have been canine tooth marks. Other than a slight irritation, the skin was unbroken.

"Unlike you." The paramedic grabbed my arm and began cleaning it. "I'd recommend rabies shots for you if we don't find the beast."

"He . . . he was almost gentle," Cynthia sobbed. She hiccuped and turned her huge brown eyes toward me, imploring me to agree with her.

"From my observation, I agree with the girl," the stranger with the clipped accent and drooping glasses said.

Tension built in my nape, rippling downward. Different from the presence of monsters and demons from other dimensions, but still alert to danger. If I'd had a tail as bony and as sharply barbed as Scrap's, I'd beat it against the ground.

I gave him another brief scan. Squarish jaw, limp blond hair, not bad looking, with a nerd's, or a scholar's (there's a difference?) pasty skin. His navy polo shirt and crisply pressed khaki slacks seemed almost a uniform. He scrunched his nose in an attempt to keep his tinted glasses from sliding off. I almost wished he had let them go so I could see his eyes better, read his emotions, maybe even figure out how he could see my scar.

A new man, in shirtsleeves with his tie half undone and a summer-weight sports jacket slung over one shoulder skidded down the embankment.

"And you would be . . . ?" he asked both me and the stranger with the clipped accent. He flipped out a notebook and licked the end of a stubby pencil. I pegged him as a police detective. A reporter would have sponged the coffee stain off the front of his shirt.

The nerdy stranger towered over him by half a head, but probably weighed less. He was downright skinny. I like a little more beef and less length on men.

I tried to melt into the background. How could I explain Scrap? How could I explain the fact that the previously gaping wounds in my arm were already closed? The virus that had caused the scar on my face had left enough anti-bodies in my system to combat anything this world, and several others, could dish out.

That dog had not been a natural creature. Neither was my infection. The itch in and around the puncture wounds told me I wouldn't get away from the encounter totally clean.

Police and paramedics did not like paranormal explanations.

The nerd gave a name. I didn't listen, trying my best to fade into the background while giving Cynthia as much support as I could.

If I stopped long enough to give a statement, I'd miss my appointment in the city. Less than two hours until I needed to be in downtown Portland for a book signing at Simpson's, the largest bookstore on the West Coast.

Autumn was at least three weeks behind schedule. It was way too hot for September. The heat beat down on my back and shoulders. Sweat trickled between my breasts and around the waistband of my shorts. A tank top, shorts, and a sports bra seemed almost too many clothes for the climate.

I wanted to leave, but I could not abandon Cynthia. We'd connected back in the cemetery. Her flower had lightened my loneliness for just a moment.

An ambulance roared up, sirens cutting through the rising noise of too many voices, too many questions, not enough answers. Attendants spilled out, grabbed a gurney on collapsible legs, and slid down the steep hill, nearly on their butts. They worked efficiently and gently to lift the injured boy onto the mobile bed. An inflatable cast contraption hid the strips of raw meat, bone, and blood on the arm that might never work properly again. The paramedics had already started an IV drip and fixed an oxygen mask to his face.

That dog had a lot to answer for.

Up on the street a woman wailed in recognition. One of the traffic cops kept her from pelting down the hill.

My heart wrenched in sympathy.

I avoided watching the turbulent emotions by turning my attention back to Cynthia. I ignored the detective. The bespectacled stranger occupied most of his attention anyway. The paramedic pumped up a blood pressure cuff on Cynthia's thin arm and frowned. He signaled a second ambulance crew to join him.

"I don't want to go to the hospital. I just want to go home," Cynthia said. She looked imploringly into my eyes, as if I could order the world for her. She tried hard to keep her voice firm, but tears already streaked her face.

"Your blood pressure is really low, honey," the paramedic said quietly. "You are going into shock. It's only natural. We need a doctor to check you out."

"Are your parents up on the hill?" I asked her. "They will go with you." I smoothed her long dark hair where it escaped her tight braids. She leaned into my caress a moment, then straightened. I wished I could accompany her, keep her safe.

"My folks are dead. My foster parents won't bother coming to the hospital. That might cost them money. They'll just expect Social Services to deal with the bills and the doctors. I wish I could go home." She began crying openly now. Her breathing became shallow and her coppery skin looked gray.

The paramedic eased her back until she lay upon the trampled grass. He checked her blood pressure and pulse again and frowned.

"Why can't you go back to the Colville reservation?" I asked, trying to calm the girl. I wished I could take her there, where she would be safe from the monsters from other dimensions as well as the ones that called themselves her foster parents.

The girl's voice and eyes brightened a little. "My parents lived here before they died, and Children's Services won't let me cross state lines to go home. No blood relations close enough to me, they say. I want to go home. The tribe will care for me. They are my people. There are no orphans among us."

I wrapped my arms around her, not knowing what else to do.

I wanted to go home, too—home to my husband. But he was dead, and no one could replace him.

The ambulance crew arrived with another collapsible gurney. I eased out of their way. The paramedic was occupied with Cynthia. I kept my left arm behind my back so no one would notice the dog bite and try to treat it. It took all of my willpower to keep from scratching it raw.

The detective seemed occupied with the tall stranger. Medical people handled the wounded. Someone else supervised putting two bodies into heavy black bags.

Two adolescent boys, cut down by a monster before they even had a chance to grow. Something twisted inside me.

"I'll do what I can to get you home, Cynthia. I promise," I bent and whispered to her.

Then the paramedics pushed me aside.

Psst, Blondie, Scrap hissed in my ear. *You're gonna be late, babe.* The imp completed his statement with a passing of gas.

I had to bite my cheeks and scrunch my nose to keep from coughing. The people around me subtly shifted position and looked away.

"Thanks, buddy," I said, not at all certain what I was thanking him for. Still, I grabbed the chance of diverted attention to sidle toward the tree line behind the church. With that little bit of cover I made my way back up to the street and the crowd of gawkers, wailing parents, and frantic authorities.

The too-observant stranger seemed to be giving a complete

statement to the police. Better than I could. I had been too busy fighting Dog to notice much else. No one needed me here anymore. Not even Dillwyn Bailey Cooper.

Except maybe one lost and lonely little girl. As lost and alone as I was.

I slumped my posture, gaped my mouth, and made my eyes a little vacant. A little twitch of the tank top made it bag and hang awkwardly. "Scrap, can you fade the colors a bit? I'm too bright and noticeable."

Sure, babe, he whispered.

I blinked my eyes and felt Scrap slide across my back. A quick glance over my shoulder confirmed that my hot pink tank top had faded to a hideous yellow-green and my lavender shorts to a bluer green. The two did not complement each other.

I sagged my jaw and let my eyes cross a little.

Again the crowd shifted away from me. People just do not know how to deal with those they perceive as deficient.

A quick dodge around the cemetery and I dove into my rental car on the side street. The white compact from Detroit looked like every other compact rental car in the country and was stifling hot inside. I turned on the ignition so I could open the electronic windows. The ninety-degree summer heat felt comfortable in comparison.

As I sat there, waiting for the air-conditioning to blast out some of the hot air, I became aware that I had been sweating. Heat, exertion, fear, all contributed to the damp, sourness of my skin. And the wound itched so badly it burned. My nose wiggled trying to avoid my own body odor.

You, dahling, are more rank than I am. Scrap appeared on the dashboard, directly in front of me. He looked gray again, but too pale and not quite healthy, like he'd been working too hard.

Got any mold I can munch on? He looked in my half empty coffee cup with hope. *Shifting into your weapons is hard work.*

"No food this trip, Scrap. I'll get you beer and OJ as soon as I can. Hang on, we've got to get out of here. And you didn't really shift into a weapon. A soup ladle, for Goddess' sake!" I spotted a uniformed cop prowling around the parked cars, looking into each one, occupied or not.

I shifted into gear and peeled out.

Turn right, right, right, right here! Scrap screeched loud enough to slice an eardrum.

"That's away from town," I objected and kept on driving straight. No left turn presented itself behind the Safeway, only the high school athletic field where a Med-Evac helicopter descended in a typhoon of dust.

Trust me, Tess. Turn right at the next intersection. Scrap shifted his black cherry cheroot from one side of his mouth to the other. Fortunately he hadn't lit it.

"Why should I trust you?" I stopped at the big red sign that said I must.

A black-and-white police car turned onto my street.

Without waiting for an answer from Scrap, I yanked the wheel right and stepped on the gas. At the next street, a broad one, but free of traffic, I turned left. I didn't see the police car in my rearview mirror.

Good move, dahling. Now just follow this road for six point five miles. Scrap jumped down onto the passenger seat and pulled a map out of nowhere. He could do that when he wanted to be helpful and not just a pain in the ass.

"Six point five miles! How far out of our way is this?" I knew Dill's hometown was removed from the city. How far removed I had not realized until I needed to be back in Portland in a hurry.

The road twisted and burst into a straight stretch. It hung on the edge of a bluff. Off to my right stood Mount Hood in all its towering splendor. The grand old man of the Cascade Mountains was a little bare of snow in mid-September, but still sported a few glaciers to take my breath away. At the bottom of the bluff spilled a long river valley full of green. Green trees, green meadows, green crops.

I wanted to linger and stare in awe at the wonder of it all. Words began to form in my head. I had to describe this scene, use it somehow. Where? Where in my book could I plant this landscape?

Wake up, Tessie, and drive. Dirty rotten copper on our tail. He doesn't like the way you weave across lanes while you gawk. Scrap bit down on his cigar. Then he reached for my coffee cup.

"Paws off my coffee!" I screeched. But I kept both hands on the wheel and my eyes on the road. "There's a ton of heavy cream in it and you are lactose intolerant, Scrap."

Not even any good mold in it yet. I hate book tours. You never stay in one place long enough for mold to grow, and I have to pick up after you before the hotel maids come to clean. Scrap turned bright red. Steam blew out his ears.

"Stop sulking, Imp, and prove your worth. I need clothes, something respectable. I need my professional face and persona."

One best-selling fantasy author coming up. Scrap faded to passionate pink. He had a job to do, he could stop thinking about his malfunctioning digestive system and perform fashion miracles.

The obnoxious scrap of an imp would rather play dress up with me than fight demons any day.

So would I.

▧▨▧▨▧

Whoopee! Time to play.

A quick slide through the car's air conditioner for another restorative bite of mold and off I go. Rapid transit for imps requires popping into the chat room, the entryway to all the portals to all the dimensions. Imps can go anywhere from the chat room. Other beings are usually limited to one or two dimensions. Humans even fewer, unless they are unusually persistent—for that, read "stupid."

Time is just another dimension, if you know how to use it. So I decided to take a moment for a quick visit to Mum. Just to see how she was doing. I hadn't been home in a while—like since she threw me out. Maybe she'd finally accept my diminutive stature now that I'd melded with a warrior companion. After all, being small made me low maintenance compared to my siblings.

"Hi, Mum, what's you up to?" I asked as I dropped in from nowhere. Nowhere being the portal.

"Out, out, out." She swished her broom at me. "I banished you yesterday and here you are back again."

Crap. There's that time thingy again. I'd been gone nearly

three years human time, barely a day by Mum's. I'd had time to grow one whole wart on my bum, but she didn't bother noticing the beauty mark.

"But, Mum, I've m . . ."

She swung the broom again.

"The least you could do is sweep up some of the dirt with that thing!" I dove beneath a pile of interdimensional garbage. I skidded, scraping my nicely rounded belly on some flash-frozen watermelon rind. Good thing my wings are dwarfed, otherwise they might have snapped off when I bumped against a cast-off 286 cpu. Goddess, there were a ton of those—literally—in our backyard alone.

Someone tossed the cpu aside. I rolled, expecting a swat from Mum's broom, but it was just a gamer treasure hunting. Did I tell you that to get out of the chat room through a portal humans have to be incredibly persistent? That's gamers for you.

I came up short with my nose on top of a pretty hair comb with only one broken metal tooth. The curved back of it was decorated with all kinds of semiprecious stones and filigree gold knotwork.

"Oooooh, Tess will love this!" I snatched it up, broke off a bit that might look like a stylized bat, and flitted back through the portal to her hotel room where I snagged some clothes and other niceties. The magic glamour of the comb shone like a pulsar in my dimension; in the mortal realm it faded to a soft patina of antiquity.

Chapter 3

Fruit bats have been known to cut and shape leaves into tents for roosting.

IFTEEN MINUTES LATER Scrap popped back onto the passenger seat carrying my favorite tote bag. A friend had machine embroidered the fabric with magicians and dragons and castles.

"Did you remember my bookmarks and autograph copy stickers? What about my favorite pen?"

Better than that, babe. Scrap glowed green with pride. *I brought a wet washrag, lightly soaped, and moist towelettes. And perfume. I'll have you smelling like a rose in no time.*

"Can you do something with the dog bite first? It burns. I'm afraid of infection."

Ooooh, that is a nasty one. Nothing like imp spit to fix you up.

"Scrap, no!"

He went ahead and licked the wound anyway. I had visions of all kinds of otherworldly bacteria having a feast on my flesh. The wound cooled instantly. Then he wiped it with the soapy washrag.

Don't even need a bandage now.

"Uh, Scrap, what did you do?" I twisted my arm, trying to look while keeping both hands on the wheel.

No need to bother looking. Imp spit is a natural antibiotic to our warriors. To anyone else, though, it's a lethal toxin. He giggled wickedly.

I didn't like the sound of that.

Then he began scrubbing the tension out of my neck with his washrag. I sighed in relief. Just that little bit of moisture and coolness made me a lot less anxious.

The road stopped winding and widened as we neared civilization. I'd seen enough nurseries and Christmas tree farms to last me the year. A gas station, a lumberyard, and a feed store looked positively civilized.

"Time?" I asked. The digital clock in the rental was positioned wrong for the angle of sunlight coming in through the windshield.

We've got forty-five minutes, Scrap replied, moving the washcloth down my arms.

I lifted my elbow so he could reach the pit.

"Time enough to get to Simpson's, not enough time to change clothes," I grumbled despite the relief of the impromptu bath.

Trust me, dahling. I brought clothes.

Strangely, I did trust the imp. When it came to clothes and makeup, he had better sense than I did.

We came to a red light beside a tractor dealership. I stared in awe at the size of the farm implements. The wheels were taller than I. More fodder for my fertile imagination. A scene began to form in my mind.

Half a mile down the road, with the entrance to Highway 26 in sight, Scrap gave me new directions. *Take a right here,* he said from somewhere around my left foot. He'd slipped off one of my pink tennies and bathed my bare foot.

I sighed in near bliss and turned away from the road I knew would take me to the freeway.

Next thing I knew Scrap had slipped a high-heeled, white sandal onto my left foot. He was working on untying my right shoe. At the next stoplight, three miles downhill and approaching a community college, I braked with my left foot and he worked on my right. By the time we reached the freeway at the base of the hill, I had proper shoes on clean feet.

"What about the rest of me?" I rummaged with one hand in the tote bag.

Scrap slapped my wrist. I felt only a swish of air.

Two hands on the wheel, babe. I don't fancy having to transport you into another dimension to free you from a car wreck.

The miracle of freeway speeds brought me through the junction with I 5 and up to the City Center exit faster than I thought. I even had enough time to throw on the denim wraparound skirt and a white blouse with blue and lavender sprigs—the long sleeves covered the still angry-red dog bite on my arm. Instant color coordination with the tank top. I threw the pink belt pouch into the tote, refreshed my lipstick, layered new makeup on the scar—the stranger had seen it, maybe someone else would, too, and ask questions.

"I'm as ready as I can get, given the circumstances."

A surge of delightful adrenaline sprang through me, lightening my step. I supposed I should get used to battling demons and rescuing damsels in distress in my spare time.

What spare time?

Your hair, sweetums! Scrap called from inside the tote. He handed me a wide decorative comb. *Your dishwater-blond curls are a tangled mess.*

"Dill used to say I had sandy-blond hair. This is new. Where'd it come from?"

Don't ask.

"Ill-gotten gains?" I hesitated. Even after two years together I had no idea if Scrap considered theft illegal or immoral. The comb looked expensive. *Very* expensive, and although lovely, not something I would indulge in for myself.

Trust me, dahling, the comb is legally and morally yours.

"But my hair is so short, I'm not sure it will hold the comb." If I didn't keep my hair cropped short, the curls became so tight the only way I could comb or brush them was if they were soaking wet. But I'd been on tour and attending science fiction conventions for close to three months with few breaks, while promoting the new book. No time for a haircut.

Would you rather I turned myself into a hat for you?

I winced at the thought. I didn't need the imp wrapped around my head all day. I was close enough to a headache without him.

I scooped the mass of curls into a twist and anchored as much of it as possible with the comb. As I walked the two blocks to Simpson's—a former warehouse turned into the biggest bookstore on the West Coast—I grabbed my cell phone out of the pouch. Two buttons connected me with Sylvia Watson, my agent. Miracle of all miracles, she answered the phone.

"Tess Noncoiré, where are you? Simpson's expected you half an hour ago," she barked into the phone.

"They can expect me forty-five minutes prior, but I don't have to show up until the scheduled time," I barked back. Then I relented "I'm sorry. I did some sightseeing and ran into a monster of a traffic jam. Listen, Syl, I don't have a lot of time and I have an important job for you."

"It's Saturday, my day off."

"You are in the office. You answered your business line, not your private one. Just listen and do. Please. This is important. I need you to find me the best lawyer my money can buy." My heart beat faster and my concentration narrowed on the cell phone, just like I did before a fight. This was right. I lost all hesitancy.

"What kind of trouble are you in, Tess?" She sounded instantly alert. I could almost see her flicking through the pages of her computerized address book.

"Not me, Syl. There's a little girl, Native American, twelve or thirteen, Colville tribe, Cynthia Stalking Moon. She's been in foster care in Alder Hill, Oregon. About now, she's being admitted to the nearest hospital. Probably in Gresham. Dog attack. She wants to go back to her tribe, but officious officials won't let her because the reservation is in a different state. I agree with the girl; she should go home to her people."

My arm began to shake while holding the phone. That dog bite had affected me worse than I thought.

How was I supposed to sign dozens of books with this injury?

"Uh, Tess, this doesn't sound like something you want to get involved in."

"I promised, Syl. It's important. Trust me, please." I owed the girl.

"Are you sure, kiddo? You haven't allowed yourself to

care about anyone since . . . well, since Dillwyn died. If you don't care about them, they can't hurt you when they leave. Why this child? Why now?"

"Because she gave me a flower to put on Dill's grave."

Sylvia was silent a moment. "Okay. Good publicity for you, championing the cause of an underdog."

I winced at the canine reference. "Sic the press on the case, but keep my name out of it. I don't want anyone to know I was in Alder Hill this morning."

She tried to talk me into a press conference.

"No. Just let me know the moment Cynthia is safe in the hands of either her tribe or a relative. And I mean safe."

We made small talk. I disconnected as I approached the bookstore.

I swept into the nirvana of Simpson's. Four stories of books, books, and more books. And today, a couple hundred copies had been written by me. I pushed aside my morning adventures and settled in to the fun part of my job. I forgot the burning ache in my arm.

Mold! Scrap crowed. He popped out of my tote and disappeared into whatever part of the old building was the dampest. He'd feast, hopefully on something that had nothing to do with milk, and leave me alone for a while.

The staff treated me like royalty. Before I could hint at the need for the restroom, they directed me. Mostly I needed to check myself in the mirror. Wow, the comb worked wonders on my frizzy mop, even if it did leave a few tendrils dangling.

When I returned to the reading/signing/lounge area, the staff had a large double latte, two sugars, waiting. I'd move to the Pacific Northwest just for their coffee, but home was elsewhere. The coffee hadn't been enough to keep Dill here. I sipped at the nectar of life and took my seat behind a fortress of books. The line of readers waiting for my signature stretched through two departments.

I smiled and poised my pen to sign the first book.

For two hours I talked to the people who made my job worthwhile. I answered the same questions over and over again.

"Where did you get the idea for the warrior Sisterhood serving a Goddess manifested in the stars?"

I directed them to the cover artist for my book and a painting he'd done years ago. Each time I answered this question I caressed the cover art.

I traced the curve of a crescent moon that defined *Kynthia*'s cheek much as I had traced the lettering on Dill's tombstone. The slash of light reminded me of the hidden scar on my own cheek. Clusters of stars revealed the Goddess' eyes and mouth, smiling in gentle beneficence. The Milky Way streamed away from her face like hair blowing in a celestial wind.

As I looked at the cover I realized that the Indian girl Cynthia's face was a younger, reversed image of the Goddess. Dark hair and eyes in opposition to Kynthia's star-bright features. Cynthia's coppery skin was alight and alive; the Goddess' face was defined by night and darkness.

"Is there really an order of Sisters who battle demons?" Usually asked by an adolescent girl or an awkward teenage boy in serious lust.

"The book takes place in the far future, after a devastating apocalypse. It's fiction," I replied. Sometimes I added, "Why don't you start your own order?"

No way could I tell the truth.

"How do I get my book published?"

I hated that one.

"When is the next book coming out?"

When I have the time to finish the damn thing. But I couldn't say that in public, so I smiled and told everyone it was scheduled for June of next year. Actually, book two was done, awaiting revisions from my editor. Book three was barely more than outline, but the publisher wanted book three done before releasing number two.

"I have some of your earlier, out-of-print works. Will you sign those, too?"

I loved that person.

Questions about where I had been for the last two and a half years, since my last book hit the stands, I avoided completely.

Scrap came back once to check on me. He bored easily and returned to his orgy of mold in a subbasement near the river that had been neglected for years. I worried then that the damp could not be good for the books, the treasure

trove of Simpson's. An employee pointed out a state-of-
the-art heat pump and dehumidifying system. I sighed in
relief.

At long last the line of people waiting for me to autograph their copies dwindled to a trickle and finally stopped.

I was free to wander through the temple of books. By
this time the comb was beginning to pull and strain my
scalp, so I released my hair and dropped the lovely piece
into the tote.

First stop, the rare book room, properly escorted by two
employees. One of them screamed "Security" in his posture, attitude, and super-short haircut. I'd be willing to bet
my next advance that he was a former Marine.

First editions and one-of-a-kind antiques did not cover
the subjects that interested me. I left the Holy of Holies
with a smile to the clerk and the guard, breathing a little
easier in the less rarefied air of the main store.

My feet took me to the myth and folklore section. Simpson's had a wonderful collection of used books stacked
cheek by jowl with newer works.

I found an obscure and dusty tome translated by G.K.L.
Smythe in the thirties from an even more obscure Italian
scroll dating to the 1540s. It listed and described a myriad
of demons. Most of them quite accurately. This should have
been in with the rare books but wasn't in the best of condition.

The original had been written during the heart of the
Reformation when Catholics accused Protestants of con-
sorting with demons and monsters, and the Protestants accused Catholics of being the tools of the Devil Pope. They
both had it wrong. The book was a true treasure neverthe-
less. I thumbed through it greedily.

"If you are looking for references to your monster dog,
you won't find it in that book," a man with a clipped accent
said from about a foot above me.

"How . . . how did you find me?" I looked up anxiously
at the nerdy stranger from the skate park this morning.

"Would you sign my copy of your book? I'm afraid it's a
little dog-eared. I've read it three times. The picture of you
on the back does not do you justice. It makes your hair look
nondescript, but it really has a wonderful golden trans-

lucence." He held *Imps Alive* open to the title page and produced a pen from his shirt pocket.

His slacks still had a sharp crease and the collar of his navy shirt lay flat and neat. He smelled faintly of a spicy and exotic aftershave. I wondered how he'd managed to remain neat, tidy, and clean after the chaos of this morning.

But then, he hadn't fought a demon in the shape of a dog. I had.

The reminder brought back the burning intensity of the bite on my arm. Not as bad as before, but still uncomfortable.

"Only once have I heard a reference to your Sisterhood, Ms. Noncoiré. Perhaps you could enlighten me on their origins." He looked over the top of his tinted, wire-rimmed spectacles at me. "Is your imp around? I would dearly love to examine him, or is it a her?"

Chapter 4

The common brown bat can eat up to six hundred mosquitoes in an hour, including disease-carrying insects, and thus are necessary in controlling the spread of insect-borne viruses like West Nile.

"*E*XCUSE ME, WHAT are you talking about? Do you see an imp on my shoulder?" I blinked up at the tall meddler in wide-eyed innocence. His broad, long-fingered hands still clutched my book with an odd intensity.

Inside, I quaked with fear that he really could see Scrap sitting on my left shoulder.

Maybe he was just an obsessive fan. I'd run into them before, borderline stalkers.

He'd seen my scar.

"Your assistant?"

"Who are you, and why am I talking to you?" I made to move around the all-too-perceptive man before he saw more of my secrets.

What kind of powers did he have? Did I need to go into attack mode?

Nice evasion, Tessie-babe, Scrap snorted in my ear. His gray skin had a faint pink tinge. He wasn't happy, but he wasn't about to transform. The base of my spine remained tingle free.

And yet this stranger knew about him. He'd seen my *scar!*

Scrap's cigar smoke wafted in front of my nose. I resisted the urge to fan it away. A sneeze began building. I had to bite my cheeks to hold it back. I wanted to wiggle my nose, but that would be a dead giveaway to my stranger that something was amiss. Or that he had touched upon the truth with his observations.

"Sorry." The man actually blushed! "Guilford Van der Hoyden-Smythe."

I stared at his proffered hand as if it were contaminated.

"Good day, Mr. Van der Hoyden-Smythe." I clutched the treasured book to my breast and once more tried to pass him. He shifted slightly to block my path.

"The book does not mention the monster dog that was in the park this morning," he said. "My friends call me Gollum." Again he held out his hand.

"Gollum, as in the Tolkien character?"

"Gollum as in . . . Gollum." He shrugged and looked uncomfortable.

"Have you read this book?" I held it up between us. Then the translator's name jumped out at me upon the cover. "G.K.L. Smythe."

"My great-grandfather. I was named for him. So, of course, I have studied the book extensively. He inspired me to get a Ph.D. in cultural anthropology. The book covers only European myth and folklore. The dog's attention to the Native American girl leads me to believe he derives from a more local tradition." Van der Hoyden-Smythe paused for breath. But before I could reply, he plunged on. "Interesting that your imp did not assume the Celestial Blade configuration while you battled the beast."

"I think you need to consult medical help for your imaginings. You seem to have lost touch with reality." I tossed him the book. While he grappled with it, I ducked beneath his arms and away from him. I'd come back later to buy the book if it was still there. If not, I'd find it on line.

"With my luck, Guilford Van der Hoyden-Smythe deals in rare and antique books and has locked up every copy of that tome," I muttered as I wended my way through the crowds of Saturday afternoon shoppers.

Hey, chickie-babe, you need a disguise? A greenish Scrap tweaked one of my stray curls, all the while puffing like a steam engine on his cigar. The smell nearly gagged me. I had to get out of the confines of Simpson's.

When had I ever hastened *out* of a bookstore? Nearest thing to blasphemy I'd ever committed.

Blasphemy is a state of mind. I didn't believe in anything anymore; therefore, I could not commit that sin.

"Just lose the cigar. Maybe that meddling stranger will follow the smell rather than me." I dodged through the security detectors at a side door. Nothing in my tote set them off. A minor miracle. They usually reacted to the metal in my lipstick case, or something in the tampon packaging. Sometimes they just did not like Scrap. I'd gladly have left the imp behind if the things had blared out their warning of theft.

I walked as fast as I could, without drawing undue attention. As I ducked into the driver's seat of my anonymous rental, I spotted Van der Hoyden-Smythe's tall figure hastening toward me with long and determined strides. Some perverse inspiration made me honk my horn and wave at him as I merged into traffic. I turned two corners at the first opportunity and lost sight of him running behind me.

His offhand compliment lingered, though. I checked myself in the rearview mirror.

"Golden translucence, my ass," I scoffed. Same old dishwater-blond curls packed into a tight mass. Though they did look a little lighter than usual in the evening light.

Now where, Tessie? Scrap eyed my cold coffee cup longingly. He'd gone back to his normal peckish gray.

I grabbed the tempting cream-laden coffee away from him and dumped the dregs out the window. "Back to the hotel and some downtime. I need to work. What's on the schedule for tomorrow?"

The imp grabbed my PDA out of my purse. He handed it to me rather than fight the electronics. He hadn't quite mastered the art of turning it on or tapping the screen with his talons. I dreaded the day he figured it out and moved on to my laptop. All I needed was his acerbic insertions into my novels.

Actually, I wondered, not for the first time, how he could manipulate physical objects in this dimension and yet weigh nothing on my shoulder and appear to have no mass.

Another mystery for another day. Scrap didn't talk about himself or his abilities often. He just did things.

"Nothing on for tomorrow but a flight home." I glanced at the schedule page while driving one-handed up Broadway. "How did that happen?"

Remember how you bitched at the publicist that you had to have a week to work on your book? Scrap said. He levitated to the dashboard and pointed excitedly at a cigar shop. He turned royal blue in anticipation of a new blend of tobacco.

I was mightily sick of black cherry cheroots. I ignored his wild gestures and salivating, though.

"I remember bitching. I don't remember getting any time off from this interminable publicity tour."

You compromised on four days. Monday through Thursday. Sunday, tomorrow, is travel day. Thursday morning we head out to the next convention. Scrap shifted his concentration to a department store with a display of perky autumn hats for ladies. He remained a happy blue, but not as intense a hue as when he wanted a new cigar.

"Then I presume I have airline tickets home tomorrow," I commented absently. My concentration centered upon finding the shadowed driveway into the hotel's underground parking garage.

Please, Tess, can we go back to the hat place? Scrap looked positively innocent sitting on the dashboard with his paws clasped neatly in front of him and his bat-wing ears folded downward. He'd taken on a lovely shade of lavender, one I hadn't noticed before. His pleading color?

"What? No sarcasm? No demands? This must be important to you, Scrap." I glanced away from the street for half a heartbeat and missed the driveway. *Damn.* Now I had to go around the block again.

My skin turned clammy and my spine crawled as if big ugly bugs skittered up and down my back. I squirmed and twisted.

What? Scrap demanded. He scrambled around and around, turning deeper and deeper red. His big eyes moved back and forth and his ears twitched.

"Just a weird feeling." I flipped on the blinker and turned right.

Park, babe. We got work to do.

"Now what?" I sighed. A car in front of a parking meter signaled his intent to merge into traffic. I let him, then twisted the wheel and claimed the spot.

The driver behind me yelled something obscene out his window and leaned on his horn.

I resisted flipping him the finger. No sense in aggravating him more.

Still sitting in the air-conditioned coolness, I unfastened the wraparound skirt and shed the overblouse. The moment the light changed and traffic eased around me, I was out of the car clad in shorts and tank top. I barely remembered to pocket the keys after locking the vehicle.

"Think you can manage the Celestial Blade this time?" I asked Scrap as I jogged back toward the underground parking lot.

Scrap did not say a word. He became so insubstantial and colorless on my shoulder I had to look to see if he had remained in this dimension.

"I can't do this without you," I said quietly, mindful of the crowds on the sidewalk.

Still no answer.

I stopped short just shy of the shadowed entrance. My skin twitched all over my body. My heart rate sped up and my focus narrowed to a dark recess just beyond the last visible car parked against the right-hand wall. A cream-colored BMW, I thought. Maybe one of the Detroit luxury cars that tried to imitate a Beemer in styling. Definitely not a Mercedes.

"Stand by, Scrap," I whispered. Slowly, I edged into the structure, keeping to the shadows at the left of the door. From there, I could keep an eye on the sleek car and not be noticed. Hopefully.

The sudden relief from the relentless sunshine brought goose bumps to my arms and thighs. I did not know if I should welcome the coolness or heed it as an additional warning.

My eyes adjusted gradually to the dim lighting. I watched a tall man, silver streaking his dark hair at his temples, emerge from the luxury sedan. Long legs, nicely tailored dark slacks, and an equally dark knit shirt. For a moment I thought it might be Van der Hoyden-Smythe, but this man had broader shoulders and wore only sunglasses, not the thick spectacles of my stalker.

My senses continued to hum. A part of me knew that the sun neared the horizon. Twilight descended.

A tiny winged shape materialized out of nowhere in the dark corner above the cream-colored Beemer.

"Yeep!" A tiny sound of huge fear escaped my lips. It overrode the humming need to confront the menace in the garage.

I dropped into a quivering crouch, my head between my knees and arms covering as much of my head as possible.

A bat! All I could think of was the animal tangling its claws in my hair and yanking it out by the handful. Or worse, nesting in there.

The logical adult part of my brain called me an idiot.

The childish nightmare fears knew better. My newly attuned warrior senses had warned me there was a bat in here.

Up, Tess. Get up. We need to do something! Scrap implored.

I peeked through my crossed arms to see what had become of my imp. Surely he'd transformed into my Celestial Blade in the face of the evil vampire bat.

It's just a little brown bat, and it's gone, Scrap said. Did he whisper out of mutual fear?

I knew that. I hated my stupid phobia. But every time I caught a glimpse of the winged mammals, even on TV, my skin crawled and I grew short of breath. Panic overrode logic.

Then out of the corner of my eye I saw the man turn around and face me. His eyes seemed to seek mine. He removed his sunglasses. Our gazes locked. He smiled at me.

All my fears dropped away like water flowing over a deep fall, leaving me almost light-headed and giddy with relief.

The bat was gone. "Stupid, stupid, stupid," I muttered to myself. "Grow up, bats can't hurt you."

At the moment I truly, I mean *truly* believed that.

I registered that the man's smooth skin showed no signs of a five o'clock shadow on his prominent jaw. A deep dimple appeared in his left cheek as his smile increased. My heart went pitter-pat in excitement.

All memory of the bat and my phobia disappeared.

He took two steps toward me.

I remembered that I had spent the morning at Dill's grave site and backed out into the evening. No man could replace Dill. I did not want any man in my life again, not even a casual flirtation.

Whoa, Tess. Scrap pulled my hair with both paws as if yanking on reins. *Why are we running from a fight?*

"Hungry yet, Scrap?" I asked rather than face my own fears. Which was greater, the atavistic fear of bats? Or the fear of finding another man attractive?

"I think we'll explore Chinatown. You need a good dose of MSG to counteract the lactose intolerance." Don't ask me why the food additive negated his noisome gas, but it did.

Can we stop at the hat place? my imp asked eagerly. *There was that rust-colored one with the long feather. It would look spectacular with your new winter suit.* He salivated into my hair. *And maybe the cigar store?*

Thank heavens he did not truly exist in this dimension and did not soak me with lavender slime.

"If you insist. I also want to go to the Chinese Gate and gardens. They are supposed to be spectacular, real landmarks. We should sightsee a little bit tonight before we pack to go home. Stay away from the hotel," and this bat-filled garage, "for a while."

If you say so, Tessie-dahling. I was born to serve. He produced a new cigar, already lit, and proceeded to blow smoke rings across my face.

"I'll believe that when I see it," I snarled at him as I pulled the car into traffic and sped away from my hotel and my phobias.

But did you stop to think long enough to wonder why your demon-sense started tingling before *you knew there was a bat inside? You normally don't react to bats until you see one.*

Interlude

IMP LORE WILL TELL YOU that what drew me to the Timber Town Bar and Grill in Alder Hill, Oregon, that slushy day in early February two years ago was the potential warrior setting herself up to contract *The Fever*. I'd been drifting aimlessly around the Pacific Northwest for a few weeks gorging on mold, replenishing my energy reserves after using all my wits and a good deal of my strength battling the Sasquatch who guarded the portal out of my home dimension.

I think it was all of the outrageous puns passed in a circle with each new round of beer that pulled me into the dim tavern that smelled of smoke, stale beer, peanut shells ground into the floor planks, and, of course, a wealth of mold. What better place to find mold than in the damp foothills of Mount Hood in February?

"Have you heard this one?" called a man with a black beard and mustache that compensated for a balding head. "I swear it's true; read it in the paper the other day."

"What now, Bob?" A collective groan went through the crowd in anticipation.

"Some guy was arrested for throwing rocks at seagulls. But the judge let him off 'cause he took a vow to leave no tern un-stoned!"

More groans and slurping of beer.

"Moldy oldy, Bob."

"I got a better one," Tess said. She slurred her words just a little and her eyes were rimmed with red from all the tears she had shed. I could tell she was hurting inside from the way her in-laws (or are they outlaws in this culture?) had cut her out of their grief. She needed to share her emotions, This crowd of her husband's friends from science fiction conventions and colleagues from the local community college where he taught geology gave her the best outlet.

"We're going to have to change all of the breakfast menus in this country. The restaurants are calling them 'Pope's Eggs' rather than 'Eggs Benedict' now."

"Booooooo!"

Someone threw peanut shells at Tess.

She ducked, laughing and crying at the same time.

"Dill told me that one just as we were going to sleep that last night. Before the fire broke out," she said quietly.

I think I might have liked this guy Dill.

The room sobered instantly.

The Bob person began singing in a gravelly baritone, "There's a bimbo on the cover of my book," to the tune of "Coming 'Round The Mountain."

"Come on, Tess, sing it, sing the greatest filk song ever written!"

Color drained from Tess' face. More so than what her prim little black dress drained from her. She looked terrible in black, and I hoped she never had to wear it again.

"I can't sing," she choked and took a long draught of beer.

I think that was the beginning of the fever.

Anyway, the party broke up soon after. By this time Tess had me hooked. I had to follow her. She left the party with only one lingering look at the substantial house on the hill behind the white church with the red door. All of her hurt and anger and guilt for living when the love of her life had died so tragically saving her was caught up in the gaze.

Then she got into her mid-sized sedan and started driving. East at first, then north over the mountain in rotten weather on tires that were in no condition to handle mountain pass snows the first week of February.

I gritted my teeth and held on as she took the curves too fast. A death wish in the making.

She couldn't see me yet, of course. The fever hadn't taken her and changed her brain enough for that. But I like to think I had a little influence on her. She slowed down and made it over the mountain, in the dark.

Somewhere along the line she stopped for food and checked into a motel. The next day she headed north with grim determination along a chain of mineral lakes in Washington, just east of the Cascade Mountain Range. She was headed back to the scene of her husband's untimely death. I know now that she was looking for answers. Answers that might not exist. But she had to look.

By the end of the second day she was within a few miles of her destination. By that time the fever had overwhelmed her. Only she knows what nightmares she endured in the grip of the virus. She doesn't talk about it. Not even to the Sisters who shared her infection and survived.

It took all of my willpower to keep her on the road that day. Six times she nearly drove into one of those mineral lakes when the fever slowed her reaction time and skewed her perceptions.

I sat in her lap and yanked the steering wheel in the right direction. When we came to the dirt track that most people don't notice, I steered us along it. I even managed to avoid most of the potholes that would rip out the undercarriage of a high-crop tractor.

Finally we stopped dead outside the citadel. The one place in the world I knew she would be safe and I knew she would wake up and claim me as her own precious imp, companion, and Celestial Blade.

<hr />

I walked hunched over, a little wary of the surgical incision beneath my belly button and the one that ran along the right side of my face from temple to jaw. Sister Serena, the only doctor in the citadel, had to cut the infection from my face and abdomen to save my life.

Spring sunshine softened the austere landscape within the citadel of the Sisterhood of the Celestial Blade. Stout stone walls made of reddish rock from the local area defined at least ten acres of land and buildings. All around me, my Sisters worked. All of them had visible scars on their faces like the one on mine. Some hoed and planted a huge vegetable garden. They tended to be the older women, middle-aged mostly. I didn't see any truly old women here. Some of the more vigorous women repaired storm damage to the roof of the refectory where we took our meals. Still others stripped down to red sports bras and shorts to practice various martial arts in a sandy area set aside solely for that purpose.

I paused about every third step to watch the bustle and to rest. I'd spent at least two months in the infirmary and still hadn't regained my strength from the wasting fever.

Sister Serena walked beside me, as she did every day I ventured outside. She stood straight and tall, mid-forties I guessed. Her muscles flowed easily beneath her bright purple scrubs. All of the Sisters wore bright colors in celebration of life. Not a sign of a uniform among them—except for the sports bras and shorts—those always seemed to be blood red.

"Don't walk too far. Even if you feel better, it is too easy to overdo," Sister Serena said. Her voice, like the rest of her, oozed soft contentment. In two months of rather intimate contact, I'd never seen anything upset her mental or emotional equilibrium. Though once I'd seen her slip on some spilled gelatin and nearly lose her balance.

"I need fresh air," I panted. Sure, I'd walked too far already, but I wasn't about to let Sister S put me back to bed in the closed and stale atmosphere of the infirmary. Not yet at least.

A bevy of children, all girls by the look of them, erupted from a small building in the corner. I stared at them in puzzlement. Only one of the girls, the eldest by the size of her and the maturity of her face and figure, had a scar.

"Future Sisters in training," Sister S explained.

"Do you kidnap children?"

"No." Sister S laughed long and loud. I noticed she laughed a lot. "The fever that marks us does not render us infertile. Nor do our vows to the Sisterhood make us celibate. We raise our daughters to fill our ranks."

"What if you have sons?" I sank down onto a conveniently placed bench in the middle of a flower garden that caught the sunshine. A small fountain burbled beside me as it irrigated the soil.

Sister S stilled in thought. "I don't think any of us have had sons, at least not in living memory. I wonder if we are even capable of having boys?"

"So not all of you come from the outside world like I did." I felt the rough skin along my face. The infection had ruptured before Sister S could lance it clean and straight.

"Very few of us have come from the outside. You are the first in living memory. You have a lot to learn before you can hope to truly be one of us." She looked puzzled, as if she wasn't sure what to do with me.

I didn't know what to do with me either. I'd managed one cell phone call to my dad to make sure my house and finances were taken care of. That was the only outside contact they allowed me. By that time the phone had a dead battery, and there was no electricity here to recharge it.

"And if the fever doesn't take one of your daughters? What becomes of her?"

"All of us go to high school and college on the outside. How do you think I became a doctor?" She raised perfectly arched black eyebrows at me. I'd give my eyeteeth to look that beautiful even on a good day.

"We board with the families of girls who were born here but elected to remain outside, marry, and have children. Usually the few women who come to us from the outside come from those families."

Again she shook her head and looked puzzled.

"So why me?" I asked the question that had burned inside me since I fell into a fever of grief and wound up here.

"The fever finds those who need to become one of us. We never ask why. We welcome anyone the fever chooses." But she pursed her lips in disapproval.

Sister S settled beside me. Her gaze lit fondly upon the oldest of the girls—the one who already had a fever scar. It looked fairly fresh and raw.

"How old are they when the fever selects them?" I waved vaguely at the girls. At twenty-six, I thought myself a little on the old side.

"Usually in their mid-twenties, when they've had a chance to taste life outside and know if this is where they belong or not."

"Am I trapped here for the rest of my life?" That didn't

sound so bad. Without Dill, I didn't have a lot left behind. Mom would take over my house, as she took over everything in her orbit. Dill's life insurance—double indemnity for accidental death—and the mortgage insurance would ensure that she could afford the place. I had completed my contracts with my publisher. Nothing drew me back to reality outside these walls.

Except the burning question of "Why?" Why had the fire started in the crummy motel where Dill and I stayed while he grubbed about looking for specific geological examples. He was due to start teaching at the community college in Cape Cod near our new home in spring quarter. He wanted special samples to take with him.

"No, dear." Sister S laughed again. "None of us are trapped. We can come and go as we choose. Mostly, we choose to stay here, where our work is, where we are needed."

"What, exactly, is your work?" My gaze kept straying to the Sisters working out with quarterstaffs and wrestling. Two of them donned boxing gloves and engaged in something akin to TaeBo.

"The same work you started when the fever took you."

"Huh?" All I remembered about that was a long and involved fever dream of fighting demons.

"Exactly," Sister S replied.

"Exactly what?"

"Think about it."

Chapter 5

Bats are not blind. Their eyes are adapted to see in the dark and some species can see in light as well as humans.

A HUGE BAT LOOMED over me screeching in my sister's voice, "I'm going to drink all your blood!" I screamed and covered my head with my arms, crouching down to make myself as small as possible.

And then the monstrous bat began pulling my hair. Great clumps of the tight curls tangled in claws as long as fingers.

I screamed again in abject terror.

The sound of my own voice croaking woke me up. The sterile hotel room with my half-packed clothes strewn about offered me little comfort. My scalp still hurt from . . . from . . . from wearing the comb. Not from a bat that had really been my older sister Cecilia dressed up for Halloween.

Funny. All these years and I'd never remembered the incident that had triggered my bat phobia.

I looked over at the clock. Not quite ten on the West Coast. I'd been asleep maybe a half hour. Nearly one at home. Would Mom be awake?

Probably. She didn't sleep much since she and Dad divorced fourteen years ago. I hit number four on my cell phone speed dial. My agent Sylvia was number two, and my editor number three. I'd never deleted Dill's cell phone from the number one position. Somehow doing that would be a symbolic erasure of our brief marriage.

"Hi, Mom. My plane lands in Providence at three. I should be home in time for dinner," I greeted her before she could monopolize the conversation.

"That's fine, dear. I'll fix a nice pot roast. I found it on sale at WelSave this morning. We'll eat early and go to evening Mass together."

Not on your life, Mom. I hadn't been to Mass in years, and I had no intention of starting now. She knew that. But she never acknowledged it. Mom and reality sometimes had only a passing acquaintance.

She rambled on with more domestic details in her Québécois accent. It sounded rather thick tonight. Like it did when she'd been alone too much and thought in the French dialect of her childhood.

Her parents had left Quebec when she was seven and never spoke French again. Somewhere in her twisted mind she had created a need for her Québécois roots and pieced together half memories of baby talk in French and called it the pure language.

Her need for the linguistic security blanket increased after Dad left. He'd brought me up nearly bilingual with a Canadian accent. I'd taken Parisian French in high school and college and tried to correct Mom once. After having my ears boxed for corrupting the language, I never tried it again.

Somewhere along the line, I figured out that Mom understood real French. She just refused to speak it. While I mourned Dill, I began to understand her need. She grieved for people and things lost in her life, her grandparents in Quebec City and her husband, much as I grieved for my lost husband.

"Mom, do you remember an incident about a bat when I was small?"

"Oh, yes. Your sister was quite naughty. But she so loved that Halloween costume I made her. She wore it for months and months every time you three children played dress up or make-believe. Why do you ask? It's been years. I thought you were too young at the time to remember. Barely three."

"I had a nightmare about it." If I was three, then Cecilia

had been a very grown-up and authoritative seven. Our brother Steph, between us in age, had defended me when he could. But Cecilia always won our sibling battles. "What triggered it, Mom? Cecilia isn't one to like creepy animals."

"Oh, we'd all taken a road trip with Chuck that summer." She never referred to my dad as the father of her children. She barely acknowledged his existence after the divorce and church annulment. "We toured the Grand Canyon while Chuck audited a client's branch office. When we got home, we found a dead bat plastered to the radiator grille. It was quite mummified from the heat of the engine I think. Just a little thing but it fascinated Cecilia. Nothing would do but she had to be a bat for Halloween, *la petite garnement.*" Little scamp, I translated the term, almost an endearment. Mom rambled on a bit more with memories from that wonderful summer trip that I could not remember.

Eventually sleep tugged a yawn from me, and I said my good-byes with assurances that I would indeed be home the next day.

"You okay, baby?" Mom finally asked.

"Yeah, Mom. I am." And I was. The dream had faded from the reality of nightmare to just another annoyance about my sister.

But the phobia? That was still something I didn't want to push.

"I'll press a dress for you to wear to Mass," Mom concluded just as I clicked off.

Mumble grumble. I settled back into sleep, satisfied that my nightmare hadn't been real.

I felt a disturbance on the mattress beside me. Dill often came to bed late after reading and studying for the next day's fossil hunt.

"Dilly," I murmured only half awake.

"Move over, love," he whispered. His smooth tenor voice caressed my mind and senses.

As I had longed to do, every night for two and a half years, I scooted to the edge of the bed. Dill lay down behind me and wrapped a light arm around me. I snuggled in, cherishing the feel of him, the smell of him, the weight . . .

He had no weight. No substance. No warmth. Only a preternatural chill.

I jerked awake. "Dillwyn Bailey Cooper!" More a plea than a question.

"Tess," he whispered. "Don't ask questions. Don't object. Just be here for me. Let me feel you."

"Talk to me, Dill," I said warily. I turned onto my back and pushed myself into something resembling a sitting position. Light creeping around the hotel room drapes and under the door showed only the dimmest outline of a man sitting cross-legged on the other side of the bed.

I ran my fingers through my tangled mop of hair. For half a moment I considered confining it in the lovely comb Scrap had given me. But it was across the room in my tote bag.

Where was the imp anyway?

Dill brushed his hand lightly around my head without touching me. My scalp tingled where the hairs stood on end.

"This is what I miss most about you, Tess," he breathed. "The sight of you all sleep tousled and adorable. Lovable."

A soft draft passed my ear. I shivered from the temperature change. The room was now colder than the air conditioner could make it.

"Don't shy away from me, lovey. You said you missed me so much your teeth ached."

Lovey, his pet name for me. Much better than *lumpy,* which the kids had called me in school.

"I do miss you, Dill. There's a gaping hole inside me that only you can fill." I reached a tentative hand out to him, not quite daring to touch in case this was only a dream. I couldn't bear to lose him again.

"Then let me fill the gap. Let me watch for you. Get rid of the imp. Keep me by your side instead." He smiled at me, as he used to.

My resistance to his ghostly presence dissolved. No man had touched me in a very long time. I ached for more than just his presence. I wanted his body. Next to me, inside me.

Bad plan, Tessie. Suddenly Scrap on the night table was more substantial than Dill at my side, in my bed. Scrap also glowed pink in warning.

"Dill, why did you have to die?"

"I told you not to ask questions." His voice rose in anger. "I can't answer questions."

He faded.

I needed to see his eyes, to look deep inside their hazel depths to understand what he was thinking and feeling.

"Dill, don't go. I need you. Stay with me."

The phone rang with my five AM wake-up call.

The mattress creaked.

The room warmed.

I fumbled for the lamp. Light flooded the room and dazzled my eyes.

The room was empty. Even Scrap had deserted me.

The ache in my gut doubled from loneliness.

"It was all a dream. I visited Dill's grave yesterday, so of course I dreamed about him." The sound of my own words in my ears convinced me that the conversation had not happened.

I was still alone and more lonely than ever.

What's up with this spook? Where did he come from? Why is he here? Imp lore tells us nothing about ghosts. When we die, we die. We do not come back as ghosts or reincarnations or anything. Our bones burrow through the dimensions to take root in the great garbage heap of the universe.

So we live a long, long time and cling to life like a hamster gnawing on a finger.

Nothing can break the bond between a Warrior of the Celestial Blade and her imp. So why is this ghost trying to oust me?

I need answers this dimension cannot give.

Do I have time to seek? And while I'm at it, I should make some inquiries into Guilford Van der Hoyden-Smythe, the scholar who sees too much.

Cookies! Scrap chortled at the smell of charred flour, sugar, and fat that greeted us upon opening the kitchen door of my rambling home on Cape Cod.

A hint of movement in the oak tree at the front of the house made my heart skip a beat. A blacker-than-black shadow. A bat.

I had to sit in the car a moment to catch my breath before I had the courage to dash for the kitchen door.

Even though I now knew why I feared the creatures, I couldn't banish the phobia overnight. If anything, it might be worse. I couldn't get the dream image of the huge bat out of my mind, twice as big as me, threatening to drink my blood and rip out my hair. My scalp hurt just thinking about it.

"Mother." I acknowledged Scrap's delight with a sinking heart. My plans for a long bubble bath, a quiet snack, and then a good workout at the fencing *salle* vanished.

I'd tried martial arts when I first left the Citadel, but all the philosophy, meditation, and breathing exercises bored me. I needed to move.

Sport fencing fit me better.

"Teresa!" Mother rushed to greet me at my own door with a fierce hug. She squeezed the breath out of me, as if she hadn't done the same thing ten days ago. "Come in, child, come in." She took the lightest of my carry-on luggage from me, leaving me with two heavy suitcases and my laptop case. Each one was loaded with books—research and my own personal reading.

I lugged the bags into my kitchen and dumped them in the middle of the floor. The previous owner of the house had run a bed and breakfast. The oversized kitchen and casual eating area gleamed with modern colonial-style furniture and lighting.

"You really should stay home more, Teresa. You haven't come to family game night in ages. You *will* be there tonight," Mom prattled. After being away for a while I noticed her French accent more than usual.

Great, another excuse to spend "quality" time with my harpy, control-freak sister Cecilia, bachelor Uncle George who couldn't tell the truth if you paid him, Mom who talked endlessly about everything and nothing whether someone listened or not, deaf and forgetful Grandma Maria, and Auntie Em . . . er, MoonFeather, as she preferred. She was from Dad's side of the family and thus not named for a saint. In fact MoonFeather was a card-carrying member of Wicca (if they have cards and membership and such) and the only relative I could describe as close to normal. We played Trivial Pursuit® for about four hours every Sunday so we wouldn't have to talk to each other, or have to feel guilty for totally ignoring each other the rest of the week.

Dad and his much younger partner Bill, tennis pro at the local country club, had a life and therefore avoided family game night.

Why had Dill and I decided to settle on Cape Cod and not in the Pacific Northwest? We'd given up wonderful coffeehouses on every other corner for this?

We'd traded his eccentric family of D. B. Coopers for my dysfunctional family. Every one of his clan, parents and siblings, were named some variation of D. B. Cooper.

I'd often wondered if his parents were related to the infamous D. B. Cooper, the first successful airplane hijacker who had disappeared with his ill-gotten gains into the Cascade wilderness back in the seventies and become a local folk hero. In the decade when baby boomers sought new and unique ways to defy authority, D. B. Cooper had bested them all at the game.

Dill had liquidated his trust fund for the down payment on the huge old house. He'd offered to sell his share of the family furniture store, too, if we'd needed it to put three thousand miles between us and his family.

My brother Stephen had been smart enough to move to Indiana as soon as he graduated from college. He'd finished his master's in organic chemistry and worked for a pharmaceutical company. Last Christmas he'd announced plans to begin work on a Ph.D. I talked to him regularly, but I don't think he called Mom or Dad more than twice a year.

"I need a nap and some exercise, Mom." I dove for the oversized steel fridge, looking for a cold drink. I grabbed the last bottle of beer. Either Mom had really cleaned house or she'd thrown a party in my absence. More likely, Uncle George had pilfered five bottles.

Mom is the only person I know who can clean more thoroughly than Scrap.

"You have time for a nap before we gather at eight. You can go for a walk tomorrow. All that fencing nonsense isn't good for you. It isn't ladylike." Mom stood in front of the center island, between me and the bottle opener in the drawer.

Fortunately, her back was to the racks of cooling cookies. Scrap scarfed up three of them. Then he disappeared— probably into the cellar.

"I have to work tomorrow." I pushed her aside to open the drawer for the church key. Where the bottle opener should be, it wasn't. I rummaged deeper, thrusting aside a myriad of cooking utensils I couldn't name and rarely used.

"Mom, you rearranged my kitchen!" I wailed.

"Well, if you'd stay home more often, you could clean your own house and keep it more efficiently arranged." She stood with hands on hips in affronted outrage. "I don't see why you have to travel so much. You never traveled this much before you met that Dillwyn person."

"Dill was my husband," I ground out for the umpteenth time.

"Humph," Mom snorted. "A quickie ceremony in Reno with no family or friends when you'd known him less than a week? I don't call that a wedding. Then three months later he takes off, just disappears. That's what you get for hooking up with a man you met at one of those weird conventions. I don't see why you can't write something normal, like romances, or histories."

"Mother, Dill died. He was horribly burned in a motel fire. I barely escaped alive. He was burned to death. TO DEATH, Mom."

"So you say. It's easier to tell people that he died rather than admit to being a grass widow like me. And he left you with this huge mortgage and tremendous debts, so you have to work too hard and can't spend time with your family."

Back to family game night.

"Dill and I bought this house together. His life insurance paid off the mortgage." Double indemnity for accidental death on the life insurance, plus mortgage insurance.

I had money left over to live off of until I finished writing *Imps Alive* and started earning money of my own. "No mortgage means I can afford to let you live in the guest cottage rent free. Mom, I'm tired of this argument."

Tired of the memories. Tired of remembering how Dill and I had planned to fill this rambling old house with children.

I worked too hard in an effort to avoid remembering.

I ran miles every day and worked out at the *salle* so I'd sleep without dreaming.

This old house had ghosts aplenty, so far none of them Dill. Would he haunt me now that I had been to his grave?

I almost hoped he would.

She cleaned with bleach! Scrap screamed in my ear. He flickered from deep orange to red and back again. *I don't need bleach to clean. She dumped all of the mold I was cultivating. The whole house reeks of bleach—even the cellar,* he wailed.

Then eat cookies, I snarled back at him. *No one else will.*

Then a new thought struck me. *Did she get into the armory?* Only I had the key to the secret room in the cellar filled with all kinds of weapons, most of them very sharp, pointy, and lethal. One hundred fifty years ago it had hidden runaway slaves as part of the Underground Railroad.

I didn't check. Scrap popped out again.

"Mom, I'm going to take a bath. Lock the door behind you."

Without looking to see if she actually left, I made my way through the butler's pantry to the dining room, then into the oldest part of the house to the steep stairs up to the suite of rooms I kept above. This was part of the original five-room New England saltbox that dated to the pre-Revolutionary era. I loved this part of the house; three rooms downstairs and two up, all clustered around a central chimney.

"Oh, and, Teresa," Mom called after me.

I froze halfway up the stairs, the part where I had to duck to keep from banging my head on the support beam. That tone of voice never boded well for me. On top of that, the base of my spine itched and my heart beat at double time.

"You might want to watch the news in a few minutes. Your face is all over the media about a strange incident in Oregon yesterday. Something about you rescuing an Indian girl from a rabid dog."

"Shit!"

Mom fairly danced out the front door at the base of the stairs.

I scrambled up the remaining steps, practically on all fours, to keep from knocking myself out on the beam. The attack of the monster dog wasn't the first item on the news. That belonged to the latest drive-by shooting in Providence. But the dog and I were second. The local anchor showed a composite sketch of the dog that looked more like the mastiff from the *Hound of the Baskervilles* than the brindled mutt that was taller than a wolfhound and broader than a rottweiler.

Then they showed my publicity photo, since no one had captured any shots of me in action. Someone in the crowd — probably that snoopy Guilford van der Hoyden-Smythe — had recognized me. At least they only talked about how I had subdued the beast with a skateboard, not how my invisible imp had become a fireplace poker.

The newscast went on to say that a similar attack had taken place near Puyallup, Washington, three days before. An adolescent Native American girl had also been the object of the dog's attention, and had not been hurt.

At last the news went on to say that the Colville tribe had filed suit for custody of Cynthia. The Stalking Moon clan claimed her even though the closest blood relation was a second cousin of her father's.

Chills ran all over my body. The name was just too much of a coincidence for me to not take heed.

Cynthia: Greek for moon. *Kynthia:* the name of the Moon Goddess in my books, based upon the Sisterhood of the Celestial Blade Warriors. My Sisterhood. The women who had rescued me from a raging infection and uncontrollable grief.

Stalking Moon: her clan. My Sisterhood worshiped a Goddess who manifested in the stars defined by a crescent moon.

The base of my spine tingled and itched. I forgot my

need for a bath. Leaving the TV on, I prowled through the sitting room of my suite and the long addition over the dining room for reference texts on Native American folklore.

Nothing. All of my work so far had been based upon European myth and legend. The American tribes had never interested me before.

Time for an Internet search and probably a hefty order from some rare book dealer.

Chapter 6

"**T**ESS, ARE YOU AWAKE? We brought game night to you," my sister Cecilia called as she tapped on the door to the sitting room, one of the two small rooms in the original part of the house. Soft Celtic ballads sung by a friend of mine from cons played on the stereo system.

I stifled a groan. I'd decided to deal with game night by ignoring it. I was curled up with a book on the overstuffed sofa in front of the fireplace. A fire crackled and lent a lovely golden light to the shadowy room. The comfortable presence of Maggie, one of the ghosts, dissolved, leaving me cold and alone with my family.

"Chicken," I muttered under my breath.

"Really, Cecilia, I am too tired," I added, slamming my book down on the end table. This was my house, damn it! Why couldn't my family respect that?

"Maybe you just need to get laid," Cecilia chirped. "Then you wouldn't be so snippy."

"A lot easier to just buy a vibrator and rent some porn."

"*Merde*, we did you a favor bringing game night to you." Cecilia stomped out toward the dining room.

Don't you just wish you could ignore them, babe? No such luck tonight, dahling, Scrap chortled from his perch on the spider—the wrought-iron swinging arm in the fireplace designed to hang pots over the flames for cooking. He always sought a heat source. I'd often wondered if his home dimension was hotter than hell and ours too cold for him.

"Sorry," MoonFeather, Dad's sister, mouthed as she bustled in behind Cecilia. She headed into the dining room—one of the first additions to the original saltbox.

I rolled out of the armchair and stretched my back until it cracked. I wasn't going to get out of this easily, and burying my nose in the book wouldn't work. I'd tried that before.

"Where's the beer?" Uncle George demanded, heading directly for the kitchen, inconveniently at the other end of the house.

"Mom, I told you I couldn't make game night. I'm too tired," I protested.

Mom flitted her hands in dismissal as she placed the game box on the long table that could seat twelve comfortably.

"Someone close the door. It's cold in here." Grandma Maria shivered in the open doorway. Stepping out of the way and closing it herself seemed beyond her faculties tonight.

But I'd almost be willing to bet my new hair comb that she'd trounce the lot of us in the game. The space in her brain she used to store vast amounts of trivia must crowd out the room she needed for short-term memory.

Since no one else seemed to think it prudent to close the door, I performed the chore myself. Fluttering shadows from the old oak tree out front sent deep chills through me and robbed me of breath. I had to make sure they were just leaf shadows and not bats.

Uncle George returned with a beer in one hand and a bag of chips in the other. He took the place of honor in the captain's chair at the head of the table with his back to the fireplace and looked around as if startled that the rest of us hadn't set everything up in his absence. My sister Cecilia began laying a fire without permission.

"I'll make coffee." I escaped to the kitchen.

"Make it decaf, dear. It's evening and we don't want the caffeine to interfere with our sleep," Mom called after me.

"Unleaded, my foot," I grumbled and started making a full pot of the real thing.

While the filtered spring water from my own well dripped through freshly ground gourmet beans, I rummaged through the luggage I hadn't taken upstairs or unpacked yet.

In the mesh bag, wrapped in your dirty underwear, Scrap said, reading my mind again. I wasn't sure I liked this new ability of his. He appeared inside the big suitcase, clawing the drawstring of the mesh bag open with his talons.

"Thanks, buddy." I retrieved the antique comb from deep inside the protective wrapping.

An argument between Uncle George and Grandma Maria erupted over possession of the captain's chair and its placement closest to the fire. I took the time to rinse the comb in cold water and let the moisture ease its way through my tight mop of curls rather than intervene in the argument.

I kind of liked the glamour of elegance the new hairdo gave me.

Then I switched the carafe of coffee for my favorite heavy ceramic cup shaped like Earth with a blue dragon circling the center while it still dripped from the coffee maker. One sip and the room seemed brighter, warmer, and friendlier.

A tap on the glass half of the back door interrupted my savoring of the second sip.

"Dad!" I opened the door and hugged him tight. He'd kept much of his rugged blond handsomeness as he approached sixty; even if Chuck Noncoiré was a serious-minded accountant who peered at the world over half glasses. Living with a tennis pro kept him lean and fit.

"MoonFeather warned me of your mother's plans. Want me to chase them off?" He stepped into the breakfast nook alone. A rare occurrence.

"Nah. They'll only gang up on me worse next time I'm home on a Sunday night. Where's Bill?"

I peered through the glass top half of the back door for signs of Dad's partner. I didn't mind Dad being gay and had accepted Bill Ikito as a member of the family long ago. But Mom had never forgiven Dad for preferring a male tennis pro—younger than herself by fifteen years—to her. I couldn't remember her being in the same room with Dad except for an occasional Thanksgiving dinner at my house since I was twelve and the scandal erupted all over Cape Cod.

"Bill's coming down with a cold. I tucked him into bed with a cup of lemon-and-honey tea and a romance novel. I'm serious, I'll send them all home if you aren't up to company. You've been on the road a lot this year." He placed a thick hand on my shoulder, squeezing with gentle affection.

"If I get too tired, I'll call Maggie to chase them off." I grinned at him.

"Tess, I don't mind that you let your overactive imagination take off in your books, but believing in ghosts is pushing the limits of true sanity." His blue eyes looked tense behind the magnification of his glasses.

"Don't worry about me, Dad. It's all a family joke," I hedged. If I ever mentioned Scrap and everything his existence entailed, Dad just might find a way to commit me.

"Besides, what am I supposed to do? When Dill and I bought this house, the earnest money agreement specifically left possession of three ghosts in the house along with the appliances and the dining table with twelve chairs." The table had come into the house through an open picture window during remodeling and was too big to get out any other way.

"I guess it is only significant that your mother believes in the ghosts. Go ahead and sic Maggie on her early. I'll call you tomorrow. We'll have lunch at the club before you take off on your next junket." He kissed my cheek and went back to his loving partner.

I was left with my . . . possessive, obsessive, wacky and . . . and yes, loving family.

We exchanged a few comments about me attacking rabid dogs. Mom muttered that should include her ex and his partner.

"Hey, Tess, I heard there was a bigfoot sighting out in Oregon. Same newscast as that dog fight. We wondered if the monster had kidnapped you," Uncle George said. He pronounced it ore-ee-gone rather than orygun. I didn't correct him. He wouldn't have listened.

He wasn't lying that the family worried I'd been kidnapped. Uncle George couldn't tell the truth if it hit him in the face. But right now I knew he spoke it. I knew it in my heart and my head.

How?

"Bigfoot might be preferable to you lot," I quipped.

They call themselves Sasquatch, Scrap hissed in my ear.

"And the proper name is Sasquatch," I added. "How many points do I get for that?"

"That isn't one of the questions, dear," Grandma Maria said, patting my hand. "We haven't started yet. We were waiting for you. Have you done something to your hair? It looks lighter, blonder." She cocked her petite head like a little bird, her soft curls looking like a halo. I'd inherited her hair and hoped mine became as soft and silky when I was her age.

"No, Grandma. I just changed the style a bit. I might let it grow out."

"That would be nice. Long hair is more ladylike." Mom patted her own coil of medium brown hair atop her head.

Bill, I might add, kept his straight black hair buzzed so short it looked like a dirty shadow on his skull.

"I'm worried about that Sachey-foot guy," Uncle George grumbled as he grabbed the dice to begin the game. "You're going to California next weekend where they had that sighting. You watch your step and don't get caught by one of them monsters."

"I agree," MoonFeather added. Her keen gray eyes pinned me with otherworldly knowledge. "I've seen in the stars grave portents on your horizon."

I don't like that word grave, Scrap added.

Interlude

*M*OONFEATHER'S DABBLINGS IN astrology looked like chimpanzee art next to Michelangelo's Pieta compared to the way the Warriors of the Celestial Blade, male and female, study the stars. Their faith, their sole purpose in life, and the reason they gather together into cloistered armies, centers on a single configuration in the sky. When the Goddess reveals her face in the skies, then Her warriors will be blessed with victory over demons and the world will be safe for another space of time.

Far be it from me to scoff. Imps have their own Gods and sacred rituals that mean everything to us. The warriors' Goddess might not do much for me, but then garbage dumps in cold storage don't do much for humans.

I've seen the face of the Goddess and so has Tess. We've seen the aftermath of a demon battle.

The first new quarter moon after Tess was up and about in the citadel, Sister S invited her to watch—not participate, just watch—as the Sisterhood gathered to pay homage to their God-dess.

A lot of cultures watch the stars, and a lot of cultures worship at the full moon, or the dark of the moon. I hadn't run into any other that worships at the new quarter moon.

As darkness fell, the Sisters drifted away from their dinner, their study, their exercise into the central courtyard. Each of them carried a lighted taper with a hand cupped around the flame to shield it from view as well as the wind. If one of those tapers ever snuffed on its own before the ceremony ended, ill winds blew for the entire Sisterhood. Each Sister had an adult imp on her shoulder to help protect the candles. They talked and joked softly among themselves, cheerful; family going to church on Sunday morning. Except this was a Tuesday night.

Tess shuffled out of the infirmary wing on the arm of her doctor, Sister Serena. She stood a little straighter today. Sister S had taken the stitches out of her belly incision the day before. Tess also took slightly firmer steps than yesterday. But only I could discern the difference, because I watched her so closely, so lovingly.

A swarm of older Sisters stood three deep in a crescent facing east, at the point where the moon would rise. The honored dozen of the leadership of the order assumed seemingly random spots within the arms of that crescent. All of the youngsters and the bulk of the warriors took their places across the top of the formation, assuming east as the top, in a scattered wash. Imp wings kind of made the entire formation look fuzzy and bigger to my eyes. Sort of like looking through an out-of-focus telescope.

Tess stood apart, on the top step of the infirmary building. Of all those present, we alone could see the pattern of lighted tapers and compare them to the miracle that was about to rise in the sky.

This courtyard, though protected by high walls—ten, twelve feet, what do I know of exact measures?—was slightly elevated and gave a clear view of the eastern horizon.

They all got real quiet, all at once.

The quality of light changed as the moon thrust one curved arm into view. One day, soon I hoped, I'd become Tess' Celestial Blade, in a good imitation of that waxing quarter moon. Sister S, standing among the leadership, began a soft hymn of praise. I didn't understand the language. I don't think Tess did either. An ancient hymn preserved through countless generations of Sisters pledged in the eternal fight to keep this dimension safe from interlopers known as demons. The others joined her song, swelling the courtyard with music that raised goose bumps on

Tess' arms and made me spread my ears to gather maximum sound.

The hymns continued, all in the haunting language that lingered in the back of the mind, almost understood, not quite discernible. Like a racial memory or an atavistic need.

The moon rose higher. The night grew darker. Overhead, the Milky Way spangled the heavens with a river of light.

And then the top of the moon touched the Milky Way. A few stars below the elliptic plane of the galaxy burst into view.

The Sisters raised their tapers high and continued singing.

"The face of the Goddess," I gasped in wonder as the constellations and moon came together in the sky. For one breath I felt a part of something bigger, something greater and more important than my solo life, the pain in my scars, and my grief.

The Sisters stood in imitation of the miracle I saw reflected in the sky. I needed to be part of that homage.

"Hush," a Sister in the courtyard below me hissed. "The Goddess has not yet appeared. Your place is to watch, not to comment."

"But . . ."

"Hush."

Of course they couldn't see Her. Kynthia. The Goddess of the Warriors of the Celestial Blade. They had their candles above their heads, blinding them to the wonders in the night sky. A kind of mist covered the lot of them.

Dimwits. They should extinguish their candles, or hold them below their faces, so the flames didn't blind them to the miracle above.

The image lasted only a moment. Clouds gathered. A breeze came up.

Spielberg couldn't have staged it better.

"There," someone shouted as her candle blew out.

Other candles extinguished. Other Sisters gasped at the fading magnificence in the sky.

"To arms, Sisters, to arms! The demons march this night."

"Inside. Stay low, stay safe. Whatever you hear, whatever

you think you might want to do, do not emerge from your room," Sister Serena commanded, suddenly appearing at my side. She shoved me into the infirmary and firmly locked my door behind me.

I pounded on the door, suddenly afraid of the darkness and the way the base of my spine tingled. Energy coursed through my blood as it never had before, demanding I take action.

No one answered my demands.

Over the course of the next several hours, I heard the clash of blades, a strange ululating battle cry, and screams of pain.

"Let me out, I can help," I pleaded over and over again.

But my Sisters had other concerns that night.

After a while, the cacophony of chaos gave way to bumps and thuds within the infirmary. Women gave orders, equipment moved. Lights showed beneath my door.

In the morning I learned a small contingent of furred demons, perhaps two dozen of them, had broken through the portal the citadel guarded. Three Sisters, including Sister Serena, had received serious wounds. A fourth had died.

But they had beaten the monsters back.

"That doesn't sound right," I said when I sat beside Sister Serena's bed the next day. "I write sword and sorcery stuff. It doesn't make sense for them to send only a small contingent against the full Sisterhood. Of what? Two hundred fifty, maybe three hundred, trained warriors?" I held a glass of water with a bent straw to the doctor's mouth and let her sip.

"Unless the demon population is way down and they are desperate to breed with humans. Otherwise, why didn't they send more to secure the portal?"

"You know nothing of demons," Sister Gert, the leader of this citadel, snarled from the doorway. "We were triumphant and suffered only minor losses."

"Sounds more like a diversion to me," I muttered. "What else were the demons up to last night?"

"You know nothing! Your place is to watch and learn, not to question." Sister Gert turned on her heel and left before even inquiring about the health of their doctor.

"She is right," Sister S said quietly. "We of the Sisterhood do not ask questions. We follow tradition, and do our job. 'Tis the only way to keep the demons subdued. You were not raised here. You have never fought a true demon."

Oh, yeah? What about the demon of grief? What about the demons in my fever dreams? No questions, my ass, I thought, but kept my mouth shut.

This time.

Chapter 7

The smallest bat, the bumblebee bat, weighs less than a penny. Its forearms measure barely twenty-five millimeters. The largest bats, the Old World Flying Foxes, have a wingspan of two meters and can weigh seven hundred fifty grams.

"YOU KNOW WHAT I LOVE about my job, Scrap?" I asked the next weekend. I threw open the French doors of my room at the Double Lion Hotel in San Jose, California. The balconied room looked out over the pool rather than the parking lot or the freeway. Such luxury! "Now that I'm really making money, I get to go to West Coast conventions as well as those closer to home."

I drew in a deep lungful of dry air scented with some desert plant I couldn't name. A touch of salt on the edge of my taste buds told me that rain would come in from the Pacific Ocean tonight.

Scrap just slithered into the air conditioner looking for mold. The little glutton.

"Time to go to work, Scrap. I'm going down to the green room to register and get my schedule." I'd also nosh on the goodies spread out for the visiting pros. Airplane food had become nonexistent in the latest economic crisis. "I'll buy you a beer later, Scrap." He still didn't answer, too absorbed in his feeding frenzy.

I'd started attending conventions—or cons—in college with friends who had grown up in the culture of fandom.

They soon became an addiction. Any weekend of the year, somewhere in the US, there is an SF convention. Three or four days, depending on the weekend, of costumes, books, writers, readers, gamers, filk—the folk music of science fiction and fantasy—nonsense, and fun.

Just because I hadn't been able to sing since Dill died didn't mean I couldn't listen to the filk concerts. But I didn't go to the filk circles and open sings anymore.

Oh, and did I say books? Book dealers, new and used, classic and potboiler, abound at cons. They tend to stock up on books by visiting writers so the fans can get them autographed. I loved the atmosphere as much as I loved the people who dashed up to me wanting an autograph or those who came and sat in rapt attention when I did a reading or spoke on a panel discussion.

During the lean years, when my writing barely put food on the table, and I had to work as a substitute teacher in Providence to keep a grubby little apartment, I had to limit my cons to New England. If I could conveniently drive there and crash with friends, I attended, had a great time, and promoted my books as much as I could.

Then there was High Desert Con in Tri-Cities, Washington. My oldest friend from college, Bob Brown, the man who had first introduced me to cons, ran programming on that convention. I always scrimped and saved or went into debt to attend his con.

I was just beginning to make more from writing than teaching when I met Dill at High Desert Con and everything changed.

I hadn't been back since.

I'd be guest of honor, or GOH, there in a few weeks with my expenses paid by the con. I wanted to see my old friend again, but . . . I just wasn't sure how I felt about going back to the place where I'd met Dill.

Would he haunt me there as he had in Portland? I almost hoped so. I desperately needed to see his smile again, feel the special warmth his love gave me.

I also dreaded the pressure he had put on me to discard Scrap.

Bright and friendly smiles greeted me in the green room. Three volunteers jumped to answer my questions, provide me with maps of the sprawling hotel, introduce me to everybody and anybody. I glad-handed my way around the room, basking in their welcome. Then I smelled the cake. Chocolate. Rich double devil's food chocolate.

I barged into the connecting room, the lounge, of the suite and made a beeline for the luscious treat. My feet came to a skidding halt and backpedaled.

The cake had come from a bat-shaped pan, Halloween orange-and-black candy sprinkle bats littered the dark frosting. It was the weekend that bridged September and October. Appropriate decorations for the season.

I lost my appetite.

What's the matter, babe, afraid of a little bat candy? Scrap goaded me.

"I am not afraid. Just turned off."

"Tess, I may call you Tess, might I? I'm Dee Dee Richardson, head of costuming." A short, blowsy, bleached-blonde held out her hand as she zoomed in on me from the registration area. "I'm sorry to impose on you and your busy schedule, but one of my judges for the masquerade just canceled out. Emergency appendectomy. Is there any way I could impose upon you to take her place? Having a celebrity like you on the panel of judges would be such an honor," she said all in one breath.

Gratefully, I turned my back on the bat cake and led her back to registration. "Of course you can impose. I love costuming. I used to do quite a bit of sewing myself and consider myself quite competent to judge workmanship as well as creativity."

The heady aroma of ranch-flavored chips and dip began to blot out the now nauseating smell of chocolate.

"Did you know that I knit and crochet as well? My Grandmother Maria taught me *la frivolité*, 'tatting' you call it. I love textiles," I blathered on.

"Yes, I noticed how your details about clothing and textile textures add so much richness to your books."

That settled, I went to find some dinner so I could enjoy the rest of the con.

I met up with some old friends from the costuming guild in the hotel garden café. I sometimes wonder if this same café teleports around the country for each and every con. It looked the same in every hotel. We had a marvelous discussion about how the development of scissors had changed clothing construction.

A few people dining near us sported *Star Trek* and *Star Wars* costumes. A few others were more creative and elaborate. I saw everything from elegant and historically accurate Regency and early Georgian wear on both men and women, to green-painted ogres wearing horns and wispy rags. I noted a lot of women and children had commercially made fairy wings stuck down the back of their outfits. Chiffon drifted and floated nicely out from a wire framework. I almost wished I had brought some of my own garb.

The best costumes would come out tomorrow night for the masquerade. I wiggled with happy anticipation at being allowed to judge them.

Then a large family group with three small children filed into the café. They all wore black leather with brown fur hoods. When they raised their arms, black leather bat wings connected them from wrist to knee. A tall man, their seeming leader, threw back his fur hood revealing a thick black braid going halfway down his back. His hair was going gray at the temples, like silver wings.

Where had I seen him before? Some con probably.

Not a con, Scrap whispered to me. *The underground garage where you cowered because a bat dared fly past you on its way to dinner.*

I shuddered in memory of my own stupid fears.

The man smiled, and the entire room seemed to go quiet, more relaxed. He raised his hand to smooth back that magnificent head of hair. His bat wings flowed out from his costume.

Breathing became difficult. I couldn't think, couldn't move. My heart beat overtime and cold sweat broke out on my brow and back.

Then the three-year-old began running around making squeaky noises. My companions all "Ahhed" at how cute she was.

I lost my appetite and pushed away the remnants of my otherwise excellent salmon Caesar salad.

My room seemed the best respite from the bats at the con. I scuttled away and turned on the evening news, something I never do at a con. Reality has no place here. But I needed a heady dose of reality right then.

While the local anchor prattled on about bank robberies, gang violence, and road rage, I yanked the antique comb out of my hair and began brushing my curls, now long enough to cover my neck. And . . . and definitely lighter in color. I seriously contemplated cutting it. But I really liked wearing that comb.

A particularly tight tangle broke off in my hand as I worked the brush through. As I stared at the near transparent gold strands, a word on the TV caught my attention.

"Another in a series of dog attacks that have plagued the Pacific Northwest . . ."

"What?"

The screen flashed briefly with a picture of the hind end of a big dog—it could have been any big dog—and then the face of the scholar with the clipped accent who had followed me from Alder Hill to the book signing at Simpson's.

The station went to a commercial.

Five agonizing minutes later, the news came back with a thirty-second story including one sound bite from Guilford Van der Hoyden-Smythe. "This dog seems to be on a mission," he said.

Time up. Old news now. New story.

The news readers reported a Sasquatch sighting in the wilds of the high desert plateau east of the Cascade Mountains. They both had to bite their cheeks to keep from laughing out loud.

The base of my spine tingled. I wanted—no—needed, to rent a car and drive up to Pendleton, Oregon, near the Oregon and Washington border and quite close to Tri-Cities, Washington. Also part of the high desert plateau east of the Cascades. Once there, I could check out the latest dog attack upon a Native American adolescent girl. Too far to go during the con. Monday would be too late.

And what was Guilford Van der Hoyden-Smythe doing there?

Needing to *do* something, I called my agent, Sylvia Watson. "What have you heard about Cynthia Stalking Moon?"

"Who?" She sounded distracted. I gulped an apology for calling so late. I'd forgotten the time difference.

"The Indian girl I wanted to help get back to her tribe."

"Oh, yeah, Cynthia Stalking Moon. Last I heard, the tribal lawyers were working on it. They'd found a second cousin willing to take her. Middle-aged man with grown children. Empty nest syndrome if you ask me."

"Is it done yet?"

"Don't know."

"Oh." The dog was still out there, and I didn't know for sure if Cynthia was safe.

Damn. No wonder my spine itched.

I gave Sylvia a brief progress report on the new book and disconnected.

I cursed and bit my nails. "Is this my fight, Scrap?" I asked.

He shrugged and dove back into the air conditioner like a ghostly cartoon.

▽▲▽▲▽

Curiouser and curiouser. There are no coincidences in imp lore. Nor are there any references to four-eyed scholars stalking a monster that should be stalked by my warrior. I need an imp version of the Internet to do some research. Lacking that, I just might have to figure out how to use Tess' laptop.

▽▲▽▲▽

I spent the next day jumping at shadows and avoiding bat wings. Those bat costumes creeped me out. Finally, after dinner—a sandwich grabbed at a nearby restaurant filled with con goers but no bats—I retreated to my room to change for the masquerade.

Dahling, don't tell me you're going to wear that *to judge the masquerade.* Scrap folded his stubby arms and looked offended. He took on a bilious yellowish-green color that made me feel sick just looking at him.

"What's wrong with this?" I twirled in front of him showing off my little black dress—which is really midnight blue since I hate wearing that much black—that I never travel without.

The skirt is too long. It cuts off in the middle of your calves and makes them look fat, Scrap sneered. He fluttered around me, sniffing and wrinkling his nose as if I smelled bad.

"Don't do that. I just had a shower."

Take it off, he insisted, tugging at the demure elbow-length sleeve that hid the lingering twin red marks left by the monster dog's teeth. They still itched but showed no sign of infection.

"No. I like this dress."

Why, pray tell?

"It's . . . it's practical."

It's ugly!

He was right. I looked ten years older and . . . heaven forbid, was returning to my former *lumpiness*.

"Oh, all right." I unzipped the soft crepe and flung it onto the bed. "What do you suggest I wear?"

Go play with your computer for ten minutes.

"I can't go out in just my black slip and I didn't bring another dress."

Hmm, that is a nice slip. Silk?

"You know it is. You picked it out." And the garment dripped lace.

I plunked down into the desk chair and awakened the laptop. I didn't dare get embroiled in my work in case I forgot to leave for the masquerade on time. So I played three hands of solitaire.

Hey, Blondie, I fixed your dress.

I groaned, dreading the result. Scrap had been known to crop dresses so short they showed my butt. While playing cards on the computer, I'd decided to wear my black slacks with the red silk blouse and black sandals with two-inch heels.

"Wow!" What else could I say. Scrap had sculpted the dress, slitting the side seam almost to my butt, removing the sleeves and plunging the neckline. I slipped into it and surveyed the result in the inadequate mirror.

"I look almost sexy. But I need makeup to cover that dog bite."

What do you mean, "almost"?

"I've got cleavage!"

And legs and a teeny, tiny waist. Every man in the room will be looking at you, babe, and not the costumes.

I turned side to side, surveying the transformation. "It needs a necklace."

Just that hematite pendant. Scrap dropped the gleaming black necklace in my hand.

Two minutes later I strolled (strutted) down the corridor to the staging area beside the main ballroom. A couple of Trekkers whistled. A pirate and his minion kissed my hand.

I tossed my loose curls and smiled.

Until I saw the bat troupe mingling with the crowd. They sported big blue ribbon rosettes—awards for hall costumes. Thankfully, that took them out of competition for the masquerade. I wouldn't have to touch their costumes to judge workmanship. The younger members had gone from furred hoods to full fur masks. I walked around them quite warily.

The tall man with the wings of silver hair paused to stare at me. He lifted his hand to smooth his braid with a wonderfully long-fingered hand (a habitual gesture?), showing the full breadth of his bat wings. He smiled.

I froze. Our gazes locked. I couldn't look away, couldn't move, totally entranced by the chocolate depths of his eyes.

That flash of teeth and the steadiness of his brown eyes reminded me of Dill.

Then he looked away.

I shivered and entered the private area as quickly as possible. Those bats could take all the fun out of this con for me.

Sunday morning, the last day of the con, when half the members walked around in zombie trances of fatigue, I slipped into a filk concert performed by a couple of acquaintances. I'd picked up their latest CD in the dealers' room and was anxious to hear them.

Scrap bounced and twitched in time to the music. *We don't have anything this good back home.*

"And where is your home?" I whispered.

Elsewhere. He never said anything more than that.

We were deep into a rousing version of a movie parody sung to a familiar tune when I felt a sharp tug on my hair. I jerked my head around. One of the bat children grinned at me. She had on black lipstick and kohl around her eyes. I glared at her and slapped her hand, with its unnaturally long fingers, away from my head.

Watch your left, babe, Scrap hissed at me. *She's just a diversion.* He bared his teeth and morphed to hot pink bordering on red.

Then I noticed a bat brother crawling up beside me, one hand (also with extra long fingers) reaching into my tote bag. I pulled it into my lap and hugged it close. What was in there to entice them, other than the challenge? Some bookmarks, autograph copy stickers, book covers minus the books, my con schedule, some aspirin, and a hairbrush. And the antique comb. I'd pulled it out of my hair an hour ago. The tines were beginning to irritate my scalp, and I noticed more very pale gold hairs breaking off every time I took it off.

Nothing of value. My wallet and room key were in a belt pack.

The children retreated.

I tried to enjoy the concert after that. But my mind kept returning to the black-clad brats. What did they want from my tote bag?

Gratefully, I flew home that night. That was the first con I hadn't thoroughly enjoyed in ten years.

Chapter 8

TWO WEEKS LATER, I had exhausted my creativity on the Internet with no luck in finding a reference to the monster dog. I spent hours looking through sixteen new research books on Native American religion and mythology. In the process I'd found a lot of material for my next book. Somehow, I'd also added four chapters to the current work in progress.

Still, I had nothing referring to a big ugly dog attacking adolescent Native American girls. Two more attacks had made the news, one in western Idaho, another near Spokane, Washington.

Sylvia Watson had not called with news that Cynthia Stalking Moon had returned to her clan. I worried about her as much as I worried about that damn dog.

Each report of a dog attack was accompanied by yet another Sasquatch sighting. An intrepid hiker had even managed some hazy footage of the beast on his camera cell phone. Those few frames could have been of a big hairy dog or a kid in a gorilla suit. No way to tell without more pixels in the pictures.

No one seemed to make a connection between the dog attacks and the Sasquatch sightings. I began to wonder if they were related. Most news readers passed the craziness off as symptoms of increased stress due to a downturn in the economy.

In order to stop the dog, I needed a cultural anthropologist who specialized in Native American lore of the Pacific Northwest. No one but me had the skills and determination to take it out. My instincts told me that. So did Scrap. He claimed that I had permission from the Sisterhood of the Celestial Blade to pursue the dog. As if I needed their permission for anything.

They'd kicked me out because I didn't conform to their ideals. I'd left their hidebound sanctuary gladly.

Hey, Blondie, Scrap called to me from his perch on the wrought iron spider hanging inside the fireplace of my office. He swung back and forth on the hook. His barbed tail twitched dangerously near the flames. It glowed red.

He jumped to his feet on the hearth and slapped his tail against the bricks. A few sparks fell harmlessly back into the fire as he blew on the burn.

I scooted my chair back to peer at him from my desk in the back parlor of the house. This room stretched the width of the house and contained an original, still-working fireplace big enough to walk into. The two smaller original rooms also had working fireplaces in the same chimney. I used the little rooms as a library and a private sitting room where I could entertain special guests or read.

"You are disrupting my concentration as usual," I replied, not all that upset.

You are turning into a computer potato, Tessie dahling. Time for a workout. Scrap had turned a pale orange all over to match his still hot tail.

Then I realized my muscles ached from inactivity. "What day is it?" I searched for the icon to open my PDA file.

Tuesday.

He came up with the information at the same moment I did.

"I'm going to the *salle*. You coming with me?" I closed down the computer and stretched my back, still seated.

You'd do better working out with the Celestial Blade in the basement. I'll coach you.

"Tomorrow, Scrap. I need confrontation with people to hone my reflexes. I also need to socialize. I'm turning into a grouchy hermit."

Surprisingly, Scrap agreed.

Before I could weave a path through piles of books and papers filed upon the floor, Scrap disappeared, then popped back with a whoosh of displaced air carrying my gym bag with two foils, an epee, and a saber sheathed and attached to the side with a special strap.

Clean jacket, knickers, mask, and glove inside, he told me. *You'll have to find your own shoes and socks.*

I looked down at my fuzzy green slippers in the shape of dragons and sighed. "Any idea where I left them?"

Your mother put them away.

I rolled my eyes upward. Who knew what interesting nook or cranny Mom had found to stow them in. Her idea of organization and mine were entirely different. At least she didn't dare clean up after me when I was home. Only when I left town for more than twenty-four hours did she ferret out all of the half empty coffee cups, dirty dishes, and laundry wherever I dumped them. Scrap cleaned, but at least he left things where I could find them!

"Okay, Coach will have to put up with my dirty running shoes and mismatched socks." Those I found on the first step. I had intended to take them up to my bedroom with me next trip. That had been last Thursday.

Twenty minutes later I walked into the *salle,* a good-sized storefront in an old strip mall. Coach had marked three lanes on the floor with duct tape. Two of the lanes were equipped with electronic equipment for competition fencers. I staked out the third lane. I didn't compete. I came here to hone my skills and reactions should I ever have to confront a demon with my Celestial Blade.

If Scrap could ever transform properly.

I had that funny feeling at the base of my spine. Something told me that I was headed for another confrontation with the monster dog.

No sooner had I stretched out and warmed up than someone tapped me on my shoulder.

A tall man with long dark hair pulled back into a tight braid, dressed in a European styled padded jacket, faced me. He smiled and showed brilliant white teeth against his bronzely tanned face. His teeth were brighter than the silver wings of hair at his temples.

Something familiar . . .

"May I have this bout, miss?" No discernible accent.

"I haven't seen you here before." I had seen him some-where else.

He shrugged. "I am visiting from . . . the West Coast."

"You look familiar."

He flashed those brilliant teeth at me once more.

My heart threw an extra beat. Soda bubbles danced through my veins.

"You signed a book for me in Portland a few weeks ago."

"Of course." I returned his smile and picked up my foil, whipping it back and forth a couple of times to test its balance. A stalling technique.

I'd have remembered him if he had stood in line at Simpson's. He'd stand out in any crowd, especially that one, which had been filled to overflowing with teenagers and young con goers, with only a sprinkling of people his age.

What was his age? His smooth face, without a trace of five o'clock shadow, and sparkling brown eyes placed him at early thirties. The silver in his hair pushed that guess up a decade or two.

I had seen him in Portland, though; driving a cream-colored BMW. He'd smiled and my fear of the little brown bat had vanished.

Then I'd seen him at the con in San Jose wearing a bat costume himself.

Something akin to warning flared at the base of my spine. But . . .

He smiled.

We moved onto the strip, four meters apart. Two more fencers took up positions on either side of the center line. My opponent and I saluted each other with upraised blades that we snapped downward with an appropriate whoosh through the air. We saluted our officials and then put on our protective masks.

The blade seemed to come alive in my grip, eager for me to use it. Niki, the assistant coach, had tweaked the alignment last time I'd been in. She did excellent work.

Gareth on my left called, *"En garde."*

I assumed the position, right foot pointed forward, left

foot ten inches back pointed outward at a right angle, both knees bent, weight to my center, foil held level, wrist straight, palm up, left arm behind my shoulder, hand up.

My opponent mimicked me. But he centered his weight over his front leg. An aggressive fencer. I watched him for other tells.

He used an Italian foil with a pistol grip that required the fencer to slip two fingers through rings. Impossible to knock the blade from his hand. Which is good if you are fighting a duel to the death. Those grips had been known to break fingers. That can ruin your day in sport fencing and knock you out of a competition.

"Fencers ready?" Gareth asked. His teenaged voice carried through the suddenly quiet *salle*.

I could hear my heart beat inside the enclosed mask.

"Ready," I replied, as did my opponent.

"Fence."

I crept forward, watching my opponent's blade and his eyes, what I could see of them through the black metal screens of our masks. He kept his head up, assessing, planning. He circled the tip of his blade, testing my reaction. I beat my blade against his once, knocking his blade aside and slid in, aiming for his *quarte*, the upper inside of his chest—the side opposite his weapon hand.

Lightning fast, he parried my attack and riposted to my exposed *sixte*, the upper outside—the side of my weapon hand. I parried that attack and withdrew one step. He followed, pressing me, rapid thrust after thrust. I gave ground, seeking a weakness, an opening.

Then before I could find a way beneath his longer reach he caught me with a *doublé*.

Did I say he was tall? Make that very tall with long arms and longer legs. He struck me at a distance that would require me to do a double advance and a full lunge. He only did a half lunge.

My heart raced. Heat flooded my face. I could learn from this man.

His broad shoulders and lean waist enticed me to explore more than his fencing technique.

"Halt," Gareth called. He recounted the last action and called the point good.

We backed apart, putting the full four meters between us. A long four meters. This time when Gareth called "Fence," I leaped forward and lunged beneath my opponent's attack while he was still planning.

My blade bent with the force of my thrust. I was close enough to smell the musky undertones of his sweat. My nose twitched and my body tightened with desire.

The score was one to one. Sometimes a surprise attack works against the most highly trained and skilled opponents. I'd have to remember that.

He countered my next lunge with one of his own. We met in the center, masks and bodies so close I could feel his heat and see his smile behind the mesh.

The bell guards of our foils clanged.

My senses sang.

"Halt. *Corps á corps!*" Gareth called. "If you two are close enough to kiss, you're too close to fence. Yellow card to both of you."

We backed apart. I had to bite my cheeks to keep a feral grin at bay.

For many long moments we battled, back and forth. My face and back dripped with sweat. The terry cloth band inside my mask caught most of it. But the occasional salty drop stung my eyes.

Every time I changed tactics, he met my attack and countered, always leading with a strong point and incredible flexibility.

If this bout were a duel to the death, I didn't know if I'd have the stamina to win through. Even with the added advantage of my Celestial Blade.

Told you, dahling, you need more work with a true weapon, Scrap whispered into the back of my mind. But he stayed away. I couldn't sense him near my left shoulder, his favorite perch.

The next clash of blades brought us *corps á corps* again, which gained us each a point but did nothing to dampen the heated sensuality of the match.

Finally, my opponent caught me with a wicked flick. He took the bout with a score of five to four.

We removed our masks and saluted, then moved together to shake hands—left-handed without gloves. Our gazes locked. His long fingers wrapped around my hand with something more than respect for a bout well fought.

We nearly exchanged promises with our eyes.

"Good bout," I said sincerely, trying not to pant.

His hand remained folded around mine. Little thrills of electricity raced up my arm to my heart. I forgot where and when I was.

"Sloppy, Tess," Coach Peterson said. He stood, hands on hips and with a deep frown of disapproval on his face. All the while his eyes twinkled with mischief and fire for good fencing.

Embarrassment burned my ears, and I finally dropped the stranger's hand. Then I pointedly stepped off the strip, clearing it for the next pair.

"You can't let a pretty face distract you, Tess. Your grip was too tight and your balance too far back," Coach continued his lecture. "Slowed you down."

"And as for you, my friend." He slapped the stranger on the back. "You overreached yourself the first three times she scored. You left your lower *octet* open and vulnerable. She caught you there on two of her points. Tess, let me formally introduce you to my old friend, Donovan Estevez. We trained together in Colorado Springs umpteen million years ago. He'd have made a good fencer if he wasn't so busy making millions in gaming software."

"Tess Noncoiré." I shook hands with him again, right-handed without gloves, needing to feel the warmth of his hand in mine. By this time we'd both opened the neck flaps of our jackets to dissipate body heat.

It didn't help.

"I know who you are. I've read all of your books—even the ones you wrote under a different name. The last one was worth the wait." Estevez smiled again, nearly blinding me with those teeth.

I slipped my hand free of his and dropped my eyes. I did not discuss the long years between my fifth book and my sixth, the most recent one.

No one knew about the year after Dill's death when I'd made myself sick with grief and locked myself away from reality in the Citadel of the Sisterhood. When I finally emerged, scarred, trained in many weapons, and accompanied by Scrap, I'd needed another half year to finish writing the book and sell it, then another nine months until it saw print.

"Enough mooning about. You can flirt over coffee after class," Coach intruded. "Drills, Tess. You need drills and concentration." He practically shoved me toward the back corner where Morgan, a twelve-year-old girl, awaited me. "Parry/riposte, until your arms threaten to drop off," Coach called after me.

I knew the girl; she'd make the Olympic team if she didn't get distracted by boys and high school in the next couple of years. No insult to drill with her. We stood nearly eye to eye.

I looked over my shoulder to see coach setting up a bout between Estevez and Gareth, the young man who had officiated for us. Gareth was quick and strong but lacked discipline and point control.

By the end of the evening, I'd fought seven bouts, winning all but that first one. I even managed a win against Niki, the assistant coach, in saber. She was the only one who defeated Donovan Estevez that night.

I dripped sweat, and was on an exercise high by the time the clock clicked over to nine. I needed coffee and carbs to replenish my body and calm my mind.

For those long two hours I had totally forgotten Scrap. But I could not forget Donovan Estevez. My eyes strayed to his whenever we had a moment to breathe between bouts.

We spent far too much time just staring at each other.

Coach gathered Estevez and me, along with three other adult students. We all headed toward the diner across the street that served the best pie on Cape Cod.

A decidedly yellow Scrap appeared out of nowhere and jumped into my gym bag, strangely subdued. He remained in the bag when I tossed it into the back seat of my car on the way to the diner. But he poked his head up long enough to hiss at me.

Watch yourself, Tess. He *smells wrong.*

Then I looked around the parking lot for Donovan Estevez. Scrap could only mean the newcomer.

Estevez dropped his gym bag into the trunk of a cream-colored BMW sedan.

My sense of danger flared at the base of my spine. At the same time, his dazzling smile threatened to swamp my common sense and willpower to resist him, or any man who was not Dill.

Oh, Tess, my love, what have we gotten into this time? I cannot come close to this man. I dare not let you get close to him. What does he smell like? Certainly not human. But not demon either. Something almost familiar. Like leather and sage and a dry musk, not acrid but not sweet either.

I need to make a quick circuit through the dimensions to trace that scent. I dare not leave my babe. Yet I cannot get close to her while that man holds her enthralled.

I wish she could find a nice, normal man to love. One who loves her as deeply as I do. One who has the right smell about him and won't be intimidated by her warrior calling. For it is a calling. A vocation. A way of life she can never give up.

Until she dies. And then I will die, too. For my life is tied to hers more completely than in a marriage or a mortal love.

For the first time since leaving the Citadel, I am truly afraid, for myself and for Tess.

Chapter 9

I WENT INTO THE diner cautious and withdrawn.

By midnight, Donovan and I sat alone, coffee cups empty, pie eaten, and totally fascinated with each other. At least he held my fascination. I presumed he was equally entranced by the way he held my gaze and looked longingly into my eyes.

He held my hand across the table. Little thrills invaded my sense of calm and rationality.

He admitted that fairly equal mixtures of Coleville Indian, Irish, Spanish, and Russian blood flowed through his veins. I confessed to my parents' French Canadian heritage, but not that Dad and his thirty-something male tennis instructor partner lived a few miles away from me, to Mom's total embarrassment.

We discussed politics, art, the state of the school system, the weather, and fencing. Often back to fencing and other blade weapons, fighting strategy, and the place of rules and honor in a battle.

The diner staff sat bleary-eyed and resentful in a corner booth, having already cleaned up and cashed out.

Scrap never made an appearance though he loved the old diner for its damp cellar.

Every time I paused to think about this oddity, Donovan smiled and I forgot to be worried.

When my yawns punctuated my sentences too heavily, Donovan paid the bill and escorted me back to my car.

"Nice car," I said when the conversation stalled, needing to become more personal or be abandoned. I didn't know which.

"It's a rental. I travel enough to reserve the same model I own. I don't want to have to think about where the windshield wiper switch is while driving strange roads." He grinned again and I forgot to breathe.

Dill had had the same effect upon me.

"May I follow you home?" he asked a bit wistfully.

"I can defend myself . . ." I replied, thinking only of the chivalrous meaning behind his words.

My body tightened with longing. Heat flashed from my breasts to my ears and downward. Could I? Dared I?

Would Dill haunt me in the middle of sex with another man?

"Oh, I'm sorry, not tonight. I have a lot of work to do before I leave town again Thursday morning." But, oh, I wanted him to take me in his arms and kiss me, lingering long, holding me tight, as we learned each other's bodies.

Some tiny part of Scrap's warning nagged at me.

"Where are you headed this time, Tess?"

"Tri-Cities, Washington. I'm GOH at High Desert Con."

"I have clients in Pascoe, Washington. Perhaps I can arrange to be there . . ."

I lifted my face, expecting his lips to meet mine.

He paused.

We looked at each other with longing.

His lips brushed my cheek.

Disappointed—and relieved—I got into my little hybrid car and started the engine before he could add any more persuasion to his request.

The moment I cleared the parking lot, Scrap popped onto the dashboard, pale red and puffing away at his smelly cigar. *About time you showed up, babe,* he snarled between clouds of acrid smoke.

I opened the window and let some chill night air in and some of the smoke out. And some of his noisome gas.

You want to do an Internet search on that guy, Tessie. He smells wrong.

"And you smell rotten from mold and cigars. Not to mention your lactose intolerance. You've been into the heavy cream again. Tonight I want to sleep in my own bed, not bent over the keyboard of the computer."

Maybe you should teach me to use the computer . . .

"Not on your life."

What if it means your life? He grinned around the cigar, showing his dagger-sharp teeth. His color paled, took on the greenish tinge of teasing.

I couldn't take him seriously when he showed his teeth and flapped his ears. He looked too much like a cartoon.

"Tonight I sleep. Tomorrow we search."

Monday, after the con, we go look at that motel. Maybe Dillwyn's death wasn't senseless. Maybe he was saving you from something worse than the fire.

"Like what?" I demanded, suddenly angry. I couldn't go back to that little place in Half Moon Lake, Washington. I just couldn't.

The tiny resort town built around a mineral lake was only a two hour drive north of Tri-Cities. I could rent a car, drive up after lunch, and be back at the con for a late dinner.

Like that guy that you left in the dust back there. Hooking up with him might be worse than burning at the stake. Scrap disappeared into that other dimension where I could not follow.

▽▲▽▲▽

"Donovan Estevez is CEO and founder of Halfling Gaming Co., Inc.," I said as I swept a wooden replica of the Celestial Blade through the air of my basement, testing the weight and balance. Each end of the quarterstaff curved into a sickle blade, one waxing and one waning. A dozen fine spikes extruded from the outside curve of the blades. Symbolically, I fought with the twin faces of the Moon Goddess Kynthia with the Milky Way flowing behind her like tresses blown in the solar wind.

I'd actually seen her face in the sky once. A considerable blessing according to my Sister warriors.

And only once. Most people never got the opportunity even if they knew what to look for.

The moment of peace, serenity, and connectedness to the universe I'd experienced in that instant of viewing the Goddess spurred me on to finish my training. Despite the tension and disagreements that grew steadily between me and the Sisterhood. All in hopes of catching another glimpse of the elusive star configuration and regaining that moment when I knew my place in the universe and why I existed.

I was still striving for that.

So you found out his company is legit. What about him? Scrap asked. He unfurled his wings. They'd grown a little and now supported him for short flights and extended his bounces. He fluttered about, daring me to catch him with the training blade.

I didn't know why he wore a pink feather boa draped around his neck. He usually played dress up with me, not himself.

He could only assume the blade's conformation when in the presence of something totally evil, like a being from another dimension—a demon. Hence the less lethal training blade that matched the true one in size, weight, and balance.

"Donovan's bio on the Web page mentioned an MBA from University of Florida. He's not married. Almost made the Fortune 500 list of most eligible bachelors."

I sensed a pattern in Scrap's movements. As he swooped up and to the right, I swung the left-hand blade to catch him on the downward spiral.

Only the boa tangled with the tines on the outside edge of my blade.

Fooled ya! Scrap chortled, yanking his garment free, scattering tiny feathers through the air and into my nose.

I sneezed as he arced farther right, almost behind me.

I spun in place and caught his tail in the spikes, dragging him away from the support beam that would hinder my swing.

"You did what?" I laughed as I released him with a twist of the blade.

Timing is better. But you can't play in the battlefield. You can't hurt me in this dimension. Attack for real. He bounced and tangled his tail around the staff at the opposite end. All of a sudden he put on weight and form, dragging my weapon down.

I compensated and flung him back toward the stairs. He landed with a gush of expelled air, odiferous from both ends.

The boa lay at his feet. He snatched it up and wound it around his neck.

"You are such a flaming queen," I snorted.

Am NOT! Scrap sounded genuinely affronted.

"Are, too! Why else would you wear a *pink* feather boa?"

Bcartlin demons have pink feathered ruffs around their necks. He fussed with the drape of the boa, getting it just right. It matched his pink skin perfectly. *You need to know their vulnerabilities.*

"And how would you know?" I stood over him, still balancing the blade.

Last time through the chat room they were on guard. He stuck out his receding chin.

"And just where is this chat room you mention but never explain?" A new tactic came to mind. I played it through three times, wondering if I was fast enough to make it work.

I'll take you there when you're ready. It won't make sense until then.

With a quick thrust I stuck the flat of the blade under his butt, scooped high, and twisted at the same time.

Scrap flew over my head and landed, face and belly flat against the far wall.

He slid down with a grunt, boa still in place.

"I thought you said I can't hurt you?" I dashed over to him, concerned when he lay there like a puddle of ectoplasm.

"Who are you talking to, Tess?" Mom called from the top of the stairs.

I cursed long and fluently under my breath as I stashed the Celestial Blade in the armory, a hidden cubbyhole beneath the stairs, and slammed the door. It latched automatically.

In the last second I grabbed the very visible boa and hid it behind my back. Nothing I could do about the flecks of pink feathers scattered around the floor. I just hoped Mom wouldn't notice them in the dim light from a single bare bulb overhead.

"I thought you went shopping in town, Mom," I called up to her. I leaned against the door to my secret room and panted a moment.

Scrap disappeared.

"I finished, dear. I hope you are doing laundry down there. You know you are leaving again tomorrow and I don't think you have a clean set of underwear anywhere in the house." She floated down the steep stairs like an elegant lady descending to a ballroom. Of course she wore heels and pearls; a lady did not shop wearing more casual clothing. I'd never be that graceful. Mostly because I didn't work at it like she did.

"Laundry's all done." I pointed to the piles of folded clothing, sheets, and towels atop the drop table across the back wall—well away from the armory. Thankfully, I remembered to use the hand that didn't hold the pink feathers. I dropped it into the shadows behind the stairs.

Damn! A glimmer of light shone beneath the door.

Scrap, please turn off that light, I pleaded silently. *If you don't, she'll be in there cleaning. Not a single saucer of mold will be left. Ever!*

"Here, Mom, will you carry these upstairs for me?" I dashed over to the laundry counter on the opposite wall and handed her a pile of towels. I'd even fluffed them in the dryer an extra time so she couldn't complain about how old and threadbare they had become.

A nanosecond before she turned back to face the stairs *and* the armory, the light beneath the door extinguished.

I breathed a sigh of relief, and Scrap returned to my shoulder. He looked his usual gray with just a hint of pink. No boa.

"Oh, Teresa." Mom turned around quickly, as she had when I was a teen and she was trying to catch me hiding a package of condoms or cigarettes.

I returned her peering survey of me with innocence.

Her gaze lingered on my left shoulder.

I knew Scrap made faces at her. The longer her gaze lingered, the more I began to sweat and the stiller Scrap became.

"Yes, Mom?"

"Uncle George just called. We've changed family game night from Sunday to tonight so you can come."

"I have to pack . . ."

"You have an hour before dinner to do that. I'm fixing my special *ragout au vin*."

"Mom, *ragout* is stew with wine, so if it's *ragout au vin*, do you double the wine?" I asked.

She snarled at me and retreated upstairs.

"I need your support tonight, Scrap," I whispered. "The only way they will let me get out of game night is if I answer every question correctly, even the sports and science questions."

You mean cheat? That's against the rules of the Sisterhood. Scrap sounded enormously happy at that prospect. *You'd cheat your own family?*

"With my family it's not cheating, it's survival. The rules of battle say survival comes first, honor and dignity second."

Donovan had said that last night.

I am not gay! What an insult. And from my babe, too. What would make her say that?

Imps can't be gay. Can they?

Ooooh, Mum would be murderously livid if she ever suspected one of *her* offspring leaned that way.

Maybe I should admit to it in Mum's presence just to put her knickers in a hot pink twist.

My babe doesn't care which way I lean. That's one reason why I love her so.

But I am not gay. I just like pretty clothes. That doesn't make me gay. I'm the weapon of a Celestial Warrior.

Tess is learning to think like a warrior. But will it be enough, soon enough? The fact that I grew a little bit after the abortive attempt to transform must mean that I will continue to grow each time we encounter evil. Each time the evil will grow worse, requiring more strength and agility from both of us.

Something looms just over the horizon. MoonFeather and her horoscopes can break through the veil of the future only a little. Only enough to see warning signs. Her talents help. Not enough.

Do I dare? Am I skilled enough to manipulate time to catch a glimpse of the future or the nature of our enemies? The least slip can trap me in that awesome dimension. The tiniest moment of inattention will make me vulnerable to the portal guardians. In the dimension of the future I have only my wits—no magic, nothing to help me.

The past is easier to view as long as I don't try to manipulate it. That leads to total disaster.

Tess needs me tonight. Any test of my skills with time must wait.

Uncle George really needs a comeuppance at game night. When he feels superior, gloating over a triumph in the game, he searches Tess' house for her secret stash of cash just so he can afford to get drunk. If we beat him at game night, maybe he'll go crawl back into his hole and leave the money and my mold alone.

Now what can I do to keep Mom out of here?

I know, I'll persuade Standish the standoffish ghost to prowl down here rather than in the butler's pantry. Mom fears that ghost more than any of the others, mostly because he wants to be alone and howls like a werewolf when we disturb him.

Chapter 10

"*T*ERESA!" MY OLD FRIEND Bob Brown greeted me at the miniscule Pascoe Airport. He enfolded me in a hug worthy of the black bear he resembled, (or was it a Sasquatch, so frequently in the news of late?). Six feet tall, two hundred twenty pounds of muscle, thinning, curly black hair against tanned skin. For once he'd trimmed his beard. He had a BS in nuclear physics and an MS in health physics. He worked at the local nuclear reservation developing shields against radiation.

"You've lost weight, kid. There's hardly enough of you to gather to my benighted bosom."

"Forty-seven-and-a-half pounds," I chortled, still proud of the fact I'd kept off the weight the fever had wasted from my frame. "I think you're mixing metaphors again, Bobby," I laughed as I extricated myself from his arms. Tears came to my eyes unbidden. I hadn't seen my friend since Dill's funeral. A lot had happened since then. Quite a lot.

"You okay? Dill went so suddenly, and I didn't hear from you for so long, I was afraid you'd cracked up."

"I nearly did. But it's been nearly three years, Bob. I've finished grieving and moved on."

Yeah, right, Scrap mumbled from atop my laptop case.

"Ready to move on to me?" Bob asked hopefully. His nose worked like it itched. "Do you smell cigar smoke?"

"Wishful thinking, Bob. You gave up smoking ten years ago." I grabbed the handle of the wheeled case and dragged it, and Scrap, toward the baggage claim area. Bob had no choice but to follow.

"How many cons have we been to together since we met freshman year at Providence U, Tess? A hundred? Two? And you still don't love me enough to marry me."

"More wishful thinking. You're my best friend. Let's not spoil it." I waved a skycap over.

"You don't even trust me enough to carry your bags?" He pouted, but a smile tugged at his mouth. We'd known each other too long for us to take such banter seriously.

"I don't travel light anymore. Especially when you are tipping the skycaps," I teased.

"You really don't travel light anymore," he whistled as I claimed two oversized suitcases and three boxes full of books fresh from the publisher.

"One of those books has your name on it, the rest are for the dealer's room. There was a warehouse glitch in getting the order here in time."

"I tried to be easy on you with the schedule, Tess, so we can go filking." Bob loved sitting up in a ballroom all night swapping parody tunes and Celtic lays with all and sundry. I did, too, once upon a time.

"I haven't sung since . . . no, Bob, I'd rather not."

"Dill was a good man, Tess. Maybe you should sing something in memory of him. Get yourself some real closure."

"What? 'There's a Bimbo on the Cover of my Book'? That was his favorite."

"Is there a bimbo on the cover of your book?"

"Not this time. My publisher went tasteful for a change. They even spelled my name right."

For my first five books I'd written as Teresa Newcombe so readers could remember it and spell it correctly, though the copyright had always been as Teresa Noncoiré. When I had reemerged from my self-imposed exile, Teresa Newcombe was a fading memory among the powers that be in the book world. My publisher wanted a new name on the book he promised to push onto the best-seller lists. I decided to stick to my legal name. I'd never planned to take on Dill's name of Cooper. Fans had no trouble pronouncing or spelling Noncoiré after the book hit five best-seller lists including the *NYT*.

"A filk would be more appropriate for Dill than a hymn or dirge. Just promise to sing at my funeral." Bob hugged me again.

"Since I plan for you to outlive me by at least a decade, that might be a little hard."

"Oh, you'll come back as a ghost to haunt me at every con we've ever been to together."

Laughing, we made our way out to the parking lot, trailed by the overloaded skycap.

Bob drove into the porte cochere of the hotel five minutes from the airport. I got out without waiting for him or the valet to open my door. Eagerly, I arched and stretched my back, checking my surroundings for unexplained shadows as I had been taught by my Sisterhood. In the still warm night air of the high desert plateau of the Columbia River, I spotted a familiar cream-colored BMW across the parking lot.

Pointedly, I did not look closer. If Donovan Estevez had followed me here, he would find me. But he would not surprise me.

"Bob, are there any anthropology professors at the community college who specialize in local Indian lore?" I asked as I registered and the bellhop struggled with my luggage.

"Excuse me, I happen to have several anthropology degrees," a clipped voice remarked at my other elbow.

I closed my eyes a moment to master my irritation. Scrap bounced around the high counter, blinking shades of neon green.

"Guilford Van der Hoyden-Smythe." I turned to confront the tall nerd who had stalked me in Portland. "If you specialized in Pacific Northwest native lore, you might have had answers to my questions three weeks ago."

My dear friend held out his hand to introduce himself. "Bob Brown, I'm guest liaison and programming chair for the con."

"Call me Gollum." Van der Hoyden-Smythe reached across me and shook Bob's proffered hand vigorously.

Just then three people, two female, one male, wearing jeans and T-shirts and demon masks sauntered past. Very good demon masks at that. One had numerous tentacles dangling from wrinkled purple skin. I could not detect where the mask ended and their hair began. The other two had the furred faces of bats.

Bob draped an arm about my suddenly cold shoulders. He knew about my phobia. As long as they didn't show their wings, I'd be okay, though.

Gape-mouthed, Gollum stared at them.

"Don't worry. That's rather mild for costuming at this con. Wait until the masquerade on Saturday night." I patted his arm in reassurance. He kept staring at the con goers.

"Part of the game is for them to stay in character, so don't be surprised if you hear them speaking nonsense words pretending it's a demon language." Bob said straight-faced. But not for long.

We both burst out laughing in memory of the time a Klingon had ordered a beer in Klingon at this very con five years ago. Bob and I had called the puzzled waitress over and suggested she serve the man prune juice. She did. No other Klingon dared order anything in any language but English after that.

I guess imitators aren't as tough as the real thing. Prune juice is, after all, a warrior's drink. They served it every morning at the Citadel of the Sisterhood.

I sobered instantly with that memory.

"I don't know any anthro profs at the college, but the guy who owns the Stalking Moon brew pub is full-blooded Sanpoil Indian—that's part of the Colville Confederation. He's full of tribal stories. We could have dinner and a tankard there," Bob suggested to both of us.

My senses flared. "Stalking Moon?"

"Yeah. Leonard Stalking Moon owns the place."

"Let the bellhop stow my luggage in my room. I'm starving. Take me to the pub now." I marched back out to the covered drive knowing both men would follow me.

Scrap landed on my shoulder, chortling and puffing away. I calmly reached up and took the cigar out of his mouth. It dripped pink slime as I tossed it into the bucket of sand placed outside for that purpose.

"Stay quiet, watch, and listen closely," I whispered to him.

I'll watch you fend off two admirers any day, he laughed. *This is going to be fun.*

"This is work," I whispered back as cold dread swept through me. I was getting closer to a battle with demons. "Special work that we have trained for."

We are never fully trained until we survive the first full battle.

"We've had one battle."

Fighting off that dog with a fireplace poker was not a true battle. Not a true test of our skills, our lives, and our vocation. But it is coming. Trust me.

Interlude

A WARRIOR IN TRAINING sends out pheromones that will attract every imp who can squeeze through the portal and all those on the loose. A kind of mating ritual was about to begin. But this joining of two beings had nothing to do with marriage and propagation. It had everything to do with survival.

Normally all the available imps will gather around the training field. The candidate bouts with her Sisters. She works up a sweat, straining muscles and ingenuity to score, something opens in her mind, and she will see an imp. Not all of them yet. But one. The special one she is most suited to meld with.

I had to be that imp. I had to fight off my bigger brethren so that I was the only imp on the field that day.

The imps who came to the choosing field that day were all fully grown, aware of their powers and their need to meld with a warrior. For imps are incomplete and without honor if they cannot bond.

But I am older than all of them. Stunted I may be in body, the runt of Mum's litters. My mind and ingenuity are far more developed than theirs. How else could I survive my one hundred two siblings? And Mum.

Life among imps is harsh. It has to be. Only the best survive. My sibs learned that from me the hard way. I knew I was something special because I had survived though I should have died a century ago when I failed to grow to full size.

Imps expect their brethren to fight fair. But life isn't fair. Demons don't fight fair. I pulled every dirty trick I could think of: gouging eyes, tying tails in knots to destroy balance, shredding wings with my hind claws while I dug out warts on faces. Whatever eliminated my competition.

When Tess walked onto the training field that day, strong, fit, and fully recovered, but inexorably scarred by the imp flu, only I awaited her. A torn ear, nearly severed tail, and beautiful bruises all over (two new glorious warts) but I was there.

"So this Citadel sits directly upon a portal between reality and the demon world," I said with a straight face. The night I had witnessed the Goddess in the sky had convinced me. The warrior Sisterhood had some serious enemies. But I had yet to see any evidence those enemies were demons and not mortal predators.

Sisters Paige, Mary, and Electra nodded.

"And we are from the world of mortals, but this Citadel exists in neither that realm nor the one of demons; somewhere in between," I continued. Just to make certain I had the facts straight, as weird and unbelievable as they might seem. Seem to them. I had yet to be convinced.

I had to concentrate. My mind had already begun constructing a new book, an entire series based upon what was going on here.

I'd started writing it on a lined spiral notebook with a stubby pencil. In the evenings, I told stories to the Sisters, making them a part of the story. Some thoroughly enjoyed the novelty. Others . . . ? Most of the older Sisters, especially Sister Gert, the leader, and those so entrenched in the life here and so long cut off from the world they had lost most of their memories of reality, scoffed and scorned and tried to get me to stop my tales. Those Sisters had no use for books, fiction or non. They had no television, no computers. No electricity to run them. And only a primitive plumbing system to provide sanitation.

I was bored out of my gourd except for my new book!

And I'd only been on my feet and training a month. A total of three months here. How was I supposed to remain here the rest of my life and stay sane?

We occupied our days with training. This morning I stood easily in the middle of a sandy square, about five meters to the side, in the middle of the Citadel courtyard. The three arms mistresses all looked alike to me: medium height and stocky build with lots of muscles in arms, legs, and torsos. Not a bit of fat on any of them. But then, I didn't have any fat left on my body either. The fever had eaten it away and no matter how much I ate, I'd only regained about two of the fifty pounds I had lost.

After only a month of working out, my entire body had become whipcord lean and strong.

For the first time in my life I was not pudgy. In fact I was downright skinny. Ten pounds underweight instead of forty over. To my eyes I looked positively anorexic.

But I was strong. And gaining fitness and stamina by the day.

Paige, on my left, had a shock of black hair pulled back into a tight bun. Mary's wispy blond curls framed her face like an angelic halo. Electra had a bigger bust and lots of fiery red hair that clashed with her bloodred workout clothes. All three had long scars from temple to jaw to match mine. Theirs had faded to a thin white line. Mine still looked red, raw, and angry.

"If there is a portal, why can't it be sealed?" I asked. "And what's to keep demons from finding and opening another?" I needed those answers to satisfy my own curiosity as well as to plot the next scene in the new book.

The arms mistresses looked at each other. Some silent communication passed between them. "No questions," they spoke in unison.

Electra stepped forward one pace, the obvious spokeswoman of the group. "You'll stop talking and learn to fight properly when you face a Kajiri demon head-on with only a Celestial Blade for a weapon." She tossed me a quarterstaff with strange hooked ends.

I caught the thing easily. It balanced well in one hand.

"What kind of wood is this?" I asked, fascinated with it. The curved blades on either end seemed just as sharp as a steel sword.

"We call it imp wood. It is an exact replica of the weapon that will come to you when you face a demon. We are here to teach you how to use it." Paige picked up her own weapon, a duplicate of mine, from a nest of them at the edge of the sandy workout plot. She took a stance, feet spread, knees bent, back straight, staff balanced easily in both hands.

I mimicked her pose.

"Copy me move for move," Paige said. She raised the right end of her staff and thrust it forward.

My move blocked hers.

"Good. Again."

We played with the staffs for a good twenty minutes, increasing the speed and force of each move until we were both covered with sweat and my arms shook with the unaccustomed activity. The most exercise I'd had since I nearly failed physical education my freshman year at Providence U.

Then Mary jumped into the square with her own staff. The two of them went at me in unison. I barely had time to wipe the sweat out of my eyes when Electra took over for the two of them. She put me through my paces at twice the speed and ferocity of the other two combined.

My knees trembled, my heart beat overtime, and my lungs labored before she let me call a halt.

She'll do, a strangely accented voice called from behind my left foot.

I looked. No one stood behind me.

"Lower," Sister Gert, the head of the Sisterhood, commanded me. She sounded . . . disappointed or disapproving. I couldn't tell which. But then she didn't much like me because I wanted to know everything and anything about this place and the people here, all at once.

I looked at my feet.

A translucent imp, tinged with the same green as the fresh flower sprouts two plots over, stared back at me with huge eyes. His bat-wing ears flapped, showing off a rippled rainbow of colors along the serrated and torn edges. He grinned, showing pointed teeth beneath his snub nose. He rested his taloned paws on his pot belly. His tiny wings fluttered in the slight breeze.

"What is that?" I raised my staff ready to smite the thing.

"No, don't." Electra grabbed the staff away from me. "That's your imp. You need to ask his name."

"My what?" I rounded on the three. Each had a similar being perched on their shoulders. The imps took on shades of lavender. They looked larger, more fully formed than the little thing at my feet. And they all had full-sized wings that rose above their heads in sharp and hooked points. The tips of the appendages dipped well down the backs of the women whose shoulders they sat upon.

Even Sister Gert had one. Bigger than all the rest.

"We all have them," Paige explained. "Our imps."

"That sorry excuse for an imp is the only one that showed up to claim you," Sister Gert snorted, as if the imp reflected the sort of Sister I would make.

My knees gave out, and I plunked onto the churned sand at my feet. Between fatigue and shock I was done in, incapable of absorbing anything more.

The little imp hopped into my lap and stared at me in frank appraisal. I couldn't even feel his weight he was so insubstantial. *Can't fight demons sitting down, babe.*

"Oh, shut up!" I buried my face in my hands, unsure if I should cry or laugh out loud.

"Ask his name!" Mary said quietly. "He's not fully yours until you exchange names, and we can't get on with your training until you have an imp."

"Okay, I'll bite. What's your name, imp?"

Scrap will do for now, he said, or sneered. I couldn't be sure which.

"Scrap? Because you're just a scrap of an imp?" The ridiculousness of the situation and my total exhaustion took me. I rolled on the ground unable to contain my laughter.

Sister Gert stalked off in high dudgeon.

I'd always wanted to use the word. Now I had the perfect example. And a place to put it in the book.

The imp—Scrap, I should say—pulled my hair and pinched me hard.

I sobered instantly.

Stop laughing, you miserable, no-good excuse for a warrior. Do you know what I had to go through to get here?

Only then did I notice just how battered and bruised he looked. I thought I was too tired to care about anything, even Sister Gert's disapproval. But my heart went out to the little beast.

"Sorry, Scrap."

"Your name," Sister Mary said gently. "You have to tell it your name."

"I'm Tess," I said, looking into Scrap's eyes. "That's Tess, not Teresa and not babe."

Right, dahling, Scrap drawled. The thing wiggled and settled himself. Then he hopped onto my shoulder with a flutter of his stubby wings. They barely aided his ascent.

"I guess we are well suited for each other," I sighed. "What is it you do exactly?"

"He becomes your Celestial Blade when you face the demons in battle." Paige prodded me with her wooden replica weapon.

"Until a demon is present, you must train with imp wood." Sister Mary took a fighting stance.

Grab your blade, dahling, they're gonna attack, Scrap warned me.

I rolled and rose to my feet, blade in hand, in one smooth move, blocking three attacks within as many heartbeats.

<hr />

The melding has begun.

Chapter 11

Vampire bats do not suck blood. They make tiny cuts in the skin of large birds, cattle, horses, pigs, and upon occasion, humans. Then they lap the blood from the wounds.

"*L*EONARD STALKING MOON, this is my good friend Tess," Bob introduced me to the owner and brewmaster of a local pub.

I shook hands with the stocky Native American, not much taller than I, older by at least a decade. Hard to tell with his near hairless mahogany skin. He wore his sleek black hair in two long braids. A harelip scar marred his upper lip.

He looked me up and down with the same intensity I gave him.

"Are you any relation to Cynthia Stalking Moon?" I asked quietly, hoping Van der Hoyden-Smythe was too occupied ordering drinks and pizza for all of us to hear my question.

"My second cousin's daughter." He finished his appraisal of me and pointed to a photo of a smiling adolescent girl behind the bar. Cynthia's picture stood out among the dozens of photos of happy patrons.

"She looks happy," I said. She also looked less gaunt and strained than she had at the park. But that was an unusual situation. "Is she with you yet?"

"Yes, thanks to you, Tess Noncoiré. I hope you know

how special is our Cynthia," Leonard replied almost in a whisper. "My daughter Keisha wanted her. She has fancy degrees and works in a museum, but she lives in Seattle. Cherry and I thought Cynthia would be happier here."

"She told you about me?"

"Everything." He looked closely at my left shoulder, then nodded.

I gulped. Had he seen Scrap? If so, did he know what the imp represented?

"My family, my entire tribe, owes you much," Leonard said, handing me a foaming glass of ale with a strange purple cast. "On the house. A very special brew with huckleberries, only for family and special friends. Very special friends who are almost family. For you, Bob, and your friend, everything is on the house tonight."

I smiled my thanks to him.

"Tomorrow, you speak to the high school and middle school English class. Cynthia will be there. She will thank you personally." He smiled hugely, showing an endearing gap between his upper front teeth and a twinkle in his eye that reminded me of MoonFeather.

Then I noticed a necklace of some sort tucked beneath his shirt. Only a little bit of knotted hemp showed around his open collar. MoonFeather had shown me a similar one in a book. That was a shaman's knot. Leonard Stalking Moon probably did see beyond this reality.

"You and I will talk more later. About just how special Cynthia is." I looked pointedly at his necklace.

He blushed and tucked it deeper beneath his short sleeved sports shirt so that it didn't show.

"Your thanks are appreciated but not necessary. I was just doing my job," I demurred.

"I know."

"Will you sit with us a few moments? We have questions about the dog."

"In a bit. I have other customers right now." He moved to the end of the bar and served several more drinks.

"What was that about?" Bob asked, jostling my elbow so that I almost spilled my mug of beer.

No way to avoid telling him at least some of the tale. He'd never believe most of it.

"Well . . . let's sit down first." I wended my way between scarred and scuffed tables to the booth Gollum had claimed. The new building worked hard at looking old and rustic with rough planked walls and floors. The many windows were high and curtained, the lights electrified oil lamps.

"What did he say?" Gollum asked the moment I sat down across the table from him, next to Bob.

"He'll join us in a bit. I think he knows something about the dog."

"What dog?" Bob asked.

I let Gollum fill him in. Thankfully, the man left out the crucial point about Scrap becoming a poker and any reference to the Sisterhood of the Celestial Blade Warriors.

As Gollum finished, he took off his glasses and scrubbed his face with his hands. He looked weary.

For the first time I could look into his pale blue eyes. Really look. Our gazes met, and trust flowed between us as if we had known each other for ages.

Or perhaps in another time and dimension.

Those thoughts shocked me. I filled my books with ideas like that. I never considered that it could happen to me. Could happen in reality, anywhere outside the pages of a fantasy book.

I leaned against the high straight back of the booth and closed my eyes. Closed Gollum out of my thoughts.

"So you followed Tess here just to find out about a stray dog?"

I didn't add that Gollum had stalked the dog across three or four states.

Bob shook his head incredulously. He also moved his hand to cover mine, laying claim.

His hand was warm and comforting. The contact lacked the electricity of Donovan Estevez's touch.

Naughty, naughty! Scrap chortled. *Letting poor Gollum believe you are taken.* He slurped some of the foam off the top of my glass.

I made a casual gesture, as if shooing away a fly, that sent Scrap sprawling onto the floor, under the feet of two couples getting up to dance. He had to scramble to keep from getting crushed.

Of course he could have popped into another dimension. But then he might miss something.

"What's so important about a stray dog?" Bob asked. He downed a considerable portion of his porter. "Send a sharpshooter after it. No more problem."

"Trust me, Bob, this is no ordinary stray dog." I considered my next words carefully. Bob might be an avid reader of science fiction and fantasy, but his belief in the supernatural was limited to his Christian religion.

"Bob, this dog is like something out of my books. Beyond the reach of an ordinary sharpshooter. Beyond the size and strength of any mortal dog."

Both he and Gollum stilled for a long moment.

A tingle grew out of the base of my spine. I looked about the pub, peering into the shadows. I expected to see the dog, green slime dripping from its jowls.

Scrap turned bright pink and took up a defensive position near my hand.

Leonard Stalking Moon narrowed his eyes and lifted his harelip in a snarl as the front door opened.

I half stood, ready to face the demon dog we had been discussing.

Donovan Estevez sauntered into the pub as if he owned it. He brought with him two young ladies and a young man. From their T-shirts, I recognized them as the kids with the demon masks. Thankfully, they'd left the masks off for a public appearance outside the con. The bartender—not Leonard—carded Donovan's friends but let them enter.

Donovan surveyed the room, flashing that brilliant smile.

I relaxed instantly, and my belly warmed. Nothing to fear here. The tingle of warning evaporated and I waved in greeting to a man I considered a friend and wanted as a lover.

Scrap remained quite bright as he popped out of this dimension. *See ya later, babe, when stinky man is not around.*

I knew I should pay attention to Scrap's implied warning. I knew it. Yet Donovan's welcoming smile and my blossoming affection for him clouded my senses. He and his friends sat at the table adjoining our booth and proceeded to monopolize the conversation. I didn't care. My weekend was complete.

Bob and Gollum faded in significance.

Leonard Stalking Moon avoided our table for the rest of the evening, and I learned nothing new about the dog.

The stinky man drove me away. He came too close to Tess and drove me away. What is he? There is nothing in imp lore to account for him or his friends.

Leonard Stalking Moon knows about me somehow. He must be a shaman. I wonder if I can communicate with him. He might know something about Donovan. He might be able to tell me how to stay close to Tess when he is around. I know that she needs me.

Even if she does not think so. All he has to do is smile and she succumbs to his every wish.

But I have noticed something. I will try something when she is alone.

Donovan escorted me back to my room when we'd all eaten and drunk our fill. I thought I'd have trouble ditching Bob and Gollum, but those two seemed to have bonded. They had role-playing games they wanted to check out.

The three young people in Donovan's wake evaporated.

The huckleberry ale was wonderful, leaving me mellow.

Now that I had him alone, Donovan filled my vision and my thoughts. Perhaps tonight I might, just might, get over my lingering inhibitions and doubts. Perhaps tonight I'd let him stay with me in the huge suite paid for by the con.

He held my hand in the elevator as it creaked noisily to the third and top floor of the sprawling hotel. At my door he lifted my hand to his lips. His eyes met mine in silent inquiry.

Heat flooded my face and a little thrill sent moisture to places in my body I thought I'd forgotten in the last two and a half years.

"Would you like to come in for a drink?" I couldn't believe my voice sounded so breathless and . . . anxious.

Inside the living room of the suite Donovan pulled me into his arms. Our mouths eagerly sought each other.

I melted under the firm pressure of his mobile lips. We came up for breath. My balance deserted me. He held me firm against his long, lean body.

We came together again in a searing kiss. His fingers tangled in my hair. I delighted in stroking the length of his black braid. No fair that his hair was prettier than mine.

In that moment I didn't care about the mystery that surrounded him. I just wanted him to hold me, make the delicious champagne bubbles coursing through my blood go on forever.

We stumbled toward the sofa, too intent on touching each other to care where we landed. He braced his weight on his elbows on top of me, eagerly exploring my neck with his wonderful mouth. The buttons of my cotton knit shirt fell open with just a touch. I yanked his shirt tails free of his jeans the better to run my hands up his hairless, muscled back to his broad shoulders.

A touch of shyness made me reach behind me to turn out the lamp on the end table. As I fumbled for the switch on the base of the lamp my fingers brushed the antique comb. It fell to the floor.

How had it gotten there? I hadn't even unpacked yet. My luggage was piled at the foot of the bed in the other room.

Before I could think of an answer, my skin cooled and my brain cleared just a little.

"Don't turn away from me now, L'akita," he whispered.

"Just for a moment. Not anymore," I answered on a spare breath. His gaze latched onto mine, and I lost whatever stray thought or doubt had flitted through my mind.

The world dissolved in a flurry of kisses and caresses. Our clothes landed in a tangle on the floor.

We came together in a glory of sensation. He coaxed and teased me into ever-heightening explosions of joy.

Replete, we lay cuddled together for a long time on the sofa. We didn't need words, we just needed to lay there with our arms about each other, my head tucked between his shoulder and his chin.

Eventually, we moved to the shower where we came together again.

Then we tumbled into the big bed, content to use only a third of it.

Sometime in the middle of the night he reached for me again. I opened to him eagerly. We slowly explored new ways to delight each other. Then as we fell asleep, he mumbled something into my hair.

I thought he said, "I love you, L'akita."

But I couldn't be sure.

I was too exhausted to react. Instead I savored a special warmth beneath my breastbone.

I might be falling in love with him, too.

Chapter 12

Scientists give bats names containing the word chiroptera, Latin for handwing. Most of a bat's wing structure is supported by the elongated five-fingered hand, including a thumb.

DAWN CREPT AROUND the edges of my perceptions. I cracked an eye half open. The digital clock showed big red numbers somewhere around six-thirty.

Donovan's arm lay across my waist, heavy, possessive, welcome.

I basked a few moments in the aftermath of being thoroughly loved by a very handsome man.

My mind spun and my fingers itched to write, as they did every morning about this time.

And my bladder was full.

Time to get up. I lifted Donovan's arm and wiggled out from under. He mumbled something, and he reached for me again.

"Later," I said as I scooted to the edge of the bed.

Something hard jabbed me. I squeaked and looked about for the offensive object.

The antique comb lay beneath me. I grabbed it with the intent of throwing it across the room in irritation.

Something in the luster of the gold knotwork grabbed my attention.

I sat up to put a little distance between Donovan and myself.

"Second thoughts, L'akita?" he whispered. He placed his hand on my thigh.

"It's been a long time. I haven't been with anyone, wanted to be intimate with anyone, since my husband died." I turned the comb over and over in my hands, examining it from every angle, falling in love again with the delicate filigree along the back. The abstract design suggested flowers, perhaps Celtic knotwork. I couldn't be sure. It seemed to change with each new slant of light.

"A long time to be alone. A woman as beautiful as you should not be alone." He lifted my hair and kissed my neck. "You aren't alone anymore."

Delicious shivers ran up and down my spine.

Not knowing what else to do, I twisted my hair up and secured it with the comb.

I shuddered as a stray draft worked its way through the French doors and wrapped around me. More than a draft. A ghostly presence. I'd lived with ghosts in the house on Cape Cod for too long not to recognize it, and I felt my mood change.

"I'm sorry, Donovan. In many ways, I still feel married to Dill. I feel like I've betrayed him." A cold lump gathered in my belly.

"A live man I could compete with. A ghost I cannot." He withdrew from me physically and emotionally. "The time will come, L'akita, when you banish this ghost. Only you can do it. When you do, I want to be the first man waiting in line for your affections. Your passions." He dropped a kiss on top of my head and departed. At the door he blew me a kiss.

Something in his posture, the swagger in his walk, something sent a frisson of fear into my throat, threatening to cut off my breathing. The indirect lighting gave him a visible aura, part a golden luster inviting trust, part black and impenetrable.

I swallowed deeply to master my fear and confusion.

"Donovan, were you one of the bat people in San Jose two weeks ago?" I knew he had been. I needed him to admit it.

"You recognized me?" He came back into the room, pulling on his clothes.

"Your posture, the way you walk." I gulped, not certain if I could ever look at him in the same light again. The delight his long-fingered hands had given my body turned to revulsion.

A bat. Anything but a bat.

How had I forgotten the bat family last night when I succumbed to the desire that still plagued me?

Two of the bat children tried to steal my tote. Had he fathered either one of them? Or both? And, if so, where was their mother?

"You had other issues. We had not been introduced. I had family with me. My family can be overwhelming." He smiled crookedly.

I laughed a little. "So can mine." I had to know. "Were any of those children yours?" I put on a bright smile, as if I had thought they were cute in their horrid bat costumes.

"No. Nieces and nephews, and one a half sister. My father took a new and very young wife. I have not yet had the luck to meet a woman I wanted to have children with. Until now."

That thought lingered between us for several meaningful, almost wonderful heartbeats. It changed our relationship completely. A quickie at a con wasn't going to be enough, or the end of it.

The blackness around him competed with the gold. What was going on? Who was he really?

"I'm glad Coach introduced us."

"A lucky happenstance."

"I won't have doubts forever, Donovan."

"I'll plan on it, L'akita. I'll catch up with you later. At the con. You have a panel at two?"

"I'll look for you."

The door snicked closed with barely a whisper.

I felt colder and lonelier than I had in a long time.

"How could you, Tess? How could you betray me with *him!*" Dill said, sitting beside me.

He didn't startle me. I knew he was a part of the cold drafts swirling around my body and my heart.

"Don't you like Donovan?" I asked. "Do you want me to be alone the rest of my life?" Anger began to boil up inside me. Anger that he still had such a strong hold on my emotions.

Anger that he had deserted me by dying.

"You promised to be faithful to me as long as we both shall live."

"You aren't alive anymore. You died in my arms, Dill!" I jumped up and threw a robe over my naked body.

I had to get some perspective, some distance from this specter.

"I'm not completely dead, Tess. I can come back. You won't have to be alone, you won't have to waste your affections on the likes of *him*. All you have to do is get rid of the imp. Then I can be with you always. I can be your weapon as well as your lover."

I paced. What did I truly want? Who did I trust? The man I had loved so well in life, and in death, or the man that sent my senses soaring and engaged my mind? Logic began to percolate in my foggy brain.

"How?"

"How what?" Dill returned.

I peered at the insubstantial form sitting on the over-sized bed in the sumptuous suite. He looked just as I remembered him from the last night before the fire; clad in jeans and a western-cut checked shirt. Hiking boots on his narrow feet and a Stetson perched on the back of his dark, glossy head. No trace of soot or of strain marred his face. His skin had color, a ruddy tone darkened to bronze by hours spent hiking in the sun in search of geological specimens.

And I could see right through him. I could never embrace a ghost as I had a living man.

"How could you become a weapon? Would you be the Celestial Blade?"

"Nothing so mundane, lovey." He gave me his special smile, the one that reminded me of Donovan.

But the sight of his grin no longer melted my knees or drove logical thought from my head. The magic was gone. My vision was clear.

He was dead.

I wanted to cry that only a ghost would call me that now.

Donovan had called me "L'akita." I didn't know what it meant, but it sounded special.

"I would be different. Better, more effective," Dill insisted. "You won't need the imp in battle or that traitor in your bed."

"Show me."

"I can't."

"Why not?"

"We are not in the presence of great evil."

"You're lying."

"Tess! How could you. I love you. I could never lie to you."

"Because I could always tell. From the first moment we met, I could tell when you stretched the truth. After that, you never dared lie to me, even when you came home late with the smell of tequila on your breath."

A memory startled me. We had both drunk a lot during those short three months of our marriage. Dill more than me, though. I could barely remember a time when one or both of us didn't have a drink in hand.

I shuddered at the thought that perhaps the great love of my life had been nothing more than a drunken haze.

"I can see that you need more time. You need to experience more evil and the limitations of your imp before you can fully embrace me. Before I leave you, remember all the books I made you read when I discovered how you felt about bats."

Knowing facts about the ugly critters hadn't helped my phobia, but I did remember odd things now and then, like the chiroptera—the handwing bone structure that supported the wings.

Donovan and the bat children all had very long fingers.

But his knees did not rotate backward like a bat's so that they can launch into flight from hanging upside down. I knew exactly how Donovan's knees were shaped. I'd kissed the back of them and tasted the salty sweat of his thighs.

Dill vanished as swiftly as he had come.

I wrapped my arms around myself trying to still the cold trembling of my limbs and my chin.

"Scrap, where are you? I miss you."

Right here, dahling. Never far. Just sometimes out of reach. That man drives me away.

"Which one?"

The one who doesn't smell right. A ghost has no smell.

"Did you ever stop to think that maybe you can't be close to us because he is meant to be my lover and we need a little privacy?"

I know how to be discreet. I know when I should pop out for a minute.

"How about for an hour?"

Lots of things I can do in an hour. Or overnight. If I thought you were safe without me. I don't think you're safe with that man. If he is a man.

"What is that supposed to mean?" Oh, how I ached for that man. I really wished now I hadn't driven Donovan away with my blasted sense of guilt and grief.

Scrap didn't answer me. I was left to shower and dress and prepare for the day alone.

Chapter 13

SEVEN O'CLOCK IN THE morning and I paced the lobby of the con hotel. I hadn't slept after Donovan left and Dill visited. Now I waited for Bob to pick me up for a breakfast meeting and then take me to the high school. My mind spun in odd loops of wishful thinking and bewilderment. Pacing burned a little adrenaline but didn't help my mind.

A battered pickup wheezed into the porte cochere. I raised an eyebrow as Leonard Stalking Moon swung out of the driver's seat and entered the lobby with firm and confident steps. He held himself erect and proud and ready to confront anyone who might try to kick him out of the lily-white establishment.

No one challenged him as he walked right up to me. "We need to talk. You need breakfast and transportation."

"Bob?"

"Is sleeping in after a long night of gaming with your friend."

I chuckled at that. I'd pulled a couple of all-nighters with role-playing games in college. Then I channeled all of that creative energy into my writing and learned to keep normal hours. Bob only indulged in the need to game at cons. But he could cope, almost thrived, on about four hours of sleep during the entire weekend. I needed my beauty sleep.

Not that Donovan and I had slept much. My body tightened in memory. Then I banished the longing. Time to investigate Cynthia and the monster dog.

Leonard drove me to a small family café across the street from the high school. We settled into a booth near the window with large cups of trucker-strength coffee. There were as many Native Americans among the customers as there were ranchers and truckers. Maybe they were all ranchers and truckers.

"I know that Cynthia is special," I began once we'd ordered. "What kind of special that the dog singled her out?"

Leonard looked out the window a long moment. His eyes focused on something I couldn't see, possibly something in his mind or another universe.

"The blood of shamans runs strong in our Cynthia." He fingered his knotted necklace.

"Why would a dog need a shaman?"

"The story is long and old. We do not share it with outsiders, or those who have no shamanic learning."

I cocked an eyebrow at him and waited.

"We do not see Warriors of the Celestial Blade outside the Citadel often. What makes you so special that you do not need your Sisterhood to guide and support you?" he countered.

Touché! Scrap mumbled around a mouthful of mold he found deep in a crevice in a broken tile in a far corner.

One good thing about my imp: he'd leave nothing behind for a health inspector to find and quibble about.

"I'm a pain in the ass who asks too many questions."

Leonard chuckled. "Estevez will like that even less than does your Sisterhood." He sobered slightly. "Be careful around him, and his companions, Tess Noncoiré. They are both more and less than they seem."

I stifled my sharp retort. No sense offending this man. He had information I needed. And, from the looks of things, I'd have to pry it out of him bit by tiny bit.

"Tell me about the dog." Better to change the subject than dwell on my mixed emotions about Donovan Estevez.

"I can say but little. But trust me. My people have more at stake than you. We work to bring the dog under our control and our protection."

The waitress delivered our food. Simple pancakes, eggs, and sausage. The huckleberry syrup reminded me of the hint of an undertaste in the ale Leonard had served last night. Flavor fit for the gods.

I used the few moments of silence to think of a way to get more information from him.

"The dog is a killer. I watched it murder two adolescent boys and maim a third trying to get to Cynthia."

Leonard blanched a little beneath his dark copper skin. "Innocents fall victim in every war. Some die at the hands of the enemy, some from friendly fire."

"What is this war? The dog is evil, and I am trained and commissioned to fight evil wherever I find it."

"We fight the ultimate war of good against evil, Tess Noncoiré. Who is good and who is evil is sometimes not clearly understood by either side."

He refused to say anything more on the subject. We left a few minutes later so that I could speak to the eight o'clock creative writing class.

▾▲▾▲▾

"Uncle Leonard says I don't need to talk to you if I don't want, but I want to. I want to thank you. I need to know that you are okay," Cynthia blurted out as I left the classroom. The third one of the morning.

I'd spoken for three hours on the joys of writing and the need to learn to express yourself well on paper in everyday life. The classes were the usual mix of bored-to-snores and enthusiastic participants. A few woke up when we started plotting a book as an exercise. I expected to see entries from them next year in the junior writers workshop at High Desert Con.

I considered my work in the schools as payback to the people who helped me when I was first getting started.

Cynthia had sat quietly in the back, the new kid in school without familiar bonds yet. She'd also had the seat closest to the door so she could pop up beside me the moment I walked past her.

"I appreciate your concern, Cynthia. Are you safe and happy with your family now?" I wanted to hug her, didn't quite dare.

"My father's cousin has taken me in. He has legal custody now." She dropped her head and a shy smile spread across her face. "I like it here. It feels like home. We will visit the reservation soon, so that I never forget that I am Sanpoil." One thing I'd learned in my reading, the people we called Native Americans preferred to be called by their tribe if possible.

"Good." I gave her a quick squeeze around the shoulders. "I need to talk to you about that dog. Something really weird is going on with it," I whispered. "Are you sure he didn't try to hurt you?"

She nodded, gulping. "He only hurt my friends because they wouldn't let him get to me. Then he just tried to pull me along with him, not hurt me."

"He tried to pull you along where?"

Cynthia shrugged and ducked her head.

Then I turned to catch the questions from the teachers and students who had followed me out of the classroom.

"Excuse me, Ms. Noncoiré," Principal Barbara Mitchell, a comfortably chubby woman in a no-nonsense pinstripe suit, charged along the hall. She grabbed my elbow and separated me from the gaggle of lingering students and teachers.

She smiled warmly as she tried to assume a casual air.

My spine flared in warning. Scrap turned a darker pink.

The moment we were out of earshot she hissed in my ear. "We are about to go into lockdown. If you need to leave the campus, I suggest you do it now."

"What's wrong?" I immediately shot an anxious look toward Cynthia.

"Some suspicious characters have been seen lurking on the fringes of the campus. They're wearing weird masks."

I started to relax. "Probably just people from the con trying out their costumes." Then my mind flashed to the too-real demon masks worn by Donovan's friends.

I kept my uneasiness and let it fine-tune my senses. Something strange was going on.

"A witness reported guns and knives. I've called the police."

Some costumes required weaponry to complete them. Con rules usually required a peace bond on them—a red twist tie or tag marking a promise not to brandish or unsheathe the weapon—while within convention boundaries. Who knew what kind of mischief they could cause near a school.

"We have a strict 'no weapons' policy. Not even toys. This is serious," Principal Mitchell continued.

"Rightfully so. Kids need to learn that weapons are not the norm, in spite of television cop shows. Good luck. I'll just slip out now and you can make my apologies." We shook hands.

Then I called over my shoulder, "Find me at the con, Cynthia. We'll talk."

But I didn't leave the area. While I waited for Bob, or Leonard, or whomever to arrive, to drive me back to the con, I circled the school campus on foot.

Too much weirdness was going on. And my spine kept up that flare of warning.

Keeping to the side streets, Scrap and I patrolled, wary, ready to fight off whatever might menace Cynthia. All of the houses dated to the World War II era, with tiny yards. A lot of them were duplexes. Clear evidence that the three cities had barely existed before the Hanford Nuclear Reservation started up during the war.

Maybe those demon kids are mutants from the radiation? Scrap mused as we peered between houses and kept our eyes open to any hint of movement.

Scrap shied at the presence of a tabby cat.

I nearly ran after a German shepherd on the loose.

Other than that, we saw nothing suspicious.

Whoever, whatever, had caused the alert had disappeared.

Bob was early for a change and had to wait for me.

"I just needed to stretch my legs," I excused my tardiness.

He shrugged and put his pickup in gear.

"How about lunch at the Stalking Moon Brew Pub?" I wanted to talk to Leonard some more about that dog.

But Leonard's assistant manager ran the pub that day. The owner didn't show the entire hour and a half we lingered over sandwiches and beer.

Chapter 14

"BOB, YOU DO THIS to me every year," I whined, looking at my con schedule.

"What?" He opened his hazel eyes wide, innocent. Innocent as a kid with his hand in the cookie jar.

"You open the con with the sex panel and make me moderate." I only half complained. This opening panel was always well attended and set a comic mood for all the other panels. At least this year Bob had put a writerly spin on the topic. "How much is too much detail?"

"Who better than you? You write some of the most sensuous love scenes in fantasy. All your male readers drool over you." He waggled his bushy black eyebrows suggestively.

I could only laugh.

Two other respected writers shared the panel with me. One male, one female, guaranteeing a mix of genders among the attendees. Surprisingly, the mix of ages was equally diverse. Maybe we could actually get a little bit serious and talk about adding sex to writing without tipping over into erotica or porn.

"What is the difference between erotica and porn?" Gollum asked from the front row right after introductions.

"Men write porn," Jim Blass, the male on the panel, replied straight-faced. "Change the author's name to female and it suddenly becomes erotica."

Big laugh all the way around. That set the stage. We kept it light and suggestive without slipping into graphic detail. A few of the questions actually focused on the writing and not the interpretation. I didn't even blush when Donovan appeared among the standees who couldn't find a seat at the back of the room.

"Where do you get your inspiration?" asked a leather-clad Goth girl at the back of the pack. She carried a copy of *Imps Alive* under her arm. Her black sleeveless vest-style blouse couldn't close completely over her ample breasts.

Then I did blush.

"I'm sure you'll have plenty of offers for a research assistant," Jim Blass said into his white-streaked beard.

"Or if that doesn't suit you, you could buy a vibrator and rent some porn," I suggested. That set off a new round of laughter and suggestive nudges. On that note we concluded the panel.

Donovan sought me out for an early dinner before the opening ceremonies and succession of parties and dances afterward. We found a small circular booth near the back of the open coffee garden of the con hotel—the same restaurant from the con in San Jose, I swear. Tall potted plants grew in a box separating us from the view of con goers outside the restaurant. People coming in to the restaurant would have to scan every booth and go around the service area to find us.

In this semi-seclusion, our hands reached for each other beneath the table. We scooted closer, forgetting to look at the menu.

He lifted my hand and kissed my fingertips. Small thrills coursed through my body. My eyes lost focus as heat and effervescence filled me. I basked in the excitement generated by our bodies pressed close together; anticipating what was to come.

I gazed into his dark brown eyes and lost myself in their depths. Every thought, every molecule of my being concentrated on him. I could almost read his mind.

A wait-person hovered on the edge of my peripheral

vision. "Chef's salad and iced tea," I said, not taking my gaze away from Donovan. Always a safe order at a con hotel.

"The same," Donovan echoed, caressing my hand, his attention solely on me.

Thankfully the waiter (ess? I had no idea which) re treated.

Donovan leaned closer. His mouth waited a hair's breadth from mine.

I closed the distance. His kiss was soft, exploratory, tentative.

I longed to deepen it. Discretion held me back. We had all weekend to get to know each other better. While the promise of sex simmered just below the surface, we both seemed more interested in the emotional intimacy developing between us.

"Hey, there you are! Donovan, Tess, can we join you?" Donovan's three young friends called from across the restaurant in voices loud enough to be heard in the next county.

"Ignore them," Donovan growled.

"A little hard to do when they are surrounding us." I jerked away from him and smoothed a napkin across my lap. A wave of cold emptiness threatened my equilibrium. I sipped at my iced tea and fussed with sweetening it and squeezing a lemon wedge over it to cover my momentary disorientation.

"Can't you send them away?" I murmured under my busyness.

"Sorry. Their parents are clients. I promised to look after them."

"They are old enough to go to a bar. They are old enough to take care of themselves."

"Not according to their parents. Tess, I'm sorry. I can't afford to offend their parents." He captured my hand again and tried to bring my gaze back to him.

I waved to Gollum just beyond the plants at my back. "Join us," I called.

"I'm meeting Bob, but we'll both be over in a minute."

"Did you have to?" Donovan asked, very much annoyed.

I heard Scrap chuckle in the back of my mind. *Keep him off balance, Tessie. He deserves it.* I hadn't seen much of the imp since returning from the high school. I wondered what was keeping him busy.

What does that mean?

No answer.

Donovan's friends—I never did learn their real names, they insisted on gibberish sounds as their con names— pulled up chairs, filling the table. I frowned at them, but they didn't budge.

Gollum and Bob elbowed them aside and slid next to me on the banquette. I felt like the filling in a cookie squashed between Gollum and Donovan.

And that set the tone for the rest of the con.

The weekend passed in a blur of activity with my entourage in tow at every event. Panel discussions, writer workshops, I judged the costume competition, no bats this time. Donovan wore jeans and T-shirts like a normal person. We all partied. Leonard Stalking Moon presided over a keg at a reception held for the visiting authors and musicians and other special guests of the con. He was always too busy to discuss anything other than the amount of foam topping each cup of beer.

No sign of Cynthia. I looked for her at every panel and party. If she came to the con, she kept her distance. I even sent Scrap to look for her. He came up empty.

Donovan and friends—he was always in the company of those blasted friends—came to my panels, my reading, and my autographing. He produced old and battered copies of my first books for my signature. Since they were all out of print, my estimation of him rose and the tension and longing between us climbed, too. He came to the parties, but was rarely more than an arm's length from his three masked friends. Bob and Gollum did their best to stay between Donovan and me.

The dance Donovan and I performed trying to carve out some time together became almost funny.

The tension between us continued to mount, along with the frustration.

I wanted him, but I knew I needed to spend more time

getting to know him before we enjoyed a replay of Thursday night.

Scrap kept a low profile.

Dill did not return, even in my dreams. Maybe I was finally moving on. Maybe the grieving process had run its course.

But . . .

Bob dragged me into the filk circle. I couldn't sing. My throat closed every time I even thought about it. Dill had loved this part of cons and we had harmonized easily, my soprano against his lovely tenor.

Donovan and friends partied and danced rather than sit still long enough to enjoy the filk.

By this time both Gollum and Bob had a few beers in them. They joined the music with lusty—and slightly off key—bravado. Their near instant friendship warmed my heart. I'd learned to like Gollum even if he was a bit stuffy and pedantic. Then someone struck up a ballad and Gollum took the lead line with a beautiful light baritone. All the singers faded out just to listen. Afterward, he blushed and stammered and kept quiet for the rest of the evening.

Sunday morning I had a few minutes to breathe, so I joined the mock battles in the hotel courtyard. All of the weapons were "boffered" or padded and blunted to avoid injury and a dozen gym mats had been duct-taped together on the ground. (Did I mention that a con cannot be run without two dozen rolls of duct tape?) I selected a quarterstaff wrapped in acres of bubble wrap and duct tape. It lacked the Celestial Blades at the ends but weighed and balanced much like my weapon of choice.

To my surprise, Donovan appeared opposite me with a long broadsword made from cardboard stiffened with a dowel down the center and wrapped in duct tape. The demon children hovered in a semicircle behind him, but off the mats.

"Care for a rematch, L'akita?" he asked.

His voice slithered over me like hot massage oil.

I focused on his mouth, felt myself pulled toward him. I needed to kiss him again. I needed to feel his arms around me.

Two hundred people around us and two meters separating us kept our mutual sizzling heat down to a slow burn.

All of the disappointment and frustration of the weekend rose up like a living entity. We wanted each other. This bout was only the foreplay.

Donovan selected a gaudy football helmet in orange and green to protect his head.

His three companions stood behind him, still masked. Outside the pub, I hadn't seen them without the masks all weekend.

I chose a helmet in pink and purple to match my lavender slacks and sweater. Bob and Gollum moved behind me, almost as if they needed to back me up in this mock battle.

Appropriately, the bloodmobile had parked at the far edge of the combat area. A lot of cons have blood drives—they aren't all fun and games—but the symbolism of the truck struck my funny bone.

"A little different this time, L'akita," Donovan said. He smiled showing his very white teeth against his dark skin. But not as bright as the silver wings of hair at his temples. He looked more tanned than I remembered, his hair darker and longer.

My focus narrowed and my heartbeat quickened. My body told me I needed the practice. My heart told me I needed a long roll in the hay with the man.

"No fencing strip and no rules to confine me." I smiled as I swung low, to my left, aiming for his knee. A quick sidestep and I pivoted out of reach of his counter attack. He thrust his sword forward in parody of the sexual act.

We both grinned and circled each other, seeking an opening.

"She looks so skinny and fragile. She'll get hurt," Bob whispered.

"She's fast and strong," Gollum answered, also in a whisper.

Only then did I realize an even larger crowd had gathered to watch the GOH in a weapons demonstration. I'd talked a lot about writing realistic battles this weekend.

Donovan came at me low. I swung the staff high, clipping his helmet as I danced out of his way.

He shook his head to clear it. "You surprise me, L'akita. Where did you learn that move?"

"Not from Coach." I engaged his sword once more.

A flicker of movement to my left, and I knew Cynthia Stalking Moon watched from the fringes of the crowd. Finally. I hoped she had something to tell me about the dog, some tribal legend or shamanistic secret knowledge.

Donovan caught my right arm with a vicious sideswipe. I went numb from elbow to fingertips and almost dropped the staff.

Dammit, I needed to talk to Cynthia, find out what she and her family knew about that dog. Donovan wasn't about to let me free of this bout until one of us lay in the dust or both us lay naked in bed.

I had to postpone any other encounters we might desire. All because of the damn dog and the near continual itch at the base of my spine.

Very well. "No more Miss Nicey-Nicey," I muttered. He tended to lean forward and overreach. I pressed him to the edge of the gym mats with half a dozen fast strokes. He met them, barely, retreating a step or two with each block and parry.

"Interesting strategy, L'akita," Donovan said. He sounded surprised at my ferocity.

Then, as he panted and considered my next attack, I caught him from behind, between the shoulder blades. He stumbled forward. I swept the staff in front of his knees and knocked his feet out from under him. He went down onto the gym mats with an "Ooh."

He lay there long enough for the officials to count him out. They began selecting and arming the next opponents.

I kept my hand on the quarterstaff. For some reason I felt I needed it close.

Gollum rushed to my side. "Congratulations!" he gushed, patting my shoulder.

"Quickly. Cynthia is over by the bloodmobile. We've got to talk to her." I glanced down at Donovan as he struggled to sit up and remove his helmet.

He cocked his head at me. "You were not so fast and sure on the fencing strip, L'akita." He flashed his teeth at me. My knees nearly melted.

"No rules and restrictions here. No sportsmanship and honor. When I need to defend myself, I fight dirty." I offered him a hand up anyway.

"Later," I whispered, then eased my way through the crowd, Gollum and Bob in my wake.

Chapter 15

MY SKIN TINGLED from the exercise, and my right arm still ached from the hard blow I'd taken. I shook it out as we moved. Surprisingly, I kept hold of my quarterstaff, as if it belonged to me. My eyes searched every shadow and between parked cars for signs of the girl. As we rounded the bloodmobile, I spotted her edging away.

"Cynthia, please don't run away from me. We need to talk." I held her shoulder gently and tried to make eye contact, tried to reestablish the fragile friendship we had begun.

"Uncle says I don't have to talk to you," she said in a meek voice.

"No, you don't have to talk to us. But it would help me find the dog that attacked you if you would tell us what you know. It would help me prevent that dog from harming another little girl. What's in the tribal legends about that dog?" I tried to keep my voice bland and unthreatening. I picked nervously at the duct tape holding the bubble wrap on the staff until I had one end exposed and a long loop of twisted padding hung free. It was sort of like the compulsion to pick at an itching scab.

Somehow, I breathed easier with every inch of tape I freed.

Cynthia pressed herself against the van, making herself as tiny as possible.

"I don't know. Those are stories told to the hunters by the shaman." She kept her head hung low and her eyes on the ground.

"But you have listened, haven't you, Cynthia?" Gollum took up the litany of persuasion. "Your encounter with the dog makes you a warrior. Warriors should not be excluded from the legends. They need to know them, they need to know how to fight the legends."

"Legends aren't real," Bob scoffed.

"Some legends are," I countered. "Some legends come to life when we least expect them."

"What are you saying, Tess?" Bob looked around warily. He shuffled and shifted as if he expected a boogeyman to crawl out from under the bloodmobile.

"I'm saying, Bob, that some of the things I write are real. It's not all fantasy. And right now, Cynthia is in the middle of something important." I caught his gaze, hoping he could read the truth in my eyes.

"I thought so. What can I do to help?" He half grinned at me and nodded his acceptance. "Gollum and I had some interesting talks this weekend."

"Watch my back."

"Always, love. You know this means you have to marry me now, to keep the secrets in the family."

I sighed in exasperation. I couldn't tell anymore if he was serious or not. I didn't have time to puzzle it out.

Finally, Cynthia lifted her gaze to mine.

"You gave me a flower for my husband's grave. That was kind and thoughtful," I whispered, strengthening our ties. "We were both lonely and grieving. That's a powerful connection, Cynthia. We have common ties to this dog."

"Legends do come to life," Cynthia whispered. "The dog and the old woman. There's a blanket that must be saved. It must be rewoven or mankind will shrivel into dust without honor."

"What did you say?" I wasn't sure I'd heard her correctly.

"The old woman weaves the blanket of destiny. The dog protects the old woman from the demons who need to steal the blanket."

"Look out!" Bob yelled as he pushed me to the ground.

Then I heard the growls and the scrabble of sharp claws on the parking lot.

"Scrap! Celestial Blade. Now!" I held out my hand, desperately hoping my imp heard my plea. All I had was the padded quarterstaff.

Even as I spoke I rolled out from under Bob. "Protect the girl."

Then I faced the dog. I took a guarded stance.

So did he.

I centered my weight.

He bunched his muscles.

I lifted my lip in a snarl of defiance.

So did he.

I twirled the staff, and circled, never taking my eyes off the dog. The staff shifted. The looping tape and bubble wrap hardened, sharpened.

Dog followed my moves until his back was to where Bob and Gollum huddled over Cynthia.

The staff lengthened, turned silvery. Twin Celestial Blades curved and flowed from the ends. Scrap's puckish face blinked at me from the shiny metal.

He'd done it! For the first time in our partnership he fulfilled his potential.

We faced a demon, the personification of evil.

We swung into action, moving the dog away from his intended prey. He leaped and reared, avoiding the blade. Came at me sideways. Green drool oozed from his long-jowled, square muzzle. Red blood oozed out of a long gash on my forearm.

I gulped and blinked. And pressed on, ignoring the burn that ran all the way to my shoulder and into my brain.

I pressed him, back and back until I had his measure.

Then I swung the right-hand blade to connect with his neck. He dashed past me. I nipped his tail and flank.

He took a piece out of my calf.

He turned and snapped at the blade. I whipped it out of his reach. And stumbled to the left, leaving Bob, Gollum, and Cynthia exposed.

Donovan's demon children edged closer to them.

Hastily, I regained my footing and swiped at Dog, moving his attention away from the others.

We circled again, feinting and dodging.

Dog bunched his muscles for a leap.

I swung the blade to meet him.

Dog dove beneath me toward Cynthia.

The demon children made the same leap. They and Dog landed upon Bob's broad back, fangs ripping through flesh, knives flashing.

Screams.

Shouts.

Blood. Too much blood.

I ran, blade sweeping toward the dog.

Gollum rose up and kicked the dog in the belly.

The monster released his grip upon Bob and turned, growling at his new enemy.

I lashed out with the Celestial Blade. Tears blinded me. I cut a long gash along the dog's ribs.

He yelped, turned on me, saw the blade. He bared his teeth and growled. But his eyes remained upon Cynthia who cowered beneath the bloodmobile. He barked once and loped off.

I threw the blade aside and reached for Bob. Blood gushed from a dozen wounds. His face looked gray beneath his tan.

Gollum ripped off his knit shirt and pressed it against Bob's jugular. Some of the blood slowed. Not enough.

The demon children backed off, looking confused. "We were trying to protect Cynthia," they protested over and over.

"Don't you dare die on me, Bob!" I cried.

"Someone call for an ambulance," Gollum yelled over the shouts and merriment on the other side of the van.

"Get a doctor. The bloodmobile. Nurses. Med techs. Anyone!" I barely dared breathe as I tried to staunch the horrible wounds.

The demon children faded into the mass of people drawn to us by the sounds of chaos and the scent of blood.

"Sing for me, Tess," Bob murmured. His lips barely moved. "Sing at my funeral."

"You aren't going to die. I won't let you." Too much blood seeped around my makeshift bandages and my hands. Too many wounds.

Too much blood.

The smell nearly gagged me. Still I did my best.

"You know which hymn to sing," Bob breathed.

"If you live, I'll marry you. But you have to live."

"Just sing at my wake." Blood foamed at his mouth. His lungs labored and rattled.

Then he smiled as he looked up into the brilliant autumn sky with wide blank eyes.

Chapter 16

"WHERE'S THE GIRL?" Gollum shouted into the chaos.

"Tess, L'akita, what happened?" Suddenly Donovan knelt beside me and enclosed me in his arms.

I leaned my head back onto his shoulder and let the tears flow.

Someone moved Bob's dead weight from my lap. All I could do was huddle in on myself; let Donovan's warmth take care of me. I couldn't do it for myself.

Gollum, thank Goddess, answered questions, organized a defensive barrier, and kept people away from me. All the while he kept asking after Cynthia.

A medic slapped bandages on my two bleeding wounds and slid a blood pressure cuff on my arm. The bite of the band jolted my senses back to reality. I had to ignore the gaping hole in my gut and do something. Bob was dead. A vicious dog from another dimension had killed him. Only I had the tools and the knowledge to keep it from happening again.

Bob was dead. Just like Dill. Was this to be a pattern? Were all the people I cared for doomed to die horrible and painful deaths before my eyes?

Did I dare care for anyone?

Cynthia was missing. And so was the dog.

Body heat returned. Clarity flooded my mind with the same tidal wave as a jolt of coffee.

Donovan must have sensed the change in my body tension. He slid away from me. I barely noticed.

"Those wounds don't look too bad. Just grazes. But you really need a rabies shot to make sure," the medic said, inspecting the areas beneath the bandages. They'd already begun to close.

"Which way did the dog go?" I asked anyone who could hear me.

Shrugs all around.

"Gollum?"

"North, I think. Forget the dog. I can't find Cynthia."

"She's with Leonard, or she's with the dog. I'm going after the dog." I jumped to my feet, knocking the crouching medic on his heels. My leg buckled, and I stumbled. I might heal fast and clean, but the dog was a demon. His bite would fell the healthiest of big men.

"Not now, miss." A deputy in a sheriff's uniform stood squarely in front of me, one hand on my shoulder steadying my balance. "That's my job. You are just a civilian who has suffered injury and a severe shock. Get in that ambulance and go to the hospital. Change your clothes, but save those. They may be evidence. Someone will come to you and finish questioning you."

"Is anyone looking for that dog? It's a killer. Six bodies in three states by my count." I shrugged off the ambulance and the rabies shot. No germ would dare infect my body after the imp flu.

Modern medicine had nothing to combat demon toxin. I needed Scrap to do that.

"It's being taken care of, miss. Now, if you refuse medical treatment, return to your room and rest. Drink some coffee and calm down." He turned his back on me.

"The deputy is right, L'akita." Donovan cupped my elbow with one hand. His fingers dug into the flesh of my upper arm painfully.

"But . . ."

"I'll look into it." Gollum speared me with an intent gaze above his glasses, which had, of course, slid down his nose. Then he grabbed me in a quick hug. "Scrap needs to recover. He needs you and privacy," he whispered.

I didn't have time to question him before Donovan literally dragged me back into the hotel.

A decidedly subdued crowd gathered as close to the doors as possible. They peered intently at the flurry of police activity, the coroner's van, the ambulance.

Halfway to the elevator another deputy appeared at my side. "Did the deceased have family?" He held a notebook in front of him, poised to write down everything I said.

"I have an address on my PDA. It's in my room." Along with Bob's work number and a myriad of other details.

Details. I could handle details. Then I wouldn't have to think, wouldn't have to anticipate adding yet another ghost to the ones that already visited me.

Cold. I am too cold. As cold as if I had returned to the realm of imps. But I'm hiding beneath the bloodmobile. I can only shiver and watch. I wounded a beast that I should have protected. A man has died. I should have protected him even more.

Donovan's demon children had as much to do with his death as the dog. They were all going for Cynthia, but Bob got in the way. I do not think the demons wanted to protect Cynthia. I do not think they are merely humans wearing masks.

Tess mourns. She's as fragile as a frozen rose and may break if I don't return to her soon.

But I am too cold. I can't move. I can't jump from here to there. I've got to eat. The thought of food turns my tummy.

We're hunting the wrong beast. I knew it the moment my blades cut into the flesh of the dog and drew blood. This is no demon. This guy's on a mission to stop evil.

So who's the bad guy who allowed me to transform? Whose evil became stronger than the barrier around Donovan that keeps me away?

Why didn't we know about the dog before?

Why did Bob have to die before we discovered this? He didn't need to die if we had known.

He did not need to die.

If I do not move, I will die.

I'm too cold to move. Too tired to comfort my warrior. Too hungry to live.

I need a cigar. And a beer.

"This is more than just a job, or a duty now. This is personal!" I screamed into the crisp desert night. The balcony railing outside my hotel suite bit into my hands where I gripped it. My leg and arm hurt like hell, but I needed the pain to take some of the hurt out of my heart. If I rested just a bit, propped the leg up on pillows, I'd relive the nightmare, watch Bob die in my arms again.

Just as Dill had died in my arms.

I stomped with the hurt leg just to make it hurt more.

I'd changed into a loose caftan that didn't rub on the bulky bandages on my right arm and left leg. My sweater and slacks were ruined by Bob's blood. So was Gollum's shirt. The police had them, testing them for DNA.

The police had asked endless questions. Donovan had deserted me to tend to his demanding demon children. I'd made numerous phone calls to Bob's family and workplace. Scrap sulked silently beneath my bed in the other room of the suite. He must have been as exhausted and depressed as I was.

Cynthia had disappeared along with all trace of the dog.

Only Gollum remained at my side.

I scanned the skies for a trace of the Goddess to tell me to go ahead and seek out that bloody dog. But it was the wrong quarter of the moon and storm clouds blotted out the stars.

Anger continued to boil through me. I'd cried my tears, nursed my wounds, washed away the stink of death with a shower. And now I had to *do* something.

But what?

"So, you finally admit that you have a duty to hunt this dog, other than your personal connection to his latest victim," Gollum said quietly. He lounged in the armchair just inside the French doors. His legs stretched out onto the coffee table. An empty beer bottle dangled from his hand. His third. Or was it his fifth?

I'd had two myself, then switched to scotch. I needed the burn down my gullet to remind me that I lived.

"You seem to know more about me than mundane people are supposed to know," I replied cautiously. Secrecy had been pounded into me by the Sisterhood. If people knew how many demons crossed the portals between dimensions, we'd have mass panic on our hands, witch hunts, and major interference from the xenophobic military.

How could we do our work properly without secrecy?

"I have made my life's work tracing folklore and legends about the supernatural back to the source," Gollum said. He pronounced each word carefully as if afraid he'd slur them.

"A little hard when most of the stories began before recorded history," I snorted. I wanted to scratch beneath my bandages but knew I shouldn't. If only Scrap would recover enough to lick the wounds, they'd heal faster and cleaner. Had he drunk the beer and OJ I'd ordered for him?

"Hard to trace, but not impossible." Gollum raised the beer bottle to his mouth, discovered it was empty, and replaced it with one from the mini fridge, then took up his same pose and the conversation as if the interruption had never happened. "It's surprising how many current stories of magic, hauntings, and miracles have their sources in the dim mists of time. More surprising how often the source has remanifested in modern times, and throughout history."

He ran the last two words together, then corrected himself, on guard against any appearance of being drunk.

How much could the man drink?

"You're a demon hunter." I'd been warned about people like him. Fanatics who misinterpreted facts, sometimes deliberately, to prove their point. They also seemed intent upon murder and mayhem in the name of ridding the world of demons.

Pity, I'd come to like Guilford Van der Hoyden-Smythe.

"You could say I hunt demons. I prefer to consider myself a seeker of the truth. An archivist. Someone needs to record this hidden history."

"Like your grandfather?" I still lusted after that musty old book. Maybe Gollum wasn't as bad as most demon hunters.

"You could call it a family tradition." He pushed his glasses up and peered at me mildly. "Much as your calling tends to run in families."

Back to the issue of the Sisterhood of the Celestial Blade Warriors, just when I thought I'd neatly sidestepped it. I thought briefly of MoonFeather. She'd understand about the Sisterhood. I didn't take her for the warrior type, though.

She fought battles against society with calm, balance, and restorative herbs. Though I'd heard stories about how she could tongue-lash officious clerics and leave them bleeding in their own aisles.

But her cats? Try crossing her threshold without an invitation and you'd swear at least two of her nine cats had demon origins.

Then again, I wasn't the warrior type before the infection had opened new pathways in my brain, and the training had awakened suppressed instincts.

I returned Gollum's stare, refusing to make a comment.

"I've seen the Celestial Blade," he commented. "I watched it dissolve when it rolled beneath the bloodmobile. I can also detect the telltale half-moon scar on your cheek."

Standoff.

"You said you'd seen a reference to the . . . Celestial Blade Warriors." There were also Brotherhoods, or so I was told.

"One oblique reference in a text that escaped burning by the Inquisition in the seventeenth century."

"And this book came into your possession how?"

"Family secret," he said on a big grin. "And I'm the last of the family." He took another gulp of beer.

"Cynthia said there was a blanket that must be recovered or humanity will shrivel and die without honor." I couldn't remember her exact words, but this sounded close. "Does that ring any bells with you?" I wandered back into the suite and headed for the mini bar. I needed more scotch. That might calm the ache in my wounds and numb the pain in my heart.

Damnation, I shouldn't drink hard stuff when I hurt so badly, inside and out. If I started drinking now, I might not stop.

I settled for a beer.

"Let me think a moment. The blanket does sound familiar." Gollum took off his glasses and leaned his head back. His closed eyes twitched as if he read the insides of his eyelids or dreamed deeply.

I plopped into the matching armchair and studied my beer bottle, a local microbrew that tasted faintly of huckleberries. I looked more closely at the label. "Stalking Moon Brew Pub." Leonard must have sent over a six-pack when I was out of the room.

Why was he avoiding me? Had Cynthia returned home safely?

Suddenly Gollum sat bolt upright, eyes still closed. He began speaking in tongues.

I grabbed my dictation recorder and switched it on. Whatever he said in this dreamlike state might be important. Or maybe he was just drunk.

After chanting a lengthy recital, he remained absolutely still and silent.

"What does it mean, Guilford?" I asked quietly, careful not to disturb his trance. I'd never seen anything like this, and I'd seen a lot of strange things over the years, feigned and real.

He opened his mouth and repeated the chant. This time in English.

"In the bad lands between here and there and nowhere, in a deep ravine that no one can find, lives a woman older than anyone can remember, older than any other person. All day long she weaves the blanket of life. She uses the old style of weaving with gathered goat wool, cedar bark, porcupine quills, and hummingbird feathers. All day long as she weaves, she imparts to mankind honor and dignity, courage and moral strength.

"Beside her sits the Shunka Sapa, her dog that is bigger than a wolfhound, uglier than a mastiff, and meaner than a pit bull.

"Each evening when the old woman puts aside her weaving to stir the stew of life that feeds her and all mankind, the dog rips out what she has woven that day. For if she ever finishes the weaving, the world will come to an end. There will be no more life to weave."

Gollum slumped down into the chair and began to snore.

I switched off the tape recorder.

"Something to think about." I went into the bedroom and switched on my laptop.

For the rest of the night I poured my grief and my thoughts into my work. I wrote and wrote until I, too, slept, slumped across the table, the cursor still blinking, awaiting my command.

Chapter 17

I'M HUNGRY, Scrap wailed in my ear.

My stomach growled as I straightened up from sleeping hunched over the desk. I automatically wakened the computer and saved whatever I had written last night to both the hard drive and the flash drive. I even e-mailed the new work to myself as a backup. Then I pocketed the little flash drive.

"Food?" I had to think about that for a moment. "I guess I'm hungry, too." I looked at my rumpled caftan. "I need a shower before I do anything."

Room service? my imp asked hopefully.

Yesterday's events came flooding back through me. Suddenly I wasn't hungry anymore. I wasn't interested in doing anything.

I slumped back into my chair and stared at the empty computer screen; my suddenly empty life.

Scrap jumped to my left shoulder and rubbed his face against my cheek, the first show of affection from him since he came into my life. *I liked him,* he said simply.

"I loved him. Best friend doesn't begin to describe what I feel."

Uh, Tess, we need to talk.

No sarcasm, no "babe" or drawled "darling." Something was up.

"Spill it, imp."

The dog is not a demon.

"What do you mean, 'he's not a demon'? He killed my best friend! He's left a string of dead bodies and maimed children across three states and a province of Canada!"

He's not a demon. I tasted his blood. He's one of the good guys on a mission. The innocents got in the way.

"If he's not a demon, how could you transform?"

I don't know. I just know the dog is one of the good guys. We should be fighting with him, not against him.

"And why should I believe you?" I stared at the translucent blue being incredulously. Heat flooded my face. Anger roiled in my stomach.

I'm your imp. I can't lie to you.

"You won't even admit that you're gay. You won't tell me anything about your home world. Why should I believe anything you say?"

Trust me, please.

I marched into the shower without answering him. The sharp spray drove a little of my indignation out of me. But only a little.

"Dog's one of the good guys, my ass!"

Dog had killed Bob. Nothing could make me believe the beast was anything other than a demon, or fill the vacancy behind my heart.

I ripped off the bandages on my leg and arm, almost welcoming the ripping hurt from adhesive resisting me. The wounds were still raw, still burning, but not weeping. I was so angry with Scrap I couldn't ask him to lick the wounds to make them heal faster. I didn't bother covering them again.

If the dog were a demon, the toxin in his saliva would make those wounds a lot worse, Scrap whispered.

"I've still got the scar from the first time he bit me."

I shut out Scrap's further protestations. He was wrong about this. I knew it in my gut and my heart.

He was just plain wrong.

With my hair still damply springing into tight curls, dressed in jeans, a long-sleeved blouse, and walking shoes, I strode into the living room of the suite and froze in surprise.

Gollum peered over a map spread on the coffee table. His

hair tumbled into his eyes and looked endearingly rumpled. He pushed idly at the glasses that slid down his nose.

I'd forgotten about him.

"Been awake long?" I asked, as if he usually slept in my armchair. I wasn't really in the mood for banter, but I didn't need to take my anger at Scrap out on Gollum.

"A few minutes. Long enough to find this map among your freebies from the hotel. Must be nice getting the best suite in the hotel. I didn't get a map," he grumbled, never looking up from his study. He acted as if he did usually sleep in my armchair.

I couldn't allow this to become a habit. He might have become a partner in my quest to find and kill the dog, but I wasn't about to let him into my life.

Him or anyone else, I thought as I remembered another man I had let sleep a lot closer to me than the armchair.

Once.

Donovan.

He might become my next great love, but he had deserted me in favor of the adult children of clients.

I couldn't bear to love another man and lose him, or have him killed.

"Tell me what's so interesting about that map over breakfast. I haven't had anything but coffee and booze since . . . since breakfast yesterday."

"Good idea." As he unfolded his gangling length, he knocked the map askew.

"Where's my dictation tape?" I scanned the area around the coffee table. The map lay flat, without a telltale bulge beneath it.

"Is it important? I might have knocked it off when I cleared the table. I don't remember."

He's as oblivious to the world as you get when you write, Scrap snorted.

"We can listen to it when we get back. It's very interesting." I didn't want to talk to Scrap right now.

"What's on it?"

Briefly I explained his trance, his speaking in tongues, and finally chanting an explanation about the dog.

"Tell me the legend while we eat. I don't remember a thing. I think I had a bit too much to drink."

He opened the door to the corridor to find Donovan about to knock. Behind him stood his three friends still wearing their masks.

A burning sensation flared up my spine. Scrap hissed and blinked out.

"The con's over, kids. Time to come back to reality," I said. All my disappointment that Donovan had left me before I was ready to cope on my own welled up.

He looked very handsome in the morning. His eyes held concern. A new spate of tears threatened.

I let the anger overwhelm them.

Donovan snapped his fingers behind his back. The kids retreated down the hall and around the corner.

"I have to explain. The kids saw the dog going for Cynthia. They were trying to protect the girl. But Bob got in the way of both of them. The police have ruled it an accident. No blame on the kids," he said all on one breath. His gaze was riveted on mine.

I gulped. The thought that Scrap might be right warred with my grief and anger.

"So? You've delivered your message." We stared at each other. Longing and disappointment poured out of both of us.

"I thought I might offer to buy you breakfast, but it seems you already have company." Donovan sneered with disapproval. He turned his back on me, his shoulders drooped a little. Not enough.

"Sorry; you lost your chance yesterday. Where were you, by the way, when a rabid dog mauled my best friend and the police interviewed me for over two hours?" He'd comforted me for an extremely short period of time, then deserted me for business reasons.

Demons take his business, Scrap hissed from the other room. He sounded peckish. He needed food. And so did I.

I pushed past Donovan, not giving him a chance to answer.

Gollum pointedly checked the door to make certain it was locked, then politely took my arm and led me to the elevator.

Over a double order of strawberry waffles with whipped cream, eggs, and bacon I related as much of the story Gollum had recited as I could remember. It filled in a few of the blanks in Cynthia's rambling version.

Scrap slurped at the orange juice and beer I had ordered for him. I might be mad at him, but I couldn't neglect him. The waitress didn't even raise an eyebrow at the order. This was a con weekend, after all.

Gollum eyed the level of the beverages as they slowly lowered without me taking a drink.

"The name of the dog?" he queried, making notes in his palm pilot.

"Shanka something."

"That doesn't sound right. No language I can pinpoint."

I watched Donovan and his friends, sans masks, come into the coffee garden and take seats at the opposite end from us. They seemed remarkably subdued.

"Just how many languages do you know?"

"English, French, German, and Latin; a smattering of Greek and Aramaic. I read Sanskrit and Sumerian."

"Is that all?" I asked dubiously.

"For now. I've never had occasion to learn any Native American tongues. Until now. I wonder if Leonard Stalking Moon could point me to a Sinkiuse tutor."

"How long will that take? In case you haven't noticed, the dog attacks are getting more frequent and more vicious."

"Two to three weeks to get a basic vocabulary and grammar. Another month, maybe two, to truly master it." Gollum seemed preoccupied with pouring huckleberry syrup on his pancakes.

"Is that all? Two or three months? Most people need years to master a foreign language."

Gollum shrugged. "When I hear the tape, I'll have a better idea of what we are dealing with."

"What were you doing with the map?"

"Tracking the dog. Are you finished? I'm anxious to hear the tape."

I sighed and signed the check. But I made sure I finished the last of the carafe of coffee. Stars only knew when Gollum would come up for air long enough to think about eating again.

"You listen while I pack. The con only pays for my room

until noon today. I have to decide where I'm going next," I said as I opened my suite door. "After the funeral on Wednesday."

I froze in the doorway. Inside, all the cushions lay tossed about the room, furniture rested upside down and askew.

"I've been robbed!"

Interlude

"GET OFF HIM, SAGE!" Before the last word left Tess' mouth, she used her imitation Celestial Blade to sweep the much larger and more aggressive imp off my back. The fricking bully landed in the dust beside the training ground with a whomp and a gush of air.

I immediately jumped to my feet and snarled at the dominant imp.

Sage flew up to eye level with Tess, teeth and talons bared.

"Enough, Tess," Sister Gert commanded.

"She's a bully," Tess defended her actions. "Where I come from, we do not tolerate bullies." She did not add that Sister Jemmie, the companion of Sage, was also a bully who cheated by sharpening her training blade. She liked hurting others but could not tolerate a single blow to herself.

I crawled across the sand of the training ground to sit at Tess' heel and nurse the bite wound on my forearm and the tear in my stubby wing tip. I'd had worse injuries from my fellow imps. They didn't like it that I, a runt, had invaded their turf. This was the first time Tess had witnessed them in action, though.

"This is not where you come from, Tess," Sister Gert reminded her. "We train for war."

"Since when are imps the targets of each other in our war

against demons?" Tess rubbed at the welt rising on her left thigh
where Sister Jemmie had slashed at her with the sharpened blade.

I liked that Tess defended me, rather than herself. I needed a
few moments to recover. Imps can push toxins into their saliva—
the better to slay demons with. Or we can make them antibiotic
specific to healing our companions. If I wasn't careful, the open
wound on my arm might fester and I'd lose the use of it.

Precisely what Sage and her ilk intended.

They'd do anything, including crippling a Sister to send me
back where we came from.

"The imps have a social order we do not understand. They
have to work it out for themselves," Sister Gert dismissed the
problem. "Now get back to work. We can't afford to tolerate
sissies in our order."

"Then why don't I see any other imps attacking each other?"
Tess muttered under her breath.

*Because I'm a runt and should have died from the cold back home a
century ago. But the Sisters will never know that if I can help it. The
other imps won't talk about it because they are embarrassed that a mere
scrap of an imp survived the portal and managed to meld. I make them
look weak in comparison.*

I took the opportunity to hop over to one of the irrigation
springs and wash the wound.

"Sage is not only a bully, she's ugly, too," Tess continued.
"Covered in green warts."

Tess had yet to learn that we imps consider warts the most
beautiful and seductive part of us. I wanted more than my mere
three. Tess could use one on the end of her nose, but humans
might object to that.

She took one step to the side and swung her blade at Sister
Gert, shouting "En garde." In one smooth move she hooked the
leader's blade out of her hand and pinned the woman across the
throat with the staff.

"We train for war, Sister Gert. Always be on your guard."

"You will regret your insolence, Tess. You are not a Sister yet."

"I'm beginning to wonder if I want to be."

"Hidebound, pretentious, cliquish, bullheaded . . . bullies!"
I exhausted my vocabulary of maledictions against the Sis-

terhood. Midnight, huddled in the gatehouse while the wind howled and dry lightning raged outside the Citadel was not my favorite time. But it was the only time I had any privacy from the Sisters. That night I needed privacy to rant and rave and pound my fists against the walls.

I no longer counted Scrap as an intrusion. In just a few short weeks he had become so much a part of me, almost like my conscience, that I felt incomplete the few times he slipped off on his own business.

I presumed that on this stormy night he returned to whatever dimension speeded his healing.

When I stopped for breath, I heard a different pounding, weak and rhythmical. Not like a tree branch scraping. There weren't any trees outside the citadel. This was the high desert of the Columbia Coulee in Eastern Washington. Tumbleweed, sage, and stunted juniper were about all that grew naturally here. Maybe a few grasses if you looked hard enough.

I braced myself for the blast of wind and opened the gatehouse door. The feeble light of a shielded lantern revealed no untoward shadows on the inside of the gate. I stepped the two yards to the spy hole in the middle of the double doors, ten feet high and six wide apiece.

A lone figure slumped against the door, pounding weakly with a loose fist. "Let me in. Please let me in," she wailed.

Red suppurating sores on her face told me more than her own words ever could.

I heaved at the crossbar that sealed the door against the elements as well as enemies.

"What are you doing?" Sister Gert hissed in my ear. She leaned on the crossbar, keeping me from lifting it.

"There's a woman out there. She's sick."

Sister Gert peered through the spy hole. "She's not one of ours." She kept a heavy hand on the barrier.

"She's infected. Just like I was. We have to let her in." I tried to open the door anyway. I didn't have the strength to overcome her pressure added to the bar's weight.

"The infirmary is full. Three of our daughters returned from the outside, and three more who haven't had the chance to go to school. We can't take in another."

"Did it ever occur to you that maybe this recent epidemic is the Goddess telling us that we need more warriors? That maybe the demons are gearing up for a major push and we need every woman who can be infected?" At least that was how I'd write the current scenario. I had yet to see a demon or the supposed portal and was more than a bit iffy on the belief business.

What kind of God or Goddess would allow my beloved husband to die after he'd gotten me to safety from that horrible fire?

Sister Gert and I stared at each other, neither willing to move.

"You know nothing about it."

"I know that I can't leave her out there. She'll die."

"She'll die if we let her in. We don't have enough medicine and caretakers to treat our own."

"I'll take care of her. I'll venture into the nearest town for antibiotics. But we can't let her die out there alone."

"Are you willing to give up your place here to make room for her?" There was more to that question than I wanted to think about right then.

"I'll move into the gatehouse. I'll tend her fever there if there are no beds in the infirmary."

"Think on this, Tess Noncoiré."

"I don't need to think. I need to help a Sister in trouble."

Sister Gert stepped away from the gate.

I shoved the crossbar out of the way with a bang and flung the gate open.

A woman about my own age with silvery-blond hair and fifty or sixty too many pounds on her fell into my arms. She was sopping wet and smelled of the heavy mineral salts in the string of lakes that used to be the riverbed of the ancient Columbia. I staggered beneath her weight as I dragged her into the gatehouse. Getting her onto the cot took more effort. Sister Gert watched but did nothing to help.

I knew nothing about medicine, only that I needed to get her fever down. Her polyester shorts and tunic would not tear. I resorted to a knife to cut away her soaked clothing. Then I wrapped her in the rough blanket and rubbed her skin dry.

Sister Serena appeared at my elbow. She still wore a sling on her right arm from the demon battle five months ago. "She's in bad shape, Tess. I can't lance those festers. You'll have to do it."

I gulped back bile. No matter how much gore I wrote into my books, when it came to the real thing, I was very squeamish.

"It's not nearly as bad as demon gore, Tess. You have to do it." She opened a sterile pack and began swabbing the woman's face and a spot under her breast with the orange stuff they use in hospitals. It smelled like a hospital at least. Then she opened a second pack containing a scalpel.

"Shouldn't I scrub or something first?"

"No time. If we don't lance it now, the infection will go inside and she'll die horribly within a few hours. Put on some gloves."

That might help. At least I wouldn't have to touch the foul-smelling goo with my hands.

"Where are your nurses? Your *trained* helpers?"

"In the infirmary, doing this same chore for another Sister. They have their hands full and then some. It's just you and me, Tess, for this outsider."

I gulped, tried not to look too closely at what I was doing as I followed Sister Serena's instructions. A neat slice along the outside of the fester that ran from her temple to the jaw.

"Have you noticed that your scar is longer and more jagged than any other Sister's?" Sister S commented. "Women who come to us from the outside wait too long. They don't know what they are dealing with. By the time they get to us, the infection is deeply embedded, the fever so high, they are on the brink of going mad." She kept up a detailed conversation as I worked, trying to keep my mind off the grisly nature of the chore.

"Outsiders are harder to treat; they have a longer recovery because they do wait too long. But it makes them better warriors in the end. The changes in their bodies and their minds are more profound."

"I was nearly mad with grief before the fever hit."

"The grief made you vulnerable to the infection." Sister S directed me to sit before my knees gave out. Then she deftly produced sterile pads to soak up the smelly residue that oozed out of the wound. She might have trouble using her right arm again, but she was getting good with the left.

"Are we all mad here?" A question I'd long wanted to ask. A psychiatrist would have a field day with every woman in the citadel as well as their stated purpose in life.

"A good question."

"Sister Gert doesn't like questions. She doesn't like me."

"Sister Gert is under a lot of stress. Not much has changed here in almost three hundred years. We don't get a lot of outsiders. Since I finished my residency in trauma surgery and returned here we haven't had many cases of infection. Rarely more than one at a time. Rarely more than one a year."

"Three hundred years? There were only Indians here then."

"You'll have to do the stitches, Tess." She handed me a curved needle already threaded from another sterile pack.

I got to my knees shakily. Stitches I could do. Just like fancy embroidery, or mending a difficult rip in upholstery or curtains. I'd done those chores often enough under Mom's direction.

"In the beginning our warriors were of native stock, women who needed to be warriors but were excluded from that occupation by their society. Later came the native widows of fur traders, their half-breed daughters, then some missionary women who did go mad on the frontier. Now we're a thorough racial mix."

I had noticed some African and Asian features among the women.

While Sister S filled me in, I set fifteen neat stitches down our patient's face and another five beneath her right breast.

"No matter what Sister Gert says, you were sent to us for a reason, Tess. The Goddess chooses wisely."

"Sometimes I think I was sent here just to shake things up."

"Change does not come easily to us."

"I've noticed." Did I accept change any more easily than the Sisters? I just wanted to go home.

Without Dill, did I even have a home?

"Change is what drives the world, Tess. Change is part of

the human condition. People change. Lives change. Lives come and go. The only constant in life is change. Without change, we do not grow, we do not evolve. The demons are evolving, and so must we. Do not allow Sister Gert to drive you away."

Chapter 18

"MY MAP!" GOLLUM CRIED as he dashed into the room.

"My book!" I headed for the bedroom and my laptop.

"Intact," we both said when we met in the middle.

"What's missing?" he asked, pushing up his glasses and peering about.

"I'll check. You call security."

I didn't dare touch anything in case I disturbed evidence. The laptop seemed intact, the flash drive was in my purse, and I'd e-mailed my latest work to myself this morning. An old habit. I backed up everything, not taking a chance on losing my livelihood. Anything else could be replaced.

But nothing seemed missing.

"Did you ever find your dictation recorder or the tape?" Gollum asked. He braced himself on both sides of the doorjamb to the bedroom and leaned forward.

"No, we were going to listen to it when we came back."

"Where did you leave it?"

"On the coffee table. Did you look under all the chairs and the sofa?"

"Yes. They've been overturned, the carpet is dusty under where they sat. Except for a rectangle about two inches by three that's been disturbed."

I gulped. "Who would want my note dictation?"

"An aspiring writer out to steal your ideas and publish before you?"

"If that were the case, they'd take the laptop with the full manuscript on it."

A knock on the open door to the suite interrupted my next thought. A man in a dark suit, crisp white shirt, and blue-and-green paisley tie entered. He took one look at the chaos and pulled his cell phone from a belt clip. "I have to call this in to the police, ma'am," he said and autodialed a number.

The next two hours evaporated under a barrage of questions and paperwork with the same city policeman I'd talked to the day before.

"Seems like trouble follows you, Ms. Noncoiré," Police Sergeant Wilkins said. He wrote copious notes on a tiny tablet.

"A string of bad luck." I smiled sweetly at him.

The hotel manager stood by, wringing his hands as another officer made a bigger mess searching through the debris for evidence. He dusted everything with a fine black or silver powder hoping to reveal fingerprints on light and dark surfaces. A useless task. I'd hosted a writers workshop in here Saturday morning and I doubted the place had been properly cleaned since.

Scrap thoroughly enjoyed following the officer about, diving into piles of clothes and blowing on the fingerprint powder. This room might never get clean again. I wanted to laugh at my imp's antics but didn't dare.

"Ms. Noncoiré," the manager said, "we will gladly move you to another suite, at no charge for tonight. We are terribly sorry for the inconvenience."

"Thank you, a regular room will be fine. I'd like to stay until the funeral." I figured the price of a regular room for three nights ought to be about the same, or less than a suite for one night.

"Of course. Of course. We hope this inconvenience in no way impinges upon your opinion of our hotel or the chain . . ." He babbled on.

Scrap, I whispered with my mind. *Find that dictation machine and the tape.*

About time you asked, babe. He puffed on a cigar that sent the police officer sniffing all over the suite for the source. This was a nonsmoking room.

"What was so special about the tape recorder?" Wilkins asked after a long pause of considering his notes.

"Nothing really. Just notes about some scenes I plan to write. Some native folklore I recorded." And that bizarre channeling episode of Gollum's.

Could someone have stolen the tape for that?

Fine, if someone else wanted to chase the dog and put him out of my misery, let him.

"Yesterday was the second time you fought off that marauding dog," Wilkins said, almost an accusation.

"And the second time the dog had selected Cynthia Stalking Moon as his victim. But Bob Brown got in the way. He died protecting that little girl." Maybe the police would give the girl some protection.

"You saying there is something special about this girl?"

I shrugged. "Ask her uncle, Leonard Stalking Moon."

"Now I happen to know Leonard Stalking Moon. And I knew and respected Bob Brown. A lot. So why don't you tell me what's going on."

"I don't know," I replied earnestly. "I wish I did. Then I could track down this monster and kill it before it harms someone else. Why don't you ask Leonard and his ward Cynthia?"

"Maybe I'll do just that, except Leonard reported the girl missing last night. We'd put out an Amber Alert, but haven't got any proof she was kidnapped. No proof of anything. She just vanished right after Bob was killed. Care to comment on that?"

My heart beat rapidly and my spine burned its entire length. My throat closed.

My fault, my heart screamed.

I swallowed back my panic. Panic would not save Cynthia.

I'd panicked the night Dill died. I might have saved him if I hadn't panicked.

My fault!

"I only can say that I believe Cynthia is in grave danger." And I had to help her. I couldn't let another person I cared about die because I failed to act.

"Where are we headed?" I asked Gollum as he turned his battered green minivan onto a state highway headed north.

"You need to get away from that hotel." He signaled a tricky merge and managed to squeeze between two SUVs that didn't want to give an inch to any other vehicle.

I grabbed the handrest and held on for dear life as he accelerated and passed the macho cars. Maybe I shouldn't watch.

"So, we are out of the hotel. Where are we going?"

"A little resort town on a mineral lake about two hours from here."

My skin grew cold and my lunch turned to lead. "Half Moon Lake," I growled. "About ten miles from Dry Falls."

"We are on the same wavelength."

"No, I've been there before."

"I drew a line connecting all of the reported dog attacks, including two in British Columbia that didn't make the local news. Dry Falls and Half Moon Lake are almost exactly dead center."

"That's in the very ancient streambed of the Columbia River. The dry coulee. Aeons ago, an ice dam backed up millions of cubic acres of water . . ."

"Lake Missoula," he interrupted me.

"Yes. Periodically, the dam would break and flood the river all the way to the ocean, gouging the terrain. The last time it changed the course of the Columbia. The coulee was left with just a string of spring-fed lakes with heavy mineral content." I recited what I could remember of the lessons Dill had taught me on our last fatal trip together.

"Why do you know so much about the local geology?" Gollum looked over at me and almost rear-ended a pickup with tires taller than me.

"My husband and I went fossil hunting in the canyon that used to be the largest waterfall in the world—four times the size of Niagara—but is now just another cliff in the desert."

"Husband? I'm sorry, I didn't realize you're married."
His face lost animation, and he shut down his emotions.

"Dillwyn died the last time we came this way."

"Sorry."

So was I.

We rode in silence for another fifteen miles. Gollum
slowed to the speed limit and obeyed all the traffic laws,
thoroughly pissing off numerous drivers who all honked
and passed us with angry gestures.

"I figure the dog is ranging around the area. The cave of
the old woman must be around Dry Falls or Half Moon
Lake," Gollum broke the silence.

"Why is the dog ranging if his job is to rip out the weaving every day?"

"The old woman must be dead and he needs to find a
new weaver . . . that's why he goes after adolescent girls of
Native American blood."

"If the old woman has ceased to weave the blanket of
life, what will happen to humanity?" My insides grew
colder than they did when I remembered that I might have
saved Dillwyn Bailey Cooper if I had acted in time.

"We have to make sure the weaver and the blanket are
restored."

What was this "we" business?

Chapter 19

"**Y**OU SHOULD WEAR your hair up in the comb more often," Gollum said an hour or so later.

The road ran straight and boring for mile after mile, and we'd run out of conversation fairly quickly.

"I like the comb, but it's not always comfortable." Self-consciously I patted the golden filigree that still held most of my curls in place. I wasn't used to compliments. Especially from geeks.

Donovan had complimented me often. From him, it seemed natural, a part of the relationship. From Gollum? I wasn't sure what kind of relationship I had with him, if I had one at all.

"You look more glamourous in it." Gollum grinned as he sped up to pass a farm truck. "Maybe it's the desert sun, but it gives you a golden aura."

Listen to him, dahling, Scrap commented from some distance. I hadn't actually seen him since I sent him to retrieve the tape. *The comb has magic in it.*

I wondered what kind of magic. Other than outdated ideals that women were more glamourous in days gone by when they wore their hair up and their skirts long.

We drove through steepening hills covered in sage and

rock and not much else. Then, as we drove around a bend, the town of Half Moon Lake appeared out of nowhere. All eight blocks of it.

The town rested at the tip of the crescent mineral lake. Along the inside curve of the lake, next to the highway, I spotted RV parks, campgrounds, and aging resort hotels, including the barren ground where the seedy Life Springs Motel had burned three years ago. New homes and a golf course spread around the outside curve up onto a ridge. Atop that ridge, new construction of a wood and stone monstrosity marred the picturesque and craggy skyline.

I studied that new construction rather than take a chance of espying the place where my husband had died. The log construction Mowath Lodge had grown up beside and around the original motel. Only a cement slab remained where it had burned to the ground. I didn't care. I wanted out of this town and away from my memories.

I'd lost two men I loved.

"There's a crowd gathering around that log building," Gollum said. He slowed the van and pulled into a parking space beside a restaurant. The last place Dill and I had eaten a meal together.

He'd had the fish. I had the steak. The buttery taste of the baked potato that accompanied the meal lingered in my mouth.

"Looks more like an angry mob than a crowd," I replied, doing my best to hold the memories and the tears at bay.

"Let's ask while we have lunch," Gollum said. He killed the engine and sat staring at the milling throng of men and women.

The pattern of their movements became clear. Two factions. One side: men dressed in slacks and knit shirts and expensive athletic shoes. The other side: all had dark hair, coppery skin, worn denim, Western cut shirts and boots.

The whites versus the Indians.

I felt like I'd been dumped into a bad B Western movie. John Wayne or Roy Rogers should ride over the hill at any moment.

"Do you see any sign of the dog?" I asked. While I made a production of stepping out of the van and stretching my back, retying my shoes, straightening my shirt, I took the time to study the faces on the tribal side of the brewing confrontation. No sign of Cynthia or the huge dog. Scrap said he was less a monster and closer to a kindred spirit, on a mission and not knowing quite how to accomplish it.

But he'd killed Bob and some innocent children. He was a monster by any definition despite his supposed mission.

I wanted to kill him, or at least take a big piece of his hide for the death and misery he had caused.

"Cynthia's not here," Gollum replied. He looked as if he'd made an inventory of every face and noted it down for future reference. "Can you make out what they're saying?"

"Not really. Something about overstepping bounds and violating permits." Food interested me less than the scent of fear and creeping violence in the air. I wished that Scrap would return from . . . wherever.

My feet wandered toward the simmering crowd. Gollum followed me. He kept pushing up his glasses and looking around as if threatening monsters could jump out at us from any of the sun-drenched buildings or from behind a scraggly tree. Ancient cottonwoods mostly, drawing moisture from the spring-fed lake.

I'd forgotten the salty, fishy smell of the place. One of the oils in the lake came from decaying and fossilizing fish left over from the flood twelve thousand years ago. That layer of oil remained fixed in the water. None of the layers in the lake mixed. No currents, no movement.

A thick crust of mineral salts frosted the coarse black sand beach; a beach that extended a good fifty yards farther back from the water than I remembered.

My fingers itched for a weapon.

"You're draining all of the wells with that fucking resort," a man wearing a shirt with the golf course logo on the left breast shouted and raised his clenched fist.

"You were only going to build a spa, not a full-blown casino," a woman accused, adding her voice to the crescendo.

The noise rose and fell like ocean waves that wanted to swamp me and drown my senses. At the same time a tingling awareness coursed through my veins.

Where in hell had Scrap gotten to? I might need him if things turned ugly.

Uglier.

Gollum edged closer to me. I didn't know if he wanted to protect me or hide behind me.

"If we want to build a casino, who are you to stop us?" yelled a slender, well-groomed man on the Indian side of the fray. "You owe us water, land, and respect for what you have done to our people."

"Respect, my ass," snorted a woman on the white side. "Lazy buggers who don't know how to work for a living. Can't even clean up your own yards."

"How are we going to feed and water our cattle if you damn Indians drain all our wells?" asked a wiry little man with leathery skin. Only his blue eyes and sun-bleached hair beneath his Stetson separated him from the "damn Indians" in appearance.

"The casino isn't even up and running, and my water's down by half," the man from the golf course said. "I'm gonna lose a million bucks in greens fees if I can't water my grass."

A younger Indian woman tugged on the arm of the man beside her. "Why *did* we agree to the casino? All we really needed was the spa. We could survive very nicely on the money we'd make from a spa."

That statement told me more than all of the shouting. Something strange had happened in this town. Something manipulative.

"Tess," Gollum said quietly, touching my arm.

I made a conscious effort to relax my fists and take the tension out of my face and shoulders.

"Look there." He jerked his chin to the doorway of the log building beside us.

A dark-haired man with the smooth coppery skin, flat face, and almond eyes so prevalent on the tribal side of the conflict stood watching every move. He remained stolidly aloof from the conflict.

"I sense a connection between him and why these people gathered here." I gestured to the octet of modern log lodges scattered around this collecting point. I didn't remember these buildings from my last visit three years ago. Each lodge appeared to be a four-plex, two rooms up and two down, built from massive tree trunks at least two feet in diameter.

I searched for a sign. The grand two-story edifice the watcher had come from announced to the world in big carved letters "Mowath Lodge. Office." It overlapped onto the foundation of the burned out Life Springs Motel.

"They rebuilt. Bigger and grander," I said quietly. My knees and hands began to shake.

If Scrap were here, would he be able to help me sort out my own emotions from those of the crowd? Would wading into the fray with fists and feet flying make me feel better?

"What?" Gollum asked.

"I've got to get out of here. Now."

He stared at my cold face. "You are looking a little pale. Let's get some lunch."

He took my arm and led me across the street to a café. It looked run down and weather-beaten, like so much of the original town. Only in the last ten years had tourism and the mineral qualities of the lake drawn outsiders to exploit the sleepy town's only resource. New Age herbal stores now nestled cheek by jowl with antiques and oddities, shamanistic counselors, and massage practitioners. The café stood out like a withered old lady among aggressive professional women. The age of the building seemed embedded in the cracked linoleum.

We took a table by the window. Gollum sat facing the Mowath Lodge. I kept my back to it.

"Do you want to talk about it?" he asked. His eyes centered on mine but flicked to the view out the window periodically.

"The foundation of the two-story office," I said flatly.

He nodded.

"That was the original motel. An old and run-down place. A firetrap." I gulped back my tears. "It burned three years ago. Dill and I were staying there. He didn't make it out."

"Oh." His eyes flicked back to the scene playing out across the street. They strayed there more often as we worked our way through huge hamburgers with homemade rolls, thick-cut fries, and milkshakes made with real ice cream.

With food like this in my system I could fight dragons. But not my own personal demons.

I felt a weight against my belt purse. Quicker than thought I slapped the thing and prepared to knock a thief flat.

My hand encountered air.

Watch it, Blondie. You almost knocked me back three dimensions, Scrap snarled.

He looked exceedingly gray and I had to peer hard to actually see his outline. He was barely into this dimension.

"Are you okay?"

"What?" Gollum asked, instantly alert.

"Scrap," I mouthed.

Hungry, my imp said in a whisper of a breath.

I searched frantically for something he could and would eat. All the food here was fresh, the inside of the building scrubbed clean, the outside so dry and dusty no molecule of mold would dare try to take hold. Desperate, I signaled the waitress and ordered a beer and OJ.

"Did he get the tape?" Gollum asked sotto voce.

"Screw that. Something more interesting just showed up." I threw a twenty on the table and dashed out the door. "You stay there until the beer and OJ are gone," I threw over my shoulder to Gollum.

Donovan in his cream-colored BMW (his own or a rental?) had just stopped in front of the Mowath Lodge. He angled his long legs out of the car and flashed his brilliant smile at the angry mob.

An immediate hush came over the noisy crowd. The smell of incipient violence melted out of the air.

What kind of magic did Donovan have?

That smile?

Very like Dill's smile.

Some kind of connection flickered across my mind. Then I lost it. So I plowed forward.

A look of intense relief settled on the face of the Indian in the doorway. I sensed then that he had been guarding the door. For some reason I did not know he feared outsiders entering the room behind him.

This was just too much of a coincidence.

There are no coincidences in imp lore, Scrap reminded me around a mouthful of liquid. His voice sounded weak, but better than when he'd first showed up.

Donovan climbed the three steps to the wide deck of the office and spoke to the guard in quiet tones before I could catch up to him. Then he passed inside without a backward glance at the suddenly dispersed crowd.

"What just happened here?" Gollum asked, out of breath as he caught up to me. Scrap hovered behind him. He looked the same washed-out orange as his juice.

"I don't know. But I think I need to find out. Something about the man doesn't ring true," I replied.

Goddess! Why had I been so dumb as to let him into my bed?

"I could have told you that Thursday night back in Pascoe," Gollum said, straight-faced.

I glared at him. Friend he might have become. But he had no right to pass judgment on the man I found very attractive. As well as mysterious and irritating.

"Donovan!" I dashed through the door before he or his guard had a chance to close it in my face.

Gollum slid in behind me.

Scrap returned to the restaurant to slurp up more beer and OJ.

Before I could say a word, I stopped short in the lobby of a small office. Inside the room containing a desk, an oversized swivel chair, and one small, straight, uncomfortable-looking visitor chair, I spotted, hanging on the wall, the most magnificent example of Native American weaving I could imagine.

Something clicked in my memory.

"And the old woman weaves the blanket in the old way. The way it was done before the white man came. She uses wool gathered from the sheddings of wild goats, cedar bark, grasses, and bird feathers. She has nearly completed the blanket except the binding for which she uses porcupine quills. Only the binding remains unfinished . . ."

"What language are you speaking?" Gollum hissed in my ear.

"English. It's the only language I know besides French."

"She speaks a dialect of the Lakota," Donovan said. His voice was as tense as his neck. His eyes narrowed to mere slits. "Are you stalking me, Tess Noncoiré?"

My senses sizzled under his scrutiny.

Goddess! He looked sexy, even strained and harassed as he was now.

"I was about to ask you the same question, Donovan Estevez." I yanked my eyes away from the blanket. But the pattern remained burned into my memory. Grayish-brown background from the goat wool with an abstract design in greens and cedar. Brilliant red, black, and blue from the bird feathers highlighted the arcane symbols within the weaving. I knew they had to be symbols. They just had to be.

"I live and work in this town. You don't." Donovan challenged me. He leaned slightly forward as if ready to engage in another duel.

That answered the car question. It was his.

The light from the window behind him made a golden corona around his head. An aura braided with black darker than his hair.

The aura I could explain as a trick of the light. But not the darkness that entwined with it. Was I seeing a true aura that reflected his personality?

I hoped not.

Our gazes locked once more. But I retained control. I clung to the burning anger in the pit of my stomach and the questions teasing my brain rather than succumbing to the weakness in my knees and the warmth in my breast.

"I brought her here as a tourist, to get away from the hotel and the scene of her friend's death. We had no idea you had any connection to Half Moon Lake." Gollum edged between me and Donovan, leaving me free to examine the blanket.

"Or the controversial casino," I added. Laid out flat and held that way by fossilized rocks and pen holders, on the desk that nearly filled the tiny room was a roll of architectural plans labeled "Half Moon Casino."

"That mob came near to exchanging blows several times in the last hour. Then you show up and they just drift apart as if drugged into a mindless trance. Care to comment on that?" I lifted my eyebrows and stared at him, but kept part of my gaze on those plans. I didn't dare study the blanket.

If it was what I thought it was, and the unfinished porcupine quill binding led me to believe it was, then the dog and probably Cynthia Stalking Moon couldn't be far away.

My spine began to tingle. Scrap hovered in the middle of the outer office, mostly recovered and glowing a pale pink.

That stinky man keeps me away from you, he glared at Donovan. *You act different around him. Let's split this scene, babe.*

When I met Donovan at the *salle* back on Cape Cod, Scrap had said that Donovan smelled funny to his imp senses.

The silent guard moved to stand in front of the blanket. He jerked his head toward the door, then looked pointedly at the plans on the desk.

"This is a private office, Tess. I have to ask you to leave now. But I'll meet you for dinner at Don Giovanni's Restaurant at eight. We'll talk then."

"I'm going back to Pascoe. If you want dinner, look for me in the hotel coffee garden about six." I turned on my heel and marched out.

Scrap thudded onto my shoulder the moment I cleared the office.

I got the tape, babe. It's damaged. But you don't need it now.

"Gollum needs the tape. He needs to know that he recited the legend in a language he doesn't know he knows."

Tough. Scrap winked out again, leaving me with more questions than before.

Chapter 20

MY BABE WOULD be horribly shocked if she ever learns where I found the tape. She would want to go charging into the lion's den, or rather the nest of the Sasquatch guarding the chat room and the hiding place of the thieves. She is not ready for what I suspect the demons are planning. The entire Sisterhood combined is not ready. The stinky man's demon children stole the tape for reasons I can only guess. They hid it near the portal to their home dimension. I don't know why they didn't destroy it.

Seems like those super-special masks weren't masks at all. They're half-bloods—Kajiri. Their proximity at the time the dog attacked was why I became the Celestial Blade so easily. The dog is no demon. The dog is the enemy of demons.

I didn't recognize one of those demons from imp lore—a dozen tentacles, four inches long at least, dangling from each purple cheek. Maybe Gollum knows. Maybe they're a whole new kind of demon mixed from several tribes with a bit of human thrown in.

They hid the tape well. I had to wrestle it away from a black Sasquatch who had sworn to protect it with his life. He didn't die. By tomorrow he will kinda wish he had. I hooked his face with the talon on my wing elbow. He nearly ripped my tail in two. The battle cost me two of my three warts, but it earned me one more.

I am worn to the bone and must recover.

Beer and OJ are nice, but they are not mold. I can't find a scrap of mold in this entire desert. Oh, for a neglected air conditioner! Or better yet, a neglected cup of coffee laced with heavy cream.

I would know heaven if only I could have a fat layer of mold growing atop a thick layer of real cream.

"Well, we found the blanket. But where is the dog?" Gollum asked as we headed south down State Highway 17.

"More important, where is Cynthia?" I replied, hugging myself against an autumnal chill that only I felt. Scrap had not returned to me. Or if he did, I could not see or sense him. Without him, I'm not whole, and I don't think properly.

There was something important just on the edge of my perceptions that I couldn't grasp. I needed Scrap, dammit!

"Cynthia is with the dog," Gollum stated with some authority.

I looked at him sharply. "How do you know that?"

"Logic. If Dog needs to find someone to continue weaving the blanket, and he's gone after Cynthia twice, then she is his choice." Dog needs to get Cynthia and the blanket together." He shrugged and fiddled with the radio.

"Cynthia has shaman blood in her. Leonard admitted as much. It must be very strong for the dog to want her so badly."

Gollum's older van had a tape deck rather than a CD player. I fished the damaged tape out of my sweater pocket where Scrap had dumped it. Without bothering to look too closely, I plugged in the tape and turned on the machine.

Sputters and pops came out of the speakers for many long minutes. Then Gollum's trance-induced voice came through speaking the alien language.

He cocked his head and listened closely. "Are you sure that's me?"

"Very sure. I was there." Some of the phrases sounded familiar.

Then my voice came through asking him what he'd said.

His voice returned in English for about two sentences. Then nothing but the whirring of the tape player trying to forward a damaged tape that no longer wanted to feed through.

"Know anyone who can fix that?" I asked.

"Not here. Back in Seattle."

"Bob will . . . would know." Damn.

"What's your connection to Seattle?"

"Are you sure the blanket is the one we want?"

We asked at the same time.

"You first," he said as he swung around a slow-moving pickup loaded with hay.

"My mom raised me to be a proper French housewife. I can cook when I want. Sew when I have to. But I also know a lot about knitting and crocheting. I can even do *la frivolité.*"

He quirked an eyebrow in question.

"Make tatted lace." I had to search for the English word. Mom never used it if she could pound the French one into me. "In short, I know about textiles. I recognized the porcupine quill band that is unfinished. And that thing wasn't woven on a modern loom."

"Okay. In answer to your question, I taught for a year at UW in Seattle. Adjunct work, no tenure track. Stayed on for a while because I like the city."

"Where's home?"

"Upstate New York when I can't go anywhere else."

I laughed. I had similar sentiments about Cape Cod. More because of my relatives than the place. "Dysfunctional family?"

"Dysfunctional mother. She wanted me to become a financial advisor for her family's investment group. I chose to follow my father's family business."

"Which is?"

He clamped his mouth shut.

He passed another car, this one going over the speed limit, rather than answer.

"You know a lot about me, even without me telling you. How about some equally shared information," I demanded.

"Your Sisterhood didn't tell you about the archivists?"

"No."

"Ask them." He punched the eject button repeatedly on the tape player until it spat out the damaged tape. Then he tuned the radio to a country and western station—the only thing we could receive out in the middle of nowhere. He turned up the volume so loud we couldn't converse if we wanted to. And he clearly didn't want to.

One thing I'd learned during my travels: when in doubt take it to the con com.

The convention committee was still in the middle of packing up from the long weekend. The computer gamers clung to their last few minutes of screen time. I poked my nose into the secluded conference room they had made their home.

"Anyone know someone who can salvage a damaged dictation tape?"

A bevy of techno-geeks swarmed around me, all begging for the chance to prove themselves the geekiest. Three of the eight were female. The gender ratios had changed in the last decade. Most were under the age of twenty.

"Hey, weren't you the babe hanging out with Bob the other day?" asked a middle-aged man with a very round belly and thinning hair, the only "adult" in the crowd.

"Yes," I replied hesitantly. Of all the children consulting over the damaged tape, he seemed the most stable.

"I worked with Bob. He was a good guy." The man shook his head and frowned. "Dave Corlucci." He offered me his hand.

"Tess Noncoiré." I shook Dave's hand with conviction. "Yes, Bob was a good man. A good friend."

"This got anything to do with the beast that mauled Bob?" one of the kids asked. He poked his head up out of the huddle for a moment.

"Perhaps."

"Then we gotta do this. We gotta crack the tape for Bob's sake." He dove back into the consultation.

"We'll have this for you tonight." Dave gave me a thumbs up and joined the consultation that made its way over to one of the computers en masse.

"Tonight? So soon?" I edged closer to the blob of helpers.

"No prob," one of the female voices piped up. She couldn't be over fifteen, with black lipstick, exaggerated black eyeliner, and ragged black T-shirt and jeans. She meandered off into a spate of techno babble that left me more confused than when I came in.

With the tape safe in their hands, I made my way back to my new room—considerably smaller than the suite—and put in a call to MoonFeather. I took the coward's way out and had my aunt tell Mom why I wouldn't be home tonight. I had no doubt that any leftovers in my fridge would find their way into the hands of one relative or the other. Dad paid my bills online for me, out of my checking account. He also kept track of my few investments.

Donovan did not show for dinner. Why was I disappointed? In my head I should have dismissed the man as a lost cause romantically. Another part of me yearned for his touch.

Gollum disappeared in search of a library, and possibly Leonard Stalking Moon.

I retreated into my work.

Once again, I fell asleep over my laptop. This time I awoke in the wee small hours of the night. I wasn't alone.

Dill, my ghostly husband, sat on the edge of the bed, not three feet from my armchair at the round table by the window.

"Have you deserted me already?" he asked.

"Wh . . . what?" I pushed tangled hair out of my eyes (I'd dispensed with the comb hours ago) and peered at him, trying to find some point of reference; something, anything that would tell me if the love of my life was truly there, or just a dream. Nightmare.

"Dill . . ." I reached out to him.

He scooted away from me.

"Don't touch me. You are tainted by that . . . that halfling." He sounded nearly hysterical. Dill, always calm, logical, organized; hysterical?

"Halfling? What are you talking about?" The only reference I could dredge up from my tired brain was hobbits. J.R.R. Tolkien had referred to hobbits as halflings.

"Don't go near him, Tess. Beloved, Tess, I can't stand to watch you ruin yourself with him," Dill pleaded.

These extreme emotions could not come from the man I loved.

Then another half-memory clicked in. Donovan owned Halfling Gaming Company.

"Are you talking about Donovan Estevez?"

"Don't even say his name. He's tainted. He's selfish. He's a traitor to everyone. He lies. Don't believe a word he says."

I'd already come to a similar conclusion but didn't want to believe it.

Either my face showed my reaction, or Dill's ghost read my mind. He calmed down instantly. "You know the truth in your heart, Tess." He caressed my hair with a translucent hand.

Frissons of otherworldly energy tingled through my body. I forced myself not to shudder. This was Dill. He'd never hurt me. He loved me.

And I loved him. Still. Even after three years of separation by death.

"Let me stay with you, Tess," he begged. "I can watch your back better than the imp. I can take care of you. If you just accept me, the veil of death will no longer separate us."

I did not want to explore that. Somehow bringing him back to life seemed a violation of . . . of life, fate, the natural order of things. That was the stuff of romantic fantasies. Even I didn't write that nonsense.

"Can you lead me to the dog and Cynthia?" I asked the only practical question I could think of when all my heart wanted was to accept his proposal.

He disappeared without a backward glance.

Someone knocked loudly on the door.

◁▽▲▽▲▽▷

"Hey, is this some kind of demon language?" the black-clad girl geek asked before I'd opened the door all the way. She and her clones surged into my room without further invitation.

"No, it's not a demon language. It's a subdialect of

Lakota," Gollum said, right behind them. He had on his "teacher" face, and I knew he'd spout a lot more information given the chance. Subjects, he'd talk about. Himself, he would not.

Dave Corlucci planted a laptop computer next to mine; a much fancier and slimmer one than mine. I was sure it had all the bells and whistles available at the moment. It booted up in a matter of seconds rather than moments. Then with a flourish and many grand gestures, he took a CD from the girl who had been first through the door and inserted the disk into his computer. It slurped up the CD like consuming a gourmet meal.

Before I had time to banish lingering questions about ghostly Dill, Gollum's disembodied voice came through the computer. I heard once again the gibberish, trying to make sense of the syllables.

Gollum made rapid notes into his PDA, shaking his head. "I don't remember any of this. How?" He looked up at me in disbelief.

"You were drunk," I replied.

Then the voice on the machine switched to English. Gollum listened more intently, still making notes.

"Interesting. I remember seeing a Masonic jewel once. It had a carved head of Isis, in black onyx, set in an ivory crescent moon. Below that, dangling within the curve of the moon, was a five-pointed star representing Sirius—the Dog Star. Isis, a form of the Mother Goddess full of wisdom, like the old woman weaving the blanket. And Sirius, connected to the dog-headed god Anubis; the god who first taught mankind language, astronomy, music, medicine and the ways of worship. This legend smacks of Universal Truth."

"Cool," from the Geek Chorus. Happy smiles spread among them along with many high-five hand slaps and other arcane gestures.

"May I keep the CD?" I asked.

"Of course. We've got a backup," Dave chortled.

"What do I owe you for this? It's wonderful."

"This was for Bob," Dave said hesitantly.

"How about autographed copies of your book?" one of the boys asked.

"One for each of us?" one of the girls looked at me hopefully.

A small enough price with my discount on the surplus books. That much less weight to haul home. "They're yours." I dug eight copies out from the box stored by the door. The dealers at the con had made a considerable dent in the copies I'd brought with me, but I still had half a box left after giving out the eight.

I signed the books and ushered the wonderful computer whiz kids out the door. The moment the latch clicked, Gollum replayed the CD.

"What am I listening for?" I asked quietly.

"This." He turned up the volume.

At the moment his voice switched to English in the background I heard the door open quietly.

I had to look to make sure the noise was on the CD and not the actual door to my room.

"Someone else heard the story," he said.

"Someone who has something to gain, or lose big time, by us investigating the dog and the blanket."

"Your friend Donovan has the blanket."

"So where is he hiding Cynthia and the dog?"

"I don't think he has them."

"What makes you say that?"

"He's still trying to keep the blanket a secret. He wants the dog to bring Cynthia to him."

"What if he wants to keep the blanket away from Cynthia and the dog?" Where did that thought come from? Dill had called Donovan a traitor and tainted. If Donovan wanted the blanket to remain stagnant, then he wanted humanity to stagnate as well.

I shivered.

"Scrap!"

No answer. Where had the imp gotten to?

"Scrap?" I called again. "Scrap, please come back to me."

He popped into this dimension, hovering on extended wings between Gollum and me.

What do you need, babe? He removed his cigar from his mouth and blew visible smoke rings into my face.

I coughed.

"Why can't I see him?" Gollum asked, coming around

Scrap to stand beside me. He peered into the air with and without his glasses.

"You haven't been infected with the same fever I had." I touched my scar tentatively. I barely remembered the lancing pain from having the infection cut out. I had full gagging memories of doing the same for Gayla, the woman I'd let into the citadel under protest from Sister Gert. Only the monsters I fought in my delirium remained real to me.

Or maybe they were real monsters. The fortress of the Sisterhood guarded a dimensional portal. I might have fought real demons trying to slip past their vigilance.

"Scrap, where did you find the tape?" I asked as pleasantly as I could. I didn't want him running away again.

Don't ask, babe. You won't like the answer. He paled and shrank in size until his wings would no longer support him in flight. He dropped to the table beside the laptop. But he did not flee.

"I need to know, Scrap."

One of the demon kids from the con had it. Scrap almost became invisible. He wouldn't look into my eyes.

I smelled his cigar as the only evidence that he remained with me.

I repeated Scrap's words for Gollum.

"If one of those brats knew Donovan had the blanket and overheard me reciting the legend, then he, or she, took the tape to protect Donovan," Gollum mused.

"Possible. But that doesn't tell us why the demon child sneaked into my room at the crack of dawn in the first place."

"Jealousy?" Gollum asked. One of his endearing smiles flashed across his face.

I snorted. But I blushed at the same time. Donovan was one sexy man. The girls in his con entourage could very well have a crush on him and want to pull some prank on me to discourage our budding romance.

A romance I seriously doubted could continue without a lot more communication between us.

Be careful, Tess. Not everything is as simple or as obvious as it seems. Scrap turned bright pink then winked out.

I took that as my cue to send Gollum on his way, and I went to bed.

Since Dill had visited me earlier that night, I did not expect him to pop up in my dreams again.

He did.

Interlude

MY BABE'S DREAMS are private. She would not allow me to enter them even if I could. Once in a while, when she is distracted, I can nudge her to certain actions.

Or I can listen to her rave during her nightmares.

I wish I had known this Dill person who haunts her. Waking and sleeping, he comes to her. I cannot see him, cannot hear him in her dreams when he is most powerful.

The other ghosts talk to me. They play with me and plan tricks on Mom.

Dill acts as if I am absent when he shows up—uninvited.

That is how I know that Dill does not mean well by my babe.

Human men talk a good line. Especially to women they want to possess. Knowing when to trust them is difficult. Trusting any human other than my babe is difficult for me. I know them too well. She does not.

How can I help when I cannot enter her dreams and he can? He has magic when she dreams. He can influence her. That does not bode well for either my babe or me.

I just hope she has enough sense not to follow him into that half world between life and death. That realm is much like the chat room that leads to other dimensions. A very dangerous place for the living and for the dead. Choose the wrong door at the wrong time and you become demon fodder.

The nightmare began again.

Once more I drove through a dream landscape that became more real by the heartbeat. I proceeded north, through the massive rock formations that twelve thousand years ago had been the streambed of a much larger and deeper Columbia River. Now only a string of mineral lakes marked the ancient coulee.

I drove and drove, barely able to see the twisting road through my tears. Paroxysms of grief racked my body and my mind.

Two days before, I had buried Dill. Two days before, I had laughed at all of his jokes recited by his friends, but not his family. Three days before, Dill's family had refused to acknowledge me as a member of the family and threatened to sue me for Dilllife insurance and his portion of the family business.

I let them have the business.

Fever sent chills through my body and distorted my vision even more. I knew I should pull off the road and sleep. I knew it. And yet I kept driving. The road was narrow and twisting with no shoulder and few gravel turnouts. Darkness fell.

I remembered seeing lights out on one of the lakes. I remembered glancing over. Oncoming headlights blinded me.

I missed the curve. My car kept flying forward, off the road, over the cliff. Into the lake.

I did not care. Without Dill, I did not think I had anything worth living for.

My car plunged deeper and deeper into the lake at the base of the dry falls. Before the last Ice Age changed the course of the Columbia River, water poured over these cliffs in the largest waterfall in the world.

Now only a small lake winds around the base of the eroded rock formations.

I plunged deeper than the water, into another world. Another dimension.

Monsters met me with clubs and poisonous talons. Tall

hideous shapes that barely resembled human beings. Short, oozing, squiggly things. Worse than the nightmares created by Hollywood.

They reached for me through a darkness lit only by the green and yellow gleams from their eyes.

I fought them off with my purse, my fists, my feet, and my teeth. I fought myself, knowing how easy it would be to die here. But if I did, then I could never return to my own dimension. I'd wander endlessly in this timeless space, always fighting off the monsters.

I'd never be reunited with Dill in any afterlife.

Gradually, my fever abated. I had periods of lucidity when the Sisterhood of the Celestial Blade bathed my brow and fed me broths. How I got there, I did not know then.

During these periods of half-waking I became aware of a searing pain along my face, across the top of my belly, and beneath my breasts. I slipped back into my fever dreams almost gratefully to escape that pain.

Doors to otherworlds opened off to my right and left. Huge bronze doors with iron bars across them. Tiny glass doors that revealed impossibly green meadows filled with flowers in bright hues never seen by a human eye. Normal wooden doors that opened an enticing crack.

I had but to choose the proper door and the nightmare, the pain, and the loneliness would end.

How could I choose? I didn't have Dill beside me to guide me.

Then he appeared, not as I'd seen him last, hideously burned with his skin peeling away, flesh cooked, blood oozing through his cracked visage, bones poking through his flesh.

He was whole, clean, handsome, and loving. He pointed to the tiny glass door that led to a fairyland of too brilliant colors and lovely dancing figures. I could never fit through the opening, even in this realm of distortions.

I stood there, long dangerous moments in indecision. All the while the monsters crept closer. I realized they had become wary of me. I knew I could defeat them, but I would not emerge from their realm unscathed. I needed to escape.

Dill beckoned to me anxiously. He mouthed words I could not hear. His gestures became more frantic.

I took one step toward him and the escape he offered me.

Then a tiny figure bounced across the landscape. It had one horn, elongated earlobes, and a hump upon its back. Other than that, it appeared vaguely human, maybe a lizard dancing on its hind legs. It kept its eyes closed as it played a haunting and wistful tune on a flute held in front of it rather than to the side. Seeds dribbled from its hump. Wherever a seed landed, light blossomed out of the darkness. The music was decidedly not European. Still it enchanted me.

"Don't listen to Kokopelli," Dill shouted to me.

But Dill didn't have his normal voice. I heard deep guttural growls beneath his words, and I knew that this was not my Dilly who enticed me into a land where I could not survive. My Dill spoke in smooth, melodic tones. Almost like he was singing to me.

And when he sang, the world stopped to listen.

"Come with me, and we will be together forever. Come, lovey. Come to me. Our love is eternal. Death cannot separate us." He held open the door to the impossibly beautiful fairyland.

I could actually see little winged beings flitting from flower to flower. I could get drunk on the perfume that wafted toward me on an ethereal breeze.

But that wasn't Dill talking to me. That was another demon who had taken on his face and form. I couldn't trust this dimension.

So, if the demons did not want me to follow the little guy with the flute, then perhaps, just perhaps . . .

I followed Kokopelli through a narrow slit of a door made of a rough deer hide. The tight confines squeezed my oversized butt and breasts.

A demon grabbed my arm, pulling me back into the darkness. I resisted. The demon pulled harder, nearly dislocating my shoulder.

Kokopelli played a faster tune that made me want to dance.

I broke through into reality, my normal reality, with a squishy sound like popping wet bubble wrap.

A woman wearing surgical scrubs and mask, (a doctor?) leaned over me. "Welcome back," she said. "I see our treatment was successful."

"What treatment? Where am I?" My voice sounded raspy. The movements of my jaw made me aware of a tightness and dull ache along the whole right side of my face.

I reached up to touch the soreness.

The doctor grabbed my hand. "Best keep your hands off the wounds for a few days. You had a serious infection with a very high fever. We had to cut out the sources of the infection. I've stitched and bandaged them, but we can't risk a secondary infection. That might kill you." Her voice was smooth and matter-of-fact. I couldn't place an accent, regional or foreign.

Fever explained the nightmare dreams. I hadn't truly battled demons. They hadn't truly slashed me with their poisonous talons.

"Where am I?" My nose detected the pervasive smell of disinfectant.

"In the infirmary," the doctor replied.

"Which hospital?" I choked the words out. My throat was too dry.

The doctor held a glass of water with a bent glass straw to my lips. I sucked greedily. She took it away from me all too soon.

"Not too much at once. We don't want to upset a very empty tummy."

She hadn't answered my first question. But I had more.

"How long was I out of it?"

"Five days."

That must have been some fever. "Recovery?"

"Oh, you will mend quickly now that the infection is gone. In fact you'll be stronger than before once we feed you up and rebuild some muscle tissue. I think you'll like the new you."

"I lost some weight?" I asked hopefully. I'd always had a rather round figure. The loss of a few inches on my hips could only improve things.

Why bother? Dill was gone. Gone forever. Keeping a

svelte and sexy body no longer mattered if he wasn't there to appreciate it.

Thus began my yearlong recovery and training to become a Warrior of the Celestial Blade.

Wait a minute.

This memory/dream was different.

Chapter 21

Of the nearly one thousand recognized bat species only three may be classed as "Vampires."

I SAT BOLT UPRIGHT in my hotel bed some three years after I had battled demons in my fever dream. I had battled those fever demons alone. Dill had not been there, either as a ghost or a corpse.

Why was I rewriting things in my memory?

Sleep fled, lost mist in the sunshine. So did any memory of why I might have added Dill to the recurring nightmare of my time between dimensions, keeping demons from slipping past the guard of my Sisterhood.

Talk to me, dahling, Scrap ordered. He shifted a very stinky cigar from one corner of his mouth to the other.

I grabbed it away from him. "This is a no smoking room, you idiot. You're going to get me thrown out of this hotel."

Then talk to me. Maybe I know something you don't.

"Fat chance." I drowned the cigar in the sink, then wrapped it in tissue. In the morning I'd dump it in the ash can outside the hotel.

You never know what I know.

"It was just a nightmare."

The same nightmare that haunts you month after month. I was there, babe, even before you could see me. Tell me about it.

Did I really want to relive that nightmare long enough to talk about it?

If you talk about it, you will purge your mind of the worst of it.

"I've heard that."

So I sat cross-legged on the bed with a glass of water and a box of tissues and talked.

Scrap stayed a normal grayish green, nodding his head as he listened attentively.

The tightness in my chest eased and my eyes grew heavy. I trusted Scrap with my secrets. Hell, he was my biggest secret.

So why couldn't I trust him when he said Dog wasn't a demon?

Because Dog had killed Bob.

Think on this while you snooze, Tessie babe: Why does Dill want you to reject me and go to him? What can he do for you that I can't?

"He can love me."

Scrap winked out in a huff.

I slept dreamlessly through the rest of the night.

Tuesday morning dawned bright and cold. The air smelled clean with just a hint of mint and sage on the wind. More than just a breeze. I'd noticed that out here on the Columbia River plateau the wind always blew. Air masses shifted from here to there endlessly, without regard for human concerns.

Bob had loved the land. A real desert rat, he backpacked through the treeless local mountains and the trackless Cascades.

I think one of the reasons I had never married him was that the desert scared me. The emptiness, the loneliness. The silence deep enough to break my heart. People and monsters I could fight. Only with Dill had I found beauty beneath the relentless sun and seen color in the barren rocks.

An empty day loomed before me, as empty as I perceived the desert. Bob's funeral was tomorrow. A funeral I had no part in planning. Bob had been my closest friend, but was not my lover or my family. I could pay condolence calls on his parents and sister. Nothing else.

You could sing at his funeral, Scrap reminded me.

I couldn't see him, but that didn't mean he wasn't close.

"I can't sing anymore." Not since Dill died.

Can't or won't?

"Is there a difference?"

You tell me.

A loud knocking at my door ended that pointless conversation.

Donovan stood in the hallway bearing a single red rose and a sheepish look. "Can we talk?" he asked.

"Over breakfast. Have you eaten?" He was right. We needed to talk.

I didn't want him in my hotel room. My bedroom. Not again. Yet.

"No. I left home before dawn and drove straight here. Breakfast would be good."

I grabbed my purse and my key card and met him in the hallway. He gave me the rose. I buried my nose in it, suddenly shy, but warm and comfortable in his presence, just like I had been back at the *salle* on Cape Cod.

In a public place I could trust him. Alone? I don't think I could trust myself.

We walked the long length of the hotel in silence, a scant three inches separating our shoulders and our hands. Together and yet . . . not yet.

We sipped coffee while we waited for our orders. Scrap hadn't showed up, so I didn't order his favorite beer and OJ.

"Tess."

"Donovan." We spoke at the same time.

"You first." I gestured.

"I reacted badly yesterday, Tess. I'm sorry." He looked up at the plants growing around the ceiling beams rather than meet my gaze.

My suspicions hovered on the edge of my perceptions. Then he smiled and I relaxed.

"The truth is, I need to know which tribe approached you to try to get the blanket away from me."

"What?" Of all the explanations that was the last one I expected. "No one approached me."

"Are you certain? Maybe that Van der Hoyden guy said

something. He's an anthropologist. Maybe one of the tribes approached him to authenticate it."

"I am certain, Donovan. My interest in the blanket is . . ." Goddess, how did I explain it to someone who didn't know about the Sisterhood and my imp? "My interest in the blanket is deeper than possession by any single person or group. It's the stuff of legends. I need to study it. Research it."

"For a book?" He looked hopeful.

"Very likely." I already had a fantasy novel outlining itself in my head. The first one in the series—the one that had made the best-seller lists—was based on fact, though I'd never admit it publicly. Why not one of the sequels?

"I'm glad. The truth is, several tribes have applied a lot of pressure to get the blanket into one of their museums. But it's a family heirloom. It's protected in a temperature-and-humidity-controlled environment, behind museum-quality Plexiglas, out of direct sunlight. I've got provenance going back to the first written records in this part of the country."

Not so long ago. Europeans didn't bring reading and writing to this part of the world until the early 1800s.

Could the old woman, the weaver, have been dead that long?

I doubted it. The dog would have been looking for a new weaver before this. And probably found one. But if he hadn't found a weaver, his activities would have passed into local legend more readily. Sort of like Sasquatch.

Something hummed along my spine with that thought.

The number of lies Donovan told me mounted up.

So why did my blood sing every time he came near?

Our food came, interrupting my train of thought. The tingling at the base of my spine calmed.

"Who is this Van der Hoyden person anyway?" Donovan asked around a mouthful of Belgian waffle. "I have to admit I'm jealous. He spends more time with you than I do."

"He's . . ." How did I describe him? "A colleague. Sort of a research assistant." I ducked my head and tucked into my omelet with Hollandaise sauce, sausage, and pancakes.

"I wish you wouldn't spend so much time with him. I don't trust him. Who is he and where did he come from?"

Good questions. I'd asked them many times of Gollum and received only vague answers.

Yet I trusted him more than I did Donovan.

"He's been a friend," I replied lamely. He had stuck by me after Bob was killed while Donovan attended to the adult children of his client.

"How about I ask around and see if I can find you a real research assistant, a grad student or something?"

"I don't know . . ."

"We'll talk about it later."

We ate in silence a moment.

"Tell me about your husband?" Donovan looked at me hopefully.

"I'm not sure . . ."

"I'd like to scope out my competition. Were you married long?"

"Not really. He died quite suddenly. A fire."

"You must have known him a long time, then. High school sweethearts?"

"No. We met here at High Desert Con three years ago. He taught geology at the community college. He transferred to Cape Cod Community College after we married, was due to start spring semester. He didn't live that long. Bob Brown introduced us."

Donovan stilled like his entire being listened for clues to something.

"Does this ghost of a man have a name?" he asked after several long moments.

"Dillwyn Bailey Cooper. Dill."

"D. B. Cooper?" he asked on a grin.

"You know the legend?"

"The first guy ever to have the audacity to hijack a plane, hold it for ransom, and get away with it. He's a local folk hero."

I laughed. "My Dill was too young to be *that* D. B. Cooper. But maybe his father, who was also D. B. Cooper, as are his mother, brother, and sister—before she married. They did come into a lot of money without explanation and bought a furniture and appliance store."

"How mundane. You'd think with a name like that they'd open a pub or a hotel, or something more exotic."

"Mundane. That's a good way of describing them." For the first time in a long time, I laughed while talking and thinking about Dill and his family.

"I have some business in town this morning, Tess. But I swear I'll be done by lunchtime. We'll spend the rest of the day together. Get to know each other better." His eyes pleaded with me as he signaled the waitress for the check. "How about we take a picnic down to the river. I'll show you where Kennewick man was found." He mentioned a thousands-of-years-old skeleton found on the Columbia River banks, almost intact. Legal wars raged for more than ten years as to tribal rights to bury the bones with respect and scientists' rights to study them.

"Sounds like fun." I smiled up at him.

"What will you do this morning?" He toyed with the red rose that lay between us on the table. Almost a pledge, certainly a token that something strong kept bringing us back together.

"Work." I shrugged. "I can write anywhere, almost anytime."

Suddenly Donovan broke off a long portion of the rose's stem and tucked the flower behind my ear. My left ear, isn't that supposed to be the side that symbolizes a woman was married or betrothed—taken, anyway?

"I like that better than the comb. More natural. It suits you." Then he kissed me lightly, scooped up the check, and left. At the cash register he blew me another kiss.

About time he took off, Scrap complained. He popped into view in the middle of the table, inspecting coffee cups and juice glasses for residue. *Nothing left for me.* He pouted.

"If you'd stick around more, maybe I'd get you something to eat. Guess you'll have to make do with mold in the air conditioners." I grabbed my purse and headed back to my room and my laptop.

I've cleaned them all out! Scrap hopped to my shoulder. *Witching into your Celestial Blade is hard work.*

I ignored him.

Maybe Gollum has some beer in his room.

"Where is Gollum by the way?" Now that Donovan had left, I wanted to discuss the blanket with my friend.

College library. Been there most of the night.

"Good place for him."

With both men out of my hair, I could get some serious writing done. And think about the questions I had for Donovan and Gollum when next they darkened my door.

Something perverse made me keep the rose behind my ear when Gollum showed up a couple of hours later with a stack of printouts from tribal databases all over the country. The jerk didn't even notice.

But Donovan frowned when I jammed the comb into my hair as we left on our picnic.

The time is coming when my babe will understand that Dog isn't our enemy. Soon she'll listen to me calmly and rationally and form a plan. Two days ago when the dog killed Bob wasn't the time for her to get what Dog's all about. Two days ago she was in danger of drowning in her grief like she did when Dill died.

She still wears her emotions on her sleeve. Only with Mom does she hide her feelings. But then she's always done that, even before she had secrets to keep. I wouldn't tell Mom anything either. She reacts more volatilely than my babe does.

But that time comes, too, when Mom will have to be told. Dad would never understand, and we'll keep him in the dark. MoonFeather, on the other hand, is a ripe candidate to help us.

That is if my dahling babe doesn't do something stupid like fall in love with the stinky man that I can't figure out.

Chapter 22

*T*EN O'CLOCK THE NEXT morning found me tearless, sitting in a middle pew of the Catholic Church in Kennewick, Washington, a few blocks west of the con hotel in Pascoe. The two cities blended into one, along with Richland, the third city in the area.

I wore the little midnight blue dress that suited all occasions and I never traveled without. Bob did not approve of black or tears at a funeral any more than Dill did. Funerals were meant to be celebrations of a life.

So I sat alone for almost half an hour before anyone else showed up. Alone with the memories of the man who had shaped more of my life than Dill had.

Memories washed over me like a sneaker wave at the coast. Good memories. Bob in our Freshman Western Civ class at Providence U, totally at sea in the mass of historical information. I helped him study. He tutored me in math. We went to our first con together in Boston. He introduced me to science fiction. I introduced him to fantasy. We went to another con together. And another. We learned to filk together.

We graduated together, then went our separate ways, only to meet up again at other cons throughout the country. He built a career at the nuclear reservation. I built mine in publishing.

Always there was that deep and abiding friendship uncluttered with sexual tension. We might have been good lovers, but knew each other well enough that sex wasn't important between us.

I breathed deeply, aware of the emptiness in my life. But I was refreshed. I remembered Bob with joy and thankfulness for that wonderful friendship. I regretted his passing, but not our time together.

Why couldn't I remember Dillwyn Bailey Cooper with the same sense of gladness and thankfulness? Whenever I thought of Dill, I wanted to cry and scream and rant, and dive into the depths of the lake at the base of Dry Falls to escape the emptiness of my life without him.

Friends from cons all over the Pacific Northwest nodded to me as they took their seats in the church. A few stopped to say "Hello," and condole with me. Bob's coworkers gave me curious looks. I heard their whispered questions. "Is she the famous one?"

None of them asked if I was the one who had caused Bob's death.

Guilt and anger gnawed at me. I should have saved Bob. If I were faster with the Celestial Blade . . . If I'd thought beyond . . . If I'd thought at all rather than just reacted.

Scrap plopped into my lap. His skin looked brighter blue against my dress. *You look bluer than I do, dahling,* he said, puffing on a thin black cherry cheroot.

"Bad pun, Scrap," I whispered to him. My anger vanished. My life wasn't so empty after all. No matter which path I took, I'd always have Scrap with me.

Where do we go from here? Scrap climbed onto the back of the pew in front of me and surveyed the growing crowd of mourners.

"I'll let you know when I know."

Further conversation was cut off by the entrance of Bob's family, escorted by a priest. The service began and I lost myself in the beauty of the familiar ritual. The responses came naturally to me. Mom and Dad had raised me Catholic even if I'd stopped attending church after Dad moved in with Bill. I even managed to choke out some of the songs and chants.

A filk group got up and played some of Bob's favorite pieces and two of the hymns. They looked meaningfully at me. I shook my head. No way could I sing the piece Bob loved above all others. "Ave Maria."

I turned and left the church before the Eucharist. I felt everyone's eyes on me. That did not matter. I'm not certain I'd have stayed even if they hadn't expected me to sing.

I didn't believe in that God anymore. I didn't really believe in anything. Music had been a large part of any kind of faith I might have had.

I doubted I'd ever sing or believe again.

Scrap remained oddly subdued.

"I think we need to go back to Half Moon Lake," Gollum said as he followed me out. "The dog is going to show up there sooner or later."

"This is my job, not yours," I snapped. I wasn't in the mood to be pleasant to anyone.

"Consider me an objective observer who will report back to the proper authorities." He remained beside me, matching me step for step.

"No." I planted myself in the middle of the sidewalk. "You aren't coming with me unless you come clean. I am sick and tired of your half statements and cryptic answers. Who are you and why are you following me?"

He clamped his jaw shut.

"Fine. You're fired." I turned on my well-shod heel and marched back toward the hotel and my luggage.

"Tess, you can't fire me. You need me."

"No, I don't."

He continued to offer me arguments in favor of us teaming up. I refused to hear a thing he said.

Righteous indignation propelled me all the way to the car rental booth. All they had left was a huge SUV. White. I took it though I hate big vehicles. Then as I signed my name to one form after another my hand began to shake.

I kept right on signing. I'd finish this on my own, with only Scrap for help. That's the way I was supposed to work. One Sister, one imp. We'd find our demons and fight them back to their own dimension, then return to our normal everyday lives. Alone.

People I cared about couldn't desert me if I never let them into my life.

❧❧❧

Locals in Half Moon Lake tended to hang out at the bar down the street from the Mowath Lodge where I booked a room—hey, it was the only lodging in town, dirt cheap, and I could watch Donovan's office from my front deck. I couldn't watch Donovan's suite from the bar. But it was dark anyway. This town rolled up its sidewalks at suppertime.

That would change when the casino opened. People could lose money there three shifts a day. The local unemployment problem would evaporate with the locals taking care of those determined to dump money into slot machines and roulette wheels and card games.

If the casino employed locals. In some places Indian casinos only hired other Indians; bringing them in from other tribes and locations rather than hire any "white" folk.

With the tension I'd witnessed earlier in this town, I guessed the casino would hire outside.

But if the casino used up all the local water, the locals would lose doubly, no irrigation for livestock and the few crops. And no golfers at the lushly green resort at the southwest end of town.

I took a seat in a booth in a back corner where I could watch the local gathering and not have to worry about anyone approaching me unobserved. Before leaving Tri-Cities, I'd stopped at the mall and outfitted myself with faded jeans, boots, and cotton shirts, the better to blend in with the town folk. A little fussing and oily hair products straightened my curls and made my hair long enough to pull into pigtails. Darker makeup and pale lipstick completed my disguise. A careful observer might recognize me, but not strangers. Scrap gave me a gentle aura of familiar friendliness.

A few people half waved and smiled as I entered, then ignored me. Hopefully, they would keep their conversations normal rather than clam up in the presence of a stranger.

I needed to hear the local gossip about the casino, Donovan, and any dog sightings.

The waitress let her eyes glaze into boredom as she took my order for hamburger, fries, and beer. No one else ordered the overpriced limp salads, so I didn't either. The chilled beer came with a frosty mug. I drank from the bottle, like the locals. It was good and slid down my dry throat like balm on a wound.

The beer was the most tasty part of the meal. I'd downed four of them—Scrap drank a fifth—before I heard anything new in the conversation that rose and fell around me.

"Those fuckin' Indians can't drain the water table if we blow up the casino," a man whispered in the booth next to mine.

"I got some dynamite left over from building my irrigation dam," another man said quietly. "Fat lot of good it did me. Ain't no water left in the creek to dam."

"Don't even have to bomb the casino. That hillside is riddled with caves. All we have to do is plant a little bit of explosive in one cave. It'll undermine the foundations. Make it too unstable to build anything up there."

I shivered with that. One cave had already collapsed and started this entire chain of unfortunate events—the one with the old woman who wove the blanket of life. I had to do something.

What could I do to stop them?

Whisper campaign, Scrap said. Then he belched, having drunk his entire beer and eaten all of my greasy fries.

"Nice to see you are back to normal," I replied sotto voce.

Nice bugs in the lake water.

"I didn't think anything could live in that heavy mineral mixture."

Microorganisms in the top layer that doesn't mix with the heaviest minerals at the bottom—sort of like the cowboys and Indians in this town.

"Meromictic," I said. "That's what Dill called it when the layers of lake water do not mix."

Anyway, the microscopic shrimp are better than mold. And there is mold in the air conditioners. I could live here.

"Don't get used to it. We're leaving as soon as I can find Cynthia and get her away from Dog."

Won't happen unless you rescue the blanket and find a new weaver. Dog is on a mission. He's one of the good guys.

I snorted in derision. "Dog killed Bob and a bunch of other innocents. He's not one of the good guys."

Sometimes innocents get in the way of an important mission. If they don't step aside, they become casualties of war.

I decided to ignore that rather than think too hard. But the idea sounded good for the book.

Don't forget that the demon children were as responsible as Dog for Bob's death.

"Let's start that whisper campaign against the idea of blowing up the hillside under the casino." Something to do rather than think too hard. I wanted to blame Dog.

Hell, I wanted Donovan's demon children to be innocent so that he would be innocent.

"If you set dynamite in one of those caves, any one of those caves, the whole hill will slide into the lake. The town will close down without the lake," I said as I slipped onto the seat next to the conspirators, beer in hand. Flirtatiously, I took a cowboy hat off one middle-aged and paunchy rancher and set it on my own head. The brim hid my eyes and shadowed my face.

The men leaned closer to me. Lust and hope crossed their faces.

"I know enough about geology to tell you, you're better off sabotaging the building materials. Then you get an inspector out from Olympia to declare the construction shoddy and unsafe."

"Estevez has got all the inspectors in his pocket. Pays them better than the state does," Paunchy grumbled.

"The local inspectors, sure. But what if we demand the state bring in someone new? This is a big construction project. Local guys don't have enough experience to know what's being done right or where Estevez is sliding beneath building codes," I countered.

Three men raised their eyebrows. "Who do we know with enough clout to get that done?" Paunchy asked.

"Let me send an e-mail." I returned the hat and slid out of the booth. Scrap clung to my back, making me look a lot broader and taller than I truly was.

No gossip about a big ugly dog in town. But he'd be here.

And I'd be waiting for him when he arrived. Then I'd let these guys blow up the whole town if they wanted.

If they blow up all the caves, Dog will have nowhere to put the blanket and the new weaver. He'll go after Cynthia again.

"Oh, shut up, I didn't want to hear that."

Chapter 23

Bats use echolocation to find food and avoid obstacles.

MY FEET TOOK ME north to the end of town and a little east to the dregs of the housing. About half the dwellings here were tiny abandoned structures—sanitariums left over from the heyday of the lake as a healing place, before modern medicine. I found the Wild Horse Bar in a ramshackle building with a stone foundation made from rocks rounded and smoothed by water action, and wooden additions that took off at weird angles.

The Indians hung out here.

Scrap, can you darken my hair and skin a bit? Few of the locals appeared to be full-blooded Indian. I could get away with Caucasian features but not my New England fairness.

A slithering like gel flowing over my head made me shiver in revulsion.

Done, dahling.

I stepped into the bar and ordered another beer, fully intending to let Scrap drink it. I'd had enough fuzziness for one night.

The jukebox played the same country western music as at the other bar, the linoleum floor looked just as ancient. It smelled of spilled beer and crushed peanuts and the ever present fishy smell of the lake. Other than the fairly universal dark hair and dark eyes, this could be the same bar I had just left.

Except the patrons were not quite as drunk. I knew alcoholism was a big problem on the reservations. I watched the bartender—who might have been a Leonard Stalking Moon clone including the harelip—cut off a sullen young man. He had three beer bottles in front of him. The well-groomed middle-aged man I'd noticed in the crowd the other day pushed a cup of coffee at the man. The waitress pulled the drunk's keys out of the pocket of his tight jeans and handed them to the coffee pusher.

These people took care of their own.

I took a table in a corner and ordered a beer.

"Estevez had no right to fire me from the construction crew!" the drunk slammed his fist on the bar.

"He had every right if you showed up drunk, Billy," Good Dresser said, plying another sip of coffee on the man.

"But I wasn't drunk. I swear it, Joe. I didn't start drinking until after he fired me." Drunk Billy looked sullen.

"Then why were you late? Two and a half hours late by my reckoning," Joe prodded.

"Mellie has morning sickness. I didn't want to leave her until her stomach settled."

"Let me talk to Donovan in the morning," Joe said. "You need to go home to Mellie. Sam will take you." Joe snapped his fingers at a youngish man hovering behind Billy. "You can come back in the morning to get your pickup."

Sam led a still grumbling Billy out the door.

A collective sigh of relief went around the room.

"Anyone else got a beef against Estevez?" Joe asked. He didn't look happy.

"The bastard promised me long-term carpenter work," the man next to Joe said. "Replaced me with one of his own cronies who doesn't know a finishing nail from a sander. Demoted me to unskilled labor at half the wages."

"Who's he?" I whispered to the waitress when she brought my foaming glass. I jerked my head in Joe's direction as he handled more complaints.

"Joseph Long Talker. He's the only lawyer in town," she

replied on a chuckle. "Even the whites have to go to him or drive into Ephrata for a more expensive guy."

Within a few minutes I understood that Donovan hadn't made himself popular with either side in this town. Arrogant and self-serving with the whites; not living up to his promises of good employment and overbearing with the Indians. My distrust of the man rose, and I vowed never to be caught in the net of his smile again.

Remember that the next time he tries to charm you.

Donovan did seem to have the ability to make me forget my resolve. All he had to do was smile . . .

Just like Dill had.

I jerked into new awareness. Dill had charmed and manipulated me much as Donovan did.

Anger at both of them seethed within me.

"What kind of magic does he have?" I whispered to Scrap, who still had not appeared.

I wish I knew.

If Scrap didn't know, then we were both in trouble.

▽�▲▽▲▽

After breakfast the next day, I sent e-mails to friends in Seattle who might get an impartial and unbribable inspector out here. I called Leonard. He sounded anxious, and weary. Still no sign of Cynthia.

"Donovan Estevez has the blanket in his office," I said.

He replied with a string of invective I didn't want to translate even if I could.

"Watch him, Warrior. Watch him close. Cynthia will come there soon. The blanket is a lodestone. The forces of good and evil will circle around it in a never ending dance. You must keep it that way. No one side can dominate. I charge you, Warrior, with Cynthia's safety until a balance is achieved."

He hung up abruptly, leaving me with more questions than when I started.

Then I decided to walk along the lake edge on the far side, beneath the casino. It was early yet, and Donovan's posted office hours were ten to two. Bankers' hours. I wondered what he did there. Maybe he spent the rest of his day at the construction site. I'd have to take a look up there eventually. Not today.

The Mowath Lodge sat at the southern tip of the lake. The golf course spread out south and east of the lodge. A dozen sprinklers watered the manicured greens. The town hugged the inside or eastern curve with its sandy beaches and easy approaches. I followed the shoreline as far as I could to the west and the outside curve of the water until the beaches became cliffs.

Houses with irrigated lawns fell away to shacks hidden behind tumbles of reddish-brown rock. A few scrawny goats and cats seemed to be the only inhabitants of these dwellings. Occasionally, I spotted a bit of laundry on a line behind the house, a diaper, dish towels, socks, not much else.

I needed to stretch my body, push it to more vigorous activity than sitting in cars on endless drives through boring country or sitting and eavesdropping. Long strides took me quickly beyond the developed lakeside into rough and rocky terrain. The salty sands became shallower. The cliffs came closer and closer to the water's edge. I looked up and up and up along water-scoured rock with deep crevices and ravines. This land was planned on the vertical.

I tried to imagine what the area would look like if the Columbia River had not changed course twelve thousand years ago. Deep water everywhere, I guessed. The river had dug channels four- and five-hundred-feet deep in places when the glacial floods happened. The amount of water needed to fill the coulee boggled my mind. I concentrated on finding some of the caves the river had carved out of the rock.

"Not much here, Scrap," I said, poking my nose into a shallow ravine. "Might as well turn around."

Not so fast, Blondie. Look up and to your right fifteen degrees.

I did and saw a shadow that was probably more interesting than the narrow crevice at beach level.

"I'll have to climb up onto rocks to avoid the water," I complained.

The old woman wouldn't live in a place accessible to just any tourist out for a stroll.

"What if there are bats living in there?"

You'll survive. They'll be sleeping now. It's broad daylight.

"Still . . ."

Climb, babe.

Scrap pulled my hair harder than any bat could. At least, he didn't tangle his talons in it.

As I pulled myself onto the first boulder, a good twenty-five feet high with convenient hand - and footholds in the rough surface, I spotted the dark shadow that had no business being on that cliff face. The sun shone directly onto that area with nothing between the light and the rock to cast a shadow. I climbed with more enthusiasm.

I'd look inside and hope this was the one. Then I wouldn't have to chance any more exposure to bats.

Sure enough, the tall, narrow shadow proved to be an opening into the rocks. Scrap scampered in ahead of me. I shifted my daypack from my back to my hand and turned sideways to slither in.

With a high-pitched screech, Scrap came tearing back out, claws extended. *Bats!* he yelled.

I screamed louder than he did and backpedaled to the edge of the rocks and almost took a dive into the water.

Just kidding! Scrap laughed. He lay on the boulder rolling around in uncontrollable laughter.

"Very funny," I snarled. My heart was in my throat and beating double time. I could barely breathe.

But I had to admit the sight of Scrap making an ass of himself was funny. I began to chuckle. And soon I had to sit while I let the laughter take control.

Eventually we calmed down.

Still friends?

"Maybe."

We trudged on, climbing three more boulders in search of the next cave.

Found one.

I pulled myself up to the next level, arms shaking to support my weight as I heaved upward, and scanned the cliff.

Sure enough, Scrap had found another shadow that didn't belong on the flat surface in full sun.

I entered cautiously, wary of Scrap's tricks. He behaved himself.

A low cave spread out just beyond the opening. I had to crouch down to avoid hitting my head while I allowed my eyes to adjust to the new darkness.

My bare arms chilled, and a frisson of . . . something crawled across my nape. The interior darkness seemed artificially deep and oppressive. A perfect home for bats.

A sense of someone—or something—else filling the cave pressed me against the wall.

I wasn't wanted here. I intruded upon someone's privacy, someone's sacred place. A sanctuary.

This place was old beyond ancient. I didn't belong here.

Take off your sunglasses and hat, babe. You'll see better, Scrap chided me. He snapped insubstantial fingers and produced a morsel of flame on a chubby pawtip. This he applied to the end of a cigar. He began puffing away, producing clouds of aromatic smoke.

That otherworldly sense of another presence vanished.

I choked and coughed. When my lungs and eyes cleared, I saw evidence of rockfall along one side and the remains of an old campfire up against the back of the cave. I touched the bits of charcoal. They crumbled to dust without the least scent of burned wood.

A very old fire.

Rock chips littered the ground around the site. They might have been detritus from arrowhead knapping. They might have been just bits of rock. I didn't have the training to know the difference.

I don't like this place, Tess. It's old. There are ghosts here, Scrap said. He radiated waves of defensive red, ready to transform if needed. He levitated himself into the cave opening, as if he intended to flee.

"Ghosts, I can deal with. It's bats that scare me."

These ghosts should scare you. They scare me.

"Any ghosts that haunt this place can't be any worse than the ghosts that terrorize my dreams," I replied. But I, too, crawled out into the sunshine. Immediately, I felt a weight lift from my chest, and I breathed deeply of the crisp autumnal air.

"I'm missing something, Scrap." I gulped greedily at one of my water bottles from the daypack.

My imp perched upon my shoulder without saying anything. But he took on shades of pink as he watched and thought.

I sat on the long bench of rock with my back against the cliff and stared into nothing. Quiet times like this were part of the everyday life within the Citadel.

Part of me longed to go back to those simple days of training and meditation, of companionship and learning. Sure I'd had my problems with the powers that be. But there were good times, too. I'd made a few friends. Serena, the doctor. Gayla, the woman I'd rescued and nursed through the imp flu. Paige, my trainer in the use of the Celestial Blade. If I sat here long enough, absorbing sunshine and quiet, maybe my mind would open up and give me some answers.

Answers to questions like: Where were Dog and Cynthia? How could I get the girl away from the monster dog when I found them?

I look three long breaths, making certain I exhaled as deeply as I inhaled. With my eyes closed and my mind open, I sent my thoughts searching for an equally open mind.

Images of the lake and shore reversed on the inside of my eyelids, light and dark swapped places, as did red and green. I let the scenes develop and dissolve, not concentrating or dwelling on any one of them.

My muscles twitched, demanding action. I let them twitch but ignored the need to stand up and move.

This was the hard part. Sister Serena had tried very hard, but in vain, to instill good meditation habits in me during my training.

You have questions, daughter. A voice came into my mind: gentle, calm, serene.

I nearly jumped out of my quiet in surprise. I didn't often manage to contact anyone at the Citadel.

Many questions. No clear path to find answers, I replied. Not so much words as symbolic images of a path broken by

boulders, booby traps, and diverging trails, all marked with
question marks.

Trust in dreams, my child.

My dreams are troubling, filled with demons.

*As are mine. We live in troubled times. We are challenged
often. Besieged. Many of us are wounded or dead. Dreams
are our only truth.* The sense of another mind in my head
vanished abruptly.

I opened my eyes, startled by the brightness of the sun
on the water. I felt as if I'd just awakened from a long sleep.

"Trust my dreams? What does that mean?" I'd had a lot
of disturbing dreams of late. Did the message mean that
Dill truly was a ghost who haunted me? Should I trust him?

Or should I be wary of the demons that stalked me in
my dreams and in real life?

Scrap shifted uneasily on my shoulder. His movement
made me lift my gaze from the depths of the lake and the
whirlpool of my thoughts to the buildings across the water
from me. About half a mile away, on the inside curve of the
lakeshore, I watched children playing on the swing set of
the public park while adults in bathing suits caked their
bodies in the salt-encrusted sand or waded in the oily water.

The salts caked the dry sands for about twenty feet
above the waterline. Another thirty feet of dry sand
stretched above that. Evidence that the water level re-
ceded? Was this a seasonal retreat after a long, dry summer,
or did the construction of the casino divert enough water
from springs and creeks to deplete the lake?

That was a lot of water. The lake was two miles long and
one across.

And the casino and hotel were still under construction.
What would happen to the water level when six hundred
toilets and showers started operating?

To my right, my own room at the Mowath Lodge sat
back from the beach. My balcony looked out over the water, as did the room next to mine. Each of the eight log
lodges contained four suites, two up and two down. All of
the rooms had lakeside views.

The old motel, where Dill and I had stayed, the building
that had burned, had been designed just like a normal

motel, a single long building, two stories, doors on the street, windows and balconies facing the lake. Just because it was built with a log facing didn't make it anything other than what it was, a motel.

I liked the new design better. It must have cost the earth to rebuild with the massive logs and unique wooden interiors. Did the insurance money cover all the costs?

Maybe someone had made a lot of money off the insurance when the old building burned. Who?

If I knew that, I might have a clue as to why my husband died.

Donovan seemed to be in charge of an office. Not the hotel reception office, though. That was in a small single room cabin at the edge of the grounds. Did he own the building and delegate hotel management? Or did he just rent office space?

Before I could follow that thought any further, a flicker of movement inside my suite caught my attention. Maybe it was just a reflection off the glass doors and massive windows. Maybe not.

I stood up and cupped my hands around my eyes to reduce the glare off the water.

Movement definitely. Reflection or inside, I could not tell.

"Time to go home, Scrap."

Home to Mom's burned cookies? he asked hopefully, glowing green.

"No, the lodge. I need to check some things out. Good thing every room has a data port and wireless Internet."

Along with microwave, mini refrigerator, and coffee maker. You need more coffee.

"You mean, you want to drink my leftovers when they get moldy."

Who, me? Scrap turned a cute and innocent lavender.

I began searching for the safest way off this rock. If I turned around and backed down . . .

A shot rang out from above me. A bullet pinged against the place I had sat seconds before.

Rock shards sprayed and ricocheted.

I ducked. Not fast enough.

Burning pain seared my upper right arm. A sharp sliver of rock penetrated my sleeve.

Blood dripped and stained my blouse.

Darkness encroached from the sides of my vision. I grew hot and chilled at the same time. Up and down reversed.

A second shot landed beside my left boot.

I barely clung to consciousness as I crawled into the cave full of hostile ghosts.

Chapter 24

I SANK TO THE ground inside the cave, clutching the puncture on my upper arm, careful not to wiggle the shard of rock. It burned all the way to my fingertips and up across my shoulder into my neck.

Damn! I still had tender wounds from the dog attack. If I wasn't careful, I might lose strength and stamina when I most needed it.

Slowly I pinched the sliver of rock and slid it out. A good half inch of the pointed edge came out red. Blood flowed freely down my arm.

Pressure, babe. Apply pressure, Scrap whispered.

I couldn't see him. But I followed his advice. Basic first aid. Pressure and elevation. No way could I lift the wound above my head. The arm was just too heavy and hurt more with every movement.

Let me help, Tess. Scrap sounded worried as he popped back into view, a pinkish haze that glowed slightly. He ran his tongue around the edges of the wound and across it.

I had to look away. Too close to vampirism for my taste.

The intense burn dissipated and retreated. Now I only ached from neck to elbow. The arm was still too painful to lift.

So I fumbled for a bandanna I'd stuffed into the pack. It

was sweaty and dirty from where I'd mopped my face and neck. Better than nothing. With only a few missed tries, I managed to wrap it around the wound. With my teeth and my good hand I tied it reasonably tight, then clamped my palm across it and pressed.

The bleeding slowed to an ooze while I leaned my face against the cool rock wall and tried to stay conscious.

"Who, Scrap?" I finally whispered. Even if I had the strength to speak louder, I didn't want the sound of my voice to carry and alert the shooter to my location. Caves did strange things to acoustics and might amplify sound in a weird direction.

Don't know. Scrap stubbed out his cigar in the remnants of the fire.

"Can you go look?"

Not with you bleeding. Can't get more than six feet from you. Even if the stinky man showed up right now, he couldn't force me away from you.

"Oh?"

Code and honor and magic tie me more closely to you when you're wounded or under attack.

"So what do we do?"

Wait.

"For what? For an assassin to come looking and find me?"

Three misty forms oozed out of the walls. No features, no definition. Just blobs of white. They hovered in front of me. My vision must have been playing tricks on me. Shock and blood loss.

I gulped. Once again I had that overwhelming sense of unwelcome.

Just then I heard small rocks falling and a body flopping around on the cliff face. "She can't have gotten far," a man said in a deep, guttural voice. He sounded like the Indian who had guarded Donovan Estevez's office.

I froze in place. Specters in the cave or an enemy with a gun outside?

The ghosts grew in size and took on the vague outlines of short, muscular humans. Male or female, I could not tell. Modern or ancient remained just as elusive.

I was betting on ancient.

"I told you, I don't want her hurt," Donovan said.

What was he doing out here?

Good question, babe. What is the stinky man up to?

More scrambling among the rocks. The voices still sounded far above me.

The ghosts shifted their eerie attention from me to the men outside.

"But she was spying on our operation," the other man replied.

"Spying on the casino from down here?" Donovan sounded a lot closer now. Closer than his guard. "Come now, Quentin. Even you aren't dumb enough to think she could see anything from below."

"The office, boss."

I didn't need to see the men to know that Quentin pointed across the water toward the Mowath Lodge. I *had* seen movement in my suite.

Donovan said something in a language I did not understand, full of hisses, clicks, and grunts.

Scrap's ears pricked and he turned brilliant red, as if he needed to transform into the Celestial Blade.

The ghosts melted back into the cave walls.

"What?" I mouthed to Scrap.

You don't want to know.

"Yes, I do!" I insisted without sound.

"Next time, ask me before you shoot. Tess Noncoiré dead is a whole lot more trouble than alive."

"If you say so, boss. I still think she should meet with an accident."

"No."

"I could make a fire look like an accident. Like when that Dillwyn person died."

Quentin knew how Dill had died. He implied that he had set the fire.

I strained to hear more. Fear kept me rooted to the spot. I began to shake all over.

"What part of 'no' don't you understand, Quentin?" Donovan's voice became strained.

I imagined the lines of anger creasing his face.

A long moment of silence.

My blood ran cold. Donovan's henchman was talking

about killing me. Just two days ago Donovan had plied me with champagne, caviar, and strawberries dipped in chocolate on a picnic.

"Well, she's long gone now. We might as well return to work. We're behind schedule as it is," Donovan said.

"You going ahead with construction without that inspection?"

So my e-mail and phone call had done some good.

"Inspectors aren't worth the paper their credentials are printed on," Donovan sneered.

"This one sounded serious and important. He can close us down if he doesn't like what he sees."

"I'll see to it that he likes what we are doing." Donovan moved away.

I counted to one hundred in the unnatural silence that followed.

"Check to see where they are," I finally whispered to Scrap.

He winked out and back in less than a heartbeat. *Half-way around the lake, still in full view of here,* he reported. He hovered close to me, wings working overtime as he peered through the gloom at my aching arm.

I leaned my head back against the cave wall while I gathered my strength.

The bleeding has stopped. You'll start to heal soon, Scrap tried to soothe me. *Imp spit does the trick every time!*

"But it still hurts. And it's weak. I'm going to have a hell of a time climbing down those rocks." I drank deeply from the water bottle.

Power Bar, babe. You need some protein.

"I need answers. What was that language Donovan spat out? I didn't think a human voice box could wrap around some of those sounds."

Absolute silence from Scrap. He tried to fade into nothingness, but I was still hurt and he was still bound to stay with me.

"Spit it out, Scrap."

You don't want to know, he repeated.

"I'm getting tired of hearing that."

His glamour of irresistible male potency is not natural.

"Tell me something I don't know." Cold fear and adrenaline washed over me, replaced by an ugly sense of—I didn't like myself very much in that moment. Donovan had *used* me. He'd used some kind of unnatural magic on me.

And I fell for it.

"I'm gonna kill that guy when I see him next," I ground out between clenched teeth.

Not a good idea, Tessie.

"I know. He's got money and connections. I'd bring a whole hell of a lot of trouble down if he turned up dead with me holding the gun. At least now I know I can't trust him."

You'd be better off with Gollum. I like him.

"Guilford Van der Hoyden-Smythe is a pest and a nuisance."

That's why I like him.

"Go check again and see if they are out of sight. I need to get out of here and then find a drugstore so I can properly clean and bandage this wound. Don't want infection setting in." My emergency med kit was in my own car, at home. Too bulky and extensive to carry with me. The small first aid kit I kept in my suitcase wouldn't cover this large a wound.

Scrap snorted even as he poked his head out the cave mouth. *You can't get infections anymore. And it's all clear.*

"Don't suppose I could go back to the Citadel and have Serena fix me up?"

We both have to earn our way back in. You haven't even killed one demon yet. We've got a way to go, babe.

The story of my life. What I truly wanted was always just beyond my reach. Like answers and saving Cynthia.

"Au revoir," I called to the ghosts as I crawled out of the cave. "Mind the store until I get back."

In that moment I knew I'd be back. With questions. Or maybe just to wait for Cynthia to show up with the dog.

◄▽▲▽▲▽►

I didn't have the energy for disguise and subterfuge that evening, so I dined in the steak house next door to the lodge. This place catered to tourists and wealthy retirees in the big houses around the golf course. The chilly evening gave me the excuse to wear a bulky sweater with my jeans to cover the bandages on my upper left arm.

Donovan apparently ate there, too. He straddled the chair opposite me, leaning over the back, without invitation.

"Why are you here, Tess?" he asked without preamble.

"Research. I'm setting a new book in a place like this. Add one monster out of local folklore to that lake and it makes a perfect setting. I like the idea of the water layers never mixing, not in twelve thousand years."

"You've been here long enough to gather all the books on local geology and take pictures of every rock formation." He tapped the book on local Indian legends I'd been reading before he so rudely interrupted me. I hadn't found anything on the dog or the blanket.

Not that I minded staring at his handsome face rather than rereading the same paragraph over and over because I couldn't concentrate.

Stop that! I admonished myself. *He's using that weird mojo again.*

"You could go home in the morning," he said with a sexy smile.

Was that an invitation to spend tonight with him before I went home tomorrow? My bones wanted to melt despite my resolution to never trust him again.

Mentally, I slapped my face to rid my brain and my libido of all those stray thoughts.

"I'm fascinated with that blanket hanging in your office. It's obviously very old. What's the story behind it?" I had to think about something other than the way his mobile mouth curved over his teeth, how that mouth tasted, and molded to mine.

"The blanket is a family heirloom."

"I'd like to buy it from you."

"It's not for sale."

"Then tell me more about it. Where did it come from? How was it woven? Why is the binding unfinished?"

Donovan looked up sharply and frowned at some newcomers at the door.

"Doesn't this town have animal control laws?" a stranger shouted. "I swear that dog was ready to chew through my *closed* car windows."

I turned around and stared. Just an ordinary middle-aged couple going to fat and wearing too much turquoise and silver jewelry with their polyester slacks and matching golf shirts.

The hostess murmured something soothing to the couple.

"I've got to go. I hope to see you in Cape Cod next time I'm there. But not around here, Tess. This town can be dangerous. We have our own monsters to deal with, and they don't have anything to do with your fantasy books. And I prefer your hair down, like it is now." Donovan slammed his chair back, dropped a kiss on top of my head, and stalked toward the door.

I waved the waitress over. "Serve that couple the drink of their choice on me," I said quietly, nodding toward the strangers who had had a dog encounter of the close kind.

When the drinks arrived, I picked up my own glass of wine and moved my chair to their table. "I'm so sorry you had such a terrible fright from that dog. He's so big and dangerous. I don't see why the authorities don't just shoot him," I said in my most sympathetic manner.

"You seen him, too?" the man asked.

"Just before I came to dinner. Bigger than a wolfhound, uglier than a mastiff, and meaner than a rabid pit bull."

"That's him alrighty. Vern and Myrna Abrams." He stuck his hand in my face for me to shake.

I took it limply. "Teresa Newcomb," I replied, giving him my first nom de plume. "Where did you see the dog?"

"On the road into town, not ten minutes ago."

Already dark out.

"Was there anyone with the dog? You'd think if someone owned him, they'd be chasing after him, trying to catch him."

"Just a little girl. Looked like an Indian, dirty and scruffy. She yelled at the dog, and he seemed to pay attention to her, but he just kept coming right at the car, like he didn't see it. Woulda run right over us if I hadn't hit the brakes."

The waitress arrived with my steak. I told her to put it on my table. I'd learned enough. No sense in disturbing this couple further.

"We're staying at the Mowath Lodge, number seven. Where're you staying, Teresa?" Myrna Abrams asked.

I gulped. They had the suite right next to me. So much for privacy. "Number six," I admitted reluctantly.

"Maybe we'll see you around, take the cure together. I hear the water works wonders on arthritis. Bet you've got a nice case of bursitis going in that shoulder the way you favor it," Myrna gushed.

I smiled and picked up the book I'd brought to read with my dinner.

At least Cynthia was still safe and communicating with the dog.

Interlude

*P*ATIENCE, DAHLING. *You need patience to survive in this world,* I counseled my babe. She sat with her legs folded beneath her, hands resting on her knees, palms up, eyes closed, and a frown upon her face. Half a dozen other trainees sat with her in a circle. Sister Martha marched around them. Her voice droned out the litany of meditation.

Concentrate. You have to concentrate.

Tess wasn't listening. She was bored. I could tell. She'd been here in the Citadel eleven months now. She'd mastered every physical exercise and blade technique they threw at her. She even threw some new ones into the mix—and got into trouble for it.

But this simple relaxation and thought mastery eluded her.

I couldn't blame her. I tended to snooze through these sessions, too.

Today Sister Gert observed. That did not bode well for us.

"Sister Teresa, what do you think you are doing?" Sister Gert demanded.

I cracked open one eye to make sure she meant me and not one of the other newcomers. The way she scowled I was pretty sure she meant me. She'd used my real name, the one I only allowed my mother to call me.

Sister Gert was *not* my mother.

"I'm trying to concentrate." That was what Scrap had advised me to do, wasn't it?

"You cannot meditate with your shoulders hunched and your face screwed up like a dried prune. Now what were you thinking about? Not the exercise, certainly." Sister Gert stalked over to my position in the circle.

"Actually I was thinking up a new plot for a book. But the character of the villain has me puzzled. Would you like to model for her?"

Not the most diplomatic thing to say. Obviously.

Sister Gert grabbed me by the collar of my cotton shirt and hauled me to my feet and out into the slightly warmer corridor. At least part of the Citadel had south-facing windows that absorbed some of the winter sunlight and heat.

Thank the Goddess. My butt was numb from the cold stone floor in this cold stone room without windows. My back ached from sitting straight for so long without support. My mind was threatening to desert me from sheer boredom.

"Insolence cannot be tolerated here!" Sister Gert clenched her fist as if she wanted to slug me.

I almost welcomed it. She wanted to hit me. I wanted to hit back. And then I wanted to leave.

"We are a tightly honed fighting unit. You must learn to obey without question in order to survive the next attack."

"An attack from what? I've been here almost a year and there has only been one fight. I wasn't allowed to watch or participate. I've never seen a demon and I've yet to see the supposed portal." My fists clenched, too.

"You do not believe?" Sister Gert looked at me incredulously.

"No. I do not believe in your demons, or your Goddess, or anything you've taught me." Except for Scrap. He was the only part of this entire experience that seemed real.

A translucent imp from another dimension was the only thing real here.

Maybe I had gone mad in my grief over Dill.

"Come with me." Sister Gert marched down the corridor toward the central tower building. I'd been in the ground floor of that building once or twice. Just an armory. Nothing more. I had my own personal replica blade and Scrap. I didn't need anything more from there.

Sister Gert yanked open the heavy wooden door with iron hinges, locks, and crossbar. The thing weighed more than the two of us combined, yet she moved it with ease.

My estimation of her strength and abilities went up, even though I'd rarely seen her on the practice field.

The armory smelled of dust and cold. Afternoon sunlight streamed in through high windows on all four walls. Bright blades in numerous shapes and sizes from ornate daggers to broadswords to scimitars to pikes gleamed. Well-oiled, sharp and deadly.

"A case of AK47s would kill a lot more demons a lot faster than blades," I said, admiring the weapons anyway.

"Wouldn't do a thing against a demon," Sister Gert snorted. "Specially forged blades are the only thing that will penetrate their hides."

"Specially forged?"

"With magic."

Can't you feel it, babe? Scrap asked. He stared at the weapons array with longing.

"Feel what, Scrap?"

"The magic. The aura. The specialness," Sister Gert answered for him. She stared at a broadsword with awe.

They looked like any other sword I'd seen at cons and SCA events. Only sharper.

Sister Gert ended her rapt study by whisking a tacky piece of dirty carpet off the floor near the center of the room. Then she beckoned me to help her lift a stone trapdoor. It came up with surprising ease to reveal a flight of narrow stone steps heading into darkness.

"From here we must have absolute quiet. Your life depends upon this." She fixed me with a stern glare.

Scrap turned bright red and gibbered something unintelligible. I guessed it was some kind of prayer, or curse, in his own imp language.

I nodded my agreement. Then I followed her down the stairs, stepping lightly, breathing shallowly of the hot moist air that rose up from the depths of the basement.

At the base of the stairs, when the diffuse light from the upper room dwindled to almost nothing, Sister Gert produced a very modern and powerful flashlight. The beam shot forth from the lens to reveal a large room, big enough for forty or fifty Sisters to swing their blades all at the same time.

I couldn't figure out what heated and humidified the room. We were in the high desert, barely fifteen inches of rain fell a year. This was the middle of December when outside temperatures rarely ventured above forty. This room should be cold and dry. Very cold and very dry.

Sister Gert shook her head and frowned a warning as I opened my mouth to ask my questions.

Scrap prodded my mind to remind me to obey.

Then the flashlight picked out iron-and-brass fittings on a round door in the wall. At least twelve feet in diameter. It looked to be one solid piece of metal. Nothing decorative about it, just a solid barrier between here and there.

As we stood there, the door began to vibrate and glow red with a new blast of wet heat.

Scrap turned scarlet.

Sister Gert grabbed my arm and we both hastened upstairs.

The cold air in the armory was a welcome relief. Briefly. Then the goose bumps on my arms rose and I shuddered with more than cold.

When the trapdoor was back in place and the carpet hiding it once more, she heaved a sigh. "That is the portal. Just going into that room was dangerous. The demons smelled us. They wanted to break through and taste our blood."

I sensed her genuine fear.

Believe her, babe, that is one mean place to be.

"What keeps them from breaking through?" I finally asked. I didn't like the way my voice shook. Something was down there. But I still didn't know precisely what.

"We do not know. For many, many generations the Sisterhood has been charged with the duty to guard that portal. All we know is that upon occasion, demons breach it. When they do, we must fight them back to their own dimension and close the portal once more." Sister Gert led me out of the armory, back into the sunlit corridor.

"Well, shouldn't we find out what seals it and what breaks it so that we can do a better job of keeping it closed?"

"Ours is not the place to question, only to fight."

"Well, that's stupid."

"There are others who keep this information. They will tell us if we need to know more."

"How long has it been since you've heard from these 'others'?" I couldn't stand still any longer. This woman had blinders on and refused to look beyond them.

"Questing into other realms is more dangerous than allowing demons to breach the portal and come into this world."

"How do you know that if you've never done it?"

She looked at me in bewilderment, not understanding what I asked or why. "We leave that to those who know better than we."

"But how do you know that these 'others' still exist? How do you know they have the best information and pass it along? How do you know . . ."

"It is very clear to me, Teresa, that you do not belong here. I hate to waste one who is chosen by the Goddess, but you must leave here. You will never be worthy of the title 'Sister.'" She marched off. I don't think she had any other gait than marching.

"Who said I wanted to be a 'Sister' in the first place?"

Time to keep your mouth shut, Tess. We're in big trouble here.

"What can they do, throw me out?"

Yes.

"That is bad how?"

We will be utterly alone.

"Sounds good to me. I could use a little privacy now and then."

Chapter 25

*S*HOUTS AND GUNFIRE awakened me just as the first rays of sunlight poked above the hills to the east of Half Moon Lake. Friday morning, my second full day in this dusty little town.

I dashed out of bed and peered out the front windows, heedless of my lack of sleeping attire. A quick glance through a slit between the drapes showed Donovan and Quentin barring their door to Dog and a decidedly grubby and disheveled Cynthia.

Quentin had a big handgun. A very big handgun.

Dog had a slight graze on his left flank, like a bullet had bounced off his hide. Bullets wouldn't touch a real monster from another realm. Sister Gert had been most adamant on that point.

I couldn't dress fast enough. Clad in jeans and a sweater, without underwear or shoes, I ran across the courtyard to Donovan's office suite.

"Don't hurt him, Sapa!" Cynthia yelled as she grabbed the dog by the scruff of the neck.

"Outta the way, girl. I'm gonna shoot the fucking dog!" Quentin yelled back.

"Forget the dog, protect the blanket, you fool!" Donovan joined the fray. He looked as if he'd slept in his clothes.

His rumpled hair and heavy eyes only made him look more attractive and vulnerable.

I couldn't let my heart stutter in utter awe of the man's beauty. I had to get the girl away from the dog.

Dog, Sapa she'd called him, looked into Cynthia's eyes with utter devotion and backed off two steps. The killer I loathed with every atom in my being looked just like any other oversized puppy in need of an ear scratch.

I came to a stumbling halt, suddenly aware of the gravel cutting my feet. "Everybody shut up and hold still," I commanded as sternly as I knew how. I put on my schoolteacher face—I had teaching credentials in history and lit, and had substituted in numerous inner city high schools in New England before I met Dill.

Strangely, they obeyed me. Even Sapa turned his attention toward me for two heartbeats. Then he looked to Cynthia once more for confirmation that he should obey me.

Good move, Tess. Stop and think before you get everyone into more trouble, Scrap said around one of his favorite black cherry cheroots. He looked mildly pink. There was evil afoot but nothing imminently dangerous. Still, he stayed back by the doorway of my suite. The barrier that existed between Donovan and him was back in place.

"Can you talk some sense into these men, Tess?" Cynthia asked. A little-girl plaintiveness returned to her voice and posture. She didn't want to be in charge, even though Sapa thought she should be. Someone needed to be in charge of that dog.

"Donovan, I suggest you allow the dog into your office. He won't hurt the blanket."

"Are you crazy, Tess? He'll steal the blanket again. It's unique, worth three fortunes. And it belongs to my family." He stood firm, arms crossed, chest heaving in agitation.

"I know how unique it is." I took my eyes off the dog and shifted my gaze toward Donovan. A glare of pure hatred crossed his face. Before I could blink, the malevolent expression vanished, replaced by his completely charming smile.

But I had seen something in his eyes that broke his spell over me. At least temporarily.

"As long as Cynthia is nearby, Sapa will merely guard the blanket for her."

"What's she mean, boss?" Quentin asked. He kept his handgun leveled on the dog. I didn't know the caliber, only that it was an automatic and the muzzle looked very large and powerful.

"Never mind. Let the dog and the girl inside, but keep your aim on the dog at all times. If he so much as drools on that blanket, shoot him." Donovan turned back into his suite.

I counted his stomping steps. Fifteen of them. Then I heard an interior door slam.

"Go with Sapa, Cynthia," I said quietly. "I'll be right behind you. As soon as we get the dog settled, I'll take you to my room. You can bathe and have breakfast."

"I . . . I don't know if he'll . . ."

"Sapa knows you need food and rest. He'll let you come with me. Won't you, Sapa?" I forced myself to scratch the dog between the ears. His shoulder was as high as my hip. But he reacted just like any other dog, sighing and leaning his weight against me as he luxuriated in the caress.

Remember, he isn't totally responsible for Bob's death, Scrap reminded me. *If the demon children didn't have knives aimed at Cynthia, Dog would not have attacked. Bob got in the way of both of them.*

"It's not over between you and me, Dog, but for now I'll let you live. For Cynthia's sake."

In moments the dog had curled up below the blanket and rested his massive head upon his paws. He looked up when I led Cynthia out the door. Then he settled down again.

"Quite a show, Ms. Newcomb," Vern Abrams said from his half of the deck that spread in front of our suites. "Thought you believed the dog to be dangerous." He looked at me with suspicion and not a trace of the previous evening's camaraderie.

"Most dogs are only dangerous when they or their pet humans are attacked," I replied. I dragged Cynthia inside and slammed my door, putting an end to the next question I could see forming on Vern's lips.

I'd figure out who he was and what he wanted from me later.

Scrap's words set me to shaking. What if Dog *was* one of the good guys?

Right now, Cynthia needed a bath, new clothes, and food. I was the only one who could give them to her.

"Interesting development, the dog and the blanket together with a new weaver," Guilford van der Hoyden-Smythe said. He'd parked his long, skinny body on the sofa in my suite and propped his big feet up on the log-and-tree-burl coffee table. The television blared the twenty-four-hour news station. He fingered my antique comb, shifting his attention between it and the TV.

Damn. I knew I should have locked the door behind me.

Chapter 26

*W*HEN I'D SETTLED Cynthia in the tub and ordered breakfast for three from the steak house,
I planted myself between Gollum and the TV that fascinated him.

"Why are you here?" I asked when he finally realized
that I blocked the screen from his view.

I smell cat. Do you smell a cat? Achoooooo!

That was the least of my worries.

"I think you'd better watch this next news segment," he
replied. ·

Frowning, I turned to watch an all-too-familiar scene.
SWAT teams camped outside a chain-link fence and a scattering of low featureless buildings. Police tape, crowds of
media trucks, and cameras littered the rest of the high desert landscape. The anchorman's voice over the live pictures
droned on about the militants inside the abandoned military facility—unnamed, of course.

I'm sure I smell a cat. Scrap turned a nauseating shade of
puce and sneezed again.

"Software mogul Donovan Estevez, as spokesman for
the C'Aquilianish Tribal Council, released this statement
yesterday evening."

Donovan replaced the unnamed military facility in an unnamed location on the screen. He stood before a bouquet of microphones, wearing a pristine white shirt and tie. His long black braid, decorated with those eye-catching silver wings at his temples looked just as respectable as the rest of him—an image I'm certain the tribe chose deliberately.

I'd never heard of that particular tribe, though.

"More than one hundred forty years of abuse of treaty rights by the U.S. government must end," Donovan said most pleasantly, as if discussing business over tea. "We of the Confederated Tribes of the C'Aquilianish Nations," he went on to name several other tribes I did not recognize. None of them resembled the Colville tribe he claimed as part of his ancestry. Each name had more of the unpronounceable clicks, pops, and hisses I'd heard Donovan use in his curses the day before.

"We do hereby declare war on the United States Government," Donovan continued. "We currently occupy this military base and have taken possession of all the weapons stored here. We have set up further defenses with armament purchased out of tribal funds."

His speech went on and on.

I stared at the TV in disbelief, mouth agape.

"They can't possibly win. What can they hope to gain? They're insane," I said over and over again.

"Or they are desperate," Gollum replied quietly.

"Or they are being manipulated."

"Those aren't any tribes I've ever heard of," Cynthia said from the doorway to the bedroom of the suite. She wore one of my jogging suits with the cuffs and sleeves rolled up.

"Me either," Gollum said, his accent more clipped than usual. He leaned forward, peering at the TV screen intently. "And I've done a lot of research into tribal legends and mythology this last month."

Breakfast arrived. Gollum paid for it out of a thick wad of bills.

I raised my eyebrows at the sight of the cash.

"Family trust fund, just kicked in," he said as he started to make coffee.

I'm going to find that cat. I hate cats. Another sneeze. *How can I scent out evil with a cat clogging my nose?*

We all tucked into the meal provided by the steak house. Steak and eggs and pancakes for Cynthia, bacon and eggs and waffles, traditional Belgians (not air-filled) for me, more sausage and eggs and French toast for Gollum. Cynthia wolfed down most of her food, including two glasses of milk and sixteen ounces of orange juice. But she barely touched her steak.

"Um, Tess, would you um, mind . . ."

"Go ahead and give it to Sapa. That's why I ordered such a big one. I figured you'd want to share."

"Thanks." She wrapped the meat in a napkin and bounded out the door, barefoot and happy.

"That's an incredible bond between her and the dog, considering he kidnapped her and killed two of her friends back in Alder Hill," Gollum mused.

"They adore each other. Sapa is the family that was stolen from her when her parents died." How did I know that? "I don't think she really fit in, even after Leonard Stalking Moon adopted her. She needs that dog as much as he needs her." And I needed to call Leonard.

"But she can't stay here. She needs adults to look after her, school, clothes, friends, all the normal things adolescents have," Gollum insisted.

"In her culture she is a woman. I don't know how this is going to turn out, and as much as I hate leaving that dog alive, right now we have to keep Cynthia and Sapa together. We also have to call Leonard and let him know she is safe."

"Are you forgetting that Sapa is a killer?" Gollum and I stared at each other. The vivid memory of two dead boys at the skate park and another maimed rose up in ghastly detail in my mind's eye. The perfect recall given me by the fever was as much a curse as a blessing.

Then I remembered Bob. My dear friend. I choked and nearly gagged on my tears. I could almost smell Bob's blood on my hands, on my clothes, in my hair, everywhere but in his body where it belonged.

The weight of his head in my lap was all too real.

Remember Donovan's demon children and their knives. Were they trying to protect Cynthia or kill her?

"Why would they want to kill her?"

She is the weaver.

I had to relate the snippet of conversation to Gollum.

"Sapa has killed, but only to achieve the mandate given him centuries ago. He had to find a young woman of tribal blood to weave and maintain the blanket—for the good of all humanity." As much as it felt like betrayal of Bob's memory, I had to acknowledge that Sapa would never hurt Cynthia, his chosen weaver.

Gollum sighed and nodded. "I can stay a few weeks and look after her." He pulled out his PDA.

"Scrap, what's my schedule?" I called into the thin air. I hadn't seen the imp since he'd gone cat hunting. He probably got distracted by hunger and was in the lake feasting on micro bugs.

Clear for most of a week. Then you have to go to World Fantasy Con in Madison, Wisconsin.

"Crap. I forgot about that." Both my agent and editor planned to attend the mostly professional con. I was up for an award. I really needed to go.

Gollum's got a cat. He can't stay if he has a cat. I won't let him.

I relayed my schedule to Gollum, remembering that he couldn't hear or see Scrap. I didn't care about the cat. "Let's just hope we can wrap this up in a week."

"Where'd you get this?" Gollum held up the comb.

I snatched it from his hand. "It's an antique I picked up somewhere." I twisted up my hair and jammed the comb in. It seemed to fit better every day. But I also noticed more and more transparent and brittle hairs came out with it each time I removed it. My scalp hurt, too, as if a cat had run its claws over the surface.

I couldn't wear it as often as I liked, or I'd lose all my hair.

"It has a glamour of magic about it. Only a few antique stores in this country would be able to handle something like that. Do you remember where in your travels you found it?" Gollum moved around behind me to study the thing.

"Magic," I snorted.

Listen to him, babe. And find out why he has a cat in his room. Scrap sounded decidedly stuffy.

"Magic," Gollum said firmly. "I wonder what sort of magic."

So do I.

Cynthia came bounding back in, still happy. "Sapa thanks you for the steak. He was really hungry." She plunked back down at the table and tucked into her remaining pancakes. "Oh, and Sapa reminded me that the mean man thinks he has a claim on the blanket, but he doesn't really."

"What?" Gollum and I said together as we stared at her.

"Long ago, in the time of our oldest grandfathers, when Coyote still walked the earth, the gods gave the blanket to all of the tribes so that they would learn honor and dignity and compromise." Cynthia fell into a kind of chant.

I thought she might be channeling this legend much as Gollum had channeled the original, but her eyes remained bright and her face animated.

"The blanket didn't always work, humans being what they are, so when the Columbia River changed course, and chaos ruled, the demons from beneath the lakes and rivers stole the blanket. Humans took a long time recovering from the awesome floods, but when they did, they missed the blanket and the honor and dignity and compromise it helped us hold onto. So three warriors from each of three different tribes went down below the lakes. The nine warriors had many adventures and six of them died. But the remaining three captured the blanket from the demons and returned it to humanity. This time it was entrusted to the best weaver in all of the tribes and she and the blanket were hidden where no man could find them with the dog Shunka Sapa to guard her and the blanket." She finished and drew a deep breath.

"I think that's everything Sapa said to tell you."

"How does Sapa communicate with you, Cynthia?" Gollum asked the question that burned in both of us.

"In my dreams. We travel in my dreams, too. I don't remember walking a step, but each night when I'd fall asleep curled around Sapa, I'd dream deep and long, then in the morning I woke up miles and miles and miles from where we were. And I didn't get hungry either."

"Cross-dimensional travel. I've read about it in a number of legends. Rip Van Winkle comes to mind." Gollum looked as if he'd embark on a lecture longer than Cynthia's story.

Time is just another dimension. Cynthia may have matured ten years or more in five days, Scrap whispered in my ear. He didn't appear.

Obviously, he was still hunting the cat. Why, I didn't know.

Trust your dreams, Sister Serena had said to me yesterday. *My* dreams, not Cynthia's.

I think that's what she said anyway.

"Why didn't we know about this part of the blanket legend, Cynthia? We only had the part after humanity got the blanket back." I diverted the conversation.

"Coyote made people forget the early part, so we wouldn't get into trouble with the demons." She finished her meal and went looking in the mini fridge for more juice. "I've got to get back to Sapa and study that blanket." Cynthia dashed out again before I could object.

"I don't like the implication that Donovan comes from a family of demons," I muttered into my coffee. But that would explain a lot. Especially his potent male mojo that melted my knees and sent my logic flying in the wind.

"What makes you say that?" Gollum asked. He got up to make a new pot of coffee. The in-house machine only brewed about two cups at a time.

"He claims the blanket is an old family heirloom and he's deathly afraid the dog will steal it. Again."

Chapter 27

"OKAY, IF DONOVAN is a demon, why don't I just kill him? That's what I'm trained to do." And that would take away the annoying temptation to jump his bones and screw his brains out.

I might also get rid of some of my own self-disgust for succumbing to him.

"No!" Gollum leaped up in protest. The table rattled. His plate rocked. The remnants of his coffee sloshed over the rim of his cup.

"Why not? He's a demon." I shouldn't have any remorse about killing a demon. I had to forget that Donovan looked and acted like a man; that he kissed me like a man in love.

Find out about the cat. I hate cats. Cats are evil. Scrap tugged at my hair, but I ignored him. Cats weren't important.

Waddya mean they aren't important. They are as evil as demons!

"We don't know for sure that Donovan is a demon, more likely a half blood, possibly only a liaison. True demons can't shape-change into human form in this dimension."

"Then how do they breed with humans?"

"They kidnap them and take them back to their own

dimension where they appear very human and very charming."

"And you know that how?"

"Old family tradition. We study demons." A long pause while he bit his lip and thought long and hard. "We also study those who can kill them."

Meaning me and my Sisterhood. Brotherhood, too, I supposed. The Citadel ruled by Sister Gert wasn't the only one in the world.

"If Scrap can transform into the Celestial Blade in Donovan's presence, then he's a demon. That would explain why he couldn't become anything more lethal than a fireplace poker when I first encountered Sapa. Sapa isn't a demon. But Scrap did transform fully when the dog kidnapped Cynthia." I had to avoid mentioning that Sapa had killed Bob during that encounter. I wouldn't be able to continue thinking, let alone talking if I dwelled on my best friend's death. "Donovan and his three demon children were right there."

"Whatever Donovan Estevez is by blood, he is a legal citizen of the U.S. He owns a business. A *BIG* business. People will ask questions if he dies. His death will be investigated. You, my dear, will be arrested and tried for murder."

"I am not *your* dear. But you have a point. So what do we do?" I paced restlessly, needing to feel the Celestial Blade or a fencing foil in my hands, needing to lash out at something. "I'm going for a run. You do what you do, like finding out how and why Donovan is involved in the casino, and the Indian movement to declare war on the U.S. Then call Leonard." I might as well make use of Gollum while he insisted on annoying me with his presence. "Oh, and while you are at it, figure out how you are going to explain to me why I've let you back into my life. I still don't want or need a partner."

I ripped out the comb, not wanting to lose any more hair than I had to. Let him study the magic in it.

When I came back an hour later, winded and glowing with sweat, Gollum had set up his own laptop—much more expensive and powerful than mine—on the coffee table and was studying an Internet page filled with arcane symbols. He was so intent upon his study that he didn't acknowledge me when I came in. Nor did he turn his head as I stripped off my sweats and wandered into the bathroom wearing only my bra and panties.

A true geek if I ever saw one.

"Guilford, this is *my* room. How about some privacy?" I poked my head out of the bedroom door and glared at him.

"I can go back to my room, directly below you, if you insist." He stretched and yawned, never taking his eyes off his computer screen. The TV continued to broadcast the world news on the tall stand above him. At least he'd muted the blasted thing.

"Oh, my Goddess!" I stared at the TV. Without regard to my dishabille, I moved to stand directly in front of it.

"What?" Gollum stood up beside me. The TV was about eye level to his tall frame. I had to crane my neck a little.

"That shot of the abandoned military facility Donovan's 'Indians' took over." I pointed at the latest account of the story.

"What about it?"

"In the background, caught in the sidelight of the setting sun."

"A lot of desert."

"And a casino under construction. The military base is right next door to Donovan's casino. Just outside the city of Half Moon Lake. I've got to check this out." I hastened toward the door.

Gollum grabbed me by the shoulders. "After you shower and you get dressed, we'll both go up to the casino and check it out." He pushed me back toward the bedroom.

I followed orders, my mind spinning with thoughts and possibilities.

"By the way, I like that you color coordinate your underwear," Gollum called after me.

I half laughed. I'd clung to the tradition of the Sisterhood. Blood red bra and panties to remind me of the demon blood I was commissioned to spill.

"But I don't like that wound on your upper arm." Gollum stopped me just before I stepped into the bathroom. He peered at the raw flesh that oozed a little blood, left over from the bullet ricochet. "How did this happen?"

"It doesn't hurt anymore, and it will heal by tomorrow," I replied defensively. "Nothing to concern you."

"But it does concern me."

"It's none of your business until you tell me why you are still here getting in my way. You find a way to tell me when I get out of the shower, or you are out of here, along with the cat that Scrap hates." Anger heated my face and pulsed through my entire being. The wound throbbed anew.

I slammed the door in his face.

"I'm waiting for an explanation," I said, freshly showered and dressed in jeans, sweater, and boots. Cloud cover had moved in and turned the high desert into a cold place hunkering down toward winter.

Ask him about the cat.

"This isn't easy for me, Tess."

"Fine. Then grab your computer and the other detritus of your sojourn in my room and get out of here. I don't want to see you again." I grabbed my purse and fished out the keys to my rental car. The big honking white SUV. I hated driving the gas hog, but it was all the rental agency had left.

Don't be so harsh on him, Scrap admonished me as he blew a particularly odiferous smoke ring into my face. Then he farted.

I had to lean away and fan the air in front of my face.

I like him, Scrap explained. *Except that he has a cat. If he stays, the cat has to go.* He fluttered near Gollum's shoulder but didn't alight. Maybe he couldn't sit on anyone's shoulder but mine.

"Okay, best I blurt it out before I lose my courage." Gollum fidgeted, shifting from foot to foot. "Secrecy is a hard habit to break."

Meanwhile, the news coverage showed a flurry of shots exchanged between Donovan's "Indians" and the SWAT team. Three military helicopters and a squad of Marines had been added to the chaos.

"Then blurt and stop hedging. I need to get out to the

casino and see what is really going on." I juggled the car keys between my two hands.

"My family has monitored the Orders of the Celestial Blade for over four hundred years. We do the research for them."

"But you never fight the demons yourselves?" Why hadn't anyone told me about this?

"Upon occasion. My dad lost an arm to a demon. He claimed he lost it in Viet Nam when I was two. Mom never quite forgave him for that. He didn't even admit it to me until last week."

I raised both eyebrows at that.

"My grandfather told me about the family trust—the trust to seek out and aid your Sisterhood any way we can. Mom insisted they were all just tall tales born of Gramps' overfertile imagination. But I knew he told the truth."

I stared at him for several long moments, not certain I wanted to believe so simple explanation.

"Have you ever fought a demon?"

I bet he lets his cat do it for him. Cats are mean.

"No."

"Have you ever seen one?"

"Just the kids at the con. By the way, they are half-blood Kajiri demons, according to my research."

I shuddered at that. Paige, Mary, and Electra, the arms mistresses at the Citadel, particularly feared Kajiri demons.

"Why didn't you just come out and tell me this when we first met?"

"I had to be sure you are what you are."

"You seemed more certain of it than I did."

I looked at my keys, wondering what to do next. What to ask next. "Are you officially attached to any of the Orders of the Celestial Blade?"

"No."

"So why are you here?"

"We . . . my grandfather and I had been led to believe that all of the initiates had died out. There haven't been any authenticated demon sightings in over thirty-five years, not since the battle that took Dad's arm."

"Of course not. They all hang out at SF cons and win prizes for their costumes that aren't really costumes at all."

Donovan had won a prize for his bat costume. Was it truly a costume?

We both sighed at our ignorance at the last con. We could have taken out three demon children if we'd only known.

"So why did you seek me out? Why didn't you just take a teaching position at some obscure college and forget about the Sisterhood of the Celestial Blade."

"I read your book."

"Crap."

"The family trust fund supports us when we are assisting members of your order. Gramps reopened it as soon as I told him about you. It hasn't been touched in decades. I can access the money for all our expenses until this matter is settled."

"Thanks, but I can pay my own expenses."

"I've already paid the hotel for our two rooms for two weeks in advance. This place is cheap."

I brushed past him.

"You need me, Tess. Not many members of your Sisterhood venture outside the Citadel once they are initiated. You are alone in this fight. You can't contact them for help. You can't go back there until you have done their dirty work for them."

No phones, no computers, no running water, or electricity in the Citadel. I had only an occasional and spotty mind contact with Sister Serena. And no true control over that.

"The Sisterhood is fully occupied in guarding the portal. They don't have time to help me."

We are challenged often. Beseiged. Many wounded and dead, Sister S had said.

Or had I imagined it.

No, the contact had been real. And clear. Demons on the move meant trouble everywhere.

"In the year you spent in the Citadel, did you even once engage in battle at the portal? Did you even hear about a battle while you were there?"

"One. But I wasn't allowed to participate. And they showed me the portal."

"But you never saw a demon or fought one. They've abandoned you, Tess. You sink or swim on your own."

A fitting metaphor since we bordered on a lake. A lake that might very well be its own portal to a land of demons. The one I crossed into when I first contracted the fever.

"You can scout with me *today* if you want. But I'm driving."

Chapter 28

*W*E FOUND AN UNPAVED road that wound up the hill on the west side of Half Moon Lake to the ridge where the partially built casino sat like a squashed spider. All of the regular roads were blocked off by state police and the military. Heavy trucks carrying construction materials had churned this rutted dirt trail into a mess. I had to engage the four wheel drive to get up the steep road. For the first time ever I was glad to have the SUV.

"I brought your comb. I think you should wear it," Gollum said, peering through the dusty windshield.

"Why don't you wear it?" I had trouble concentrating on getting through the next pothole that looked big enough to swallow a tank. Thankfully, the SUV was bigger.

"Because it is *your* comb. However you came by it, it was meant for you. The rightful owner is probably the only one who can access the magic."

He's right.

"Okay, okay. But not right now. I need both hands to get us up this hill."

The main casino building in the center rose two full stories with framing for another two atop it. A number of satellite buildings sprawled around it with only the skeleton of connections among them. Construction trailers, heavy machinery, stacks of wood, and other construction supplies lay scattered about as if a tornado had hit the area. I couldn't see a sign of activity or people anywhere near the place.

I stepped out of the car. Even the ever present wind had stilled, waiting in ambush for the unwary. I could have written this scene. And I didn't like what I did to my characters when I did.

I don't like this, Tess. No sarcasm, no cigar, no "babe." Scrap was worried.

"Let's do this when there are people around to ask questions of," Gollum said quietly. He stood with the door open, ready to duck back into the car at the first portent of trouble.

I'm made of sterner stuff. Or maybe I'm just stupid.

I stepped away from the car and walked around the first pile of construction debris. It smoked. The crew burned the scraps as they went. I hadn't been around construction projects much, but that seemed wasteful. At least in textile projects you never knew when a small leftover piece would correct a mistake or fill an unexpected gap, or highlight a finishing touch.

I kicked at the smoldering mess. It wasn't all wood pieces. Something metallic caught my eye, and something else . . .

"Tess?" Gollum called.

I whirled to face him.

"Can we go now?"

"No. Something is wrong. It's the middle of the day, not yet lunchtime. It's not raining. Where is everyone?"

"Maybe they are with the 'Indians' taking over the abandoned army fort."

I could see the ten-foot-high chain-link fence topped with rolls of razor wire a mile or more behind the casino. The horizon was a long way away up on this plateau, distorting my sense of distance.

I looked across to the back side of the abandoned—and now reoccupied—buildings. Even they seemed stagnant, waiting for someone to move, or fire the next shot.

"Do you have any binoculars in the car?" Gollum asked very quietly.

"Emergency travel bag behind the driver's seat," I replied in a whisper. I didn't need the binoculars. Scrap fluttered before my eyes, beet red, ready to transform.

We'd all spotted movement along the back of the buildings. Hunched-over forms that moved with a stiff gait and heavy fisted hands that brushed their knees. Thick fur, both dark and light, covered their bodies.

Sasquatch.

Demons.

My skin prickled, and tension built along my spine. The otherworldly figures opened a door by scratching at a keypad near a seemingly blank space of wall. They slipped through the opening, then closed the door. It blended into the gun metal gray walls so well, I doubted I could find it if I stood directly in front of it.

Scrap faded a little. But he still retained a battle-ready attitude and redness.

The air thickened. Then I heard the distinctive *whopp, whopp* of a helicopter flying low and close. The stealth-black vehicle was above me before I saw it.

The wind from its blades tried to push me flat against the ground.

Scrap winked out.

I held my ground.

"You have entered a restricted area. Get into your car and leave immediately," a voice boomed from speakers mounted on the skids of the helicopter.

I stared at the black whirling machine above me, slightly stunned by the wash of noise and that we had seen no signs restricting the area outside the fence.

"Come on, Tess, we've got to get out of here." Gollum beckoned me.

Of course, the military and the SWAT teams would have cleared the area if they expected a firefight to remove Donovan's "Indians."

I took one step toward the car.

The demons emerged from the hidden door once more.

I pointed furiously at the activity, willing the officials in the helicopter to look in that direction.

A hideous buzzing noise erupted from a bulb on the front of the helicopter along with a sizzling blue light.

Incredible lancing fire assailed every muscle in my body. I collapsed in a writhing blob of pain.

Disaster! I can't find my babe's mind.

Medic!

Oh, my, what do I do?

She's gone. I can see her body. But her mind is gone. Worse than before she had the imp flu. She can't reach me. I can't reach her.

It's as if she no longer exists. Has she died?

Without her I will die.

Without me she will die.

I feel myself fading.

Is this the end?

Chapter 29

"LIEUTENANT, THIS REACTION isn't normal," a disembodied voice said into the chaos that had become my mind.

"Keep her restrained, corporal. Medics are on their way," a deeper voice growled.

I tried to ask what had happened. My mind and voice seemed disconnected. Every muscle in my body seemed disconnected from the rest of me.

If this was a dream, I didn't want to trust it.

"She's still twitching and unresponsive, lieutenant," the first voice said. "That's not normal. Instructions on that weapon say that victims should return to normal within thirty seconds of the blast."

"This is a prototype, not the standard police issue taser," the second voice, the lieutenant's, said.

Okay. That sizzling blue light and hideous buzzing was a taser. Some kind of super-duper taser designed for military use. I made that much sense of the conversation.

Coherence began to return to my thoughts. But my muscles still twitched and ached and refused to listen to the rest of me.

Muffled grunts and thumping came from my left. I tried to turn my head but failed to make the connection.

"Lieutenant, the other vic is trying to say something. He might have information as to why the lady had such an abnormal reaction to the taser."

"Keep him restrained and gagged. These two are obviously terrorists connected to the hostiles inside Fort Snoqualmie." The lieutenant brooked no interference with his orders.

The other "vic" must be Gollum. I wasn't alone. But where was Scrap? I could really use his ears and eyes right now.

A door opened and then closed. I managed to focus my eyes long enough to see a rectangle of brighter white around the door for just a few seconds. Then there was a shifting of bodies, a rustle of clothing, and boots scraping on a vinyl floor.

That told me I'd been moved from the casino site. Indoors somewhere. That would account for the lack of background noise, especially the roar of helicopters.

Hands upon my wrist. The cold metal mouth of a stethoscope on my chest beneath my sweater.

"Vitals are normal," a new voice said. Probably the medic the lieutenant and corporal expected. "Must have been some strange and individual neurological reaction to the taser frequency. She'll come around eventually. I'll shoot her full of tranquilizers before she hurts herself with those convulsions."

No drugs! Scrap screeched in my ear.

"No," I managed to squeak. "No drugs." I had strange reactions to drugs since the fever that marked me as a Warrior of the Celestial Blade. Maybe the fever had changed other things in my brain as well.

Tranquilizers will kill us, babe.

I couldn't see Scrap. I should. Why couldn't I see Scrap?

Because you're only half alive and so am I.

"Sorry, miss. This will make you feel better, and keep you from hurting yourself."

I concentrated very hard on getting out the next few crucial words. "Drugs make worse. I'm weird," I choked.

"Huh?"

"The lady said no drugs. Now put that syringe away," Gollum said in his most clipped accent, as if speaking to a child.

How did he get loose from the gag?

"Really, sir," the medic protested.

Then I heard the sounds of someone choking, a scuffle, shouts. A clump. A body fell hard across my middle.

I forced my eyes open. Gollum lay across me, glasses askew, silver-gilt hair tangled, muscles limp.

Suddenly my body stopped twitching and my mind connected everything up.

I rolled out from under Gollum and came up to my knees, elbows out, ready to jab someone in the throat. Handcuffs hindered my movements but didn't stop me.

The medic and the lieutenant lay collapsed upon the carpeted floor. The corporal—I presumed the youngest of the trio with two stripes on his camouflage jacket was the corporal—cowered against the metal wall of the small room. He held his pistol—a long and wicked-looking instrument—by the barrel. He must have used the butt to hit Gollum over the head.

An ugly lump bled a little on the back of my friend's head. Gollum's face looked a little raw, like someone had rubbed it with sandpaper—or ripped off a wad of duct tape.

Corporal Bolo, at least I thought that was the name embroidered on the pocket of his fatigues, gulped and tried to disappear into the wall.

He was mortal and mundane and couldn't get any farther away from me.

"Don't let him hurt me, lady," he pleaded.

What had Gollum done to put the fear of God into this boy? This military corporal who still had a gun!

"Get these handcuffs off me, and we'll leave you mostly intact," I replied, trying to sound a lot fiercer than I was. He had the gun after all, even though he still held it by the barrel.

Nice try, babe, but I wouldn't be afraid of you, Scrap sneered from the region of my left shoulder. He was back.

I'd never been so grateful for his smelly, rude, nosy presence in my life.

Glad to have you back, babe. Wondered if we'd survive this.

"Who . . . who's smoking?" the corporal asked. "This is a nonsmoking area. We've got a lot of sensitive equipment and . . . and firepower stored here." He stared at his own gun and fumbled it around until he finally pointed the business end roughly in my direction.

I rolled my eyes at Scrap. *Toss the cigar, imp. You're more trouble than you're worth. Where have you been?*

No answer, but the cigar smoke disappeared.

"Just get these handcuffs off me. Please."

I looked down upon Gollum's sprawled figure. He'd be uncomfortable with his restrained hands tucked under him in that awkward position. If he were conscious. That lump on the back of his head looked painful.

"And off my friend, too."

"Look, lady. We were just doing our job. You're terrorists. We can't let you loose." Corporal Bolo's chin quivered a bit and his voice threatened to crack.

"What makes you think we're terrorists, Bolo?" I asked as I did my best to stand up. My knees were still a little weak and my balance sucked, but I made it upright without falling over. I held out my hands as if I expected the man to produce a key and release me.

"You . . . you sneaked up behind us in a white SUV rental. That's a profile car."

"Sheesh!" I rolled my eyes and stared at the ceiling.

"I'm a novelist doing research. The white SUV was the only rental available in Tri-Cities."

"Is that why you had a case of books in the back of the SUV?"

"Duh."

Gollum groaned. His eyelids fluttered open. He looked at me, unfocused and puzzled. Then his face cleared of befuddlement and he reached a hand to touch his wound. But his hands were still cuffed together. He moaned and lay still again. But his eyes remained open, searching, taking in every detail within his range.

He was no normal professor-type geek. I knew he hadn't told me his entire life story and I began to wonder just what he wanted to keep secret. And why.

The medic and the lieutenant also began to wake up. They grabbed their throats and coughed shallowly several times before completely rousing.

Before I could think of a way to talk myself out of this mess, the door to the outside banged open.

"Get in there, you terrorist bastard!" a Marine sergeant shouted as he shoved Donovan inside the tiny hut. A quick glance told me this was a portable trailer moved on site—probably painted camouflage—as a command center.

Donovan stumbled up the one step to the inside, cursing and spitting blood. His shoulders hung at an awkward angle with his hands cuffed behind him. Blood dripped from his split lip, his left eye had nearly swollen shut. The bruising would become a rainbow of colors before long. His white shirt was ripped at the shoulder seam and filthy. A jagged cut showed through the torn knee of his dress slacks. He looked like he'd been beaten, rolled in the mud, and hung out to dry.

Couldn't happen to a nicer guy.

So why was he still the sexiest man in the trailer?

Ta, babe! Too much demon smell in here. He's been around demons. I gotta go find them. Scrap winked out.

"Tess, thank God you're okay," Donovan gushed. He winced as he dropped to his knees beside me.

"Traitor!" I hissed. Hard to do without any esses in the word, but I managed.

Gollum grinned, then quickly blanked his expression again. He still surveyed the room warily from his position at my feet.

Scrap pressed his nose against the tiny window above the door from the outside.

"What?" I mouthed to him.

I'll say something when I've got something to say, babe. He chomped on a cigar but didn't light it. *You're not bleeding, I can go scout around for you.*

Stay right where you are, I ordered him.

He left anyway. But that's Scrap, as independent as I. He couldn't get along with the other imps any better than I got along with the Sisters who partnered them.

"I couldn't help it, Tess. They kidnapped me. They forced me to be their spokesman," Donovan continued his litany of innocence.

He was so sincere I almost believed him. Almost. We had a lot of trust issues to work out.

"Define 'they,'" Bolo barked, finally gaining courage in the presence of backup.

"That mob of crazed youngsters who think they can take on the world and win," Donovan spat, literally. A wad of blood and spittle and a tooth came out of his mouth. It looked like a normal human tooth.

"So why didn't they keep you?" I asked.

"I don't know." He had the grace to look abashed and drop his gaze.

"Did the demons do this to you or the Marines?" Gollum whispered.

"The Marines." He was silent a moment, then looked at us both in surprise. "Demons?" he mouthed.

"They aren't exactly Indians." I smiled too sweetly.

Donovan shook his head. "They are Indians. I've known a lot of them all my life."

"I don't doubt you've known them most of your life." Standoff. "How'd they force you if they didn't beat you?"

"They threatened to burn the casino. I've got every dime I own tied up in that project. One more delay, one more bad inspection and I'm ruined." He looked up with those big dark eyes framed by beautifully long lashes and pleaded with me to believe him.

My heart, and my innards threatened to melt under those eyes.

"Don't believe him," Gollum muttered as he struggled to sit.

"Well, I don't believe any of you," the lieutenant sneered. He sat on a typing chair in front of a console full of monitors and keyboards.

I ignored the tactical displays because I didn't understand them and didn't have the concentration to figure them out.

"We've got to bust out of here," Donovan whispered.

I was sure everyone in the trailer heard him. The sergeant just leaned against the door and grinned, inviting us to try. He wanted to hit someone almost as much as I did.

"Not on your life, Donovan. We stay put until these people realize that they made a terrible mistake and release us. I'm not spending the rest of my life on the run from the U.S. government. I have a life and a career." I sank down to sit cross-legged next to Gollum.

He still didn't look real healthy. His complexion remained pasty, and his eyes still rolled out of focus occasionally.

"If you two are so innocent, how come tall and lanky attacked us?" The lieutenant leaned forward, almost falling off his chair.

"The medic wouldn't listen. He was going to give Tess a drug that would kill her," Gollum replied. He looked the lieutenant directly in the eye. Few people could do that and lie effectively. "Sweetheart, we've got to get you a medical bracelet so emergency personnel know which drugs you're allergic to." Gollum patted my cuffed hands with his own cuffed hands.

I wanted to snarl at him that I wasn't his sweetheart.

He frowned at me until I almost heard him beg me to play along.

Reluctantly I decided to let him lead the way. Maybe he had a plan. I sure didn't.

Chapter 30

*T*HE DOOR RATTLED. We all looked to see how many more bodies wanted to squeeze into the trailer.

"Background checks coming in on monitor four, lieutenant," a private said as he poked his head inside. He looked askance at all of us, counted bodies, sitting and standing, on the floor and at the workstations, then backed out.

Lieutenant Vlieger (thank the Goddess these guys all wore name tags) swung around on his chair and clicked a mouse. The center monitor flashed a picture of me—my most flattering publicity photo with soft lighting and fuzzy edges that disguised my untidy hair and imperfect makeup—along with a bunch of text.

Vlieger switched his gaze from me to the monitor, peering ever closer to both. "I guess that could be you," he finally admitted.

"Well, thanks," I said. Sarcasm dripped from my words thicker than it did from Scrap at his most polite.

"Your hair is quite a bit lighter now," he said half apologetically.

"Women dye their hair," I returned. Only I hadn't. It had only gotten lighter since I'd been wearing the comb. I wondered if the translucent hairs it pulled out were the transformed darker strands, leaving only the fairer blond ones.

That comb was certainly weird. Wish I knew what its magic purpose was.

Vlieger scrolled down the screen until he came across the cover to my book. "You wrote this?" He pointed.

"Every last word."

"Guess that explains the case of them we found in the back of the SUV."

I rolled my eyes. "Don't think I'm going to give you an autographed copy," I muttered. "That is, if you can read."

"Easy, Tess, we want him on our side," Gollum whispered and patted my hand. He was getting too used to that proprietary gesture.

"May I check your blood pressure again?" the medic asked, almost meekly. He held up a cuff.

I nodded and held out my arms.

He maneuvered around our sprawled legs until he could crouch beside me. While he pumped up the cuff and monitored a digital readout, Vlieger continued to read every word of my bio.

"Sheesh, not even a traffic ticket," Vlieger said out loud. "What are these organizations you belong to? They might be subversive."

"A bunch of writers banding together so they can have legal advocacy funds and medical insurance are very subversive," I replied.

He scrolled further down. I guess he found explanations for the acronyms for romance authors, science fiction writers, and novelists in general.

"If you are so squeaky clean, Ms. Noncoiré, then why did you disappear for a year?" He tapped a blank portion of the screen.

"I was in retreat while I researched and wrote that damn book."

"Right after a dubious marriage."

"My marriage to Dillwyn Cooper was legal, binding, and . . ." I choked. "And real."

"Easy, Ms. Noncoiré," Medic Lawrence soothed. He pulled me back down into the sitting position. "Your blood pressure just rose sixty points. That's not good."

"Did her blood pressure go up because she was lying?" Vlieger looked hopeful.

"This isn't a lie detector," Lawrence said. He was too calm, too collected, too bland.

I didn't trust him. That blood pressure cuff just might be the latest thing in lie detection.

"She was really mad at you for questioning her marriage. My educated guess is that she was telling the truth." Lawrence kept his eyes on his equipment, not meeting Vlieger's malevolent gaze.

Vlieger turned back to his screens. "Homeland Security says you're clean, Ms Noncoiré. I trust that you aren't a terrorist or security risk. Take the cuffs off her and let her go."

"What about Gol . . . Guilford?" I figured they wouldn't appreciate his nickname. Or understand it.

"We'll get to him." Vlieger clicked the mouse and read silently.

We waited.

He muttered and snarled to himself.

We waited some more. And fidgeted.

"What haven't you told me about yourself?" I asked sweetly. Too sweetly.

Gollum shrugged. "I practice tai chi every morning." He smiled weakly, apologetically.

Scrap peered through the window again. *Gollum smoked marijuana in college. Says so right on the screen,* Scrap chortled. *They're gonna put him away for ten years for that!*

Scrap, we all smoked marijuana in college. Probably even the lieutenant there.

Oh. Scrap sounded disappointed. *Even you, babe?*

Even me.

"There is a little matter of two years in Africa working for the Peace Corps," Vlieger turned back to pierce Gollum with his gaze.

"I gave back to the world." Gollum shrugged.

"Says here you come from old money in upstate New York. Why'd a guy born with a silver spoon in his mouth condescend to grub in the dirt with a bunch of primitives?"

"Like I said. I felt I needed to give something back to the less fortunate. Money isn't always enough. Besides, it gave me a chance to study some of their myths and folklore firsthand. I wrote my master's thesis on what I learned." Gollum's grip on my hands turned fierce. He was hiding something. Possibly something even Homeland Security couldn't find.

Something I needed to know.

Vlieger gave his attention to the screen once more. "Two Ph.D.s and you haven't even applied for a tenure track position at a college or university?" He raised his eyebrows.

"Old money from upstate New York. I don't have to work, so I take on short-term teaching positions in interesting places. When I find the right place to settle down, I'll consider something more permanent." His grip on my hand softened. Whatever he had to hide was in those two years in Africa, not in his recent career.

"So why are you here?" Vlieger kept up his interrogation.

"Helping Ms Noncoiré research a new novel." Gollum grinned and scrunched up his nose in an effort to push up his glasses.

"Why were you both poking around the casino construction site? Today? When we'd closed off the entire area because of terrorist activity nearby?" Vlieger was out of his chair and grabbing Gollum's shirt at his throat in less than a heartbeat.

No one else moved.

No one breathed.

Except Scrap. He lit his cigar with a flamelet on the tip of his thumb. Then he blew a huge smoke ring toward the sergeant at the door. Good thing the door was still closed and Scrap on the outside.

"We need to speed this up or turn on the air-conditioning." The sergeant fanned the air in front of his face. Some of Scrap's smoke did get through. "The air's getting stale in here. Smells of old cigars and . . . oh, my God, who farted?"

This time he did open the door and let in some of the cool desert air.

Scrap remained outside, eyeing Donovan with a fierce hatred.

Donovan eyed the door longingly.

"We did not know the area was closed," Gollum explained patiently. "There were no signs on the construction road, no roadblocks. We wanted to talk to some of the people in favor of the casino. Heaven only knows we've talked to enough people in town who are against it."

"All fodder for the writing mill," I chimed in. "Conflict is the essence of plotting. I need more conflict in my new book."

Donovan shifted as if ready to get his feet under him and dart out the door.

I kicked him. He glowered at me.

I wondered what he had to hide that he didn't want to stick around for the revelation of his background check. Even if Vlieger kicked me out right now, I doubted I'd go. I needed to know more about Donovan Estevez.

We waited. Corporal Bolo took the handcuffs off both Gollum and me, but left them on Donovan. Vlieger had said we were free to go, but he didn't kick us out and neither of us made a move toward the door. Lawrence kept fussing over me with his blood pressure cuff and stethoscope.

Scrap popped up and down by the window, laughing at us mere humans.

It's a circus out there. Neither side seems to know how to fight this war, he chortled. *Some of the media trucks are packing up and going home. Not enough action.*

Finally, Vlieger's computer beeped. "Took long enough," he muttered.

We all leaned forward.

Vlieger read the screens without comment. Screen after screen rolled past. I saw blurred photos; some looked like they'd been downloaded from news services.

"Homeland Security wants us to hold on to you a while longer, Mr. Estevez. You two can go."

Did I dare ask what was on those computer screens?

"I'm ruined." Donovan slumped. He looked smaller, more human, and more vulnerable than I'd ever seen him before.

And sexy as hell.

"Come on, Guilford." I didn't want to raise questions by calling him Gollum in this crowd, and I certainly wouldn't call him sweetheart. "We need to check on Cynthia."

"Don't even think about stealing the blanket," Donovan snarled. "My people are armed and guarding it with their lives."

"I wouldn't dream of committing a crime." I opened my eyes wide, trying to look innocent. Though that was precisely what I was thinking. "But who will defend your claim to the artifact in court while Homeland Security has you locked up on suspicion of terrorism?"

I grabbed Gollum by the elbow and decamped as quickly as I could.

Fresh air never smelled so sweet as that windy hilltop in the high desert on a cloudy autumn day.

A series of pops and bangs sounded off to our left.

The sergeant pushed us down one step into the dust. "Down! Those damn Indians are trying to break through our lines."

Bullets whizzed over our heads. They pinged against the trailer and smacked into the dirt.

I cringed and cowered with my arms over my head, trying to make myself as small a target as possible.

Gollum landed on top of me. His weight became a reassuring barrier between me and a weapon I could not counter.

Scrap, what do we do now?

Hide! He turned bright red and elongated, thinning, ready to transform.

Another spate of gunfire. I couldn't fight guns with the Celestial Blade. Scrap and I were useless.

The bullets intensified on both sides.

I watched in stunned horror as a bullet crashed into Corporal Bolo's forehead.

He looked stunned for half a heartbeat. A dark hole appeared between his eyes. His blood and brains splattered against the trailer wall. Then he slumped to the ground, dead before his knees crumpled.

Chapter 31

Up to twenty million bats have been known to live in a single colony inside a cave—Bracken Cave in the central Texas hill country.

DONOVAN BURST OUT of the trailer, automatic weapon blazing like some movie action hero. I half expected him to spout words in Austrian. He aimed at the figures gathered on the other side of the fence. "Stupid Kajiri fools. Too impatient. Too violent. Too young to know your ass for a hole in your heads. Everything I've worked for—ruined!" he screamed as he marched forward.

Young men and women on the other side of the fence fell bleeding. Crumpled rag dolls thrown into the dirt. Their blood smelled like water tasted when tainted by heavy mineral salts—like the lake.

That's what these demons smell like, the lake. Donovan smells different, Scrap said, puzzled. *Demons are close, their evil counters Donovan's mojo. We need to go into action, dahling.*

Not until they stop shooting! I protested.

"Stand down, Estevez!" Vlieger shouted. Wisely, he stayed in the doorway of the trailer, ready to duck back inside the dubious shelter should Donovan turn that horrible weapon on him.

Donovan paused. His gunfire sputtered to a stop. No one was firing back. No one was left inside the compound to fire back.

"Stand down and hand me the weapon, Estevez," Vlieger ordered, like he was speaking to one of his own Marines gone berserk.

An ugly sneer marred Donovan's handsome face. But the tip of his gun lowered. His finger on the trigger went slack.

"Hand me the weapon." Vlieger stepped down from the doorway. He placed a gentle hand on Donovan's shoulder as he eased the heavy gun out of his hands with the other. Keeping his eyes on Donovan, Vlieger handed the gun to the sergeant.

"Let's go back inside and talk."

"Just lock me up and throw away the key," Donovan said sadly. He looked toward the half-built casino with longing near despair.

"I'm sure you can work something out, Donovan," I said as I crawled out from under Gollum. "The siege of the fort is over." So why was Scrap still hovering so close to me? Donovan's presence should chase him away.

Already I could see Marines breaking through the front gates, weapons at the ready. No one stirred among the fallen defenders.

"Your crews can get back to work. You've only lost one day of work." I kept up my soothing tone.

He turned his bleak gaze back to me.

"Promise you won't steal the blanket until I get clear of Homeland Security?" He flashed me one of his charming half smiles.

That might be a very long time. I couldn't promise him that. I clung to my doubts and distrust with a will as strong as imp wood.

"We'll talk when Lieutenant Vlieger is done with you. I'm sure he'll understand that you couldn't have been part of the takeover." He wouldn't kill his own people just to prove his own innocence, would he?

A demon would.

Shaking and numb at the same time, Gollum and I stumbled to my rental car, or what was left of it. The Marines had been very thorough in their search for anything incriminating. The seats lay strewn about the ground. My books had been ripped to shreds. The vehicle sat on its axles, the wheels and tires stacked nearby.

"Who's going to pay the damage on this?" I screamed. My usually healthy checking account suddenly seemed vastly inadequate to deal with this. I sank onto the ground and stared dumbly at the mess.

Tess! Scrap screamed at me.

Before my butt hit the ground a long arm wrapped around my neck and pulled me back.

I leaned into the arm, thinking it must be Gollum come to console me.

Scrap dropped into my hand and began to stretch and thin and . . . and solidify.

Alarmed, I slammed my left elbow backward. I connected with hard cartilage and bone. And fur. Not a normal chest.

Curved blades extruded from Scrap's head and feet. Close enough.

I flipped the Celestial Blade over my head and stabbed the blade into what should be a demon head.

I missed.

A thick gun barrel pressed into my temple.

"Put the blade to rest, or I kill you before you can breathe again," a deep bass voice growled at me.

◁▽▲▽▲▽▷

I can't risk it, babe, Scrap apologized and winked out of view.

"He was hiding behind the tires, Tess," Gollum explained. He fidgeted and tried to ease around behind me.

"Stay put, teacher man," the demon said, pressing the gun tighter against my skull.

I gulped. Sweat broke out on my brow and my back.

How could I fight a gun?

"Everybody stay put, or I waste the chick," the demon shouted.

I felt him shift his grip on the trigger.

Instantly, every Marine within view froze. Even those behind the fence.

"What does he look like?" I mouthed to Gollum. He may have crept closer. I couldn't tell. My whole being shook so badly the world seemed to tremble in fear.

"He's human," Gollum replied in a whisper.

I glanced sideways at the pile of bodies on the other side of the fence. They looked human, too. And there seemed to be a lot fewer of them than when Donovan had first blasted them with his automatic weapon.

"Wh . . . what do you want?" I asked the man who held me hostage. My brain finally kicked in, though my feet and hands itched to take him out any way I could, despite the risk to my own life.

"I want all those fucking Marines out of our home base," he yelled.

My ears rang from the volume of his demand.

"And I want everyone to clear a perimeter half a mile from the fence."

The closest Marines edged away from us. Gollum stayed put. He might have come an inch or two closer.

I couldn't see how he'd do any good with that honking big gun muzzle pressed against my head and probably a hair trigger for a jumpy guy.

Prayers. I should have said a prayer. My mind remained blank. I didn't believe in God anyway. Why should I call for help now when He or She couldn't give any?

"And we want a million dollars and Fort Snoqualmie declared an independent and sovereign nation, separate from the rest of the country," my captor added.

"I'm not worth that much," I said, wishing I could joke my way out of this.

"Someone will come up with the money. You're a celebrity, after all."

"The U.S. government doesn't negotiate with terrorists. They'll kill me when they storm the fort just to get rid of you."

"Let 'em try," my captor chortled. "Now everyone out of our way. I'm taking her inside. All those Marines in there need to get out now."

"Take me instead of her," Gollum said. He stepped a little closer.

I gulped. I tried to shake my head no, but the gun barrel kept me immobile.

"You ain't worth a damn, teacher man."

"My family has money, influence in government. I'm more valuable than she is."

"But she has fans that will make a big stink in the press." He prodded my back and pushed me toward the gate.

Again I noticed the pile of bodies was smaller, down to two or three. Where had they all gone?

"Gregor, no!" Donovan called from the trailer. "This is about our people, not about any of them. Do you really want to involve outsiders?" He stepped down the one step to the ground and approached us.

Gregor swung me around, putting my body between himself and Donovan. He began backing up until we pressed into the fence. "This has gotten bigger than you, Estevez. Bigger than me. We have a homeland now, right here at Fort Snoqualmie. No one will dare take it away from us. This woman is our guarantee of that."

He pushed and pulled me along the fence until we reached the gate.

A dozen Marines filed out, all holding their weapons away from their bodies, hands away from the triggers.

My heart pounded so hard and fast I couldn't think beyond keeping my knees locked and my body upright. I could almost taste the metal of the gun and bullets.

Gollum and Donovan kept pace with us as we sidled along.

"Gollum, go take care of Cynthia. And call Leonard. Oh, and call my agent. And I guess you should call my mother. But whatever you do, don't speak French to her. The numbers are on my cell phone."

"Got it. Why shouldn't I speak French to your mother?"

"Just don't."

Scrap, what the hell do we do? I implored my imp.

We play along until the moment is right. I'll be right here with you, every step of the way.

"Don't try anything, lady," Gregor whispered. He yanked me into the compound. One of his friends—risen from the pile of bodies?—slammed the sliding double gate closed.

"We've got guns trained on you from every corner of the compound. And we've got this." He held up a long rope of mistletoe and holly twined together by vines of ivy.

"So?"

Scrap gagged and held his throat as if strangling. He turned a sickly neon yellowish green, then winked out.

"Scrap!"

"Didn't know about imp's bane, lady?" Gregor laughed. He released his death grip on me.

I sank to my knees. Tears streamed down my face and my body shook uncontrollably. What else could go wrong?

Chapter 32

Bat mothers nurse their young. Specially adapted milk teeth in the young—teeth that are shed after weaning—allow the babies to cling to Mama's nipple even during flight.

"EVERYBODY BACK INSIDE," Gregor commanded. "They've got snipers all around, just waiting for the right moment to pick us off." He grabbed my hair in one of his oversized fists and dragged me back to my feet.

I stumbled along in his wake, too shocked and numb to do anything else.

My total awareness centered on the gun barrel now pressed against my spine.

And my thirst. I hadn't eaten or drunk since breakfast. How many hours ago?

"You guys got any beer in here?"

"What do you care, writer lady? You aren't going to live long enough to appreciate our beer," one of the resurrected demons off to my left said.

Gregor jammed the gun tighter against my spine. I raised my hands in surrender, but couldn't keep my mouth shut.

"The whole point of taking me hostage is to keep me alive so that those on the outside have hopes of getting me back." I stopped short of the doorway into the main building. A gray, squat, ugly place with few windows and no grace. "Kill me, and they have no reason to answer your demands. Kill me, and you give them an excuse to nuke the entire place."

"She's right, Kaylor," Gregor mumbled. "Gotta keep her alive and happy until the outsiders do something smart or incredibly stupid. Then we kill her."

"Then bring out the beer, boys. How about some sandwiches, too?"

"Better than that. We got pizza."

My mouth watered.

Okay, I'm a slave to my stomach. I think better when I've been fed.

As they shoved me against a pile of packing crates that held a microwave and mini fridge, I remembered to pull the comb out of my pocket and jam it into my hair.

The world seemed to tilt, and colors jumped out at me as if I was tripping on LSD. I saw a halo or aura of fur surrounding each of the demon faces.

Sasquatch.

The boys, they all looked to be in their late teens, maybe early twenties, had made a cozy nest for themselves out of brightly striped blankets in a ghastly color scheme, oversized pillows, and packing crates. The place had probably been a warehouse or a hangar originally.

I arranged a couple of pillows to support my back and butt. My captors faced me in a semicircle, boxes of pizza and six-packs between us. The smell of warm bread and tomato sauce made my stomach growl.

"I bet you boys don't have food this good where you come from," I said, offhandedly, as I drowned my third piece of pizza with my second beer.

Kaylor stilled and stared at me with a what-do-you-know-about-that expression. He wasn't the brightest bulb in the pack.

"Hey, I'm a Warrior of the Celestial Blade. It's my job to know where you boys come from."

"We aren't 'boys,'" Gregor said. He sounded very offended.

"No, you're not." I'd seen their like at hundreds of cons over the years, too old to have a parent in tow, too young to truly be ready to face the world on their own. But they had enough experience to think they knew everything there was to know.

They all looked smug and satisfied, and ever so macho.

"You're demons, halflings, really."

"Don't call me that!" Kaylor screamed. He crouched, ready to spring at me, paws and talons at the ready.

Gregor had to hold Kaylor with both hands to keep him from climbing over the pile of pizza boxes to rip my throat out. He hadn't managed to morph his hands/paws completely. His fingers looked preternaturally long, tipped with talons as long as my hand.

"Writer lady, we don't like being called 'halflings,'" Gregor warned. His canine teeth elongated, hanging down below his lip. "We eat humans for lesser offenses."

None of these guys had a lot of control over their morphing.

"Well, I don't like being called 'writer lady.'" I stood up, hands on hips, glowering at the contingent of young demons. "And I thought you kidnapped humans for breeding purposes, not food."

They all exchanged uneasy glances.

Gregor's eyes slitted vertically and turned yellow before he regained control over himself. "We are Kajiri. What are you?" he finally spat. His saliva was still green, but his eyes and hands returned to a more human appearance.

My heart flipped and beat a few extra beats. Kajiri? Could that be just the name demons gave to half-breeds?

"I'm Tess. A writer by profession." *And a Warrior of the Celestial Blade by a fate I didn't choose.*

I sat down again on a fuchsia-and-pea-green blanket on the cement floor, feigning casualness.

Gregor reached for another piece of pizza. His eyes dropped out of confrontational mode. "Pizza and beer are better than human blood," he muttered. "Most of the time."

Kaylor still looked ready to pounce and eat me.

"So, Donovan is also Kajiri?" I might as well make use of my time here.

"Yeah, Kajiri, like us. But he ain't Sasquatch. He's Damiri. They're pansies. Disdain eating humans, pride themselves on their ability to maintain a human form and get educated in your universities. They like blending in with the enemy. Some even try to forget where they really come from," a shorter and lanky fellow from the back of the pack said with derision. "And they're all richer than Bill Gates."

"No one is richer than Bill Gates. How would an ignorant human tell the difference?"

"The Damiri are tallish by your standards, about six foot, and darker. They tend to go to fat if they don't watch it. But they are more deadly in a fight." Gregor seemed truly interested in educating me. "Their natural form is similar to your bats."

I blanched and lost my appetite.

"Donovan is tall and dark, but he certainly hasn't gone to fat," I choked out. But he liked bat costumes at cons. Was it all a costume?

"He works out," the short and lanky one said.

"They get those silver wings of hair at about age thirty, but the rest of their hair never goes gray."

"Their names always start with a D and end with an N."

In less time than it took me to inhale, an image of Dillwyn flashed before my mind's eye. He'd just turned twenty-eight, a year older than me, when I met him, and lost him three months later. He had about two graywhite hairs on each side of his full head of dark hair. Right at his temples. The same place Donovan had silver wings of hair.

He'd been about an inch taller than Donovan, too.

I'd fallen for him within minutes of meeting him.

No.

Impossible.

My imagination running overtime. I am a science fiction/fantasy writer after all.

"Where'd the pizza and beer come from?" I asked rather than think those horrible thoughts. They had a microwave and mini fridge plugged into the wall. "Come to think of it, where is the electricity coming from?"

The first thing the Marines and SWAT teams outside would do is cut off electricity and water.

"We've got our own sources," Kaylor said smugly. His eyes dropped to the floor.

"From underground. You're bringing up resources from the underworld."

Silence.

I'd hit the nail on the head.

"I don't remember seeing any pizza parlors or bars the one time I ventured into the underworld."

"You only made it as far as the chat room. That's a scary place if you aren't used to it," Gregor said.

"Chat room?" I raised both eyebrows in astonishment. I'd heard Scrap use that term before.

"That's what we call it," the short and lanky one said. Short being relative. These guys were big. Sasquatch. All of them well over six feet. I wondered if full-blooded Sasquatch were in the eight-foot range as legend suggested.

"It's the room just beyond the portal where you get to choose which dimension to go to. Anybody can get into the chat room. Getting into a dimension not your own takes real talent. Never known a human to manage it," Gregor said. He seemed to be warming up to me.

I wanted to ask if this chat room was where demons seduced their breeding partners. That might explain the Beauty and the Beast legend. But I didn't want these angry young men to think I was coming on to them by asking too many questions about breeding.

"Time to set the watch," Gregor changed the subject. Then he switched to that strange clicking and hissing language as he pointed to six of his fellow demons.

Those six rose reluctantly, each grabbing another piece of pizza and an extra beer. They disappeared into the shadows. Within a few moments, six different demons reappeared, all carrying new stores. They settled in to eat with only a quick glance and dismissal of my presence.

They all wore jeans, western-cut shirts, belts with big buckles and boots, much like the Indians I had seen in town. They all had dark hair, but not the jet black I expected of Indian genetics. And they all smelled of the oily, mineral-laden water, including the ancient fish oil, from the lake.

"Mind if I go off into a corner and sit by myself for a while?" I asked.

Gregor waved me off to the left, away from the microwave and fridge.

I took the bright pink blanket and a pillow with me. That cement floor was cold. Once I'd made myself comfortable,

I closed my eyes and breathed deeply. Maybe, with luck, and a lot of concentration I could reach out with my mind and find . . . "Sister Serena?"

The fuzzy image of my friend and doctor at the Citadel appeared before my closed eyes. The image came and went sporadically, like a hologram shorting out in an SF movie.

"What ails you, child?" she asked into my mind.

"I am a hostage of two dozen Kajiri demons. They have strung imp's bane around so Scrap cannot find me. I need help getting out of here."

"Kajiri demons!" She sounded alarmed, looking about frantically. "How did two dozen Kajiri slip past the portal?"

"I think they came through a long time ago. They are very familiar with this world, very comfortable here. They admit to being half-breeds."

"Impossible. Demons cannot breed with humans. Your information is faulty. Perhaps they are Kmera demons. Our brothers to the east have been lax in guarding their portal. They age and do not recruit new members."

"No. They definitely said Kajiri."

"I have to go. There's more activity around the portal." She snapped out of my awareness so fast I thought she might have panicked.

That was a concept I had trouble getting my imagination around. Sister Serena never panicked. She was always calm, always clear-headed, always willing to answer my questions.

Now what did I do?

Wheee! Tessie, look at me.

I swung merrily from rafter to rafter. Lighter than air. Hardly any wing needed at all. Whee!

Hey, babe, you aren't looking at me.

Oops, forgot. She can't see me through the miasma of imp's bane.

I jumped onto a rafter beside a bat. A big fella. We stared at each other for a while. Kinda hard since he was upside down.

So I went upside down, too, clinging with my toes. What a rush. Blood in my head and in my eyes. Everything looking weird and wonderful.

Bat got bored. I think he said his name was Morris or was that Morrissette and a she? Anyway, he went back to sleep. Too bad. He was kinda cute. So I tried watching my babe for a while. She wasn't doing much, meditating. How boring.

Time to slide down the walls and give those Kajiri a scare. A tweak to their ears here, a pinch to a bottom there.

But they don't scare easily.

So I hang in front of one of the guards and make ugly faces at him. He can't see me either. He's got a braid of mistletoe, holly, and ivy around his neck.

Weird. None of those plants ever put a foggy wall between my babe and me before. She's a nut at Christmas and drapes the whole house in greenery. Must be the way they braid and knot the stuff.

Who cares. I'm going back to the rafters. I can see the world from here. The world could come to an end—and I wouldn't care!

Interlude

*S*OON AFTER I'D begun training seriously, a night
of a waxing quarter moon came around. The Sisters all gathered in the courtyard for their ritual. I stood
aside with a new initiate, Alunda, still recovering from her
fever. We wouldn't be allowed to participate until we finished our training and went through some kind of ritual
blessing from the Goddess.

This night the Goddess did not appear. The portal had
not been breached.

I helped Alunda back to her infirmary bed. Her black
skin glistened with sweat from the effort of standing. Sister
S hastened in and fussed around her, taking her temperature and blood pressure, clucking her tongue, and showing
her best bedside manner.

The warm, cozy, charming atmosphere Sister S created
tugged at me. I wanted to linger, be one of her patients
again. Not because I was sick. Because I was lonely. And
bored. I needed mental stimulation, a book to write, animated discussion on hot topics. Even the evening news on
TV would help.

None of that happened at the Citadel. Here, life revolved around training, recounting past battles, working in the garden, and sleeping.

Reluctantly I retired to my solitary cell in the dormitory. No books. No radio. No CDs. No TV. Nothing but myself and my purloined notebook and pencil.

Trouble was, I had no idea where the story was going. I needed an ending to drive the story forward. So I played with words and graphs and character development until loud voices and laughter drew my attention.

A party seemed to be growing in the common room. I slunk out of my cell and down the hall to the big room where twenty women lounged about on sofas, overstuffed chairs, and big cushy pillows. A keg of beer stood in the corner. Sister Paige played bartender, drawing glass after glass.

I joined the line for this rare treat. Sister Gert probably allowed the keg in this one dorm because the Goddess had not appeared. The rest of the dorms were on watch. I wondered if the single keg just wandered from dorm to dorm each month.

The beer tasted funny, too heavy and yeasty for me with bits of floating vegetation. Homemade with a crude filter. Maybe they'd used the recipe found in the Hammurabi Code. Maybe the Sisterhood had written the code for the ancient king of Babylon who codified every aspect of life he could think of, including how to make beer.

Don't you like beer, babe? Scrap looked at me wistfully. He snuggled next to me in the armless chair I found off to the side.

"Sure I like beer. Just not this beer." I didn't have to whisper to keep this conversation private. The stories and songs in the center of the party had become rather raucous. No one could overhear us unless they sat in the narrow chair with us.

Can I drink it? He looked hopefully lavender.

I held the glass for him. The liquid disappeared at an alarming rate.

I wondered if there was a limit on refills. Then I noticed a lot of the Sisters fed beer to their imps.

More, Scrap demanded.

"Say please."

He stared at me malevolently. *None of the other imps have to be polite.*

"But you're my imp, and I like to live life in a somewhat civilized manner. That requires a degree of politeness just to get along."

Scrap fumed in silence a moment.

Oh, okay. May I please have some more beer?

"Sure, pal. I'll get it for you."

I had to duck beneath swooping imps to get back to the keg. Sister Electra had taken over at the tap. Her flushed face matched her flame-colored hair, and her eyes glazed over a bit. Her imp hung from a drawing of dry falls on the wall by one elbow talon. Electra and the imp swayed in rhythm to a discordant tune the imp sang.

I looked back at Scrap. He perched on my chair, hands crossed over his pot belly and tiny wings folded neatly against his back. He swiveled his bat-wing ears, catching every nuance of the conversations. Oh, well, if he got drunk and had a hangover in the morning, maybe he'd learn not to indulge. I let Electra refill my glass.

The party went on and on. I told story after story, each more fantastic than the last, fishing for the right ending for the book I wrote. Nothing worked for me. My audience seemed to appreciate them, though, singing battle songs in the right places and dirges in others.

Scrap drank glass after glass of beer, keeping pace with the other imps.

"Why aren't you as drunk as those idiots?" I asked, leaning back to avoid two imps fighting a mock battle using plastic straws for swords. (Some modern conveniences made their way into the Citadel. Sister Gert made a trip into the nearest town once a month in an unobtrusive four-by-four pickup. I had no idea where the money came from.)

Because you aren't.

Interesting. "So if I'm hungry, so are you. If I'm tired, so are you. If I get drunk, so will you."

Yeah, something like that. He belched and let out a huge yawn.

I couldn't help but echo that.

We retired long before the party even began to wind down. I was still bored to tears. And I hadn't learned anything new. The Sisters drunk told the same stories they told sober. And frankly, I could write more exciting stuff with one hand tied behind my back. If I could just find the right ending.

Chapter 33

Some bats can live up to thirty years. Even small bats live considerably longer than other small mammals.

S ITTING IN THAT DRAFTY warehouse in the middle of abandoned Fort Snoqualmie, I'd give my eyeteeth for a cell phone. Or my laptop. Or even a PDA. But the Marines were probably jamming cell phone signals, my laptop was back at the lodge, and my PDA was in my purse, which Gollum had, along with my cell phone.

How many minutes was he running up explaining the unexplainable to my mother and my agent.

"Close the door, dammit," I snarled at the young Sasquatch who escorted me to the restroom.

He snarled back, showing his teeth.

"At least turn your back. Don't you guys have any sense of privacy?"

"Can't have you climbing out the window, writer lady."

"Fine," I growled back at him. I stomped into the middle stall which had no window above it and slammed the door. The catch was broken. Somehow I managed to hold the thing shut with one hand as I crouched over the throne, not letting my butt touch the stained and broken seat.

My headache throbbed, worse than any hangover I could imagine. What do you expect? All they had to drink around here was beer. And the fumes from the joints they smoked were thick enough to swim through.

No wonder I was cranky.

And I hadn't seen Scrap for hours. I missed him. Part of me wanted to wither up and cry from missing him.

My mind began to spin with new ideas for my book. My fingers wanted to beat on the keys of the computer. I needed to get this down before I lost it.

The adrenaline rush from new ideas cleared my head some.

That made me want to write even more.

"Gregor, I don't suppose on your next trip out for supplies you could slip into the Mowath Lodge and liberate my laptop? Or a pad of paper and a pen." I asked as nicely as I knew how. All those years of Mom beating good manners into me must account for something.

"I'll try." He shrugged and curled up on his pillow and promptly went to sleep.

They all went to sleep.

I paced, trying to keep the words and images in my head. As I paced, I managed to kick a couple of the braids of imp's bane into the fire they kept burning in the middle of the warehouse. The smoke vented naturally through the original heating ducts.

Autumn had settled in, and the desert air grew cold at night. The cement floor and vast open spaces held the cold. I hated to think how hot and stifling this place would be in summer.

My head cleared a little. I tossed another bunch of mistletoe, holly, and ivy into the fire, curious at how they'd bound the three plants together.

My head cleared a little more. I caught a glimpse of movement in the rafters. Scrap.

Plans flashed in and out of my head.

After about an hour I decided I should sleep, too. I might never know when I'd need to be rested and ready to roll.

◁▽▲▽▲▽▷

"Tess, you have to help me," Dill whispered in the dead of the night.

I stilled every muscle, every thought. Had I truly heard the soft voice next to my ear?

Then I felt him, a warm, comforting, solid body curled up against my back.

Another dream?

I pinched my thigh hard enough to bruise. The old superstition proved true. My leg *hurt* and Dill remained.

"Dilly, my love." I rolled over, throwing my arms around my husband. Desperately, I wanted to submerge myself in his dominant personality, give over all the troubles and decisions to him. As I had when he lived.

"Make it all go away," I cried.

"We can do that now, lovey. The imp no longer stands between us. All you have to do is renounce your vows to the Sisterhood of the Celestial Blade, and we can be together again. Just like this. Together we will be invincible." He kissed me hard upon the mouth.

I melted into him, opening my mouth to his demanding tongue. He held me tight. I drank in the touch of his hands against my back. Too long we'd been apart. Too long I'd been alone.

"Where have you been, my Dilly?" I kissed him hungrily on cheek and neck and mouth.

"Drifting, lost. Wanting you. Join me now. All you have to do is renounce . . ."

Something in the desperate pressure of his fingers against my back sent warning tingles up and down my spine. The fine hairs in the small of my back stood straight out.

His hands were cold as ice. Literally. Cold enough to burn through my sweater and cotton shirt. The place on my neck where his tongue made enticing circles just beneath my ear was cold and dry. Not the cold of chill air touching a wet spot. It was the ice of another world.

"Don't pull away from me, Tess. Please," he pleaded.

I pulled my head back enough to look into his deeply shadowed eyes.

"I can't bear it if you reject me just because I'm dead, Tess."

That sentence chilled me more than his touch.

"What is this about, Dill? Why now? Why didn't you come to me three years ago when I cried myself into a fever in my grief?"

"I wasn't offered the deal until now." His gaze dropped away from my face.

I lifted his chin with one finger. His skin felt dusty and fragile, as though if I pressed too hard it would slough off like the layers of a fine pastry.

"What deal?"

"If you get rid of the imp and renounce your vows, you and I can be together. Forever. I get out of limbo. You won't be alone anymore."

In other words I had become a threat to some . . . *thing* since surviving the imp flu and acquiring Scrap.

"I can't trust that kind of deal, Dill. I'm sorry. But you are dead. Giving you life again is . . . wrong. There aren't any 'get out of jail free' cards once you're dead."

"But I'm not dead, Tess. Not completely anyway. Can't you feel how alive I am? It's the imp. He's tricked you into thinking I'm dead."

"You died in my arms, Dill. You said you loved me with your dying breath. I held your body until it grew cold. I buried your ashes in the pioneer cemetery in Alder Hill." I choked on a sob. This was it. I had to finally admit to myself and to the ghost of my husband that Dill had died.

I traced the lines of his face lovingly one last time. "Good-bye, my love."

Resolutely, I turned my back on him and closed my eyes. The solid presence evaporated.

I took one last tear-filled glance over my shoulder. A man-shaped column of black mist drifted away and passed through the solid cement block walls.

This isn't the end, Tess. I won't let you get away from me. Ever. You're mine in this life and the next.

◄▽▲▽▲▽►

I awoke with a start near midnight as the watch changed. I shuddered in memory of the all-too-real nightmare. As I shifted position, the new bruise on my thigh reminded me of every last touch and word of Dill's visit.

New loneliness and despair opened holes in my soul.

A band of Sasquatch had taken me hostage. Imp's bane

kept Scrap from my side and made him drunk. I was on my own with little hope of seeing tomorrow, let alone living out the rest of my life.

Maybe I should have taken Dill's offer.

But that grated on every nerve and scruple I had.

New supplies of pizza and beer arrived with the change of guard. A repeat of lunch. Couldn't these guys find some steak or tacos or even peanut butter and jelly? Would a glass of water or cup of coffee kill them?

My bad mood and headache returned. I tore the comb out of my hair, bringing a handful of crystalline strands with it.

Immediately, the room dimmed, colors faded. The boys looked like normal boys. The aura of fur, talons, and teeth became echoes of my former vision. After a few minutes they faded altogether.

But my headache didn't.

I stuffed the comb back into my hair. Everything brightened and the auras came back.

So that was the magic of the comb. That was why I'd felt the chill of the grave in Dill's touch and seen it in his eyes.

I couldn't wear the blasted comb all the time because of what it did to my hair and scalp.

I stuffed it back into my pocket. I knew these guys for what they were now. I didn't need it.

Now that I knew what to look for, how would Donovan appear with my vision cleared of demon glamour?

"Any news?" Gregor asked the newcomers. I hadn't seen Gregor take a watch yet. Maybe he was the leader.

"All quiet out there. Marines, SWAT, and press still camped just outside the fence. A lot less press. The news is absolutely quiet after one mention of our demands. Heard one of the Marines say they'd put a clamp on coverage," the underling replied.

Gregor cursed long and fluently in his own demonic language. Then he cast me a malevolent glare.

After the meal we dispersed to our separate nests again. The boys slept as if they were just normal teenagers, sleep, eat, eat, sleep, occasionally take responsibility for a watch, nothing more, nothing less. If they'd had video games, a few would probably zone out on those, taking breaks only to eat, sleep, and take a turn at watch.

I have a very low boredom tolerance. I'd reached mine several hours ago. I tried calisthenics until Kaylor yelled at me to quiet down.

Another day passed without change. Was this the second or third? I'd lost track. More pizza and beer. I wanted coffee. I needed coffee.

I feared for how Scrap managed without me.

I feared for how my mother reacted to Gollum's phone call.

I feared I might go insane.

I kept the fire going with the piles of brush the boys brought in and an occasional braid of imp's bane. Couldn't burn it all at once in case they noticed. It was something to do and dispelled some of the autumnal chill settling into the room.

Hey, babe, I'm drunk and you're hungover! Scrap's voice came through the thickness in my brain. *And our best friend is a bat named Morris. A mighty cute bat at that. We might get somthin' goin'.*

I rolled my eyes at his rambling. "How can I have a hangover and you don't? You can't get drunk unless I get drunk, and I'm not drunk."

Great, just what I needed. A drunken Celestial Blade when I was going to need it most.

Who cares. Whoee!

I sensed a rush of movement like riding a roller coaster. The vertigo made me stumble. I caught myself just before I stepped into the fire.

The imp's bane burned brightly. That must be it. The stuff that kept my imp away from me made him drunk. Either the plant combination or the separation gave me all the symptoms of a hangover.

Yuck. I went back to my corner and tried to sleep.

Then, around noon, the watch changed again, and new supplies of pizza and beer arrived along with my laptop.

"Thank you, thank you, thank you," I gushed all over the young demon who carried the black sanity saver under his arm. "And the flash drive, too! You are wonderful." I kissed the boy's cheek, and he blushed a bright purple.

I fell upon the computer with a vengeance, totally ignoring the greasy aroma of fresh tomato sauce and cheese with too much garlic in the sausage and pepperoni. Not a vegetable in sight.

Idly, I munched on a piece of lunch while I plugged the thing into the only outlet I could find. The boys didn't really need the microwave. Then I booted up the computer. Within minutes I was so absorbed in writing that I didn't notice the beer shoved into my hand or the second piece of pizza someone handed me.

My conscious brain remained paranoid enough that I set the computer on automatic backup every five minutes. That way, if the power blew, I'd still have most of my work. No telling how reliable the electrical source was coming from the other side.

Twenty pages and several hours later I came up for air. My watch said midnight. Not a demon was stirring.

I got up from my blanket and packing crate and began to prowl and stretch. The pizza was cold, but the microwave took care of that once I switched plugs. The beer was warm but there was more in the fridge. I wandered around the warehouse of a room inspecting my captors for more individual characteristics. True to type they were all leanly muscled, well beyond medium height for human males.

I stuck the comb into my hair for a moment.

Their skin and hair colors . . . At first glance their skin ranged from palest Nordic Caucasian to the dark olive of the Mediterranean, with a suggestion of Negroid in a couple of them. Upon closer inspection I saw that they had no beards. By this time all of them should have needed a shave. We had basic plumbing and most of them showered and used the toilets—utilities purloined from the underworld. But I'd never seen them shave. What I saw as skin was actually a light fur, mottling from cream to black.

Not human. I had to remind myself that none of these "boys" was human. They were demons, unpredictable, probably violent.

I backed off from my inspection of Gregor and stumbled over a clump of plants. The imp's bane. It had begun to wilt and lose its brightness. What did these guys expect? They hadn't watered the stuff.

I threw the wilting branch into the fire. It burned rapidly. Several more of the bunches joined it. I left enough scattered around so my current depletion of it wasn't too obvious.

Time for a snooze.

Chapter 34

A drug company has recently patented a new blood thinner called Draculin, developed from research on natural anticoagulants in vampire bat saliva.

"HEY, LOOK WHAT we found!"

I woke up, still groggy, headachy from the lack of caffeine and fresh air.

And from Scrap's absence.

The boys gathered around the watch change near the back entrance to the warehouse.

I checked the laptop and pocketed the memory stick out of habit before rolling to my feet.

The ebb and flow of bodies changed enough to reveal a smaller figure huddled in on itself in the center.

"Leave her alone!" I screamed, dashing forward. I ripped young men out of the pack until I could wrap my arms around Cynthia Stalking Moon.

"Out of the way, bitch. She's fair game," Kaylor snarled.

"She's too young for you, Halfling," I sneered back at him. The fine hairs along my spine stood on end. Scrap was close and ready for a fight.

Kaylor's eyes morphed to yellow with a vertical slit. His fingers elongated and grew horny nails. His mouth and nose grew into a long muzzle with way more teeth—very sharp teeth—than most primates had. His posture crouched and his paws brushed his knees. Black fur shone through the brown glaze on his head and on his body.

Cynthia screamed.

I slapped the demon's muzzle. What else do you do with a beast that refuses to obey?

Startled, Kaylor sloughed off some of his demon aspect. For half a moment a bewildered teenager stared at me.

"We don't take women below the age of consent," Gregor snapped at Kaylor. "That's the rules. Good rules. They keep us safe." He elbowed his way to Cynthia's other side. "Take the kid over to your nest and keep her there," he hissed at me.

His clenched fists and authoritative attitude kept the beasts at bay. For a moment. Long enough to drag a sobbing Cynthia over to my corner.

Halfway there I kicked another bundle of imp's bane into the fire.

The demons were too busy snarling and snapping at each other to pay attention.

"How did this happen?" I whispered to Cynthia the moment we had an illusion of privacy.

"I don't know," she wailed, clinging to me. Fat tears slid down her cheeks and made her dark eyes look overly large and bruised.

"Where is Sapa?"

"I don't know." She buried her face against my chest, fists wrapped in my sweater as if she clung to a lifesaver.

Maybe I was a lifesaver for her. I had to be. No one else was left.

"Let's just sit here for a while and think this over while we calm down."

The demons began to circle us. Feral. Hungry. Growing bolder by the minute.

"Back off, boys," I ordered.

They paused in their cautious circling. But only for a moment.

"Hey, she unplugged the microwave for her stupid laptop!" Kaylor snarled. He ripped the wires from the outlet. He held them up and ripped the plug free of the connection with a twist of his large hands.

I swallowed the gibbering fear that wanted to climb out of my throat into a screech that would put a banshee to shame.

"Into the corner, Cynthia. Stay right by me." Cautiously, I moved us to a place where walls protected our backs.

"Scrap, you available yet?" I kept my eyes on the Kajiri. They took on more and more aspects of their demon nature, the Sasquatch of legend. But more deadly than imaginable.

Not yet, babe. Getting there.

Shit. No weapon but myself, and a little girl to protect. From rape. Or worse. From being eaten.

Tall cement block walls comforted me where I could feel them behind me. A smaller flank to defend and protect.

Cynthia still sobbed.

Kaylor edged closer. He kicked my laptop aside. The machine crashed into the wall. The case split down the lid.

Another demon jumped on it until it shattered.

"Now that makes it personal," I snarled. Boiling hot anger replaced the sinking emptiness in my gut. At least I had the flash drive to continue the project.

Provided I lived through the next ten minutes.

Kaylor laughed and dropped all pretense of humanity.

I kicked his snout with the heel of my boot. Then stomped upon his foot. They get the nickname "Bigfoot" for a reason.

He backed off, snapping and snarling.

A second demon lunged for my throat. I twisted and hit his chest with my shoulder. The jolt raced through my body. My head ached and my left arm went numb.

He landed heavily and yipped.

Before I could catch my breath another dove for my leg. He grabbed my calf in massive jaws and sank in his long teeth.

Green saliva burned through my jeans to my flesh, like acid in chem class, only worse. My leg threatened to crumple. Already weakened and off balance from the shoulder, I knew I'd not last long with six demon bigfoots ready to attack.

"Forget the bitches. I found something better," the youngest of the pack announced from the main doorway.

The demons turned their attention toward him—all except the one worrying my leg.

I slammed the side of my hand across his spine, just behind his head. He let go.

We both stepped apart, nursing our hurts.

Cynthia gulped and clung to my belt loop. The small warmth of her body cowering in the corner eased my heavy breathing.

Then we looked to see what had distracted the demons.

The young one held up the raggedly severed head of a man by his long black braids.

A look of horror and pain was frozen into the tired face. A harelip scar split open.

Fresh, bright blood dripped onto the floor where it pooled and spread.

"Uncle Leonard," Cynthia whispered through a new spate of tears and choking sobs.

The smell of blood filled the warehouse.

Two dozen demons gathered around the boy with the head, drooling green ichor as they licked at the dripping blood.

I gagged and nearly lost two days' worth of greasy pizza and beer.

Chapter 35

Spectral vampire bats make a purring sound when held.

"THE BODY IS OUTSIDE. We got fresh meat for dinner!" the boy chortled.

All of the demons surged out the door.

"Come on, Cynthia, we have work to do to get out of here." I grabbed her by the hand and limped toward the nearest clump of imp's bane. Damn, that leg hurt. I needed Scrap to lick it before the boys returned and I had to fight. "Gather up all of these and throw them in the fire. Quick."

She stood beside me paralyzed with fear and shock.

"Move, kid, or we die with your uncle." I slapped her face just hard enough to get her attention.

Her big brown eyes teared. She gulped but nodded.

We ran, well, she ran, I had to drag that leg, about the huge room, collecting the bundles of twined mistletoe, holly, and ivy. Dozens of them. And I had already destroyed dozens. What had the stuff done to Scrap?

My plodding footsteps drowned out the sound of two dozen demons slurping and slathering over the dead body of a man who deserved more respect and honor in his death than this.

I cast the last bits of trailing ivy leaves into the fire just as Gregor wandered back into the room, back in human form. He wiped blood and flesh off his mouth with the back of his hand.

Even he, the leader and most reasonable of the pack, was not immune to his nature when presented with a fresh kill.

"You will be the first of your kind to die." I snapped my fingers. Scrap appeared on my palm, already half extended into the Celestial Blade.

"Can you help the leg first?"

No time, dahling. Do the best you can.

I twirled the shaft in both hands, like a baton while my imp completed his transformation. His grinning face leered back at me from the shining metal of the curved blade on the right side.

Let's kill the bastards, Scrap said with morbid glee.

"My thoughts exactly." An invigorating tingle started at the base of my spine and shot up and out, filling me with resolve and purpose. Adrenaline overcame the need to favor my leg.

A bat swooped across my field of vision.

I screamed and tried to hide beneath the Blade.

It's just Morris come to help, Scrap cajoled. *Isn't he cute?*

I whimpered.

Morris won't hurt you, but that blond Sasquatch will!

Gregor dropped to all fours and leaped across the room in three bounds. The last one launched him up and forward, directly at me.

I had no choice. I had to swallow my fear. Murmuring prayers to any God or Goddess that might hear, I met his attack with a curving swish of the staff. The right-hand blade sliced neatly through his neck. His body collapsed and twitched. I yanked the blade free of muscle, bone, and gristle.

Green blood dripped onto the floor.

"Oops! I'm wearing the wrong color underwear."

Kaylor appeared at the door at the head of the pack. Two or three could enter at a time, no more.

I had my work cut out for me.

The lead demons saw Gregor's still twitching body and snarled a warning.

Too late. The left-hand blade severed Kaylor's spine in midback. He yowled in pain and confusion as his body convulsed. He scrabbled around in a circle lying on the ground. A stench arose as he lost control of his bowels and bladder.

He didn't stink any worse dead than alive.

"Next time, take a shower before you attack someone."

Another circle of the blade to adjust my grip while the surge of demons halted just outside my range.

The bat flew back and forth between us.

I clenched my jaw and locked my knees so I wouldn't run screaming into the corner. Not that I could run. But I could stand, as long as I watched my balance and locked that left knee.

"What's the matter, boys, afraid of one angry human bitch?" Sarcasm always hid my fears and hurts best.

A third demon tried to slip under the twirling blade. He lost a leg and rolled out of the action.

Behind you, babe.

Without thinking, I extended my twisting of the shaft to my back and clobbered a lurking demon.

Four down, only twenty to go.

We can hold out longer than they can, Scrap reassured me.

I wasn't so sure.

Three of the demons melted away.

Three more jumped forward. I shoved the staff to meet their chests. They dropped back, winded but still breathing.

The bat dove and tangled its claws in their head fur, yanking hard as it flew up.

The Sasquatch squealed loud enough to wake a Marine out of a dead drunk.

Better them than me. I had no hope that the Marines would come in time to rescue me. Their weapons wouldn't do more than bruise these guys.

"Left!" Cynthia screamed.

My blade flew back and forth, up and down. Two more stinking bodies littered the ground. Exhaustion crept up my arms to my shoulders and back. My leg burned all the way to the hip. I paid heed to only the next demon. My vision narrowed and turned red.

I even forgot the bat.

And then my swirling blade bit nothing more substantial then air. I stumbled at the lack of resistance.

The Celestial Blade lost substance.

Eight demon bodies lay piled around me. I caught a glimpse of a cinnamon-brown fuzzy butt tucked between hind legs disappearing out the back door as the last of the Kajiri slunk away.

Energy and strength drained out of me. Scrap disappeared. I bent double, hands on knees, gasping for breath.

Cynthia touched my back. "Tess, there's a commotion at the gate."

"Of course there is. Rescuers always come a day late and more than a dollar short." I rose to my knees. Cynthia helped me stand. I stiffened my spine and turned to face the Marines pouring into the compound.

To mask the shock and horror tremors that filled my body and mind, I whistled a jaunty tune that I couldn't name, placed Cynthia's arm around my waist while I leaned on her shoulder. Together we marched (limped) out to meet the Marines.

I stumbled at the doorway and fell into Gollum's arms.

Totally off balance, I dragged us both to the ground. He rubbed my back and held my shoulders while I vomited and retched way beyond empty.

Chapter 36

"HOW DID THE DEMONS get Cynthia?" Showered and dosed with three cups of coffee, I sat on the sofa in the living room of my suite with Gollum. Cynthia stretched out, sound asleep, with her head in my lap. Neither one of us wanted to let go of the other.

Scrap had shown up long enough to lick the hideous wound on my leg. My blood revived him a little. Enough for him to take on color and pop out to feed elsewhere.

"I don't know what happened. I'm sorry. I should never have left her alone," Gollum apologized for about the fiftieth time. "She was with Sapa over at the office. She must have been returning here, after dark. They grabbed her between the two buildings."

He took a big gulp of coffee. "Leonard showed up. I called him like you said I should. We went over to the office to get Cynthia. She wasn't there. Sapa was agitated. Pacing, growling at everyone, unwilling to leave the blanket to Donovan's goons. Leonard took off."

"He must have hiked up the hill to Fort Snoqualmie and sneaked in under the radar of the Marines," I said on a regretful sigh. "The boys caught him inside the fence and . . . and their demonic nature took over. They couldn't stop themselves." My coffee threatened to come up again as I remembered all the gory details.

We endured an eternity of silence, wrapped in our own thoughts and horrors.

"Is this what my life is going to be like from now on? Horrible deaths and torture for people I like and respect, and then I have to go out and kill monsters who appear to be just misguided teenagers on the outside."

"Innocents you don't know will die, too. More of them will die if you do nothing. The demons are on the move. Somehow, they've found a way around the guarded portals. This rogue portal must bypass the chat room." Gollum stared into his coffee cup as if startled that it was empty. "Either that or the Warriors of the Celestial Blade have become incredibly lax and complacent."

"I don't think so. From what little communication I've had with the Citadel, they seem besieged. Under heavy stress and pressure at the portal they guard."

"Feints to keep the Sisters from noticing their use of the rogue portal?"

I shrugged. We sat in silence a while longer. Chills took over my body, upsetting my stomach again.

"I quit. I've had enough blood and gore to last a lifetime. Cynthia is safe. The blanket is safe. This job is done. I quit." I rose, settling Cynthia's head on a pillow, then headed toward the bedroom, still limping. I needed another shower.

"I don't think it works that way, Tess," Gollum said quietly. "What are you going to do about Scrap?"

"Send him back to his own dimension. He can pick a new warrior." A hole opened in my emotional gut. Scrap had filled a big part of my life in the last three years. He'd helped me stop thinking about Dill every minute of the day and get on with my life and my career.

"I've got a book to finish. The demons destroyed my laptop. Can I borrow your machine?" I'd lusted after the top-of-the-line computer since I first saw it.

"No backups?"

"Backups!" I dashed for the pile of dirty clothes in the corner. A search of my jeans pockets turned up the flash drive. "Thank Goddess for long habits." I sank to the floor

• in relief. For a minute I'd feared it lost or destroyed in the battle.

A bit of my depression left. I could work. I'd forget while I worked.

For how long?

"You are wrong about Cynthia and the blanket. Neither of them is safe as long as Donovan Estevez has possession of the blanket," Gollum reminded me. "Humanity may not be safe while Estevez has possession of the blanket. I think the blanket is the seal to the demon portals. No one is working on it, so the seal is weak."

"Where is the bastard, by the way? Do the Marines still have him, or has Homeland Security taken over?"

"He's free. They let him go. Apparently, his story of being blackmailed by the 'terrorists in search of a homeland' held up. I believe he went back to his house."

"Which is where?"

"On a lake island between here and Dry Falls. I hear it's guarded like a fortress."

"How . . . how did the Marines explain the demon bodies I left behind?"

"I don't think they did. They probably swore themselves to secrecy and burned the remains before the press showed up. What little press they allowed in. Most of the reporters—the legitimate ones anyway—packed up and went home with a story Vlieger spun and altered dramatically."

We sat in silence again, I on the floor by the dirty laundry, Gollum in the armchair with his big feet on the coffee table.

"You should get some sleep," he said quietly.

"I don't think I dare." Every time I closed my eyes for the briefest of moments, I lived again the sickening sight of demon Sasquatch lunging for me, their fangs dripping green saliva; their dead bodies dripping green blood; Leonard's severed head dripping red gore.

I lunged for the toilet, vomiting again. The stink nearly set me to retching again.

Vaguely, I heard a telephone ring. I didn't care. I just wanted everything to end.

"Your mother," Gollum handed me a cell phone while I lay on the floor, resting my cheek against the cool tiles.

Limply, I held the tiny receiver to my ear.

A spate of angry, garbled French stabbed at my brain.

"You spoke French to her!" I accused Gollum.

"What was I supposed to do? She reverted to it when I gave her the news that you'd been kidnapped. Really weird dialect of it, though." He shrugged and left me in private with my mother and the crude invention of a language she thought she spoke.

I let Mom babble on for several minutes, picking out an actual phrase now and then. When she finally wound down, I replied in English, reassuring her that I was indeed safe, I had not been harmed. But no, I was not coming home on the next plane.

After a bit of negotiation, she agreed to ship me some clothes so I could attend the World Fantasy Convention in a few days. And yes, she would file a claim with my insurance company for the loss of my laptop.

Or rather she'd tell my sister Cecilia to tell my dad to do it. Maybe I should call him in the morning and make sure the message got through. Cecilia was good at "forgetting" things that might help me.

We talked for a long time. Slowly, I absorbed my mother's love for me. Warmth returned to my limbs. My stomach settled, the horror began to fade.

Despite her eccentricities, her irritating habits, her need to manipulate and control, my mom loved me. And I loved her.

When my world and balance tilted back toward normal, I allowed her to hang up.

"Scrap?" I called when we finally disconnected. "Scrap, what's my schedule?"

No answer.

The imp, my best friend, had to recover in his own way, much as I did.

"Gollum, get on the Internet and order me a new computer. My credit card is in my purse. I'm going to bed."

Only then did I notice the fat, fluffy white cat sitting in his lap. The beast blinked green eyes at me. It opened its mouth in a satisfied grin as if he'd just swallowed the canary.

I hate cats, Scrap whimpered into my mind. He sounded stuffy and insecure.

Chapter 37

"**I**F THE BLANKET is a metaphysical seal on the demon portal, why don't the demons just burn the blanket?" I asked at dawn as I stretched out in preparation for a run.

Gollum roused himself from where he'd fallen asleep in the armchair, his laptop across his knees, the screen gone black in sleep mode. He looked all tousled and vulnerable, approachable, likable.

Then he adjusted his glasses back onto his blade of a nose and put an impenetrable emotional barrier between himself and the world.

His cat peeked out from beneath the chair. I hissed at it. It hissed back at me.

If the beast was keeping Scrap from me, then I wanted it gone. I'd spent too much time without him in that creepy warehouse at Fort Snoqualmie up on the plateau.

"You say something?" Gollum looked just a little baffled and confused, but his eyes focused clearly.

I wondered briefly if he truly needed the glasses.

I repeated my question.

"For the same reason they didn't destroy it the first time they took possession of it." He straightened up and placed the laptop on the coffee table. Idly, he reached down to scratch the cat's ears. It leaned into his caress and purred.

"Which is?" I asked, ignoring the interplay between the man and his pet.

For a moment I wished Scrap were more tangible so we could pet and cuddle like Gollum and his cat.

"I haven't figured that out yet. But there has to be a reason why the demons protect the blanket even if they work just as hard to keep it out of the hands of a weaver."

"I'm going for a run. You might wake Cynthia. We'll go to breakfast when I get back."

Our charge still slept on the sofa. At some point he'd placed a blanket over her and she had cuddled into it, looking once more like the child she was rather than the tortured adult she had been forced to become yesterday.

"Breakfast, yes. Good idea," he mumbled. The cat meowed, demanding its own meal.

"And you might go back to your own room and clean up. You know you could have slept there last night. And take the cat with you."

"You might have needed me. I expected you to have nightmares." He lifted the cat and held it close to his face, all the while scratching its ears.

"Well, I didn't." I'd had nightmares. But I'd dealt with them in my own way, by outlining the next scene of my book in my head. If all those horrible things happened to my characters, then perhaps I could persuade myself they hadn't happened to me.

I couldn't dismiss the burning demon wound. It would leave a scar. I was growing a collection of them. I'd run on it anyway. If I let it interfere with my life, then the demons had won.

"I want the cat gone by the time I get back. Scrap hates it and Scrap is more important than your pet."

My slow run through town and along the lake, with frequent breaks to rest my leg, cleared my mind. While my feet made slight indentations in the salt-encrusted sand I looked for traces of the cave I had found across the water. Too many cracks and crevices defined the landscape for me to find the specific spot where ghosts had loomed over me and Donovan's minion had shot at me.

All the while, the briny scent of the lake water filled me and refreshed me. People had been coming here for many generations to find healing in the waters. A lot of them had stayed to continue the beneficial effects of both the lake water and the slow, low stress, pace of life here.

Until Donovan decided to build a casino.

I could see men swarming over the half-finished structure today. He hadn't wasted any time getting back to work.

Maybe his primary concern was merely the financial commitment to the casino. Maybe he was merely another victim of the overzealous demon children.

Maybe he was more.

I had no way to tell at this point. My focus had to be to keep Cynthia and the blanket safe. Permanently.

I turned away from the lake, crossed the deserted highway, and sent my feet pounding along a dirt trail. Memories of my first visit to this area flooded through me.

Dill grubbing in the dirt for a choice geological specimen and coming up with a near perfect arrowhead. We'd exclaimed over the treasure, hugged, and kissed.

Sister Mary showing me how to properly hold a bow and nock the arrow with a similar broad arrowhead. "It won't kill a demon, but it will slow him down while your imp rests," she explained patiently as she guided my hands to find a proper aim for the straw target fifty yards distant.

Dill patiently climbing a rock face, expertly seeking hand- and toeholds. I waited anxiously at the base of the cliff, my heart in my mouth as he braced himself with one hand and his feet, tiny pickax in his hand. Dirt fell into my face as he chipped away the effluvia that held a fossil in place. Then his wild and exultant slide back to me with an ugly lump of rock in his hand that looked like every other rock but delighted him.

Sister Electra sparring with me, forcing me to push myself beyond my physical and mental limits. Me shouting in triumph as I finally found an opening in her defenses and sent her sprawling on the ground, both of us panting from the effort and wiping sweat from our eyes.

My ankle twisted on the uneven trail and my weakened leg nearly gave out on me. I turned around and headed back toward the lake. My body told me I'd had enough exercise. My mind rebelled, wanting more physical effort to help banish the memories.

Little puffs of red dust sprang up with each pounding footstep. The dust was real. Here. Tangible. Just like the black clouds scudding across the sky to the west, obscuring the top of a nameless peak. A flash of lightning revealed jagged and tortured rock formations. The sharp smell of ozone replaced the dusty dryness, purging the air and my mind of the past that tried to rule my thoughts and actions today.

My rental SUV was parked in front of my room at the lodge when I returned. Lieutenant Vlieger in crisp fatigues, along with a man wearing a dark suit and sunglasses, sat on the steps leading to my room. The suit positively screamed Homeland Security or FBI. They rose, as one, at my approach.

"Ms. Noncoiré, on behalf of the Marine Corps, I extend to you an apology for the ill treatment we gave you. We have restored your car and offer you a check for the destruction of your personal property." Vlieger almost saluted as he proffered a slim white envelope.

"Thank you," I replied. What else could I say?

"Tell me," I said after staring at the envelope for a moment. "Why did you have to trash the car?"

"Profile vehicle. White SUVs are a favorite among certain terrorist groups," the suit replied.

"My Marines were careful to disassemble the vehicle and keep the parts in order. We put it back together without damage," Vlieger added. "You should not have to pay for any damages to the rental agency."

"Whatever." I tried to push past them.

"Ms. Noncoiré, we do have a few more questions for you." The suit snaked out an arm to block my passage.

"Your questions will wait until after breakfast." I stared at his arm as if it offended me and smelled bad.

"The security of our nation may be at stake."

"It will wait until I've eaten. Or do you want me fainting in your lap from low blood sugar?"

"The lieutenant and I will join you."

"Does he have a name?" I asked Vlieger.

"Ben Miller," snapped the suit. He had fewer manners than Scrap.

Ten minutes later, Gollum, Cynthia, and I took places in a booth across the street at the steak house. I wore my hair twisted up in the comb. I wanted to see everything and everybody for what they were.

An aura surrounded Cynthia's head. In just the right light I almost detected an ancient woman of great wisdom overlaying her personality. Scary and yet satisfying. She was easing into her role as the weaver. Or her shamanistic heritage was showing through.

The suit and the Marine were forced to take places at a table adjacent to us. They had no compunction against moving the table so that it butted up against our booth and effectively blocked our exit.

Miller finally removed his sunglasses and placed them in his breast pocket. He turned pale brown eyes on me, assessing me, trying to peer past my reserves into my soul.

That was something I allowed no one. Not since I'd left the Citadel anyway. I forced my face into neutral, but felt my spine stiffen and tingle with wariness.

Where the hell was Scrap?

At least I couldn't see anything unusual or otherworldly around either of them.

"Ms. Noncoiré, explain to me the significance of the—er—rather interesting bodies we found inside Fort Snoqualmie," Miller stated rather than asked the moment the waitress had taken our orders. He didn't seem concerned that she hovered nearby with full coffeepot ready to pour while she eavesdropped.

I looked at Gollum for inspiration.

He shrugged. "You might as well tell them the truth. They'll put their own spin on it anyway."

Cynthia and I both raised eyebrows at him.

"Illegal genetics experiments that failed. The monsters ended up killing each other."

"That's what we thought," Miller said, taking a long drink of the super-strength coffee, black, no sugar.

The waitress must have used the pot they reserved for

local law enforcement rather than the milder one she used for tourists. I had to dump extra cream and sugar in mine to make it palatable. Scrap would have loved the leftovers.

Where was the imp anyway? I'd never known him to stay away this long. Even when the imp's bane separated us, he hovered close by. Or, rather, played in the rafters. I had a brief vision of him swinging from them like Tarzan swooping through the trees.

But then he'd never had to recover from such an extensive battle with demons before.

I missed him.

"What about the bodies of the men we, er, Estevez shot?" Vlieger burst into the conversation. He, too, took his coffee black with no sugar.

I wondered if coffee had become the new contest to prove manhood.

"More genetics experiments and Kevlar, or maybe the new carbon fiber armor. You didn't kill them. In the confusion they melted away to nurse their wounds. They'll be back to fight another day."

Thank Goddess our food arrived. The waitress took her time refilling coffee cups.

"What about the kid? What's their interest in her?" Miller spat. Or was it an accusation? Every statement or question seemed to be an accusation.

"My name is Cynthia Stalking Moon," the girl jumped in. She faced the man defiantly, demanding he acknowledge her as a person and not just a victim, or thing.

"Where do you fit into this puzzle, Ms. Stalking Moon?"

"I . . . I don't know for sure. I think they want my DNA. I come from a long line of shamans. We have . . . powers." She lied. I knew it. Gollum knew it. Did Miller?

On the other hand, maybe she didn't lie. Maybe Sapa singled her out because of her genes; more than just being of Indian blood, she might be a direct descendant of the old woman who had originally woven the blanket. The old woman had to have been a shaman to maintain the power of the blanket.

Curiouser and curiouser.

"I'm the last of my line," Cynthia added. That was true enough. "The last of the great shamans with special powers of insight and prophecy." She fell into the now familiar chant of her people reciting old legends.

Miller looked askance at that statement.

"There are more things on this earth than you can perceive with your limited imagination, Miller," I added, trying to sound spooky and cryptic like an old horror film. Then I took a big bite of toast so I wouldn't have to say more.

"The study of anthropology has revealed a number of instances when humans have been able to reach beyond the realm of what we call reality to tap powers and secrets." Gollum put on his professor face and proceeded to expound in big words and the most boring tone I'd ever heard. Usually he had more animation with his favorite subject.

But then, this was information that Miller didn't want.

Vlieger, however, looked very interested. He'd been there and seen some pretty weird things yesterday.

"As you explore Fort Snoqualmie, you might be looking for a back door, probably underground," I said casually. "The boys kept bringing in fresh pizza and beer. And pot. Lots of pot. And Cynthia." And they always smelled like lake water.

I examined Cynthia speculatively.

She shrugged and mouthed, "Later."

"Where is this genetics lab?" Miller demanded. He'd barely touched his sausage, pancakes, and eggs.

"I have no idea. Why don't you ask Donovan Estevez?"

"Maybe we will. In the meantime, don't leave town." Miller pushed back from the table, giving me an exit.

"Sorry. I have professional commitments in Madison, Wisconsin. I'm flying out of Moses Lake with connections to Seattle on Wednesday." I sat placidly eating my own meal. "I'll be back Sunday night unless my agent has other plans and projects that demand more time."

Miller threw a twenty on the table and stalked off.

Vlieger scooted closer, all traces of yesterday's antagonism vanished. "So what really happened up there?"

"My kidnappers are demons who came through an underground portal. I allowed them to keep me hostage so I could learn their true motives for claiming the fort. When they kidnapped Cynthia and tried to molest her, and killed and ate her uncle, I called up my imp from another dimension and slew them one and all," I said with a straight face. "Well, maybe not all of them. I think a few retreated back down the portal."

Vlieger burst out laughing. "Good one. I can see why you write fantasy fiction. With your imagination, you'll go far. I kept one of your books by the way. One of the damaged ones that we paid for. Not bad. Not bad at all."

He, too, threw a twenty on the table and left.

Gollum and I breathed a big sigh of relief in unison.

Chapter 38

I'M GOING TO KILL that cat.

Cats are evil.

I'd just finished a good feed in the lake and returned to my babe to find the cat crouched in the middle of Tess' bed, waiting for me. If I dare move from this shelf above the bed, it will attack. If I leave the shelf, I have to abandon access to the box of tissues. The longer I stay the more my nose runs. My eyes are swelling shut.

I can't smell anything!

I don't have the strength yet to fly.

It just stares at me, unblinking, with those vicious green eyes, like I'm a mouse or something. It won't even tell me its name.

"That's a secret," it says. "That's precious," it says.

Big honking deal. How important can a name be? I mean, even the demons tell people their names.

Gollum has been duped by this cat. It is not a pet. It keeps Gollum as a pet. Gollum is not evil. But that damned cat is.

If I could transform, I'd kill the beast.

Not enough strength or rest. I need to eat more. Where is my babe? She'll give me beer and OJ. That always helps.

But I can't get past the damn cat. Achooooooo!

"You know, Tess, if I don't start weaving on that blanket, humanity is going to lose its integrity, dignity, and honesty," Cynthia asserted, hands on hips, feet grounded soundly, and head cocked in that all-knowing teenage way she had.

I'm afraid I snorted at her statement. "When have you noticed a lot of integrity, dignity, and honesty in humanity? Have you watched the news lately?" I mimicked her stance.

"My point exactly. Sapa should have gone looking for a new weaver a century ago. But the old woman was still alive, just not very effective."

We entered a staring contest. All the while, my feet itched to show her the cave where I believed the old woman had lived and worked.

"Those qualities are already woven into the blanket," Gollum said, peering up from a book. He had a pile of them around "his" chair in my living room. And the bloody cat in his lap. He seemed to have moved in, except for his clothes and toiletries. "Humanity can still tap into those qualities, if they choose. The blanket has another, deeper purpose that we need to address."

"Such as?" both Cynthia and I asked.

"Such as sealing a portal to the demon dimensions. It is precisely the integrity, dignity, and honesty of humanity that allows the portal to be sealed." He returned to his book as if he'd had the last word.

"A rogue portal that the Citadel doesn't know about because it was sealed centuries before the Citadel was founded, and bypasses the chat room," I mused. That would explain a lot.

"That still doesn't explain why Donovan doesn't destroy the blanket," I said.

"Because he's half human," Cynthia replied.

Out of the mouths of babes.

Gollum put down his book and stared at the girl. His hands stroked the cat in rhythm with his breathing as if the action helped him think. Or maybe the cat's purr soothed and ordered his thoughts. "Of course. If Donovan destroys the blanket, he destroys half of himself. He's not trying to go back to the demon world, nor is he trying to integrate completely with the human world. He wants a homeland for half-breeds, like himself."

"There's a story in history . . ." The brief glimpse I had of an answer passed. "Come on, I need to show both of you something."

"I need to start weaving."

"You need to come with us." I threw Cynthia my running jacket and grabbed a sweater. Gollum could fend for himself.

An hour later Gollum boosted Cynthia and then me up the last boulder to the ledge outside the cave. Cynthia had delayed our trek by constantly stopping to gather bits of grass and plants, bird feathers, a tuft of animal hair, anything that might enhance the blanket when twisted together into a rough yarn.

Instinctively I looked up the cliff face, ready to duck at the first sign of observers with guns.

As Gollum hauled himself over the edge of the rock, he paused, still supporting himself with his arms and shoulders at an awkward angle. He was stronger than I thought. He studied the rocks beside his hands for a long moment before continuing up to our level.

"Looks like a bullet hit the dirt right there," he commented casually.

Automatically, I touched my arm where a rock chip had sliced me on the ricochet. It had healed cleaner and faster than the two dog bites. I didn't want to think about the demon bite. Scrap's ministrations helped, but it would still take a long time to heal. I had needed Gollum's broad shoulders and well-muscled arms to help me over the last barrier.

Why hadn't I noticed his strength before? He had to do more of a workout than just tai chi.

Gollum raised his eyebrows, keeping his eyes on my arm.

I nodded briefly, then turned to face the crease in the cliff. "In here."

"Doesn't look like much of a cave to me," Cynthia said skeptically.

"Trust me. It's bigger than it looks."

I paused before ducking inside. "Please do not reject us," I pleaded with the unseen guardians of this place. "We mean you no harm. We honor this place and will not desecrate it."

Then I swallowed deeply and entered the narrow defile. I didn't really expect the ghosts to heed me, but it couldn't hurt.

Goose bumps rose on my arms and back the moment I moved from sunshine to shadow; far more than the change in temperature from outside to inside would account for. Gollum shivered as well the moment he stood upright within the dim confines of the cave. Cynthia, however, poked into the ashy remnants of the fire without visible concern.

"An old campfire. So what. It could be two weeks or two centuries old." She shrugged and scuffed the dirt.

"Can you tell if it's old or new?" I asked Gollum.

He was already on his knees, sifting through the rockfall. In moments he had collected a hand full of . . . of pottery sherds. They looked like rock chips to my uneducated eye.

"This looks precontact, but I'd need to do some tests in a lab to be sure. People are turning out some great fakes these days." He held up one of the larger sherds with traces of pigment on it that might have represented a lizard, or a snake, or rippling water. Or it might just be a squiggle.

"If it's precontact, and the construction above caused the rockfall, can we get the casino shut down?" I asked.

"Probably. There's enough here to call the state archaeologist and get an investigation started." He came to one knee, ready to rise to his full height.

Suddenly, the temperature in the cave dropped at least another ten degrees. We both froze in place.

"What?" Cynthia asked, still oblivious to the eerie chill.

Mist developed around the fire, drifted a moment, then coalesced into three vaguely human forms.

I caught glimpses of long dark hair and feathers, bone beads and leather.

Pressure fell on my chest. My breathing came in short sharp pants. I had to leave. I had to go outside. There wasn't enough air in this place.

Gollum, too, breathed with difficulty.

"Leave the sherds. We've got to get out of here," I panted.

"What?" Cynthia protested. Then her eyes grew large. I saw understanding dawn in her gaze.

She smiled hugely and walked right up to the trio of ghosts. "Hi, guys, are you here to protect me?"

Tess is in danger. I can feel it. I have to brave the cat to go to my babe.

I have battled and bested all forms of demons in the chat room. I survived my Mum. I can handle one lowly cat.

"I am not a lowly creature," it deigns to advise me. Its tail swishes and churns. It narrows its eyes and bunches its muscles, ready to pounce.

"Tell me your name and I won't kill you, this time," I snarl at it.

"Sit still so I can kill you, imp."

That's it. I take a deep breath, unfurl my wings—grown quite a bit after the last battle, and I got six more warts—and leap.

I skim past the highest reach of the cat's paws, lean down, and grab a pawful of tail hair.

Gleefully, I pop over to my babe, trophy in hand.

Chapter 39

The Incas and Aztecs used slave labor to collect bat
fur as clothing decoration. They probably used only
pelts from large fruit eating bats as most do not have
enough fur to make collecting economically viable.

*T*HE CAVE MIGHT HAVE warmed a degree or
two. Nothing more. Cynthia might feel at home
here with the spectral guardians. Gollum and I still were
not welcome.

"What?" Cynthia turned her big dark eyes on me once
more. "They won't hurt you."

"Tell that to them." I jerked my head in the direction of
the three solemn figures who had moved into a semicircle
around the rockfall.

I heard mad laughter in the back of my mind. It sounded
a lot, more than a lot, like Dill when he'd told one of his
outrageous puns that insulted the entire world without being totally offensive because he touched a universal truth.
He was good at that.

Suddenly I wondered why I had found his humor so endearing. In retrospect, he seemed immature and unsympa-
thetic, almost racist. And definitely insulting.

The three native ghosts remained the only ones I could
see. If Dillwyn was present, he wasn't visible. I chose to ignore him.

"Listen, guys, these are my friends. They take care of me

in the outside world. I welcome them, so you should, too,"
Cynthia addressed her new friends.

They remained implacable.

"You might be a little more respectful of them," Gollum
whispered. "Ghosts are not usually in tune with teenage flip
attitudes and vocabulary."

Cynthia rolled her eyes. But she turned back to the
ghosts and bowed ever so slightly. Just a token, barely a
show of respect at all. "Listen, my friends, I'm the new
weaver. Times have changed. I've got to live out there as
well as weave the blanket."

"If we ever get our hands on it again," I muttered.

"*When* we get our hands on it again," Cynthia insisted.
"The dog, Shunka Sapa, chose me. I am the new weaver. I
need Tess' and Gollum's help. I invite them here. You have
to accept them."

*Where is the Shunka Sapa? Only the dog of the ages may
reveal this cave to the weaver.*

The feeling of menace increased. I really wanted out of
the cave. More than that, I wanted Scrap to recover and
return to my side. I didn't feel safe without him anymore.

"The dog is protecting the blanket. It was stolen from
you when the old weaver died," Gollum answered for Cynthia.

*Many times over the centuries the dog and his descen-
dants have brought new weavers to us. Always the dog.
Never has a weaver been disrespectful to us. Never has the
weaver needed assistance beyond what we can give.*

"Well, times have changed, guys," Cynthia retorted. "It's a
whole new world out there. I'm about the only one Sapa could
find who will respect you and the blanket and everything it
stands for. Now either get with the picture or get lost."

Out of the mouths of babes. Or did I say that already?

The misty ghosts faded for a moment. I sensed, could
almost hear, an indignant conversation among them.

Abruptly, the cave warmed. Air returned to my lungs.
The lifting of the pressure of unwelcomeness made me feel
so light I almost lost my balance. Gollum staggered, too. I
grabbed his arm and kept him upright.

I may have leaned in to him, holding myself vertical as
much as helping him.

If you are to be the new guardians of the weaver, then you must dream and learn.

My knees turned to jelly, and I found myself on the cave floor, fighting a huge yawn.

I opened my eyes to find myself, Gollum, and Cynthia in a green landscape filled with sharp contrasts of rock and prairie, river, cliff, and plateau.

A steady rain pounded us yet didn't seem to get us wet. The sky looked black and ominous, but it was full daylight—or as bright as those clouds would allow.

"Where are we?" Nothing looked familiar. My sense of direction, up and down, right and left, forward and back, tilted about five degrees to the left. The colors altered by the same measure as well. And I didn't even have the comb with me. The slight tug by the North Pole on my senses had disappeared as well.

I shivered a little from the bite in the air. Early spring. I guessed the season by the depth of the green and the chill.

"I think the better question is, when are we?" Gollum replied.

Found you! Scrap chortled. He bounced into view, more solid and bigger than I had ever seen him. He stood about four feet tall instead of the eight inches I was used to. His wings had grown, too; they reached high above his head and draped below his four-taloned feet. Something else was wrong, but I couldn't pinpoint it.

He waved a fist full of white hairs, then let them scatter to the rising wind.

"So that's what he looks like!" Gollum gasped.

"Hey, he's cute. Can I pet him?" Cynthia asked.

"He's a pain in the ass and not normally this big or solid," I snarled.

"As solid as you, babe," Scrap chortled out loud. "But only in this dimension. Time warps things."

"What is happening, Scrap?" My senses remained distorted, but Scrap was here. With Scrap, I could defend myself and my companions.

"You jumped a couple of dimensions," he replied.

"Where's your cigar, Scrap?"

"Wrong time, wrong dimension. No tobacco here."

"Then what do we have here?"

"Floods!" Gollum shouted. He grabbed Cynthia by the elbow and began running uphill.

I didn't wait to see what had alarmed him. Hot on his heels I registered a roar in the background. A roar that had been there ever since I arrived, but I hadn't noticed it as separate from my other disorientation.

We crested the closest hill. Instinctively, I looked toward the river that wound around the hills below us. If anything, the water level seemed lower than my first glance moments ago.

"Gollum, what's happening?" I pointed toward the water.

Sure enough, more and more damp rock on the cliff sides was exposed.

And the roar came from behind us.

I whirled around. Off in the distance, many miles away, I caught a hint of rapid movement.

A brown wall of water raced across the landscape, gouging out a new riverbed. It leveled hills. Boulders as big as houses tumbled like feathers. People, animals, villages—everything was swept up in the relentless surge of water.

"I think we are watching the flood that nearly destroyed my people twelve thousand years ago," Cynthia whispered in awe and terror.

"The ice dam over in Montana must have broken, releasing more water than fills all of Lake Superior in one gush. It's forging a new riverbed," I quoted one of the pamphlets I'd picked up in Half Moon Lake.

The old river behind us continued to drain away. Soon, only a necklace of mineral lakes would be left. We were probably standing on the site where Donovan Estevez and his demon cohort would build a casino twelve thousand years in the future.

"The real question is, why are we here?" Gollum asked. He peered through the onslaught of rain.

"Over there," Scrap said. He pointed north.

Movement. A long line of people trudging along the ridgeline, perhaps two miles away, approached us. Too far to see details.

But Scrap elongated and thinned. His head and wings took on a metallic cast. His wings became curved blades with spikes sticking out of the outside edge.

"Those are demons," Gollum informed us.

"I guessed. Scrap doesn't do his Celestial Blade thing unless a demon or great evil is present."

"Sasquatch demons," Cynthia breathed. "I bet they've got the blanket. Maybe we can keep them from stealing it."

"No," Scrap spoke from within the blade that balanced so easily in my hand. His voice sounded deeper, more solemn and filled with portent. "We can only observe the past. We cannot change it. In this dimension we are all as transparent to the inhabitants as I usually am in your true time and place."

I gulped and began swinging the blade, ready to defend myself and my companions.

"Won't work, babe." Scrap sounded his usual sarcastic self. "You can't touch these guys in their own time. They belong here. You don't."

"If it won't work, then why did you transform?"

"Because it is his nature," Gollum said.

The demons came closer. True demons rather than halfbreeds, close to twelve feet tall.

I drew Cynthia and Gollum behind me while I continued to keep the blade in motion.

Sure enough, the lead Sasquatch, obviously male with huge testicles hanging between legs half hidden by auburn fur, clutched the blanket to his chest.

I peered closely at the textile as the demons passed us, seemingly oblivious to our presence. But some of the smaller Sasquatch, possibly half-breeds, looked about nervously.

The blanket looked more vibrant than I remembered, full of color from dried grasses, tree bark, bird feathers, and multicolored wild goat wool. Especially the bird feathers.

Maybe the blanket rippled because the demon who clutched it bounced as he jog-trotted along the plateau. Maybe.

But it looked to me as if it vibrated with life.

Three of the demons pushed ahead of their leader. They joined hands (paws?) in a circle and began chanting something in a weird language full of pops, clicks, and grunts. A very similar language to the one the demons who'd kidnapped me had spoken.

The ground beneath my feet rocked. I fought for balance. The land heaved. I had to jab the Celestial Blade into the rain-slick turf to stay upright.

Gollum and Cynthia flopped facedown, clinging to the grass with desperate fingers.

The demons seemed unaffected by the quake. But the three chanting ones broke their circle and stepped back. A jagged hole opened where they had been standing. A metal ladder led down that hole deep into the earth.

"The demon portal," I breathed. "Did you get that invocation, language guy?" I asked Gollum.

Abruptly, the world went black, and I tumbled into nothing.

Thank the Goddess I still had my hands on the blade.

Chapter 40

I CAME UP BLIND and swinging.

"Easy, Tess. Back off." Gollum's voice.

Light glimmered around the edges of my perceptions.

"Did they get you, too?" I asked. Why did my hands feel numb and empty?

"We're back home, Tess. Back in the cave."

"Scrap?"

"I can't see him," Gollum said.

"I can't either," Cynthia chimed in.

"I can't see anything." I rubbed my eyes. A little more light. Concentrated in a vertical line off to my left.

Dimension blindness. It will pass. That was one of the Indian ghosts who had started this nightmare.

I closed my eyes and thought for several moments. *Yes!* The tug of the North Pole on my nerve endings was back. My feet found a rock-solid balance. I breathed normally.

Then I opened my eyes. I picked out a few more details in the cave. Rockfall, the pile of sherds Gollum had collected, the remains of an ancient fire that had burned for millennia until the cave-in killed the old woman and sent her dog in search of a new weaver.

That rockfall was the beginning of this entire adventure. A collapse caused by construction of the casino above.

Construction directly on top of a demon portal that the Sisterhood of the Celestial Blade didn't know about.

They didn't need to know about it until a few months ago because the weaver and the blanket sealed the portal.

The blanket still existed. We had a new weaver. So why wasn't the portal closed?

Because Cynthia wasn't actively weaving the blanket and Sapa wasn't ripping out her new work each day so that the blanket was never finished. Finish the blanket?

The world comes to an end.

Stop weaving the blanket?

The demon portal opens and demons return en masse. That might well be the end of the world, too.

"I need a drink," I muttered.

"It's almost dark. I think we can safely go outside now without being blinded by the sun," Gollum said.

"Did you remember the incantation the demons spoke to open the portal?" I asked.

Gollum looked at me, puzzled. "I can't learn any language that quickly."

"But you spoke Lakota dialect when you channeled the legend." The myth might belong to all of the Indian tribes, but apparently only the Lakota had recorded it and allowed the outside world to think it their own.

"I don't remember a word of it other than what I've learned from listening to the tape."

"Shit. I think we're going to need that incantation."

"But we don't want to open the portal, we want to close it, and keep it closed," Cynthia said.

"Demons aren't very smart," Gollum said, adopting his professor tone. "They probably can't remember two different chants. They'd use the same one to open and close the portal. Like the word 'Aloha' means both hello and goodbye."

"What day is it, Scrap?" I asked, stepping out into the twilight, grateful that the cave mouth faced east, and not west where the sun set. I couldn't find Scrap with my eyes or my other senses. He must have done his disappearing act again after transforming.

"My watch says Tuesday, October twenty-seven," Gollum replied.

"Shit. I've got to leave in the morning for the con. Let's go get a little bit drunk while I pack."

Three hours later, as I filled my suitcase with the clothes Mom had sent to me and drank from a bottle of single malt scotch I'd found in the local liquor store, Gollum entertained Cynthia with stories of ancient man in Europe. The cat perched on his lap as if it was seated on a throne.

I half listened, marveling at the man's talent for dealing with an adolescent who would really rather be with her monster dog.

Sapa still guarded the blanket over at Donovan's office. The guards with guns kept Sapa and me from stealing the blanket. The dog kept Donovan's goons from damaging or removing it to another location.

So why didn't the goons just shoot the dog? Because he'd been touched by the otherworld. Bullets would bounce off his hide, like they did with demons.

Balance, Scrap reminded me from his hidey-hole. *Even demons respect the need for balance.*

A loud argument next door interrupted my errant thoughts. I thought I heard echoes of Donovan's voice in the verbal melee. Specific words eluded me.

Anything that concerned that man now concerned me.

I placed a glass from the bathroom against the wall and pressed my ear against it, hoping to use the old movie detective trick to pick out the nature of the argument. The volume rose, but the words did not become any clearer. When I stepped away from the wall, I noticed the volume had risen even without the aid of the glass.

Gollum and Cynthia were engrossed in an argument over the intelligence of Neanderthal Man versus Cro-Magnon. Gollum sipped at his glass of scotch quite regularly, and he slurred his words. Between the two of us, we'd drunk over half the bottle. I hadn't had more than one glass. No wonder Cynthia seemed to be winning the argument that Neanderthal was smarter than normally given credit for.

I stepped out onto the back deck overlooking the lake. A tiny slice of a moon drifted in the autumn sky surrounded by a blanket of stars. A fresh breeze ruffled the lake and brought the sharp scent of mineral salts to me—an odor I would now always associate with Sasquatch demons rather than the healing attributed to those mineral salts. The window in the suite adjacent to mine was open. About two feet of space separated my deck from theirs.

If I climbed onto the railing, I could step over the space and get directly beneath that window.

"We're cutting you off, Estevez. No more delays, no more money. We're through. If you don't come through in two weeks, we take over," Vern Abrams shouted.

"If you'd only listen," Donovan pleaded.

"We've listened enough to your platitudes and innuendos. No more," Myrna Abrams added. Her strident voice nearly pierced my eardrum.

Someone shoved the sliding glass door open, then rammed it closed again. Donovan stood at the railing gulping air. Even in the dim light, I could tell from his posture that he wasn't happy. Then he slammed his fist into the top rail. The varnished cedar pole, nearly three inches in diameter bent, almost buckled.

I stepped back into the shadows, unwilling to be a part of or witness to his violence. His physical strength alarmed me.

"Who?"

My movement must have alerted him.

"Just me. Tess. I couldn't help but overhear. I'm sorry. I wasn't deliberately eavesdropping." Like hell I wasn't. But I couldn't tell him that.

"Abrams is my banker. He's just refused to extend the financing on the casino. There's no way I can finish on deadline, thanks to those impatient and stupid fools. Homeland Security still has the construction site roadblocked until they finish their investigation. Heaven only knows when that will be." He took a deep breath to steady himself.

Did he mean that Homeland Security were the impatient and stupid fools, or the Kajiri—the half-blood demons?

"I'm ruined, Tess."

"Your software company?"

"Mortgaged to the hilt to finance the casino. My house, even the car. I . . . I'm . . . I need to be alone. I can't hope that you will learn to love me when I'm broke." He vaulted the railing, landing softly on the sand, then ran off into the night.

I gulped, more than a little confused. There was that "L" word. Call me a sucker, but there was more between Donovan and myself than I wanted to admit. He hadn't pulled the trigger or authorized Quentin to. But still . . .

I could never trust him enough to love him as he wanted me to.

Did he love me as he hinted?

I needed to break the spell that man had on me. Until I figured out how to do that, I needed to stay well away from him.

Maybe all I needed was to buy a vibrator and rent some porn.

Would I ever dare love anyone again? Dill had so dominated my emotions I hadn't thought I'd be able to look beyond the too-short time we had together.

Only now, after three years, was I able to look more closely at the whirlwind love affair, the blind devotion, the all-consuming love . . . or was it just lust?

I went back inside rather than face my own emotional demons.

Gollum sat straight up in his chair, eyes focused on something too far in the distance for me to pinpoint. A stream of nonsense syllables streamed from his mouth.

Cynthia tried to write down the sounds on the tiny sheets of memo paper provided by the lodge. I grabbed my brand new Dictaphone and turned it on.

Only then did I note that the bottle of scotch was nearly empty.

Gollum had been almost as drunk the last time he'd channeled a legend in a foreign language. No wonder he didn't remember it.

Chapter 41

Fruit eating bats drop seeds far from the source, thus increasing the number of seedlings away from the mother tree.

MADISON, WISCONSIN, IS a lovely city. What I saw of it. Flight options out of Moses Lake, Washington, connecting to Seattle were limited. I flew in during the wee small hours of Thursday morning. The hotel was . . . a hotel. I've seen too many of them to get excited about any of them.

"Tess, you look wonderful for having been kidnapped by terrorists," my agent Sylvia Watson gushed when we met for brunch that first morning. I'd had a few hours of sleep. She hugged me to her ample bosom. I found my face nearly smothered in her shoulder. She's *that* tall and she was wearing four-inch heels. I had managed to find a pair of flats that actually matched in my luggage when I stumbled awake ten minutes before. That left me at my normal five foot two.

"Wonderful?" I blinked at her blearily. "Where's the coffee?"

"Same old Tess. Brush it off, hide your pain, and pour it into your work. Makes for wonderful novels, Tess, but I worry about you. You need to talk about this, maybe see a counselor. Posttraumatic stress syndrome."

"I have talked about it, Syl. Endlessly. To the Marines, to Homeland Security, and to my research assistant."

"That cute-sounding gentleman who called me? What is his name? Gordon?"

"Guilford."

"There something going on between you two? About time you found someone new. You've mourned Dill long enough."

"There is nothing going on between me and Gol . . . Guilford." Not while I lusted after Donovan, even though I couldn't trust the bastard any farther than I could throw him.

My cell phone bleeped out the opening phrase of the *Star Wars* theme.

Sylvia raised her eyebrows.

I turned away from her as I answered.

"Tess, you didn't call me. Are you okay?"

"I'm fine, Gol . . . Guilford. I'm getting ready to eat brunch with my agent. I need to talk business with her." In other words, go away.

"I made some progress on the tape you made Tuesday night."

"Was it only yesterday?" My time sense and balance were off. This was . . . what, Thursday? So day before yesterday. Yesterday had evaporated in long waits for airplanes, flurries to get onto airplanes, then long waits while flying. Over and over again.

"I think we've got the incantation to open the portal."

"Fine. Memorize it and translate it. I'll check back with you later."

"In an hour, Tess. I'm serious. You are in danger."

"I'll check with you *later*." I disconnected.

"What was that all about?" Sylvia asked, too curious to be polite. Maybe too pushy to care about being polite. That's why she's such a good agent.

"He was just giving me a progress report."

"Making sure you aren't with another man?"

I picked up my menu and pointedly ignored her comment.

Before we'd done more than order, three other writers stopped by our table to say hello. By the time our food arrived, we'd waved and exchanged distant greetings with an editor and another agent. Over the course of the next two hours I connected with almost every person I knew attending the con.

The tension of the last weeks dropped away as we discussed business and gossiped about the publishing industry and our genre. Once more, I was one of them; nothing special about me or my life other than the success of the latest book, the upcoming release of the second in the series, and my progress on the third.

Scrap remained elusive, though I caught whispers of cigar smoke now and then, like he was near, just not interested enough or strong enough to show himself. I hoped he was having as much fun in his home dimension as I was in mine.

"I want to do an anthology on the etiquette of first contact," Julie Jacobs said over drinks before dinner.

Five female authors from an e-list had gathered so we could get to know each other in the flesh after communicating only by e-mail for years.

"Got a publisher interested?" I asked. The most important question. An anthology without a publisher had no life.

"Working on it. He says I need ten more recognizable names committed to it before he can push it through marketing."

"I'm in," four of us said together.

Then we laughed about possible story ideas that got more outrageous with each drink.

I wanted to stay, but dinner with my editor called. This was a private meeting, just the two of us, to talk about my books and my career in general. I ran story ideas past him. He countered with issues I could explore with those scenarios. We parted with me promising him an early draft of book three by the first of the year.

Friday morning I sat on a panel discussing heroic characters from mythology and literature. Since most of the attendees were professionals, there were always more writers willing to do panels than panels to do. So we each only got one. Two at the most.

That left me the rest of the day to play in the dealers' room and hang out in the bar with friends. I excused myself for a much needed nap about two, and reemerged ready for dinner with Sylvia and some of her other clients. I wore the little dress Scrap had altered for the convention in San Jose. I got a few whistles from male writers and editors who knew me. A lot of makeup hid the still healing demon bite on my leg. Dark nylons couldn't cover it adequately.

Sylvia introduced me to her newest client, Val White, and Val's husband George. "I just sold her fat fantasy trilogy to Gryffyn Books," Sylvia preened.

I shook hands with Val. She gave me a limp and sweaty grip with a hand as pudgy and pale as the rest of her. George, on the other hand, presented an exact opposite. Tall, lean, dark-skinned. He vibrated with energy. She tended to hide behind him.

We sat down together in a private corner of a Mexican restaurant three blocks from the hotel.

"I thought Howard Ebson was supposed to be here," I said as I looked around the small circle.

"The famous recluse?" Val gushed, the most animation I'd seen from her.

"Infamous is more like it," replied Dave Fischer, a professor of psychology from out west somewhere. He wrote psychological thrillers with futuristic backdrops.

"He promised he'd show up on Sunday for the lifetime achievement award." Sylvia shrugged. "At least his lady friend promised she'd get him here. He doesn't talk on the phone to anyone anymore, not even me." Sylvia pouted, offended that her most famous client had shut her out along with the rest of the world.

"When did his last book come out? Ten years ago?" I asked, amazed that anyone could remain viable in today's publishing industry without producing something every year or two.

"Two short stories last year," Dave said. "Both got nominated for every award there is. Wish I could write that well."

"Nominated but didn't win," Val offered tentatively. She acted afraid to enter the discussion in this rarified company.

"Token nominations by his longtime friends because they can't stand to see a short list without his name on it," Sylvia grunted.

I raised my eyebrows at that.

The discussion went on to the validity and ethics of campaigning works for awards versus just letting them happen.

Scrap finally showed up on the walk back to the hotel. I hung back a little to assess his color. Still a bit gray around the edges, but definitely closer to normal.

I don't like it here, babe, he said, chomping on his cigar. *Great dress by the way. New designer, dahling?* He winked at me.

"What's wrong?" I whispered, very aware that Dave also hung back from the crowd.

Don't know. Just feels colder than it should.

I'd noticed that the wind out of the north bit through my nylons to the still healing demon bite on my leg. I snuggled deeper into my wool coat.

We continued on in silence.

Gotta feed some more. The moment we stepped into the brightly lighted hotel lobby, Scrap winked out.

"Time to party!" I called to the others. I suddenly needed a lot of people and noise around me. Body heat and the hot air from too much talk sounded wonderful.

My cell phone sang. Gollum checking in. His concern warmed me even better than the party. Make that parties. I hit three that night before my body's demand for sleep overcame my need to keep people close and unseen enemies away.

Chapter 42

SATURDAY BECAME A close repeat of Friday. I pitched book and story ideas right and left, made one firm deal, and got tentative commitments on two others. Life can be good when you are on a roll. I began to believe that life could become normal once more. Demons and Native blankets and pesky anthropologists had no place here.

Especially the pesky anthropologist who called far too often.

Only the hotel staff wore costumes on Saturday—Halloween. We were professionals after all (at least we pretended to be). I couldn't tell if Val White's flowing caftan in glaring colors was a costume or her normal style of dressing.

I saw some great costumes on the street Saturday evening while I walked to a restaurant with friends and colleagues. Thankfully, none of them wore demon masks that might not have been masks at all.

The parties were fun but much more subdued than those at cons run by fans for fans.

For some reason I kept looking for the contingent of bat people. And not with my normal trepidation. Maybe the Morris critter back at Fort Snoqualmie had helped me get over my phobia. Maybe. I didn't count on it.

I think I was just lusting after Donovan. Dammit! One night in bed with the man, and every other man paled in comparison.

I kept remembering the feel of his slick skin under the shower spray, all lean muscle, not a bit of fat on him.

So was he truly a half-Damiri demon? Gregor said they tended to fat. . . .

By Saturday night I had convinced myself that the past few weeks, *the last three years,* had all been a dream. Just to prove it to myself I dialed Bob's cell phone, his work number, the one he always kept with him.

"We're sorry, the number you have dialed has been disconnected. No new number has been assigned," the automated voice blared in my ear.

Tears nearly choked me. I hadn't even been able to sing at Bob's funeral, as he requested.

Would I ever sing again?

Not if my new life kept putting the ones I loved in the way of demons and monsters.

Resolutely, I went off to the next party, this one at the overflow hotel two blocks away. I needed to party, to reaffirm that life existed beyond the realm of demons and imps and secret warrior Sisterhoods.

I took a shortcut through the back parking lot since I was running late, no thanks to yet another call from Gollum. With a quick dash, I shouldn't need a coat.

This party was hosted by my publisher, so I wore a brand new black sheath covered in gold and iridescent sequins. Since this was the end of October in Wisconsin, I slung a lace shawl woven with metallic gold threads around my shoulders. Not much protection against the wind, but I should be okay outside for a few minutes. Tiny glass beads weighted the fringe of the shawl. The entire ensemble glittered gaily in the subdued light. I could hear the noise from the party in the small ground-floor ballroom half a parking lot away.

The soft grass verge between the two parking lots absorbed the sound of my high-heeled footsteps. It absorbed the raucous voices and music from the party as well.

Streetlights didn't penetrate here.

A hushed barrier grew between me and the rest of the world. The hairs along my spine tingled.

Mist covered the few lights I could see.

"Scrap?"

More silence. No cigar smoke. I couldn't even smell the booze, smoked salmon, and cigarettes from the party.

"Where the hell are you, Scrap, when I need you?"

A shadow appeared beneath a spindly tree to my right. It looked like it stepped right out of the tree. A shadow that had no being to cast it. I stopped and placed my feet *en garde,* or at least as close to that position as the straight skirt of my dress allowed. I hiked it up, almost to my hips to give my legs moving room. While I debated kicking off my shoes, another shadow appeared out of the matching tree on my left.

Retreat or advance?

Right shadow took the decision away from me. It moved away from the wall and placed itself between me and the party. It had three dimensions now, roughly humanoid in shape, though with no substance.

Left shadow crowded behind me.

What could they do to me if they had no substance?

The temperature dropped to freezing. Ice crystals formed on the grass and in the mist around the lights.

They could freeze-dry me and crumble me into stale coffee grounds.

I took off the shawl and whirled it over my head like a toreador cape. The weighted fringe made the thing bell out. Front shadow ducked.

Every creature is vulnerable in the eyes and in the groin, Sister Paige's voice came to me unbidden. *The trouble with demons is finding the eyes and the groin.*

Since these guys looked vaguely human, I kept the glass beads on the fringe as close to their eye level as I could—a full head above me. Were these guys more Sasquatch only halfway into this dimension?

Back shadow moved off to my side.

Still whirling the shawl, I lashed out with my left foot toward backside shadow. The spike heel landed near its groin.

It grunted painfully.

Before I could take satisfaction in landing a good one, front shadow advanced. It grabbed the shawl in one hand and reached for my throat with the other.

I ducked and plowed forward, ramming my head into its middle. It stumbled and went down.

It had substance after all.

Back shadow recovered. It lunged for my knees.

"Goddess, Scrap, where did you get to?" I evaded the tackle, just.

Right here, babe. The smell of cigars sharpened in the frigid air.

I snapped my fingers. Scrap appeared in my right hand, elongated and sharpened in the blink of an eye.

I twirled the blade, cleaving mist. It hung in tattered streamers like shattered silk in a circle around me.

Shadows backed off.

I kept up my circular pattern, over my head, down low, in the middle, never giving them a chance to touch me.

They kept moving around and around me, looking for an opening, reaching to touch me so they could freeze me.

I kept edging closer to a tree, to protect my back.

Could they lose their third dimension and slip between me and the trunk?

I gulped, hesitated.

One of them dove low toward my ankles.

I stomped on its hand with my heel. It yelped and flowed backward, half mist, half solid.

Gut one of them, Scrap chortled gleefully.

"Bloodthirsty little imp, aren't you?" I followed suit with a long lunge and backhanded slash with the spikes on the outside curve of the blade. My skirt ripped.

Damn. The dress had cost a fortune.

I cleaved in two the shadow demon in front of me.

It screamed. The high-pitched shriek stabbed at my hearing and my sanity.

My shoulders hunched in an attempt to cover my ears. I couldn't drop the blade to use my hands.

The two parts of the demon toppled to the ground in opposite directions. Black liquid pooled out from both halves. The grass absorbed it like nourishing water.

I gagged on the scent of burning hospital waste mixed with sulfur and disinfectant.

The other shadow came at me from the left with a roar that could shake the eight-story building in front of me to dust.

I swung the blade. It backed off, turned to mist, and disappeared within itself.

The parking lot brightened. The temperature rose. Noise from the party oozed out of the French doors.

My teeth stopped chattering. But the base of my spine still tingled.

Using my Celestial Blade as a walking staff, I sauntered on toward the party, pretending nothing had happened, that the rip in my skirt seam, halfway up my thigh was intentional.

"Hey, Tess, cool weapon," Steve Littlefield, one of my fellow writers called. He squeezed between people to come examine my blade. He wrote sword-and-sorcery fantasy and had a collection of blades, real and fanciful.

"Hi, Steve. I had this made up as a wall ornament, but it works really well as a prop at cons," I hedged.

Steve touched the spikes with tentative fingers. "Those are really stable. Surprising. You'd think metal that slender would wobble." He made as if to take the weapon from me.

I jerked it away from his reach. "I know you, Steve. You couldn't resist trying it out and it's way too crowded in here."

I propped the blade behind a potted palm and took Steve by the arm, steering him away from the Celestial Blade. Scrap could use the privacy to return to his usually invisible self while I particd.

But three hours later, the blade was still intact.

Scrap couldn't dissolve because a demon was present.

"Steve, walk me back to the hotel," I suggested around midnight. I knew almost everyone in the room. Who among my colleagues led a double life as a demon and a writer?

If that was the case, who was missing? Besides Howard Ebson and his lady friend. They were always missing. Val and George had said Thursday night that they didn't party. They got up early for a refreshing swim before breakfast.

"Sure, I'm about done in anyway." He eyed my Celestial Blade with longing. I kept it close by my side.

"So who's going to win best fantasy novel tomorrow? You or me?" he asked.

"There are three other nominees," I hedged. I really wanted that award. I'd never won anything before.

"Token nominees to fill out the field and pretend it's a real contest," Steve laughed. "Everyone knows its between you and me and no one else."

First I'd heard that rumor. "May the best woman win." I grinned and offered him my hand.

"May the best *man* win," he countered as we shook hands.

"Where's Val, your wife?" Valeria Littlefield as opposed to Valerie White. I suddenly went cold again. What if . . . ?

"Oh, she's tucked up in bed with a cold and the copy edits of my next book. She should be well enough to attend the awards brunch tomorrow."

I hid my sigh of relief. I'd known and liked this couple for a number of years. Who else did I need to be suspicious of?

Goddess, I hated suspecting my friends.

Chapter 43

"GOLLUM, I'M SCARED," I whispered into my cell phone at two in the morning. Only midnight back at Half Moon Lake, Washington. He was still awake, still working on the translation of the demon language he'd channeled.

"What happened?"

I could almost see him straightening from his slump in the armchair of my suite, pushing his glasses up his nose, and planting his big feet firmly on the plank floor.

"What do you call a shadow that takes on three dimensions and freeze-dries everything around it?" I tried for a flippant tone but failed miserably.

"I don't know. What do you call it?"

I rolled my eyes. He couldn't be that oblivious to my emotions. Could he?

My gut still churned with fear. Why now? Why were demons coming after me now? I'd been going to cons this last year, promoting the new book. Were the shadows local and opportunistic?

Or were they in communication with the Sasquatch and out to get me wherever they could?

"A pair of demons who tried to kill me," I informed Gollum. Sarcasm helped me quiet the roiling acid in my stomach.

Dead silence.

"Are you there, Gollum? Is the line still open?" Cell phones had a bad habit of dropping calls in Half Moon Lake.

Well, cell phones had that bad habit everywhere.

"Yeah, I'm still here. Describe them." He sounded clinically detached, once more the anthropologist deep into research.

I knew he opened files on his laptop—a twin to my new one. Trying to separate myself from the awful reality and fear, I matched his tone, giving him as much detail as I could. Surprisingly, I had observed more than I thought. I described shades of black, height, estimated mass, a clear description of how the surviving demon dissolved, and how it grunted when my spike heel connected with its groin.

"You have to get out of there, Tess. Come back now. Take whatever flight you can grab."

"This is Madison, Wisconsin, not Chicago or New York. Planes don't come and go at all hours here. I'd be stuck in the airport. Alone. For hours and hours."

"Better the airport with lots of people around. Demons won't attack where there are witnesses."

"I'm not alone here, Gollum. Any one of a hundred people could have stumbled across that attack."

"Get out of there, Tess. Rent a car and drive to Chicago."

"Alone in the middle of the night on the road? You call that safer? Besides, I have to stay for the awards banquet. My publisher paid for it. I'm up for an award. I have to stay for that. This is my career."

"I mean it, Tess. You aren't safe there."

"I have to be. Scrap just crawled into the temperature control unit under the window. He'll gorge on mold and be fine in a couple of hours," I said too brightly. Actually Scrap had resembled a wounded mole limping back to his dark tunnel.

"I don't like this, Tess."

"I don't like it either, but I have to do this. Tomorrow evening I'm on the seven o'clock flight to Chicago, then to Seattle and Pascoe. I should be back in Half Moon Lake by midafternoon."

"Call me. Every hour."

"In the morning, after I get some sleep."

"Every hour, Tess. In the meantime, I'll see if Gramps can call in some favors and get you reinforcements."

I snorted at the idea of two octogenarian anthropologists hobbling into a battle with canes against demon claws. "I'll call you when I wake up."

I did call him. But first I called Donovan to see what information I might pry out of him. If I admitted to being a Warrior of the Celestial Blade, would he admit to having demon ancestors? Not likely, but I felt like I had to talk to him.

He didn't answer his office or his cell phone. My heart sank toward my belly.

Being really stupid where he was concerned was getting old.

▽△▽△▽

"Eat something," Sylvia admonished me at the awards brunch the next day.

I'd picked out crepes and eggs and sausage rolls from the better-than-average buffet. The fruit had tasted good and three cups of coffee had helped make up for the hours of lost sleep. For a few moments I felt almost human, almost normal. Then I remembered freeze-dried grass and tree bark. My appetite vanished. I kept harking back to the feel of the Celestial Blade biting into demon flesh and the sight of black or green blood spilling on the ground with the horrendous scent of sulfur and other noxious things.

I kept wondering who in the room might be a demon and who I had killed last night. I scanned the crowd constantly, wondering who was missing. The comb in my hair revealed only normal auras. No extra shadows or braids of black within the variety of colors.

The awards portion of the day wouldn't start until after we'd all eaten, about an hour from now. It couldn't come soon enough.

"I wonder where Val got to?" Sylvia asked, looking toward the untouched place setting across the round table from me.

"Val Littlefield? Steve's wife?" I gulped. No wonder

Steve had had such an intense interest in the Celestial Blade. But he'd touched it. I didn't think a demon—even a halfling—could touch it with impunity. And I'd asked him to walk me home last night!

"No. Valerie White. The new author I introduced to you. You two share an editor as a matter of fact. Gryffyn Books bought her ticket to this brunch. The least she could do is show up." Sylvia searched the room, her mouth turning down in distress. "There really is no excuse for not showing up for a free meal with your agent and publisher."

Tom Southerby, the publisher of Gryffyn Books, wandered around the large room, networking rather than eating. We'd be lucky if he sat anywhere long enough to do more than say "Hi," before he took off again.

My stomach sank. I knew of a very good excuse why a new author might miss a free meal that could make her memorable to the publisher and launch her career to a new level. I'd killed her last night.

My cell phone sang again. Gollum, of course. I leaped to take it outside the banquet room.

"Jealous Romeo again?" Sylvia leered at me knowingly. "Who else?"

The hush of the lobby outside the banquet room came as a relief from the constant noise of conversations and cutlery clanking against fine china.

Gollum continued his litany of complaint that I had not checked in with him every hour. I apologized and cut him off.

Then I stepped outside for a breath of fresh autumn air, lightly chilled and redolent with the scent of fallen leaves. I missed the trace of stale cigar smoke that used to pervade my life. Scrap's failure to recover from last night's ordeal added on top of everything else that had happened to us recently twisted my gut with apprehension.

Demons all over the country wanted me dead.

After about five minutes, the bite in the wind penetrated my good wool rust-colored suit—the one Scrap had wanted me to buy a new hat with a feather for.

Damn, I wish the imp would come back from his hidey-hole. There was still a shadow demon out there who wanted my blood.

I yanked open the door and stepped back inside, grateful for the relief from the wind.

Maybe my eyes took longer than usual to adjust from bright autumnal sunshine to a remote inside corridor of a hotel. They shouldn't have. Since the fever that had made me a member of the Sisterhood, my senses reacted more quickly than those of a normal person. The moment I stepped inside, I felt shrouded in shadows, chilled beyond the seasonal temperatures, dull and heavy.

Just like I'd felt before I cleaved shadow mists with the Celestial Blade.

Quickly, I inventoried my assets for another fight. No heels. No shawl weighted with glass beads. No energy.

And no Scrap.

The shadows began to coalesce around me.

"You killed my mate," someone whispered through the growing darkness. An androgynous voice. Menacing.

"Your life is forfeit."

"Not today, buddy." I turned on my flat heel and dashed back outside into the minimal shadows of noon sunshine.

Half running, I made my way around the hotel to the main entrance. Knots of people laughed and joked and talked very loudly in the lobby.

If any shadow demon followed me, I denied it privacy for the kill.

Hunching my shoulders a little and dropping my head, I assumed a posture of meekness. One group of seven people had two other hangers-on who listened intently but offered no contributions to the conversation.

I joined them, sidling closer to the center, using these people as a human shield.

"Hey, looks like they've finished serving the overpriced brunch and will let us poor peons in now," Suze Naggar said. I'd known her for years. A marine biologist by day, she wrote hard science fiction and had a small but solid corps of fans. She only produced one book about every two years and had yet to break into the big numbers of publishing.

Feeling like part of the wallpaper, I followed her back to the banquet room. Even Sylvia didn't notice me until I sat heavily in my chair and nibbled at a cold crepe stuffed with strawberries and cream cheese.

"Have you been running?" my agent asked. "You're breathing heavily."

"Sylvia, I think I just had a panic attack. Post-traumatic stress and all. Would you . . ." I gulped and swallowed heavily. "Would you stay with me while I pack and check out? Maybe ride to the airport with me?"

"Honey, I'll stay with you until you get on your plane. I'm scheduled to leave an hour after you, same airline. No problem." She patted my hand and waved my publisher back to the table as the organizers began the award ceremony.

Val, the missing new author, breezed in wearing swaths of floating rayon and more bracelets than I could count. She glittered and clanked and gushed apologies. Something about a panicked phone call from her teenage son who thought the microwave had died.

I had trouble deciding if the layers of floral prints and garish background colors covered a fat body or disguised a thin one. Her middle-aged face sagged at the jawline but not badly. Her hands were pudgy—and heavily beringed— but that didn't mean the rest of her was. My hands used to swell at that time of the month and during the summer when I ate too much salt and drank too much iced tea.

"Where's your husband?" Sylvia asked, after she'd hugged Val and kissed her cheek.

I'd had to publish three novels before I got that kind of affection from our agent.

"He'll be along in a minute. There's a glitch with our flight reservations." Val dismissed his absence with a wild gesture that almost took out the publisher's eye with one of her rings. It looked like a hinged casket, one of the "poison" rings so popular with the con populace.

This woman's style was very different from mine and not what I considered professional. Some writers could carry off flamboyance. I'd never tried.

Steve Littlefield, the toastmaster and previous winner of the World Fantasy Award, finally wound down his humorous speech. Most of it went over the top of my head. I was concentrating too hard on who was missing—besides Val's husband—and who I might have killed last night.

If Val and her husband were the shadow demons, she

might decide to eliminate me now that I was competition to her own career. Any con we had been to together before this, we weren't in the same league.

I kept looking around, too nervous to pay attention to the ceremonies that captured the attention of the entire room.

The presenters went through the long list of publications up for awards, short stories, novelettes, novellas, editors, artwork, anthologies and collections, even industry magazines. Finally they came to the last and most coveted category, novels.

I gripped my chair with white knuckles and bit my lip. I'd never been nominated before. I'd never had a work sell well enough to gain this kind of recognition before. I really wanted to win, though I knew the voters in this contest favored obscure literary pieces over commercial successes.

"Ladies and gentlemen, I don't remember this happening before. For the category of Best Fantasy Novel of the Year, we have a tie," the presenter, an editor from a rival publisher announced. "The winners are . . ." dramatic pause while he opened the thick cream-colored envelope. "The winners are, Steve Littlefield for *The Dragons of Banesfield Manor* and Tess Noncoiré for *Imps Alive!*"

I sat there numbly, not daring to believe what I heard.

Sylvia pounded my back. Tom pumped my hand and pushed me up to the dais. I bowed to the thunderous applause as Steve grabbed the microphone. He said a few words I couldn't hear over the roaring in my ears, then he handed the mike to me.

"I . . . uh . . . I need to thank my agent Sylvia Watson, my editor and publisher Tom Southerby, and um . . . and my mom, as well as all the readers who voted for me," I stumbled.

I had to give credit where credit was due. Editors and publishers invested a lot of work and money in putting a book on the shelves. This was a big feather in Tom's hat.

Scrap loved hats with feathers. He should be here to share the moment, too.

I gave the mike back to Steve. He rambled on quite nicely, covering for me.

My attention riveted on the tall black man who took a seat next to Valerie White. He had to be at least seven feet tall and wore a conservative business suit.

Was he the shadow demon? If so, then who was his mate? Certainly not pudgy and flamboyant Caucasian Val.

I couldn't see their auras even wearing the comb.

If the Whites weren't the shadow demons, then who were?

Eventually the crowd let me sit down again. One more award, the previously announced lifetime achievement award to Howard Ebson. More speeches and intros.

Finally Lilia David stood up to accept the award for Howard. She wore jeans, a flannel shirt, and hiking boots. Very inappropriate to the occasion. She mumbled some kind of apology for Howard. Everyone knew his reclusive nature. He hated crowds and ceremonies.

I barely comprehended a word she said. Her aura revealed layers upon layers of shadow shifting in the wind.

Last night, I'd killed her mate, Howard Ebson, the shadow demon.

▬▽▲▽▲▽▬

While my babe is safe aboard the airplane, I have a little freedom to roam. I'd like to bust into the chat room and put the bad guys on notice they've caused a Sister enough grief. Next time we stop pussyfootin' around. Next time I won't be showin' no mercy.

Speaking of pussycats and no mercy, I've made plans for Gollum's little playmate. That cat is goin' down. I've earned a couple of new warts and my wings actually look like wings now instead of stubs. I've taken out shadow demons and I've neutralized a tribe of renegade Sasquatch. I'm ready for that cat.

But first I think I'll just zip back home for a moment and see if the garbage dump holds any more little treasures for Tessie-babe. She needs a little gift to make her feel better.

But I've got to be careful. She won't appreciate an old 286 CPU, like some people. Nor will she want a leather leash and slave collar with metal studs. Some of the Sisters might like them. But not my babe.

My babe has class. Like the comb. Now what other useful little talisman can I find?

Interlude

*T*HE ENTIRE SISTERHOOD filed out of their various quarters. Each woman wore a red gown, all different designs, revealing or hiding cleavage, clinging or full, but all long and flowing. Each woman carried a red candle, not yet lit. Quite an impressive display when they gathered in the courtyard on the night of a waxing quarter moon. Seven initiates stood to one side, on a little dais. They all wore white.

Except for me.

Sister S had given me a new pair of jeans, a flannel shirt, low-heeled boots. Clothing for the outside world.

Sister Gert stepped forward. She wore her gown cut low on the bodice, empire waistline, and falling in straight folds to her feet. Thus clad, she looked younger, more vibrant, less stern than I knew her to be. She'd swept her short, blunt-cut hair behind her ears and secured it with a glittering barrette that might have diamonds and real gold in it. It looked very elegant and expensive. And old.

"Before we induct seven new members into our order, we must deal with one who is not suitable, but has certainly been chosen by the Goddess." Sister Gert's voice rang out, caught and echoed on the stone walls, compounding in volume and authority.

I firmed my shoulders and faced the assemblage with defiance. I'd not conform to their rules, so they wouldn't let me play their game. Fine. I didn't like them or their game. But I respected their dedication and their training. Even if I did feel like the entire thing was a bogus excuse to withdraw from reality.

A little more sanity, and they'd probably all fit in nicely with the con culture.

Easy, babe. There's a time to speak out and a time to hold your tongue. Scrap stuck out his long forked tongue and grasped it between two talons.

I bit my cheeks rather than laugh at him, and thus at the Sisterhood.

"Teresa Noncoiré, you have been privileged to share many secrets with the Sisterhood of the Celestial Blade," Sister Gert said more quietly. But still her voice carried to the far corners of the Citadel. "We charge you to keep those secrets close to your heart, nurture them, and be aware that evil walks abroad, enemies to those secrets and all we fight for and hold dear."

Oh, my, she was serious.

I could only nod mutely. Otherwise I might laugh out loud. This was more solemn than the most serious of cults within fandom.

"Do you swear by all that you hold sacred to keep the existence of the Sisterhood secret?"

Swear it, Tess, or we'll never get out of here alive.

If the matter was so important, why was Scrap making faces at Sister Gert from his hiding place within the folds of her skirt on the ground?

"I so swear." In the face of the solemnity that graced every face and demeanor I could see, I had to agree.

"Do you swear to nurture your imp and prepare for the day you must combat evil and protect the innocent from its ravages?"

"I do so swear." And I did. Those were ideals I could agree with and follow.

"Then we send you forth into the world, a more complete and better woman than when you came here."

That was certainly the truth.

In the middle of the crowd, a Sister lit her candle and lifted it high. Then another and another of them saluted me.

Gulping back a sob, I held my head high and marched out the huge double gate of the Citadel. Alone except for Scrap. More than a little scared at having to face the world again. Saddened that I had to leave friends behind.

I had made friends within the Citadel. Friends I would cherish for a long time to come.

And we cherish you as well, Sister Serena whispered into my mind.

Thank you for championing me when no one else would, came a farewell from Gayla, the woman I'd pulled in from the storm.

Keep your guard up on your left. Demons will know it's your weak side, Sister Paige reminded me.

Remember to give your imp an occasional beer, Sister Mary added.

Thanks for telling us stories in the dead of night when our nightmares became too real. That was Sister Electra with her flaming red hair.

Questions have their place. Learn when to ask them, and when to accept what is, Sister Gert got in the last word. She even had a bit of a chuckle in her voice. *You gave us many things to think about, even if you are rash, impudent, and disrespectful.*

I laughed out loud and started up the refurbished car I had arrived in eleven months ago.

Chapter 44

"**W**HERE'S CYNTHIA?" I asked Gollum the moment I entered my suite at the Mowath Lodge. Why was the place starting to feel like home?

Thanks to Sylvia's mother-hen presence, my return trip had been free of incidents, shadows, and other boogeymen. I wasn't ready yet to face them here where I knew they hovered.

"She's with Sapa. They are out collecting grass, bark, and feathers to weave into the blanket," Gollum replied, not even looking up from his computer screen. As usual, he was sprawled in the armchair with his laptop. I had no idea what the arcane symbols on the screen meant. The cat had squeezed itself around the computer and still managed to occupy most of his lap.

"If Cynthia and Sapa are out collecting, who's guarding the blanket?" I turned on my heel and began the march back to Donovan's office and the precious artifact. I couldn't stand still anyway. Something drove me to keep moving. Unpacking wasn't enough.

"The blanket is under lock and key and I have the key. I can't get into the office to take it. They can't break into where the blanket is without setting off an alarm." He held up a shiny brass key no bigger than his thumbnail.

"Who set that up?"

"I compromised with Estevez."

"How'd you twist Donovan's arm to get him to agree?" I couldn't imagine Gollum so much as threatening the man, let alone forcing a compromise.

Although I had a fuzzy dream image of Gollum near strangling a Marine medic to keep him from giving me lethal tranquilizers. That must have been a hallucination induced by fried synapses from the super-industrial-strength tazer.

But then I had a flash of remembrance as he hoisted himself up rocks by the strength of his arms alone while Cynthia and I had to scramble with footholds and elbows and knees to get over the obstacles in front of the cave even after he boosted us up.

"I got the phone number of the state archaeologist and put him on speed dial." Gollum grinned and finally looked up at me. Even through his glasses, I could see the smile light his eyes with mischief.

"And Donovan will do almost anything to keep the state archaeologist from prowling around the caves beneath the casino." Part of me was delighted. Only part.

Goddess, I wished I could get over that man. Why couldn't I just admit to myself that he was half demon and not attractive at all?

Sad and vulnerable Donovan was more attractive than strong and confident Donovan. I still lusted after both of him.

One night with him didn't seem like enough.

And yet it was too much.

I'd never chosen bed partners indiscriminately before.

Dill, my husband, was the only man I'd slept with before a long series of dates and inner debates. With Dill, it was love at first sight.

With Donovan, it was lust at first sight, nothing more. It had to be.

"Tess, look what we found!" Cynthia bounded into the suite looking flushed, windblown, and happy. Happier than I'd ever seen her.

Once more my heart swelled with . . . with love for her. She had given me a flower for Dill's grave. Now she held out a pretty feather for my inspection.

A longing opened in my soul. A longing to keep this child/woman close and cherished; to protect her as a mother as well as a friend.

Possibilities . . .

"Let me see." I held out my hand for the long, dark tail-feather that looked black upon first inspection but glimmered iridescent blue when the light shifted.

"Magpie," Gollum said and went back to his computer.

A strain from "The Thieving Magpie" by Rossini drifted through my head. I couldn't think of a more appropriate feather to add to the blanket that had been stolen and recovered so many times in the past.

After a light supper at the café—I'd eaten so much restaurant and airline food in the past few weeks even Mom's cooking was beginning to sound good—Cynthia went back to the office and the blanket to sleep with Sapa. The two of them truly belonged to each other now and I had no idea how I could arrange for them to stay together with the blanket once we closed the demon portal.

She was still only twelve, and the state had very serious issues with a child who didn't have adult supervision and school.

"The blanket belongs in a museum," I muttered. An afternoon job demonstrating weaving in the old way might be the solution. If we could find foster parents and a school for her close to the museum.

"But there is no museum close enough to the portal to be of any use," Gollum reminded me.

An idea itched in the back of my mind but slid out of reach every time I tried to grab it. My body twitched more than the idea.

"Let me think about this for a while. Come on, let's take a walk." I grabbed Gollum's hand and hauled him out of his chair.

He slid the laptop onto the coffee table. The cat humphed and took up a roost under the highly varnished slab of burl wood.

We walked in silence a few moments, comfortable with each other and with the silence.

"If Donovan is keeping his office in town open, then he

must be working on refinancing the casino," I mused as we climbed the steps to my suite an hour later.

I was beginning to wonder if Gollum actually had the suite below me. He didn't seem to use it at all.

The night was too fine, and I was too restless to stay inside. I wandered out onto the back deck, pacing. Inside, outside.

Maybe if I went for a run around the lake, I'd settle down. I hadn't had any serious exercise other than the treadmill at the hotel gym in nearly a week. The demon bite was healing, though it itched abominably.

My skin felt like it didn't belong to me. A run didn't sound right. I wanted Scrap beside me. I even missed his smelly cigar. My fashion sense wasn't complete without him.

I grabbed the deck railing with both hands and forced myself to breathe deeply. Three breaths in, exhaling completely each time. I tried a standing meditation to clear my mind so that I could pinpoint the source of my agitation. No way could I sit still long enough to do a proper meditation.

Three more deep breaths. I couldn't get rid of enough air. Everything clogged in my body and my mind.

Something outside myself nagged at my soul.

This was like PMS magnified by ten, except that I didn't get PMS anymore. Not since the fever.

Only once before had I felt this extreme and uncalled-for agitation . . .

The night I witnessed the Goddess manifest in the stars while I was still at the Citadel.

I looked up to where the waxing quarter moon floated in the sky. It cast a diffuse reflection across the surface of the murky lake.

The stars shone so brightly behind the moon I felt as if I could reach up and touch them.

A river of light streamed away from the top of the moon. The Milky Way.

The constellation jumped out at me. The moon defined the curve of a lady's cheek. The Goddess Kynthia. The Milky Way became her flowing hair, drifting in a celestial wind. Two bright stars with a blue cast twinkled at me like eyes trying to communicate wordlessly.

Even as I blinked in wonder, the rest of Kynthia's face filled in with more stars. Her mouth quirked up in a knowing smile, reminiscent of the *Mona Lisa*.

"Guilford, get your butt out here!"

He slammed open the sliding doors and appeared at my side before I finished speaking. "What? What's wrong?"

"That!" I pointed to the wondrous event in the sky.

"The moon's up. So?"

"Can't you see her?" I couldn't take my eyes off the Goddess. "She's so clear, so dominant in the sky!"

"See what?"

"Oh, My Goddess!"

Kynthia only showed her face when the Warriors of the Celestial Blade needed to gather in defense. She warned us that the demons were on the move.

Quickly I scanned the horizon, wishing for supernatural vision or at least infrared goggles.

"There!" I pointed up and across the lake. In the few security lights around the casino on top of the ridgeline I saw movement. Many figures. Many figures carrying torches. Live fire in a desert that hadn't seen any rain in months.

"I need binoculars."

"Your binoculars won't help. But these will." Gollum produced a pair of the night vision binoculars.

I didn't waste time asking him where they came from.

"Two dozen beings up there. I can't tell if they're human or Sasquatch. How do I increase the power of these things?"

Gollum adjusted something on top of the heavy binoculars.

Images jumped into focus. "Sasquatch!"

"Tess?" Donovan called to me from the front of the lodge, followed by fierce pounding on the door. "Tess, where are you?"

"Back here!" I didn't move, didn't dare take my eyes off the demons until I figured out what they were up to.

"Tess, they've stolen the blanket. They've got Cynthia and the dog, too." Donovan rounded the building and stood below me on the verge of the beach.

I vaulted the railing and landed lightly, ready to run. Kynthia imbued me with power I didn't know I had.

"Scrap, get your ass back in this dimension. Now!"

"I didn't hear the alarm," Gollum said accusingly.

"They smashed it and cut the wires before they entered the office. They ripped the blanket off the wall, glass case and all. The dog attacked them. They just clubbed him over the head and picked him up. Cynthia, too. We've got to get that blanket back!"

Chapter 45

"WE'VE GOT TO SAVE Cynthia." Images of Cynthia proffering me a flower for Dill's grave cleared my priorities.

"We'll help." The banker and his wife appeared on their deck.

"How?" I asked Donovan.

"They know everything. They can help."

"Number crunching won't help." I was already running to my rental car, another SUV, red this time.

Gollum grabbed the keys from my hands. "I'm better qualified at off-road driving," he informed me as he started the engine. I had no choice but to claim the seat beside him. Donovan and his friends piled in behind.

I burned with questions about the bankers. We rode in silence. Gollum took the rough back road up to the casino way too fast. My teeth jarred until my jaw ached. We bounced over ruts and dipped into potholes only to climb out the other side with speed and dexterity I'd never have managed.

Gollum certainly had more talents than I suspected.

I gripped the seat with white knuckles. The drive went on forever.

All I could think about was Cynthia alone and frightened. Kidnapped a second time by demons.

Demons who had clear access to a portal beneath the casino.

The road leveled out abruptly as we topped the ridge. Gollum jerked the emergency brake on before we came to a complete stop. I was out of the car and running a heartbeat later. Donovan came hot on my heels. The bankers and Gollum were only a step behind.

"Scrap, where the hell are you?"

I ran into a solid wall of Sasquatch. The stench nearly gagged me. My head felt too light and my knees too heavy.

I bent my head and rammed straight forward into the gut of one. He grunted as the wind whooshed out of him.

More bad breath.

But he backed up, giving me access to the backs of his comrades.

They must have been Kajiri—half-bloods. Not a one was over six-and-a-half-feet tall. Judicious kicks to knees and groins helped clear more space. I needed fighting room, with or without my Celestial Blade.

"Scrap!" I continued to call, whenever I had breath enough to spare.

Then, at last, a familiar whiff of cigar smoke cut through rancid BO and lack of mouthwash.

Scrap landed in my outstretched hand with a thud, already halfway into transformation. He clutched something bright and shiny, but I didn't have time to wonder about it. Whatever it was, it became part of the blade.

I cleared more space twirling him, giving him the centrifugal force to elongate. Together, we cut a swath through the Kajiri.

Over to my left I saw Donovan fighting tooth and nail with a pair of full-sized Sasquatch. He stayed human, no trace of bat wings. Why?

No time to wonder. The Sasquatch came at me thick and heavy.

The banker couple engaged their own pair. They'd grown teeth that might have looked adequate on a saber-toothed tiger, and long purple tentacles sprouted from their faces, like the kids at the con.

I didn't care as long as they helped me rescue Cynthia.

I caught a glimpse of Gollum wrestling another full-blooded demon for the blanket, still in its glass case. Cynthia clung to the monster's back while Sapa worried its feet. That was one big Sasquatch. It dwarfed all three of them combined.

Then the herd was on me. They brandished torches, trying to force me to back away from the casino building. I had no time to think. No time to worry.

But I did worry. There were hundreds of them and only a few of us.

I had to save Cynthia, and Gollum, and, yes dammit, Donovan, too, because I cared for them. Losing them would hurt worse than losing Dill.

My blade sang as I cleaved the space around me. The Sasquatch jabbed their torches at me. They had me on reach. I had them on reaction and timing.

I whirled right and caught a torch, spinning it up into the air like a fiery baton. The second half of my blade ripped out the throat of that demon.

The others backed off.

I breathed deeply, grateful for every lungful of precious oxygen.

Then I noticed the heat from the torches. Like a ring of fire, the demons closed upon me. My skin blushed red in the first stages of burning.

A jab from my left. I thrust and swung. One demon backed off, another replaced him.

And so we danced.

My shoulders grew tired.

The heat increased.

Scrap began to blur and lose his edge.

Desperate to end the fight, I lunged forward, thrusting out and back in one smooth move.

I gutted one demon and nearly fell onto the torch of the other.

Then I danced with my blade. Forward, back. High, low.

Two more demons met death. My blade darkened with their blood. The heat lessened. Scrap brightened.

The sage and tumbleweeds burst into flame, giving me brief flares of light to kill another demon. That one fell upon his own torch and screamed.

The stench of burning flesh and fur grew thick as fog.

I gagged. My shoulders grew heavy and felt as if they'd dislocate if I had to swing the blade one more time. My ears roared with blood pounding behind them.

The roar grew. Not just the laboring of my pulse.

A dozen pickups crested the ridge behind the casino. Their headlights blinded me.

"Who?" Donovan shouted above the noise of huge diesel engines.

"I don't know!" I shouted back. My heart stuttered a moment in fear. What if the Kajiri had called for reinforcements?

Then dozens of women swarmed out of the oversized pickup beds and out of the cabs. Imps filled the air, their wings beating furiously as they, too, elongated and transformed.

"Cavalry to the rescue!" Gayla shouted above the melee. "We figured out that the assaults on our portal were diversions against something bigger. We came to help."

My knees nearly melted in relief. My Sisters had seen the light and joined me in this battle.

New strength invigorated me. My heart swelled with gratitude and . . . and love.

Well, let's leave it at gratitude.

Gradually, we pushed the never ending tide of Sasquatch back and farther back toward the empty casino buildings. A few dozen against two hundred. With the help of our imps, we prevailed as we were ordained to prevail over demons and evil forces.

Gulping air, foul as it was, I chanced a look around to see how my companions fared.

Donovan was down and bleeding but breathing. I couldn't find the bankers.

Sapa ripped at the throat of a full-sized Sasquatch. That demon clutched a hunk of hide and a hank of fur from Sapa's hip in its dying fist.

Cynthia and Gollum? I couldn't find them. Dared not take the time to look for them.

Then I heard Gollum's blessed voice. "They're going back down the portal. Quick! We have to close it!"

"How?" Cynthia asked weakly. I think she sobbed.

My heart cried out to her. I needed to hold her tight, and reassure her.

I needed to keep these last three demons from ever touching her again. My Sisters fought mop-up actions, finishing off the downed and wounded Sasquatch with bloodthirsty glee.

"The blanket, Cynthia! Weave the feathers into the blanket," I yelled.

One more demon down. Two left.

They threw their torches into the open piles of timber stacked beside the building and dove for the region of the portal.

Smoke and flame billowed up. The hungry flames licked greedily at this new fuel. The fire became a living wall between me and the last of my victims.

Then Cynthia and Gollum were beside me. Cynthia grabbed bits of Sapa's hair from the fist of a dead Sasquatch. Rapidly, she rolled it between her palms along with some tree bark and one of her treasured feathers. A crude thread extruded from her makeshift spindle. The quill tip of the feather became a primitive shuttle.

Gollum jumped upon the protective case of the blanket. Glass shattered upon impact. Not bothering to clear away the shards, he plunged his hand into the mess. He emerged with a bloody arm. The sharp edges of glass snagged the blanket, ripped holes in it, and finally released it.

Cynthia grabbed a hunk of fabric and began weaving her feather thread through one of the snags.

"The incantation," I panted. The smoke thickened making it harder to breathe.

"I need three people to say it," Gollum said. An edge of panic touched his eyes and his voice.

"I know it." Donovan half-crawled, half-stumbled beside Gollum.

"So do I," said Vern Abrams.

"Are you sure, Estevez? You know what will happen." Gollum looked him in the eye levelly.

Donovan swallowed deeply, closed his eyes, and grimaced.

"I know. We've got to do it. We can't let those stupid fools loose again in this area. Not any time soon anyway."

Gollum dropped the blanket across Cynthia's legs. She continued her weaving.

Sapa limped over to her and lay his great head in her lap. He was hurt badly, but I thought he'd live.

Myrna Abrams staggered over to me. Blood dripped from a nasty gash in her forehead. Her teeth, like her husband's, had retreated, along with her tentacles.

My Sisters gathered behind me, leaning on each other in exhaustion. Some had taken wounds. I barely registered that they all had survived.

Gollum took the hands of Donovan and the banker. They circled again and again as they chanted the weird language full of pops and clicks and unpronounceable syllables.

"What are they doing?" Gayla whispered.

"Sealing the rogue portal," I replied and draped an arm about her shoulders.

We stood there, propping ourselves upright with our blades, trying to breathe the heavy air through exhausted lungs.

The land heaved beneath my feet. A great rumbling roar near deafened me. I let go of Gayla and braced myself.

I blinked in the fiery light as the casino crumbled and imploded. A gaping hole in the earth opened and swallowed the entire building, extinguishing the fire.

Then the earth settled back into place.

In moments all that was left of Donovan's empire was a pile of ash and shattered dreams.

Chapter 46

*H*ERE, BABE, I FOUND *a new treasure in Mum's garbage dump.* I dropped the shiny bit of metal into Tess' outstretched hand the moment I managed to shrink back to my normal self. A little hard with the bankers still hanging around, but they are good folk even if their great-granddads were demons. And their two kids didn't kill Bob. It was the bat child. I remember it clearly now. The bat had the knife. Tentacles tried to pull her back.

"What's this?" Tess asked. She turned the jewelry over and over, examining the curved shapes by the light of the headlights from the pickups.

Most of the Sisters stumbled and limped over to their transport, packing up to go home and nurse their wounds now that the excitement was over.

"That looks like real gold," Sister Gayla said, peering over my babe's shoulder.

Of course it's real gold, I snorted disdainfully. Mum's garbage dump is high class. Not like the homes of some imps I know.

Ginkgo, Gayla's imp, took exception to that remark as well as my diminutive size.

I flashed my array of warts at her, and she subsided into a pout. I might be small, but I've now slain more demons than five of these so-called proper imps put together.

And I'll admit that the females don't interest me at all. Even the one going into heat. But the males now . . . Pine has a most interesting array of warts on his backside.

My babe found the loops on the back of the jewelry for either inserting a chain or attaching a brooch pin to the talisman. She hefted the weight of it and smiled.

"It looks a little like an abstract Goddess in the sky."

Did you notice how she capitalized the G in Goddess? She's beginning to believe.

I puffed out my chest with pride.

"If that's the face of Kynthia, then these indentations must be places to set precious stones," Gayla mused. She used the full name of the Goddess. I guess that means she believes more than my babe does.

Jewels, right, I added, wondering when and where I could find some fine diamonds in just the right size.

"I count twelve settings," my babe said. "They feel rough, like stones have been ripped out."

"Oh, my Goddess!" Sister Electra gasped. She'd wandered over to see why Gayla hadn't climbed into a truck with the rest of them.

"What?" Tess asked.

"That's—that's—" She just pointed and gasped.

"That's what?"

"We need to get that back to Sister Gert. It's been missing for centuries."

Not on your life, Sister, I snarled. *I found it. I gave it. It stays with Tess.*

Arborvitae, Electra's imp, Ginkgo, and I got into a snapping match. I settled it, and they backed off. I guess we imps aren't meant to get along outside of the Citadel. That's how we survive in the wild. We earn our warts and seniority.

"But that is the talisman of the senior Sister. She gets to put a precious stone in it for every battle she survives." Electra tried taking it from Tess.

Tess snatched it away and held it close to her heart. "Tell Sister Gert to come get it herself. The Goddess chose me for a reason. She helped Scrap find this for me for a reason. Sister Gert and I will settle this between us."

I whipped out a cigar, lit it, and blew the smoke into Electra's face. Then I passed some gas. She backed off, coughing and fanning the air.

Take *that,* Sisters. My babe is gonna be top dog some day, and there's nothing you can do about it.

And I'm gay!

▰▰▰▰▰

"I don't see why I have to go to school," Cynthia whined.

"You go to school because the state says you have to," I tried to soothe her.

We'd retired to the Mowath Lodge, slept, showered, and eaten. Now it was time to settle some things.

"But all I'm going to do all day is weave the blanket," she continued her litany of grief, all the while rubbing Sapa's ears.

The big, ugly dog licked her hand and settled back into a light doze. He hadn't done much but sleep and eat since the final battle with the Sasquatch. But he was healing fast and had found a girlfriend, an English mastiff, in town.

I suspected there'd be new puppies in about two months, an heir to Sapa's duties among them.

"You will not just be weaving the blanket," a tall and absolutely gorgeous Indian woman informed us as she entered my suite, followed by a google-eyed Gollum and an openly drooling Donovan.

Some men have no loyalty whatsoever.

"You will have to learn to weave it properly and conserve it for future generations. Those fibers will not last long in an open and unstable environment," the woman announced. Pronounced. Assumed authority anyway.

"Excuse me?" I took a defensive stance between Cynthia and this stranger. Somehow, I'd come to think of Cynthia as mine. I'd even toyed with the idea of moving to Half Moon Lake so I could adopt her and keep her, and therefore the blanket, close to the demon portal.

But then, what would I do with Mom?

I didn't trust her living on her own without supervision. I didn't trust any of the motley crew I called family alone without supervision.

"Tess, I'd like to introduce you to Keisha Stalking Moon," Donovan said, never taking his eyes off the woman's finely honed features, full lips, and liquid chocolate eyes. Not to mention a more-than-adequate bosom beneath her crisp red wool business suit. The tight skirt was slit halfway up her thigh, revealing legs that seemed to go on forever.

She should have been a model.

Then her name struck me.

"Stalking Moon?" I think my heart forgot to beat.

"Yes, I'm Leonard Stalking Moon's eldest daughter, and Cynthia's new guardian." She appraised me with the same scrutiny I'd given her.

I had the feeling I came up short in more than just height. My faded jeans, threadbare cable knit sweater, and dirty running shoes just didn't cut the fashion mustard anymore. Let alone my rather tangled curls and lack of makeup.

Obviously Scrap was missing again, or I'd have dressed better.

I scooped my hair into a twist and inserted the comb.

The world brightened, but nothing about this woman changed. She was still gorgeous, sexy, smart, and an alpha bitch—meant as a compliment if you know dogs.

"Dr. Stalking Moon is also going to be the curator of the new museum," Vern Abrams said, joining us with a sheaf of papers beneath his arm. "Keisha has an impressive array of degrees that qualify her for the job."

"Museum?" I'd only slept a night and a day, yet I felt as if I'd missed some major world events.

"The land beneath the casino still has value, but I think a less ambitious project is more in line than Donovan's original," Vern said, settling at *my* table with his papers.

"We are starting over with a spa, hotel, and museum. We'll pipe lake water up into hot tubs right over . . . right over . . ." Donovan trailed off, not knowing quite how to phrase the words "demon portal" in mixed company.

"We are also bringing in a consortium of tribes to run the place. This will no longer be a one-man operation or financial burden," Vern added. "Now I need some signatures, Donovan. And witnesses." He held out an expensive looking fountain pen.

I wondered if the ink was really Donovan's blood.

"What about the lake water?" I asked, remembering the complaints of the locals. "The lake levels are already too low . . ."

"But rising," Myrna Abrams said from the doorway. The suite was large but getting *way* too crowded. "Last night's rain broke a three-year drought, which accounted for part of the lower levels. I wonder if the open portal had something to do with that. Anyway, the portal was draining water out of the lake. That's why you smelled lake water every time the demons came and went. And the owner of the golf course was hoarding his share of water from irrigation, getting ready to sell it back to the ranchers at a profit. We've put a stop to that."

"We estimate the water table should be back to normal by spring if we have decent rainfall this winter," Vern continued brandishing his papers at the assemblage.

I wanted Scrap there to clear the room with his cigar smoke and a judicious fart or two.

Then I spotted him beneath the armchair teasing Gollum's cat with a feather stolen from Cynthia. Scrap, wearing something like a surgical mask, twitched the feather. Gandalf the cat swatted it and earned a smack across the nose for his efforts. He jumped back and hissed. Scrap waved the feather again, and the stupid cat tried to grab it, earning another swat.

Sometimes cats are victims of their own hunting instincts. Or just plain stupid. I hadn't figured out which.

Donovan grimaced as he signed in about fifteen places. The ink was black. But that didn't mean it wasn't his blood.

When I'd added my own name to appropriate places as witness, and so had Gollum, I looked around at the polished log walls, the burl wood tables, and the people who crowded around me.

"I guess there is nothing left for me to do but go home," I sighed.

"Until the next time," Gollum whispered.

"Tess, I'll call you the next time I'm on the East Coast," Donovan said. His warm brown eyes pleaded with me.

My knees wanted to melt. I scanned him for any sign of demonic genetics. Only that strange golden light with coppery overtones and the black braid writhing in the light.

"We'll see." I shrugged. "You'll keep in touch, Cynthia? I want to know how things go with you and Sapa. I need to know that you are safe. Thriving."

"Of course!" She hugged me tightly. "You're the best, Tess. I love you." She pulled another feather out of her pocket, along with a wildflower I didn't recognize.

I took them from her with shaking hands and blurring eyes.

"Don't let yourself get too lonely," she said quietly.

"Not anymore. I don't think I'll ever be truly lonely again."

▽▲▽▲▽

"Somewhere on the high desert plateau, between here and there, yesterday and tomorrow, a walled fortress houses the Sisters of the Stars; devoted followers of a Goddess who holds the world in balance between good and evil. When a waxing moon caresses the Milky Way just so, the Goddess shows her face in the heavens. The Sisters know then that trouble is brewing." I read the opening lines of my newest book to a group of gathered fans, Gollum among them.

But Donovan was missing from this gathering of fans at a con. I wasn't sure yet if I truly missed him or not.

Only a few weeks after leaving Half Moon Lake, I found myself at yet another con on the West Coast. This one in Portland.

Donovan had sent me a couple of e-mails reporting on the good progress of the new spa and how well the town cooperated with the new building plans. He'd also sent a dozen red roses to my room here at the con hotel. Cynthia e-mailed me every day and we chatted on the phone at least once a week.

Other than that, my life had returned to normal.

Nice job, Scrap said from the region of my shoulder.

I'd persuaded him to leave his cigar behind. This con frowned deeply on any smoking inside the hotel. If Scrap wanted to smoke, he had to go outside, just like everyone else. He'd learned at least a few manners in the past months.

A round of applause erupted when I finished the prologue and closed the book.

As a group, the fans and I made our way from the small reading room down the hall to a larger meeting room. I still checked the walls for signs of shadows that didn't belong there. In this crowd I should be safe.

And Scrap was back, bigger and uglier than ever. And openly wearing his favorite pink feather boa.

Don't tell me he's not gay.

A larger group of people greeted us at the party already well underway. A lot of Bob Brown's friends had gathered to hold a wake for him in true con fashion. I couldn't think of a better way to finally say a proper good-bye to my best friend.

Gollum handed me a glass of single malt scotch. I climbed up onto the small dais and held my glass aloft.

"To Bob, may we always remember him with the love, the respect, the liquor, and the puns he deserves!" I toasted my best friend.

The crowd grew hushed as we downed Bob's drink of choice.

Gollum handed me a live microphone. Just like we'd planned.

I gulped and swallowed with uncertainty. Then the words in my heart made their way to my mouth.

"I knew Bob for a long time. We shared many things in common, including a love of filking. Which we will get to in a moment. But first, when Bob was dying in my arms, he asked that I sing at his funeral. I'd know which hymn."

I had to gulp back a spate of tears before I could continue.

"I couldn't bring myself to sing at the funeral." Just as I had not sung at Dill's funeral or his wake. Now I had to do it for both of the men I loved in very different ways. Maybe once I'd sung for them, as they both requested, I'd be able to say good-bye and move on with my life.

"Knowing Bob, and how much he loved a good con, I think this is the better place to celebrate his life with a hymn that meant a lot to him."

I opened my mouth and the beloved words of "Ave Maria" flowed from my soul. For both of the men I loved. For every person I had lost.

My voice soared, my heart swelled, and my tears fell.

Everyone in the room joined me in the last chorus.

After several long moments of grieving silence, someone in the back of the room, maybe Gollum, maybe someone who'd known Bob longer, struck up a rousing chorus of a folk song on a guitar. A flute and drum joined him.

Then we all burst into the best filk song ever written.

There's a bimbo on the cover of my book.
There's a bimbo on the cover of the book.
She is blonde and she is sexy;
She is nowhere in the text. She
Is a bimbo on the cover of the book.

There's black leather on the bimbo in my book.
There's black leather on the bimbo in my book,
While I'm sure she's lot's of fun,
My heroine's a nun
Who wears black leather on the cover of my book.

There's a white male on the cover of the book.
There's a white male on the cover of the book.
Though the hero-INE is black
With Art that cuts no slack. So
There's a white male on the cover of the book.

There's a dragon on the cover of the book.
There's a dragon on the cover of the book.
He is long and green and scaly,
But he's nowhere in the tale. He
Is a dragon on the cover of the book.

There's a rocket on the cover of the book.
There's a rocket on the cover of the book.
It's a phallic and a stout one,
But my novel was without one.
There's a rocket on the cover of my book.

There's a castle on the cover of the book.
There's a castle on the cover of the book.
Every knight is fit for battle,
But the action's in Seattle.
There's a castle on the cover of the book.

*   *   *

There's a blurb on the backside of the book.
There's a blurb on the backside of the book.
There's one story on the cover;
Inside the book's another.
There's a blurb on the backside of the book.

And my name is on the cover of my book.
Yes, my name is on the cover of my book.
Although I hate to tell it,
The publisher misspelled it,
But my name is on the cover of my book.

They reviewed my book in Locus *magazine.*
They reviewed my book in Locus *magazine.*
The way Mark Kelly synopsized it,
I barely recognized it,
But they reviewed my book in Locus *magazine.*

Well, my book won the Nebula Award.
Yes, my book won the Nebula Award.
Still it ended in remainders,
Ripped and torn by perfect strangers,
But my book won the Nebula Award.

So put that bimbo on the cover of my book.
Put a bimbo on the cover of my book.
I don't care what gets drawn
If you'll just leave the cover on.
(Don't remainder me!)
So put that bimbo, dragon, castle, rocket, vampire, elf, or
magic locket—
Please put a bimbo on the cover of my book!

Epilogue

$\mathcal{G}$OLLUM AND I FLEW to Seattle together the next afternoon. He stayed there. I flew on to Providence. As the plane circled Mount Rainier, the setting sun caught the folds of the uppermost glacier in a peculiar light.

"Is that what I think it is, Scrap?"

Might be. Y' never know, dahling.

"Can you sense anything?" I checked him for signs of solidifying and transforming. He remained a translucent pink.

The plane's in the way.

And then we were past the strange phenomenon.

The moment the captain cleared us to use the built-in phones, I dialed Gollum's cell, heedless of the hideous price they charged per minute.

"Gollum, have you ever noticed that the glacier on top of Mount Rainier looks an awful lot like Cthulhu, the alien god in Lovecraft's novels?" Cthulhu had become a cult figure, and most dealers at cons featured stuffed animals shaped like the multilimbed squid-faced embodiment of evil. "Do you suppose that Cthulhu is alive and well on top of that mountain?"

"Of course he is," Gollum replied nonchalantly. "The mountain claimed the lives of fifteen climbers and three skiers already this year. Can you think of a better explanation?"

MOON IN
THE MIRROR

To Heather Alexander: friend, musician, collaborator, and bard; the only person I know who can filk herself and come up with a song that is as good or better than the original two. How many of you can catch a fly?

Acknowledgments

Lyrics for "Playmate" by Philip Wingate, 1894 as found http://ingeb.org/songs/idontwan.html

"March of Cambreadth" music and lyrics by Heather Alexander and "Courage Knows No Bounds" music by Heather Alexander, lyrics by Philip R. Obermarck used with permission from Sea Fire Productions. Copyright Sea Fire Productions, Inc. © 1997.

Both of Heather's songs can be heard on the CD "Midsummer" by Heather Alexander which is available at *www.heatherlands.com*. I have loved Heather's music for many years and am very happy to find a place for it in my work. I own the entire set of her albums and frequently buy extras as gifts, or to replace my own when children and nephews come to visit and abscond with them.

Sitting at a con and shouting the lyrics to "March of Cambreadth" with two hundred other audience members sends chills up my spine every time.

My amazing husband, Tim Karr, spent an evening educating me on the wonders of single malt scotch. This is one commodity where the price of a bottle is directly proportionate to the quality of the "water of life." I have thanked him privately.

Many thanks also to Deborah Dixon, Lea Day, Maya Bohnhoff, Carol McCleary, Sue Brown, and Bob Brown for their untiring help and thoughtful critique of this manuscript. You keep me going with encouragement and prudent kicks where I need it most.

Much appreciation has to go to Sheila Gilbert, editor extraordinaire at DAW, for guiding the vision of this series.

And I can't forget Carol McCleary of the Wilshire Literary Agency for believing in me when no one else did.

Chapter 1

In African folklore, trickster Hare was sent by Moon to first people with the message: "Just as the moon dies and rises so shall you." But hare confused the words and said: "Just as the moon dies and perishes so shall you." Thus trickster Hare cost humankind its immortality.

*T*HE WIND CIRCLED and howled. It wailed with the pathos of an errant spirit trapped between heaven and earth with no hope. No end to its torment. It rattled the window latches and whistled down the chimney, seeking haven inside my old house.

My benign resident ghosts retreated, leaving me utterly alone.

That was all I needed. Another storm to knock the power out and trap me indoors with several feet of snow blocking the doors. I saved the latest draft of my novel to a flash drive and switched to my laptop.

Finished or not, I had to e-mail it to my publisher first thing in the morning. If I had power and phone lines. Maybe I should do it now before the storm robbed me of access to the world outside. I had a reputation for punctuality to maintain. I also had a reputation for meticulous editing before I allowed the name Tess Noncoiré to appear on the cover.

I sent the e-mail, with the promise to polish the last four chapters and resend them as soon as I was sure of power.

The wind increased its tortured moans.

I shivered in the preternatural cold. "Old houses are drafty," I reassured myself. If this kept up, I'd start believing my own prose.

Unconsciously, I edged my chair closer to the huge hearth opposite my antique rolltop desk. My eyes strayed to the book on the plank floor, propped open with two other books. A research text on the folklore, monsters, and demons of the New World.

Research.

"Windago," I read and shivered. I'd encountered a mated pair of real Windago last autumn. Once human, they became one with the frigid northern wind, reclusive until they needed to hunt. Then they turned cannibal. They craved the blood of other humans, ever seeking to replace the souls they'd lost.

The book went on to theorize that the myth developed as an explanation for people of the north woods having to resort to cannibalism to survive especially harsh winters. If a monster bit them and they lost their souls, then humans hadn't done the unthinkable. Replace internal demons with external monsters.

Yeah. Right. The author hadn't ever encountered a Windago. I had. And I didn't want to do it again.

Ever. I'd come this close to becoming freeze-dried coffee grounds. All from a single touch of a shadow.

What the research book didn't say, but I'd learned on my own, was that Windago always hunted in pairs. To propagate, they had to bite a victim and leave the person living. The victim in turn had to bite a lover from his or her former life to maintain a pair.

Last autumn I'd killed one Windago. His mate still hunted me.

Was she the ravening wind that sought entrance to my home?

Did she seek a new mate or stalk me until one or both of us died? I didn't know.

"Damn it, go away," I shouted into the big empty house.

Not even my resident ghosts replied. I think they decamped to warmer climes along with my mother. After the third month when the temperature on Cape Cod didn't break freezing, Mom suddenly found a third cousin twice removed she hadn't seen since childhood who just happened to live in Florida.

Stay inside, Tessie babe. Demons can't violate the sanctity of a home, Scrap, my otherworldly companion and weapon, whispered to me across the dimensions. From very far away. Too far away to come help me fight off a Windago.

Goddess only knew what Scrap was up to. Or where.

I'm stuck in the chat room. Big nasties trying to separate us permanently.

"Take care, buddy."

A pang of loneliness stabbed my heart.

Coffee. I needed more coffee. Well, maybe I should switch to decaf. My nerves were jittery enough with that wind preying on my sanity.

I wondered if the tension in my neck was the precursor to a migraine. Normally I didn't suffer from them like Mom did. The wind often triggered them in her. Something about changing air pressures.

This wind was more than changing air pressure.

I coaxed my shoulders into a more relaxed position. No way would I fall victim to my mother's ailments. I was just worried about finishing the book. And staying free of the Windago.

I applied myself to the keyboard once more. Just a couple more hours of work.

If the damn wind would shut up.

The window rattled again, sounding very much as if a human hand tried to open the latch.

"Stay inside. Keep the doors and windows latched. Wait for dawn. Windago can't survive daylight," I repeated to myself over and over.

I dashed to the window anyway and checked the aging latch. Still closed.

Who could I call for help? My Aunt MoonFeather, the Cape's resident witch, didn't answer her phones. Gollum—Guilford Van der Hoyden-Smythe, Ph.D.—knew a lot about magic and demons and he'd helped me defeat the Sasquatch last autumn. Last I'd heard, he was still in Seattle teaching anthropology in some community college. Too far away to do anything but talk. He was good at talking and not much else.

Then there was Donovan Estevez. Handsome, sexy, a fantastic fencer, and knowledgeable about demons. Too knowledgeable, probably from firsthand experience. No. No way would I make myself vulnerable to him by asking for help.

Something crashed in the kitchen. I jumped. My heart lodged in my throat.

"Scrap?" Please, oh, please, let it be the mischievous brat returning from wherever.

No answer. I crept from my office through the long dining room and adjacent butler's pantry, keeping well away from the walls and any shadows that might lurk there. At the entrance to the modern kitchen and breakfast nook, I paused and peered out.

No pots and pans littered the floor. The curtains lay flat against the windows.

Bang!

I screamed and leaped back at least six feet. Freezing air whirled around me.

Bang.

"Scrap, where the hell are you? I need help."

Distant mumbling and grumbling in the back of my mind.

Creak, creak.

Was that someone twisting rubber soles on wet linoleum?

I grabbed a butcher knife from the utility drawer and inched forward again.

Creak, creak.

A quick glance through the narrow archway. The back doors, which opened into the mudroom, swung in and out, in and out in the freezing wind.

I wrapped my arms around my shivering body and cowered there in indecision for several moments.

Opening! I heard the wind wail.

Not daring to wait any longer, I ran with every bit of strength I could muster through the mudroom and slammed the outside door closed. I twisted the lock and the dead bolt for good measure, something I rarely bothered to do. Then I shoved the heavy boot box across it.

A wicked laugh. *Not enough to keep me out.* An almost

face appeared through swirling snow and shadows in the glass top half of the door. Frigid air made the aging wood pull away from the fragile pane. Shadows cast from the streetlight across the yard played tricks on my senses.

I couldn't tell if the Windago pressed close or not. Didn't dare wait to figure it out.

I darted back into the kitchen and closed the inside door. A chair from the nook braced beneath the latch held it.

The laugh came again. This time singing a ditty from my childhood. A song my best friend Allie and I had cherished since kindergarten.

> *"Playmate, come out and play with me,*
> *And bring your dollies three*
> *Climb up my apple tree,*
> *Holler down my rain barrel*
> *Slide down my cellar door*
> *And we'll be jolly friends forever more."*

Cellar door! Oh, my God, were the slanted doors attached to the outside foundation latched? They'd been covered with snow for so long I hadn't checked the padlock on the outside, or the crossbar on the inside for months.

No way was I going down the dark, narrow cellar steps with only a single bare bulb down there to light my way. No way in hell.

I jammed another chair under that door handle. "No lock!" I screeched. Why wasn't there a lock on this door?

Because that would make it too easy to get locked in the cellar while doing laundry. Damn.

Three phone books on the seat of the chair anchored it better.

I sang the alternate version of the childhood ditty to bolster my courage.

> *"Enemy, come out and fight with me.*
> *And bring your bulldogs three,*
> *Climb up my sticker tree.*
> *Slide down my lightning*
> *Into my dungeon door*
> *And we'll be bitter enemies forever more!"*

It didn't work. I still trembled in fear.

Not enough! A really cold gust whooshed down the chimney. The flames died. Coals faded from glowing orange and red to black.

I whimpered and threw some kindling into the grate. A cascade of sparks shot up the chimney. I added a log of heavy maple. Bright flames leaped and licked at the new fuel.

An otherworldly screech of pain responded to the fire.

You murdered my mate, an almost feminine voice snarled into my mind. *I will have retribution. A little fire won't keep me away for long.*

"Scrap, get your sorry ass back here," I screamed into the night. If he'd just come back, he could transform into the Celestial Blade and I could defend myself.

Ordinary blades might slow down a Windago. All my mundane weapons were locked in a special closet in the cellar. Only the Celestial Blade could kill a monster.

The lights flickered, faded, then came back on. I bit my lip, waiting.

A crashing boom outside.

Dark silence. Not even the comforting hum of the refrigerator.

The wind kicked up three notches into a hysterical laugh.

I dashed from room to room replenishing every fireplace. In the parlor I used the very last piece of pine in the stack. Soft evergreen. It wouldn't burn long. I didn't dare close the damper or I'd smother in the smoke.

Ruefully I looked around, assessing the burnability of every bit of furniture in the house. The dining room table would last all night if I could break it up, along with the twelve chairs. Fortunately, I had a hatchet beside the big hearth in the office, to splinter kindling if I needed.

I double-checked every window and door. Prowling the house all night. Never once relaxing my vigil.

Neither did the Windago.

Chapter 2

DAWN FOUND ME still wandering the house, testing window latches, keeping the fires roaring, starting at every noise and shadow. Somehow, I managed to stretch the last of the firewood in the house and didn't have to start on the dining table. I kept the hatchet or butcher knife in my hands at all times.

As a sullen gray light crept across the land, the wind faded. The temperatures plummeted. A new depth of cold descended upon Cape Cod.

My yard looked like a hurricane had hit. Broken tree limbs, roof shingles, and the neighbor's garbage lay strewn about.

A magnificent patriarchal oak tree leaned drunkenly against the power lines, pushing the supporting pole to a dangerous angle across my driveway. I could still get my car out if I had to. I didn't dare leave the house.

Windago weren't supposed to come out in daylight. The sky was so leaden it made the entire day one huge shadow. Lots of places for a Windago to hide.

Why hadn't I headed south with Mom?

"It's the friggin' vernal equinox," I moaned. "Where are the sunshine and spring temperatures?"

My cell phone chirped the theme from "Night On Bald

Mountain." I jumped and trembled a moment before it registered. "I think I need to change that ring tone."

No power. No telephone. Cell phones only working communication.

"H . . . Hello," I answered, half expecting that whispery voice born of the north wind.

"Tess, you've got to come. Right now," Allie Engstrom pleaded desperately.

Not much fazed Allie. She stood nearly six feet tall, and had the breadth of shoulder of her Valkyrie ancestors. She was also our local cop and packed weapons comfortably.

"Calm down, Allie. What's wrong? And why can't you just call for backup? An entire squad of constables should be on duty."

"I can't call them. They wouldn't understand. You've got to come. And bring MoonFeather." Anxiety drove her voice up an octave.

"MoonFeather? What can my aunt do that you can't?"

"She's a witch. They're both witches. You've got to hurry. Before they attack!"

"Witches. Plural. Who's attacking?"

"Sh . . . she just came out of nowhere. Right in the middle of the street. I crashed my cruiser swerving to avoid her. And she's naked." Allie gulped air. I heard the boom of a fired gun. "My God. The bullets bounced off them!"

"Off of what?" Not who. What. They weren't human.

"Garden gnomes with teeth!"

I skid to an abrupt halt inside the chat room. This is the place that opens the doors to every universe. A big white room that stretches so far into infinity normal eyes can't perceive the dimensions and curves.

Each species calls the chat room something else. The Waiting Room, Limbo, Purgatory, Avalon, Oblivion. A rose by any other name . . . You know what I mean. Call it what you will, it's the same place of transition.

Easy to get lost here. Any being can get into the chat room. Getting out again is a different matter indeed.

Late March and still two feet of snow on the ground with a

subzero wind chill in Cape Cod. I may be the imp companion to the greatest Warrior of the Celestial Blade ever born, but I'm just a scrap of an imp. I don't like having my tootsies frozen to popsicles. My barbed tail is so frizzed it feels like it will fall off my cute little bum.

And I've got five beee-u-tee-ful warts adorning my backside. Another one dead center on my chestie. Hard-earned beauty marks they are. Can't afford to have them fall off.

Even my favorite perch on the cast iron spider hanging over the fire in the fireplace can't keep me warm. So, I make tracks for Imp Haven. To get there I have to cross the chat room.

My warrior companion, Tess Noncoiré, is just finishing a manuscript and is looking for some downtime. She won't need me for a few days. She can handle just about any crisis that isn't demon inspired if she keeps her head on straight.

But when she's deep in a book, I keep her inspired and on her toes. I clean up after her and make sure she eats. Without me, she'd be a total wreck instead of only half a wreck.

Her fashion sense is . . . well let's just call her challenged and be polite about it.

Our bond goes deeper than that. She is my warrior, I her blade. Neither of us can exist without the other now.

The Powers That Be dictated long ago that only demons should guard the chat room. They are nasty enough to keep everybody in their home dimensions unless they have a special pass from the all-powerful PTB. Hard to get a pass. Harder to slip through the chat room to someplace else, somewhen else.

Unless you are an imp. Even imps don't have *carte blanche*.

On this day Windago guard the chat room. The howling wind you hear in the middle of the night when storms rage is just their chatter. The misty black shadows swirling up to greet me feel familiar. I've fought these shadow demons before. I'd rather not have to do it again without Tess. Only when I'm with her and in the presence of a demon or tremendous evil can I transform into the Celestial Blade.

Damn, I wore my feather boa as a disguise, hoping to run into Bcartlin demons. Think a cerulean Michelin Man with a hot-pink ostrich draped around its neck. Such a passé color scheme. I mean bright blue and pink went out with . . . well I don't know for sure that they ever were in fashion.

Now if they'd go with the country blue with hints of gray

and maybe a touch of yellow accent, I could do something with them.

I digress.

Two human larpers—that's live action role playing gamers to the uninitiated—in search of magical artifacts have wandered into the chat room, unaware of what they're doing or how they got there. These guys are trying to engage the Windago in conversation, asking directions to *The Comb*.

Give me a break. If you need to ask directions you have no business in the chat room. You have no business talking to a Windago, let alone six Windago, at all. The poor saps are doomed—I don't mean just their garish costumes—unless I do something.

But maybe I should let them meet the fate of the foolish.

Ever since I liberated a particular magical hair comb from freeze-dried storage—aka my home in Imp Haven—for my Tess, the Powers That Be have put a bounty on it. Word gets out, especially among wanna-be witches and sorcerers, and the search goes far and wide. One of these days Tess and I will have to fight off all kinds of nasties—some of them human—to retain possession of *The Comb*.

The Comb allows her to see through magical glamour when she wears it. But she can't wear it all the time because it turns her hair translucent and brittle. She'll go bald in a month if she wears it too often or too long. We can't allow her distinctive springy sandy-blonde curls to thin, straighten, and break off.

Six Windago—they always hunt in pairs—reach out with spectral shadow hands that can freeze-dry the larpers.

At least the humans have the sense to hunker down and cover their vulnerable heads and necks with their arms.

I whistle sharply between my two outer rows of teeth.

The bad guys hardly notice. They have a job to do, keeping beings in their home dimensions.

I wave my pink feather boa at them. Full-blooded demons—Midori as opposed to Kajiri half-breed—aren't real bright. It takes them a few moments to figure out I'm in their territory. These guys obviously don't have any human blood in their family shrubs to give them any smarts.

I'm on my own with six shadowy black whirlwinds, each the size of an industrial refrigerator. One of them turns away from the whimpering humans to see me full on. Most demons have no neck and have to turn their entire body to see beyond the end of their nose. This particular beastie has no shoulders either. Just an amorphous mass of black wind swirling ever faster into a tornado.

Demons may be dumb. But they are always hungry. Blood-thirsty. They'll eat anyone. Simply anyone. Even imps wearing perfectly wonderful pink feather boas.

The other shadowy masses spiral to their left and pin me with malevolent gazes. Glowing red coals burn through the dust storms.

The larpers make a judicious retreat through the nearest door-way. Fortunately for them, it's their home dimension. They never really got far enough away from it for it to close properly and seal their fates.

Meanwhile, I have six Windago to dupe into letting me back into my home dimension before they bite me and turn me into an antisocial cannibal. Mum would never forgive me.

Not that she approves of me much anyway.

"Get him. No imps allowed out of impland," screams one pair of the ravening horde.

"We must kill all imps on the loose," chimes in a second pair.

"Imps are dangerous to the dimensions," adds the third pair.

I flit above their heads. "I love my wings!" I crow to them. They'd grown enough to actually be useful—though still not up to snuff, just like the rest of my body. There's a reason Mum named me Scrap.

Blood-red talons at the end of a misty black fist reach higher than I guess possible.

"Yeow! That hurts." I yank my tail up and out of the way. But I now have gouge marks its full length to the arrowhead tip. And worse! They left red nail polish embedded in the furrows. Not quite the fashion statement I'd hoped for.

And then my stunted wings give out. I drop into the middle of the cold black crush.

Six churning storms of frigid air steal my breath and crumple my precious wings.

I gasp and nearly swallow half my weight in black dust and fur. It tastes of . . . you don't want to know how stale cigars sweet-ened with licorice and a touch of sulfur taste.

Black stars blossom before my eyes. "Oh, Tess, I'm sorry. I

shouldn't have deserted you just because of a little frostbite on my tummy. Can you ever forgive me? For when I die, so will you."

Maybe Cape Cod isn't so bad after all. Tess does keep lovely fires in the hearths of her two-hundred-fifty-year-old home. And her mom might come home and burn some cookies for me.

Chapter 3

"Please hurry, Tess. I don't know what to do," Allie whispered. Two more shots sounding too loud across the airwaves.

A naked woman who stepped out of nowhere. The Windago in human form come to plague me?

What about garden gnomes with teeth? Where did they come in?

"Great, just great." I couldn't ignore Allie's call for help. She was my best friend. I knew her crushes and the color of her footed jammies. When we first met, at the age of five, she'd been too tall, and I too fat and bookish for either of us to be popular. So we'd bonded and found we had more in common with each other than we did with our families or anyone else at school.

She'd been an important part of my life for twenty-three of our twenty-eight years.

I pulled on heavy boots, sweaters, a coat, hat and gloves. Some things were more important than avoiding trouble. Then I dashed for the basement armory. I kept a key around my neck for emergencies like this. Without Scrap I needed a mundane weapon. A very sharp mundane weapon.

On my way, babe. This may take a few moments, Scrap reassured me.

But he wasn't here right this minute. No way to know if he'd make it back in time to help. I grabbed a broadsword off the rack though the replica of the Celestial Blade beckoned me. Made of imp wood, I knew it was sharp. Effective against monsters?

I stuck with the broadsword. The door closed on its own, and the padlock snicked shut. "Thanks, Godfrey," I called to the ghost who haunted the basement. He'd stashed runaway slaves in that closet and guarded it more zealously in death than in life. And that was as good a guard as I could get. No one knew he ran the local Underground Railroad until his memoir was published ten years after his death in 1893.

With fresh snow on the roads and no plows out yet, I decided to drive my mom's black baby SUV rather than my cute, midnight-blue hybrid. Mom's car had a better niche for stashing the broadsword under the driver's seat.

In four-wheel drive, with studded tires, I inched the car beneath the listing oak tree. Low dragging branches grabbed at the car, scratching paint off the roof. Mom was going to kill me. Each scrape had me wincing and imagining the Windago opening the metal with her talons.

As I turned left onto the road, my rear tires slid on the icy surface. No new snow here. Just the arctic cold. Strange. I had almost a foot of white fluffy stuff around my house.

I steered into the skid until I had traction again, then crawled forward toward the Old King Highway. Reluctantly, I stopped at the intersection to check for traffic.

"Go ahead, gun it," my husband's ghost said from the passenger seat. He wore a western-cut plaid shirt, sleeves rolled up, blue jeans, hiking boots, and a white Stetson pulled low over his hazel eyes and sleek black hair. Like he always did. Before and after he died.

I sat back and closed my eyes. "Now what do you want, Dill? Where were you last night when I could have used some company while monsters raged?" As much as I missed the man, he had a strange habit of showing up when I finally thought I could move on. Weird things happened when he was around. I wanted done with weird.

Maybe all I needed was a vacation in sunny Mexico.

"Take a chance, lovey. Why freeze our fucking asses off trying to stay safe. Your imp isn't around to tattle on you."

"You shouldn't use that kind of language, Dillwyn Bailey Cooper," I reprimanded him in death as I hadn't dared to in life.

After three years on my own, I wasn't sure I'd fall for him again. Wouldn't let myself become dependent on him.

But, oh, how I missed him. I longed for the mental intimacy we'd shared as well as the physical. He shared my love of science fiction/fantasy. His fascination with geology satisfied a lot of my curiosity. We even agreed politically. I'd never met another man I bonded with so quickly or so well.

Fighting demons with a Celestial Blade had given me confidence and self-assurance I didn't know I was missing when I married a handsome man who looked past the fifty extra pounds I carried then to the woman I was inside.

I'd lost the weight and kept it off for three years. Grief will do that to you. That and the rigorous martial arts training of the Sisterhood of the Celestial Blade Warriors.

For my newly fit and trim figure I really had to thank the otherworldly infection that had laid me low with delirium for weeks on end. The fever had opened new pathways in my brain that allowed me to bond with Scrap. I'd been with the imp nine times longer than I had been married to Dill.

"As much as I love you, Dill, you are dead. Isn't it time we both moved on?" Did I really want him gone?

"Can't do that, lovey. You and I were meant to be together. Forever. So you can't move on without me." His skin was smooth, nicely tanned, and free of the charring from the fatal fire.

The fact that his ghost showed no signs of his painful death always made me suspicious. Was this specter truly my husband or a demon wearing his face and form? Either way, he asked the impossible.

"Accept it, Dill, you are dead. I have."

"Have you, lovey?" He quirked an eyebrow at me just like he used to. "I've tried to pass over, Tess. Really tried. But the Powers That Be have decreed I can't completely die without your help. But I can come back to life if you just get rid of the imp."

"Not on your life! Or death. Or whatever. People don't come back to life, Dill. There are no 'get out of jail free' cards for dead people." I shuddered with more than just the cold. "Besides, if you were serious about replacing Scrap, you'd have come to my aid last night and we could have slain that Windago."

"How do you know people can't come back to life?"

He ignored my second statement. He'd had a bad habit of bypassing what he didn't like or didn't want to deal with when he was alive. I guess bad habits don't die.

Instead of replying I gunned the engine and shot onto the main road.

"It's the scar that keeps us apart, Tess. It's an inter-dimensional reminder of imp flu. If you hadn't gotten sick and had to have the infection cut out of your face, you couldn't see the imp. Go to a plastic surgeon and have it removed," Dill pleaded. He traced a ghostly finger from my temple to my jaw.

The scar burned beneath his ephemeral touch.

"A little hard when the scar isn't visible to mundane humans," I snapped.

Flashing blue-and-red lights atop Allie's monster white four by four with blue *Police* lettering came into view less than a block away. The front end teetered in a roadside ditch. A venerable maple as wide as the cruiser pressed deeply into the radiator. Steam hissed, froze, and fell back onto the hood as snow.

I slowed and skidded to a halt. I let loose a string of curses as the rear end fishtailed.

A dozen or more little beings in overbright clothing and mouths over-full of sharp teeth paced around and around the vehicle. A hideous replica of "ring around the rosie."

"Language, Tess. Watch your language," Dill chuckled, reminding me I had just reprimanded him for doing the same thing. "Your vocabulary has deteriorated drastically since I died. You'd think a writer would be more inventive."

"Shut the fuck up!"

You talking to me, babe? Scrap popped into view, his translucent gray-green body already turning vermilion and elongating into a solid shaft.

Dill popped out of view. "You don't need me for this fight, lovey." He sounded hurt and . . . and lonely.

"Glad to have you back, buddy. I was afraid you were trapped in the chat room."

Your call is stronger than the bad breath of six Windago.

I didn't like his metaphor.

No time to think. No time to mourn Dill. A gnome was gnawing away at the tailgate of Allie's cruiser. An industrial-strength can opener on the move.

"Scrap, now." I held out my palm for him while I released the seat belt and opened the door.

By the time my feet hit the ground, Scrap had thinned to a four-foot shaft with twin curved blades extruding from each end. Dozens of razor-sharp spikes flowed away from the outside curve of each blade.

I twirled him about like a baton around my knees. The swarm of bad guys backed off. Except for the one chewing through metal.

Nasty bastard, Scrap growled. His reflected eyes blinked in the right-hand blade.

An easy wipe separated the beastie from the cruiser. Dark, dark blood, almost black, spurted from where his pointed nose should have been. It steamed when it hit the ice. The rear lock of the vehicle filled the gnome's mouth. Still he smiled around it, showing acres more teeth.

As he bounced across the road to the embankment where his cohorts huddled, the blood ceased spurting. His nose grew back, longer and pointier than before. It almost reached his long chin.

My scar throbbed. I only hoped it remained invisible. Allie was watching me too closely from the inside of her cruiser.

I stood guard over the SUV with my constantly moving blade. "Get over to my car now!" I yelled to Allie and the figure huddled in the back seat.

"Tess, what's going on here?" Allie asked, opening her door.

Her passenger remained inside.

"Shut the fuck up and get your girl over to my car. Now."

"I beg your pardon!" Allie said, blinking in startlement.

"You heard me. Do it. I can't hold them off much longer." Even as I spoke, the gnomes edged closer. Only one lane of blacktop separated them from me and my blade. Their jester-styled shoes with the upturned toes didn't slip on the ice.

My boots had problems with traction.

Allie's hands trembled inside her heavy leather gloves as she fumbled with the door. She wore a dark blue down uniform parka over her blue shirt, sweater, and Kevlar. I spotted the telltale ribbed neckline of silk long underwear at her throat. And she still looked long, slim, and feminine.

I could never carry off that look. Being vertically challenged and short of leg always made me look broader at the shoulder and hip than I really was.

Underneath the uniform, her height, her butch short hair, and her bravado, Allie was a shy little girl.

I made sure I stood between her and the bad guys. They grew braver and crossed the yellow line.

Allie grabbed at a lumpy figure huddled beneath a blanket in the backseat of her cruiser. They hesitated as two long, slim legs extended from the blanket. She stopped moving with just inches between bare feet and icy road.

"She'll be fine for ten steps," I reassured my friend.

They ran for my car. I sidestepped along with them. The gnomes respected my blade. But they followed our movements, staying just outside my reach.

Three gnomes took two steps closer.

I slashed right and left. Two tiny backbones severed. The top half of each gnome plopped sideways. Black blood shot up and out. The feet kept coming forward.

"Svargit! What does it take to kill these guys?" I cursed everything in sight, and a few things that weren't, in Sasquatch. That was the only word of Sasquatch I'd learned. It fit everything.

With one last vicious swipe, I leaped into my car and slapped the locks closed. Scrap shrank to normal size and disappeared in the blink of an eye.

I threw my jacket to Allie, adding it to the scant protection the blanket offered the shivering blonde woman. Woman? Girl? She couldn't be more than eighteen.

"Here. Use this if you need to. More effective than bullets against these guys." I hauled the broadsword free and handed it to her grip first. "This is the only blade you saw me use," I added, capturing her gaze with mine.

She nodded and gulped, standing the sword between her legs, point down.

"Where did she come from?" Allie asked after a long moment while I coaxed the engine to life. "I looked. No one was in the street. She just appeared out of nowhere. Out of *nowhere*. I looked. I swear I did," She shook her head as she peered over her shoulder at her precious wounded vehicle, guilt and pain shrouding her eyes.

"And then those gnomes walked out of the woods as if they owned the road." She kept blinking as if to clear her vision of the memory.

Then I realized she was looking at the center of the street, not her car or the troop following us. Was she hoping to see a doorway into Neverland?

"This isn't your fault," I reassured her as my heart raced and heat flooded my face. Bodies coming out of nowhere *shouldn't* surprise me. Garden gnomes with teeth *shouldn't* surprise me. I wrote weirder stuff every day. I considered an imp my soulmate. My husband's ghost haunted me for weeks on end. A bereaved Windago stalked me.

But it did surprise me.

"She came out of nowhere," Allie insisted.

Or another dimension.

Did she have to go through the chat room to get from one dimension to another? If she had, maybe Scrap knew something. No access to him for a while until he'd recovered from our battle. Nothing a full dose of mold wouldn't cure.

Rogue portals existed. Direct transport that bypassed the guarded chat room. They were rare. I'd closed one last autumn.

"Now you're in a dilly of a pickle!" Dill chortled from the backseat.

"Here we go again," I groaned.

The young woman crumpled in a faint. Bright blonde hair draped about her shoulders like a living curtain.

One look at her sweet face and I knew she wasn't Lilia David, the human persona of the widowed Windago.

(What a wonderful title. *The Widowed Windago.* I filed that away in the writer portion of my brain before the ideas could start tumbling around and blot out reality for me.)

"Where the hell did you come from?" I asked. "And why the fuck are those guys chasing you?"

"Tsk, tsk, language, lovey," Dill said, only half joking.

"Cold. So cold. Where did all the pretty flowers go?" the woman whispered.

"What?"

"I'll call ahead to the emergency room," Allie said. "I don't dare go through Dispatch. I'm going to have enough trouble explaining the car." She fumbled for her cell phone.

"Trippin' car," the stranger murmured, without opening her eyes. "Boss ghost."

"Haven't heard that word in a while," Dill said peering at our guest. "Oh, dear. She's an interdimensional refugee. I can't be here right now."

Dill vanished. Did he imply that he, too, was an interdimensional refugee? As good a description of a ghost as any.

Or was there more?

Chapter 4

The March full moon is sometimes called the Crow Moon because the cawing of crows signals the end of winter. It is also called the Crust Moon because the snow cover becomes crusted from thawing by day and freezing at night.

"**W**HAT ARE WE DEALING with, Tess? Do you think MoonFeather will have any answers?" Allie asked, her voice more gravelly than usual. She shifted her utility belt, a habitual gesture of domination, piercing me with her tough-broad glare.

"You tell me what you saw. Every last detail." I put the car in gear and eased off the shoulder onto the street, without bothering strapping the girl in. The emergency room was only a half mile up 6A, the official name for Old King Highway. Nothing is very far away on Cape Cod.

"The street was clear. I swear it. It was six AM. Rush hour not started yet. Anyone who doesn't have to be out in this cold isn't. Then she just appeared," Allie insisted.

"Just appeared? Any misting or morphing?" I knew how I would write the scene. That didn't make my description correct.

I ransacked my memory for a clue, a hint of what she might be. Besides human. Demons could assume human shape in this dimension, but only if they had some human blood in them. Kajiri, they called the mixed-bloods. More dangerous than full-bloods because the human half gave them the ability to think and hold a grudge.

Like my Windago stalker.

"Maybe the light shifted. Like a halo. You'd call it an aura," Allie said. She tugged on her earlobe while she thought. "Sort of like a door opening from a dark room into a darker room. Not a change so much as a shift. And then she was there. Running, looking over her shoulder. Then she froze in place. A naked and unprotected living statue."

Scrap, if you are anywhere near, I need you! I called with my mind. Fat chance of that happening any time soon. I knew he needed downtime after transforming and fighting.

"Sounds like the lady dashed out of the chat room in fear for her life. Or her immortal soul," Dill said. He lounged in the backseat again. Had he dashed off to consult with his Powers That Be?

I was about to say the same thing, but Allie wouldn't understand what I meant. I'd never consciously been in the chat room, the empty space between dimensional portals, and couldn't say for sure what it looked like. My nightmare visits there while in the throes of a horrible fever didn't count.

"And the gnomes?"

"They showed up about a minute, maybe a minute and a half later. Just walked out of the woods."

"They didn't come from the same portal as the girl?"

"Maybe. I dunno. I was busy getting a blanket around her and hustling her into my vehicle. Warmer there even if the engine didn't run. My poor car. The chief's going to kill me for wrecking my car."

Did I say that Allie loved her cruiser like a pet dog?

"Tess, this is like something out of one of your books. What's going on?" Allie looked worried.

"I want to go back to the faeries and the flowers. It's warm there. And pretty," little-miss-drowsy-and-half-naked mumbled. Her head nodded forward. She threatened to tilt into the space between the front seats.

Shit. I knew I should have taken the half second to strap her in.

"We'll talk later, Allie," I stalled, negotiating the ruts and snow drifts as rapidly as I dared.

"Promise?"

"Promise." I hid my crossed fingers inside my clenched fist on the steering wheel.

Allie grabbed my hand and opened my fingers. "Promise?" She knew me too well.

"Promise," I sighed. Then I turned to our mystery woman. "What's your name, honey?"

"Names are like dandelion fluff. They scatter in the wind and only take root in places that give them meaning." She drifted off again.

"Sheesh, she sounds just like MoonFeather," Allie sighed.

A flicker of movement in my peripheral vision froze my thoughts.

Off to the left a flash of impossibly bright green against the dirty snowbank. The fine hairs at the base of my spine stood on end. Alarm spread across my back.

You anywhere close, Scrap? I called into the ether.

No answer.

"Of course you aren't around. I need some answers, so you take off," I muttered low enough Allie couldn't hear me. She was busy trying to keep our nodding guest in her own seat while holding on tight to the sword. As if her life depended upon it.

It might.

Motion on my right. I got the impression of vivid red.

"Wrong time of year for Christmas colors, guys. If only you were garden gnomes blowing around in the wind," I said out loud. Some of their black blood had landed on my parka and was eating away at it like acid. Hopefully, the blood wouldn't manage to work its way through both the parka and the blanket the girl was wrapped in.

Mom's garden club had sold lawn monuments to bad taste as a fund-raiser a year ago. Because of the political prominence of a number of the club members, everyone on tasteful Cape Cod had a dozen of the tacky things on display.

"At least Dill's disappeared," I subvocalized, hoping Scrap would hear my mutterings better than my mental voice. I didn't need my husband's acerbic comments at the moment.

But, Goddess, I missed him.

"Not so lucky, lovey. I'm right behind you."

"Well, stay there. Out of the way." Again with the barely audible grunts.

"Your ghost isn't warm. He's colder than cold," the girl said. For a brief moment her eyes cleared, and she looked almost alert.

How come she could see Dill? Allie couldn't. Or, if she did, she didn't acknowledge that she could see a ghost.

"Don't move about so much. You don't have a seat belt on," I replied.

"Seat belts aren't groovy. They restrict our freedoms."

Both Allie and I rolled our eyes at that one.

"She has a point," Dill added. "People should have the choice to die or not."

"Why don't you go back to whatever ever after you came from?" I muttered, louder than I'd intended.

"Don't be rude," Allie admonished me. She must think I spoke to the girl.

"Love to move on to the ever after, lovey, but I'm stuck in limbo until you and I are truly united forever," Dill said.

"Not in this lifetime," I mouthed.

"That's what I mean." I didn't have to see his grin in the rearview mirror—couldn't see him at all in the mirror—but I knew it was there.

"I didn't come from the ever after, I came from Paradise," the girl whispered. "I want to go back."

"Looks like you got kicked out of Paradise, kid. If I remember my folklore right . . ." And I did. "Wrong time of year for easy passage between dimensions for humans. You need the solstice and a massive ritual for that," I told her, trying to figure out what was going on.

Something, an old story, tickled my mind then vanished.

"Kicked out of Paradise?" Allie repeated. She pulled on her earlobe again, thinking hard.

I grabbed her hand. "You'll end up like Carol Burnett with a long and drooping lobe," I chided her.

We grinned at each other.

I proceeded forward at a crawl that seemed breakneck on the snow and frozen ruts.

Try All Hallows Eve for dimension moving, Scrap chimed in. He popped into view leaning on the dashboard, feet braced against the center console, one wing folded neatly around his shoulders. The other wing canted at a strange angle. It looked like it hurt. He looked more faded and washed out than usual. The aftermath of a fight without a full dose of mold or, lacking that, beer and orange juice to restore him. If he started to glow pink, I needed to be wary. When he got full red, we'd both need him to transform into the Celestial Blade.

Not likely to happen for a while, until he recovered. *Not to worry, babe. I found a stash of mold along the upstairs bathroom floor trim.*

About time you got back from kissing the ass of that golden weasel you worship, imp. There's more trouble brewing. I had no idea if that was where he'd been. But he was always on me to believe in something, anything. Lots of Gods and Goddesses out there.

Yeah. Right.

I caught a flash of a little being pacing me on the left. Green cap and tunic. Yellow leggings and pointy shoes. The cheap plastic statues that littered the Cape were just that—cheap. Their colors had faded in the long harsh winter. This guy was impossibly bright.

Same for the red one on the other side.

Greenie grinned at me with a mouth full of far too many dagger-shaped teeth. Three rows of them up and down. The flare of warning along my spine became full fledged ripples of alarm.

"You see that, Allie?"

"See what?" All her attention was on the girl in the back.

On it, dahling, Scrap said. *By the way, that bulky sweater over jeans is so not you. Black may be classic, like this car, but it drains the color from your face. You need the teal cashmere sweater Dad gave you for Christmas and a lavender turtleneck—silk, I think—in this weather. Such a nice insulator silk is.* He disappeared with only a little whoosh of displaced air.

"I'll worry about my fashion sense later. Tell me about the garden gnomes, one right, one left."

Allie turned pale.

That told me a lot.

"Pretty little imp," the girl crooned. She reached a bare arm out of my parka to grasp a handful of air where Scrap had been.

"What's she talking about?" Allie asked.

"She's hallucinating." No one but me, or another Warrior of the Celestial Blade should be able to see him. And most of the warriors were locked up tight in their Citadels. I was the only reject on the loose that I knew about.

They'd have taken Scrap from me if they could when they kicked me out. But our bond was too deep. Metaphysical ties knotted and tangled us together for life.

I took my eyes off the road for half a second to stare at the girl. An icy rut grabbed my tire and swerved me toward the curb and a parked car.

Cautiously, I corrected before my tires skidded and I totally lost control.

The two escapees from the trailer park say they came for the girl, Scrap said, popping back into view and chomping on a black cherry cheroot. Out of respect for Mom, he never smoked in her car. *They say they'll take down anyone who stands in their way. We're on the hit list now, babe.*

I tensed my shoulders and clenched my hands tighter on the steering wheel.

"Don't let them take me back," whispered the girl. "They're mean and they hurt me."

"No one's going to hurt you, honey," Allie reassured her. "We'll take care of you."

"What's this *we* business?" I raised my eyebrows at Allie. "I'm going to Mexico, just as soon as I e-mail the rest of my book to my editor."

I didn't think the Windago could find me on a sunny beach south of the border.

Ahead I saw the blaring red neon arrows pointing to the ER. Two more blocks. Get the girl safely inside, then I could get on with my *normal* life. In my head I made vacation plans.

I slid into the covered entry of the ER. Allie stashed the broadsword beneath her seat and hopped out before I came to a complete halt. Using the authority of her uniform, as well as her intimidating size, she grabbed two orderlies and a gurney.

Gratefully, I let them ease my passenger into the welcome warmth of the ER. I retrieved my jacket the second they covered the girl with another blanket. Then I followed, keeping my eyes and other senses open and wary. Scrap hovered above my head and off to my right, stubby wings and wide ears flapping. (The left wing was still drooping unnaturally. Where had he been playing? Or rather who had he been playing with?) His pug nose worked overtime seeking hints of demon blood. Shades of pink outlined his edges. He'd lost the cigar, ready to work his magic.

The moment the automatic doors whooshed shut behind me the warning flares across my back soothed.

Hospitals are sacred. We're safe here. Scrap paled and dropped back to his normal pudgy grayish-green form. He flapped his wings once and landed on my shoulder, as substantial as dandelion fluff.

The kid had mentioned dandelion fluff when I asked her for a name. Now the admissions people were asking her the same question.

"Names have meaning only to the person owning them," she said on a breathy sigh.

Allie looked at me and tsked in disgust. "Want to get your aunt down here? Maybe she can make sense of this."

"Not yet," I replied. "Stow the New Age crap and give it to me straight, lady. What's your name?" I ordered the girl. I'd learned long ago, when I made my living as a substitute teacher, that sometimes kids will only respond to direct commands snapped in an authoritative voice.

"WindScribe." Her eyes rolled up into her head and she lost consciousness.

Allie choked.

"What?"

"Weirdest story ever to come out of the cold case files. We pass it around the station about once a year." She swallowed heavily. "Twenty-eight years ago, about the time you

and I were born, twelve women from the same Wiccan coven disappeared. All on the same night. No trace of them
ever found. We presume they ran away to California where
witchcraft is more acceptable. But the case file is still
open."

There went that flare of warning up my spine again.

Chapter 5

It was once believed that the Moon was a gem worn by the Goddess, and that the stars were decorations upon Her Gown.

"TWELVE WICCA WOMEN?" I thought I knew where this story was going. No one on Cape Cod talked about it much, but kids whispered it around the campfire when they wanted to scare the youngest members of the scout troop.

"A Wiccan coven celebrating the sabbat of summer solstice," Allie added.

I caught a glimpse of the red-and-green gnomes peering in through the glass doors.

"A coven has thirteen members. MoonFeather says the rituals always need thirteen," I insisted, ignoring Dill. Maybe he'd go away.

Part of me hoped he wouldn't.

"But that night MoonFeather didn't attend. It was her coven," Allie said. "Her father—your grandfather—locked her in her room and tried to get the family priest to perform an exorcism on her, to cure her of her devilish ways. She missed the sabbat, so only twelve were there. Only twelve went missing."

"And WindScribe here was one of those women." Hard to believe, she looked so vulnerable, innocent, and young. Way too young to have gone missing thirty years ago.

Time is just another dimension, babe, Scrap mumbled

around his black cherry cheroot. *Those who know how to manipulate it can flit hither, thither, and yon in a single night while decades pass in their home dimension.*

"Rip Van Winkle in drag. Times twelve," I said. "I think my vacation in Mexico just vanished into Neverland when it dumped this broad in my lap."

▽▲▽▲▽▲▽

The sounds of coughing, hacking, retching, moaning, and crying filled the ER lobby. The cold weather took its toll on the health of the community. With disease and accidents.

The place was full to overflowing.

"I'm going home," I told Allie. If I was on anyone's hit list, I wanted to fight on my own turf. Without an audience or endangering bystanders.

"Not yet you don't." Allie grabbed my arm and steered me toward the desk. "I want your statement, in writing. Before my boss gets here."

"But I wasn't there. I didn't see her appear."

Allie bit her lip. "But you heard her talk about paradise and flowers. You saw that she was naked. You heard her say her name. You made those garish apparitions bleed. Who's going to explain the blood?"

"Um . . . Allie, is this a good idea? Can't we just put the whole thing in the X-files or the UFO folder or whatever you call it?"

"No. I was there. I saw something really strange, and I want explanations." She stood between me and the door.

The gnomes continued making faces at me from the other side of the glass. They also shook their tiny fists and bared their rows and rows of teeth.

"Come on, Allie, what am I going to put into that report? That you told me you saw a beautiful blonde step out of nothing directly into the path of your car and that she claims to be a witch who disappeared thirty years ago but hasn't aged a day? That the garden gnomes that litter the Cape came to life and tried to chew through your bright and shiny new cruiser to get to that girl. If I wrote that anywhere but as fiction, we'd both be laughed off the Cape. Or into the loony bin."

"I've got to have something to tell my boss."

Anything resembling the truth was suspect.

"Coffee. I need caffeine before I can think this through." I jerked away from her in search of the cafeteria, or (shudder) a vending machine. "The Pacific Northwest has great coffee on every corner, and I bet the weather behaves itself, too," I grumbled. Dill's folks lived in Oregon. Maybe I could take refuge there from the Windago and garden gnomes with teeth.

Not a great idea. My in-laws were weirder and more suspect than Dill's ghost.

Allie followed me to the cafeteria where they had an espresso machine. Over hazelnut lattes we tried to find a way out of the dilemma.

"They call hazelnuts filberts in Oregon," I said, still daydreaming of a refuge elsewhere.

Then Joe Halohan, Chief Constable for our township, wandered in. "Thought I'd find you two in here." He pulled a chair up to our miniscule table and straddled it. He draped his portly frame over the back, chewing on a toothpick. "Care to give me a saner explanation than the doctor and the naked woman did?" He raised bushy gray eyebrows at us both.

"Can't find anything saner, sir," Allie reported.

"Then until you do, I suggest our novelist here takes the fictional character in hand." He heaved himself off the chair, the matter concluded.

"What does that mean?" I snapped at him.

"Very simple. The hospital doesn't have any spare beds. The jail is full, too, with all the bums we've pulled off the streets to keep them from freezing to death. There is nothing visibly wrong with the woman who calls herself Wind-Scribe. Someone has to take her in. Until the FBI gets here. I elect you, Tess."

"FBI?" I gulped.

"A cold case of kidnapping warming up. It's their jurisdiction."

"But . . ."

"No buts about it. Either take her in, or find a logical explanation for where she came from, who she is, and why she's totally naked in subfreezing weather." This time he escaped me.

"Shit."

"You don't *have* to do this, Tess." Allie didn't look convinced.

"He's right. Who better than me? I've got that big rambling house that used to be a bed and breakfast. I just finished a book, so I'm not on deadline. I only have to e-mail the last four chapters as soon as I get power and phone lines back. And I've got MoonFeather to help us untangle this. Come on. Let's take WindScribe home. The sooner we get answers, the sooner I can take off for vacation in warmer weather." I needed at least a couple of days to make reservations and pack. And do laundry, check my stacks of unopened mail, take out the garbage, and wash four days of accumulated dishes before I could leave.

Then I was outta here.

If the gnomes let me.

An hour later, I zipped up my parka and huddled into it a moment. A bewildered WindScribe sat beside me in the car clutching a little white paper bag with two vials of tranquilizers. She huddled into a hospital blanket draped around her hospital gown and robe.

The garden gnomes were nowhere in sight. Scrap remained a peaceful gray, and the hairs on my spine lay flat. We were safe.

For a while.

"You can't imprison me with that," she protested the seat belt, swatting at my hands.

"It's the law, kid. Strap in or walk." I glared at her.

She stared out the window a moment at the frigid weather. The wind had picked up again, bringing the wind chill even lower. The lowering skies threatened to dump more snow.

Born of nature or the Windago?

"If you insist. But I want it on record that I protest this infringement upon my rights."

"At the moment you don't officially exist, so you don't have any rights," I said sweetly, putting the car into gear.

Allie had gone back to the station armed with fingerprints and dental X rays to try to match WindScribe to any *recent* missing persons reports. A DNA swab would take three days to process. Too long for me to wait. Allie also promised to notify any relatives the original WindScribe had left in the area.

Scarcely noon. Would MoonFeather be up yet? I needed to call her. She'd want to know about her Wiccan sister from thirty years ago. A woman who hadn't aged a day while the ravages of time had worked on my aunt. Though if the phrase aging gracefully applied to anyone, it did to MoonFeather.

Damn, I wanted a vacation. Two weeks alone on a warm beach sipping *piña coladas*. Maybe find a luscious man who had no connection to demons and monsters and witches who fell out of another dimension. Someone more satisfying than the vibrator I'd considered buying. Almost any man would prove more interesting.

Silently, I drove home. The short distance seemed to take forever with the scowling presence beside me. Even Dill was cheerier than this unexpected and unwanted passenger.

"It's all so different," WindScribe murmured. "So different and yet so much the same."

"Not much changes on Cape Cod. Just the latest tech toys."

Power company crews packed up their chain saws, having cut up the fallen oak and repaired the lines. My twisting driveway was clear and lights blazed from my kitchen. I pulled into the gravel parking area outside my kitchen door with a sigh of relief. Heat. Hot coffee. Internet!

Not everything was bad.

"I think I know this house. A lawyer owns it." WindScribe peered through the windshield, leaning forward as far as the seat belt would let her. She released it and twisted around, surveying my entire property.

"I own it now." All two and one half acres. No mortgage, thanks to Dill's life insurance.

"Houses are sacred. No bad guys allowed," I reminded myself. "We'll be safe here. Or should be."

Braced for the blast of frigid wind born over arctic snows, I opened the car door and moved around to help

WindScribe into the house. "Tomorrow's the first day of spring, for Goddess' sake!" I protested to the charcoal-gray sky.

Something rattled in the shrubbery. Hopefully, just the wind.

The wind came in gusts that shook everything in its path.

Only a single bush rattled.

I didn't want to battle demons outside in this weather. Even demons should have the sense to stay home today.

Maybe it was an animal. Stupid people let their dogs and cats wander in this weather.

Not with my luck.

I caught a flicker of movement out of the corner of my eye. I paused for just a moment, waiting to see if the base of my spine flared in warning again.

Only a tingle of watchful waiting.

Good. I could outwait the best of them.

The storm door to the mudroom stuck. Cursing in Sasquatch again, I kicked the metal door. My big toe threatened to fall off inside my boot and wool sock from the blow. But the door unstuck.

I hustled WindScribe through the kitchen to the butler's pantry into the dining room. Then up the new staircase (added on in 1850 as opposed to the old staircase from the original building in 1743 between my office and the parlor) to the long attic room. My nose wiggled. The house smelled different. Clean and fresh rather than musty and moldy. Maybe Scrap had done a hasty cleanup.

Normally, I used the attic over the dining room as book storage. It still had a double bed with a brass frame tucked into the corner, left over from the previous owners.

WindScribe wilted with every step. I'd planned to put her in the guest room on the other side of my bedroom above the office. She wouldn't make it that far. So I tucked her into the bed. Got her a glass of water from my bathroom and left her sleeping peacefully with one tranquilizer in her. The bottle said she could take two every four hours. One seemed more than enough. She was confused and stressed, not suffering panic attacks.

"Woo wee, it is colder than a titch's wit out there," I said to no one as I headed for the coffeepot in the kitchen. I rubbed my hands together.

The smell of burning sage stopped me in my tracks. The strains of Heather Alexander singing a Celtic lay about a stag hunt played on the stereo.

"MoonFeather," I greeted my father's sister. She must have been in my office or parlor, so I didn't notice her when I hastened upstairs with WindScribe.

I like my aunt. She's the closest thing to normal in my life, less than twenty years older than me and ten younger than Dad, we're closer in age and philosophy to each other than to most everyone else on either side of the clan.

My aunt is *only* MoonFeather. She'd never taken the names of any of her four husbands when she dropped the family name of Noncoiré. That was thirty years ago when she embraced her true calling as a witch, just before her coven disappeared on the night of the summer solstice.

I needed to talk to her about that.

"Is it family game night already?" My odd assortment of relatives on Cape Cod gathered every Sunday night to play Trivial Pursuit®. We didn't have to pretend we liked each other the rest of the week because we had spent four hours of quality time together.

Their presence might make talking about WindScribe difficult.

"It's only Thursday, Tess. I decided to clear your house of evil spirits now that you have finished that manuscript. You need to invite good spirits back into your home. You drive them away with your foul moods when you are on deadline."

"Foul moods on deadline are part of the job description."

"Yes, I know, but this is something . . . different. More intense." She scowled and added lavender to the burning sage wand.

A waft of smoke brushed my nose. I jammed my finger under it to keep from sneezing. This smoke smelled more like Scrap's black cherry cheroot than MoonFeather's herbs. First time I could remember welcoming his bad habits. I wanted the imp close right now.

"How did you know I finished the manuscript?" Despite myself, I found my foot tapping the rhythm of the next tune on the CD.

MoonFeather gave me *that* look that said I was stupid for asking how she knew.

She knew things. I had a lot of trouble keeping Scrap a secret from her. She was the one person who might believe my tale of spending a year in a hidden Citadel learning to be a Warrior of the Celestial Blade.

I'd fallen to pieces after Dill died and the Sisterhood welcomed me, nursed me through a near-lethal fever, gave me a reason to live beyond my grief. Our purpose was to keep demons from crossing into this dimension. Good thing they kicked me out of the Citadel for questioning too many rules and asking why ten times too often. If I'd still been stuck there guarding a single doorway to another dimension, I'd never have been available last autumn to close a rogue demon portal they missed.

I wouldn't have been under WindScribe when she fell out of Paradise.

Maybe it was time to use the ultra secret, in life or death, emergencies only phone number Sister Serena had given me.

Probably no one would answer the damn thing.

Chapter 6

"**Y**OU READ A completion or closure for me in the tarot, MoonFeather." I was sure I hadn't said anything about my progress or my deadlines last Sunday at game night. Uncle George, my sister Cecilia, and Grandmother Maria never paid any attention to my career anyway. The money I earned just made it more convenient for them to gather in my big house.

Dill and I had bought it right after our marriage. He'd liquidated his trust fund for the down payment. Then we'd returned to central Washington to collect his stuff and gather a few more rock samples before he began teaching at the local community college. He'd died before we could get back here. His death was another convenience for the family, if not for me. He had a Ph.D in geology and usually beat the pants off the entire family combined against him on game night. They wouldn't allow me to team up with him; the two of us together made an even more formidable team.

I really needed the last cup of coffee in the pot.

But not garden gnomes with ten extra sets of teeth.

Or a Windago with a grudge.

"I saw the end of a segment in your life and the beginning of a new one in the cards. So of course I knew that you finished a book and I knew you'd need help cleaning house." MoonFeather waved the glowing sage wand at a dark corner where a cobweb had taken up residence and threatened to engulf the refrigerator.

I knew it was there and meant to clean it out when I finished the book, when I had a few spare minutes, when I couldn't find anything better to do.

Or when Mom came home and cleaned it out for me.

"You made a new pot of coffee," I sighed in relief.

"I also scrubbed the pot," MoonFeather said emphatically.

I cringed. I hoped she hadn't collected all my discarded, half empty mugs with a thick patina of mold growing in them. I was saving those for Scrap when he got back from wherever. Beer and orange juice might revive him after a battle, but he craved mold like I crave chocolate and coffee. Only mold was more essential to his metabolism than chocolate and coffee were to mine.

Maybe not.

"You washed the dishes." So much for the mold farm for Scrap.

A chuckle in the back of my mind told me that Scrap had gotten to a couple of them before MoonFeather did. I relaxed with a sigh.

Now how to ask her about WindScribe.

"I also took a bunch of messages for you," MoonFeather continued. "Two of them from men I don't know." My aunt raised her eyebrows in speculation. She might be nearing fifty, but she still had a fine figure and great legs. She'd divorced three husbands, buried a fourth, and now lived with a man fifteen years younger than herself. She'd raised two daughters, mostly on her own, who were now off at college. She knew every eligible man on Cape Cod and a good many more throughout New England. With way too much info on each one.

And she didn't like sharing.

I poured coffee, thick cream—the real thing—and three sugars into my favorite cup; heavy natural-colored pottery with a bulbous center and a blue dragon circling it. Then I reached for the notepad hanging on a string beside the telephone.

"Donovan Estevez?" My heart went pitter-patter. I'd met Donovan last autumn and slept with him. Once. He was the sexiest man alive and he had the hots for me. He'd make a good diversion on that beach in Mexico. . . .

At the same time my spine bristled with anxiety. I couldn't trust the man. No, I'd never invite Donovan to meet me anywhere. Well, maybe on vacation if no demons threatened.

"Mr. Estevez is a very spiritual man. Is he part Native American?" MoonFeather gazed into the ether as she drew information into herself.

I nodded. Part Sanpoil Indian, Russian, Dutch, and a few other ancestors, as well as possibly Damiri demon. I didn't know about the spiritual part. I'd leave that assessment to MoonFeather. I don't do spiritual or religious.

"He says he will be on the Cape tomorrow on business and hopes to meet you at the *salle d'armes* for a fencing bout in the evening." MoonFeather read her scrawled handwriting over my shoulder.

"And Guilford Van der Hoyden-Smythe." I looked at the next message. Gollum to his friends.

"Quite a nice and scholarly gentleman. Isn't he the one who called to reassure your mother when you were kidnapped by terrorists last autumn?"

I nodded again. Those terrorists had been Sasquatch demons. I didn't like talking about that episode. That's where I learned to curse in Sasquatch.

"Mr. Van der Hoyden-Smythe says that he is lecturing to the National Folkloric Society in Boston tomorrow night and requests that you attend."

"Can't," I said. I didn't want to explain about the two men who were almost in my life. For various reasons, neither one of them was always welcome.

Should I invite Gollum to join me in Mexico? He might be a comfortable companion, but a sexy one . . .? Tall, lanky, with glasses that slipped down his nose, he always looked crisp and pressed. He also had a tendency to drone on and on and on about obscure topics of interest only to himself. A true nerd—um—scholar.

Gollum's expertise might be valuable in figuring out what happened to WindScribe and where the garden gnomes with teeth came from.

MoonFeather added her sage wand to the fire in the breakfast nook. "Do you want me to exorcise your ghosts?" she asked.

I needed a moment and several sips of coffee to jump thoughts with her.

"Why would I do that? I'm comfortable with them and they with me." Except for Dill. I wasn't sure if I wanted his ghost in or out of my life. Pretty soon there wouldn't be room for me in the house with all of the ghosts.

"They bother your mother."

Since Dad moved in with his much younger tennis coach, Bill Ikito, the rest of the family tried to take care of Mom. They failed, and most of the responsibility fell to me.

"Mom isn't here."

"But she is coming back. When the weather breaks. Soon, I think."

"It's my house. She lives in the guest cottage, which is not haunted."

"That's what you think."

"Have I acquired a new one?" Half jokingly—but only half. The previous owner had included the ghosts in the earnest money agreement along with the monster dining room table and twelve chairs as part of the sale.

If I did burn the table and chairs, I could turn the dining room into more library space and not have room for family game night. Hmmm. Something to think about.

"I'm not certain. There is a new presence hovering nearby. It could be a ghost returned to a place of comfort or something else. The air tastes of . . . I don't know what. Something odd."

"Uh, MoonFeather, we need to talk about something odd that happened today. Or, rather, thirty years ago . . ."

Her eyes narrowed in speculation and . . . did I detect worry behind her scrutiny?

A flicker of bright red and green flashed before my memory.

That's right, babe. We're about to have a close encounter

of the weird kind, Scrap laughed in my ear as he settled into my hand, flashing neon red, ready to transform into a weapon.

Why couldn't these guys wait until I was safely snoozing on a sunny beach somewhere?

Chapter 7

It was once believed that the Moon was a spinning wheel, upon which the Goddess spun the lives of Men and Women.

"TESS, WHAT IS happening?" MoonFeather stared at the elongating staff that suddenly materialized in my hands. Then her eyes shifted to my face. "When did you get that scar?"

"Later," I snapped at my aunt. Damn, the scar pulsed and burned as if it were a newly opened wound. Maybe something about Scrap transforming and the presence of an enemy brought it into the real world.

I twirled the shaft, giving Scrap centrifugal force to continue his transformation. Between one eye blink and the next, mirror-image, half-moon blades extruded from the ends. Metal spikes grew out of the outside curves. They mimicked a special configuration in the sky when the Milky Way touched the top of a waxing quarter moon and revealed the face of the Goddess Kynthia.

The music on the stereo kicked up a notch. Throbbing drums, rousing pipes, a husky alto singing/snarling:

"Axes flash, broadsword swing
Shining armor's piercing ring
Horses run with polished shield
Fight those bastards till they yield
Midnight mare and blood-red roan,

Fight to keep this land your own
Sound the horn and call the cry,
How Many Of Them Can We Make Die!"

"Stand back, MoonFeather."

The mudroom door burst open. A gush of frigid air blew at me along with a ravening horde of tiny beings, all gnashing their nasty sharp teeth.

The first wave lunged for my bare ankles.

I swept the blade down and sideways. Three were caught up in the curve, swinging from the blade. They clung with their gnarly fists, using my weapon as a swing. One of them laughed at me.

I hadn't cut a single one of them.

Then I backhanded and impaled two more on the spikes. They died instantly, spewing black blood and a ghastly smell.

Holding back my gag reflex, I flipped the blade and attacked again with the spines.

Caught another one! Scrap chortled.

"Bloodthirsty imp," I growled. A little bit of relief washed through the tension in my shoulders and in my gut. These guys could hurt and die. I had a chance.

"Follow orders as you're told,
Make their yellow blood run cold
Fight until you die or drop
A force like ours is hard to stop
Close your mind to stress and pain
Fight till you're no longer sane
Let not one damn cur pass by
How Many Of Them Can We Make Die!"

The second wave of invading gnomes backed off. They stared at their fallen comrades, then up at me. Clearly, they were reconsidering their attack—or their strategy. I had surprised them. They didn't know who they faced.

A screech of pain came from behind me.

I whirled, flashing the blade right and left.

MoonFeather stood atop the round table in the nook. She fended off a gnome with my dagger-length dragon-grip letter opener.

As I watched, a gnome grabbed the blade in his fist and grinned. No blood oozed from his grip. With a laugh that welled up from the depths of hell and reverberated around my kitchen, he yanked the dagger away from MoonFeather.

Damn, these guys were hard to kill.

MoonFeather retaliated with a frying pan, flattening the little guy with quiet efficiency. But another one clung to her calf with its teeth. As I watched, it tore a chunk of flesh out of one of my aunt's gorgeous legs and spat it out. Blood gushed everywhere.

She cried out in shock and pain as her leg crumpled beneath her weight.

> *"Guard your women and children well,*
> *Send these bastards back to hell*
> *We'll teach them the ways of war.*
> *They won't come here anymore*
> *Use your shield and use your head,*
> *Fight till every one is dead*
> *Raise the flag up to the sky,*
> *How Many Of Them Can We Make Die!"*

I stomped my feet in rhythm with the drums and bagpipe and swung my blade in time with the lyrics. Then I dispatched the offending tiny monster attacking Moon-Feather with a clean sweep and spun again to make sure no others slipped by my guard.

"Perhaps we should talk." A little man held up his hand, palm out. He had a nose that met an elongated chin Jay Leno might envy, and a few scraggly whiskers. His equally ugly fellows cowered behind him.

"Talk about what? Maiming my aunt—my favorite person in the world?" I swept the blade back and forth between us.

MoonFeather whimpered something behind me.

I gave her half a glance, not daring to take my eyes off the enemy.

> *"Dawn has broke, the time has come,*
> *Move your feet to a marching drum*
> *We'll win the war and pay the toll,*

We'll fight as one in heart and soul
Midnight mare and blood-red roan
Fight to keep this land your own
Sound the horn and call the cry,
How Many Of Them Can We Make Die!"

The flattened one, now looking more like a two-dimensional cartoon than the menace I knew him to be, slid off the table and sidled along the wall until he could meld into the pack of miniscule invaders.

With a popping sound he puffed out and filled normal space again.

What would it take to off these guys?

"You have felled several of Our subjects. We do not forgive easily," the leader said.

Was that the royal "We"? The little fellow did sport a tiny bit of gold around the rim of his peaked cap and a golden feather stuck jauntily into the folds of red fabric.

"You're the king of garden gnomes, so what?" I sneered. "You invaded my home without provocation. Aren't there rules against that?"

"You attacked us first."

"Because you were menacing my friend. A policewoman doing her job!"

"We sympathize with the one you call Allie. We respect her duty. But we have a mission. You stand in our way."

"You're in the wrong dimension to be dictating anything."

"You harbor an escaped prisoner."

I raised my eyebrows at that. "You look like something an escapee from a lunatic asylum might dream up."

"You know better than that, Teresa Louise Noncoiré, Warrior of the Celestial Blade."

The Blade vibrated in my hands. Scrap had something to say but was having trouble communicating in this form.

"So you know my name. What's yours, and why are you crossing my threshold without an invitation?" I dredged up a fragment of a folk memory. "Homes are sacred. Invitations and hospitality a requirement." Out of doors was where the battles took place.

Only outside today was a frozen hell for both of us.

I kept the blade moving, not daring to give these guys an opening.

"Names are a source of power. Not to be given lightly."

WindScribe had wandered all around that subject.

MoonFeather moaned again. I hoped she'd managed to find a dish towel or a place mat to staunch the flow of blood.

"You forfeited your right to secrecy the moment you crossed my threshold, you little piece of trailer trash." I increased the arc of the blade, coming within a hair's breadth of the gnome king's chest.

"Yeep!" He jumped back, plowing into the crowd of his minions like a ball and ninepins. Among much jostling and staggering and muttering of curses in an oddly fluid language, the king righted himself and faced me once more.

"Give us the dangerous prisoner and we will depart your presence, never to bother you again," he offered. But his eyes wouldn't meet mine. I also suspected he crossed his fingers behind his back.

Tricky little bastard.

"I don't know what you are talking about," I lied.

"Windscribe," he said, slowly.

"WindScribe? Dangerous? She's a ditzy hippy." She was also human, one of my tribe. I wasn't about to give her up without a fight.

The king advanced one step. "You do not know the dangers you court. We will have the prisoner."

I gave him a taste of my blade.

The entire horde popped out with a whoosh.

The vacuum resulting from their departure brought a ringing to my ears and a new rush of arctic air into my kitchen.

The music faded to a poignant ballad.

My bloodlust died with the music.

"Oh, my," MoonFeather groaned. "I think I need more than a poultice on this wound."

No amazement. No protestations of the unreal. No questions about Scrap becoming the Celestial Blade.

That's my Aunt MoonFeather.

Nasty little beasties. Nasty. Nasty. They taste worse than their blood smells.

My babe needs answers. Like little Mr.-more-important-than-Ghod's name, rank, and serial number.

We need help. Help Tess won't ask for until she's desperate. Just once I wish she'd put aside her stubborn independence and ask. Gollum is nearby. But will she call him?

No.

Will she even think about it?

No.

Instead, she'll moon over that stinky Donovan. That man does not smell right. Old dust and sage and copper. Not fully human, but not a demon either. What is he?

Old. He's old. I can smell that much. But how old is old when one hops dimensions? Time is just another dimension.

I don't think my babe wants to know what he is. Then she'll have to feel even more guilty for sleeping with him.

Now if she'd just use a little common sense and hook up with Gollum . . .

I need a bath.

I need some mold and a nap.

Chapter 8

"YOU AGAIN?" a tired orderly in the ER asked. "What have you got this time, Snow White and the Seven Dwarfs?"

I grabbed the wheelchair from him and dashed back to the still running SUV. "My aunt is ensanguining while you malign my veracity!" I deliberately used words I didn't think he knew.

WindScribe dozed in the backseat, tranked to the gills. And hadn't I had a lovely time getting her back into the car. But I didn't dare leave her alone in a strange house.

MoonFeather was so absorbed in her own pain and staunching the torrents of blood from her wound she barely noticed the extra person in the car.

"Hey, how many of those pills did she take?" the orderly asked, checking WindScribe's neck for a pulse and shaking his head at her pale skin.

"I gave her one." I hadn't bothered to check the bottle in my hurry to get my aunt to the hospital. I could move faster with four-wheel drive than the local ambulance.

"Looks like she took half the bottle."

"She's not the patient! My aunt is bleeding to death." We'd managed a crude pressure bandage on her leg. Blood saturated it and seeped down her leg.

A nurse appeared, took one look at the blood that spattered both MoonFeather and myself, and started barking orders. Life sped up to fast forward. Medical professionals whisked MoonFeather off to surgery, leaving me with the paperwork and a dreaming WindScribe.

I'd managed to call Josh, MoonFeather's current significant other, and begun to fill in name and basic information when Allie returned.

"Now what?" she asked.

I shrugged and dredged a few more pieces of vital information out of my tired brain. Date of birth. Current residence. Contact phone number. Had to check the call list on my cell phone for that.

"Hospital said violent wound. I've got to investigate," Allie persisted.

"A raccoon got into the kitchen seeking warmth. It bit MoonFeather before we could evict it." That sounded more believable than the truth.

"That the truth, Tess?"

I looked her square in the eye. "You want the truth or what sounds logical?"

"Is this day going to get weird again?" She sat down beside me with a sigh. Her long legs stretched into the aisle between chairs, blocking my exit.

The place had mostly cleared out since this morning.

"Probably get weirder yet." Especially if both Donovan and Gollum came to town. "Weird describes my life."

"Shit. Do I need to find a new best friend?"

"I'd rather you stuck by this one."

We grinned at each other and touched fists, knuckle to knuckle, thumbs extended and entwined.

"You want to know how weird this day is?" Allie asked.

I groaned.

"They gave me a rookie for a partner."

"You don't usually partner."

"Didn't think I needed one. Boss Joe says no one goes out alone anymore." She shook her head, then jerked it sideways.

I noticed the uniformed man leaning on the reception counter. He didn't look much bigger than me.

"Rookie, indeed. Still wet behind the ears," I said. "What is he, twelve?"

As if he heard me, the young man swaggered over, thumbs hooked into his belt. A classic stance of a scared little boy trying to make himself look bigger and older. He'd be almost handsome if he didn't try so hard.

"Tess, meet Mike Gionelli." Allie gave no further explanation.

"Pleased to meet you, Mike." I politely held my hand out to shake.

He grabbed it eagerly and firmly with dry palms. His smile spread from ear to ear and lit his eyes. "I've read your books. I'm really looking forward to the next one."

"Flattery will get you everywhere, young man."

An hour later I got MoonFeather ensconced in a private room—amazing what good insurance will get you. The hospital wasn't as full as they pretended.

WindScribe, who had no insurance that we knew of and therefore no hospital bed, dozed in a chair in the corner.

"A garden gnome came to life and bit me with dagger-sharp teeth," MoonFeather told the intern, keeping a straight face and her eyes wide open in innocence.

"Why that's . . . that's . . ." the young man spluttered. He looked cast from the same mold as Mike Gionelli, far too young for the responsibility he wielded. "Must be the pain meds." He shook his head and left us.

"Did you see his face?" MoonFeather giggled through her intravenous drugs.

I sat on an uncomfortable stool, holding her hand. I told her the raccoon story.

"They're afraid of rabies. If we don't come up with a better explanation in the next few hours, the doctor's going to require shots. They aren't pleasant." I tried to keep my voice calm and low. Too many people ran about eavesdropping in this small but well-appointed hospital.

Cape Cod may be small, but we have some of the priciest real estate in the country. Our local billionaires demand state of the art medical care whenever they need it. So the rest of us peons benefit from the facility.

"I can't lie, Tess." MoonFeather's eyes cleared of the drug haze a moment. "Everything we do—good or bad—comes back to us threefold. I won't lie."

"Then let me do it for you." I should have built up a fair amount of good karma to make up for a little white lie when I dispatched a couple dozen Sasquatch. Besides, a lie couldn't be *too* bad if I told it to protect the innocent from information they wouldn't believe and couldn't process.

"Something will turn up." She dismissed it all with an expansive gesture that nearly dislodged her IV. Her eyes glazed over and drifted closed.

"MoonFeather, before you drift off into the land of nod, we need to talk."

"Hmm?" She cast me a beatific smile.

"MoonFeather." I jostled her arm a little to get her attention. "Your friend WindScribe has come back." I pointed to the witless lump in the corner. She'd roused enough to hum something I didn't recognize.

"WindScribe. Such a beautiful girl. Blonde hair as light as a feather in the moonlight." She paused long enough that I thought she'd gone to sleep.

Odd that she would describe another witch with the attributes of her own craft name. When people join Wicca, they often take a name that describes themselves better than the name their parents gave them. I'd seen Moon-Feather dance nude in the moonlight. She moved as gracefully as a feather drifting in the wind.

Would she ever dance again? I hoped so.

Those gnomes had a lot to answer for.

She mumbled something I couldn't catch. Then she swallowed deeply and stopped slurring. "I always thought you'd take the name WindScribe if you ever embraced your true calling. Your spirit is as free as the wind and you are a scribe." Something more unintelligible. Then, "Society didn't grant as much religious freedom in those days as they claimed. We had trouble keeping a sacred thirteen."

MoonFeather opened her eyes and sat up abruptly. "Have you called Josh?"

"Yes. He's in court and will be here as soon as he can. He has to clear his schedule so he can stay home and take care of you. But I think you should plan on coming to my house. So he can work." Josh's law practice was just starting to take off. He needed to be in the office, or the courtroom, as much as possible. He also needed to make money to keep up his health insurance premiums to cover MoonFeather and this hospital visit. Hospital administrators do not look kindly upon people without insurance.

Like WindScribe.

Besides, those little beasties had tasted MoonFeather's blood. They'd be able to find her anywhere, in any dimension. I needed to stay close to protect her.

"Your mother is coming home."

I groaned. "But the weather hasn't turned yet."

"She's still coming home. You need to think about protecting her. Until I can devise a ritual to banish the bad guys. You'll need help. You need an apotropaic."

I knew that archaic word. It meant something designed to avert evil, like a gargoyle protecting a cathedral. How did she know it?

Yeah, I needed a gargoyle. A live one with a sharp and pointy weapon.

"I always need help with Mom," I said instead. But I didn't like the idea of my naïve and defenseless mother all the way across the yard in the guest cottage. Alone.

So much for two weeks in Mexico, or Southern California, or San Antonio . . .

With a weary sigh, I dug out my cell phone. Gollum wasn't the first on my speed dial, but close. (That spot was reserved for Dill's extinct cell phone. I'd never allowed myself to delete the number. Too final an admission that he was truly gone forever.) Gollum was the closest thing to a gargoyle I could think of.

I'd never seen him fight, but he knew things about demons no mortal should. He had access to more information from arcane sources he never talked about.

Come to think about it, he didn't talk much about himself. Just myth and legends and demons. About those, he talked endlessly. And he hid behind his scholarly tinted glasses so that I couldn't read his eyes.

Maybe he was busy, and I could just leave a voice mail.

No such luck. He answered on the first ring. "Tess, good to hear from you. Are you coming to my lecture tomorrow?" His clipped upstate New York accent sounded all too comfortable and familiar, even though I hadn't heard from him since I left him in Seattle last November, other than a generic holiday card with a scrawled signature I could barely read.

I easily imagined him stretching his long legs and lanky frame, then folding himself into the nearest armchair and setting up camp with his laptop, his cat, and *my* beer.

"I don't think I can make it." I glared accusingly at WindScribe. If I took her with me maybe. "Um, Gollum, what's your schedule like while you're in New England?"

"Actually, I've taken a teaching gig at your community college. Seems like your anthro prof has complications in her pregnancy and has to take to her bed for four months or so. I'm filling in."

"Oh." He'd be on my back step for months. He and his cat. Scrap hates cats. He's also allergic and can't smell evil when the cat is around. "Um, do you have an apartment yet?"

"Got a line on two but haven't committed to either yet. I'd planned to do that this weekend and move in next week during spring break."

"Would you like to stay in my guest cottage?" I had to grit my teeth to make the offer. But I needed his expertise in dealing with flesh-eating garden gnomes.

"What about your mom?"

"I'm moving her into the mother-in-law apartment attached to the house." No way would I leave her alone out in the cottage, easy prey to my latest supernatural enemy.

Dill had set up an office in the house extension. I'd locked the connecting door after his death and never looked inside since. But it had three good-sized rooms, a private bath, and a kitchenette.

"I'll meet you at the house in an hour," he said on a chuckle.

"Where are you now?"

"Halfway between Boston and Cape Cod."

"Like you knew I'd make the offer?"

"Like I hoped you would when you saw my smiling face."

"House rules. You sleep in the cottage, not the armchair in my living room. You drink your own beer, eat your own food, and keep your cat out of my house and Scrap's way. And you never, ever, under penalty of death, speak French to my mother."

Chapter 9

*In old Alchemical prints, the lion and the unicorn
are frequently used to describe the opposing forces
of sun and moon.*

I LEFT MOONFEATHER in Josh's loving arms a few
minutes later and returned home by way of the liquor
store—for empty boxes to move Mom's things. And a bottle of single malt scotch. I had a feeling I was going to need
it if Gollum was moving into the guest cottage. The scotch
was for me.

WindScribe brightened enough to notice the booze. I
think she wanted to start in on it the moment I set the bag
in the backseat of the car.

"Not yet, kid. You're still drugged. Can't mix booze and
pills."

"Why not?"

I rolled my eyes at that.

"Makes for a boss trip." She started humming something catchy about a white rabbit.

Oh, boy. I was going to have my hands full with this one.

I knew that tune. Where? The only lyrics that came to
mind were filk, parodies of the original with a science fiction or fantasy twist. I spent a lot of my time at the SF/F
conventions, or cons, filking. We'd sit up half the night singing the parodies, or Celtic lays, and punning ourselves to
sleep.

Dill's death had closed my throat, seemingly forever. I

couldn't even sing at the funeral of my best friend, Bob Brown, though he'd asked me to with his dying breath. Then, last autumn, I'd finally let the songs within me bubble up and out.

I could use a rousing round of filk about now.

By the time we got back to the house, WindScribe was swaying on her feet.

The moment I got her back into bed, she reached for the vial of tranquilizers. I grabbed it away from her. "Well, I guess you can have one. It's been over four hours since I gave you a dose." I shook a few tablets into my hand.

The bottle seemed fuller than before. I counted. The label said thirty tablets, should be twenty-nine now. I counted thirty-three. And some of them looked suspiciously like aspirin.

"How many did you take before?" I demanded, not at all happy with my unwelcome guest or the way my life had slid downhill since . . . since last night when a Windago tried to gain entrance to my home—against the rules of hospitality.

WindScribe answered me with a snore. No wonder she was so spacey and incoherent.

Then she twitched and thrashed. "Don't lock me under the stairs, Mama. Please don't. I'm afraid of the dark."

I thought about waking her from her nightmare. Then she settled down and smiled. "Pretty flowers. No darkness in Faery."

Shaking my head, I took the pills with me and stashed them in the downstairs bathroom on my way to clean the kitchen.

I downed one small shot of the scotch while staring at the bloody mess and scrunching my nose against the stench of dead gnome and drying blood. In the movies no one had to clean up the mess. There's no *smell* in the movies.

Three, no, four miniature bodies lay scattered about the breakfast nook along with blood spatters and gore. On the walls. On the table. All over the muted blue-and-brown calico café curtains and chair pads Mom and I had lovingly made when Dill and I first bought the house. I wanted eight chairs so that we could seat an entire family here to start each day.

Together.

Ruined. Both the furniture and my dreams.

I'd have to get a new table and kitchen chairs along with some new dreams. No way would I ever be able to eat at this table again.

Those garden gnomes had a lot to answer for.

"It's just a table, lovey. Don't cry." Dill enfolded me with almost tangible arms. Instead of warmth and comfort, I felt cold.

An ache opened in my gut.

"If you trade in the imp and come to me, we can still have all those children together and get a new table."

"Don't start on me, Dill. I'm not messing with fate and death. That's too weird, even for me. I won't write it. I won't write vampires either, so I certainly don't want to live with it."

Maybe a shot of scotch would numb my gag reflex, my anger, and my grief long enough to fill a basin with bleach water.

I was still stalling when I heard a car pull into the driveway, idling roughly before it backfired and cut off. Then a brisk knock sounded on my kitchen door.

That could only be Gollum. His rattletrap van always sounded as if it was on its last legs, held together with rubber bands and chewing gum. But it kept going, and going, and going.

Dill faded into the woodwork. Not totally gone, not totally here.

I dashed to the door. Gollum would know what to do. Despite my grumblings about him and the way he tended to invade my life, I did like the man. I trusted him.

More than I could say for Donovan Estevez, the other man almost in my life.

The grin froze on my face as I looked through the glass half of the back door. A cold knot of suspicion formed in my stomach. Followed instantly by warm relief and a need to give all my troubles to the man smiling at me on my back stoop.

"What can I do to help, L'akita?" Donovan Estevez asked the moment I opened the door. He traced the worry lines away from my eyes and mouth. His hand felt warm and inviting even without gloves on this frigid day.

More real than Dill. More alive. And sexy as hell.

"You're a day early," I hedged.

"Yet obviously you have need of me. Now what brings a frown to your face and makes your shoulders reach for your ears in tension, hm?" He edged closer.

I had to back up or fall into his arms.

"Donovan Estevez, why are you driving *that?*" I pointed over his shoulder at a mud-and-salt encrusted yellow Subaru station wagon.

I didn't want to look at his handsome face with the high cheekbones and chiseled jaw, at his sleek black braid that hung down between his shoulder blades, at his long legs and broad shoulders. I didn't want to feel the warmth and strength of his embrace.

Yeah, right.

His black leather jacket and tight black jeans only emphasized his fit physique, making it harder for me to hold my distance.

"Economizing," he growled. "Had to sell the Beemer when the casino and my economic empire imploded down a demon portal."

That about explained what happened last November.

"You're a day early." I closed my eyes to override the magnetic pull of his smile. My head cleared the moment I shut out the vision of his face.

I couldn't bring myself to move aside and invite him in. Unlike Gollum, I didn't dare trust this man. I had evidence that he had demon ancestry as well as sympathies.

I also had evidence to the contrary. Until I knew more about this enigma of a man—a mysterious and wildly handsome man—I had to keep my heart intact.

I'd lost my heart and my will to Dill. When he betrayed me by dying, I'd fallen apart. My extreme grief had left me vulnerable to the imp flu. I wasn't sure I could survive that kind of loss again. Having his ghost around reminded me to keep my resolve to resist Donovan firm.

I dared open my eyes.

"Mind if I come in anyway?" He flashed me one of his famous grins, and my knees forgot to hold me upright. "It's a bit brisk out here."

"Yeah. Oh. Sorry." I stammered something and stepped aside with a sweeping gesture.

"Help yourself to coffee." I couldn't help but stare at the

horribleness just to the left of the door beneath the broad bay window. "I'm kind of busy at the moment."

He muttered something in a strange language filled with clicks, pops, and hisses. "No wonder you look worried. What happened here?" he finally asked jerking his gaze away from the bloody mess to me.

He pulled me against his chest, letting me bury my head in his shoulder. At five feet two, against his nearly six feet, I didn't reach any higher.

Faced with the task of cleaning up the gore, I chose to embrace a demon instead.

I told him, the last part of my day's adventures, not the part about WindScribe stepping out of Neverland.

"Well, you can't bury the bodies," he said. "And you don't want to burn them in your fireplace, they'll stink up the place something horrible."

"I figured I should leave them where they are until Gollum gets here."

Donovan snarled something else in his demon language.

He had nothing to be jealous about, but until I knew enough to trust him implicitly, I figured I'd let the emotion simmer between the two men.

"He'll know what to do."

"*I* know what to do. We build an equinox bonfire in the backyard and burn the critters. Where's your woodpile?" He eyed the vastly diminished stack of split firewood beside the kitchen hearth.

"Around the corner of the house, toward the woods." Half of which I owned. I stepped away from him. "Wait a minute. Why can't we just wrap them in plastic bags and dump them down a deep hole?" That sounded more sanitary to me than burning the carcasses.

The scotch I'd drunk for lunch threatened to come up. I had to turn my back on the nook.

"You have to burn any corpse from another dimension to make certain it's really and truly dead. Besides, the ground is too frozen to dig." He touched my shoulder with reassurance and affection.

I wanted to lean in to him again, let his arms enfold me and make all this horror go away. My body and my instincts craved a deeper intimacy with him.

Not until he comes clean about who and what he is, my logical brain kicked in just in time.

"But I speared them with the tines of the Celestial Blade. They are well and truly dead," I protested, making my way toward the coffeepot on the other side of the kitchen island, a full ten feet away from the nook and the stench that had begun to rise.

"Then they probably are dead. But we have to make sure." He followed me across the kitchen, staying far too close. I could feel the heat of his body along my back.

All too easy to lean back, just a little, and snuggle into his arms . . .

Stop that! I admonished myself even as my nipples puckered in anticipation of feeling his touch on them.

"Fine," I snapped. "You and Gollum take care of it when he gets here. I have to clean an apartment and move Mom's things." I walked stiffly to the right, away from him. Away from my own stupid desires.

"I'll call the firehouse and get a burning permit for a bonfire. Equinox. Religious purposes. They should grant it," I continued.

"Tess . . ." He reached out to me with a fine-boned hand and his very long fingers.

I remembered seeing him at a con in California last September. He'd worn a bat costume.

I hated bats. I feared bats to the point of phobia. Illogical and unlikely, but I couldn't overcome my panic at the merest thought of a bat touching me.

When Dill had learned of my fears, he'd made me read up on bats, learn just how harmless they were. It hadn't helped. But I did learn that the bone structure supporting a bat's wings were actually super elongated fingers. Donovan's fingers weren't *that* long, but they were long enough to remind me of one of the reasons I couldn't trust him.

"Just take care of the bodies. And . . . and the table and chairs. I'll clean up the mess later." I stalked off toward the opposite end of the house and the attached apartment. It would be cold back there with only minimal heat all winter. I'd have to turn up the thermostat, mentally calculating the increased heating bill. Those rooms had their own furnace, a much more modern and efficient one than I had in the cellar for the rest of the house.

If Donovan followed me, and I half hoped he wouldn't, he'd have to stay close on my heels to keep from getting lost in the maze of rooms.

My home had started as a standard New England saltbox. Three rooms down and two up, all clustered about a central chimney. I kept those rooms as my office, library, and parlor, with my bedroom and a spare upstairs.

Succeeding generations had added on to the house starting with the dining room and the attic over it that was now WindScribe's room. The huge kitchen and breakfast nook at the opposite end of the house and the mother-in-law apartment off the dining room were the latest additions. Bathrooms were odd shapes cobbled out of old nooks or closets or attachments on the outside walls.

Donovan didn't even trip on the odd changes in floor level. Each addition changed up or down an inch or three depending on the lay of the land.

If I didn't look at Donovan, I could almost resist him. Damn it, I needed help fighting my own lust.

Where was Scrap? He couldn't get close to Donovan for some mysterious reason. Still, he should be able to communicate from a distance.

"Scrap?" I whispered into the ether.

No answer.

El Stinko is here. He doesn't smell right. I know he's not human, but he doesn't smell like anything I've ever encountered before. As long as he is near my babe, his smell and an invisible barrier keeps me at bay.

How can I protect and comfort my babe when she insists on keeping him around?

She knows this, but when he smiles at her, she falls victim to his magic. A demon glamour. It has to be that. But he doesn't smell like a demon.

I wish she'd kick his butt back to Half Moon Lake in Washington where he belongs.

I don't think he belongs there either.

What in the six hundred sixty-six dimensions is he? The air around him tastes almost familiar, yet totally alien at the same time.

I think I should go diving in Mum's dump for another talisman to protect my babe, though I shudder to face the cold of Imp Haven. Freeze-dried body parts are not comfortable at all. But is Cape Cod any warmer?

Then, too, I'd have to traverse the chat room again. I wonder who's on duty today? Maybe the faeries have posted the j'appel dragons there. Pocket-sized flying mites that they are, I can flit past them with no trouble. They are actually smaller than me. Unless someone calls them by name. Then they jump to full size in two heartbeats. Can't get more than one full-sized dragon in the chat room at a time.

Trouble is, you never know what name a dragon is using today. It could be Hello. Or Jackknife. Or even Because. And just because he didn't use that name yesterday doesn't mean he's not using it today. Gotta keep my mouth shut around these guys.

I can't stay close to Tess while El Stinko is around, so I might as well try something useful at Imp Haven.

Chapter 10

*It was once believed that the shadowed areas of the
Moon were forests where the Goddess Diana hunted,
and the bright areas were plains.*

*L*OUD VOICES OUTSIDE drew me from the apartment back to the kitchen. I watched through the
window of the back door as Donovan and Gollum stood on
opposite sides of an unlit bonfire in the middle of the gravel
drive with my round maple breakfast table upside down on
top of the pile. The eight chairs and their bloodstained pads
stood around the fire in a circle, inviting people to sit and
toast marshmallows.

"What the hell do you think you are doing, Estevez,
burning up Tess' furniture and half her woodpile?" Gollum
screamed at Donovan. He flung his long arms about wildly,
his fist almost connecting with Donovan's jaw. His silver-
gilt bangs flopped into his eyes as his glasses slid down his
nose. At six-feet three-and-a-half inches, he towered over
Donovan's more modest five-eleven. But I was willing to
bet they weighed about the same. Gollum stood with his
big feet braced and fists clenched. Not a good sign from the
most nonviolent person I knew.

"Go back to your books, Smythe, and leave the real
work to those who were invited," Donovan sneered. He
kicked a loose log toward the pile.

"Invited? When were you invited. I live here!"

"Where, in the root cellar?"

"No, in the guest cottage, where I can watch her back."

"Fat chance she'd let you back into her life, let alone live here."

They both looked toward the house. By the light dawning in their eyes, I knew they could see me standing in the window. They both puffed out their chests in high dudgeon. (I love that phrase and use it in my books whenever I can.)

The schoolteacher in me knew I should break it up. I needed both these men at the moment. Having them at each other's throats wouldn't help.

But a perverse imp of mischief deep inside me made me step back and watch the fireworks. The bonfire wasn't even lit yet.

Donovan took one aggressive step closer to Gollum. "Get off this property, van Der Hoyden-Smythe, before I throw you off."

"I'd like to see you try." Gollum unzipped his down parka and eased his shoulders. He shifted his feet to a balanced stance, not quite an *en garde,* nor did it look like a standard martial arts stance. Something more esoteric. Probably just as effective.

Uh-oh. Time to intervene.

"We can't light the fire until Allie gets here with the burn permit," I called, descending the two steps from the mudroom to the yard. "In the meantime, I could use some help taking down the soiled curtains so we can burn them, too."

I turned back toward the kitchen, hoping the circling dogs would declare a truce before they engaged in an all out territorial battle. The alpha bitch had spoken.

I hoped.

"What's going on, Tess?" Gollum asked the moment we all stepped into the warmth of the kitchen.

I avoided looking at the bare nook. "Grab some coffee and meet me in the parlor. It's the warmest room in the house."

They followed me, still keeping a substantial distance between them while trying to stay closest to me. A little hard in the narrow confines of the butler's pantry between the kitchen and the dining room. Dill danced around all three of us, fading in and out of the woodwork to keep from having to share space with our bodies. He frowned during the entire trek.

Gollum tripped on the two-inch step down into the dining room. He flopped around but strangely did not spill a single drop of coffee from his cup.

Donovan grinned and didn't offer to steady his balance. They stared at each other suspiciously as we passed the entrance to the apartment.

We twisted past the chaos of my office, the long room of the original saltbox. The front door of the house that faced the street stood between the office and library, but I'd sealed it for the winter. No one used it anyway since the driveway and gravel parking were closer to the kitchen door. The very steep old stairs opposite the entry led to my bedroom. I led the men to the other side of the office and into my parlor.

I checked for a sign of Scrap swinging on the spider over the fire, his favorite spot. He was still AWOL.

Finally we came to a halt in the sitting room that shared a chimney with the office and the library.

"Now isn't this cozy. Your own private harem, Tess. Oh, do they call men a harem? If I'd known you were into polyandry, I'd have killed you before I died. Isn't that what they call divorce Italian style?" Dill sat stiffly in a corner of the sleeper sofa. No humor lightened his quips. His eyes glowed red with anger.

Donovan peered around as if mapping an escape route. Gollum settled easily into the wingback chair closest to the fireplace and plunked his feet onto the matching ottoman. Just like I knew he would. I took the matching chair. That left Donovan with the sofa beneath the window that overlooked the side yard and a screening copse between the house and Old King Highway. He'd have to share it with Dill. Did he sense the ghost's presence? Why else would he press himself into the arm, occupying as small a space as possible.

"Want to talk about it?" Gollum asked casually, as if he were a psychologist and I his patient.

For all I knew, he might have a psychology degree among the long list of academic letters after his name.

I took a deep breath, closed my eyes, and told them

everything from the moment WindScribe ran out of nowhere into the freezing street, stark naked. They didn't need to know about Dill. If they stayed long enough, I was sure they'd see his ghost eventually.

And the Windago? Not now. Later. I wasn't alone and vulnerable with these two around.

Donovan whistled through his teeth and shrank back as far as he could into the stiff cushions of the country style blue-and-cream sofa.

"What do you know?" Gollum pinned him with an accusing glare.

"That we don't want to wait for that burn permit." Donovan jumped to his feet and stalked back toward the kitchen. Dill followed close on his heels, as if tied to him in some way.

"Why?" I inserted myself in front of his broad frame. Too close. The heat of his emotions—anger, worry, and something else I couldn't identify—nearly swamped my senses. I gritted my teeth and held my ground.

"Because those garden gnomes are Orculli trolls. If we don't burn the bodies quickly, they'll reanimate and with twice as many teeth and less sense. You've also got to get some bleach into the spilled blood fast to keep it from re-animating on its own."

"And if we burn them?" Gollum had also regained his feet. He pushed his glasses back up his nose and focused his eyes on something beyond my shoulder.

A quick glance where he looked confirmed that he really gazed into another world, or deep inside himself, not on me or Donovan.

"If we do it right now, then the bodies and the spilled blood will remain dead." Donovan pushed me aside, grabbed his leather jacket from where he'd dropped it on my desk chair and a box of matches from the mantel and stalked back the way we'd come.

The phone on my big rolltop desk chirped. I cursed and thought about ignoring it.

"Better grab that. With all that's going on, you never know who it might be," Gollum advised quietly.

"Yeah?" I barked into the receiver.

"Teresa Louise, I'll forgive your rudeness this time, but

only because I'm sooooooo happy," my mother crooned in her light Québécois accent. She sounded excited. Soon she'd devolve into the bastard French she had made up out of childhood memories and called a pure language but wasn't much more than baby talk.

She didn't need much provocation.

"Mom?" This didn't sound like my mother, the control freak harpy who hadn't been happy a single day since Dad left her and their three children for Bill, the love of his life.

"Yes, Teresa, your mother. Your wonderfully ecstatic mother." She said something else in French that I couldn't catch. I speak, read, and understand Parisian French. Mom's dialect had little in common with it.

"Mom, what's going on?" I crossed my eyes and tried to picture my mother ecstatic, or anything but disapproving.

"I'm getting married!"

My knees gave out. I fumbled for the rolling office chair.

Gollum guided me. "Breathe, Tess," he whispered. "In on my count, one, two, three. Out, one, two, three. That's good. Again. Keep breathing."

"Who?" was all I could manage to ask. I waved Gollum off.

"The most beautiful man in the world, Tess. He's tall. He's dark. He's handsome. And he loves me!"

"When did this all happen, Mom?" She'd only been in Florida three weeks. I had visions of a Latino Lothario out to marry Mom for my money. I might not have a lot of cash on hand, but my royalty checks twice a year had started looking very pleasing. And I owned the house and land, which was worth a whole lot more than it was when Dill and I bought it.

"Time means nothing when you're in love, Teresa. You taught me that when you ran off and married Dillwyn."

That was a first. She usually refused to acknowledge that Dill and I had even legally married. Just because we ran off to Reno for a quick and private ceremony, the same weekend we met at High Desert Con, didn't make the union any less legal.

"Um, Mom, this doesn't sound like you."

"I've never been more me in my life!"

Now I really was worried. "When am I going to meet this man, Mom. You haven't even told me his name."

"Darren. His name is Darren Estevez. And we'll be there in an hour. Your sister Cecilia is driving us home from the airport in Providence now."

I gulped and jerked my head toward the kitchen, wishing I had a window through three rooms to the drive where *Donovan* Estevez lit a cleansing bonfire. *Donovan* Estevez who might be half demon.

"And I think you know Darren's son, Teresa. His son is Donovan Estevez. That casino owner you met back in Washington."

So what did that make his father? He couldn't be a full demon and take human shape in this dimension. He'd need to be in the chat room or his home dimension to do that. Maybe Donovan inherited his demonic tendencies from his mother. A mother very much out of the picture for Darren, Mom's fiancé.

Now I was totally confused.

Chapter 11

*F*RANTIC DOESN'T BEGIN to describe the next hour.

"New plan," I announced to the two men in front of the bonfire. "Donovan, you and your father get the guesthouse. Gollum, take the apartment. MoonFeather gets the sleeper sofa in the sitting room, Mom goes upstairs in the guest room next to me." I wanted my mother as far away from the demon contingent as possible.

If Darren had even a fraction of Donovan's charismatic charm, she was easy bait.

I already had WindScribe in the attic. I doubted the house was this full when it was a fully functional bed and breakfast.

Maybe if I charged them all rent . . .

"Won't your mom want to sleep with her fiancé?" Gollum asked, seemingly innocently. His glasses, firmly on the bridge of his nose for once, hid his true emotions. Then he flashed a goading grin toward Donovan.

"My mother is a French-Canadian-Catholic-June-Cleaver. She sleeps upstairs. Alone," I snarled. I seemed to be doing a lot of that lately.

Then Allie showed up with the burn permit. Sans the infant Mike in tow. She stepped out of her squad car and surveyed the landscape and the two men with the keen interest of both a woman and a good cop. Her beloved monster SUV was in the shop. She had to settle for a sedan with studded tires.

"Did you get the permit for me?" I asked anxiously. "And where's Mike?"

She pulled a folded piece of paper out of her inside jacket pocket as she approached, long legs eating up the distance at about twice my speed though she looked casual and unhurried. When she got within three feet of me, she carefully returned the permit to her pocket.

"Allie?"

"You promised to tell me what is going on, Tess. I left Mike doing paperwork, so feel free to tell me anything. *Anything.* Now would be a good time." She raised her eyebrows at the sight of the table and chairs, the curtains, and my parka on and around the bonfire. "That's good furniture to waste on a pagan religious rite. And I happen to know you are pretty agnostic if not downright atheist."

She gulped and her eyes went wide, fixed upon the splotches of blood on the chair cushions.

"Do I need to get a crime scene team out here and arrest somebody?" Her hands hovered over her radio and her weapon.

"Um . . . No more than you did this morning." I tried to signal with my eyes and my chin that I'd faced down alone the same unexplainable bad guys she'd seen before.

"And just what did happen this morning?"

"Um . . ."

Donovan fixed her with a feral grin. "This is what happened." He reached into the guts of the bonfire and delicately withdrew one of the Orculli trolls. He held it gingerly by the coat between his thumb and index finger, careful not to let any of the blood touch him.

"That's not a run-of-the-mill plastic garden gnome, is it?" Allie gulped. She looked a little pale, as if she could no longer dismiss this morning as a nightmare that didn't really happen.

"Let's go inside and talk about this. . . ." I grabbed Allie by the elbow and tugged.

She planted her feet and hitched her utility belt.

"I've got to call someone with more authority. We have to alert the feds. There is a paranormal unit in the FBI even though they don't advertise it. They should already be on their way to investigate this WindScribe person." She grabbed her radio.

"Allison Marie Engstrom," Donovan said quietly. How the hell did he know her full name? "Look at me." He smiled that wicked grin of his.

Allie's face went slack, and her eyes glazed over.

"If word of this gets out," Donovan chanted, "people will panic. The roads are a mess. How will you safely evacuate the Cape if people can't drive? How will you explain this to normal God-fearing people? Think about the chaos and the danger if you tell anyone."

"I can't tell anyone," Allie agreed in a monotone. Her eyes glazed over. Her lips moved, but her voice seemed to come from Donovan.

"Now come inside and help me clean up while Donovan lights the fire." I tugged on Allie's arm, and she docilely followed me into the kitchen.

The moment we cleared the threshold and got out of range of Donovan's smile, Allie's face cleared. Panic filled the blankness. "Oh, my God! We have to stop him. We can't let him burn the evidence." She turned to dash out the door again.

A whoosh of rapidly heated air pressed against the windows. Flames exploded into life and hungrily ate at the bonfire.

Not a natural fire. More of Donovan's demon magic?

"Too late, Allie. He's already started the fire. The bodies are at the heart of that conflagration." Sure enough, an awful stench filled the air. I slammed the door closed once more.

Goddess, my heating bill was going to eat up most of the money the publisher owed me for turning in the book if people didn't stop coming and going, leaving the door open. And Donovan had pilfered most of my remaining woodpile. Could I get another cord of wood this late in the season?

"But . . . but . . ."

"No buts about it, Allie. We can't let this information

past the door. Even to the FBI. I have to have your promise that you won't breathe a word of this to anyone." I stood solidly in front of the door, feet braced, hands on hips. I automatically shifted my weight, ready to launch myself into a wrestler's lunge to stop her if I had to.

Allie seemed to shrink in on herself. "This isn't right, Tess."

"You don't have any evidence anymore."

"I'd call the blood painting your kitchen evidence."

As she spoke, one of the splotches began to move, slithering into the rough outline of a gnome, complete with hat, coat, striped stockings and pointy shoes. And teeth. Lots and lots of teeth. They took shape before the rest of the face.

From one heartbeat to the next it took on three dimensions.

Heart in my mouth, I threw an entire basin of bleach at the thing. "Please, oh please, let this be enough. I don't have the energy to fight them again," I murmured.

The blood dissolved into a pink puddle. Was that a screech of a death rattle humming behind my ears?

I sank to the floor with a sigh of relief.

Allie stood there for a long moment, mouth agape, eyes wide and horrified. Then she swallowed heavily and regained a bit of composure. "So what do we do next? You know you can't exclude me. I'm part of this."

"The next step is to clean up this mess and con Zeb Falwell into letting me have that antique pine table in his showroom for a decent price, and deliver it within the hour. It's been sitting there for two years. He should be anxious to get rid of it. He's only three blocks away. Maybe Gollum can fetch it in his van."

As I filled the basin with fresh bleach water, I related the latest development with my mother. I didn't tell her that I assumed Darren Estevez was part Damiri demon.

"I can't believe Genevieve is really going to put the past behind her and marry again." Allie shook her head as she shed her jacket and donned rubber gloves.

"It will seem kind of strange for Mom not to have a reason to complain about Dad deserting her, leaving her dependent on her ungrateful children." Financially, she didn't have to be dependent. Dad paid gobs of alimony every month. He and I handled her bills. Emotionally, she had reverted to the age of thirteen.

Come to think about it, on the phone she sounded like a giddy adolescent with her first crush.

I handed Allie the basin and then dialed the local antiques emporium.

Somehow in the next hour we managed to get enough of the bonfire burned to disguise the fact that I'd trashed my own furniture, I conned the local antique dealer into delivering a plank table with six chairs for two thirds the asking price, stuffed Mom's clothes into the guest bedroom next to mine and installed Gollum in the apartment. Donovan unloaded his own gear into the cottage, grumbling all the while. I didn't catch his exact words but got the impression he wasn't happy about sharing digs with his dad. I also made up the sleeper sofa for MoonFeather even though she wasn't due to be discharged from the hospital until the next day.

WindScribe drifted downstairs three times, trailing her fingers along the wainscoting or pieces of furniture as if checking for dust.

I figured she was too wobbly to stand on her own two feet and was keeping something close at hand to catch herself. She continued to hum that white rabbit thing. A promise of more pills—that I never delivered—got her back into bed and out of the way.

"WindScribe—if she truly is the woman who disappeared twenty-eight years ago—her real name is Joyce Milner," Allie said after the first appearance of the girl. She poured lemon oil onto the faded and worn tabletop, rubbing it in with an aggressive stroke.

I sensed a lot of frustration in her work.

"Can we send her home to her parents?" I asked hopefully. "If you haven't noticed, my house is full to overflowing." I scrubbed the walls around the table, trying desperately to get out every trace of the dried blood. I'd have to run to the new discount store on the highway to find something resembling curtains, chair pads, and coordinating place mats and napkins. Nothing less would please my mother. Or me. I like a coordinated and well ordered kitchen when I'm not ignoring reality while on a tight deadline.

Speaking of which, I still had four chapters to finish editing.

"Presuming she really is Joyce Milner/WindScribe—we don't have any fingerprints or DNA samples in the cold case file, and we didn't get any hits on her prints on any of the networks. I've ordered a DNA test to match her against Milner's father. But that's going to take to the middle of next week, with the weekend coming up and the backlog. Dental records came up blank. Seems Milner's mother didn't believe in dentists." Allie shook her head and applied more of her considerable elbow grease to the table.

"Milner Dad is in a nursing home with Alzheimer's," she continued with grunted punctuation. "Milner Mom hasn't been heard from since she locked up her husband two years ago. Local opinion is that he's better off in the nursing home without her."

"That good a marriage?" I quipped. The particularly stubborn stain beneath the table must be Orculli troll blood rather than MoonFeather's. It was as big as my fist and *would not* come out. I could barely keep enough bleach on it to keep it from reanimating.

"We do have a medical record of WindScribe having a broken arm at age ten. Possibly caused by the mom. They took a couple X rays this morning to rule out injury under her bruises. Our WindScribe has an old break in the same place. Little enough evidence to claim she is who she is, though."

"My wireless card isn't talking to your router," Gollum said from the doorway. He pushed up his glasses and peered appreciatively at Allie—who was still in uniform and officially supposed to be supervising the burn.

Something bitter twisted in my midsection.

"If it can't wait, then boot up my computer and get the protocols off it. It's not password protected," I snapped rather than deal with strange and unwanted emotions. "Is your cat locked in the apartment?"

"Of course. Gandalf is very well behaved."

"Like hell he is," I muttered.

He wandered off.

"So that's the new anthro prof at the community college," Allie breathed through her teeth. "Where did you find him? And why didn't you tell me about him?" She preened a bit, smoothing her uniform over her lush figure.

"He found me. And if you can drag his attention away from his books and the Internet, go for it, Allie." I redoubled my efforts with the scrub brush on the stain, not certain if I felt relief or anxiety at my last comment.

"He's so . . . tall," she said with a sigh and dumped more lemon oil into the pine. Tall was definitely a priority for Allie in her search for her soul mate. She had a hard enough time finding any men she liked and she could trust, who were not criminals or fellow cops. Allie did not mix her personal and professional life. Ever.

She'd told me once that she got to know her workmates too well and often saw the ugly and brutish side of them when handling lawbreakers. Dealing with scumbag criminals brought that side of her out too often, and she didn't want to have to live with it or be reminded of it during her precious free time.

"So, you want to tell me now what's going on?"

"My mom is returning home suddenly with a surprise fiancé."

"That's not what I mean. Like where WindScribe came from? Like why you are burning garden gnomes that came to life? Really ugly garden gnomes, not those cute things the garden club sells. And why your kitchen was smeared with enough blood to overload the blood bank?"

The blood that was still left must be MoonFeather's since it stayed in place.

"You don't want to know, Allie." I couldn't meet her gaze.

"But I do want to know. I have a right to know." Allie abandoned her polishing and hunkered down beside me. "I'm more than the local cop. I'm your best friend, Tess. There's a lot of strange in your life, I've seen some of it, and you need to talk about it."

"Trust me, Allison Engstrom, you do not want to be dragged into the strangeness that is my life now." This time I pierced her with a firm glare worthy of Miss Wilcox, our third-grade teacher.

"In case you haven't noticed, I am involved. I got you the emergency burn permit so you can destroy the evidence of weird bodies. I'm helping you scrub blood off the floor and walls. I *saw* WindScribe step through a doorway from . . . elsewhere. A woman who should be as old as your aunt but looks ten years younger than you or me. I watched you attack those gnomes with a really weird weapon that appeared and disappeared in an eye blink. So what's going on, Tess? Or do I have to take you down to the station?"

"This isn't a Saturday night brawl at McT's Bar and Grill."

"I'm a cop, Tess. Not much in this world scares me."

"This should. It isn't part of this world."

She sat back on her heels a moment, thumbs in her gun belt, thinking. "Okay. Shoot. I'll believe weird. Couldn't be much weirder than skinny little you tossing McT's bouncer over your shoulder last January when he got a little too fresh."

"That was balance and training, not supernatural."

"And the other stuff?"

"Read my books."

"I did."

"They're real."

"Not the post-apocalyptic world part, I'm guessing."

I kept my silence.

"The Sisterhood with the imps and enchanted blade weapons?"

Again I let silence speak for me.

"You one of them?"

I nodded.

"Of course you are. That's where you were during the year you went missing after Dill died. Okay. So how come you've got *two* luscious men drooling after you, and I don't have one?" She cocked me a grin and returned to her lemon oil and rags. But she was really looking out the window at Donovan and Gollum at the bonfire.

"I don't have two. And I'm not sure I want the one. He doesn't always tell the truth, and when I do get a few words out of him, it's only half what I asked." That could apply to either Gollum or Donovan.

"Look again, Tess. They're both in love with you. Let me know which one you really want and I'll take the other."

Before I could issue a sharp retort, gravel in the drive crunched under the heavy tires of my sister Cecilia's double cab pickup.

Chapter 12

The term "Honeymoon" comes from the custom of providing the bride and groom a moon's worth of mead, a honey wine, to ensure fertility.

*E*L STINKO DONOVAN doesn't smell like anything normal on this plane, if you can smell anything beyond his cloying cologne—too much is not better than nothing, dahling. So how can he and Darren be related, if they don't smell alike? Mom and Tess have smells of kinship. Cecilia belongs in the same circle. Tess and Cecilia have a similar bond with Moon-Feather. All born of common factors in their blood.

Darren, the dad, is part demon. I know it. I feel it in my bones and in my nose. My internal combustion engine pumps overtime and flashes me bright red. I want to witch myself into the Celestial Blade the moment he steps out of Cecilia's truck.

Cecilia likes the big tires and heavy engine truck so she can blow lesser vehicles off the road. It makes her feel like she is in control. Now, if she'd just gain control over her figure and her clothes, she wouldn't need to drive that phallic symbol. You'd think if she needed to make such a bold statement, she could pick a pretty color for the truck, like pink or basic black. That dirty mustard yellow makes her skin look so sallow she can't do anything with it.

She should have paid more attention to her mom.

Mom does classic so well, you'd think her daughters would have inherited *some* fashion sense.

Back to D & D. D the dad has the classic silver wings of hair at his temples, and the portly figure of a Damiri demon. His name begins with a D and ends with and N. He even has that extra flap of skin under his arms where he hides his batwings when he's in human form. The whiff of ultra dough I get from his titanium credit cards and the gold chain about his neck also tell me he has Damiri connections. They are all as rich as Bill Gates. They just don't advertise it.

At least he dresses well. I love that microfiber jacket. Looks like brushed silk, or maybe very fine suede in a lovely buff color. I'd forgotten how beautiful men can be. (purr) But his khaki slacks and pink-and-green-flowered shirt won't cut it in Cape Cod. Especially in this weather.

Donovan has decent fashion sense if you go for that brooding all black look. He's got the hair of a Damiri. He's got the name. But he's lean and fit and he doesn't have a trace of wings beneath his arms.

And he lost all his money last year when the casino imploded down a rogue demon portal.

"What is that!" Mom exploded the moment her feet touched the gravel. She pointed over the kitchen door. She didn't even notice that the melting snow soaked her casual shoes, or that the wind must be cutting through her light sweater like a broadsword through leather armor.

I spun to see what strangeness had offended her. At least she hadn't pinned her attention on the bonfire.

A bleached white bone skull, bigger than a dead steer's in the desert, with spikes that would put a Texas longhorn to shame protruding from its head. Eight horseshoes ringed the skull, all with their open end pointing up so the luck wouldn't drain out.

It's your new gargoyle, Scrap whispered in my ear from the top of the chimney. The closest he could get to Donovan.

"Why, Mom, it's nice to see you, too." I gave her a hug and ushered her toward the door. "You must be freezing. Come inside and get warm. We'll do introductions there. Your friend can unload the luggage. I've put him and his son in the guest cottage. You're bunking with me."

Good move, dahling. He can rest in his natural form out there. Keep him happier and less mean during the day. Scrap yawned, exposing three rows of teeth that rivaled those of the dead gnomes for sharpness and plentitude.

"Really, Genevieve, I knew your daughter was rebellious, but that pagan idol is too much." Darren shuddered and looked at the sky rather than the house. "I cannot enter such an ungodly house."

The gargoyle! Scrap chortled. *He can't enter the house.*

Scrap, what is it and where did it come from?

I grabbed it from Mum's home in Imp Haven. You can find anything in the freeze-dry garbage dump of the universe.

He wiggled all over in delight.

"So they're demons," I muttered sotto voce.

"Did you say demons?" Mom asked. Her eyes narrowed and I could almost see her running calculations in her head. "I'd say that skull is demonic." She dug in her heels and refused to budge.

"It's just a resin sculpture, Mom. I picked it up at a con. And I said lemons, not demons. We need lemons for the fish sauce I'm planning for tomorrow night."

"Speaking of food, what are you planning on feeding this crew *tonight*?" Cecilia asked. A malicious gleam in her eyes told me she knew the state of my refrigerator. Empty.

"We can have pizza or Chinese delivered. That is unless you plan on cooking," I replied sweetly. I met my sister's gaze.

Pure malice poured from her. She was older than me and our brother Stephen, shorter than me by almost one half inch, and heavier by fifty pounds. She resented every breath I took, and had ever since I was born. Especially since I lost my extra poundage when I had the imp flu three years ago. Now I ate everything I wanted and didn't gain an ounce.

Staying thin was part of my revenge for the horrible trick she played on me with a bat costume when I was three. She was the source of my phobia.

"Genevieve," Darren pointed to the dragon skull over the door.

"Tess, be a dear and take that horrible thing down."

I jerked my head and Donovan leaped to obey. Donovan? How could he touch the damn thing if his father couldn't even get close to it?

A memory of something back in the Citadel . . .

Sister Gert had just said prayers for the newly repaired refectory roof. She'd invoked the powers of the dozens of copper gargoyles to keep out all those who harbored evil in their hearts.

Before I could remember what had happened next, Donovan climbed onto an overturned half barrel that had once held potting soil and tulips. His long arms reached the skull easily. "I'll just put this somewhere safe," he muttered after he had lifted it free of its supporting hook.

"Like over the old staircase?" I quipped. That ought to keep Darren out of my mother's bedroom. So how did I keep her out of his?

"You really should consider your obligations as hostess, Tess," Cecilia admonished me as we trooped inside. She already had her head in the refrigerator and half the cupboards open. They really were empty.

"Actually, I'd planned to take Tess out to dinner tonight," Donovan jumped into the conversation. "Since you didn't give us any warning, I'm sure you can fend for yourselves."

"I'm sure I told you I was coming when I called you last night, D," Darren said. He clapped his son on the back hard enough to make Donovan stumble.

"No, you didn't," Donovan growled. "I thought I had Cape Cod to myself."

"Why don't Allie and Gollum come with us?" I returned Donovan's smile, trying to hide my grimace and my questions at his last comment.

Scrap said that Donovan's father reeked of demon scent. Therefore, Donovan must also be a demon. I couldn't trust him alone. I'd seen what demons—even half-blood demons—did when their natures overcame the thin gloss of civilization a human form gave them. So why did my insides still turn to liquid and my skin tingle in anticipation of his touch?

I needed a buffer between us. I also needed a breather from my mother. Why not do a little matchmaking between Allie and Gollum on the side?

But that would leave Mom alone with Darren. Presumably, she'd been alone with him down in Florida.

I gnashed my teeth in indecision.

He won't hurt Mom yet, Scrap whispered from the far reaches of the house. *He wants something, so he can't dispose of her until he gets it.*

I really didn't like the idea of any of us being disposable.

"But if you all aren't here, it will spoil our surprise," Mom whined. "I want the whole family together tonight."

The crowd had stalled in the kitchen. Like they always did. It was usually the most inviting room in the house. But I couldn't get beyond the stench of bleach and blood; the image of an Orculli troll taking a hunk out of MoonFeather; the crunch of breaking bones as I impaled one of the beasts with my Celestial Blade.

"Dinner sounds good to me. Pick me up at six-thirty," Allie called as she hastily exited. She'd disposed of the evidence of our speedy cleanup. "Much as I'd love to stay and watch the fireworks, I've got to file some reports and clock out at the station." She waved jauntily and closed the door firmly behind her. Leaving me alone with my family and assorted extras.

"Surprise isn't always good, Mom. Tomorrow we'll invite Dad and Bill and Cecilia and Jim and their kids to come, too, make a big celebration of it. MoonFeather will be here, too. She's been hurt. I offered to take care of her before I knew you were coming home."

We settled around the new table with coffee and some stale cookies I found in the freezer and hastily nuked. Mom and Darren scooted their chairs so close together they might have been made from the same boards. They held hands atop the table and rubbed thighs beneath it.

"We met at a dance in Cousin Clothilde's condo on the beach," Mom gushed.

"She was the prettiest woman in the room. I couldn't look at anyone else," Darren picked up the story. He spoke with a faint accent that I couldn't place. It might have been

Spanish, from Spain with the Hapsburg lisp not generic Mexican, but I couldn't place it exactly.

I watched Gollum mouth the words, a puzzled look on his face as he, too, tried to place the accent. Professor Guilford Van der Hoyden-Smythe spoke four or five living languages and read a couple of dead ones. He claimed he could learn an American Indian dialect in six weeks. He also claimed that his family had studied and archived demons for generations. Surely he'd find the origins of that accent if anyone could. Any human, that is.

"It was love at first sight," Mom sighed.

"True love, everlasting love," Darren echoed.

I'd known that kind of love. With Dill. How could I fault Mom for falling head over heels for such a charming man?

A demon. I had to remind myself. Darren was a demon. And he was using my mother.

Donovan smiled at me, and I grew hot all over. That was his magic. He could calm a riot with that smile. I'd seen him do it. He'd lulled Allie's cop instincts and suspicions. He could also make a woman fall in love with him.

The only time I could resist him was when I wore a magical hair comb Scrap had given me. It allowed me to see through demon glamour to the man beneath. Except with Donovan I saw only a man, no demon hiding beneath the surface. I'd never figured out his strange aura though: an inviting golden glow laced with a tight black chain. Darkness and light. Good and evil.

Most people had both elements in their souls.

"Mom, I have an engagement present for you. I want you to wear it on your wedding day." I kissed the top of her head as I retreated to my bedroom where I'd stashed the comb. Right now, Mom needed it more than me.

The best offense was a good defense. Mom needed all the help she could get defending herself from that man . . . demon.

A quick check on WindScribe showed her dreaming happily in her bed. With the vial of tranquilizers beside her.

Damn. I knew I should have flushed them. But right now, having this extra guest sound asleep seemed advantageous. I pocketed the tranquilizers.

When I returned to the kitchen, I paused a moment in the narrow entry from the butler's pantry. Curious, I gathered up my mop of sandy-blonde curls and jammed the comb into them.

Instantly colors shifted and intensified. My balance tilted as well. When the moment of disorientation cleared, I peered closely at Darren and Donovan. As I expected, Darren assumed an aura with a bat's sharp features and furred face overlaying his handsome human countenance.

Now that I knew for sure, I had to stop this marriage. One way or another, even if I had to kill Darren. In open battle or by stealth.

Donovan remained enigmatic. I could see layers of energy radiating out from him, red and orange swirling together in an angry mix above the gold and black I'd seen before. At no point did his aura touch Darren's. Indeed, they seemed to repulse each other.

On the other hand, Mom and Cecilia seemed joined. Their energies reached out to each other in a blood bond. They also included me. No matter our likes and dislikes, the baggage of sibling rivalries and parent child differences, we were family.

Darren and Donovan were not related.

But I still couldn't figure out who or what drove Donovan.

<hr />

"How sweet of you, Teresa Louise," Mom gushed as I fitted the comb into her French roll. Her hair was thinning and quite straight, as was Cecilia's, but she insisted a lady always kept her hair long and wore it up. My mop of tight curls tended to tangle and frizz if I let it get too long. Mom'd look ten years younger if she cut hers properly and let it frame her face.

I tried to be gentle with the metal tines, but still Mom grimaced as the comb took hold. I'd experienced the same thing the first few times I wore it. The comb grabbed hold of more than just hair.

Darren clenched his fists tight. He looked as if he was about to launch himself over the table to strangle me.

Come and get me, big boy. I've taken out more hideous critters than you.

Donovan just grinned.

"There now, that looks lovely, Mom," I said as I settled in my chair with my cold cup of coffee.

"It's going to take some getting used to," Mom said. She tugged the magical artifact free of her hair, keeping her eyes closed.

Damn!

"But it will look nice supporting a veil. I do so want a traditional wedding gown and veil." She sighed and placed both her hands on Darren's. "Will you mind terribly, *cheri*, if we wait a few weeks to book the church and send invitations?"

"Not too long, *querida*," Darren murmured. "My love burns with impatience." He leaned over to kiss her. Their lips met in an explosion of passion. Arms around each other, they lingered and tongued, and explored.

I had to look away in embarrassment. Even Cecilia had the grace to blush. An unnatural silence descended upon the table as that kiss went on and on. Well beyond the bounds of propriety.

Anyone else and I'd have told them to get a room.

The comb sat on the table in front of Mom. The gold filigree sparkled in the reflected light from the hanging milk glass lamp. I stared at it mesmerized, even after Mom and Darren broke their teenage-style clinch.

The conversation resumed and flowed around me, I continued to study the tiny gold flowers interlaced with Celtic knotwork on the comb. I picked out stylized symbols from an assortment of cultures: Russian, Irish, French, Italian, Jewish, Arabian, and even an Aztec feathered something. In my perusal, I noticed a blank spot with a few rough edges. An important piece had broken off.

What? Possibly whatever was missing kept me from identifying Donovan.

Scrap and I needed to talk. But Scrap wouldn't, or couldn't, come near me when Donovan was in the room.

If Darren's demonhood ever overrode Donovan's barriers, I wanted to save it for a real fight.

Tonight I'd leave Scrap to keep an eye on Mom and Darren, WindScribe, too, while I went to dinner with Donovan, Gollum, and Allie.

Chapter 13

"THE SUMMER I GRADUATED from high school, Dad and Bill took me and my brother Steph to England. I loved the gargoyles on the cathedrals. Much to my dismay, no one would let me climb onto the roofs to examine them more closely," I explained to Gollum.

I held the dragon skull. He measured the support beam across the old stairs. The steps rose so steeply that even I had to duck beneath the upper story where it cut across them. Gollum had no problem reaching the beam with tape measure and marking pencil.

"Have you ever heard gargoyles gargle?" he asked in all seriousness.

"Actually, I have heard gargoyles gargle," I replied, handing him a hammer and the hook to hang my new treasure.

A blur of white movement behind and below me. Gollum's cat, Gandalf, had got loose. As long as Scrap didn't complain, I'd leave the beast free for a while. At the moment Scrap was busy playing voyeur on Mom and Darren while they ordered pizza in the kitchen. Donovan had retreated to the cottage across the yard with a scowl on his face and his fists clenched like sledgehammers.

"The term gargoyle comes from the Medieval French _gargouiller,_ to gargle." He pronounced the long word melodiously.

I'd read it but never heard it before. "Because of the sound they make when rainwater funnels through them, as they drain it from roofs and spit it out in arcs to the ground below," I completed the lecture for him. "Their primary purpose is a kind of decorative gutter and downspout. The idea of using grotesqueries to repel evil came later."

He looked at me strangely. Then a big grin spread across his face. "A woman after my own heart," he sighed. "I heard them during an autumnal thunderstorm in Notre Dame de Paris. I have friends. Next time you go to Europe, I'll see about getting you a pass to explore the gargoyles more thoroughly."

"I heard them at the Citadel. The refectory roof had copper gargoyles. But one of them was broken. I noticed the tracery of a wing left behind when I helped repair the roof. It might have been a bat."

"Bats are a quite common form of gargoyle. Your phobia against bats has roots in ancient times." Gollum actually stopped speaking for a few moments while he hammered the hook in place. "Did you know that the Native American totem pole can be considered a form of gargoyle?"

"Actually the totemic animals are more clan symbols than wards against evil."

I handed him the dragon skull. Then a bit of mischief lightened my mind. "The gargoyles at the Citadel did have apotropaic qualities. Sister Gert invoked them to repel all those who held evil in their hearts and darkness in their souls."

That was it. That was the memory that had eluded me. When I tried to enter the refectory after the prayers of dedication, Scrap disappeared for a time. I remembered thinking I'd heard something splash in the puddle directly behind me. But it could have been anyone. In the middle of the prayers a thunderstorm had hit and the gargoyles did their job of channeling the runoff out and away from those of us huddled under the eaves. Except where the broken bat had been. Water cascaded straight down on top of Sister Gert's head.

"If you know that word, I'll have to challenge you to a game of Scrabble later," Gollum said. He kept his eyes focused on getting the dragon straight and keeping it from drooping any lower than the already low support beam.

"If you know that word, you'll have to join us for family game night. We play cut-throat Trivial Pursuit every Sunday."

"It's a date. Um . . . I mean . . ." he blushed.

"Don't worry. I know what you mean."

We'd decided to put the dragon head in the corner where it was shadowed. Mom wouldn't be as likely to notice it there.

"Do you think this gargoyle will really keep Darren from sneaking up the stairs?" I asked, admiring the stately proportions of the thing.

"It should. Given its position, on the main support beam of the original 1753 house, it might also keep him from doing harm to any human inside the entire house."

"Let's hope so."

"Interesting that Donovan had no trouble holding it," Gollum mused. He stepped down six steps to admire his handiwork. That put him two steps below me and close to my eye level.

"What is Donovan? Scrap says he's not a demon, but Darren is."

"Not one of the usual suspects. I'll put some feelers out into the community, see if my colleagues have any ideas."

"There's more than one of you? I thought the archivists who follow a rogue Celestial Warrior were rare."

"We are. As rare as you. But that number is increasing, or so I'm told. More and more rogue portals have cropped up in the last fifty years. The Warriors of the Celestial Blade have to spread out to cover them. Isolated Citadels aren't enough." He covered the intensity in his gaze by pushing up his glasses. "That aside, there are always scholars interested in obscure tales and legends though. I know most of them. My grandfather knows more. We'll find out what Donovan is whether he wants us to or not."

"Darren is not my father," Donovan growled. We sat in the front seats of Mom's car while Gollum escorted Allie from her apartment.

"I know," I replied, keeping my eyes straight ahead.

"How?"

I turned an enigmatic smile on him. Let him wonder about the powers of a Warrior of the Celestial Blade. At least I'd managed to change into tailored slacks and the new teal V-neck sweater Dad had given me for Christmas. Paired with the lavender silk turtleneck that Scrap recommended I presented a less scruffy image of a true warrior than usual.

Of course, a down parka over it all kind of marred the image.

But then we were all bundled up to combat the weather. So far it was all natural weather. The Windago hadn't shown up. Maybe she wanted me alone. Or whatever kept Scrap away from Donovan, also kept the Windago at bay.

"So if you aren't Darren's son, what are you?"

"I . . . was orphaned. As a teen. Darren took me in."

Too many pauses in there. Maybe the truth. But not all of it.

"So who was your father?"

"Don't know."

"Your mother?"

He rattled off a long string of liquid syllables. I didn't recognize the language.

"And that translates as . . ."

"No translation available. Her tribe has been absorbed by the Okanogan peoples. Just a few words of the original language exist."

"I thought you had Sanpoil Indian in you. They're part of the Colville Confederation, not Okanogan."

He didn't answer.

Gollum and Allie emerged from the apartment building's exterior stairwell onto the parking lot. They were laughing. He took her arm to steady her on the ice. The temperature had actually reached thirty-six this afternoon, melting a little snow, but quickly refreezing and becoming treacherous as soon as the sun went down.

Allie and Gollum laughed at something. She leaned

closer to him, almost resting her head on his shoulder. He didn't react to her attempted affection. But he didn't push her away either.

Something inside me twisted at the easy way my two friends seemed to fit together.

"The Orculli trolls won't give up, Tess. Everyone in your house is in danger. What are you going to do about your mother?" Donovan changed the subject.

"What are *you* going to do about your father?"

"Actually, the garden gnomes are after WindScibe, not Genevieve," Gollum said, handing Allie into the backseat. He gave my mother's name the proper French pronunciation, *Jahn-vee-ev* with the soft G. "Between the new gargoyle and the wards I set, I don't think they'll hit the house tonight."

Maybe they'd keep the Windago away. Forever.

"What makes you think that?" Donovan asked, immediately defensive.

"Because there is a strange sort of twisted honor among demons on a mission. And these guys sound like they are on a mission. Tess is the vowed protector. The Orculli will honor that and wait until Tess is there to defend the girl before taking her. We have until tomorrow." Gollum climbed into the car and closed the door on the weather and the subject.

A fat waxing moon three days off of full broke through the cloud cover, promising an even colder night.

Well past the waxing quarter moon when the Goddess Kynthia was wont to show her face in the sky in warning. I'd seen it twice. Special moments when I felt connected to the entire universe. A demon attack had followed immediately after. Both times.

Somehow, I didn't think the Orculli were limited to moon phases for their entry and exit from this realm. They might not even need the chat room.

"When they come, they won't be frightened off by a few whacks from your blade, Tess," Donovan warned. "We need a plan."

"We need fire," Gollum added.

"We need barricades and AK47s," Allie grumbled.

"Not enough," I mused. "We need the most elusive

defense of all. Information and logic. We have to know why they want WindScribe and what we can do to counter their motives."

So Darren the demon and Mom take over the sitting room, smooching and cuddling in front of the fire.

I assume my usual perch on the spider, swinging in time to the lilting waltz playing on the stereo. Show tunes. Stories and good music all rolled into one. What more can you ask for? I love them. So does Mom. That's one reason we get along so well, though she doesn't know I'm here.

Tess' taste runs to filk, New Age, and Celtic. Not bad. But nothing beats a show tune.

"I don't want to wait to make you mine, *ma petite chou chou,*" Darren whispers as he nuzzles Mom's neck.

I'll never figure out why the French think it's romantic to call each other little cabbages. Mom eats it up as if it was candy, practically purring like that wicked cat Gollum keeps in his rooms.

"I didn't get a church wedding the first time around," Mom pouts.

Liar, liar, pants on fire. Oops, that's my tail on fire. I jump down to the hearth and beat my poor mangled appendage against the hearth. A few embers fly free and die on the bricks.

Tess says Mom burned all her wedding photos when Dad walked out with Bill. Tess remembers seeing photos of a lavish wedding with lots of heavy white satin and banks of red-and-white flowers. They got married on Valentine's Day.

I'm pushing for April Fool's Day for this wedding.

"I will wait, if that is what makes you happy," Darren sighs as if he's making a huge sacrifice.

Mom soothes him by running a delicate finger along his cheek. Is that a hint of red in the glaze that comes over her eyes? She blinks and it's gone.

"Being married in the church with a priest officiating is very important to me. It makes the entire thing more real, a sacred bond."

Is that a shudder I detect running through Darren? Oh, my, I think he's afraid to step foot inside a church, sacred ground and all. Doesn't bother me. But then I'm not a demon, though my past isn't lily white. Just ask my one hundred two siblings. Darren is part demon, and I sense his past is darker than mine. That takes some doing.

"We could drive to Maine and get married tonight. I know a city clerk who can do the paperwork after hours and a lawyer who can perform the marriage. Any officer of the court can do that in Maine. Then we can have the priest bless the marriage later. Perhaps here in this beautiful old house," Darren said. A smile lit his face like he'd just thought up this brilliant idea.

Yeah, right. The conniving bastard's worse than a Barrister demon.

"But . . .?" Mom has to think about that one.

From the flush on her face and the way her hands keep wandering down his torso, she doesn't want to wait for the wedding night either.

I've got to stop this. Right now. Before Mom actually brings a demon into the family. If only I could force him to transform in front of her. But he's an old demon, well in control of his urges and his form.

What to do? What to do?

I know, I can let the cat loose. Gandalf will hiss and snarl at Darren. He doesn't like demons any more than I do.

Chapter 14

The oldest ring of holes at Stonehenge may have been used to mark the nineteen year cycle of lunar eclipses.

"*A*S WORRIED AS I AM about the Orculli return-ing and taking a hunk out of our flesh," Gollum said, resting his elbows on the round table in the corner of Guiseppe's Restaurant, "we also have to do something to prevent the impending marriage." He pushed his glasses up onto the bridge of his nose and blinked rapidly.

I knew that gesture. The eye blinks were his way of re-calling something he'd read. I think he sort of replayed a videotape in his brain.

"Waiting for the church and the priest will delay it until we deal with the garden gnomes," I replied.

"But aren't your parents divorced? Will the priest even allow your mother to remarry in the church?" Donovan jumped into the conversation. He and Gollum sat on oppo-site sides, as far away from each other as they could get and maintain this temporary truce.

"Mom had the marriage annulled in Rome. Seems that since Dad turned out to be gay, his marriage to Mom wasn't a real marriage after all," I replied studying the menu rather than look too closely at Donovan and be lost in his eyes and his smile. Without the comb to strip away some of the glamour of humanity, I could fall into his arms and his bed all too easily.

From the look on Allie's face, she wanted to fall into Gollum's bed. She just needed to find some way to let him know. But he was concentrating on the problem at hand. None of us mattered while he did that.

"Speaking of gay men," Allie whispered and jerked her head to the left toward the entrance.

Sure enough, Dad and Bill waited for the hostess to seat them. I waved to them.

Dad wandered over, leaving Bill to deal with the hostess. Bill was better with people than Dad. Dad prefers things he can reduce to a column of numbers with debits and credits. People outside his circle of family and a few close friends have too many variables for his taste. Even so, he manages to put on a polite and friendly, if baffled, face in front of strangers.

He gave me a hug, and I introduced him. He shook hands like a polite little puppet. Then he surprised me beyond measure. "Aren't you the friends who helped rescue my little girl from those terrorist kidnappers last fall?" He pulled up a chair from the adjoining table and sat between me and Donovan.

"Uh, yes," Gollum replied, trying to be truthful.

Actually I'd rescued myself and a Native American girl from tribal mythology come to life. But if we told the truth, we'd have to explain the unexplainable in Dad's black-and-white world of numbers that have to add up.

"Well, I want to thank you both for bringing my baby back safe and sound." Dad reached across the table and shook first Gollum's hand, then Donovan's.

We sat and made polite chitchat, wondering if the weather would break in time for an upcoming tennis tournament. Then Dad stood up and planted a kiss on top of my head. "Have a good dinner and try to stay out of trouble."

"Oh, uh, Dad, some family matters have cropped up that require your attention," I mumbled.

"You mean about your mother remarrying?"

"Cecilia called you," I replied flatly.

"Yes. She wanted to upset me. I refused to play her game. If your mother can find happiness with another man, more power to her. I certainly did." He turned a fond gaze upon Bill, a wiry Asian man who kept fit as the tennis pro at the country club. His boundless energy pushed Dad to stay on his toes and active, even after sixteen years together. "Maybe the wedding will give Steph a chance to come home."

"Maybe," I hedged. My brother had split to Illinois the day after he graduated from college and only came home once a year if he had to. I talked to him on the phone every week and I saw him every time I was in the area. He talked to Mom and Dad less often. A lot less often.

"If Genevieve remarries, I don't have to fork out alimony every month," Dad half laughed. "Might think about retiring."

From what I understood of their relationship, Dad didn't mind supporting Mom. He did love Mom and us. He just couldn't live the straight life with the narrow world view dictated by Mom's church.

We exchanged a few more pleasantries before he re joined Bill at a table on the opposite side of the dim restaurant.

"One major hurdle behind us." I breathed a sigh of relief.

"Might be easier to postpone the wedding if he did object," Donovan growled.

"Why do we have to stop the marriage?" Allie asked. "If Genevieve is happy . . ."

"Darren is half Damiri demon," I hissed at her.

Her eyes widened in wonder. Then she turned a frightened gaze upon Donovan. "What does that mean?"

"It means that he sleeps hanging by his feet with his wings wrapped around him," Donovan replied. "He drinks pig and cow blood instead of milk."

I sensed the anger rising in him before his face flushed and his fists clenched.

"And I'm not one of them," he insisted.

But you are something. Something strange and wonderful and ever so scary, I thought.

"Darren Estevez gave me his name and an education after he manipulated . . . made a patsy of me. But that is all he gave me."

"Is he like a vampire bat?" Allie persisted in her questioning.

"Bats aren't truly vampires," I said, as much to convince myself as her.

"The Damiri were among the first of the demon tribes to infiltrate humanity," Gollum jumped in. He put on his professor face.

I prepared to sit back and let him ramble on.

"Besides their need for blood for sustenance—they prefer human but will resort to animals if they can't get it—they are extremely long lived. I remember reading that they can adapt to daylight, but they are normally nocturnal."

"Could these Damiri demons be the origins of the vampire legends?" Allie asked, clearly fascinated by the topic. Or by Gollum.

A primal response deep inside me wanted to growl at her.

I took a sip of wine instead. "Allie has read every vampire book printed," I said quietly.

"Pity there is no such thing as vampires," Gollum took off his glasses and polished them on his napkin. "No one comes back from the dead."

Tell that to Dill, I thought.

"One thing the legends are consistent on is the vampire's ability to mesmerize its prey. And there is frequently a sexual aspect to the exchange of blood." Allie settled back to discuss her favorite topic in depth. She couldn't understand why I wouldn't write about vampires.

I found nothing sexy about bleeding or giving over total control of my mind and body to another. Like I almost had with Dill.

Did I really love him? More and more I resented him. Resented his haunting me, resented him dying. Resented . . . too much.

Still the gaping hole of loneliness in my gut that he'd created by dying gnawed at me. I couldn't move on while he haunted me. Maybe that's why I held Donovan at arm's length.

I still didn't trust him.

"Damiri have that hypnotic ability," Donovan said quietly. "It would explain the love-at-first-sight aspect of Genevieve and Darren's romance."

"Is Genevieve in danger from your . . . er . . . foster father?" Gollum asked.

"I don't know."

"Of course she's in danger!" I insisted. "The question is: how is he going to use her before he disposes of her?" I borrowed the phrase from Scrap.

"I don't even know why he's here." Donovan shrugged his shoulders.

"He's after me." I began to shake. "He's the latest in a pack of demons that are hunting me. I'm a rogue, outside the protection of my Sisterhood or a Citadel. I'm vulnerable. But, I'm also outside the hidebound rules of the Citadel, and therefore unpredictable, a serious danger to them all."

"And you are a danger to the demons who are living among us. A lot of them are just trying to get by, settle in to a human lifestyle."

"Until their craving for blood overcomes their human gloss and they kill," I reminded him.

"You're the only one around who can defeat them in open battle." Donovan moved closer, as if to put his arm around me.

I told them about the Windago.

Gollum whistled through his teeth.

Donovan sat up straighter, worry creasing his brow and around his eyes.

I held myself stiff and aloof, distracted by a flurry of activity near the entrance. Flashes of vivid red and bright green darted around people's ankles.

Chapter 15

The Masons who laid the cornerstone of the Washington Monument in Washington, D.C., chose the date July 4, 1848 because the moon went into Virgo at noon of that day.

"**D**ONOVAN, I WANT you to finish your dinner and then take Allie home in a taxi. Quickly."

By the pricking of my thumbs, something wicked this way comes. Actually it was a tingle at the base of my spine.

"Tess . . ." Allie and Donovan protested at the same time.

"I'll take her home," Gollum said.

"Don't argue with me. I know what's best." I fixed them all with a glare that had been known to quell a classroom full of rowdy seventh graders.

"Scrap can't come near me with Donovan around. I'm going to need Scrap very soon."

"What?" Gollum asked. He stretched casually, using the gesture to look around the crowded restaurant. Tall plants and a scattered seating arrangement gave the illusion of privacy. It also blocked a clear view of the enemy.

From my place in the corner, with my back to the wall, I had a better line of sight to the hostess podium at the entrance.

"From ghosties and ghoulies and long legged beasties, and things that go bump in the night, good Lord deliver us," I quoted an old Scottish prayer attributed to Robert Burns but really much, much older. I must be nervous if I started spouting literary citations. "Ankle biters hiding in the shrubbery at your seven o'clock."

"Those are just statues," Allie protested. But there was a note of question in her voice.

"Not statues. Just very good at holding still as stone when someone is looking. Now get out of here."

"You'll need help." Allie set her shoulders stubbornly. She reached for her capacious purse. Allison Engstrom always carried a weapon, on and off duty.

"Allie, I need to know that my best friend is safe." I grabbed her hand and pleaded with her through my eyes. "Please let Donovan take you out of danger. Conventional weapons and tactics won't faze these guys. Leave them to me. Please. I know what I'm doing."

"I'm armed." She patted her purse. No room for a shoulder holster beneath her good tweed blazer.

"Won't do any good. You know that bullets bounce off them. You tried that already."

"Are the bullets silver?" Gollum asked. His raised eyebrows almost hiked his glasses up onto the bridge of his nose.

"Plain old lead."

"Won't do any good," I repeated. "I've seen a man shoot a dozen demons with a military automatic weapon." That man was Donovan, and he might have been aiming over their heads to make them take dives. Then, again, maybe he had been aiming for their hearts knowing the bullets wouldn't penetrate demon skin, even in human form.

Donovan had the grace to blanch.

"The bullets just bounced off demon hides," I continued. "I tried slicing these garden gnomes with the Celestial Blade, which is sharper than any mortal-made razor. They used the curved blades as a swing. I had to pierce them with the tines."

Gollum whipped out his PDA and started taking notes.

"Donovan, take Allie home and keep her safe. I'll call if we need reinforcements back home."

Donovan reached for his wallet. I stayed his hand. "I'll take care of it. Just get Allie out of here and keep her safe.

I trust you to do that." I fixed him with a look that brooked no defiance.

"You can trust me, Tess."

I kept my mouth shut.

"At least let me leave the tip." He tucked a ten under his water glass, flowed to his feet, and held Allie's chair for her.

While he was occupied helping my friend into her parka, I slipped a twenty into his pocket for the taxi. I didn't know just how strained his finances were and I could afford to help a little.

He reached into his pocket and took out the bill. Without really looking at it, he pressed it back into my hand. "I may not be wealthy anymore, but I'm not broke." He bristled with affronted pride.

They left without looking back.

I didn't take the time to breathe a sigh of relief.

"Scrap, you around?" I whispered into the air.

I am now, babe. Now that you've ditched El Stinko lover boy. My imp settled onto my shoulder. His skin took on a pink cast as he surveyed the remains of our dinners. *You could have left me something,* he wailed. *I'm wasting away to nothing and you didn't even order me a beer.*

"Can the crap, Scrap. Keep an eye on the Orculli hiding in the shrubs."

"So what's the plan?" Gollum asked, all business. He hadn't even looked twice at Allie when she left with another man.

Part of me sighed in relief.

"Plan? You don't have a plan?"

"I'm just the archivist. I research. You fight. That's the plan."

I snorted something disgusting and waved the waiter over for the check. Gollum paid out of a thick wad of bills he always seemed to have hidden somewhere on his person without obvious sign of a bulge.

"More of the archivist's trust fund?" I asked. Gollum's family had a history of working with rogue Warriors of the Celestial Blade, male and female. When they were on duty, they had access to a seemingly limitless bank account.

"Moving money and apartment deposit that I won't

need now. I'll reopen the trust tomorrow after I check in at the college."

"Provided we survive the trip across the parking lot." As we moved toward the exit, with studied good-byes to Dad and Bill and a few patrons and staff, I caught flashes of bright colors around the edges of my vision.

"I really don't want to fight these guys on ice with an arctic wind blowing."

You don't? I'm the one with a bare tushie hanging out. I could lose a wart to frostbite.

"Nice to have you back, Scrap." I suddenly felt more complete, more confident, ready to tackle this world and several others. "Stay behind me, Gollum."

We made our way across the parking lot with an escort that kept a six-foot circle around us. One cute little guy in blue and yellow—almost surreal colors in their brightness— strayed inside that perimeter. Scrap growled and bared his teeth. He had almost as many as the bad guys. The gnome jumped back to his place, eyes wide and frightened.

Okay, so they respected the Celestial Blade. What else could I fight them with? Flattening them with a frying pan barely set them back. But if I spilled their blood and didn't burn the bodies, they'd reanimate. What would work?

Fire.

"Scrap, can you light a little fire?"

Sure, babe. What's up? A tiny flamelette appeared at the end of his finger.

"Point it at the bad guys."

The gnomes scuttled backward, giving me a wider circle to work in.

Mom's car sat beneath a light—no shadows for the Windago to hide in.

The little king of the Orculli trolls perched on the hood of the vehicle, the gilded braid perfectly straight on his sagging pointed cap. Bright gold buttons also gleamed on his red-and-green tunic. He held a miniature white flag on a chopstick.

An honor guard of three in green stood behind him, arms crossed and elongated chins jutting aggressively.

I stopped at the rear door, finger poised on the unlock button on the key chain. "You mind getting off my car?" I glared at the pushy troll.

"I request parley," he said, as arrogant as ever.

"Talk to him," Gollum whispered in my ear. I hadn't realized how close he had come to me. The warmth of his long body against my back reassured me.

"What do you want?" I extended my left hand, palm up. Scrap jumped onto it, skin turning redder than the fire that bounced from pudgy fingertip to palm and back again. He stretched and thinned, halfway into a transformation.

The king jumped to his feet and scrambled to the center of the car hood.

"Call off your imp," he demanded.

"Answer my question first."

"The girl. The one you call WindScribe." The king's voice sounded a little squeaky to my ears, without the resonant tones of the otherworlds.

"Not an option. She's under my protection."

"Then we are at war."

"Sorry, I've already got a war with a Windago Widow." There was that title again that demanded attention. A scrap of an idea whistled around my brain louder than a Windago generated wind.

"My mission takes priority over Windago revenge. You will deal with me first and if you survive, then you are at the mercy of Lilia David. Choose the time and place for our battle."

I raised an eyebrow at that.

"Noon, three days hence," Gollum hissed.

"Why?"

"Just do it. I'll explain later."

"Okay. Noon."

The king winced.

"Three days hence." On the day of the full moon.

He nearly gagged. "So be it." The entire troop disappeared in a poof of displaced air.

Now what have we got ourselves into, dahling? I sure hope Gollum pulls some magic out of his computer and lets me know. I can stab these guys and kill them, but there are so many of them, Tess and I just might wilt in the middle of the fight. I can hold a tiny bit of flame in my hand, enough to light a cigar. Not enough to wipe out this herd.

We need help.

But not from Donovan.

I'm sure if I just knew what he was, then I could overcome the barrier that keeps me away from my babe when he is near. He's like imp's bane, but I don't get tiddly from him. He's more like a lock on a dimensional portal.

But locks are just puzzles if you know the key.

Hmm . . . this will take some thought.

And I don't have enough time to do any research!

But time is just another dimension and can be manipulated by those who know how.

When I got home, I tiptoed up the stairs so as not to disturb Mom and Darren in the parlor. They were curled up like two puppies, arms and legs tangled, almost indistinguishable from each other.

I knew my mom. She wouldn't do anything stupid, like sleep with the guy. He might be half demon with a talent for mesmerizing his prey, but my mother was an old school French-Canadian Catholic. I'd bet her church upbringing against his seduction any day.

WindScribe sat cross-legged on her bed, playing cat's cradle with a piece of decorative braid from my sewing bin. I cursed. That bit of brocaded ribbon had cost several bucks a yard!

"Good night," she called to me cheerily. Her eyes still looked glassy, her expression dreamy.

I dashed downstairs to check on the vials of tranquilizers. Damn. One vial was all aspirin, the other still sealed. I flushed the lot.

As an afterthought I locked the now empty vials inside my rolltop desk and pocketed the key. I'd be interested if my guest managed to find them.

Mom and Darren didn't even acknowledge me standing in the doorway.

Fuming at life in general and the host of predatory guests that had landed in my lap, I slammed back into the kitchen. I needed a snack to make up for the skimpy dinner I'd barely eaten. Not even any desert.

Empty fridge. Empty jar of coffee beans. Not even any peanut butter.

"Gollum, I'm going to the grocery store," I called down the hallway to the apartment. "Do you need anything?"

I heard a series of grunts and nothing more. Nothing from the lovebirds in the sitting room.

"Keep an eye on WindScribe," I called to Gollum.

Another series of grunts.

So I trundled to the discount store down the Six A. I still wanted Scrap watching Mom and Darren. He'd pop over to me if I ran into trouble of the demon kind.

The wind remained calm, the sky clear. The waxing moon kept a lot of shadows at bay. I'd be safe if I hurried and stayed near crowds.

Eggs, milk, bread, the cod (I do live on Cape *Cod* after all) the lemons I'd promised for dinner tomorrow night, and a bottle of white wine for the sauce. The pile in my cart kept growing and growing. I could see the balance in my checking account dropping rapidly. While I was there, I checked on table linens for my kitchen. Nothing I'd spend money on. Just cheap and tacky prints with pigs and kitties in ugly light orange or uglier dark orange.

I was not a happy camper.

I may not have the fashion sense of Scrap or my mother, but I know what I do and don't like in décor. And I don't like orange.

When I stepped outside the store with a cart full of bagged groceries, the wind bit through my gloves and slacks. Litter whipped about the parking lot in sudden frenzy.

"Scrap, I may need some help," I whispered into the night.

On it, babe. My imp flew three circles, deosil or clockwise, around my head, then lighted on the handle of the cart.

I couldn't discern his color in the weird blue-white fluorescent light circles around the poles. First time I noticed how many dark spots lay between those lifesaving circles. Did they grow darker and denser as I watched?

"Are there any Windago lurking about?" I kept looking over my shoulder and peering into the distance. Anxiety crawled up and down my spine. No way to tell if that was the flare of warning of demons present or just my own nerves.

I had been on edge pretty much all day and the night before.

Scrap wiggled his pug nose and slipped his forked tongue in and out, like a snake tasting the air. *Naw, you're safe from demons for the moment. But I'm not too sure about those three thugs hugging the shadows behind that black van next to your car.*

"Probably just teens out after curfew sneaking smokes or drinks." This parking lot had a reputation as a cool place for boys with aggressive tendencies to hang out.

As I stowed the multifarious bags in the hatch of the SUV, the light directly above me spat, fizzled, and winked out, plunging me into shadow.

I swallowed my curses and slammed the door down. I kept the key in my hand, letting the long, sharp prong of it extend through my clenched fingers.

"Nice purse, lady. Got anything in there for me? Like your wallet?" A male voice oozed menace from the area around the driver's side door. A glowing cigarette butt in the region of his mouth provided the only indication of where he stood.

No way was I going to press the unlock button on my key set with him standing between me and the dubious safety of the interior.

"Nice car, lady. We think you need to share your wealth with us downtrodden poor folk," another male voice said from behind my right shoulder. Stale alcohol on his breath.

"Need a little Dutch courage to harass a defenseless female?" I asked mildly. Judging by the price of their athletic shoes, these kids weren't poor by a long shot. I could buy two weeks' worth of groceries for the cost of one pair of their shoes.

Oh, this is going to be good. Scrap dissolved into laughter. He found a new perch on the luggage rack, swinging his bandy legs.

"What's that supposed to mean, lady?" Cigarette Guy

snarled. He moved three steps closer, blasting me with his bad breath. "We ain't Dutch."

I sensed a third presence on the other side of the car. They hemmed me in, my back against the hatch. My butt resting on the bumper.

Right where I wanted them.

Chapter 16

In the late nineteenth century, Sir John Herschel supposedly discovered a winged batman Vespertilio Homo on the moon. In 1874, Richard A. Proctor wrote a book that treated the story as science rather than science fiction.

"**Y**OU REALLY DON'T want to do this, guys," I warned them. "I'm not in the mood to take your crap."

"Oh, yeah? What's a little bit of a thing like you gonna do to us?" Cigarette Guy puffed out his chest and pressed closer to me.

"This!" I yelled.

Before I could think about what I was doing, I balanced against the bumper and lashed out with both feet. I connected with a very satisfying thunk. Cigarette Guy and Beer Breath grunted and staggered backward, clutching their bellies.

Adrenaline flowed through me and lit my senses like fine single malt scotch.

Unseen Guy launched at me, fingers extended toward my eyes. I barely registered long nails and a hint of feminine curves beneath her baggy jacket.

Instantly, I was back in the Citadel with Sister Paige screaming at me. She wanted no mercy.

I gave none to this wanna-be bad girl. She got a sweep of my leg behind her knees and my key raking her cheek.

It came away dripping blood. "Oooh, you're gonna have a scar just like mine!" Speaking of which, the scar pulsed hot and angry. I wondered if it was visible.

The first two were up and coming at me again. Backward kick to the balls of one. Then I kept turning and jabbed my fingers in the throat of the other.

A siren erupted at the far end of the parking lot. Blue-and-red lights strobed the kids.

The girl took off. The other two curled into fetal balls, choking and gasping.

"You didn't have to hurt them!" Allie yelled from the safety of her cruiser.

"You want a piece of me, too?" I snarled at her.

"Easy, girl," she said holding both hands up, palms out in a universal gesture of surrender. "What'd they do to you?" She wandered over.

I told her.

Mike crept forward in her shadow. He knelt down and examined the two youths. "This one may never contribute to the gene pool and the other might not talk again," he said with more humor than I gave him credit for.

"There was a third one. A girl. She's bleeding on the cheek," I advised them, holding up the stained key.

"I've been wanting to nail these kids for weeks. Had six complaints from women shopping alone at night, but the kids always disappear with purses, groceries, and cars before we get here. Then they abandon the cars a few blocks away, taking the food and the cash and not much else. Not smart enough to figure out how to do identity theft, I guess."

"How come I haven't heard about this, Allie?"

"Because you've had your nose in a book on deadline for the last month and haven't even turned on the TV."

"Oh."

Mike radioed for an ambulance. Then he leaned over the kid I'd struck in the throat. "Oh, my God! You broke his trachea. Allie, get that ambulance here fast. The kid's not breathing."

He was choking and gasping, clawing at his throat. Panic turned his face white. Lack of air had turned his lips blue.

"CPR?" I knelt beside the kid, prepared to go into action. Damn. Damn. Damn. I hadn't needed to hurt these guys, I just needed to work off some frustrations. And now I'd killed one of them.

"CPR won't work. He can't get air through his throat. I'm going to have to open him up." Mike pulled a jackknife and a ballpoint pen out of his pocket.

"Aren't you going to sterilize that or something?" Allie asked. She'd already added an ASAP to the ambulance call and closed her radio.

"With what? You got any matches?" Mike asked.

"I do." I made a show of fishing in the pocket of my slacks. *Scrap, I need a little flame,* I begged. With a little sleight of hand . . .

I grabbed Mike's open knife and cupped my hand around the blade, shielding it from the wind. Then I spun around on my knees, turning my back to the two cops.

Scrap landed on my shoulder and touched the blade with a blue-white light. He ran it back and forth, both sides, until my hand felt as scorched as the blade.

"Hurry up, Tess. He's beyond panic, gone into stillness," Allie warned. She blew ink out of the pen cartridge.

Calmly, I returned the knife to Mike. "If you know how to do this, go for it."

Mike breathed deeply, closed his eyes a moment, then slashed the kid across the throat.

Blood flowed along the line of the cut. Quickly, Mike separated the folds of flesh with the fingers of one hand. He probed a few seconds, found something white and gristly. Another quick cut with the knife, then he plunged the ink tube in.

Instantly, air whistled through. The kid's chest moved.

We all sat back and breathed a little deeper ourselves.

Sirens penetrated the sound of the wind, still blocks away.

"You saved the kid's life, Mike. Thank you." Energy left me in a flood. I hadn't murdered the boy.

"Cool thinking." Allie slapped him on the back. "We might make a good cop of you yet."

"Three years on the Miami force didn't do that?" He raised his eyebrows and quirked a smile.

So he wasn't a raw rookie after all.

"Can I go home now?" I didn't think I had the umpf to deal with the rest of this emergency.

"No. I need to file paperwork on this. You don't go home until I go home."

"Allie, I'm done in. How about tomorrow? I can come down to the station and give an official statement."

"Nope."

My shoulders sagged in defeat. I was very, very tired. "How come you're back on duty? I sent you home from dinner over an hour ago."

"Somebody called in sick. I was wound up after our . . . um . . . meeting." She looked pointedly at Mike, acknowledging her need for . . . er . . . discretion. "So I volunteered to come in."

"So why are you here?" I gestured around to the sparsely occupied parking lot.

"Customer heard an altercation and called 911 as they peeled out," Mike said. "We were cruising close by and answered the call."

The kid with his hands wrapped protectively around his balls moaned and opened an eye. His gaze lit on me. He slammed his eyelids closed again and groaned even louder.

"Remember that, Beer Breath. Maybe you've learned a lesson that mugging ladies in the parking lot doesn't pay," I snapped at him.

"Julie's idea," he rasped around his aching groin.

"Julie? Typical. The kid with the ideas is the first one to hotfoot it the minute the action gets tough," Allie said. "Shouldn't be hard to pinpoint her at school tomorrow. Only kid with a bloody cheek."

The ambulance arrived and carted the kids off. They glad-handed Mike and offered to write up a commendation. Allie rolled her eyes. "No living with him now. First day on the job, and he saves a kid's life." She presented me with a clipboard filled with official looking forms.

"You know all this information," I whined. "I just want to go home."

Not yet, dahling. Scrap took possession of my right hand. He pulsed a bright vermilion as he stretched longer and longer.

While I'd been occupied with Allie and the muggers, I'd ignored the way the wind had jacked up the pitch of its wail and how the bottom had fallen out of the temperature.

The Windago scented blood.

No wonder my scar pulsed and the nerves along my spine tingled.

"Windago," I breathed. I had no adrenaline left. "I really don't want to do this now."

"Windago?" Allie mouthed, eyes wide with wonder and a touch of fear. She reached for her holster.

You've got me, babe, Scrap sang.

At least the parking lot had been scraped clear of ice and heavily sanded. I had traction.

I took a deep breath as I began twirling Scrap like a baton. He solidified and extruded sharp, half-moon blades.

I stepped out into the clear space between parking aisles.

"What do we need to do?" Allie asked. A note of panic and awe squeaked out of her.

Mike's mouth hung agape. "I never thought it was true," he whispered, pointing to my now visible Celestial Blade. Then he clamped his jaw shut and drew his weapon.

Allie already had hers out.

Mine. You are mine, the wind howled.

"Wanna take a bet on that?" I called back. I swung my weapon in a full circle over my head, around my knees, and back and forth at waist level.

Vengeance is mine! the Windago screamed. *The Orculli don't order me around.*

The real wind swallowed her words.

A shadow coalesced between the puddles of light. Tall, bulky, vaguely humanoid. At least it had arms and legs. And lots and lots of unkempt, smelly fur.

No wonder these critters became antisocial. No one would come near them until they bathed.

Mike emptied his weapon into the shadow. The bullets passed right through it.

Silly human. You can't hurt me. But you can become my new mate. The shadow advanced on Mike.

He shook so badly he dropped his weapon. A dark stain spread downward from his crotch.

Now that's irony. He could coolly perform an emergency tracheotomy but wet his pants in the face of a demon.

The Windago kept coming, pressing Mike farther and

farther into the darkness. She reached out one long arm and grabbed for the poor man.

He screamed and backpedaled.

"Shit! Leave the poor guy alone. He's too young for you, Lilia David." I took a chance that there was still a morsel of humanity left in the creature. I had no proof that she and her mate were the reclusive author Howard Ebson and his longtime companion. But I had killed the mate last autumn and Howard hadn't shown up the next day to receive a lifetime achievement award. Lilia had accepted it for him with bad grace.

The Windago hissed and turned her attention back to me. She reached spectral hands toward me.

"Don't let her touch you. She'll freeze-dry anything she touches." I could see ice crystals forming in the air around me. I stayed firmly in the center of one circle of light.

Allie dragged Mike into another. He held his arm awkwardly, cradling it against his body. He whimpered in pain.

Damn. I really hoped he hadn't been bit. If he had, I'd have to kill him before three days had passed and he became a Windago.

Anger shot liquid fire through my veins.

The Windago paused at the edge of the light.

I could see the fuzz around the edges of her shadows. Hair. Akin to Sasquatch.

I'd killed a dozen Sasquatch in one battle. There was only one Windago tonight.

"Come and get me, Lilia. I dare you." I swung the Celestial Blade closer to her.

She snarled. Red pinpoints of light in the region of her eyes glowed brighter.

Before she could think about risking the light, I took the last step I needed. My blade whisked across her middle, slicing through fur.

But not hide.

She retreated with the wind and disappeared behind a spindly little maple at the verge of the parking lot. *You killed my mate. Now I'll replace him with yours!* she screeched.

"Laugh's on you, Lilia. I don't have a mate anymore."

So you think now.

An unearthly silence followed her pronouncement. My gut grew cold.

That was hardly any fun at all, Scrap complained. He dropped back to his normal form, tinged only a little bit pink.

"There's beer and OJ in the car. Meet me at home and I'll feed you," I whispered.

He popped out.

"You didn't see anything, Mike. You hear me, Mike?" Allie demanded her partner's attention.

"But . . . but . . ."

"You didn't see anything. You didn't hear anything."

"But . . . but . . ."

"If you say one word, you'll be strapped to a desk from here to eternity filling out paperwork. You got that?" She held him upright by the lapels of his jacket. He nodded, eyes wide in fear.

Fear of her, or of the Windago?

I pulled on his left arm, the one that hung limply at his side. Slashed jacket and shirt sleeve. The skin beneath looked an angry red, like a cat scratch. No trace of blood.

"You'll be okay. But watch that for traces of infection. See you tomorrow, Allie. I'll fill out your forms then." Jauntily I waved and climbed into my car for the short drive home.

Exhaustion, mental and physical pulled at my limbs and my eyelids. I wanted nothing more than to crawl under the down duvet and sleep for a week.

I really needed that vacation.

So, of course, Scrap chose that time to sit on the bed-stead and lecture me for two hours about the dangers of letting the Windago get away. About letting Donovan come too close to me. About our need to call on the Sisterhood for help. About my need to do more research. About the dangers of letting Darren stay in the house too long. About his need to choose my wardrobe. About my failure to provide him with enough mold to sustain life. About the lack of beer in the fridge.

Dill added his own litany of grief. He was running out of

time in limbo. His Powers That Be demanded I get rid of the imp and embrace Dill. He ran the same arguments over and over.

"Dill, you used to have a sense of humor," I reminded him. And myself. "Time was you'd belittle those Powers That Be with puns and scathing commentary on their pompous attitude and useless pronouncements."

Silence.

Could he be just a construct trying to force me to get rid of Scrap for a demonic reason?

I clenched my teeth and repeated Gollum's statement. "No one comes back from the dead."

Smelling of sulfur and brimstone, Dill vanished in a huff.

"I can't go back, Dill. I have to move forward," I whispered into the silence.

And then Scrap started to clean. He was very frustrated that he'd gone to the trouble of transforming and hadn't even gotten a taste of Windago blood.

Dust and stray socks flew through the air. The sharp smell of pine cleaner filled my head and made me sneeze. Mom is the only person who can outclean Scrap. And she prefers bleach.

On and on he went until the drone of his voice finally lulled me to sleep. I think he moved on to the kitchen then.

I did not sleep well. My dreams took me back to the Citadel. Back to a time when I still grieved for Dill so heavily I could hardly think. Back to a time when Scrap was new to me and I had yet to build enough confidence in myself to understand why *we* must be the ones to fight to preserve humanity from demon invasions.

My nightmares back then had repeated themselves often. They went on and on until I could no longer tell if I remembered a dream, or remembered reality.

Face your personal demons in your own reality and they might go away, Scrap had whispered to me in the dead of night when I dared not sleep.

He had a point.

"Sometimes they are like huge gorillas, but more human. Bigfoot?"

Sasquatch. Big, ugly, hairy, with fists like clubs and teeth like daggers.

"Yeah."

What else?

There were more. There were always more. Every time I dreamed, my fertile imagination came up with a different demon. Big ones, little ones, humanoid ones, squid ones, bug ones. I described a few.

"They come out of doorways into a big featureless room. It's all white and round and I can't see its limits unless a door opens. And all the doors are different."

That's the chat room. You can pass into any dimension from there.

"Is that like the eleventh dimension?" That wasn't the right term. I couldn't remember the details of the program I'd watched on TV about String Theory. Or was it Membrane Theory? Some scientists apparently had begun to believe in alternate universes. Ghosts could be explained as a temporary overlap of those universes.

That pushed more of my creep buttons. What if in another reality Dill had not died?

I think I cried myself to sleep both that night back at the Citadel and this night snug in my own bed on Cape Cod.

Chapter 17

I AWOKE FRIDAY morning feeling heavy and groggy. The clock told me it was pushing nine. The telephone beside my bed rang seven times. I ignored it. Too wrapped up in my own fog to bother.

It rang again. Another seven times. Its shrillness cut through the cobwebs in my brain.

"What?" I snarled on the sixth ring.

"This is James Frazier of the *Cape Gazette*. I'm looking for a Miss WindScribe."

What? How?

"Wrong number." I slammed the receiver back into its cradle.

It rang again. "Ugh," I groaned and dragged myself into the shower. The sharp sting revived me a little. Nothing really helped until I stumbled downstairs—careful not to bump my head on the overhead beam that crossed the steep flight that was little more than a broad ladder—and dove into my first cup of coffee.

Everyone in the family knew my habits and I found a stack of notes propped up on the coffeepot.

Idly I wandered back to the closed door leading to Gollum's apartment. He opened the door on my first knock looking fresh and alert. He'd traded his summer uniform of pressed khakis and polo shirt for crisp cords and turtleneck. With his glasses perched atop his head, I could see his mild blue eyes. I read concern there and something else I wasn't sure I wanted to identify.

"Mom and Darren headed for Boston, at some ungodly hour this morning. If I heard her correctly when she tried to wake me, I think they are looking for rings. She made coffee if you want some," I croaked, cradling my cup of the life-giving substance.

"Thanks, but I've already made myself a pot here. About an hour ago Allie took WindScribe down to headquarters to question her about other relatives who might take her in."

"You look ready to tackle the world."

"Which you don't. I have a meeting at the college at eleven. Then I need to head up to Boston for the lecture tonight. You coming?"

"Wish I could. But I don't quite dare leave with Moon-Feather coming this afternoon. And WindScribe. I'm wondering if she has a drug problem. What are you lecturing on?"

"The Windago."

"Aren't they a Midwest phenomena?" One of them had followed me from Wisconsin anyway. That area had about the coldest north woods I could think of to harbor those nasty critters.

"Originated here in New England, then moved west with the native tribes." Gollum looked like he might settle in for a prelude to tonight's lecture.

"What got you started on that horror story? I thought European demons were your specialty." I needed more coffee if I was going to let him get started.

"I began looking for the shadow demons who freeze-dry their prey that you stumbled across last autumn in Wisconsin."

I suppressed a tremble in the back of my knees. Then I gave a brief recounting of last night's adventures.

"Damn. I knew I should have gone with you."

"What could you have done?" Somehow I just could not imagine Gollum fending off three teenage muggers or a vengeful Windago. He researched. I fought.

"I don't know that I could have done anything other than deter the muggers just by being male and you not being alone. I feel useless. I could have collected more data on the Windago so that you could be better prepared next time."

"Next time I don't think she'll come alone," I mused. But who among my acquaintances would she claim as her new mate. I didn't think Dill's ghost would satisfy her.

Something in Gollum's expression as he looked at me shocked me to my core. "Lilia will come after you next," I said quietly, not sure I wanted to face any side of that issue. "Do you have some kind of charm or ward to keep her away from you when I'm not around?"

"I think I can manage." He quirked me a lopsided grin and gestured me into his new lair and retrieved a sheaf of notes from the desk. "Windago victims are said to have their hearts frozen." He perused the papers with only half his attention. Unusual.

The other half of his attention seemed to be on me.

Way outside my comfort zone.

"Lucky I didn't let one of those things touch me," I said. Once again I saw in my mind Mike cradling his arm against his chest. "We may have a problem. I think we need to keep an eye on Allie's new partner. He may have gotten tagged."

"If he was, you know what you have to do." Gollum looked me square in the eye.

I nodded and shivered with more than just the cold drafts that plagued my house and eluded my caulk gun. The enormity of my task as a Warrior of the Celestial Blade hit me anew.

I was charged with keeping these horrors away from humanity, killing them when I could, driving them back to their own dimension when I couldn't.

Alone.

Without the support of my Sisterhood.

"Looks to me like your heart has been frozen," Dill quipped from his post by the desk. He leaned against it casually, long legs stretched out. "If you had a heart, you'd take pity on me and let us be together as we are meant to be."

I ignored him.

Just then Gandalf, Gollum's long-haired white cat

darted between his legs and squeezed past me and out the door.

"Sorry," Gollum apologized as he dove for the errant beast.

Scrap swooped down the stairs and brushed past the fleeing cat. He came up with a pawful of white hairs, laughing inanely. Then he sneezed. Green slime sprayed the walls. I hoped it was invisible to everyone but me.

"You're going to clean that up," I admonished my imp.

He just laughed some more, flitting in a circle above the cat's head.

Gandalf snarled and swatted Scrap, claws fully extended. He drew blood from Scrap's butt.

This means war! Scrap yelled. He sounded decidedly stuffy.

"What's going on?" Gollum asked, scratching his scalp.

"Ongoing feud between our familiars."

"Did Gandalf hurt Scrap?"

I forgot that Gollum couldn't see either Scrap or Dill.

Yes, he did. I'm bleeding!

"Put some iodine on it," I snapped. "And leave the cat alone."

"I'll just put him back where he belongs." Gollum scooped up the cat and threw him into the apartment, closing the door sharply behind Gandalf.

I heard the cat's smug purr of triumph through the closed door.

"I need to show you something." I led Gollum back into the kitchen. From there, I showed him the door hidden behind some pantry shelves that opened onto the cellar steps. "There's another entrance from the outside, but that's covered with snow at the moment." I led him down the freestanding wooden steps, added many years after the root cellar was dug.

"This place is really old," he said, caressing ancient beams and drinking in the dank smell of mold and laundry, counting rows of preserves.

"Mom cans every scrap of fresh fruit she can find." I picked up a jar of peach jam.

Gollum inspected it as if it held demon brains. He opened it and jerked his head away from the stench. The preserves had a thick skin of mold on the top. "She used old paraffin to seal it. You'll have to toss the whole batch."

"Nah, Scrap will love it." I put it back on the painted shelves with more chips than paint. "No dairy in peach jam to aggravate Scrap's lactose intolerance. What's important about the cellar is back here," I continued.

I ducked behind the wooden steps to a thick old door made of many two by fours. "Here's the spare key," I said as I used it to open the heavy padlock on a reinforced crossbar. Then I handed him the little piece of brass. -

"What do you have to keep locked up and hidden?"

"Originally this was a place to hide from Indian attacks, then a priest hole for the few Catholics in a very Puritan neighborhood. During the Revolution it hid American spies from the British. Later it was a way station on the Underground Railroad. Now it's my armory."

The light came on automatically as the door swung open.

Gollum whistled through his teeth. He eagerly grabbed an elaborate German short sword with gold on the curved guard and etched along the slender blade. "Is this real?"

"Yeah. Seventeenth century. A collector's item. Weighs about fourteen ounces. I really liked the metalwork." Something else had drawn me to the blade when Scrap and I found it in a back alley pawnshop in Boston. I couldn't explain it. So I didn't.

I remembered clearly the store where I'd found it while Christmas shopping last December. Scrap had tugged my hair and urged me out of the crowds and the noise of holiday shoppers. Away from clanging bells, and unrelenting cheerful carols played over clashing store sound systems. I'd wandered reluctantly off the main streets into a long, dark alley filled with litter and smelling of stale beer and urine.

Scrap had pushed me urgently, not giving me enough time to think about where I was going or why.

The sword shone brightly in the dingy window display of the shop. The sword was the only thing of interest or value to me in the jumble of "collectibles."

The blade called to me. I had to have it. I couldn't go home without it. The shopkeeper had charged me a bloody fortune for it. But I knew it would cost double that on the open market.

"More important than the beautiful craftsmanship, it's a working blade, as is every piece in here." I swept my hand across the neat racks of swords, battle axes, and crossbows with quivers full of broad-tipped arrows. I could bring down a charging boar with one of those.

None of the weapons would stop a demon. But they would slow them down if Scrap needed a break in a pitched battle.

"This is absolutely gorgeous." Gollum tested the balance of the blade expertly, then snapped it through the air listening to it sing.

I wondered where he'd learned that technique, or why he should use this as a test for the temperament of the blade. I could do it, but only after months of practice with a foiled weapon. This man had as many secrets as Donovan, and was just as mute about them.

Gollum sighed and replaced the short sword. Then he reached eagerly for the most important weapon of all, hanging in pride of place dead center in the rack.

I stayed his hands. "Yes, it's an exact replica of the Celestial Blade, but made of wood."

"What kind of wood? It looks like metal."

He'd seen me wield the Celestial Blade; he knew what it looked like.

"The Sisters call it imp wood. I've never seen the trees they make them from. It holds an edge forever. I've never had to sharpen it. Want to train with me?"

"Wish I could." He looked at his watch, an elaborate hunk of metal with numerous dials and buttons. I think it could do everything but whistle "Dixie." Maybe it could do that, too.

"I've got to get to the college. Maybe later." He made to return the key to me.

"That's the spare. I want you to keep it while you are here. We don't know what we're getting into, and I want someone I trust to have access to weapons in case of emergency."

"Where's the other key?" he asked, slipping it on the same key ring as his car keys and the house key I'd given him.

"In a zipped pocket within a zipped pocket in my purse."

"Not someplace a stranger could stumble on it. Even if they stole the purse."

"Not likely. And there's another copy of it on a chain around my neck. Now go to your meeting before I decide the Windago really did touch me and I eat your arm off. Time for breakfast."

I hate cats the same way Tess hates bats. Only I know that bats are benign and cats are truly and totally evil. Gollum only thinks he locked the cat in his apartment. I know the beast turned invisible and slipped out again before the door fully closed.

So I hunt the cat. Upstairs and down. I stalk by smell and by sight. Meaning I can't smell anything when I'm near the cat, and my eyes water heavily when I get even closer. Hearing is no good because cats are totally silent unless they want to be heard; then they sound like a troop of elephants thundering across the plains.

Oh, no! He's down in the cellar, working at opening the door to the armory. I'm not sure my babe locked it properly. The padlock is in place, but the light is shining beneath the door. That only happens when something lodges between the door and the jamb.

Good thing that cat doesn't have opposable thumbs. I've got to warn Tess about this.

But first I'm going to torture that cat. Serve him right for decorating my bum with claw marks. He scratched off one of my warts. I worked hard to earn that one!

When I'm done with the cat, I must paint the scratches with iodine. War paint. Or makeup. Anyway, I'll make myself look pretty. I might even get a new wart when I win this battle.

Chapter 18

In esoteric cosmology the sun and moon pictured together represent the extremes of creative solar power and undirected lunar imagination.

WITH SCRAP BUSY stalking the cat, I decided on a trip to a home furnishing store. I really needed to do something about the kitchen. The only other rooms in the house big enough for everyone to gather was the dining room. Too formal. Or my office. Too cluttered with my private things. No one messes with my office and lives. Not even Scrap dares to clean it.

Bright sunlight and no wind. Safe to step outside. I hoped.

Mom and Darren had taken the SUV to Boston. That would cost them a small fortune in gas even though that car got better mileage than most in its class. But Darren could afford it. Maybe the SOB would top off the tank. But I doubted it.

That left me with Donovan and his four-wheel-drive station wagon. Not a heavy car but safer than mine. That would also give us some private time on neutral territory. Maybe I could pry some personal information from him. Like what kind of being he truly was.

I braved the cold and armored my defenses against his seductive charm. Then with teeth gritted and eyes half closed, I knocked on the cottage door.

Donovan greeted me with a high-pitched growl that

sounded so much like an angry bat I almost went scuttling back to the house.

Steeling myself to face my fears, I knocked again.

"What!" Donovan yanked the door open.

"Sorry." I backed down the three steps and lost my footing on a gloss of slick dew.

Before I could fall flat on my butt, Donovan reached out demon-quick and grabbed my arm. In the next instant I found myself upright again, in his arms, our bodies pressed intimately close. His mouth hovered scant inches above mine.

The world disappeared. I saw only his handsome face, felt only his arms holding me tight, knew only that I wanted him. Desperately.

He felt like the other half of me.

Lilia's next target?

We clung together for endless moments.

Eventually, the cold penetrated my awareness. As sanity filtered back into my mind I noticed something else.

"Who hit you?" I traced an ugly red-and-blue bruise around his left eye. Red lines marred the white around his warm chocolate-brown eyes.

"It doesn't matter." He blushed. I didn't think a man as coolly self-possessed as Donovan Estevez could do that. The infusion of blood highlighted the sharp planes of his cheekbones and intensified the coppery tones of his skin. He looked more Native American than ever. I wondered what the Dutch and Russian ancestors in his lineage had contributed.

"But it does matter. You are a guest in my home. I'm responsible . . ."

"D doesn't care about responsibility or hospitality or anything but his own agenda."

"And what is your stepfather's agenda?"

Stone-cold silence.

"Okay." Inside, I burned with curiosity and anger at his silence. Then I put on a bright face, totally false. I had my own agenda that included a trip to the mall. "Give me a ride to the mall, and I'll buy you brunch."

"I have appointments. Work."

"Have you eaten?"

"No."

"Then let me buy you breakfast, and you can drop me off. Pick me up later."

His stomach growled. "You know I can't resist you." He flashed me his grin.

I forgot to breathe. If only he'd kiss me.

Stop that! I slapped myself mentally. "Donovan, we need to talk. Just the two of us. We need to clear the air between us before we do something stupid."

"Like fall into bed together again?" He kept grinning as he grabbed his leather jacket from the back of the nearest chair.

"Yeah. Like that."

We went to the I-Hop on the fringes of the mall parking lot. They served breakfast all day. When the waitress had our orders and I had a steaming cup of coffee in front of me—Donovan had opted for an anemic looking herb tea—I looked him square in the eye and broached the subject uppermost on my mind.

"Why did Darren hit you?"

"I tried to warn him off your mother." He ducked his head, trying to hide the hideous bruise.

"Why did you let him hit you?"

"I didn't *let* him. D is fast. But believe me, he didn't come off unscathed."

I raised an eyebrow in question.

"Let's just say I don't think he'll be thinking fondly of the wedding night for a couple of days at least. No visible bruises, though. I'm more subtle than he is."

"Wait a minute. He called you D when he arrived. You just called him D. You just want to confuse us?"

And Dill's parents had called him *and* his sister Deborah *and* his brother Dylan "D." A cold more frigid than the weather knotted in my belly.

"His people think it's hilarious to all call each other D, so normal people don't know who they are talking to or about."

"But his 'people' aren't really people, are they?"

"Partially. Only mixed-bloods get out of their home dimensions in human form. Full-bloods can't transform anywhere but their homes."

"So they have to kidnap humans to breed Kajiri—half-bloods—who can come and go across the dimensions with impunity."

"Something like that."

"Explains the beauty and the beast legend."

"Yeah."

"So what are you if you don't have Damiri blood running in your veins?"

"I am fully human now. Mortal, too."

"And before?"

"Don't ask, Tess. I can't tell you. I want to. I want you to trust me enough to love me, to be the mother of my children. But I took vows, signed them with my blood. If I tell anyone my origins, I have to answer to the Powers That Be, probably with my death, a very long and painful death."

I digested that for a bit. He'd come close to admitting the truth of his origins. That was better than the nonanswers I'd got before.

"What are these infamous Powers That Be? Anything like God, or the Goddess Kynthia worshiped by the Warriors?"

"All of that and more. You don't want to be called before them. No human has ever survived a summons. Few other beings do either, come to think of it."

"But you did."

Again that stone-cold silence.

The waitress interrupted with our food: pecan French toast with eggs and sausage for me; cholesterol-free scrambled eggs and whole grain toast for him with a glass of OJ. Like the Damiri demons, he had to watch his weight. Another contradiction.

"Why can't Scrap come near me when you are around?" I blurted out when the first hunger pangs had been appeased.

"How can you get away with eating all that fat and starch?" he asked in turn.

Stalemate.

Again.

"Can you see my scar?"

"I'm mortal, remember. The scars left by the imp flu aren't visible to my eyes. But I felt them with my fingers the night we made love." His eyes grew warm with memory.

Heat spread delicious languor through my veins.

"I would love another opportunity to explore . . . new heights with you, Tess."

So would I.

"Not yet, Donovan. When I know that I can trust you."

Which meant I had a lot of research and discovery to do since he couldn't and wouldn't tell me about himself.

<hr />

Two and a half hours later, Donovan dropped me off at the house laden with bulky packages of curtains, cushions, and tableware to complete my kitchen. I'd gone with hunter-green prints dotted with images of mallard ducks. Totally different from the neutral blue-and-brown calico Dill and I had chosen four years ago. I'd also found a set of juice and water glasses, napkin rings, and salt and pepper shakers with the same mallards.

Scrap and I had barely set the table and I was ripping open the café curtain packages when Josh Garvin arrived with MoonFeather wrapped in blankets and pillows in the back of his sedate sedan. He carried my aunt into the sitting room with gentle ease. Only seven years older than me, he was absolutely devoted to MoonFeather. His hands gripped her slight form with an intensity that said more than any protestations of love.

MoonFeather looked a pale shadow of herself. In twenty-four hours she seemed to have lost ten pounds she didn't have to lose, and her skin had paled to the color and texture of old parchment.

I couldn't help a muffled gasp at first sight of the ravages of pain and hospital food on her. Scrap paled to a translucent gray, about as thick as cigarette smoke.

"I'll mend quickly now that I'm out of that hospital," she said as Josh deposited her on the sleeper sofa I'd just pulled open for her. "I need clean air away from the psychic waves of pain and fear, and some decent natural cooking." She settled back against the cushion, head drooping in exhaustion.

Josh grabbed an extra pillow and stuffed it beneath her heavily bandaged leg. "Keep it elevated and force fluids," he said in his melodious tenor, handing me a printed sheet of hospital instructions. He'd had some success in the courtroom with that voice lulling juries into trusting him implicitly.

Good thing Donovan didn't have that voice.

"I'll get her crutches out of the car. But she's not supposed to be up and about, only trips to the bathroom." He looked sternly at MoonFeather.

We both knew she wouldn't obey those instructions unless we tied her down. I wouldn't have either.

I left them speaking softly, lovingly, to make some herb tea, a restorative concoction of MoonFeather's rather than the pathetic stuff sold in stores and served in restaurants. I didn't know what all my aunt put into this brew, but I smelled mint and mullein and chicory root. Maybe it had some magic in it as well. I never knew with MoonFeather. The infusion made a dark and thick liquid. Coffee addict though I am, I was almost tempted to try some.

The teakettle had just boiled when Allie drove up with WindScribe in tow. The girl looked as pale and insubstantial as dappled autumnal sunshine deep in the woods. She wore a set of my sweats and one of Allie's civilian parkas that hung to her knees. She looked about her with wide and bewildered eyes.

Clear eyes. No drugs glazing them today. With luck, she wouldn't find any more. I'd made sure Mom's migraine meds were in the cottage. Nothing stronger than aspirin left in my house.

I opened the door and ushered them into the warmth of my kitchen. Mike remained outside, wandering the fringes of the parking area, examining the lumps under the snow that might be real garden gnomes. Then again, they might not.

I wondered what he'd do if one of them kicked back when he got a little too enthusiastic about removing snow with his boot.

WindScribe got the first cup of tea. She looked like she needed it more than my aunt. Allie settled in with a cup of coffee, strong and black.

"You going to be okay here alone?" Allie asked as she downed the last drop of scalding liquid. "We've got to get back on patrol. The snow is melting and the traffic is getting thick and dangerous."

"We'll muddle through. Mom and Darren should be back any time. You want to come to dinner? Gollum's in Boston, but I'm fixing cod sautéed in wine and lemon for the rest of us."

"Love to, but I'm going to Gollum's lecture in Boston." With a wicked smile she ducked out.

Why did I feel so empty inside?

Before I could figure that one out, WindScribe raised her head from her mug of tea and fixed me with a clear and determined gaze. "I'm going up to my room. I need some privacy for a change."

Probably to find a way to do more drugs.

So much for wispy and vague helplessness.

Chapter 19

THE HOUSE GROWS quiet. MoonFeather naps under the influence of pain meds. WindScribe shuts me out of her room. My Tess settles before her computer, staring at a blank screen or playing solitaire. Frustration and depression grow in her as she accomplishes nothing. Her emotions are my emotions. I have to do something or sink ever lower into darkness and drag her with me.

I could help her finish those last four chapters, or write the two short stories commissioned for anthologies. But she won't talk to me while anyone who doesn't know about me is in the house. Secrecy is more than an oath to the Sisterhood. Secrecy is our protection from superstitious mundanes who will look upon us as minions of the devil rather than their saviors from the depredations of demons.

MoonFeather would understand.

WindScribe is a puzzle. She still smells of tranquilizers and Tess' clothing rather than herself. I can't sniff out her motivations.

Of course, if that damned cat weren't around, I could smell more of everything. I alone know just how much evil oozes out of the cat's graceful fur and wide eyes. Everyone else thinks he's pretty. Or cute. Or that his purring will help MoonFeather heal.

Bah! It's all an act to cover up his plot to take over the world. Or at least this house.

Meanwhile Tess pounds her rolltop desk and stares at the fire. We really need a vacation.

An aura of menace hovers around us like a miasma of sewage. I dare not leave long enough to do some research. Fifteen garden gnomes litter the yard, ready to attack the moment we let our guard down.

The j'appel dragons are in charge of the chat room today. I could easily slip by them. But where would I go? How do I call the Windago away to another, easier prey? Or track the puzzle that is Donovan?

I think I'll search his luggage. Darren's, too. Who knows what demons pack for a week in the country.

The cat will do as fine a job of searching as I could. Now all I have to do is herd him over to the cottage.

"Tess!" Donovan called as he burst into the house unannounced.

I'd been so absorbed in a Mahjong game on the computer I hadn't heard his car.

"Tess, my love, where are you?"

"In the office. And I'm not your love." I yelled back at him. From here I could keep an eye on MoonFeather and monitor both staircases for signs of WindScribe emerging from her "privacy." Both sets of steps had unavoidable and distinctive creaks and groans. Not to mention the crossbeams waiting to conk the unwary.

I had a lot of hard questions only she could answer. Best she be in a good and gracious mood and totally clear of drugs when I tackled her with them.

"Oh, Tess, wonderful news." Donovan grabbed me out of my chair and twirled me around the cluttered room.

Dizzy and laughing, we kissed. And stilled. And kissed some more. The simmering passion between us exploded. His mobile mouth softened against mine.

I was lost in his magic.

I melted against him, too overwhelmed to care about my reservations and lack of trust. My arms crept around his waist, pulling him tighter against me. Eagerly, I ran my hands up the lean muscles of his back, reveling in his fitness and strength.

His fingers tangled in my hair.

Our tongues met, twined, explored.

"Let's celebrate and go fencing," Donovan breathed when we finally came up for air.

"What are we celebrating?" I rested my forehead against his chest, not trusting myself to look into the warmth of his eyes.

"I just cut a deal that's going to save my computer gaming company and get me back on solid financial footing once and for all." He rained kisses on my cheeks, my chin, the corners of my eyes.

"That's good. What kind of deal?" I could manage mundane details. Thought beyond that was more than my passion-fevered brain could handle. Born of our natural chemistry or his magic? I couldn't tell and, at the moment, didn't care.

"The largest maker of arcade games in the country just bought the rights to ten of my computer games. I've already got arcade versions programmed. All I have to do is deliver the sets of CDs and collect a whopping big check and continued royalties." He kissed me again.

"And you want to celebrate by engaging in fencing?" I laughed beneath his mouth.

He swung me around again. "We could go back to the cottage and lock the door . . ."

"I shouldn't leave. My aunt . . ."

"Where is everyone?" He lifted his head finally, looking as if he sniffed the air. Maybe he just listened to the quiet. The only sounds in the room were the crackle of the fire and the rasp of our breathing.

I told him the distribution of bodies.

"D called me about a half hour ago. He and Genevieve are headed back from Boston now. They'll be here in another hour or so. Surely you can leave two adult women alone for that long."

"It's nearly rush hour. Darren and Mom will be at least three hours . . ."

"We've got cell phones. MoonFeather or WindScribe can call us. The *salle d'armes* is only ten minutes away."

"I need some exercise. Let's do it. But I'm calling Dad to come sit with MoonFeather until Josh gets off work. They can eat the damned fish." Decision made, I felt lighter, freer. And much happier.

I didn't care that Donovan hung out with demons, had worked to make a homeland for the half-bloods, and wouldn't tell me a damn thing about himself. All I cared about was the fact that he made my blood sing and we were going fencing.

Still laughing, I dashed up the old stairs to my room, careful to duck beneath the crossbeam. I reached out and patted the dragon skull on the way. The murmur of a soft voice stopped me short three steps down. The top of my head barely cleared the landing.

WindScribe sat on my bed cuddling Gandalf the cat. "You understand the need to be free, my friend," she said. "Freedom belongs to all creatures, even you. That horrible man Gollum should never have locked you up in the teeny tiny apartment, should he?"

The cat yawned and purred as he plucked at something shiny on the bedspread with his fluffy white paw.

WindScribe shuffled several other objects around, her fingers never idle. Her bare toes also fidgeted and clenched to a rhythm only she could hear.

I crept up one more step to see better. The witch had scattered the contents of my purse over the candlewick bedspread and examined every coin, every dirty tissue, and credit card with intense scrutiny. She wore my favorite mint-green wool slacks and sweater set, too.

"I've made it my mission in life to free all the captive creatures. What is so wrong with that?" she said in her wispy voice.

"What's wrong with that is that dogs and cats aren't street smart and get hit by cars. They don't know how to feed themselves, so they raid garbage cans and eat things that make them sick and kill them," I said. "What are you doing with my purse?" I climbed the last two steps and yanked my wallet and car keys out of her hands.

Anxiously, I checked to make sure all my credit cards were in place. Car and house keys: check. Key to the armory still secreted in its zippered pocket. Cash intact.

Coins? Who knew. I rarely counted it except when I needed it. Was there a check missing from the book? Maybe. I might have written one and forgotten to record it.

"The lipstick you wore yesterday was so pretty, I thought you wouldn't mind if I tried it." WindScribe opened her eyes wide in innocence.

"Ask next time. Now get out of my room. I'd like some privacy while I change." I glared at her. My exuberant mood vanished, replaced by a simmering boil.

"There's no need to be so uptight. I didn't mean any harm." She slunk back to the connecting door to her attic room, gathering the cat against her chest, almost as a talisman.

"The road to hell is paved with good intentions." I grabbed the corner of the missing check that stuck out of her pocket.

"I've been to hell. And I won't go back," she announced firmly as she slammed and locked the door.

Interesting. Very interesting.

Darren is a worse slob than Tess. Clothes strewn about. Used tissues on the floor nowhere near the trash basket. Snack crumbs scattered about and crushed. He even missed when he used the toilet. And he left the seat up. Mom is going to love this. She lives to be a martyr to other people's messes.

Donovan, on the other hand, is so neat it looks as if he hasn't been in his room at all. His duffel bag is still packed, and I can't open it. His laptop is still in its case. I can't even smell him on the bar of soap in the bathroom. The only shaving tackle around the sink belongs to Darren.

If Donovan did not have a scent that I cannot identify, I would believe he doesn't exist. He leaves no taint in the air where he has been. Only where he is. Or does the reek of demon in Darren merely overwhelm the faint traces Donovan leaves behind?

I have heard nothing of his kind in all of imp lore. Imps have to know about many demons cataloged in the ghetto census. How else can we fight them when we become our true selves in the form of the Celestial Blade?

I light a cigar and blow smoke all over Darren's dirty laundry.

Mom hates tobacco smoke. If she thinks Darren has a habit, maybe she'll call off the wedding.

Oops! Got to scram. Donovan comes. His aura fairly pushes me out the back window as he enters the front door. I flit around to the front and peer through the windows.

And wouldn't you know it, just when I've finished searching, the blasted cat shows up.

Donovan pushes open the door, and the cat dashes into the cottage, purring and drooling.

See! I told you that cat was evil. If Donovan and the cat cozy up, it proves they were both spawned in some dark recess of one of the hells.

Wait. What is this? The cat strops Donovan's legs, leaving long white hairs on his black pants.

Donovan curses in that curious language of his, full of pops and clicks and hisses. Definitely a demon tongue. "Why couldn't you wait until I had my white fencing knickers on?" Then he kicks the cat. It flies out the still open door and lands on its feet. Then it struts over to me with that smug look on its face.

I retreat to my babe's gym bag, giggling all the way.

Maybe the cat isn't *too* bad. Sometimes. I'll have to cure it of its attitude problem, though.

Achoo! But not now. I can't breathe.

Chapter 20

"**B**LADES DOWN!" I screamed as the tempered steel foil shattered in Donovan's hand. My arm grew numb from fingertip to shoulder from the force of his blow. Then I began to shake and ache.

A spot of red appeared on the right arm of my fencing jacket, just below the elbow and the extra padding of the underarm protector. Donovan's foil had shattered, and he'd continued the attack with ragged steel. My parry had diverted his touch to my forearm, away from a potentially dangerous wound to my breast, even with a plastic chest protector.

I stood staring in shock at the jagged end of his considerably shortened foil. It had torn through my jacket and left a bleeding gash. Eventually, I gulped and dropped my own blade on the floor. Basic safety precaution.

After nearly an hour of warming up with other fencers, and winning those bouts, we met on a strip with no one else to fight. I simmered with adrenaline and sexual tension.

We'd been sparring back and forth for close to the fifteen-minute limit with a score of three to three. We'd each received two points from red cards—penalties for fighting *corps á corps,* body to body. If you are close enough to kiss, you are too close to fence.

Then I parried his next attack on my sixte, the high out-side line, and cut over for a solid riposte. A move he hadn't expected. His surprise and frustration at being unable to score on me must have made him lose his temper.

His counter parry was hard. Far too wide a movement with far too much force behind the blow for ordinary sport fencing with foils. Sabers maybe. But not these slender fourteen-ounce blades.

His riposte had been too fast to register the broken blade before it struck and drew blood. The fact that he'd hit off target on the arm showed how much his temper had robbed him of point control.

The clatter of wary fencers dropping their blades on the floor sounded loud in the sudden hush. Only after safely downing all weapons did they look around to find the cause of my alarm.

Just because sport fencing weapons have been foiled, or blunted, does not mean they are entirely safe. The whole reason for the padded jackets, masks, gloves, and rubber tips on the blades is safety. We wouldn't use them if we didn't need them.

Coach Peterson stomped over, shaking his head and muttering something about untamed Indians with more money than sense and not enough discipline.

In his current temper, that described Donovan perfectly. Behind my mask, I swallowed a shaky smile.

"Oh, my gosh, Tess! Are you all right?" Donovan ripped off his mask and grabbed my bleeding arm. The fierceness of his grip only made me hurt worse.

He'd struck with more than ordinary human strength. He shouldn't have been able to hurt me like that wielding only foils.

Coach continued to grumble as he picked up the broken pieces of Donovan's foil and retreated to the benches along the far wall of the *salle d'armes* where he kept a tackle box of tools and spare tips.

Donovan helped me remove my mask and escorted me to the coach's side, clearing the strip for the next pair of fencers. I still trembled with shock—both from the blow and the knowl-edge of just how short Donovan's temper was. I'd seen what happened to demon halflings when they lost their temper.

They transformed and ate people. Innocent people. Honorable people I liked and respected.

Donovan's computer game company was named Halfling Gaming Company, Inc. for a reason.

"Jacket off, Tess. Let's take a look at that," Coach ordered.

My hands shook too badly to manage the left side zipper. Donovan gently opened it for me and helped me shed the tight garment.

"Not too bad. Bleeding's slowing down. You'll bruise pretty bad, though," Coach said. He held my arm from wrist to elbow. Gentle. Reassuring.

"I'm so sorry, Tess. I know better than to let my temper rule me on the strip." Donovan guided me to a bench and urged me to sit.

I continued to stare at the splotch of blood, that had spread out from the jagged inch-long cut.

"Cold water, antiseptic, and a bandage will take care of that," Coach said. "Staring at it like a couple of moonstruck lovers won't. And ice for the bruising," Coach added. "Should be a disposable pack in the first aid kit in the back."

"I'll get it," Donovan hurried away and was back in seconds. He slapped the pack against the bench to send the catalyst into the slush and freeze it.

"No fixing this blade, Donovan." Coach shook his head. "After a blow like that, I wouldn't trust Tess' blade either. You've probably weakened it."

"I'm so sorry, Tess," Donovan apologized again, kneeling in front of me while he held the ice pack on my wound.

"If I were you, Tess, I'd hit up Mr. Estevez for a replacement blade. Make him get you a de Paul, or one of those new Italian blades everyone is raving about. The more expensive the better," Coach said and glared at Donovan. He carefully put the broken pieces into a long canvas bag for safe disposal.

"Hey, Gareth," he called to a lanky youth hovering nearby. "Run a broom over that area and make sure we got all the slivers."

I think I giggled. My usual reaction to shock. One that kept me from crying at the sharp pain that now invaded my entire hand and shot up to my shoulder.

"There's gauze pads in my purse," I said. "Two or three should cover this until I can get home and properly bandage it." It would probably be three quarters healed by that time. The imp flu had left me with all kinds of antibodies and extraordinary powers of recovery.

"Let me," Donovan said. His slow, sexy smile brightened as he removed the ice pack and kissed the wound. While he was at it, he licked it clean of blood. He ran his tongue along the gash, savoring the taste of me.

The whole move could have been extremely sensuous, a prelude to long, slow lovemaking.

So help me I couldn't break his magical hold over my senses.

Then last night's dinner conversation slammed into my memory. Vampire bats licking tiny cuts in their prey. Feeding off of their blood. Returning to the same victim time after time. Damiri demons becoming the source of vampiric legends. Drinking blood.

Only then did I notice that the dark bruise around Donovan's eye had almost completely healed.

Yeah. *Tell me again you aren't a demon.*

I yanked my arm away from his touch and dashed for the restroom, suddenly sick to my stomach and shaking all over. I splashed cold water on my face and neck. Then I washed the injury over and over with soap and hot water. Public restroom, antibacterial soap. Was it enough?

He'd tasted my blood. He could find me anywhere in any dimension to drink again.

"Scrap," I whispered, hoping against hope I was far enough away from Donovan for him to come to me.

Right here, dahling. Oooh, that's a nasty scratch. He hovered over the sink.

"D . . . Donovan licked it. Can you please clean it. Make sure you get rid of every molecule of him."

Don't know. He dropped to the counter, cocking his head and peering intently at the angry red gash. The skin already tried to knit closed. I pressed on either side to make it open again. Making it bleed again. I didn't want so much as an atom of Donovan's DNA inside me.

Scrap flicked out his tongue and jumped back, nearly crashing into the mirror.

"What?"

His saliva is poison to me. He spat and gacked.

I turned on the cold water. He drank and spat three times.

Then I stuck my arm under the stream. The water flowed over the wound, taking away the fresh blood. Then I soaped and rinsed it three more times.

"Does that mean he's poisoned me, too?"

Doubt it. But this gives me an idea. Mind if I duck out for a few? I need to do some research.

"If you've got an idea about what Donovan is, then go for it. But don't be gone long. I don't intend to stay close to him any longer than I have to."

Scrap popped out. I breathed deeply. Eventually I gathered enough courage to face him again with a calm visage if not a quiet gut.

Donovan had already fished the gauze pads and tape out of the zipper pocket in my purse for me. I bandaged it myself.

▬◣▽◢▽◣▬

Poison. What is poison to me besides demon toxin? Donovan carries no trace of demon in that bit of saliva I tasted. I'd know. Believe me. I'd know if he tasted of demon.

An old memory tickles my brain. I may have tasted something similar before.

I hop over to Lincoln, England, for a chat with the father of all imps, the one carved in stone inside the cathedral.

He's not inclined to chat. Turning into stone will do that to a body.

I've been in modern churches. No problem getting in or out. Same with this cathedral. Because of the imp glaring down from his perch? Does his presence get me past the gargoyles?

Just to test my theory, I scoot across the Channel to Notre Dame de Paris. This place has more than its fair share of gargoyles. Old and venerable ones with a great deal of power. I stand outside on the porch for a long time. Eventually, a human comes along and opens one of the doors. I follow nearly on his heels, walking every step. This is hard for me. My legs are bandy and short. They hardly support my weight. Imps are meant to fly.

And fly I do. Backward. The portal to this church repels me.

Above me, a particularly ugly gargoyle laughs when I land on my bum in a mud puddle.

Why? What have I done to offend a hideous gargoyle?

Disaster. My fall has stripped me of two of my warts. How *humiliating*.

I am so ashamed of my loss that I cannot bring myself to share this experience with anyone. Not even Tess.

Chapter 21

"**I** NEED A FAVOR," I stated as Donovan pulled his car out of the *salle* parking lot. What better time to ask than when he'd just inflicted bodily harm?

"Name it, L'akita." Worry pulled the corners of his mouth down. "Do you need to go to the ER?"

I inspected the swelling beneath the ice pack I still held against my arm. I slung my parka over my shoulders so I could keep it there along with some pressure. Hardly any redness left at all.

"No. I need backup when I confront Allie's new partner."

"Confront? Sounds ominous." An almost grin. I could tell his blood was still up. He needed a fight.

"About twenty-four hours ago, my Windago may have tagged him. If he's going to turn, he'll be showing symptoms by now."

"Got a cover story if we have to kill him?"

"He attacked and tried to rape me. I fought him off in self-defense."

"Local courts and cops going to buy that?"

"I hope so. He's new to the area. From Miami. Not well enough known to be one of the 'good ol' boys.'"

"From Miami?" Donovan's face took on a new rigidity.

"What do you know?"

"Suspicion only."

"Spill it!"

He looked away, swallowed deeply, made a big deal of using his turn signal at the next corner.

"Stop stalling and tell me."

"D's headquarters is in Miami. He has fingers in a lot of different pies. I find it too coincidental that a new cop from Miami shows up in a small town at the same time as D announces his engagement to a local woman. Then he gets tagged by a Windago? Too much."

"Yeah. If he'd come from Boston or New York, he wouldn't look so suspicious. Allie's in Boston with Gollum. This will give us a chance to talk to him without her interference."

I called police dispatch on my cell. "Hi, Millie, this is Tess." Right person on duty for this kind of call. Millie was the secretary for Mom's garden club.

"Yeah, what ya need? Allie's off duty," she said around a wad of gum. I knew from experience that she chewed and chewed on grape bubble gum for hours without blowing a single bubble. When the flavor ran out, she added more.

"I know Allie's in Boston for the evening. But I'd like to talk to her new partner, Mike Gionelli."

"Gionelli?" Donovan mouthed in surprise.

My curiosity level rose three notches. He knew the name. Too many coincidences.

"Whas up, eh?" Millie sounded relaxed, ready to settle in for a good gossip.

"We're having a party in the next few days. I wanted to invite Mike to meet the neighbors socially before he has to meet them professionally."

"Yeah, I heard about your mom, eh. When's the wedding?"

"A few weeks. But we want to have an engagement party first. Know where I can find Mike?"

"Long Wharf Café. He's got an apartment nearby and takes most of his meals there. You tell your mom I wish her the best, eh. I can run a background check on her new beau if you need me to."

"That would be . . ." Underhanded. Sneaky. Yeah, all

that and more. Necessary. "Could you do that, Millie? Legally?"

"Sure. No problem. Can't have some furrener making time with one o' our own now can we, eh?"

"Good idea. Go ahead and start the process. And report back to me, Millie. Just me."

"Even if it's bad news?"

"Especially if it's bad news." Then, as an afterthought, I asked, "Did anyone do a background check on Dill when we got married?" He was a "furrener," too.

"Just your dad. We figured he had a right to."

"Yeah, he did, I guess."

"We didn't find anythin' on him, though, eh."

"Didn't think you would." And I doubted they'd find anything on Darren Estevez either.

"Say, you ever find that raccoon what bit Moonfeather? I thought she had some kind of special connection with critters and they left her alone, eh."

"Uh. Yeah. My out-of-town friends found it, dead on the road."

"Found on road dead. Just like my old Ford, eh. Glad I finally got rid of it."

We both chuckled at her tired joke. "MoonFeather whacked him good on the head with a cast iron frying pan. Must have given it a concussion and it got confused. Someone ran over it. We had it tested. No sign of rabies."

"Good thing. I hear those shots ain't fun, eh."

Another moment of chitchat and I closed my phone.

"Must be a slow night," Donovan chuckled.

"About usual. Millie always has time to gossip."

"Even on a Friday night when the bars are hopping and the parties going strong?"

"Yeah." I told Donovan how to find the Long Wharf, three blocks behind us. He made an illegal U-turn, skidding the tires. Another driver yelled and shook his fist but didn't stop.

We found Mike in a corner booth with his back to the wall and his nose in a book. Not one of mine.

"Mind if we join you?" Before he could object, I scooted in next to him. Donovan frowned at me as he took the bench seat opposite. We blocked the guy in. He couldn't run if our conversation became uncomfortable.

I waved to the waitress, signaling a need for coffee and pie. She brought it right away along with water. She refilled Mike's ice-tea-sized glass with more ice water.

"So, Mike, where'd you come from?" I asked, in my friendliest down-home, folksy way. I'd learned a lot from Millie over the years.

"I told you. Miami." He folded down a page corner to mark his place and closed the book.

I scowled. That was no way to treat a book. So I dug one of my own bookmarks out of my purse, placed it neatly inside and smoothed out the corner. "What did this nice innocent book do to you to deserve that kind of treatment?"

"Um . . ."

Donovan just laughed. "Books are sacred to writers," he half whispered as if confiding a deep secret ritual to an initiate.

Keep it friendly. Let him relax. He'd be more likely to confide in friends.

Only he didn't relax. His slender body tensed as he drank half his water.

"Why are you here?" Mike asked, staring directly at Donovan.

"You know who I am."

"Yes."

"And you know what I am," I added, more a statement than a question.

"I've heard."

"Then you know you can't lie to us," Donovan persisted. "You can try, but you know we'll see through it."

Mike looked at the cover of his book, suddenly fascinated by the minimalist artwork and lettering of the latest thriller. My books sold well. I'd be extremely happy with a quarter of that man's numbers.

"He's not in your league for world building and emotional depth of character," Mike mumbled, still tracing the book cover with his finger.

"Thanks." Damn. Hard not to like the guy.

"I have a better question for you, Mike," Donovan stilled the man's hand with his own fierce grip.

Mike was forced to look into Donovan's eyes. He remained calm. I knew the strength in Donovan's hands and arms and winced inwardly for Mike.

"The Windago tagged you last night. Any swelling, signs of infection?"

"No. It didn't break the skin."

"Irritability? Sensitivity to light? Overwhelming desire to get lost in the woods alone?" I added my own questions.

"No."

"He's clean." I sat back and sighed with relief.

"Not entirely." Donovan maintained his hold on Mike.

I suddenly wished I had the comb. Then I could read Mike's aura clearly and know for certain who, or what, he was.

"How well do you know my father?" Donovan continued his interrogation.

Mike gulped hard. I watched his Adam's apple bob and his tanned face pale a bit. "Hardly at all. I've barely met him."

"Perhaps I should ask, how well your *family* knows Darren Estevez."

Mike yanked his hand free and sat as far back in the corner as he could squeeze his slender frame. He reached for his glass of water and downed the remainder of it in one gulp. Then he signaled the waitress to bring him more. She refilled his glass and my coffee cup then retreated a bare few feet, cleaning an already clean table.

I jerked my head toward her to make certain the two men were aware of her eavesdropping.

"So, there is a connection," I said quietly.

"A loose one," Mike admitted. "Look, I'm just an average guy trying to get by, do my job, and go home at night with a *clear conscience.*"

How should I read the emphasis of that statement? Or his body language? Or Donovan's for that matter?

"In other words, your family owes D something. He pulled strings to get you sent here as his spy as repayment," Donovan spat.

"I didn't want to do it," Mike insisted. "But I had to, or stand by and watch . . ." He shuddered and downed another glass of water.

I shoved mine toward him and he gulped that, too.

Donovan looked as if he wanted to strangle the man.

"I'm not one of his followers," Mike insisted. He drank Donovan's water and looked as if he needed more.

Our helpful waitress showed up with a pitcher. She poured water and ice ever so slowly. Watching the three of us more than the tall glass, remembering what she was doing, just before the glass overflowed.

"I know how D can manipulate things, make you feel as if his agenda is your own idea, then leave you to face the consequences alone," Donovan admitted once the waitress had retreated. "Believe me, I know. He's a master at making other people take the blame for his actions. So what are you supposed to report to him?"

"Anything I can find out about Tess and her family. But I haven't said anything yet. I haven't told him about . . . about . . ." he looked around cautiously. "About the Celestial Blade."

"And you won't," I whispered.

"Ever," Donovan emphasized.

"Ever," Mike repeated, almost mesmerized by his gaze.

"And you'll run by me anything you tell Darren before you tell him," I insisted.

"O . . . kay." He licked his lips. "Okay. I can do that, let you help me frame the words so I don't tell him anything of value while making it sound like some deep dark secret."

"Good man." I patted his shoulder. "You watch Allie's back and do as you're told, and we'll all be best friends before this is over." I slid out of the booth. "Oh, and remind Darren that I have killed before. I don't like doing it, but I can and will to protect my family and friends. I just added you to the latter list."

At least I wouldn't have to kill him forty-eight hours from now.

Mike nodded, looking relieved and grateful.

Donovan followed me. He tucked a generous tip in the waitress' pocket to buy her silence.

"What kind of demon is he?" I whispered once we were safely locked inside Donovan's car.

"Doesn't matter. He wants to be mostly human. How'd you guess?"

"If he weren't already a demon, the Windago tag would have turned him. I'm almost glad he's Kajiri. I like him."

"He's the kind of guy I'm trying to help. The trapped ones who don't belong on either side of the chat room."

Admirable. If that was *all* Donovan wanted for the half-lings, I might learn to trust him.

I really wanted to. My body cried out for his touch. My mind longed for the mental intimacy of long heartfelt conversations with him.

I'd get none of that until he told me the truth. All of it.

Chapter 22

Hey diddle, diddle, the cat and the fiddle, and the cow jumped over the moon. The little dog laughed to see such sport, and the dish ran away with the spoon.

"WHERE'S MOM? I don't see her car," I said the moment Donovan and I entered my mostly dark house. A new nervousness felt like a lead weight in my stomach.

The light over the stove and a dying fire in the hearth showed an empty kitchen. Clean dishes in the drainer. I opened the fridge to find remnants of the cod in wine and lemon sauce. Someone had cooked and eaten dinner.

Both Dad and Bill were decent cooks. I snitched a bite. Even cold it tasted wonderful. MoonFeather must have supervised.

"D said they'd be back about an hour after he called me, and that was three hours ago," Donovan mused. He whipped out his cell phone and punched a number. After an endless ten heartbeats he shook his head and pocketed it. "Either the phone is off, or they are in an area with no service."

"I don't like this." I stalked through the house, checking for signs of invasion.

We found Dad, Bill, Josh, and MoonFeather playing Scrabble in the dining room. The four of them plus Wind-Scribe could have polished off the fish easily. Bill would have washed the dishes even if he hadn't eaten.

"You are supposed to be in bed," I greeted my aunt. She looked pale and drawn, but better than I expected.

She grimaced. "I'm getting bed sores from that mattress," she grumbled. At least MoonFeather had her leg propped up on a pillow on one of the extra chairs. A small concession to her injury.

"Where's WindScribe?" A bubble of panic threatened to burst in my throat. I hadn't counted the mounds of garden gnomes in the yard when we came in. They'd promised me two more days to prepare.

When I thought with my head and not my hormones, I realized I didn't totally believe Gollum when he said the Orculli trolls would honor the temporary truce until the declared day and time of battle.

"She's in there." Bill jerked his head toward the sitting room, now MoonFeather's bedroom. He looked a little disgusted.

Then I heard the faint strains of a TV show theme song. I grimaced when I recognized a slightly obscene and totally inane animated feature of a science fiction show. It had a big cult following, but I refused to watch more than the first five minutes of the first episode.

WindScribe laughed loud and long at some piece of dialogue or slapstick action.

I grimaced.

"How did the reunion go?" I asked MoonFeather. "Did she deign to recognize you?"

"Hmf," MoonFeather grunted concentrating on her letter tiles.

"WindScribe called her old and the puppet of male politicians, then turned up the volume on the TV," Dad grumbled.

MoonFeather wouldn't say anything bad about our guest, even if she deserved it.

"Any phone calls?"

"Just James Frazier of the *Gazette*. We told him wrong number," Bill said, not lifting his eyes from his tiles.

"Good. I don't want him talking to WindScribe yet."

"Actually, she refused to speak to him," Dad said. He quickly rearranged his tiles, his eyes glowing with triumph.

"Any word from Mom?"

Dad shook his head. "Haven't see or heard from them," He yawned. He didn't look overly concerned, engrossed in compiling ever more complicated words out of his tiles. A peek at the score sheet at Dad's elbow showed that Bill was winning for a change. Probably MoonFeather's pain meds and Dad's concern for his only sister were interfering with their concentration. Josh looked like he'd rather be holding MoonFeather's hand than playing a game.

"I don't like the idea of Genevieve marrying a man she just met," MoonFeather said quietly. "We know nothing about Darren Estevez. He gives off a strange aura that makes me suspect they are not compatible." The closest I'd ever heard her say anything negative about a person.

"I'll say they aren't compatible," I agreed. "Maybe I should call Allie and see if there are any accident reports . . ." Then I remembered that Allie was in Boston with Gollum. I didn't expect them until after midnight. Another three hours from now.

But I could call Mike or Millie if I really wanted to know. Could I trust them to keep my anxiety a secret? Not Millie. Maybe Mike.

"Your mother is a grown woman, and I presume her fiancé is a responsible adult as well. Let them worry about themselves," Dad said. He placed three tiles on the board. "That makes your 'vamp' my 'vampire' with the e on a triple word!" he chortled, adding up his points.

I nearly choked. I'd had too many reminders of vampires and other undead creatures in the last twenty-four hours. I edged away from Donovan. Before I knew it, I had the entire length of the dining room table between us.

A car door slammed. I gasped and started.

"That's probably them now," Dad said. He stretched his back and added up the score again. "I'm ahead by ten points."

"I think I'm done in. Can we evict the little . . . lady from my room now?" MoonFeather asked. "Even the ghosts don't like that TV show. They're hovering outside their usual places," she whispered in an aside to me.

"I'll persuade WindScribe to find another entertainment," Donovan said and retreated into the sitting room.

I left them to turn on the kitchen lights and start a new pot of coffee.

A second door slammed. Masculine and feminine chatter. I turned to face my mother, trying desperately for a smile and a welcome. Instead, a stern frown overrode my emotions. I felt like the disapproving parent with an errant daughter who'd broken curfew.

I wasn't ready for the role reversal.

Gollum and Allie wandered through the mudroom into the kitchen.

"What are you doing here?" I blurted out.

Gollum blinked behind his glasses. I couldn't read his eyes, but his posture screamed surprise. "The lecture was from six to seven," he said blandly.

"Oh," I said flatly. I sagged. All my righteous indignation flew up the chimney. "I thought you didn't go on until eight or so and didn't expect you until midnight."

"What's wrong?" Allie asked. She stepped lightly, almost warily, eyes searching the shadows.

"Mom and Darren aren't home yet. They've been gone since early morning and they aren't answering the cell phone."

Gollum's eyes opened wide, and his glasses nearly slid off his hawkish nose. "You don't think . . . no, he wouldn't . . . would he?"

"Would he what?" I snapped.

"Kidnap her. He must want something from you. Maybe he figures holding your mother for ransom will be more effective than marrying her to get to you."

I gulped. "She had her heart set on a church wedding . . . Could he be so cruel as to crush her hopes like that?"

"He's Kajiri." Gollum sounded so matter-of-fact and emotionless I almost slapped him.

This was *my* mother we were talking about.

"Scrap, can you find Mom?" I called into the ether. I had no idea where the brat hid. With Donovan occupied with WindScribe at the other end of the house, my imp should be able to come to me.

No need, dahling. Scrap appeared in front of me, hovering on his tattered wings, sporting a fair amount of iodine on his bum and streaked lavishly around his eyes in a weird makeup job. He waggled the end of his pink feather boa at me.

I had to bite my cheeks at his garish appearance. Then I

had to pinch my nose as he farted and blew black cherry cheroot smoke in my face.

"You've been into some milk," I gagged.

Whatever. The cat didn't want it. At least not after I painted his nose with iodine. Scrap flashed his bum toward me and waggled his barbed tail. *Mom and Darren are driving down our street as we speak. They should be pulling into the drive about . . . now.*

Sure enough, I heard the crunch of gravel under tires.

Again, I sagged. This time in relief.

"Tess, sweetie," Mom gushed as she practically flew through the door.

"Mom?" Was this young, vivacious, attractive woman with short, highlighted hair and a new stylish suit with—gulp—*slacks* really my mother?

Mom always wore skirts and pearls and kept her hair in a tight French roll.

"Mom?" I choked out again.

"Oh, sweetie." She lapsed into the slight lisp of her French-Canadian accent. "You'll never guess. We drove to Maine and got married!"

Chapter 23

The word lunatic comes from the Latin lunaris for Moon. A lunatic exhibits the kind of insanity that waxes and wanes with the phases of the moon.

*E*l Stinko comes into the kitchen, but he does not eject me.

The presence of Darren, a true demon, overrides Donovan's power. Just like when we fought the Sasquatch last autumn.

I turn a bright vermilion. I lengthen and twist. My need to slay Darren consumes me. Only when he is gone from this life will Mom and my beloved Tess be safe.

Yet Tess does not command me to transform. If we attack Darren, he can only defend himself by becoming a giant bat. That would appall Mom. But would she believe that her new husband could actually be a demon? Would she trust her own eyes? Her faith would not allow her to believe the truth.

Then again, Darren might remain in human form and allow Tess to kill him, forever driving a wedge of unforgiveness between her and her mother. Is that his goal? Weaken Tess by separating her from her family.

Or, worse, having her condemned as a murderess.

Her wise head prevails.

Still, the need to become a weapon, to taste his tainted blood on my blade becomes a burning ache. If I do not change soon, I will burst into flames and consume us all in the fires of the six hundred sixty-six levels of hell.

I must duck into the chat room to douse the flame within me.

◣▽▲▽▲▽◢

"Married! How could you be so stupid?" Donovan yelled from the butler's pantry entrance.

Scrap was nowhere in sight.

"Marrying Genevieve was the smartest thing I could do." Darren smiled in a sickly-sweet sort of way that told me he didn't mean a word of it.

Mom, however, drank it in like iced sparkling water in the desert. She couldn't take her eyes off him, as if she needed his direction to breathe.

"That tears it. I'm going to a motel." Donovan plowed through the kitchen. "Let the lovebirds stay in the cottage. I'm out of here. It's been fun, Tess. *L'akita.* We'll talk tomorrow." In a flurry of cold air and slamming doors he was into the mudroom.

"Come back here, son," Darren ordered. He dropped a bundle of shopping bags and blocked the outer doorway.

"I am not your son. I was your ward. And only because you manipulated my naïveté. I do not have to obey you like that tribe of gangbangers you sired," Donovan snarled. He raised his clenched fists.

"Now, boys, there is no need to fight," Mom said. She fluttered around the inner door, looking pale, fragile, helpless, and more beautiful than I'd ever seen her.

"There is every reason to fight if this undisciplined child refuses to obey," Darren said. His eyes narrowed and he, too, brought up his fists. "You've only been mortal for fifty years, hardly enough time to learn the proper ways of the world," he said, so quietly I'm not sure anyone but me heard.

"Oh, a fight. I do so love a barroom brawl," Dill drawled from his post in the kitchen nook. "'Bout time someone showed D what it feels like to be on the receiving end."

Did he mean Darren or Donovan?

Why had he shown up now?

My head started to hurt. Like when I'd worn the comb too long.

Or not enough.

"I'm here to help you out, of course, lovey. I don't see an imp around, and there is a fight brewing," Dill answered one of my unvoiced questions.

"I have tasted the blood of an honest warrior tonight, D. Do you still want to fight me?" Donovan squared his shoulders and took on an aura of calm authority.

Darren blanched. He dropped his hands back to his sides, but he kept his level gaze on Donovan.

Until that moment I hadn't realized how much they looked alike. Or how closely Dill resembled them.

My mind whirled in confusion.

"We will finish this later, D. For now I thank you for the offer of privacy with my bride." Darren stepped aside.

Donovan stomped past him and down the two stairs. Before his foster father could gather the bags and enter the kitchen, we all heard Donovan's car backfire and gravel spray beneath his speeding tires.

"Oh, dear, I was hoping we could all be one happy family. I do so miss having all my relatives around." Mom pouted prettily. She did it well and I often wondered if she practiced it before a mirror.

Darren took his cue and enfolded her in his arms. "There, there, *querida*." He patted her back affectionately.

"Dad and Bill are in the dining room with MoonFeather. Don't you want to share your good news with them?" I asked.

"You can tell him. Right now I'm just going to slip upstairs and fetch my toothbrush and my nightie." Mom kissed Darren long and passionately.

I rolled my eyes upward.

Allie caught my expression and shared it with me.

Gollum looked like he wanted to take notes.

"Well, if we aren't going to open a bottle of champagne, I'm going home," Allie said.

Darren and Mom didn't look up from their lingering embrace.

"I'll call you in the morning," I said, escorting her to the door. "I had an interesting conversation with Mike tonight."

Allie raised her eyebrows in question.

I shook my head, indicating I wanted privacy for that discussion.

"And I believe I shall retire to my own rooms," Gollum added. "Gandalf will need his supper and I have some notes to record. I'd like to share them with you, Tess, when you get a minute."

"Sure. I'll be in when people are settled." Oh, for the days when I lived all alone and dreamed of going to Mexico for my vacation!

At last Mom broke the clinch worthy of a romance novel cover. "I'll just be a moment, *cheri.*" She positively skipped toward the stairs.

I made to follow her.

"Wait a moment, Tess," Darren said. He grabbed my arm, right over the healing wound. His grip would leave bruises. More bruises.

I couldn't help but wince and try to pull away. He held me firmly. Easily.

"Get your hand off me." Mom wasn't around. I had no reason to pretend politeness, or that I liked this guy.

"Let's get a few rules straight first." Darren tightened his fingers on me.

I nearly dropped to my knees in pain. Only extreme willpower kept me upright.

"Scrap?" I called. "I might need some help here."

"He won't help you, lovey," Dill said. He didn't move from his lounge against the wall by the nook. "But if you banish the imp, I'll break this guy's neck. Been wanting to do that for a decade or more." Dill's eye sockets glowed red. He loomed larger than life. But he remained across the room, as separate from Darren as Scrap was from Donovan.

That was something I needed to explore. Later.

"First off, since your mother and I are now married, I think it more appropriate that you move into the cottage and leave the house to us." Darren's dark eyes turned steely.

"Not on your life, buddy. In case Mom hasn't told you, the entire property is mine. She lives off my largesse, not the other way around." I held his gaze, promising him retribution if he didn't let go of my arm. My fingers were already turning numb.

He looked surprised. Then his eyes narrowed. "That can be changed. We will live in this house. With the ghosts and all of the other garbage you've collected. It will make a nice retreat for my people. Good thing you left the zoning for a bed and breakfast intact."

"You are welcome to the ghosts. But the house is mine. In fact, I think you should start looking for new accommodations immediately. You aren't welcome here. So make the new house big enough to host family game night. Surviving that is more challenging than fighting a Warrior of the Celestial Blade."

Darren smiled knowingly. Like he knew he'd get the last word. "And another thing. I'll take the comb."

Everything inside me froze. So this is what it was all about. The Kajiri wanted the comb and the magic it gave me.

"The comb is mine."

"Not anymore. You gave it to your mother, in front of witnesses. I am now her husband. What is hers is mine. Legally and now metaphysically."

"Over my dead body."

"That can be arranged."

"Are you forgetting who and what I am?" *Scrap, dammit, get your ass back here.*

"Never. But I have you in a bind. Hurt me, and you destroy your mother."

"She'll recover."

"Will she? Look how long it took her to recover from your father's betrayal. How much worse will it be if her beloved daughter hurts or kills her new husband. No, I think I'm safe. Safe enough to take the Kynthia brooch as well as the comb."

How did he know about *that?* Scrap had found a gold brooch in the shape of the Moon, Star, Milky Way configuration the Goddess assumed in the skies. Only after he gave it to me did I discover that the brooch signified leadership of the Sisterhood of Celestial Blade Warriors. It was mine now, not that I lead the Sisterhood, but because of some metaphysical law of finders keepers.

"The entire otherworld knows you have those two artifacts of power. If you want your mother safe, *alive,* and happy, you will turn them over to me."

"I'll kill you first."

"Tess!" Mom screamed.

Darren dropped my arm as if I'd burned him.

"Take that back," Mom raised her voice further. "You just don't want me to be happy. You want me dependent and needy so you can have control over everything you touch."

Psycho babble from Mom? What had Darren done to her? Again, she gazed soulfully at him rather than look at me.

Probably just the dim light, but I thought her eyes reflected red for a moment, like a flash in a photo. Gone the moment I thought I detected it.

"I told you that all that mucking about with fencing would come to no good." Mom stamped her foot in a most unladylike manner. "You were never a violent person until you started playing with swords. Now take that back, or I'll never speak to you again."

"Promise?" I smiled sweetly to cover my own amazement. How much had she heard? Not enough if she still defended Darren.

"I meant what I said, Darren." I left the room as fast as I could and still maintain a fragment of dignity. I nearly ran through the house and upstairs, frightened out of my wits, for myself and my mother. What could I do to separate her from Darren now that they were legally married?

Killing Darren seemed the only way.

Too late. Too late. I return to Tess, cooler, composed, ready to do her bidding and not mine.

Too late. I should never have left. Then we could have slain Darren out of hand. I would have tasted his blood and known that I had done a good thing. Mom would have seen Darren for what he truly is, a demon bat who sucks blood.

I know now that Darren must die. For Mom's sake. For Tess' safety. For my own satisfaction.

Chapter 24

*T*IME TO CHECK ON all my responsibilities. Josh tucked MoonFeather into her bed. Dad and Bill packed up the Scrabble game, kissed me good-bye, and went home. That left WindScribe. I wondered why she had refused to talk to our local pest . . . er I mean reporter. She seemed the type to want to flaunt her "otherness." Why not to the press?

"We need to talk, WindScribe. Or should I call you Joyce Milner?" I said as I topped the stairs and entered my room.

"Joyce is dead," she said from her perch on my bed in front of the blaring television.

I switched off the set.

"I was watching that!" she protested and pouted as prettily as my mother.

What is it with these ditzy dames that they always look beautiful when their petty emotions should make them ugly?

"Now you and I are talking. We can't do that with that mindless stupidity intruding."

"It's not stupid. It's funny!"

I let that one pass. "WindScribe, I've promised to go into battle for your freedom. I'm putting my life on the line to keep you here in your home dimension. I need to know something before that happens." I remained standing, in a position of authority. She didn't strike me as the kind who would open up to a friend sitting next to her.

Reticence and evasiveness are habits long learned and hard to break. I realized she needed time to formulate her story before going public to James Frazier, or even private to me. She'd had all day. What else had she been up to?

Maggie, the upstairs ghost who usually flitted from room to room, seemed entrenched in the guest room where Mom had slept last night, refusing to come near WindScribe.

"I don't know anything." She suddenly found the candlewick pattern of my bedspread fascinating.

"Then tell me about Faery. What's it like?"

She shrugged. "It's just another place." She still wouldn't look at me.

"Must be a special place if your coven put together a tricky and dangerous spell to take you all there." I let my voice go soft and a bit dreamy. "When you first stepped into this world, you said you'd been kicked out of Paradise and wanted to go back. So tell me about it."

"It's pretty there. Lots of flowers. Always warm so we didn't need the artificial confines and pretenses of clothes." Her face took on a wistful look.

"What kinds of flowers?"

"All kinds. Some from here. Some from every other dimension in the universe. Everything grows and flourishes and becomes better than they are in Faery."

"Sounds lovely. Healing. You needed healing when you went there," I said. From what Allie had said, Joyce had suffered a difficult life with an abusive mother.

"Wicca healed me," she asserted. Finally she looked me in the eye.

"MoonFeather says Wicca offers spiritual healing to any who ask." I doubted WindScribe had healed as much as she claimed. Not with her drug-induced nightmare of being locked in a closet beneath the stairs. Some nightmares we never recover from.

"I couldn't have gotten into Faery without healing."

"Did something happen in Faery that allows you to see Scrap?"

"I can't see him anymore." She looked off into space beyond my left shoulder. "The touch of Faery that allows you to see things as they truly are lingers in your perceptions. But not for long."

She's lying, Tess. She sees me now. Look at the way her pupils contract and the lines around her mouth tighten.

"Can you hear him?"

Of course she can't. We're communicating on a tight beam rather than a broadcast.

"I didn't know he talks."

Lying again. We had a talk about her choice of lace over brocaded ribbon to lengthen your blue slacks.

Traitor! I slammed back at him. *Couldn't you have talked her into asking my permission or for a loan of other clothes?*

"I never see . . . saw his mouth move."

"Sometimes Scrap talks way too much." I glared at him before turning back to WindScribe. "Who rules Faery these days?" I asked more gently.

"Some silly king. He had lots and lots of rules that were impossible to learn. And he kept changing them without telling anyone." The pout came back.

"Did you break one of his rules? Is that why he kicked you out?"

"I'm tired. I want to go to bed." She slithered off the bed and ducked around me so fast I couldn't catch her.

My protest was still forming in my mouth when she slammed the door to her attic room. The lock snicked closed like a period at the end of a paragraph.

Desperate for answers, I used my cell phone and dialed the secret phone number of the Citadel.

A phone on the other end rang once. Then the signal died, cutting me off from help.

<hr>

"Where is the brooch now?" Gollum asked when I'd told him about my conversation with Darren.

Talking to WindScribe wasn't doing me any good. So I decided to brainstorm with Gollum. He might not talk about himself, but he'd talk endlessly on a variety of other subjects.

"In a safety deposit box in Providence," I replied quietly,

in case anyone was listening outside the apartment. Actually the repository for the sacred brooch was a jeweler in Boston who specialized in storing valuable pieces and heirlooms while providing good replicas for everyday wear. My replica was in the bank in Providence.

Paranoid? Me?

Of course. I feared retaliation from the Sisterhood who felt that the piece belonged to their elected leader more than I feared a demon would steal it. Until tonight.

"You might look for a different repository. If it gives off a magical aura, a gifted hunter could home in on it with no trouble." Gollum's eyes lit with a bit of excitement. Was he a "gifted" hunter?

"Scrap tells me there are a couple of other pieces in the vault with a stronger magical aura than mine." The jeweler's vault, that is.

"Then keep it there," Gollum replied on an equally quiet whisper. He turned up his small stereo. Opera, a light aria I couldn't identify, filled the apartment and masked our voices. "We don't know what kind of metaphysical or magical authority the piece grants. We don't want it falling into the wrong hands."

"I agree. Darren is getting nothing from me. And as soon as I can convince my mom that he is a con man through, and through, he won't even have my mother."

"Good thinking. But we have another more immediate problem."

"WindScribe and the toothy garden gnomes." I just couldn't think of those little guys as Orculli trolls. Trolls are big and hairy and live under bridges.

Gollum pulled a book from his briefcase. The fat, trade-sized volume looked well worn and had a dozen Post-it notes protruding from the pages.

I read the title. "A Field Guide To Wild Folk: Faeries, Gnomes, Pixies, and Sprites." The author's name was long, unpronounceable, and Italian.

"A year ago I would have laughed out loud that someone actually needed a field guide for critters out of fairy tales," I said on a nearly hysterical giggle.

The music shifted to something militaristic, right on cue. I paced in time to it.

"And now you know that fairy tales sometimes come true. The grim ones, not just the cleaned up versions published by the brothers Grimm. Did you know that their original manuscript was quite accurate and quite dark, but the Church ordered revisions more consistent with their worldview?" He thumbed through the yellow flags, reading a few lines on each page.

I nodded. Of course I knew that. The gesture was lost on him. His entire attention belonged to that book.

Gollum thumbed through more pages, finally stopping about two thirds of the way through. "Sit down and then look at this."

I plopped onto the cushy sofa that threatened to swallow me. Dill had picked out the furniture in the apartment. I had never had the chance to spend any time in here. Before or after he died.

We'd headed west on that final, and fatal, trip less than a week after we moved into the house.

Now I wondered at the rather feminine choices of overstuffed furniture covered in bright floral chintz. I liked it. I doubted that Dill would. Who had he chosen the furniture for?

Where was he anyway? If he haunted any part of the house, it should be here.

"I haunt you. Not the house, lovey," he reminded me from his casual slump against the computer desk that Gollum's laptop now occupied. "And I kind of resent your new boyfriend taking over my office."

I ignored him rather than retort that Gollum was not my boyfriend. Colleague; yes. Friend; yes. Lover? I didn't think so.

"What do you think of this guy?" Gollum held the book out for me.

Right there, in full color, sat an excellent watercolor print of the little king of the garden gnomes; complete with droopy red hat and golden feather. The bit of gold braid around the crown was more elaborate in the picture, more crownlike and brighter. I wondered if losing WindScribe had given his gold a bit of tarnish.

"That's our guy." I peered at the microscopic print beneath the picture. "King Scazzamurieddu, a Laúru of northern Italy."

"This is a bad translation," Gollum said. He sat down next to me, pushing his glasses on top of his head. He took the book back. "I have an original Italian version in storage. The names are all mixed up. He should actually be an Orculli of the Tyrol district. But they did get the hat right. It's his most prized possession. Some folklorists believe the hat is the secret to his magic."

"So why is he here?"

"What this book doesn't say, but a friend of mine in Boston told me, is that the Orculli were drafted to be pandimensional prison guards. Their punishment for stealing the rest of us blind is to imprison more dangerous beings. They also are accused of bringing freezing temperatures and icy roads when in a bad mood. King Scazzamurieddu is the prison warden."

"What kind of crime warrants pandimensional imprisonment?" Darren had spoken of metaphysical laws of possession. Was there really a codification of laws that applied to all races in all the many universes?

"I don't know. But apparently WindScribe committed a big crime if Scazzy is willing to cross dimensions and battle a Warrior of the Celestial Blade to get her back." He lost himself for a moment reading more about our foe.

"Somehow I don't think petty theft is involved." I remembered the contents of my purse scattered across my candlewick bedspread. "WindScribe is spacey and immature, but she doesn't strike me as a hardened criminal."

"Beware of first impressions, lovey." The music went cold and eerie like a ghostly wind in bare trees. "I caught her picking the lock on your desk. Expertly. She was looking for drugs. Lucky you flushed the lot."

"Do you feel a draft in here, Tess?" Gollum heaved himself up and inspected the windows.

I immediately thought of the Windago. My spine remained free of the typical warning flares and I heard only an occasional gust whipping through the woods, not the wail of a demon.

"It's an old house full of drafts. Feel free to build a fire in the wood stove in the bedroom. It's probably more efficient than the fireplaces in the rest of the house."

"I don't think Donovan left you a lot of wood."

I heaved a sigh and laid my head back against the very soft cushions. With my eyes closed, I could almost believe I was somewhere else, far away from the problems that had descended on me.

"Mind if I stay here a while and pretend I'm on a beach in Mexico sipping *piña coladas*?"

"Sure go ahead. I'm going to see if anyone knows how to fight King Scazzy."

"Simple: steal his hat."

"If only it were that easy."

<hr />

A gentle kiss to my forehead awoke me. I left my eyes closed, drifting in a warm, safe cocoon of wool blankets and a long hard body pressed next to mine.

"Dill?" I murmured and reached to hold my husband close.

"Sorry," Gollum grumbled. "Wouldn't you be more comfortable in your own bed?"

I'd fallen asleep on Gollum's cushy sofa.

I opened my eyes a crack and groaned at the loss of my wonderful dream and having made the *faux pas* of all time.

"Yeah, I guess I'd better."

"What happened to the house rules? We sleep in beds and not on the furniture?" he quipped. A half smile tugged at his mouth.

"That rule was for you. You don't sleep in *my* armchair." I twisted to untangle my legs from the lovely blanket he'd wrapped me in. "What time is it anyway?" I couldn't get my arm free to check my watch.

"About two. The house is quiet, and all the lights seem to be out."

"Did you find out anything more about our Orculli trolls and King Scazzy?"

"Nope. All of my colleagues agree that he's the prison warden, but no one knows what kind of criminals he guards. Amazing what kind of information is available in a chat room. I met the most interesting man from Russia. I knew of his work, but had never had the opportunity to chat with him before."

"I guess we'll have to have a long heartfelt talk with WindScribe in the morning." I yawned and stretched. If we tied her to a chair and threatened her with hot coals, we might get some straight answers. I would never torture her with imprisonment in a dark box like her mother had.

That kind of abuse might explain her need to set things free and avoid constraint by a seat belt.

"Thanks for letting me nap. I feel much better than I did when I came in."

"Any time, love."

Chapter 25

NOW THAT IS MORE like it! In time Tess will realize that her best interests lie (or is that laid) with Gollum and not Donovan and his ilk.

Maybe if I pretty her up a little, Gollum will be more bold. That's the only thing that will penetrate her thick skull. Let's see now, a little makeup wouldn't hurt, and some nice wool slacks rather than sweats—she'll never go for a skirt unless it's one hundred degrees outside with an equal humidity, or she's going to a place that almost requires a dress. Let's see what we can find in the closet. I'll just lay it out for her, maybe help her get the hint.

What! The sapphire blouse and sky-blue pants are missing. I can smell them in the house. Where can they be?

That thieving, conniving bitch! WindScribe has stolen half of Tess' best wardrobe! And she's altering them. Taking in seams to fit her willowy figure, adding trim and lace to pant legs to lengthen them!

That look is so passé. But then the waif has been out of the loop for thirty years or so. She needs an education in fashion as well as manners.

"Tess dahling, wake up. I've got some things to tell you about your guest and the monster cat. I forgot to tell you about the cat and the armory door yesterday. Sorry. I got busy. Tess, stop swatting at me. Tess, will you please wake up."

Finally. She sits up and listens. Then she glowers. Then she sets her chin.

Ooooooh, there's going to be trouble. Maybe a fight. I can't wait.

Then she plops back down and covers her head with a pillow. I don't think she heard me at all.

Much to my surprise, Mom and Darren showed up for breakfast Saturday morning just as I started fixing johnny cakes—a kind of cornmeal pancake—sausages, and eggs. I expected them to sleep in, or go out, or do just about anything to avoid me after my confrontation with Darren the night before.

A light New Age instrumental played in the background. Nothing that demanded we listen, an easy accompaniment to life. Just as Darren entered the kitchen, I noted a muted bass string underlying and adding tension to the melody.

There was a new strain about Mom's eyes and mouth, but she put on a good show of being the happy bride, sitting close to her new husband and chattering brightly and sipping coffee and orange juice. But she didn't touch him like she had the last two days. She didn't meet his silent and penetrating gaze. Even when he spoke the bastard French Mom had invented as a child. (How'd he learn it?)

And she had reverted to her dress and pearls. The only remnant of the makeover was her short hair and brighter makeup.

Maybe there was hope for an annulment yet.

Especially if Darren's fight with Donovan had made the wedding night less than expected.

My mind shied away from the intimate details that might cause this kind of tension between them when they'd only been married less than a day. I remembered my own honeymoon with Dill and sighed with regret that I'd never share that kind of closeness with him again.

"You can, lovey," Dill whispered. His voice was a near caress on my ear. "You know what you have to do."

He asked too much. Too late. If he'd started haunting me

right after his death, I'd have given anything for us to be together, even my own life. But he hadn't shown up until last autumn, right after I'd had my first otherworldly fight. Right after I'd asked Scrap to transform into the Celestial Blade for the first time.

There was something fishy about the deal Dill offered and the timing, and I don't mean last night's supper of cod with lemon and wine sauce.

Gollum came in just then with a bag of fresh apples and oranges and made a second pot of coffee.

MoonFeather hobbled in on her crutches, grumbling about not spending another minute in that bed and what could she do to help. I set her to putting together a fruit plate. She sat at the island in the middle of the kitchen, out of my way yet still close enough for me to fetch things for her.

WindScribe drifted down wearing my blue outfit all tarted up with lace and braid trim from my bag of scraps for costumes. I ground my teeth together, determined to speak to her the moment we had a speck of privacy.

Manners were universal. Or they should be. If she'd borrowed some sweats, I'd have bought her some clothes at the mall today. But no, she went for my expensive clothes. I didn't feel like I owed her a thing.

We ate together at my new table with the new linens and things. I was happy with the décor. It gave us something to talk about to cover the false brightness in Mom's voice and posture. She fiddled with her pearls, and ran her hands uncertainly through her short hair.

"I hope you haven't made a mistake, Genevieve," Moon-Feather whispered to Mom during one of the lulls in conversation.

Mom glared at her. I could almost hear her mental shout: *Mind your own business, witch.*

MoonFeather reared back as if slapped.

I swear no words passed between them. Only negative energy. Extremely negative energy.

"What are we all doing today?" Mom asked. She sounded brittle and fragile.

"I'm searching the Internet for a good price on a trip to

Mexico," I said quietly. The clouds and wind and icy temperatures had come back. No shadows. Was that good or bad for drawing Windago out during daylight?

"I'll be setting up my office at the college," Gollum said.

Coward, I mouthed at him for deserting me with this mob.

"I guess I won't be doing anything but reading in bed," MoonFeather grumbled.

WindScribe looked a little panicked. What was she going to do with the day? With the rest of her life?

"I'd like to see a bit of Cape Cod. Never been here before," Darren finally said.

"Fine. We can find a real estate agent to take us around and look at properties." Mom didn't sound fine. She sounded angry. With him?

Hopefully.

Then they all dispersed. Except WindScribe.

"Would you help me with the dishes, please?" I asked her. I'd made quite a mess. I always did when I cooked. For the last two years Mom had done most of the cooking and all of the cleaning. I couldn't expect her to do that anymore. At least not until she got rid of Darren and life got back to normal.

Normal? What is normal? Not my life certainly. What with a grieving Windago stalking me, Orculli trolls, strangers stepping out of Faery, Mom marrying a demon, and me all hot and bothered for a different demon . . .

And then there was Dill. Could he really come back to life?

No. I wouldn't go there even in my imagination. Some things were just too creepy.

"I guess I can help. There isn't much else to do. The only TVs are in MoonFeather's room and your bedroom." WindScribe sighed as if prison shackles weighed heavily upon her soul as well as her shoulders.

"What are your plans, WindScribe?"

"What do you mean?" That panicked look was back, like a wounded bird ready to flee.

"I mean, you can't stay here forever. You need to find a job, get an education, do something with your life."

"Isn't there some kind of cosmic law that says, since you rescued me, you have to take care of me?"

"You aren't a lost puppy, WindScribe. You are a person. You have to take responsibility for yourself."

"You're just mad that I took your lipstick without asking." The limp, frightened child vanished from her countenance, replaced by a wary fox.

"I'm mad that you have so little consideration for everyone around you." I drew on every skill I had learned in my years as a teacher to maintain a calm demeanor. Anger only begat anger. "You've taken my clothes and altered them so that I can never use them again. You monopolize the television so that others are forced out of the room. You don't seem interested in communicating with me or anyone else in the house."

"I've been through a traumatic experience," she whined. "It's like . . . like battle fatigue. Or that Stockholm Syndrome or something."

"We call it posttraumatic stress syndrome now. And you need to talk about it. To me, to a social worker, to a psychiatrist. To MoonFeather. Someone."

"No one would believe me." She pouted prettily.

I was getting tired of that expression. On her. On my mother. Even Donovan looked like he'd practiced it.

"Try me. I've had some pretty weird experiences. I doubt even you could top them for strangeness."

"My coven was kidnapped to Faery. They have so many impossible rules no one could learn them in a hundred years. They threw me in prison with trolls as guards, and I escaped." She threw out the explanation as if it was a fast ball.

Was that movement outside the window? Like a face peering in, then ducking down?

I chilled, waiting for the wind to howl like a Windago.

Nothing. The weather remained calm. Cold, but calm.

"I know some of what happened. Gollum and I talked about it last night. I've fought your prison guards and killed a couple of them. They wounded MoonFeather. She's my aunt and a dear friend. What I don't know is which rule you broke to send you to cosmic prison." I threw the ball right back to her. "It must have been a bad one."

"You know?"

"Yes."

"How?"

"Because I am a Warrior of the Celestial Blade. It's my business to know. And I have to fight your prison warden again for your freedom tomorrow at noon. A fight that may cost me my life, and Gollum's as well if he helps me. So you might think about giving me a damn good reason why I should take on that horde or I just might let him have you."

"You . . . you can't do that." She looked truly frightened now.

"I can and I will if you don't come up with some explanations."

"But . . . but . . ."

Before she could come up with another excuse, Donovan walked in without knocking. WindScribe took one look at his scowl (or was that the infamous pout) and fled.

We had only washed half the dishes.

"There's a reporter skulking about outside. I evicted him. Forcibly," he reported.

<hr />

"Make yourself useful." I tossed Donovan the dish towel.

"Look, I . . ."

"You don't have a choice. If you stay one more moment without helping, you are out of here. Permanently." I applied my emotions to scrubbing an already clean skillet.

Donovan rolled his eyes and wiped the oversized fruit bowl that wouldn't fit in the dishwasher. We endured several moments of silence that became almost companionable.

"I like this," he said quietly while pouring soap in the dishwasher. "Domestic cooperation."

"It's nice to have help. For a change," I replied noncommittally. I tucked the last of the juice glasses into the rack. Dried tomato juice coated the sides. It looked like blood. Darren had drunk from that glass. The rest of us had OJ, including Scrap. Only the imp's glass was half beer.

Should I set the glass aside and have the crime lab test it? What if he'd tapped one of Mom's veins for it?

No. I'd poured the tomato juice myself. I was overreacting.

"Why are you here, Donovan?" I was so tired of waltzing around half statements; not saying what I knew about him; not getting answers.

"Because you are in danger and I worry about you." He draped the towel over his shoulder and grasped my arms, turning me to face him. He didn't turn on the magic mojo, but he was still a damned attractive man.

"Not good enough." I looked up into his eyes, trying to force the truth, the whole truth and nothing but the truth out of him. "I've been in danger before. Scrap and I came through it okay."

"D will suck you dry and spit you out into the garbage heap of the universes if I don't do something. He tried with me, but I escaped him." His eyes burned with an intensity that frightened me. I had no idea how deep or dangerous his anger was. I did know that, when enraged on the fencing strip, he could knock me flat, disarm me, and then laugh about it as if breaking rules and codes of honor was just a joke.

"I've already told him he can't have what he's looking for." I gave him my own version of an intense gaze. He needed to know I was serious about this.

"Which is?"

I held my tongue. I could play this game of secrets as well as he.

"I should know what he wants, why he came here. But I don't. I'm not in the loop like I was last year." He shook his head and looked away.

I'd won that staring contest at least.

"And which loop is that?"

Silence.

I wrenched myself out of his grasp and began scrubbing the now empty counters.

"Tess, I've never made any secret of how attractive I find you." He touched my shoulder gently.

"Thank you."

"I've also told you that I've never met another woman I'd be willing to settle down with, have children with. Our babies would be beautiful, filled with strength and talents way beyond that of normal humans. We aren't normal, Tess. Neither of us could be happy with a mundane human. We belong together. We owe it to the future of all the races to have children that will carry on our legacies." He dropped his head as if to kiss me.

I backed up a step, putting as much psychic distance between us as physical.

Though I wanted to kiss him. I longed to hold him close and just feel good for a change.

I held off. He'd tasted my blood. Savored it.

"That's all? You want me to be your brood mare. No ring, no marriage, no honesty. *No* communication. Just go to bed with you and push out a dozen brats for posterity! No, thank you. You've said your piece, now get out. I have work to do and a battle to prepare for."

"Tess, that's not what I meant."

"Well that's the way I interpreted your half truths. Now get out. Just get the hell out of my house and out of my life." I instantly regretted my words. A vast lonely gulf opened up in my heart. But I wouldn't take it back. I couldn't. Not until he told me everything.

Including why it was so important to create a homeland for half-blood demons that he'd mortgaged his entire financial empire for it. He'd lost everything when we destroyed his casino in order to close a rogue demon portal. Yet as far as I knew he hadn't given up on that homeland.

For the Mike Gionellis of this world, I could understand. He seemed like a good guy despite his demon heritage.

But he just wanted to fit in with humans, not separate himself in a halfling homeland.

So the great project was to create a halfway house for Donovan and Darren as much as the lumbering Sasquatch and other uncivilized beasties who couldn't just get along.

What about the Windago and whatever else was out there? What did they want besides *my* blood?

In the nook Dill silently applauded me. "He's not good enough for you, Tess. Besides, you still belong to me."

"You can get lost, too, Dillwyn Bailey Cooper."

"He's here?" Donovan's beautiful brown eyes opened wide. Panic flashed across his face before he mastered the errant emotion.

"Yeah, the ghost of my husband still haunts me. You'll have to stand in line with all the other supernatural beings who want a piece of me." Disgusted with them both as well as myself, I threw the sponge into the sink and nearly ran back to the sanctuary of my office.

I passed WindScribe at the far end of the butler's pantry. As I wound through the dining room I heard her say, "I'll have your babies, Donovan Estevez."

Chapter 26

"SCRAP!" TESS CALLED ME.

I could tell by the tone of her voice that she was not happy.

"Cellar. Now. Work out."

Oh, boy, she is not happy. I can smell her anger even over the cat, and . . . is that jealousy oozing out of her skin? Crap. I'm in for a tough time as she flings the Celestial Blade around. She gets so erratic she has no control when she's this mad.

I follow her down the steep steps to the cellar. Her sandy-blonde corkscrew curls bounce and fly about as if attached to her head by small rubber bands. I reach out and tweak one, trying to lighten the mood.

My babe just snarls at me. Then she flings herself off the last three steps, bracing on the banister and landing neatly in a tight turn next to the armory door beneath the stairs.

Oops! I forgot to tell her when she was awake about the faulty latch and the nosey cat trying to get in there. It's not my fault. I got caught up in keeping that horrible cat in his own domain and out of mine. I have a job to do, too! Besides, I had to cover the scratches on my tail with iodine, like Tess told me to. And a little red paint here led to a little more there, and so on and so forth.

It's not my fault.

Well, mostly not.

Maybe partly.

"Babe?" I probe delicately.

She mumbles something even I can't decipher as she fumbles inside her sweatshirt for the key.

No light shows around the doorway. I breathe a big sigh of relief. The cat probably pushed the door closed while it was playing with the latch. Or the ghost did. I'm safe from a tongue-lashing at least.

But not safe from the replica blade. Tess reaches into the armory and grabs it without looking. She's on me in less than a heartbeat, swinging the twin moon blades right and left, up and down, circling, twisting.

"Maybe you should try meditation," I suggest. Then I have to jump hither, thither, and yon trying to stay above her, below her, just out of reach. She can't hurt me. Much. I'm only partially in this dimension. But the blade is made from my essence. It is an exact replica of me when I transform. A part of me had to go into the crafting of that blade. I don't know what will happen if she actually connects with me on the cutting edge of one of those blades.

Too close. She snags my tail in the tines of the left-hand blade and flings me in a dizzying circle.

I pop out of this dimension and back again behind her in half a breath. I tweak one of her curls. "The Sisterhood might have some information on WindScribe and the Orculli trolls."

"I called, they didn't answer." Another vicious slash with the blade.

I jump high and cling to a ceiling beam while I take a breath. "You could try reaching out to them from a deep meditative trance. You've done it before," I say.

The blade comes back over the top of her head and nearly cleaves me in two.

Pop out and then in again, this time in front of her. My stubby little wings fight the air keeping me aloft. I'm getting tired.

But so is Tess. She has burned too much energy out of anger and not spared enough for calculation. When she fences, she *thinks*. Now she is just reacting.

I can use this. I fly right high, left low. She follows me with wild and wide swings of the blade. I flit back to the middle, then, just as she rears back for a hard blow, I dart high left and she misses. When she recovers, I'm already at the low left and tying the end of my pink boa around her knee.

She sees my decoration and begins to laugh. Hysterical, high-pitched gales of laughter. She is out of control.

I'm worried.

"Is something wrong, Tess?" Gollum asks from the bottom of the stairs. We'd been so preoccupied neither of us noticed him come in.

Bad move. We have a battle to fight tomorrow. One moment of inattention will be the death of both of us. If I die, she dies. If she dies, I die. For imps, there is no ghostly half life like Dillwyn Bailey Cooper has. No afterlife with a benign deity. Nothing. Death is the end. I do not wish that to happen.

A Sister at the Citadel—Jenny, I think—lingered in a wasting half death for nearly six months after her imp, Tulip, got tagged by a demon claw. Jenny clung to life; so did her imp. Until they were both bare shadows. I had to do something, I couldn't let their torture go on.

I gave them both mercy.

Tess was there. She knows how horrible that time was for Jenny and Tulip. She didn't argue with me. She just held Jenny's hand at the end, letting her know she wasn't alone. If that's not faith, I don't know what is.

We both mourned them.

Neither of them came back to haunt us. Tulip can't. He's dead and gone for good. Sister Jenny is at peace.

If Tess dies tomorrow, neither one of us will have peace.

I choked on my own laughter at the sight of Gollum appearing so suddenly in my cellar. How did he open the door and get down the stairs without either me or Scrap noticing?

Three deep gulps of air and I thought I had my breathing under control again. I'd worked off a goodly portion of the steaming anger that drove me. Now I had only aching shoulders and cramping fingers where I gripped the blade too tightly. White knuckles and trembling knees betrayed my weaknesses.

"What's wrong, Tess?" he asked again. "You usually fight with more . . . aplomb than brute force reaction."

"What's wrong?" I hate it when I parrot back a question to avoid answering it. Kids used to do that to me all the time in the classroom.

Remembering why I still boiled, Donovan's arrogant assumption that I'd be willing to become his brood mare without a thought for why I resisted a relationship with him sent new waves of adrenaline through my body. And this time my brain received some of it, too.

Faster than thought I whipped the blade up to his throat, spun him around, and pinned him to the door of the armory with the shaft across his throat.

"Don't suppose you want to talk about this?" he asked in a choked gargle.

"No, I don't want to talk. I want to fight. I want to kill that little bastard of an Orculli so that I can kick a dozen people out of my house and take a much needed vacation in Mexico." I pressed harder against the shaft of my weapon.

Gollum's face turned a little purple. He inched his hands up to grasp the staff and lever it away so he could breathe.

His strength and coolheadedness surprised me. I was dealing with Guilford Van der Hoyden-Smythe the nerdy scholar, wasn't I?

Wasn't I?

Something in his eyes sent frissons of alarm up my spine.

Before I could register the emotion, I found myself propelled backward and pinned to the opposite wall in the same manner I'd imprisoned him. Shelves pressed awkwardly into my spine.

Gulp.

And Scrap had the nerve to roll on the floor in a fit of giggles.

"You do more than a tai chi regimen every morning."

"I have studied a number of martial arts. You'd be surprised and horrified at what I can do." He eased up on me a little. His face went blank, telling me more than he wanted to.

He'd done something awful with his martial arts and regretted it daily.

The Gollum I knew didn't fight. He observed others fighting and took notes.

But there was the time last autumn when Marines and

Homeland Security had arrested us. I was in trouble from a strange reaction to their tazer. The medic wanted to give me tranquilizers to calm my convulsions. The drugs would have killed me. My brain operates a little differently since my bout with the imp flu.

I came back to consciousness to find three Marines down and Gollum's hands on the throat of the medic.

"How'd you do that?" I choked out.

"I work out." He shrugged off my query into his abilities. As he shrugged off any questions about his past. "Mostly aikido these days."

I'd heard of that martial art but didn't know much about it. Something about using an opponent's energy against them.

"Maybe I shouldn't ask you what is wrong, Tess," he said quietly. "So I'll just tell you to talk. What happened to get your knickers in such a twist?" Steel entered his voice, like I'd never heard before. What had happened to the Casper Milquetoast I thought I knew so well?

Homeland Security had asked a lot of questions about the time he spent in Africa while in the Peace Corps. He'd just admitted to knowing martial arts. Something had to connect the two. I knew it in my gut.

Shocked into truthfulness, I blurted out my conversation with Donovan and . . . and WindScribe's infuriating response to it.

"So are you considering having children with Donovan?" he asked, blinking away the scary stranger he'd become and replacing him with the familiar quirky nerd.

"Not on your life! What's my guarantee that they'll be human? What's my guarantee that he's not some kind of black widower who will kill me—most horribly—as soon as I push out the required number of brats?"

"Good points. So do you feel the need to have children any time soon? Because if you do, we could do it together." He blinked again, and something I couldn't identify crossed his face.

"Children? The way my life is going, I have no guarantee that I'll still be alive twenty-four hours from now. I'm not about to bring a kid into this crazy life with women falling from the sky, a demon marrying my mother, pandimensional prison wardens challenging me to a duel."

"None of us have a guarantee that we'll still be alive in the morning, Tess. Life is uncertain." That blank face again. Like he needed to forget something to keep his sanity.

"So, eat dessert first."

He grinned.

We both relaxed. The terrible pressure of the shaft relaxed against my throat.

"Want to let me go?" I asked, gesturing to the Celestial Blade. "I'm calm now. I promise not to hit you."

Don't believe her, Scrap chortled.

I stuck my tongue out at the imp.

"Just remember that when you do feel your biological clock ticking, I'm available." He gently traced the scar on the right side of my face from temple to jaw with the little finger of one hand while still holding the staff in place.

I didn't yet understand how he could see the scar when no one else could. It was as otherworldly as Scrap. He couldn't see Scrap. Very little about Guildford Van der Hoyden-Smythe made sense.

Maybe the aikido had some spiritual discipline that gave him insight into the otherworldly but not full access.

So what do you say to the man's proposal? Scrap took flight, dusting himself off from the dirt on the floor and the bruises of our fray.

In my mind's eye, I could more easily picture Gollum as a father of my children than as my lover. The idea didn't suck, though.

A gentle warmth trickled through my breasts and down between my legs.

Would he be a kind and considerate lover? Or was he a slam-bam-thank-you-ma'am-think-only-of-himself lover?

That question brought memories of the one night I had spent with Donovan, before I knew of his nefarious schemes and questionable heritage. Warm and delicious memories of passion shared. We'd taken hours to explore each other's bodies, culminating in explosions of multiple orgasms. I smelled again the dry musky scent of his skin. Felt the strength of his hands as he kneaded my breasts. Tasted the saltiness of his . . .

The anger wanted to boil in me again. I didn't have any left.

I had only Gollum's mild blue eyes, magnified by his glasses, staring at me, demanding some kind of answer. Not daring to hope.

I couldn't hurt him.

I couldn't encourage him either.

"I'll think about it. When my biological clock ticks loud enough and long enough, I'll let you know and we'll make a date with a turkey baster." Ungently, I thrust the staff back at him.

He stumbled just enough for me to slip free and bound up the stairs.

I trusted Gollum to put the thing away and properly lock the door. That was more than I could say for anyone else in my life at that moment.

Chapter 27

Celtic people of Europe revered rivers, lakes, and ponds, and in particular springs. They were especially sacred to Eostre, the Goddess of the Moon, fertility, and healing. They cast votive offerings to the Goddess into water sources, a tradition held over in the wishing well.

AFTER MY ENCOUNTER with Gollum in the cellar I didn't want to be alone, where I'd have to think about our conversation. So I stopped in to see my aunt.

"I want to go home," MoonFeather stated the moment I poked my head inside her door.

"That's not such a good idea, MoonFeather." I sat on the edge of her mattress and looked deeply into her eyes.

She'd banished the fogginess of the pain pills. New creases at the corners of her mouth told me she still hurt. A lot. But didn't want the drugs to interfere with her thinking.

"I can get around my house as easily as I can here on crutches. More easily since my floors are level and I don't have to go up or down two inches every time I move from one room to the next." She crossed her arms in a huff.

"That's part of the charm of living in an old house." I tried to dismiss her concerns with a blasé gesture.

"It's a pain in the ass," she snorted. Her sense of humor began to shine through. It still had several layers of pain and willfulness to peel away though.

"I may be able to speed the healing a little if you will trust me," I offered cautiously.

558   *P. R. Frost*

"How?"

"Scrap."

"The imp?" Her focus narrowed to my left shoulder, and I wondered, not for the first time, if she could see him.

This was getting spooky. I wondered if our lengthy stay in the world outside the Citadel thinned the layers of invisibility around Scrap.

"Yes," I said cautiously. "Scrap, can you lick MoonFeather's wounds to negate some of the Orculli toxins?"

Don't know, babe. I can do it for you. We are bonded.

I translated for my aunt. "MoonFeather and I share common blood origins. Will that help?"

I can only try.

"Just a little to begin. How long should we wait to see if it affects her negatively?"

Not long, dahling. If I'm toxic to her, she'll feel the first drop of imp spit.

"Go for it, Scrap. Remember, just a little around the edges to begin." I lifted one corner of her bandages, exposing two stitches that closed the horrible gash. A little blood seeped around the sutures and a surgical iodine solution stained her skin a hideous orange-red.

Scrap dropped to the mattress. He cocked his head, staring at the wound for three long heartbeats. His little snubbed nose worked, separating the individual scents of blood, skin, antibiotics, painkillers, and whatever mixed in MoonFeather's blood. Then his forked tongue whipped out and in. One drop of dried blood disappeared.

Tastes weird, Scrap confessed. *It's you but not you.* He looked immensely satisfied.

I watched MoonFeather's face for any trace of change in color or texture.

"Well, what's happening?" she asked impatiently.

"I think Scrap can continue. But take it slow, buddy, in case we've missed something.

Too eagerly, he lashed the wound with flicking lick after long savoring lick.

I exposed the entire wound.

"That feels good. It needs air to heal. Doctors don't always know what's best," MoonFeather sighed and leaned back on her pillows.

I plumped them a little for her.

"So, will you take me home, or do I drag Josh out of his office and make him come get me?"

"MoonFeather, can you wait one more day? Please?"

"Why?"

I closed my eyes, gritted my teeth, and told her about the upcoming battle with King Scazzy.

"Noon on the day of the full moon. Palm Sunday. Good instincts on Gollum's part. Two forces draining energy from the prison warden."

"How did you know about him being the prison warden?"

"I have my own research tools." She pointed to a load of books Josh had brought her now scattered across her bed. "I also spent some time talking to your Gollum in the middle of the night."

"He's not *my* Gollum." Or was he? Our strange conversation in the cellar seemed a whole lot stranger now that I thought about it.

I shuddered and shivered and banished any thoughts I might harbor of taking Gollum as a lover. Or a husband. Or as the father of my children. We were friends. Why complicate and possibly endanger with sex my only normal relationship?

"So what is your strategy for fighting off this King Scazzamurieddu?" MoonFeather brought me back to reality.

"I'll fight him like I did the Sasquatch. He's a demon. Right."

"Not quite," Gollum added from the doorway. His face reflected some dark emotions. How much was left over from our encounter in the cellar I couldn't tell.

Scrap, having finished his ministrations in short order flitted behind Gollum's left shoulder, in the place tradition assigned to death. The imp looked just as grim and subdued.

If Scrap was worried, I should be, too. My stomach cramped with anxiety.

Both MoonFeather and I looked to Gollum for an explanation.

"King Scazzamurieddu is the prison warden of the universe. He has a job to do. He's doing it in trying to retrieve

WindScribe. He doesn't judge her. That's for other powers. He enforces that judgment. By thwarting him, we are going up against some mighty powerful forces, disrupting the cosmic balance."

MoonFeather blanched. "That, Tess, is something you do not want to do."

"What can I do? I'm pledged to protect the girl. In a way, I rescued her. Therefore, I'm responsible for her." WindScribe's words came back to me. Yes, there was some sort of cosmic law that made me feel as if I had to defend her. Once she was safe she had to look after herself. Until then, I had to protect her.

"You must look to your Goddess for inspiration," MoonFeather said solemnly.

"But I don't believe . . ."

"You may not believe in your Goddess, but she believes in you."

A sense of power and mystery swirled around us. Reality tipped slightly to the left. The subdued colors in the room took on more vivid hues.

"Tonight, at midnight, just before the moon sets, it will be close enough to full for our purposes," MoonFeather whispered in that otherworldly voice that carried the wisdom of the ages.

Chills ran all over me. I sat, awestruck, listening.

"Go out to Miller's Pond where it marks the edge of your property," she continued. "There you must cast into the deepest waters that which you treasure most. Murmur a prayer, any prayer that feels right, conclude the prayer with the words 'Blessed Be.' When the moon sets, it will look as if she has eaten your votive offering."

▰▱▲▽▲▱▰

I returned to my kitchen to find Mom fixing lunch. A rich soup filled with vegetables and chunks of chicken simmered on the stove. She sliced cheese and bread at the center island with her back to the table where Darren and Donovan glared at each other.

I flipped on the radio to the easy jazz station. I didn't like the house too quiet. When only silence surrounds me, I listen for things that are not there, like Dill's step or a Wind-ago hovering in the wind.

"Thanks for cooking, Mom." I kissed her cheek, and took the opportunity to scrutinize her expressive face.

Like me, she wore her emotions openly. I sensed less strain in her than this morning. The tension was across the big room in the nook between her husband and his foster son. And her eyes were clear. She was happy for herself, not because Darren commanded it.

"Did you have a successful morning?" I asked her brightly.

Behind me, Gollum helped MoonFeather navigate the narrow butler's pantry with its tilted floor and then the two-inch step down into the kitchen.

I had no idea where WindScribe had taken herself. Silence above stairs, so she wasn't watching television.

Scrap, check on her for me, please.

She's rooting around the medicine cabinet in the bathroom. Won't find anything stronger than aspirin in there.

Mom's migraine meds?

In the cottage and her purse.

I sighed in relief.

"We found a darling house," Mom said. She turned the full force of a genuine smile on me.

"Damn near as big as this place," Darren added. His smile looked like a gloat. "Newer, too." Like that was a plus in a historic area where status came with the age of one's dwelling. "More efficient design, doesn't ramble like this one. Not hard to change the zoning if we decide to do that B&B thing."

"But it's not in as good a shape as this house." Mom handed me the platter of bread and cheese to put on the table. "D, will you help me with the soup pot?" The look in her eyes was as full of infatuation and admiration as it had been yesterday.

Darren had worked his mojo on her again. I wondered why he hadn't this morning? Maybe he needed time between bouts to recoup his powers. A weakness, perhaps? I'd need every advantage when it came time to fight him.

"It's the old Milner place," Darren said, lifting the big kettle from the stove and carrying it to the table as if it weighed no more than a loaf of bread.

I paused to breathe. WindScribe's name before she took a craft name had been Joyce Milner. I looked around for evidence of her presence and her reaction to that bit of news.

A flicker of movement in the dining room might have been her. Then again it could have been one of my ghosts, benign or otherwise, or even Scrap. No telling among these creaking old timbers.

"We'll need to do some remodeling, since the house has been empty for almost three years and hasn't been updated since the forties," Mom continued. "But we can get it for far below market value."

"We're going to make a cash offer this afternoon." Again Darren nearly gloated. "As soon as I call my banker."

I wondered if he used the same banker as Donovan. Vern and Myrna Abrams had demon connections but fought on the side of humanity with me last autumn. They'd also required Donovan to sign his mortgage papers in blood.

"I can have the kitchen I've always dreamed of," Mom sighed. "And I'd love to cook for all of D's family when they come to visit. Did we tell you that he has seven children besides Donovan? I love a big family. Always wished I had more than just you three." She nearly floated to the table and took her place at the head—the place where I should sit since I owned the house and was officially hostess.

I let the slight slide. This time.

Or was that every time?

"While you take care of the financial things, darling, I'll call on Father Sheridan and make arrangements for us to have a church blessing of our marriage," Mom added.

Did Darren forget to breathe?

"I can design invitations and announcements on the computer for you," I offered. "I'll send a bunch of them by e-mail to our relatives and friends. We should have a reception at the church. The parish hall will host a lot more people than we could have here." I narrowed my eyes and watched Darren's reaction. I needed to know what he'd do if he actually had to enter a church. I'd even show up to watch.

Donovan hid a smirk behind his hand.

"I've already told James Frazier from the *Gazette* about the engagement. He said he'll print an announcement tomorrow." Mom looked incredibly proud of herself.

"When did you see James?" The pest hadn't called today . . . that I knew of.

"He was just driving by the Milner place and stopped to chat," Mom replied.

"He asked a lot of questions about your other guests," Darren said, watching me closely. "Like how MoonFeather really got hurt and how you know Miss WindScribe, where she came from, that sort of thing. Sounded to me like he knew things he shouldn't and wanted confirmation."

"Strange that he'd be driving past the Milner place. If I remember the house correctly, it's on a dead end." I smiled sweetly at Darren, letting him know I would not be drawn into his probing conversation.

"Did . . . did you say the old Milner place?" WindScribe whispered from the doorway.

"Why, yes, my dear," Mom replied. She looked a little puzzled, as if she couldn't remember who WindScribe was. I'd only told her that she was a friend, temporarily homeless. "Do you know the house?"

"Yeah. Why is it empty?" The girl looked terribly young and frightened. One of those amazing shifts she did from vicious to vulnerable in an eye blink.

"Old Mr. Milner developed Alzheimer's. I believe he's in a nursing home," I told her. She didn't register the medical term. I'd forgotten that it had only entered our everyday vocabulary in the past decade or so. "Such a shame when people forget everyone around them."

Mom jumped in to fill in gaps in the story. "I heard tales that he confused his wife with his mother. He had to be put away when he began accosting every teenage girl he saw on the street, demanding to know where she'd been and why she ran away from home. He thought that every one of them was his missing daughter."

"How awful," WindScribe choked. "Wh . . . what happened to his wife?"

"No one knows. She just locked the house and walked away the day she put her husband in the nursing home." Mom shook her head in dismay. "Such a waste. Janice

Milner was quite an asset to the garden club. She got a little tiddley at parties, but no one minded. She was a happy drunk."

I almost gagged on that statement. I remembered the old bitch from some of Mom's garden teas when I was in high school. Janice Milner had a tongue on her that could flay a person alive. Then she'd laugh herself silly, totally oblivious to the embarrassment she caused.

No wonder her daughter had turned to the local Wicca coven as an escape. She'd probably have chosen to stay in Faery forever just to avoid her mother. Except that she'd broken a rule and wound up in an otherworldly prison.

What had she done?

"That family's tragedy is our good fortune." Darren didn't rub his hands together in glee, but he might as well have. "The township just put the house on the market. It's going for back taxes and the residual on the mortgage."

Legal wheels grind slowly. It took three years for foreclosure and confiscation.

"But the house was badly neglected even before it was abandoned." Darren narrowed his gaze to me. "We'll have to impose on your hospitality a while longer, Tess, until we can get the roof repaired and the plumbing updated. I'll find a contractor to redo the kitchen to your specifications, *querida*." He kissed Mom's palm, pausing to lick and nibble on her fingers.

Yuck.

"In the meantime, we can plan an exquisite wedding reception," Mom sighed. She blushed prettily.

"We'll have to find the perfect dress and veil for you," I said. I tucked into my soup so I wouldn't have to engage Darren's gaze any longer. Something about his eyes unnerved me. They looked human and yet . . . there was a redness to the brown iris and a slight misshapen quality to the pupil—like it wanted to shift to the vertical from round.

Oh, yes, this man was part demon. I wondered that everyone he met didn't notice it.

But not everyone knows that demons exist. And not everyone is on the lookout for them.

I checked Donovan's eyes for any hint of otherworldliness. Nope. His pupils were perfectly round, and the iris remained that rich chocolate brown I'd almost fallen in love with. Damn, I wished he weren't so attractive.

Time to change my attention.

"A pity about the Milner daughter," Darren pushed, shifting his attention to WindScribe. "She'll never get to go back home now."

"If she's even alive. Thirty years is a long time to go missing." Mom's gaze turned wistful and she turned an unfocused stare out the window toward the garden gnomes that had multiplied in the yard between the house and the cottage.

"Maybe she had a good reason for running away and staying away," WindScribe whispered. She kept her eyes down as she tiptoed to the table.

"From what I heard, she was running with a bad crowd, a bunch of witches intent on disrupting the town." Darren fixed WindScribe with an intent gaze. "Bad thing, witches and black magic. I think the Milner girl did something terrible, committed some crime, so that she shouldn't come home, even if she could."

I don't think I could have kept my head down and my eyes averted under such scrutiny.

MoonFeather gasped. "Have you ever heard of the threefold law, Mr. Estevez?" she asked sweetly. Too sweetly.

He blinked and shifted his attention.

"Whatever you do in life, good, bad, or indifferent comes back to you threefold," MoonFeather continued. "I believe that firmly. I make a point of never saying anything bad about someone, even if they deserve it."

Silence rang around the table at my aunt's oblique put-down. She hadn't said anything bad, yet still she'd let the man know he'd stepped over the line.

"Now, now, no fighting while we eat. It upsets the digestion. We should say grace, even if it is a bit belated." Mom held out her hands to join with Donovan and me.

I grabbed one of Mom's hands eagerly and took Gollum's in my other. He joined the circle to WindScribe. Would she, in turn, take Darren's at the end of the table? Donovan reluctantly placed one hand in MoonFeather's. She extended hers to Darren.

I bit my lip, wondering if he dared exclude himself from

a family tradition. A family he'd joined by marriage. He was a part of us whether he liked it or not.

Whether I liked it or not.

I wondered if he'd survive family game night tomorrow. Sunday, with Uncle George, Grandma Maria, and my sister Cecilia. Maybe Dad and Bill would show up for a change.

Just when I thought Darren would push back his chair and leave us, rather than say grace, he clutched hands with MoonFeather and WindScribe and bowed his head. His lips even moved as Mom recited her favorite prayer and invoked her Christian Trinity.

Chapter 28

Highly prized among Masonic memorabilia is a jewel of black onyx with a carved head of Isis set in an ivory crescent Moon. Below that, dangling within the curve of the Moon, is a five-pointed star representing Sirius—the Dog Star.

"TESS, CAN I talk to you a moment?" Mom asked from the doorway to MoonFeather's room.

"Sure. Just a minute while I finish changing this dressing," I replied. I steeled myself to look at the angry and seeping wound. The doctor had packed it with collagen to fill in the gaping hole left by the gnome ripping a chunk out.

The skin knit cleanly beneath the stitches. Scrap's ministrations had worked miracles in just hours.

"It doesn't look too bad," Mom said, peering over my shoulder.

"It's a mess," MoonFeather grunted.

I'd done my best to keep from hurting her when I ripped off the old bandage, but I could tell from the strain around her eyes and the whiteness around her lips that all was not well yet.

"I need to go home," MoonFeather continued. "I need to poultice this with special herbs and spells to negate any . . . foreign infection."

Demon venom, in other words.

"I wouldn't worry about that," I said looking directly into her eyes. "Much of the infection is gone."

"Actually, what I have to say might be better said in front of witnesses. D is very big on witnesses to this sort of thing," Mom said, hardly pausing for breath.

That surprised me enough to look up from placing new gauze over MoonFeather's war wound. This sounded akin to the argument I'd had with Darren.

"Since I cut my hair, and I've already married D, I won't be needing your comb to hold my wedding veil. I know you treasure this and I want you to have it back." Mom thrust the antique into my suddenly shaking hand.

"Mom, I wanted you to have this for a reason." I examined her expression, posture, and her eyes for signs of what was truly going on and found only my Mom.

"I know. And I want you to have it back for a reason. Now put it away before D stashes it in a safety deposit box or finds a more obscure hiding place. You need this." Mom turned abruptly and flounced away.

"My, my, my. So my ex-sister-in-law has a spine after all," MoonFeather mused.

"Or was that a plea for help?" I asked, more worried than ever.

"I give this marriage three months max before she dumps him."

"Maybe not quite so long," I returned. "She's seeing him for what he is." I held up the comb and nodded to it.

"And that is?" MoonFeather raised her thick eyebrows at me.

"Would you believe me if I told you he's a half-blood Damiri demon?"

"From the dangerous energies that swirl around you, and the evidence of garden gnomes come to life with more teeth than a shark, I'd believe almost anything, Tess. Now why don't you sit and tell me precisely what is going on. Maybe I can help."

And so I told her the entire story. I spoke of my time in the Citadel learning to be a Warrior of the Celestial Blade. My adventures on the high desert plateau of central Washington last autumn came out a bit more hesitantly. Then the words flooded out in a torrent. I felt lighter and freer with each revelation.

Her brows sank lower and lower as she narrowed her eyes and tensed her shoulders.

"Make certain the votive offering you give to your Goddess is something you treasure above all things. Not because of monetary value, not because the world is jealous you possess it. Give what your heart clings to. Nothing less will ensure your safety tomorrow in battle," she whispered as she clung to my hand. "The world cannot afford to lose you."

MoonFeather's advice to make a votive offering to a Goddess I didn't believe in was just too weird. Even for me.

Scrap's suggestion to seek advice from my friends at the Citadel sounded more logical. They didn't answer the phone, so I had to revert to other methods that didn't rely on technology.

But where in this very full household could I find the privacy to properly meditate?

Gollum's apartment of course. He was still at the college. I called his cell for permission to take refuge there.

"My door is never locked to you, Tess," he said quietly. "Do you need some background music. I can recommend . . ."

"Thanks, but I have my own."

"You might let Gandalf help."

"The cat? How can that pesky critter . . . ?"

"Take him into your lap and let him purr. You'd be amazed at how much easier it is to meditate with that rhythm echoing your heartbeat."

"But Scrap is allergic to cats."

"Does Scrap help you reach out through the ether beyond mortal awareness?"

"Noooo . . ."

"Then try Gandalf. If it doesn't work, lock him in the bathroom."

That sounded like a wonderful idea. So I grabbed a CD from my collection, a couple of blue candles, and a stick of incense in a scent compatible with the candles. I chose these because I liked the color, not because of any spiritual symbolism.

"Are we having a pot party?" WindScribe asked when she saw me lugging my stuff out of my office.

"No." I didn't feel like explaining myself to *her*.

"I'm bored. What am I supposed to do all by myself?"

"Read a book. I've got lots all over the house. Take your pick." Then I slammed the door to the apartment in her face.

Deep within the apartment I found some cherished peace and quiet. The sounds of life from the house and the road remained outside these insulated walls. I set up my candles and incense on the coffee table in front of a worn leather recliner. Why fight an uncomfortable posture with no support sitting in the middle of a cold floor? The idea in meditation was to relax. So I stretched out and let the chair cradle me.

The upholstery still smelled of Dill's aftershave and his unique male scent. I drank it in along with the incense. A gentle throbbing drum and wordless chant from a Midwestern tribe wafted over me from the stereo.

My body eased immediately. Some tension lingered across my shoulders and my fingers still clenched.

Starting with my forehead, I consciously tensed and relaxed each muscle group until my entire body felt more liquid, my spirit lighter. Then a series of visualizations stripped more and more tightness from my psyche.

Gandalf levitated to the arm of the chair. I reached over and ran my hand the length of his silky body. He vibrated from head to toe in a pleasing rumble. I didn't have to look at him to invite him closer. He stepped lightly into my lap, circled once, and stretched out with paws and head on my chest. That rippling purr caressed my soul.

With a sigh I let my mind drift in ever expanding circles. Gradually, I sent those circles west, across mountains and plains, jumping mighty rivers and climbing bigger mountains and plunging down to the high desert plateau of the Columbia River Basin. Mile by mile I sped across my memory of the route to the Citadel hidden in a deep ravine not far from Dry Falls.

A question mark appeared in my mind. Telepathic contact is not exact, often symbolic.

"Who?" I whispered.

An image of a bubbly blonde. Gayla, the woman I had dragged in out of a thunderstorm and nursed through the imp flu. Sister Gert had tried to refuse her entrance, the infirmary was full, resources stretched to the limit. Maybe Sister Gert sensed that this bright and bubbly personality would become a rival for the leadership of the Sisterhood. Whatever, I couldn't leave her out there to die alone. Under Sister Serena's direction I had lanced the festering wounds of the infection. Our kinship went deeper than our scars.

What followed wasn't truly a conversation, but it's easier to convey in that manner.

"I need advice," I whispered with voice and mind.

"Should I get Sister Serena or Sister Gert?"

"Let me talk to you first." I sent a flood of information about WindScribe, the Orculli trolls, the Windago. At the last second I tucked in a bit about making a votive offering.

"All other dimensional beings are evil! You must kill all you encounter." Sister Gert's voice blasted across the miles in an almost physical manifestation.

I winced at her volume and intensity.

"But the prison warden of the universe?"

"He's a troll. He's evil."

I always knew the leader of my Sisterhood was single-minded, with blinders on. Was that a redundant statement? Well, Sister Gert embodied redundancy.

"What about my leadership brooch, Teresa?" Sister Gert continued, barely stopping for breath. "When are you going to return my brooch?"

I let a long chasm of silence come between us. Scrap had given me the brooch. I wasn't about to give it to a woman I didn't like and barely respected.

"Don't worry about the right or wrong of the Orculli trolls," Gayla intervened. "Just do what you have to do."

On a more private line of communication I sensed an upcoming vote between her and Gert about leadership of that particular branch of the Sisterhood.

"Okay. I can handle a fight with the trolls, though I'd like backup. Any chance of linking me to another Citadel?"

"I'll see if there are any rogues in your area," Gayla said.

"Rogues? I thought I was the only one."

"Not anymore. Things are changing. New portals opening. A lot more traffic back and forth. We can no longer work in isolation."

"And Gert doesn't believe that," I confirmed. "The old ways have worked so long she can't envision any kind of change."

"Correct." Hesitancy, like there might be an eavesdropper.

"Good luck with the election. The Sisterhood needs you."

"They need you, too. My first change will be to open communications."

"Then make sure someone answers the telephone." I felt a lot more comfortable and less alone with Gayla in charge.

"Gotcha."

"What about the votive offering."

"You have to question that?" Gayla came through almost as strong as Sister Gert had before. "I would think that would be the obvious course of action."

"Obvious to you. I'm not sure I should bother . . ."

"Bother, Tess." Gayla's tone turned soft, confidential. A friend giving sound advice.

"If you think it will help . . ."

"I know it will."

"How do you know?"

"Because I believe."

Scrap believed in a number of Gods and Goddesses. Mom had a deep and abiding faith.

I wished I could believe in something bigger and better than just my own strength and resolve.

Chapter 29

GRADUALLY I ROSE up through layers of meditation to an awareness of reality. I felt refreshed in mind and body, as if I'd slept deeply for an entire night.

Not for long.

A crash of cast iron frying pans hitting something metallic brought me the rest of the way back with a jolt. My temples throbbed. Candlelight pierced my eyes like a laser strobe. Too fast. I'd come out of the trance too fast. I don't think my soul had a chance to catch up with my body.

I leaned forward and blew out the candles.

Another crash from the region of the kitchen, muffled by distance and thick walls.

I winced and tried to huddle back into myself.

I crawled out of the recliner, my joints just a little liquid with languor. Time to be the adult in the household.

I trudged through the house toward the kitchen, making my way by feel more than sight. I could too easily tip over from extreme relaxation to headache.

Blinking against the glare of sunset coming in through the bay window, I stood stock-still in the doorway from the butler's pantry. WindScribe stood in the middle of the kitchen with a small saucepan in her hand, ready to throw it. Moon-Feather sat at the island, out of the direct path of the girl's aim.

Allie held a defensive position in front of the refrigerator, ready to duck or retreat when the next missile flew. A pile of heavy cookware lay at her feet and a big dent shadowed the fridge door behind Allie.

Damn, that would cost a mint to repair. I couldn't afford to replace it.

Mike skulked at the breakfast table, not much more than a shadow, recording everything in a notebook as well as with a small digital recorder.

"What is going on here?" I asked as mildly as I could while I wrestled the pan out of WindScribe's hands.

She whirled on me with hands extended like claws, ready to rake my face with her broken nails. For all the time she spent primping with my lipstick, she could have borrowed a nail file and used it.

"She's lying!" WindScribe screeched. At the moment she sounded akin to the Windago.

I reared back.

"She's spreading vicious lies about me."

"Want to explain that?" I asked Allie.

"Actually, I am the one guilty of speaking too frankly about the WindScribe I knew in the past," MoonFeather said. She sounded calm, but her eyes held shadows of inner pain.

"So why is she attacking Allie?"

"Because I tried to get her to speak honestly." Allie shrugged and took a cautious step toward MoonFeather at the island.

"They both lie. I never did those things. Never, never, never," WindScribe insisted. Fat tears welled up in her eyes and she . . . pouted.

That convinced me she lied. Her pout was too studied, too pretty. A mask.

"What did you accuse her of?"

"According to the old police records, the night before the coven went missing, WindScribe broke into her neighbor's house and stole a diamond pendant and three valuable cocktail rings. Then she took a false prescription for Darvon to the pharmacy and had it filled—which she didn't pay for. When she left, she shoplifted a bunch of candles and incense."

"Lies!"

"Darvon?" I asked.

"It's rarely used now," MoonFeather said. "A powerful painkiller. Too addictive and too many abuses."

"So, thirty years in Faery didn't cure your addiction?" I cocked an eyebrow at the girl.

"I'm not addicted." She stamped her foot like a two year old. Physically, she might be eighteen, but I don't think she'd matured beyond twelve.

"Then what happened to an entire bottle of thirty tablets of tranquilizers?"

"I'm not addicted. I need help opening my mind to the wonders of the universe. Only when we break through the barriers that society imposes upon our psyches can we experience true vision. But I'm not addicted. I'm not. Only losers get addicted."

I let that one pass.

"Speaking of losers, we picked up the girl from the mugging last night, Julie Martinez," Allie said. "She really was the ringleader behind the muggings. And the boy Francis Jorgenson is recovering from his broken trachea," Allie told me. "The DA says you acted in self-defense. No charges against you. All three kids are facing trial in adult court. They're seventeen and high school seniors."

That was a relief. And a sadness. Those kids had destroyed their promise of a future. Much as WindScribe was doing, or had done.

"So, Allie provides the police record from thirty years ago, and I'm guessing you, MoonFeather, corroborated the story from personal experience. You'd seen her stoned more than once."

"I will not lie. I had witnessed WindScribe indulging in her little . . . hobby too many times. Not always in her quest for enlightenment. I'd noticed her wearing expensive jewelry and exotic perfume I did not believe she or her parents could afford. As much as I believe in the threefold law and refrain from speaking ill of anyone, I felt that Allie needed to know the truth."

"What happened to the jewelry?" I asked.

WindScribe clamped her mouth shut and shot me a mutinous glance.

"I'm guessing you used it as bribes in Faery. Maybe one of those shiny baubles got you out of King Scazzy's prison?"

"That would mean . . . no, I won't believe it. I can't believe you'd actually do something so . . . dangerous." Moon-Feather shook her head, grabbed her crutches, and made to leave the kitchen.

I stopped her by simply removing the crutches from her grasp. She had to remain sitting.

"You won't believe what?" I asked.

MoonFeather kept shaking her head.

WindScribe edged sideways toward the outside door. Mike shifted position, ready to grab her as she passed him.

"Let me guess," I said trying to capture MoonFeather's gaze. "The coven planned a different spell. They wanted to invite some of the faeries here. For enlightenment. Maybe to improve Earth in some way. But WindScribe deliberately altered the ritual. They all got whisked away to Faery instead."

WindScribe gasped.

MoonFeather's silence confirmed my suspicion.

"A dangerous thing to try, WindScribe. But stealing the jewelry and stocking up on pain pills before going makes it premeditated, not an accident."

"I didn't think she was that stupid," MoonFeather whispered. "Perhaps desperate is a better word." She looked up, having found a way to avoid saying anything bad about the girl.

"Stupid is the right word," I said. The threefold law was MoonFeather's path, not mine. I didn't believe in Gods and Goddesses and karma and destiny and such.

If I told myself that often enough, I'd believe *that*. And I wouldn't do something useless like make that votive offering tonight at moonset.

"The statute of limitations has run out on the theft," Allie said. "I can't arrest you, WindScribe. But I have to warn you that I am watching you. Anything like that happens again, and I will put you away. Our prisons are probably just as nasty as anything King Scazzy can come up with." She turned abruptly and left. Without saying good-bye.

She was pissed. Really pissed. I hadn't seen her like this since junior year in high school. She'd caught Zach Halohan—

the chief constable's son—cheating on a final exam. Then she got into more trouble than he did for tattling.

"How's your arm, Mike?" I called after him as he tried to slip out the door unnoticed.

"Fine. You don't need to worry about me."

"Was he hurt?" Allie poked her head back inside from the mudroom.

"Ask him."

"I will."

"You had better clean up the mess you made, Wind-Scribe. If you want anyone to cook for you, those pans all need to be washed and put away properly." I turned on my heel and exited as well.

Maybe I could justify having Gollum pay for the repair to the fridge out of the trust fund.

"I suppose you are going to desert me, too?" WindScribe sneered at MoonFeather. "Of all these losers and control freaks, I thought you would understand."

"I understand. I do not approve. I've learned a lot about freedom and the responsibility that comes with it. Running away is not the answer. Drugs are not the answer."

"Then what is!" WindScribe demanded.

"That is something you have to figure out for yourself. Me telling you won't help at all. I'd help with the washing up, but as you see, I cannot stand. Tess, will you help me back to bed?"

"Your ghosts are afraid of her," MoonFeather whispered as we negotiated the step down from the butler's pantry to the dining room. "They are all huddled in the library, as far from her as they can get."

"What can frighten a ghost? They're already dead?"

"What is dead but another transition? Ghosts have more transitions to make than most of us."

Another pan hit the floor.

The sun set. We all gathered for a dinner of stew and fresh rolls in the formal dining room—except Donovan. He seemed strangely silent and absent. WindScribe had managed to put enough stuff away to give me enough pots to cook with. But the kitchen was still a mess.

The wind came up. I jumped and started at the first rattling window.

Gollum didn't come home.

I picked at my food, listening diligently for the sound of his van wheezing across the gravel drive. No one else talked much. We watched each other and waited for someone else to make the first move into or away from politeness.

Finally, my cell phone rang. I breathed deeply for the first time in an hour at the caller ID.

"Gollum."

"Tess, I think I need your help."

"What's up?" I couldn't disguise my instant alertness from anyone. They all seemed to listen in, with different intent.

"Have you noticed the Wind?" He spoke cautiously, as if aware of listeners.

I caught the special inflection. "Yes. Where are you?"

"Just about to turn in at your street. But this van is top-heavy with a high turning radius. I'm afraid she'll tip over."

She as in the van or in Lilia David the Widowed Windago?

"On my way."

"Tess, what can possibly be more important than finishing your dinner?" Mom admonished me. She looked at Darren rather than me.

"She's an adult, Genevieve. Let her run her own life," MoonFeather came to my defense.

"A little politeness toward your mother is expected," Darren said. He smirked, as if he were my real father and not an unwanted step.

"My house. My rules," I gave him back the same sickly sweet smile. "I'm done. I cooked. Someone else can clean up." I stared meaningfully at WindScribe as I dashed for the kitchen.

Scrap turned scarlet and began stretching before I got my jacket zipped.

By the time I reached the gravel, he was fully extended and ready to taste monster blood.

The wind whipped my breath away and tangled my hair.

I twirled the Celestial Blade above my head, cutting through the suddenly warmer air.

No change.

Then I spotted Gollum's van inching around the corner to the drive. The wind buffeted the big vehicle. It shook and rocked back and forth.

Mine! The wind whistled. *My new mate.*

"No," I screamed. My heart beat overtime. I couldn't run fast enough to Gollum's side. "Leave him alone, bitch." I slashed the blade at every shadow.

YiiEeeeek!

Scrap hit resistance.

I followed that particular shadow toward a bank of azaleas. Brittle branches broke beneath our feet as I forced Lilia to retreat.

He's mine, she insisted.

I had trouble seeing which shadow she might have blended with. The security light didn't penetrate this far.

Then I heard the ominous sound of Gollum opening his car door.

"Get in the house now," I ordered him. "She can't violate the sanctity of a home."

I can now. You killed one mate and now you steal another. He's mine. By cosmic law I claim him.

"Halt." King Scazzy popped between us. He held his hands up.

Suddenly my blade froze in place. I glanced up. Scrap's eyes blinked at me in bewilderment from the right-hand blade.

Lilia stilled as well. The sound of the wind roaring in my ears dropped down several notches.

"Lilia claims that man as mate," King Scazzy said in his most authoritative voice.

Deep in my gut I knew I had to respect his authority in the matter. He was the prison warden of the universe after all. He had the power to force me to keep holding my weapon in one position, high above my head.

I do.

"I can't allow that," I replied. My arms ached to move again, to lower the blade. To—Goddess forbid—drop it.

But I knew if I did drop Scrap, then I forfeited my right to defend myself and Gollum.

"Do you have a prior claim?" the little king asked.

The universe stilled. My perceptions tilted a little to the right. I fought for and found a new balance. The strain in my arms and shoulders lessened.

"Do you have a prior claim?" King Scazzamurieddu repeated his question.

"Answer him, Tess," Gollum whispered behind me. "Please answer him. I think we're dealing with cosmic justice here."

"I told you to get into the house." What was I supposed to do?

I knew. Still I wavered in indecision, unwilling to make the commitment demanded by these otherworldly creatures.

"I can't retreat. The king of the Orculli has blocked my passage with some kind of force field."

I chanced a quick glance at him. His glasses drooped and I saw concern in his mild blue eyes.

My mind whirled through several scenarios and probable outcomes.

"I claim this man as my own," I said boldly. I didn't specify what I claimed him as—mate or friend.

"Very well," King Scazzy said. "My battle with you tomorrow at noon still holds precedence. Lilia David, you must wait until the outcome before pursuing your vengeance for the death of your mate."

Nooooooo, she wailed and faded into the distance, taking the wind with her. *I need a mate. I cannot hunt without a mate. I will not be denied.*

"You will wait," Scazzy commanded.

I have waited long enough! Suddenly, the wind intensified. It gained a new depth of chill that turned my sweat to frost.

"You have violated the sanctuary of this home. Do so again and I will have no choice but to invalidate your claim."

I will have justice. Next time I do not come alone. This last came as a mere whispered promise from a great distance.

I lowered my blade in relief. My arms trembled from the strain of holding it up in one place so long.

"Never thought I'd thank a troll," I said by way of backward obligation.

"Do not thank me yet. We still have a rendezvous at noon." Scazzy popped out, leaving me alone with Gollum.

Heat filled my face with a blush. What exactly had I claimed, and what did I do next?

A flash nearly blinded me.

Gollum ran with wicked speed behind the sole remaining oak guarding the entrance to my drive. He emerged a heartbeat later with James Frazier. He held the reporter by the collar of his down jacket in one hand. In the other, he carried a huge and complex camera.

James looked entirely too smug.

Chapter 30

"**D**ON'T YOU DARE publish that photo," I warned James with deadly menace. Once more I raised the Celestial Blade.

We can't do this, babe. He's human, Scrap moaned deep inside my mind.

"He may be human but he is evil."

A faint chuckle from Scrap. *Not evil enough.* The weight and balance of the blade began to fade.

I made a tossing movement, so that the reporter would think I'd dropped it instead of it disappearing into thin air.

"You can't stop me, Tess. The public has a right to know that you harbor monsters in this corner of Cape Cod."

"I don't believe your outraged indignation, James. We went to high school together. You were a sneaking tattler then, and you're a stalking, evil snake now." I shook my fist in his face.

He gulped and flailed as Gollum lifted him slightly. He had to stand on tiptoe to maintain any balance.

"I have taken a vow of nonviolence," Gollum admitted. "But you strain my willpower, Mr. Frazier."

That was new information. I filed it away to pursue later. Presuming we had a later.

"I have rights," James insisted. "Give me back my camera."

"In a moment." Gollum dropped him.

He stumbled and almost fell to his knees. His awkwardness gave Gollum time to fiddle with the camera.

"Fortunately, he's gone digital. I just deleted an entire series of photos of our little encounter." Gollum grinned hugely as he handed the camera back to James.

A safe and sane solution. But I really wanted to break the damn camera. And James' head.

"I doubt your reading public will be interested in our rehearsal for live-action role-playing games," I told him. "We're going to a con soon." As good an explanation as the truth.

"Con?" Ever the reporter, James whipped out a notebook and pencil.

"Short for convention. Science Fiction and Fantasy Convention. I attend five or six a year to promote my work and meet with other writers, editors, fans."

"And will Miss WindScribe attend with you?"

I glared at him. Gollum reached for his collar again, his other fist clenched.

"I found her high school photo. She hasn't changed in twenty-eight years. Do you have an explanation for that?"

"Her daughter," I said with finality and marched back toward the sanctuary of my house.

I heard James fumbling through the brush. Then Gollum caught up with me and slipped a supporting arm about my waist.

"You need to rest before the moon sets at midnight. I know that even a short fight takes a lot out of you."

"We need to talk about what happened."

"Later. When the rest of this is settled."

Hours later, at eleven-thirty, the house was quiet. The only light spilling out the windows came from my bedroom in the loft and from the tiny light over the stove in the kitchen. Mom and Darren in the cottage had doused the lights and grown silent. I'd turned off the stereo, the better to listen for eavesdroppers and unseen watchers.

Even Scrap kept his mouth shut. He hovered somewhere nearby, but he didn't sit on my shoulder like he usually did. After two beers with OJ he had a slight orange tinge and droopy eyes, like he needed sleep. Elsewhere.

I missed the reassuring almost weight of him.

The wind retreated. Barely a breeze ruffled the upper branches of the trees. No Windago nearby at the moment. I had no doubt she watched me from a distance.

Using a penlight, I made my way carefully out the back door and over ice and slush along a faint trail in the woods behind the house. I carried the magical comb with me. A heaviness surrounded my heart and threatened to bring tears to my eyes.

"Tess, wait up," Gollum called softly.

I heard him shuffle along the path. I couldn't bear to turn and face him. I wouldn't let him see me cry over what I knew I had to do.

"You shouldn't have to do this alone," he said quietly, draping a long arm around my shoulders. "We belong together by some cosmic law I don't understand, so please, let me help you."

"Thanks." I leaned into him, just a little. His friendship as well as his body helped warm the ice crystals that threatened to shatter inside me.

Too soon, we broke clear of the patch of forest and emerged into the clearing made by Miller's Pond. Centuries ago, someone had dammed the creek that ran through here and erected a grist mill at the west end. Only a few foundation stones remained of the mill, but the dam and the pond lingered, reminders of our pioneer ancestors.

As kids, my friends and I used to sneak out on hot summer nights to gather here and tell ghost stories. We invented tales of seventeenth-century witches thrown into the depths to test their powers. If they rose to the surface and survived, they must be witches and so were taken away and burned at the stake. If they sank and drowned, then they were innocent and buried in holy ground.

But what if one of them swam away over the dam and disappeared where the creek entered the sea less than a mile away? We shivered and made up tales of the witch's curse over all who tried to profit from the pond ever afterward. Because the witch's accuser received all of her property as a bounty.

Made for a lot of false accusations. A threat to make sure women "behaved" so they wouldn't invite the lust or envy of a malicious neighbor.

I trembled with my own fears that night.

The setting moon, just a hair off full, dipped into a small gap in the trees. Its silvery light made the pond ice shimmer with an unearthly glow. A black splotch in the middle showed where the ice had begun to break up. It looked like a black hole in space—an entry to another universe.

Maybe it was.

I shivered with more than just the cold, remembering the witch's curse that none would profit from this pond again.

Making a votive offering here might be a bad idea.

Gollum looked just as uncomfortable as I felt. But he stood stalwart beside me.

"I know the water is only ten feet deep at the most. I've swum here in the summer." Dill and I had giggled together over the prospect of skinny dipping in the pond on hot summer nights. He hadn't lived long enough to share that experience with me.

I almost wished he would show himself tonight, let me know he approved of what I did.

"Do you have a prayer or invocation?" Gollum whispered.

Neither one of us seemed willing to disturb the unearthly quiet surrounding this ritual.

"Nothing special. I've always felt that if there is a God or Goddess, they'll know what's in my heart. I need help tomorrow. I'm obligated to protect WindScribe, to keep her here in her home dimension. The Orculli trolls are obligated to fulfill their destiny as the prison guards of the universe. We are both right. They are too numerous for me to count. I don't really know how to fight them, other than with the Celestial Blade. Will it be enough?"

I turned the comb over and over in my hands. Regretting the loss of its beauty as well as its powers to allow me see through a demon glamour. I also regretted losing this because Scrap had found it for me. He gave it to me out of love.

Before I could change my mind, I drew back my arm and hurled the comb toward the black depths of the pond.

I lost sight of it flying through the darkness. Then I heard it clank and skitter against the ice at the edge of the hole. It bounced and slid back toward me.

"Yeep?" I squelched a cry of surprise.

You throw like a girl! Scrap laughed. He sounded relieved as well as his usual sarcastic self.

"Oh, my," Gollum said, adjusting his slipping glasses. "I do believe your Goddess has rejected your offering." He ventured two steps upon the ice, clinging to a sapling for support. With his long arms he stretched and retrieved the comb from its landing place, practically at our feet.

"I don't understand . . . this is the most valuable thing I own."

But you don't truly treasure it, Scrap reminded me.

I repeated his comment for Gollum.

"He's right. There is something more important to you."

"I don't treasure *things*. I treasure people. My mom, my aunt. My friends. Even my nasty sister is more important to me than any of the possessions I've accumulated."

Gollum raised one eyebrow and captured my gaze. The moonlight made angles and hollows of his face. An image of his skull, frozen in horror nearly covered the face I'd come to treasure almost as much as my family.

"Okay, there is one thing. But I'd hoped . . . Goddess, don't make me do this." Crying quietly, I drew a picture frame from inside my parka.

"Tell me about it. Let me treasure the memory as much as you do," Gollum whispered.

"Dill made the frame." I traced the rough carving of the wooden edges.

And with the memory came his presence, leaning against a tree. Tension nearly vibrated from his ghostly form.

"Don't do this, Tess. Don't throw me away."

"Dill embedded special agates and arrowheads he'd found into the wood."

"Making a choice to let me die, so you can move forward, I can understand," Dill said. Then his tone turned bitter. "Throwing me away like this is cruel, Tess."

My fingers caught on a rough edge of knapped flint.

"That's a bird point from the predecessors of the Okanogan peoples," I heard him say, both in my memory and from somewhere amidst the trees.

"And the picture?" Gollum pressed.

"Our wedding photo. In Reno. We both wore jeans and western shirts and Stetsons. Mine was white. His was black." Two fat tears landed on the glass covering the photo. "It's the only picture I have of him. We were together such a short time."

"Have you made a copy of the photo?" Gollum asked gently.

"Of course. But it's not the same. Not the actual photo of our wedding. Not in the frame he made especially for it."

"This is very important to you, Tess. I don't think I could make a votive offering to any God of such a treasure."

"And that's why I have to do it."

"Please, no, Tess," Dill pleaded. "We can be together. Let me fight the Orculli with you instead of the imp. Please, Tess, don't throw me away."

"Don't, Tess." Gollum put his big hand over mine where I held the picture and frame. "We'll find another way for you to defeat the Orculli."

"I might defeat them, but will I survive?" I whirled and shouted in the direction of Dill's ghostly presence.

Silence.

That was my answer. Dill wanted me to die, so we could move onto some other plane of existence together. Or have our spirits cease altogether. He didn't care if I lived or died. He was already dead. Why shouldn't I be as well?

This time I flung the photo and frame away like a Frisbee. It bounced against the ice, slid and slithered to the edge. There it teetered a moment.

"I can't believe you did this!" Dill protested. "I may not be able to hit you, but I know things that can!" His form flickered in and out of view.

My heart rose in my throat, almost hoping the Goddess would reject this offering as well. Had I ever truly been happy since Dill died? Would I ever be a complete person without him?

Remember the times he told you to stop writing to go rock hunting with him? Scrap whispered. *Remember how often he found other things for you to do rather than write? He didn't want you to be complete. He wanted to own and control you.*

A puff of wind caught the frame and made it sway. Back and forth it teetered on the edge of acceptance, on the brink of rejection and reality.

I think I gasped. My drying tears burned icy trails on my cheeks.

Then with an audible sigh, the wind let the frame go and it plunged into the water.

The moon sank below the horizon, gobbling up the thing I treasured most. The thing I needed to let go of most.

Chapter 31

DRAINED AND EXHAUSTED, physically and emotionally, I let Gollum lead me back toward the house. I rested my head against his shoulder. His arm enveloped me, warming me against the chills that racked my body, inside and out.

Maybe I cried.

Maybe I was beyond tears.

Scrap settled on my free shoulder, rubbing his insubstantial face against mine.

They knew what this had cost me.

I wasn't certain I did. Yet.

Dill remained anchored to the edge of the pond, staring helplessly at the black hole in the center of the ice.

As we stepped free of the woods, a little more light filled my side yard, between the house and cottage.

I straightened away from Gollum. The lawn should be in total darkness. The moon had set and a fine mist covered the stars.

The mounds that had been ugly garden gnomes were missing. Had the Goddess banished them when She accepted my votive offering?

I should have such luck.

Gollum pointed to the cottage where a dim light seeped

beneath the blinds in the living room. A vague shadow stood under the window.

I must have made a noise. The shadow turned and beckoned us forward.

Senses alert, Scrap on my hand, ready to lengthen and sharpen into the Celestial Blade, I shifted my balance to an aggressive stance and stepped into the shadows.

"Listen!" WindScribe hissed with a finger to her lips.

I just barely heard her.

Gollum stayed close behind me as we pressed ourselves against the rough siding. His head remained a scant three inches beneath the window ledge.

Angry whispers drifted to my ears.

"You have to do your part, D," Darren demanded. Though of a similar mode, it was deeper and more commanding than Donovan's.

"No. You've stepped way beyond the bounds of decency on this one, D," Donovan returned. I could imagine well his tense stance with fists clenched, shoulders hunched, and head thrust forward. I'd seen him on the edge of a fight before. I'd also seen him dissipate strong emotions in a crowd ready to turn into a riot.

Why wasn't he doing that to his foster father?

Maybe he couldn't. Darren had his own talent to lull fears and calm anger. He was probably immune to the same magic in others.

"What does decency have to do with it?" Darren said casually, no trace of emotion. "We are pledged to a mission. The end is in sight."

"Not this way. Not with Tess' life in jeopardy."

"If she needs to be eliminated, like that worthless traitor Dillwyn Bailey Cooper, then she will be."

I nearly choked on my own breath.

"Tess, no," Gollum stopped me with panicked words and a fierce grip on my arms. "If you charge in there now, your mother will hear everything. Are you ready for that? Scrap may not be able to help you. He can't get near Donovan."

Rational good sense. I didn't want to hear any of it.

"He knows something about Dill's death. He suggested

that he *murdered* my husband." I was shaking again. My teeth chattered.

Where was Dill at this moment of truth? He should be in on this.

I needed to *do* something.

"Hush, they're still talking," WindScribe said. That girl was starting to unnerve me. She was everywhere, sticking her nose into everyone else's business but her own.

And she never wore a coat or shoes. How much of Faery still clung to her?

I wondered if there was a lock that could hold her. I really wanted to put her away somewhere secure until this was all over.

Gollum pushed me back to our place beneath the window. I dragged my feet, looking over my shoulder to the front steps. Ten paces away. I could bolt and run.

"What about the witch, WindScribe? You going to kill her, too?" Donovan demanded.

"No need. She's so stupid and naïve she'll end up getting herself killed. King Scazzamurieddu needn't be so diligent in his duty. She'll be a lot less trouble to the universe meddling in this dimension, than bribing prison guards with sex and diamonds." Darren yawned. "She barely needed my help to escape."

My ears pricked. Darren had aided her prison break! He also sounded like he knew why my charge had been imprisoned. Donovan probably knew, too.

"I went along with you on the necessity of eliminating Cooper. He was a loose cannon, ready to spill our plans to the wrong people. I am as committed to your Great Enterprise as you. I was committed before I fell! That's why I did fall," Donovan ground out.

Fell from what? I wanted to scream. But I didn't. I needed to hear more.

"Then act like you think this is important."

"I won't let you hurt Tess. Or her mother," Donovan insisted.

"You don't have a choice. I am head of this clan. Leader in the Great Enterprise of creating . . ."

"I am not part of your clan. I never have been. I was

given to you because I resembled your bat form. You manipulated the Powers That Be to see things your way without a thought for what was best for me. Nothing binds us. And I will stop you from hurting Tess."

"Not bloody likely, boy. I am stronger than you. And I have the backing of the clan."

"The clan is scattered. Your children are more interested in staying human, blending in. They're too inbred to have the intelligence to be useful."

"My children are dedicated!" Darren wailed. "They would never deny their true heritage."

Sounded like rationalization to me.

"Your children are dedicated to fast cars, skiing in the Alps, snorkeling in Fiji, and electronic toys," Donovan laughed. "Who do you think are my biggest customers for computer games? Your children."

A long silence followed. Long enough that I wondered if I should retreat while I could.

"It's just you and me here, D," Donovan said. "You don't have the clan to back you up."

"You've been spoiling for a fight for a long time, D. If I didn't find you useful upon occasion, I'd take you down right now," Darren replied.

"Name the time and place. But not here. Not where Tess and her mother could be caught in the backlash."

Darren laughed. An evil, hideous sound that echoed around the cottage and the immediate environs.

New chills ran up and down my spine. I wondered that Mom didn't hear it and cry out in alarm.

"I'll find you, when I'm ready, D. Until then, watch your mouth and watch your back." The sound of a fist hitting flesh. Someone stumbled. A lamp crashed to the floor.

What little light there was vanished.

Before I could react, Donovan stormed out of the cottage and over to his car. He raced the engine and skidded on the gravel as he turned onto the main road.

"Next time, D. Next time I'll be the one who does the hitting, and you the falling," Darren chuckled. "But then you've already fallen once." He silently closed the door.

Time for answers. I marched up to the worn wooden steps of the cottage.

Both Gollum and WindScribe caught me.

"Not now, Tess. Wait until morning when you have a clear head," Gollum insisted. "And Allie to back you up."

"I'm cold," WindScribe whined.

I could see tears in her eyes and moisture gathering around her nose. She was my responsibility—at least until noon tomorrow—even if she didn't have enough sense to get in out of the cold.

Had my mother ever felt this exasperated, frustrated, aching with grief and bewilderment when she had to deal with three fractious teenagers alone, after her divorce from Dad?

Most likely.

If she could cope, so could I.

But first thing in the morning I was going to corner Darren and demand explanations. With or without my mother present. A violent showdown was coming. Soon. I felt it in my bones.

Silently, the three of us trooped back to the house. I sent WindScribe up to my bathroom to take a hot shower and go to bed. I didn't want to follow her. I wasn't ready to close down my mind and body for the night.

"I've got a bottle of single malt," Gollum offered.

"Did it start as my bottle?"

"Nope. Bought this one all on my own. Highland Park, you usually go for the more expensive stuff."

"Tonight I'll take it. Even if it isn't as complex as Lagavulin."

"I'd call Highland Park a full and robust flavor, without the taint of iodine from exposure to the sea," Gollum said. He kept his arm around me as he guided me toward his sofa.

"But Lagavulin is the fire of the gods wrapped in velvet."

The sharp amber liquid he poured for me burst upon my tongue like something magic and wonderful, then warmed me all the way to my toes as it slid down my throat. Sipping scotch is a three-step process. First the sniff. Highland Park has a flowery touch to the nose. Then roll the sip around the inside of the mouth. Here the flavors of peat and salt and other good things come into play. Then the swallow and the whiskey explodes like fireworks against the taste buds.

"Usquebaugh!" I sighed. "The water of life."

"Whiskey. The only word in the English dictionary acknowledged to have come from the Gaelic," Gollum said. For once he didn't have his professor face on. "Although I have my own theories about the word quaff. Is it derived from quaich, a footed beer cup? The only proper beverage one quaffs is of course beer. Quaffed from a quaich." He sounded a little tiddly on only one shot. Usually he needed more. A lot more to get drunk.

"Do you ever turn it off?"

"Turn what off?"

"Your head. All the vast quantities of esoteric trivia stashed there."

"Upon occasion."

"Like when?"

"When I'm making love to a beautiful woman," he said in a rush, then blushed.

"What did you say?" I couldn't have heard him right. I didn't want to have heard him right.

"Well, uh . . . um . . ."

"Never mind." Dangerous subject. Even more dangerous the way he looked over the top of his glasses at me, then hastily looked away, afraid I might catch his gaze. And hold it.

"Well, hit me with some more trivia. Like anything you've learned about the Orculli trolls that will help me fight them. Anything you've gleaned about the Great Enterprise of the demon world. Anything you might have heard on your occult grapevine about my dead husband."

Chapter 32

A child born on the first day of the full moon is said to enjoy a long and healthy life. But those who take sick on this day are in for a lengthy and serious illness. Possibly fatal.

ONCE MORE I WOKE up on Gollum's couch. This time morning light streamed through the windows. It looked like the weather had finally broken and we might, just might, be headed for a warming spell.

Could this be the Goddess breaking the hold of the Orculli on our weather? Gollum had said that unseasonable cold was often attributed to the little trolls.

The Windago also brought unseasonable freezes.

Whatever. I welcomed the warmth and basked in comfort for just a moment.

Gollum had pulled a soft open-weave blanket over me and tucked it under my chin. I was fully dressed and he was nowhere in sight.

I breathed a sigh of relief. I may have spent the night with him, but I hadn't slept with him.

"Coffee," I sighed as the rich scent wafted in from the main house. The door was open, and I heard muted conversation.

Yawning and stretching, I wandered through the house, checking for signs of anything out of place on my way into the kitchen. Sleep still made my eyes and limbs heavy. Or was that the aftermath of too much scotch?

Gollum was making a huge pot of coffee, humming along to a CD of filk. He had a fine tenor. The first time we'd gone to a con together he'd bonded with my filking friends. He'd also pushed me to sing long before I was ready. When I finally did, at a belated wake for a dear friend, he'd been as responsible for freeing my voice as anyone.

For a moment I was glad I had claimed him in front of the Windago and the Orculli.

Mom manned the stove. The enticing scent of sizzling sausages wafted toward me. I also caught the rich doughy smell of steaming waffles. Heaven.

Gollum handed me a large glass of orange juice and a fistful of vitamins.

"Thank you. Bless you. How did you know?"

"I had more scotch than you did." His eyes twinkled behind his glasses. He looked good this morning. Freshly showered and shaved, in a forest-green silk turtleneck covered by a Nordic sweater in more shades of green and brown and his usual chocolate-colored cords.

He looked better than I did with my tousled curls and splotchy eyes.

"You look like you slept in those jeans, Tess," Mom said sharply.

Well, I had.

"Breakfast is ready. You'll have to change later." She was back in her new white pants suit with the ruby blouse. Her inevitable pearls graced her neck. Every hair was in place, and her makeup was perfect.

She had a tightness about her eyes and a tremor to her hands that told me she'd had a migraine and taken heavy drugs to combat it. The pain might have vanished, but the pills left her fragile, almost frail.

No wonder she hadn't intervened in the argument between Darren and Donovan last night. An elephant gun exploding next to her ear wouldn't rouse her from those drugs.

"You're all dressed up," I said as I slid into a kitchen chair facing the bay windows and the cottage across the yard.

"D and I have an appointment with Father Sheridan after Mass. To arrange the blessing of our marriage." She actually preened as she set a plate before me filled with a succulent waffle. Melting butter flowed out from a fat pat in the center. Then she plunked a second plate on the table overflowing with sausages and fried tomato slices.

I reached for the maple syrup—the pure stuff from Vermont.

Gollum slid into the chair next to me and stole half the waffle.

I considered slapping his hand, then thought better of it. We'd shared a lot last night. Personal stuff, wants and desires, politics to religion to fashion to education. I knew more about him as a person but still didn't know much about his history and family. That would come. Some barriers had fallen between us.

"Is Darren going to Mass with you?" I looked at the clock on the microwave. Nine-thirty-five. They didn't have much time to get to church.

"Of course," Mom replied sharply. She stared out the window, worry creased her mouth and her eyes. "I'd better go hurry him along." She marched out the door, leaving it open and letting in the cold but not frigid air.

"Do you think Darren will actually set foot inside a church?" Gollum asked.

"That is something I'd like to see. Will he disappear in a cloud of smoke? Will he meet a force field that throws him out?" Like had happened to Scrap once when he tried entering the newly blessed refectory back at the Citadel.

That was something I'd have to ask him about. It reminded me of how he'd been blocked from entering a room with Donovan.

But Donovan wasn't blessed. If anything, he was as much a demon as Darren.

What had he said last night?

I was committed to the Great Enterprise before I fell.

"What do you suppose Donovan fell from?" I asked.

Gollum chewed in silence for a moment. Then he got up and poured more batter into the waffle maker. "From grace?" he replied.

"But that would mean he'd been in a state of grace at one time. Like an angel. He's no angel. That I'm sure of. Could a demon, even a half-blood, enter a state of grace?"

The Church didn't think so. That was one reason they littered their cathedral roofs with gargoyles.

"Depends on the human half of his blood. If that ancestor had been up for sainthood, maybe the spiritual quality they imparted to their offspring . . ."

An ear-splitting screech tore the air.

"Mom!" I pelted toward the cottage.

She screamed again and again. I felt the sky might tear open from her anguish.

My heart beat overtime and climbed to my throat. I couldn't cover the one hundred yards to the cottage fast enough. The distance seemed to grow longer, my goal farther away with every step.

"Scrap? Where the hell are you? I need you now!"

Right here, babe. He flitted ahead of me on wings that beat faster than my racing pulse. He flashed between curious yellow and happy lavender.

No demons or evil lurked close by.

What was going on?

Finally, I reached the steps. Gollum overtook me and yanked open the storm door. The main door swung free.

We came to a skidding halt. Mom stood in the middle of the room, hands covering her face, eyes wide in horror.

Darren lay face up on the floor, dark blood pooled around him from a deep and long gash through his chest. Death had glazed his eyes and turned him blue with cold.

▽▲▽▲▽

The sweet smell of blood and death filled me with longing. I needed to stretch and sharpen, to taste this demon blood myself.

But there were no live demons present. I took no part in this death.

Never truly sated, I dropped down beside the corpse. My tongue lapped at the chill, stale blood. Instead of satisfying my thirst, it tasted sour. He'd been dead too long. I spat it out in disgust.

My internal combustion engine remained well below the boiling point. Nothing changed in my normal cute self, gray green with six lovely warts.

Curses. I can't earn any more beauty marks from this death.

Chapter 33

GOLLUM MUST HAVE called 911. I sure didn't.

Allie and Mike roared up the drive in a four-by-four rig, followed closely by Joe Halohan, the chief constable, in his unmarked sedan, and by a third officer in a squad car. Followed by an ambulance. Followed by the tiny compact of James Frazier, reporter for the *Cape Gazette*.

I had my hands full with Mom's hysterics. She wouldn't leave the cottage. She wouldn't stop screaming. Finally I grabbed both her arms and frog-marched her outside.

Once free of the sight of her dead husband, Mom's screams reduced to sobs that shook her entire body. I feared she'd pass out from lack of breath. Or hyperventilate.

Somehow, I got Mom into the house and plied her with a cup of tea.

WindScribe ate the waffle Gollum had started a lifetime ago, hardly noticing the noise and fuss around her.

"Take a plate to MoonFeather," I finally snapped at her.

"Oh." She looked up with wide, innocent eyes as if I'd disturbed some deep and meaningful meditation. Her eyes were glassy. Had she found Mom's migraine meds?

For once, she obeyed without questions or whines.

Allie and Chief Constable Halohan trudged across the

melting snow—completely free of gnomes—each with one hand resting on their weapons and notebooks in the other. Mike trailed behind, head twisting right and left, looking at everything and . . . and . . . was he sniffing?

First time I'd ever known a cop to use his nose with the same intensity as his eyes. I didn't think smells were admissible evidence.

He swung his arms freely, no trace of a wound from the Windago. He looked so very human I doubted demon blood in him. And Scrap didn't react to him. Must be pretty diluted demon blood.

I braced myself for the torrent of questions. Who was the victim? What was our relationship? Why was he in my cottage? How did we come to discover the body? I answered them all as simply and honestly as I could. I had nothing to hide.

Right?

"And where were you at three this morning?" Allie finally asked. Her eyes constantly shifted, searching for something or someone.

Scrap flitted about making faces at her. He knew she couldn't see him. Did she sense his passage through the air? Perhaps she was looking for one of my ghosts.

Dill had remained absent since I threw his picture into the pond at midnight.

"I was asleep at three," I replied.

"And you, Mrs. Noncoiré, I mean Estevez?" Allie turned her attention fully on Mom.

"I . . . I was . . ." Mom choked and fell into another spate of sobs. "Will someone turn off the damned music. It's giving me a migraine!"

"We might as well give up on her for a while. She's in shock. Won't get anything out of her until tomorrow at best," Halohan grumbled.

I watched Mom visibly gather the ragged pieces of her psyche together. "I . . . I had a migraine last night. I took my pills. Darren was considerate enough to sleep in the spare room so he wouldn't disturb me." That could be the truth. When Mom had one of her "spells" and took her meds, nothing could wake her for close to twelve hours.

No wonder the quiet music on the stereo grated on her

fragile nerves. I always had music on the stereo. In the aftermath of the drugs was the only time she complained.

"How did you get out of the cottage without stumbling over his dead body?" Mike asked. Anger tinged his voice. He stood with his feet braced, knees locked, and his body tilted forward in an aggressive stance.

I'd seen Allie confront traffic violators and belligerent drunks before. But never with as much violence simmering beneath the surface as Mike displayed.

As if he were taking the murder personally. How close were his family ties to Darren Estevez?

Both Chief Halohan and Allie looked askance at him.

"I woke up about seven-thirty feeling quite well and refreshed," Mom explained. "The cottage was still dark and quiet, so I crept out without turning on any lights. I wanted to surprise everyone with a big breakfast before we went to Mass. Oh, my gosh, it's gotten so late. What will I tell Father Sheridan?" Mom threatened to fall back into her hysterics.

I couldn't tell if she lied or not. She'd dissembled for years, covering up for Dad's sexual preferences. I'd learned to lie with a straight face from the mistress of untruth. She was so good I think she truly believed her altered view of reality.

So many emotions crossed her face and filled her eyes with new tears I couldn't delve beyond the surface to find the truth behind her words.

"The body wasn't in the direct path from the back of the house to the front door," Halohan said, making notes.

"Still . . ." Mike persisted.

"Give it up, Mike. This thing isn't going to be settled in an hour," Allie warned.

"Isn't it?" Mike turned to me. "The victim was stabbed. Lots of blood. No weapon on the scene. We need to search both the cottage and the house." He locked his gaze on me fiercely as he kept his knees from bending.

"Mike," Halohan protested. "We know these people. We should be looking elsewhere, into Mr. Estevez's past."

"His foster son maybe?" I prompted. I'd watched Donovan leave in a huff near midnight. Who was to say he hadn't come back? Gollum and I had been at the other end of the house, in the apartment. We probably wouldn't have heard him.

Should I volunteer that information?

Never volunteer anything to the dirty rotten coppers, Scrap snarled in his best Chicago gangster voice.

"Good idea. Any idea where Donovan Estevez is?" Halohan glommed onto that tidbit eagerly.

"He said he was staying in a motel nearby," I offered. "I don't know which one."

Speaking of the devil . . . Scrap popped out as we heard the crunch of gravel under tires and a car door slam.

"Chief Halohan, do we really know anyone here?" Mike asked. His voice remained cold and unfeeling. But I sensed heat behind it, waiting to explode like Mount St. Helens.

"There have been a lot of strange reports and complaints by the neighbors the last year or so," Allie said hesitantly.

"And I find it too coincidental that both mother and daughter married someone they barely knew and then became widowed shortly thereafter. There's money involved." Mike continued.

That stopped me cold. How did he know that? Only Allie could have told him. Or Millie, chief gossip and police dispatch. But she'd only say something if Mike asked.

That was something to think about.

Rather than address that issue, I rounded on Allie.

"Allie, how could you? You're my best friend. You *know* me."

"Does she?" Mike snarled.

Allie swiveled her head looking into the empty air, a silent signal that she searched for Scrap—a big secret I'd kept from her for three years.

"Lots of nooks and crannies in these old houses," Halohan mused, scratching his chin. "Wouldn't hurt to look. The perp could have stashed the weapon close by to avoid getting caught with it."

"There is that room under the cellar stairs you keep locked," Mom volunteered. She wouldn't look directly at me. I had no idea if that statement came from her or from some lingering influence of Darren's.

My throat froze in horror. The armory. Stashed with more than a dozen very sharp and lethal weapons, new and antique.

And the Celestial Blade.

Scrap, wherever you are, get the blade out of there!

"You don't have to be so helpful," I hissed at Mom.

"I was only being honest. Which is more than I can say for you," she replied in a huff.

What had got into *her*?

A demon still influences her, Scrap whispered from somewhere else. *Look at her eyes. That's not a drug haze. It's demon glamour.*

"Let's have a look," Halohan said. He aimed for the kitchen access to the cellar. "You have a talk with the son, Allie."

"I have to get the key to the priest hole." I stalled and remained sitting at the table. If I called it the armory, they might arrest me before they even looked.

Halohan halted in his tracks. "Where?"

"In here," I sighed. Then I led him through the maze to the office and my purse inside the desk drawer. A quick search of the zipped pocket came up empty.

The copy around my neck I wanted to keep secret.

My heart raced in panic. I fumbled around inside the black hole of a purse and found only the fairy key chain with house and car keys — both my hybrid and Mom's SUV. Then a slow and methodical grope into the corners at the bottom. Still nothing.

Finally, I dumped the contents out on the desktop. As wallet, comb, sunglasses, PDA, and cell phone tumbled over the surface, I spotted the elusive key to the armory on its gargoyle chain with a mini flashlight attached. Someone had tucked them into a corner behind the computer.

Not me. Even in a hurry I'd not be so careless. I said so to Halohan.

He scrawled another note. "Who else has a key?" he asked, not looking up from his hen scratching.

"I gave a copy to Gollum."

Halohan looked blank.

"Guilford Van der Hoyden-Smythe. The gentleman who met you at the cottage."

"The nerd. Yeah. Why him?"

"I trust him."

"And not your mother?"

I just rolled my eyes. He knew Mom well. His wife belonged to the same garden club—the one that sold hideous garden gnomes to raise money.

"Yeah, I guess not. If your mother had a key, the whole garden club would, too. In fact, since she knows about the room, they probably all do, too. Not hard to have a locksmith out and make a duplicate." He took the key from me.

I noted that he'd donned latex gloves.

"Anyone else have access to *this* key?"

"You saw where I keep my purse. I don't lock it up in my own house. But I didn't think anyone else knew to look inside a zipped pocket inside another zipped pocket."

Donovan had dug through the purse in search of a bandage for my cut forearm.

"You've got a lot of people visiting. Lots of strangers wandering in and out." He made another note.

WindScribe poked her head out of MoonFeather's room. I waved her back inside. No sense involving them until we had to. MoonFeather was innocent. I knew that. She could barely hobble about on her crutches let alone get across the yard quietly in the middle of the night, stab a full grown man/demon, and hobble back quietly.

WindScribe? She'd dumped the contents of my purse onto the bed. She could have looked further. Last night I'd sent her to a hot shower and bed at midnight. I didn't think she could creep down the noisy stairs without me hearing her.

Both Gollum and I had drunk a lot of scotch. Would we have heard anything?

We trooped down the cellar stairs, collecting along the way a squarely built woman wearing a forensics team jacket and carrying a huge black case.

Cold sweat trickled down my back. I kept telling myself that I had nothing to fear. I was innocent.

But the clock kept ticking, and the number of people in various uniforms in my house and my yard kept growing.

How was I supposed to meet King Scazzy in battle in less than an hour with all these authorities hanging around?

Scrap, where are you?

Keeping away from Donovan.

Great. Just great.

Too many bodies filled my cellar. I was supposed to be the only one who came down here. Mom did to do laundry and select preserves, but that was it. Scrap and I trained down here. No one else.

No one.

Gollum and I had sparred down here once.

The forensics woman dusted the padlock with a black powder. "It's clean," she grunted.

"Wiped?" Halohan asked.

"Looks like it." She didn't clean the powder off. "Some scratches around the keyhole. Might have been picked. Can't say for sure. Could be just wear and tear."

Halohan used my key to open the lock, still wearing his gloves.

My teeth wanted to chatter. I clamped them shut.

A bellow and a slamming door stopped us all. "Tess, what the hell is going on?" Donovan pounded down the stairs.

"Donovan," I said gently, stopping him from barreling into the overcrowded cellar. He seemed to fill the room all by himself, the top of his head nearly brushing the ceiling beams. The dirt and cement block walls crowded closer using up all the air.

"It's D. All they'll tell me is that he's dead." Donovan dipped his face close to mine. The gesture was oddly intimate and conspiratorial.

I blanked my mind to the allure of his scent, his heat, his charm. Easier now. All I had to do was remember how he relished licking my blood off a wound he'd inflicted on my arm.

"Chief, I understand that I need to talk to you about viewing the body before the autopsy. There is a ritual . . ."

"Don't you worry, young man. We'll get a rabbi or priest or whatever you need to oversee the autopsy, make sure everything is done correct and respectfully." He placed a big hand on Donovan's shoulder in reassurance.

"I doubt you'll find a shaman from *his* religion," Donovan snorted in disgust. "No. I must see the body *before* the autopsy. The ritual must be performed before you cut him open."

"Can't let you alone with the body. Might destroy some clue."

"I don't need to be alone. I just need to perform a ritual," Donovan insisted.

"Donovan, your foster father was stabbed in the middle of the night. This is a criminal investigation," I tried to explain to him. All the while my mind whirled with questions. What kind of ritual? Would Donovan do something so that all vestiges of demonhood disappeared?

I really wanted to be there when he did whatever he needed to do.

"Stabbed? I don't understand." Real bewilderment clouded Donovan's eyes. "No ordinary blade . . ."

"That ain't no ordinary hunting knife," Halohan whistled as he pointed to the replica Celestial Blade. He ran a fingertip along the curved cutting edge and yelped. His finger bled through the gloves. He popped it into his mouth, glove and all and sucked on it.

"Holy shit," the forensics woman said. She took two steps into the armory and stopped dead in her tracks. Her head bounced around like the oversized bobblehead of a doll in the back window of a car.

"So that's where you keep it," Donovan whistled through his teeth. "Can I hold it? I didn't get a chance to examine it the one time I saw you use it."

I tried merging with the wall. Somehow this wasn't going to turn out pretty.

"You use these things?" Halohan looked at me with new respect and deeper suspicion.

"I collect blades. A hobby I picked up after I started fencing. You'll find my sport gear upstairs in my bedroom. I don't like displaying sharpened blades on my wall. Someone could easily slice off something important if they tried playing with them. Or steal them to commit a crime. So I store them here."

"Oh, we'll look upstairs, too. But I don't think we'll find anything more interesting than this." The forensics woman backed out of the tiny room carrying a bloodstained weapon very gingerly.

"Careful, that's a seventeenth-century German short sword. Very rare and worth a small fortune," I protested. A long thin blade with a gold etched bell guard. It weighed fifteen ounces and was perfectly balanced. It sang when I snapped it through the air. It very closely resembled a modern sport fencing foil. Except this one wasn't foiled. The point was lethally sharp. And now covered with blood for about ten inches from the point up the blade. From the foible almost to the forte.

I wanted to grab the antique away from these people who had no respect for its place in history.

"We'll take care of it, all right. What's this?" The forensics woman looked closer at the bloodstain. "Strange metal that's being eaten by the blood as if it were acid."

"More likely strange blood," Donovan muttered.

Heat flooded my face and made my knees weak. She'd found the murder weapon. And it probably had my fingerprints all over it.

Chapter 34

"*Y*OU HAVE THE right to remain silent . . ." Allie began the ritual of arrest up in the kitchen. She looked happy about it.

"What about fingerprints, Allie?" I protested, tensing my muscles against her grabbing my wrists and pinning them behind my back with her cuffs. "Your tech said it had been wiped clean of prints."

"What's going on?" Mom asked. She looked dazed and confused. Very much herself.

I would be bewildered, too.

"Tess? Tell me what's happening." Now she chose to take her gaze out of hiding and fix me with a stern look.

I opted on my right to remain silent. Anything I said at this point might get me into deeper trouble.

"You didn't kill him, did you?" Donovan asked on a whisper.

I was sure Allie heard him. Mom, too.

"Oh, my!" Mom placed one well-manicured hand over her mouth. Her nails matched her blouse. Instead of ruby, they now looked blood red.

Allie clamped handcuffs on my wrists. I couldn't feel more awkward.

"Oh, Tess, you shouldn't have. We'd have worked out

any differences you and D had," Mom added more fuel to the fire.

I almost caught a hint of a glowing ember from hell deep behind her eyes.

"Mom, don't help!"

"This is stupid," Gollum bellowed from the doorway.

At last, the voice of reason.

Everyone paused to look at him. Fury splotched his bony cheeks and made his glasses slide all the way to the end of his nose. For once, his mild blue eyes blazed with emotion.

A new fear crept through me. I'd never seen Gollum angry before. Suddenly the strength in his shoulders and the clenching of his fists alarmed me.

I had a wisp of a memory: *A Marine lieutenant and a corporal lying unconscious on the floor of an office trailer with thick bruises on their necks that looked like fingerprints. A Marine sergeant held a gun to Gollum's temple shouting at him to back off.*

But I'd been barely conscious at the time, with severe muscle spasm from an industrial-strength military-grade tazer gone astray in my wacky nervous system. I couldn't be sure if it was a memory or a dream.

Just as I could never be sure whether my nightmares of demons were real or the product of a wasting fever. Scrap said they were both. . . .

Either way I didn't want to be on the receiving end of Gollum's anger.

"Tess couldn't have killed Darren Estevez. She spent the entire night with me," Gollum stated with a straight face and a fierce look.

"Tess, you didn't!" Mom shrieked, as if sleeping with a man outside of marriage was worse than killing her husband of only thirty-six hours.

Allie inhaled sharply. Her face looked hurt. Then she hardened and yanked on my handcuffs so that my shoulders threatened to dislocate. "That tears it. You're coming down to the station, right now."

Jealousy. Allie and I had never had that between us. We'd always liked different boys in school. Always backed off when the other showed signs of interest in someone.

"Allie, it wasn't like that," I whispered desperately.

"Wasn't like what?" Halohan barged into the conversation. "You sure she didn't sneak out when you were asleep, young man?"

"We didn't sleep much." Gollum held Halohan's gaze steadily, not blinking.

"You slept with *him!*" Donovan exploded. "You slept with that bastard. Doesn't our relationship mean anything to you?"

"It's none of your damn business, Donovan. We only slept together once. Then you turned into someone I'm not sure I want to know."

"I'm still the same man you couldn't wait to fall into bed with," he ground out.

"Are you? We have no relationship, Donovan. We've made no commitments."

"I asked you to bear my children."

"And I declined. Commitment, marriage, and happily ever after weren't part of the offer. I'm free to choose any man I like as a bed partner. And I don't choose you."

He bolted out the door, knocking police people aside in his angry hurry. WindScribe appeared out of nowhere and followed him. She climbed into his car while he was backing out into the lane. Then he peeled out like a devil was after him.

"That true, Tess?" Allie asked. "You slept with Gollum?"

The hurt in her voice almost broke my heart.

"We slept the entire night together, in my apartment," Gollum insisted, daring anyone to contradict him.

"We'll sort it out down at the station." Halohan jerked his head for Allie to take me out to the squad car.

"Don't worry, Tess. I'll have a lawyer down there in minutes," Gollum called after me.

"What about my noon appointment?" I dug my heels into the slushy grass. Allie yanked again on my arms.

"Can't you see I'm trying to save your life? If you are safely locked in a jail cell, Scazzy can't kill you," Allie snarled at me. "Though why I should bother saving your traitorous hide is beyond me."

"That isn't the issue."

"It's the only issue that really matters. I'm still your friend, I guess. Sometimes, like right now, I wish I weren't." Allie looked back at Gollum standing in the doorway with longing and pain. Then she leaned her greater height and weight into propelling me forward. I had no choice but to climb into the back of her huge four-wheel-drive rig. Not a graceful maneuver with my hands cuffed behind my back.

"Does this mean we have to cancel family game night?" Mom called after me.

Tess isn't going anywhere, anytime soon. I should go hold her hand, so to speak, but there are things happening that tweak my curiosity.

There are too many people in uniform at the house to sort out the emotions and the tensions. If they find anything interesting, I can discover it, too, by peeking at their reports. I'll wait to go home until the police decamp.

So I pop over to Donovan's motel room.

I have to watch from outside the window. I think I know the source of that forcefield. I've felt something similar before. Twice now. But that theory is just too outré for words. Too humiliating to admit.

He and WindScribe are going at it hot and heavy. Oh, my, he does have a beautiful body. Lovely muscles ripple beneath his smooth skin. Not a lot of body hair. I do so admire lovely men. No wonder Tess turns to pudding every time he walks into the room. The only thing more beautiful than this man naked is an imp covered in warts.

Now, WindScribe is just another female to my jaundiced eye. Too skinny with hardly any boobs. He takes his time, working with hands and tongue. He captures WindScribe's gaze with his as he slowly, ever so slowly enters her.

She squeaks in passionate wonder. Her eyes glaze and her muscles ripple all the way to her curling toes.

She is transparent to me. I can see through her skin, to all her inner workings. And young as she is, she hasn't kept fit. Too much fat under the skin. Few females can measure up to Tess for beauty and muscle tone. She doesn't think so, but she doesn't look at her own soul. I love Tess more than life. She's my warrior, and I her blade. Our lives have melded to the point that if she dies, I die. If I die, she dies. That is an intimacy far deeper than mere sex.

Speaking of which . . . where did WindScribe learn to do that? She isn't the innocent teenager she pretends to be. Before she went off to Faery with her coven, she'd been around. Several times. Either that, or she spent her time with the little folk servicing the king . . . and all of his minions.

Oooh, so flexible. And Donovan measures up to the task, in more ways than one. He is so virile and potent. He is like the Damiri. They breed and breed and breed. She's ripe. And eager.

They reach their peak at High Noon Exactly. How appropriate.

She's following through with her offer to bear Donovan's babies.

I don't think Tess is going to like this even though it will be weeks before anyone but me can know for sure if the pregnancy will hold.

It's over all too soon.

A cold wind blows up. I have felt this wind before. Icy, bitter. It smells of Windago.

Goose bumps appear on WindScribe's skin. She cuddles close to Donovan and burrows beneath the covers. He takes longer to notice, merely accepting her desperate seeking of warmth as the prelude to more sex.

I turn blood red without bothering with any shades of pink. My body stretches and sharpens. I need to transform. But I have no warrior nearby to handle and control me.

Without Tess, I can do nothing. I am nothing. I am useless.

I bang on the window and shout at Donovan. Beware. Hide. Get ready to fight.

He can't hear me.

WindScribe jumps and starts.

"It's just the wind banging a branch against the glass," he soothes her.

No, no, no! It's more than that. Danger.

Why do I bother? Donovan out of the way will make life easier for Tess. I've fulfilled my obligation to warn him.

Three swirling black forms made of air and ice catch hold of me and slap me away. I fight for control with inadequate wings and insubstantial weight. A real imp would have enough weight to work with gravity to fly into the face of these demons.

There just is not enough of me.

Three Windago. They always hunt in mated pairs. But Tess killed the mate of one of them back in Wisconsin. They'll not let go of that grudge easily. Lilia has found reinforcements for her vengeance.

If she can't get to Tess, she'll humiliate her by taking the one she has vowed to protect. They have the backing of someone, *something* very powerful if they are out during daylight. Are the Windago WindScribe's punishment for escaping her cosmic prison?

Before I can claw my way back to the scene of action, the Windago blow down the motel room door. Cheap plywood has no resistance.

WindScribe screams. Something heavy hits the wall. A stream of Damiri curses spew from Donovan.

Finally, I am able to cling to the window frame and watch. Only watch. I ache to transform. I thirst to taste Windago blood.

Without Tess, I can do nothing but watch.

The Windago grab WindScribe by her long blonde hair. She fights them with teeth and nails and feet and fists. Her blows strike only moving air and freezing cold.

Donovan rights himself and grabs a lamp. He turns it on and breaks the bulb. Then he jabs the nearest Windago with the weapon. Sparks fly. The demon crackles with electricity gone awry. He jerks and spasms. His semihuman form is outlined by lightning. He becomes a storm.

Thunder rumbles around and through him. Lightning strobes the room and nearly blinds me.

Then he stops and crumbles to freeze-dried coffee grounds.

Now the Windago are down another mate. They will double their efforts at revenge. They will not remate from within. They must each turn another human.

His companions flee, dragging WindScribe by her hair. Where her heels touch the ground, sparks shoot out like fireworks on the fourth of July.

Donovan drops to his knees and pounds the floor in his frustration. The boards warp from the force of his blows.

I creep away. Useless. A normal imp would retreat to Imp

Haven to gain comfort and succor from his Mum. I can't. My Mum would grind me to a pulp for my failure.

So I slink back to Tess, doing my best to hide the truth from her. I would die if she rejected me.

But I am a failure.

Chapter 35

In a 1744 hieroglyph by de Hooghe, Virgo represents ever germinating life under the dominant influence of the Moon.

AN HOUR PASSED in my holding cell. Then two. Noon came and went.

I hated to think what would happen if I didn't show for my battle with the Orculli trolls.

I rattled the cell door, uselessly. I screamed to be let out. I cajoled and offered bribes to my guards. Nothing worked.

I couldn't see if anyone occupied adjacent cells—the intervening walls were solid cement. I couldn't hear evidence of occupation either. Sunday midday; last night's drunks had cleared out, and no one else was likely to need incarceration until later.

Where was Gollum with his promised lawyer? Or my dad, or anyone who could help me?

Where was Scrap? Probably off indulging in a feeding frenzy of mold. He'd be fat and limp and useless from overeating when he returned.

Even Dill had not returned since . . . since I had thrown him away last night. I wasn't sure I truly wanted him gone now that he was.

My heart sank. My whole life seemed one big failure. I'd committed myself to saving WindScribe from her fate and failed. What good was being a Warrior of the Celestial

Blade if I let a little thing like arrest for murder and jail interfere with my duty?

Slumped into a corner on the low cot, I stared at my hands, worrying the calluses I'd built up on palms and fingers from training with the blade.

"Mom always did blame me for everything that went wrong, even when I was Cecilia's scapegoat," I grumbled. "Now she blames me for murdering her husband. How could my own mother think I did such a thing?"

That set me to prowling the cell again. My muscles ached with the need to *do* something. Anything.

"Maybe she is still in demon thrall." I plopped down again, too depressed to think straight. "I detected hints of red embers in her eyes when he was around."

Scrap slid down the wall and sat next to me, silently chomping on his cigar. He looked a peckish gray.

So he hadn't had an orgy of mold. What had he been up to?

The guards kept wandering through, sniffing the air for evidence of violators of the no smoking rules. I couldn't summon enough humor to laugh at them.

"We're in trouble, Scrap."

You think this is trouble? I think this is a nice quiet vacation. He leaned back against the wall, both paws behind his head and blew fanciful smoke rings around the end of his black cherry cheroot. But there was a wary edge to his voice and his posture.

"What if . . ."

Not to worry about the long term. The murderer will be found, and you'll be released. In the meantime, you get to relax and let them feed you. Nice and warm in here.

"What about WindScribe?"

Worthless bit of trash. Let the Orculli have her. She had to have done something hideous and dangerous to the entire universe or they wouldn't want her back so bad.

"No human is totally worthless. And if she is so dangerous, why won't anyone tell me what she did?"

A whoosh of air displacement announced the entrance of an otherworldly visitor. My curiosity woke up and banished some of my worry-induced depression.

King Scazzy popped into the cell just inside the door. He

waddle-rolled over to the cot and jumped up beside me, a higher jump than I thought possible for a twelve-inch-tall garden gnome. Make that a semilevitation, semijump.

Then he wiggled between Scrap and me, sitting on the edge of the cot with the aura of assuming his throne.

I bunched my muscles, ready to fight the guy with teeth and nails and willpower. I didn't have anything else handy.

Except Scrap. And he didn't seem inclined to transform. He continued to lounge on the cot blowing smoke rings as if we didn't have a care in the world. Though he did darken from gray to flame orange. He needed to go vermilion in order to become the Celestial Blade.

"Greetings, Tess Noncoiré." Scazzy inclined his head graciously.

I snapped my gaping jaw closed. "Greetings, King Scaz-zamurieddu." I kept my head rigidly upright.

"The Orculli honor you, Warrior of the Celestial Blade."

Scrap turned his back on us. At the moment I didn't have a blade to be warrior of.

"You do?"

"Of course. We share many duties and purposes."

"Such as?"

"Keeping the demon world in check."

"Oh." Such a brilliant conversationalist! I searched my brain for something scintillating and important. All I came up with was another "Oh."

"I have come to tell you that, much to my dishonor, the one you call WindScribe, but that is not her true name, has escaped me once again."

I breathed a sigh of relief.

"Who you talking to?" The policeman in charge of guarding these cells wandered by, peering into the corners of my cell.

The place was free of shadows and hiding places. Still King Scazzy managed to fade and blend into the walls. He took on the translucent aspect of Scrap, a little fuzzy around the edges, with the wall showing through from behind him.

"I'm so bored I'm talking to myself. Can I have a maga-zine or a book or something to read? Please?" Before the prison warden of the universe showed up, I had been going stir crazy. In stir.

Hey, is that where the term originated? I'd have to look it up when I got out of here. If I got out of here.

"Sorry, Miss. No reading material in holding. You'll have to wait for an arraignment and more permanent accommodations." The officer wandered off, shaking his head.

King Scazzy brightened back into view.

"So WindScribe is on the loose again," I picked up the conversation where we'd left off before we were so rudely interrupted.

"Not exactly." The gnome had the grace to blush a little.

"What happened?" My heart sank once more. Scrap turned an embarrassed green and nearly disappeared.

"She ran to the fallen one, Donovan Estevez, for refuge."

Again a reference to Donovan Estevez falling. From what? I didn't have time to think about it.

"The Windago found them together," King Scazzy continued. "The demons born of the north wind hold a fierce grudge against you, Warrior, and took WindScribe in revenge. I do not know what force gave them the power to appear in daylight."

"Windago!" I bolted for the cell door, ready to storm through it by sheer force of will if necessary. "They'll freeze-dry her." I couldn't imagine a worse death. I'd faced it myself.

First, they will dance her through the forest until her feet light sparks, Scrap said, huddling into the corner, as far from Scazzy as he could get and remain on the cot.

"You have to help her." I rounded on King Scazzy, full of fury and anxiety.

"The Windago have their orders. They will return her to my custody once she is exhausted and so full of pain she cannot escape again."

"Alive or dead?"

"It makes no difference to me. Dead, she will be less trouble. Alive, I will fulfill my duty." The gnome jumped down from the cot and looked ready to disappear again.

"Just a minute." I grabbed for him.

He eluded me. All I came up with was his cheerful red hat with a bit of tarnished gold braid.

Scazzy whirled on me, covering his naked head with his hands. He had about three hairs, each the length of his body, growing out of his bald pate. I'd cover that head, too.

"My hat!" he wailed. "You have to return my hat."

These nasty little critters valued their hats above all else, even their freedom. The hat was the source of their power. Maybe it was only vanity. Maybe the hats were like Scrap's warts, earned in battle at terrible cost.

"Tell me something first." I held the hat on one finger, twirling it idly.

"Anything. Please. I'll do anything short of releasing my prisoner to retrieve my hat."

"Interesting. The hat is almost as valuable as your honor."

"My hat is my honor. My life is pledged as security to my duty as Prison Warden."

"That, too, is interesting. But what I want to know is why is WindScribe considered such a dangerous prisoner? She's a ditzy teenager with a lot of lessons to learn, and a craving for drugs, but she's basically harmless." I hoped. But I was seriously doubting that statement myself.

Even Scrap sat forward with interest now.

"Not harmless. In her misguided naïve belief that all creatures deserve freedom, she loosed some Midori, full-blooded demons, from their ghetto. Without restrictions. Without wards. Without thinking." Scazzy hung his head and shuddered.

"How is that different from Donovan and Darren working to make a homeland for demons?" I sat down again and continued to twirl the hat.

"The Damiri work for a homeland for Kajiri, *half*-blood demons." Scazzy looked at me as if I were stupid.

"Enlighten me."

"Have you ever encountered a Midori?"

Nope, Scrap added. *I'm smart enough to keep her away from them.*

"What about the Windago we met in Wisconsin last year?" I still shuddered in memory of the fear they'd put in me.

Scrap rolled his cheroot around in his mouth as if tasting

the memory of that fight. *Nope, they were human turned Windago, not Windago released from their own world. Lots of human hormones and enzymes in their blood.*

"And how would you know that?"

"Your imp lacks honor in his past. Do not probe too deeply if this troubles you. The darkness in his past is perhaps why he cannot remain in the same room as Donovan Estevez," Scazzy warned.

Scrap turned so pale a gray I wondered if he would disappear.

A long moment of silence passed around the room, each of us trying to break it. But with what?

"I admit that there is severe prejudice against the Kajiri," Scazzy finally spoke. "They are dangerous, but they also can be controlled with logic and intelligence. They are capable of leading almost normal lives among the race that is their other half, if allowed. They have no real place in the universe, living in the demon ghettos, or among their other ancestors. Outcast and shunned by both."

"And full-bloods, Midori, aren't intelligent or logical?"

Both Scazzy and Scrap shook their heads with horrified expressions.

We keep them locked up in their ghettos for a reason, Scrap said.

"If Midori demons are so dangerous, how did Wind-Scribe get close enough to let them out?"

Scazzy shrugged. "I am not privy to how the crime was committed. Only that she did it, was judged guilty, and is now my responsibility to imprison. I suspect she had help but do not know who would have the audacity. Or the stupidity to foment such a plan."

"Darren Estevez, for one." I reached forward, almost willing to give him his hat back. He raised his hand to grab it from my finger.

Then I jerked it away again. Other pieces of information eluded me.

"How well did Constable Mike Gionelli know Darren Estevez before the murder?"

Scazzy clamped his mouth shut. He looked longingly at his hat.

I wadded it up and contemplated eating it. Not that I would, but he didn't know that.

"The one you know as Michael Gionelli is Kajiri," Scazzy admitted.

"Half Damiri?"

"No. He belongs to another tribe."

I moved the hat closer to my mouth.

"He's of the Okeechobee. A water demon. His home is the swamp in Florida near where Darren Estevez has his headquarters. In his natural form Mike looks rather like an alligator. He, or his tribe, probably owe Darren Estevez something. A lot of money or a debt of honor. Something big enough for Darren to call in his marker by making Mike spy upon you, Tess Noncoiré."

"Ironic that a water demon pissed his pants in fear of the Windago," I laughed.

"He does not spend much time with his demon kin. He is one of the ones who try very hard to remain human, and protect humanity from others of his kind. He is not happy to be Darren's patsy."

"If he's part demon, even just a little bit, then getting bit by a Windago would have no effect on him."

"If the one you know as Lilia David tagged him to become her mate, her venom would have no effect on him. If she sought to kill him, she could."

"Okay. One more thing. Donovan claims he's not Damiri. That he was adopted by Darren as a teenager. After he fell. Fell from what? What is he? I know he's not fully human."

"He is fully human now. Very long-lived and hard to manage, with many Damiri characteristics, but human." Scazzy dropped his hand back to his side, meek and cooperative.

The lack of his hat must be preying on his arrogance and self-righteousness.

"How long is long?"

"The one we now know as Donovan Estevez was originally created eight hundred years ago. He fell and became human a mere fifty years ago."

"Weird, he looks maybe forty human years . . ." I mused.

"What was he before he fell? And what does the darkness in Scrap's past have to do with Donovan?"

"I cannot say."

"Cannot or will not?"

"Both. My life is not worth that bit of knowledge." Faster than I could react, he jumped up, grabbed his hat, and bolted into the otherworld with a pop and a foul wind that smelled of sulfur and burning sewage.

Chapter 36

*J*osh and Allie arrived on the heels of King Scazzy's departure.

"You're free to go, Tess," he said, standing taller and more confidently than I'd ever seen him. But I'd never seen him in court. Rumor had it he was a formidable presence before a jury.

Allie unlocked my cell door, keeping her gaze on the ground. I pushed past her roughly.

"Tess?" she said quietly.

I raised my eyebrows but said nothing.

"Tess, I acted in haste in arresting you. I had my reasons." She finally looked me in the eye, defying me to unleash my anger.

"You interfered."

"I saved your life."

"You don't know that."

"You aren't invincible, Tess. And there are others, too many others, who might have been hurt in the fray."

She had me there.

"Tess, I need to get you home," Josh said anxiously.

"We'll talk later, Allie." How was this going to affect our friendship? Was twenty-three years of relying on each other enough to overcome the breach in our trust?

It had to. It just had to. I couldn't lose Allie. Not now. "I'll call you, Allie. We have to talk."

"Tomorrow night at Guiseppe's as usual? It's Monday cannoli night."

"I don't know. Depends on a lot of things. But we'll talk."

I followed Josh out of the police station, drinking in the fresh air and warm sunshine.

A wild wind blew from the south bringing rapid changes in the weather. About time. But I knew my mother hated the wind. It often triggered her migraines. Like the one she had last night.

The snow melted rapidly, leaving a slushy mess. I spotted a few crocus and snowdrops poking their shy heads into the spring brightness. The grass looked a brighter green than normal. Almost surreal. A sign of new life and hope.

A camera flash exploded in my face.

"James Frazier, do I have to break that thing to keep you out of my life?" I clenched my fists and jumped at him, ready to rip the camera to pieces. And maybe him, too.

"Tess," Josh's voice ripped through my pent-up anger like a broadsword through cotton. "Not now. He is within his rights."

"See, I told you I have rights. The public has a right to know what's really going on in our quiet little peninsula. Did you know your house is haunted, Tess?" He whipped out his notebook.

"Of course. It's a matter of public record. The ghosts were included in the earnest money agreement when I bought the house. Along with the dining table and twelve chairs, the appliances, and the curtains." I did my best to swallow my emotions and present a bland face to him.

"But did you know there's a ghost standing between the police and the closet full of weapons?"

Hmm. WindScribe wasn't around, so Godfrey was back doing his job.

"I haven't been home in several hours. How could I know?" I marched over to Josh where he stood by his car. An upscale midsized sedan.

Now I just had to face my mother. She'd be in a rare temper what with the wind and Darren's murder.

"Did Donovan get to do his ritual over Darren's body?" I asked.

"Don't know." Josh shrugged and held the car door open for me. He wouldn't meet my gaze.

"Tess, I can't continue as your lawyer," he said the moment we closed the doors and locked them against James trying to jump into the backseat, notebook and camera in hand. "I got you released because Halohan and Allie Engstrom arrested you without enough evidence to back it up. But you can't leave town, and they will be watching you closely until they find the murderer."

"Thanks. But why can't you . . . ?"

"Because I'm too close to you and your family. I can't examine evidence and testimony objectively. I've left messages with Marsha Thompson. She's the best criminal defense attorney on the Cape. You should hire her. She's expensive, but she's the best."

"I understand."

"MoonFeather took a phone message for you. She told me to tell you about it but not mention it to anyone else."

"This sounds ominous."

"I hope not. Gayla says she found you some help, but it's not close. Will come as soon as possible."

"That is good news. Even if it is a bit tardy."

"There's something else." He looked hesitant again. Not good in a lawyer. "I have to go up to Boston for a week. I've taken on a big case. An important case. This could really make my career. I've got to go. Can MoonFeather stay with you while I'm gone? She's not as strong or as well as she likes to think. The wound isn't healing properly. I spotted signs of infection when I changed the bandage just before I came to get you. I'd take her with me, but . . ."

"Of course she can stay. You go do what you have to. And I'll call Marsha Thompson first thing in the morning."

"Thanks. I'll see if Marsha will give you a discount as a professional courtesy to me."

"Good. Now take me home. The best way I know to keep her fees from bankrupting me is to find out who really did kill Darren Estevez." I set my jaw and stared straight ahead, letting my mind whirl and spin, trying to find something out of the ordinary to settle on. Something I should know but didn't yet.

"Leave the investigating to the police, Tess."

I smiled and nodded but didn't commit.

From the quiet anxiety of the police station, I stepped into the roaring fury of my mother and aunt in a territorial dispute over my kitchen.

MoonFeather stood tall, braced on her crutches with her wounded leg tucked behind her. Mom set her much shorter, squarer body directly in front of her.

A burning branch of sage in MoonFeather's hand was the obvious source of contention.

Gollum's cat, Gandalf, sat in a puddle of sunshine watching the two women as if he waited to pounce on the victor and consume her for his dinner.

Scrap blew a smoke ring in the cat's face and dodged into a high corner. Gandalf hissed and batted at the imp with bared claws.

The cat was loose. Where was Gollum?

"I will not have you taint this house with your devil worship!" Mom screeched.

"The devil? Satan! I don't even acknowledge the existence of such a being. How can I worship him?" Moon-Feather retorted with more venom than I'd ever heard in her voice. She waved the aromatic smoke in Mom's face.

Mom launched herself at MoonFeather with nails extended and teeth bared.

Josh yanked his love out of the way. I barely inserted myself between the two women in time to catch Mom's arm just shy of her target.

"Quiet!" I screamed in my best schoolteacher voice.

Quiet hummed against my ears.

"Last I knew, this was *my* house," I snarled at both women. And it would stay my house despite Darren's attempts to get it away from me.

"We need to call Father Sheridan," Mom panted, still glaring at her sister-in-law.

"Maybe I should wait to perform my cleansing ritual until after *he* leaves!" MoonFeather said, straining against Josh's strong arms.

"You need an exorcism. You and that piece of teenage trash Tess dragged home. I'm calling Father Sheridan right now," Mom's face had the pinched look of the onset of another migraine.

Rebound headaches were worse than the original. She was not well.

She's still got a bit of demon thrall coloring her aura. Scrap told me blowing another smoke ring—not directly at the cat but close enough to set it hissing. *The evil wants to cling to her, so it sets her against the cleansing.*

MoonFeather blanched. She retreated rigidly against Josh. "Don't bring that foul pervert anywhere near me," MoonFeather said, her voice deadly calm.

"Pervert?" I asked. I'd never heard my aunt say anything remotely negative about anyone before. What did she have against gentle old Father Sheridan?

Mom spun on her heel and reached for the telephone before I could grab her. "About what I'd expect from a whore of Satan."

"No." I yanked the receiver out of her hand. "This has been a strange and upsetting day for all of us. Why don't you go upstairs and lie down, Mom." I herded her toward the stairs. "Josh, put MoonFeather to bed."

"I'll not spend another minute under the same roof as that woman," MoonFeather protested. She resisted Josh's urging. He simply picked her up and carried her down one side of the butler's pantry.

"I want to sleep in the cottage." Mom dug in her heels at the foot of the new stairs in the dining room. "I won't sleep in a house with that heretic!"

"You can't, Mom. It's . . . the police haven't finished cleaning up the cottage yet." Another shove toward the back of the house.

"They . . . they wouldn't let me see Darren. I need to go to him. He can't rest peacefully until I see him." She tried to flee out the door. Tears splotched her cheeks.

I held on tight. "Mom, you aren't making sense. When

you've rested and gotten rid of the headache, we'll call Father Sheridan and make funeral arrangements. He can take you down to the morgue to view the body."

"Call your father. He'll know what to do." This time Mom went meekly upstairs to my spare bedroom.

<hr />

Finally, the house quieted. I took a long hot shower and settled down to some lunch, leftover breakfast actually. No one had cleaned up the kitchen, and the waffle batter looked close to fermentation. But it tasted good, along with the sausage patty and fresh coffee. Lots and lots of fresh coffee with thick cream and three sugars. I might even leave an inch or two in the bottom of the cup to grow mold for Scrap. He deserved a treat as much as I did, even if he was lactose intolerant.

Gollum returned bearing thick deli sandwiches. I ate one of those, too, just to keep him company. He'd brought in a couple days' worth of mail as well.

Such a nice man. I could get used to having him around. Would he be so kind as to take out the garbage? A brief check showed me he already had.

Definitely worth keeping around.

"Did Donovan get to do his ritual over Darren's body?" I asked around a mouthful of rye bread and pastrami.

"Don't know. Halohan did take him over to the cottage. Two officers kept me from following or peeking through the window."

"Damn. I really wanted to know what that ritual did."

"So did I. Totally esoteric and undocumented rituals. I could write an academic paper on it. A secret religion existing right here in the U.S., not in some hidden Third World country. Do you think Donovan would tell me about it?"

I glared at him. He did get carried away sometimes.

Finally, he wound down and looked a bit sheepish. He pushed his glasses up onto the bridge of his nose.

"I've got bad news," he said taking my hand across the kitchen table.

"I know about WindScribe." I left my hand in his. It felt good, natural. Undemanding. That was something Donovan would never allow to happen. He always pushed and wanted more than I was willing to give.

"How?" he asked, allowing his glasses to stay on the end of his nose so I could see the sincerity in his eyes.

"King Scazzy popped into my jail cell and told me. Something about honoring my status as a Celestial Warrior." I recounted our conversation.

"Did he tell you that the Windago took her from Donovan's motel room?" His grip on my hand grew tighter, more reassuring. "They were in bed together. Naked."

"She didn't waste much time." I drew a deep breath, wondering what I truly felt about that bit of news. Not as hurt as I expected. I was the one to reject Donovan, not the other way around. He wasn't here to work his magic on my emotions.

"Well, she returned to this world starkers, only fitting she be taken from it again the same way," I said.

"Good girl." Gollum patted my hand and returned to his sandwich.

"Do we have any chance of getting her back?" I got up to refill our coffee cups. "Is there such a thing as a cosmic lawyer who can defend her?"

"Not that I've heard," Josh said returning from Moon-Feather's room with their empty plates. Gollum had brought enough sandwiches for everyone. Only Mom's remained untouched. Last I looked, she was sleeping with enough drugs in her to knock out an elephant.

"How much do you know about WindScribe?" I asked warily.

"Enough. Your aunt and I came together through a pagan circle. I believe there is a lot more to the universe than we can observe through the normal five senses."

"If we find a precedent, would you argue in her defense?" Gollum asked. His expression looked brighter than it had since we'd discovered Darren's body. "Donovan's case might give us some clues, if he'll give us some details."

"That would be the case of a lifetime." Josh's face turned wistful. "As long as it doesn't interfere with my case in Boston. I've got to get on the road. Thanks for looking after MoonFeather. Don't let her do too much. And I'd recommend you keep the priest away from her. In her current mood, there is no telling what she might do. She's looking for spells to ward the house against invasion."

"What is that all about?" I asked. "I've never heard MoonFeather say anything against anyone before. And she called Father Sheridan a pervert!" I couldn't imagine the short, slender man with a kindly twinkle in his eyes harming anyone. In his late fifties, he'd only been Mom's parish priest about ten years.

"That is not my secret to reveal." Josh looked at his shoes. "Suffice it to say that her anger is not against Father Sheridan personally. And her anger is *for* someone else."

Gollum waited until we were alone again before speaking. "I'll do some research, call Gramps, see if there is a precedent for retrieving the girl."

"I want to talk to MoonFeather. There's more to this than just a misguided teenager trying to act out her ideals of freedom."

Chapter 37

*T*HE DAY DRAGGED on and on. Mom slept. MoonFeather pretended to sleep rather than answer questions. Gollum holed up in his apartment with the telephone and the Internet.

Sunday quiet ruled.

Donovan stayed away. The police came and went from the cottage. They strung their bright yellow crime scene tape and they ignored me. The bugaboo of a false arrest lawsuit hung over them. One more wrong step would land all of their butts in deep trouble.

I hated that Allie would be caught in the aftermath of this. She'd only been trying to help, keeping me from my scheduled battle with King Scazzy and his minions.

She'd saved my life, but she'd probably cost WindScribe hers.

I sat at my desk staring at the computer screen and the bright wedding announcement I'd created. Was it just yesterday? Or the day before? I couldn't remember. Events merged and splashed into each other in my memory.

With a flick of the mouse I deleted the invite and began a new announcement. How did I word the death of a man I barely knew, who'd been married to my mother for barely thirty-six hours before his murder? Did I need to send it to the entire list of people Mom wanted to come to the wedding?

I should be doing something. Talking to Father Sheridan, making funeral arrangements, writing an obituary, consulting Dad. Calling a lawyer.

Instead, I finally finished those last four chapters and e-mailed them. That took hardly any time at all.

Twilight lingered as long as the day, stretching into nothingness. I wandered about the house I'd so lovingly decorated together with my own husband. Our marriage had lasted longer than Mom's. An entire three months before Dill died horribly in a fire.

I'd escaped by the skin of my teeth. Dill hadn't been so lucky.

Donovan owned the hotel that had blossomed from the ashes of the place where Dill died. A much bigger and classier lodge than the original generic and cheap motel. The place had been over insured, and he profited well. I'd heard rumors that the fire was arson. Murder.

Darren had suggested that he'd started the fire just to kill Dill.

Too many parallels in names, in physical appearance. In whirlwind romances.

In death.

"About time you started making connections between me and Darren Estevez and his clan," Dill said. I couldn't see him among the shadows of the library, one of the three rooms on the ground floor of the original house that shared a chimney.

The house suddenly seemed darker. Full night had descended outside. And in my heart.

The moon had not yet risen. Would it shine through the clouds in the sky and in my life?

Half of me sighed with relief that Dill hadn't disappeared completely from my life. The other half screamed in frustration at the questions he forced me to raise.

"Were you a half-blood Damiri demon?" I finally asked the question that had plagued me for months. I'd never had the courage to face the issue.

Never dared wonder if our love had been merely the reflection of demon magic on my emotions.

"You know I can't answer that question," he said, still not showing himself. "You aren't smart enough to deal with the truth."

"Can't or won't?" I'd had this conversation before. With King Scazzy. With Donovan.

Silence.

I slammed my fist against the mirror that hung over the fireplace. The glass tilted, swinging on its wire support. Moonlight shimmered across the silvered glass.

A full moon rose outside. Reflected in the mirror, I saw it as clearly as if I was standing by Miller's Pond.

A full moon. The time when a demon or a troll or a ghost, any otherworldly being was at his weakest. I could hear Dill, but I couldn't see him because of the timing.

Gollum had selected today for the battle with the Orculli trolls for WindScribe's body and soul because they were vulnerable near the full moon.

The Windago would be just as vulnerable. Perhaps more so, since they consisted primarily of wind and shadow.

"Gollum!" I cried running down to his apartment. "How do I find the Windago? Scrap, get your sorry ass away from stalking the cat. Time to go to work!"

I skidded to a halt in Gollum's living room. He sat in the armchair, feet on the coffee table, surrounded by a bevy of beautiful women, all draped in bedsheets, blankets, and towels and nothing else.

<hr />

"Nine, ten, eleven," I counted the half-naked bodies. An occasional leg or breast kept peeking out from the casual covers.

Gollum had a goofy grin on his face and for once kept his mouth shut.

"No. Oh, no. I can't take these women in. I'm not running a frigging boarding house for refugees from Faery!" I wailed. They could only be the missing coven. Why were they here? Why had they come back now?

WindScribe. It all came down to WindScribe. Somehow everything that had happened this weird weekend came down to WindScribe.

"Windago?" A tall brunette with skin the color of moonlight asked. She seemed to be the oldest of the missing coven, not more than twenty-four. Probably their priestess or whatever title a leader of a Wicca coven took. She had a classic beauty with a tall forehead, long face, and slender nose.

"Ooh, you don't want to mess with Windago. They are so mean," whispered a stout blonde in a pouting little girl voice. Her hair was as vague in color as her voice.

"What do they look like?" a third young woman asked. Her hair and eyes were a medium brown, medium height, a little pudgy. The sparkle of curiosity that lit her face and posture changed her from utterly forgettable to quite attractive.

"Dangerous is the word," the brunette added, frowning at Little Miss Curiosity.

"I have to deal with the Windago. They kidnapped WindScribe," I insisted. I didn't want to face them. Again. I wanted to hide in hot and sunny Mexico. But I couldn't. I owed it to WindScribe to bring her back.

Hell, I owed it to humanity to reset the balance of demons in this dimension.

I heard the clump, clump of MoonFeather's crutches coming down the hall from the main house. The sound stopped abruptly at the doorway.

"Oh, my," she gasped. One crutch clattered to the floor.

Gollum ducked and dashed to help her. He looked almost grateful to free himself from the press of lovely pulchritude.

As one, the coven turned to face my aunt. Some of them weren't exactly careful about keeping their drapes secure. Gollum blushed.

I was beyond being embarrassed by them.

"MoonFeather?" the tall brunette asked. "What happened to you? You look so . . . old."

"Because I am old, FireHind. You've been gone for twenty-eight years." MoonFeather made her cautious way into the little room. Gollum trailed in her wake.

"I've never known you to lie, MoonFeather," FireHind replied indignantly.

"I still don't. You've been gone for twenty-eight years. Time runs differently in Faery. Everyone knows that."

"Twenty years." FireHind sank onto the sofa, her sheet billowing around her.

"Twenty -*eight* years?" Miss Curiosity bounced. Her ample breasts, belly, and upper arms wobbled with her excitement. This one looked more solid than the other. More alive and less . . . wispy. "Have we entered into a true Age of Aquarius? The world should be at peace and plenty now." She clapped her hands and nearly dropped her beach towel. The terry cloth would have wrapped around me twice but barely covered her once.

"I'm Larch, by the way." She held out a hand to me.

I shook her hand, trying not to snort at her comment. In answer, I flicked on the TV with the remote. CNN came up automatically with their headline story of the latest terrorist bombing in Iraq followed by an in-depth report on the ongoing civil war-induced famines in Africa.

"Peace and plenty are still elusive, ladies. Politics are dirtier, drugs more pervasive, and crime more rampant than ever. You missed a lot."

Gollum grabbed the remote and turned off the blaring ugliness of our lives.

"Get rid of these chicks," I told Gollum, not bothering to lower my voice. "It's the night of the full moon. This is our one and only chance to get WindScribe back from the Windago."

"Oh, you mustn't confront the Windago," FireHind said. She seemed to have recovered from the shock of the time difference a little faster than the others.

"They have WindScribe, one of your own!"

Silence.

"WindScribe has chosen her own path," a small voice whispered from the rear.

"No one chooses to be kidnapped by the Windago," Gollum nearly shouted. "Do you know what the Windago will do to her?" he asked peering over the tops of his glasses.

Silence again.

"They will drag her by the hair, making her dance faster and ever faster until her heels strike sparks from the Earth. They will dance her through the heavens until she literally dies of exhaustion," he explained, straining to retain something of his calm teacher demeanor and failing.

"Even so. Violent confrontation is never justified," the dark-haired leader pronounced. She sat back as if uttering an imperial edict from a jeweled throne.

"After what she did in Faery, I'm not surprised," Larch whispered.

FireHind glared at her fiercely. "Shut up, Larch."

What did she do in Faery? No time to pursue that snippet of information.

"I don't intend to confront them. I intended to kill them," I snarled.

"Violence is never the answer, dear," FireHind admonished me as if I were a child. Looking at her, and hearing her, she seemed much more the child than I.

"Nearly thirty years in Faery, and you still haven't grown up," MoonFeather huffed.

"I beg your pardon! I am an adult."

"Yeah, right."

"Yes, she is right," the blowsy blonde replied. "She is our leader and much older than the rest of us."

MoonFeather and I rolled our eyes. "She chose her name correctly. MilkweedFluff," my aunt whispered.

"If the Windago have kidnapped WindScribe, then we must perform a ritual. We must bring balance and harmony back into their lives so that they will release her," FireHind said decisively.

This time, Larch rolled her eyes in concert with Moon-Feather.

As one (Larch a little belatedly but not much), the women shifted into a lopsided circle facing inward. They raised their hands, palms out to shoulder level, keeping their elbows bent. A solemn hum wove out of their throats.

"I have learned that I can bring harmony and balance into my own life. I can teach others who *want* to learn to do the same. But no one, *no one,* can impose their beliefs or their lifestyle on another. We do not have that right, even with demons." MoonFeather thrust her right crutch at me, thus freeing her hand. Which she used to swat FireHind's hands down.

"What has happened to you, MoonFeather? You've grown hard as well as old." Tears appeared in FireHind's eyes.

"I've grounded my hippy ideals in reality rather than a cloud of marijuana smoke," MoonFeather replied. "And I've learned that some things we can work to change, others we can only pray about. Knowing the difference is the true source of wisdom."

"Demons know nothing of wisdom, nothing of peace or harmony or balance," I added. "They know only how to breed and how to feed themselves. Part of their dietary needs are to torment their prey on the way to their stomachs."

Gollum nodded at that. "Kajiri demons—those of mixed blood with humans—have some reasoning ability. They have to in order to blend in with us. Midori demons—full bloods—act only on instinct." He was back into his professor mode, his comfort zone.

I had the bad feeling that the Windago who had captured WindScribe were Midori, enlisted by Lilia David. They'd respond to the instinctive need for revenge for a lost mate. Respond with violence against any target she directed them to.

I had the fight of my life ahead of me, and I was running out of time.

"Deal with them, Gollum. I'll find the Windago myself."

"You don't find them, Tess. They find you. All you have to do is step into the woods on a windy night," he said. A note of warning and worry crept into his voice.

"I'll deal with the ladies, Tess," MoonFeather said. "I'll send them back to Faery so fast, they won't have time to be missed. They have no place here anymore." With that, my beloved aunt rounded on the eleven women, a steely glint in her eyes.

What if Faery won't have them? Can I give them to the cat as toys? Scrap giggled. *Ooooo, this is getting fun.*

Chapter 38

The Inuit moon spirit, Tarqeq, a mighty hunter, has been given the difficult task of watching over human behavior. When Tarqeq sleeps during the dark of the moon, humankind can exceed their bounds of propriety and misbehave, often in disgusting ways.

COPS OUT FRONT. Cops out back. Someone watched every exit from my home. I really didn't want them following me, asking questions and seeing things they couldn't understand. Otherwordly things they must discount.

I couldn't ask Allie for help. She was in enough trouble as it was.

Backup from the Warriors of the Celestial Blade hadn't shown up yet.

I had to do this. And it looked like I would have to take on a tribe of Windago by myself. I shivered with preternatural cold even before they touched me.

"You're going to need help," Gollum said, following me from window to window.

"You volunteering?" I almost wished that he would. But I also wanted him left behind, safe. Guarding Mom and Moon-Feather and the errant coven if things went terribly wrong.

"No. I was thinking you should call Donovan. He has some experience in this field. And I believe he needs a distraction. He blames himself for WindScribe being taken." Gollum closed the curtains behind me as I moved to the next window.

He picked up the walk-around phone from my office so that he could continue following me. "We need to talk," Gollum said into the telephone. If the line was tapped, we didn't want the cops to think I was doing something untoward. "Come over now."

I listened in on the kitchen extension.

Donovan grunted something.

"It involves your girlfriend."

"Which one?" Donovan still sounded disgruntled and reluctant.

"Take your pick. Just get over here."

Within five minutes, I heard his car on the main road. He walked up the long lane to the front door from the street rather than drive past the cottage and into the gravel parking area by the kitchen.

I met him at the front door—hastily unsealed for the purpose. In his black leather jacket, black jeans, and a black turtleneck, with his hair a little rumpled, the wings of silver hair at his temples glistening in the porch light, he looked good enough to eat.

I'd never know if the chemistry between us was natural or a product of his demon upbringing and sympathies. Teenagers absorb information like sponges—even when they want you to think they aren't listening. Who knew what skills he'd learned from Darren.

He accepted my plan for getting WindScribe back with a curt nod. "I want a piece of those demons. A big, lethal piece," he said.

"Take your pick of weapons," I told him as we descended to the cellar. Halohan had only taken the German short sword. (I cursed every time I thought of demon blood corroding the metal while it sat in an evidence bin somewhere.) The other weapons had all turned up free of fingerprints and signs of recent usage.

"The Celestial Blade?" he asked hopefully.

"Since I'll be using the real one, I suppose you could take the replica. That is—if it will let you hold it." I flashed him a wicked grin. "Oh, and you have to stay ten yards away from me until we actually find the Windago, otherwise Scrap can't get close enough to me to be of any use. Once we are in the presence of demons, their essence overrides your barriers."

As I opened the armory door, a jolt of memory surfaced. Donovan making a half-statement when Halohan found the short sword with blood on it.

"If an ordinary blade couldn't kill Darren, then what did?"

"That was no ordinary blade." Donovan stood in front of the replica Celestial Blade, hands firmly clasped behind his back.

"Meaning?" Of course it wasn't ordinary. Real, not replica, seventeenth-century pieces were rare and hard to come by. I knew of only a handful of that particular model designed for dueling, in this country.

"It had an otherworldly aura about it." Donovan looked pleased that he had information and power that I did not.

"We had specially forged weapons at the Citadel. For when imps got tired or sickened. For novices who hadn't bonded with imps yet. Forged with magic. Scrap could smell it, but I couldn't."

"The short sword was akin to those. Forged with magic."

"Scrap?" I called into the ether.

As close behind you as I can get, babe. He sounded closer than usual when Donovan stood beside me.

"Did you have anything to do with me buying that particular sword last year?"

Meaning?

"Don't get evasive and noncommittal. You've given me a couple of otherworldly artifacts. The comb and the brooch. And the dragon-skull gargoyle. Did you direct me to that blade in particular?"

Maybe I sensed something down that alley. In that pawnshop, Scrap admitted. *It is a pretty sword. I do like pretty things. Shiny.*

"Origins?"

Unknown.

"Uses?"

Obviously it can kill a demon. Something special in the forging of the metal.

Good enough explanation for me. In the seventeenth century witch hunts happened in Europe every other year or so. A lot of them in Germany. Witches got blamed for crop failures during the Little Ice Age from the fourteenth century well into the eighteenth century. Maybe someone had a reason for imbuing special qualities in that German blade. Like real witches and demons mucking with the weather.

"Anything else in here that appeals to you?" I asked Donovan. I didn't think any of the other blades were special in the same way as the short sword. I'd bought or traded for them on the open market, through usual channels.

"Just the Celestial Blade." Donovan grasped the shaft with a tentative hand. The imp wood glowed red where he grasped it. He kept his hand there.

"Is it burning you?"

"No. It tingles all the way to my feet. I think it's recognizing me." His voice shook.

Slowly he placed his other hand on the shaft. The glow expanded to engulf both hands and arms, up into his bunched neck muscles and over the top of his head. His coppery skin pulsed and darkened to a burnished sheen.

For a half a heartbeat I caught an aura of a bat surrounding him. I backed off before the revulsion could shake my resolve to work with him during this fight.

But he had to be human now, or the blade would repulse him or burn him up.

A flash of jealousy heated my face. "The imp wood never did that with me," I grumbled.

Not that you noticed anyway.

"Were you there, Scrap, even before we bonded?"

I was with you from the moment you contracted the virus, he said softly. *I was with you when you lost your way getting to the Citadel. I kept you from driving off the road into the lake at the base of Dry Falls. I directed you to the Citadel. I licked you where Sister Serena cut out the infection, to help you heal. I watched over you in the night so that you would not be alone during your time of trial.*

I gulped. Most of that terrible journey was a blur of nightmare images.

You fought your first demons during those nightmares.

"Thanks, buddy. I appreciate you being there." One of my biggest fears was to die alone, without family or friends nearby. I'd sat vigil with Sister Jenny while she and her imp Tulip died. Tulip had gotten tagged during a battle while I was still in hospital recovering from the imp flu. He could not live. She could not live if he died. They lingered for months, neither one willing to let the other die.

The Sisters left her alone with her misery. It was their way.

But not mine. I held her hand as she died.

Ever afterward, I wondered if Scrap had held Tulip's paw in those moments. Or if he'd delivered a *coup de grace* to free them both.

I had to shake off those paralyzing memories and get back to the task at hand. Still, my body chilled and my innards began to shake in fear. And in grief.

All of it triggered by Dill's death. Would I ever be free of that?

"I hope not," he said from the corner of the cellar. "When you stop grieving, I go back to . . . whatever. But while you keep me alive in your heart, I'm stuck here and we have a chance to be together again."

"I can't, Dill. I just can't," I whispered in my mind.

"Can't or won't? Is Donovan a better lover than me? If you think you've found someone else, forget it, Tess. You and I are bound together forever, in life and in death. You are mine, and I'll never let him have you."

My blood ran cold at his words. What if he followed through with his threats out there, with the Windago, when I had my hands full and needed all of my wits?

"Will the blade glow like this with anyone?" I asked instead of dwelling on useless emotions.

I don't know. Scrap sounded chagrined.

"If you two don't get a move on, you're going to lose the moon," Gollum called from the top of the stairs. "I removed the padlock from the cellar door. No one saw me do it."

So Gollum had some covert skills. Why was I not surprised?

"This way." I led Donovan over to the shallow steps cut through the dirt and only recently made of cement. "I'll need some help."

Donovan put his back to the slanting cellar doors that lifted upward onto a shadowy corner of the yard. A tall and ancient oak sheltered us from view of any but the most probing of observers.

"Nice hidey-hole," Donovan whispered, as aware as I of potential watchers.

I shrugged. My house had a lot of history. I hoped I didn't have to add hiding place from demons on the hunt to the long list.

As an added safety precaution, I jammed the magic comb into my hair. Instantly, the shadows came alive. I probed the depths of each of them and found them empty.

Silvery moonlight dappled the lawn. Nearly twilight. Who needed flashlights on a night like this? A night made for lovers. Or hunting demons.

My blood ran hot with anticipation. And fear.

We separated as we headed for the woods. Scrap settled comfortably on my shoulder. A friend. And a weapon. My fears abated. A little.

I took the right-hand path, Donovan the left. Scrap and the magic in the comb kept my feet on the path. I barely needed the glimmers of moonlight through the canopy of new leaves popping out to guide me. The dark took on layers and shades. Nothing hid from me.

We made our way slowly around Miller's Pond. On the far side, the forest was deeper and darker. I hadn't explored this area much as a kid because it was scarier, more prone to ghostly imaginings. Now this area was beyond my property line. I had no idea who owned it.

I smelled the dank pond and the fresh green in the ground cover. And then I caught a new smell, something old and rotten and swirling around me.

Yeep! Scrap yelped and instantly glowed red. He elongated and thinned from one eye blink to the next.

I braced my feet and clasped Scrap in the middle. With a flick of my wrists I set the Celestial Blade to twirling.

Donovan leaped out of the low shrubs, his own blade twisting and turning, biting into the suddenly freezing wind.

Burning cold surrounded me and lifted my hair. Sparks flashed near the ground. My hands went numb, and I dropped the Celestial Blade. A dozen Windago reached for me with their freezing hands and souls of ice.

Chapter 39

"AT LAST, I WILL have my revenge and a new mate," Lilia snarled at me. She almost took human form within the black swirling mass of wind and smelly fur.

Each rotation of air seemed to suck more and more warmth and strength from my body. My willpower faded equally fast.

Where the hell was Scrap? I really needed him here, in my hands to give me a boost out of this mess.

"Take Donovan, for all I care. Return WindScribe to me," I said with as much strength and conviction as I could muster.

"WindScribe will be my new mate," a second form whispered from behind me. That must be the husband to the one Donovan killed in the motel.

"Isn't that shredding some cosmic law?" I asked. My knees wanted to give out. All I had left to fight with was my brains. And they wanted to melt out of my ears. "You have orders to return WindScribe to the Orculli."

"We take orders only from ourselves," Lilia hissed.

"Don't tell that to the Powers That Be."

"Fight it, Tess," Donovan called to me. Dimly, I knew that he swung the replica blade in efficient circles, keeping the Windago at bay, yet never quite connecting with them.

Lilia tangled her paw/hand in my hair and yanked. The comb flew free. My scalp burned.

Sparks flew from my heels where they dragged on the ground.

I clawed and kicked, tried to dig in my heels.

No, babe. Don't fight, Scrap countered from off in the bushes. The barest hint of moonlight glinted off his blade ends. *Windago draw energy from your struggle. The moon nears its zenith. Wait a moment.*

I held my breath. A lessening in the cold. A moment of cessation of movement.

Another heartbeat, dahling. That's my babe, Scrap coaxed.

Sure enough the edge of the moon cleared the treetops.

Then, before I could think twice about a plan, Scrap hopped to my hand, all red and stretching, and became my blade once more.

I swung blindly behind me. The blade bit into something. A grunt.

Tension released from my scalp. Lilia screamed in pain.

I dropped to the ground. Instantly, I caught my balance, rolled to my knees, and swung the blade again—right left, up down, fore and aft.

With each swing I pushed myself back onto my feet.

Twisting right and left, whirling my head to keep everyone within sight.

Each blow caught . . . resistance.

"Yeehaw!" Donovan chortled behind me. "Finally got one."

A long, mournful moan followed his glee. I hoped he got the lonely male.

A heavier contingent of freezing shadows pressed me closer.

I flipped the blade into reverse and used the tines on the outside of the blade to pierce and rake ahead of me. One, two. They went down.

A third got under my guard and raked my left forearm with a frigid talon.

I suppressed a moan and clung tighter to the shaft though my left arm felt numb and heavy at the same time. I'd have a scar from that one.

Not on my watch, babe, Scrap growled. For three heart-beats he took control of the blade. I could only follow his motions, keeping a fierce grip on the weapon and on my pain.

A cold shadow shifted to my side. Scrap and I followed it. Lilia. Her eyes glowed red. She reached for me with a new desperation. Part of her fur sloughed free. Her grief and aloneness twisted her face into a grotesque mask worthy of a gargoyle.

Feeling returned to my arm in sharp pinpricks that burned all the way to my spine. I used the pain to propel the blade into a wild twist and thrust.

Lilia's head tumbled to the ground. Dark blood spurted upward. Then all turned to dust, falling back to Earth in a frozen black shower.

Four down, at least eight to go. They paired off, coming at me in twos. My arms grew listless again. Sweat dripped down my back and into my eyes. My heavy sweatshirt dragged at each movement, became too warm. But the air around me dropped below freezing. My blade lost some of its luster in the moonlight. It felt dull and heavy. The balance was off.

And they kept coming at me. I lost sight of them. Freezing tendrils of air reached for me. Every place they touched, bare skin burned with frostbite. Blood dripped from the wound on my left arm.

A few inches to the left of my foot I saw the comb, moonlight giving it an amazing luster. If I could only get my hands on it, I could see the enemy. Fight them better.

They gave me no time, not a single millimeter of space to catch up my treasure.

Exhaustion and defeat dragged me down, made me clumsy.

A Windago chortled with glee and lunged for me.

In the distance a raw hum cranked louder. Gollum or MoonFeather had turned my stereo up full blast. Bright blessings on them both.

Throbbing drums, rousing pipes, a husky voice.

I didn't need to hear the words clearly. At this distance I couldn't. But I knew them.

"Axes flash, broadsword swing.
Shining armor's piercing ring
Horses run with polished shield
Fight those Bastards till they yield
Midnight mare and blood-red roan,
Fight to keep this land your own
Sound the horn and call the cry . . ."

"How many of them can we make die!" I screamed and swung the blade with renewed vigor. I lashed out. The blade brightened and sharpened.

Then I saw her. WindScribe lay huddled in a fetal ball at the base of a tree about two meters from me. She whimpered. I saw her naked back move as she breathed.

She was alive!

New desperation to save my charge flooded me with adrenaline.

Donovan crowed again as he felled a demon. I took out two more.

The enemy faded into the wilderness. The wind died. The temperature rose a few degrees. Scrap shrank back to his normal body and collapsed facedown in the leaf litter.

I dropped to my knees, nearly sick with exhaustion and blood loss. The warming air sent a heavy languor through me. All I wanted to do was fall over and sleep.

Not yet, dahling, Scrap urged. *We've work to do still.* He tugged at my aching scalp to keep me awake. His tongue stroked the bleeding wound on my arm. The burn dissipated. Some. Not much. Enough.

Half stretching, half falling, I found the comb and stuffed it back into my hair. The world brightened. No trace of a lurking Windago. Using a ragged stump as a prop, I dragged myself to my feet and limped over to where Donovan knelt at WindScribe's side. I'd lost a shoe at some point. I was so tired I didn't care.

Scrap faded and lost substance. He needed to eat and sleep as much as I did.

Without a word, Donovan lifted WindScribe into his arms and carried her. I grabbed the replica blade and followed, wincing with every step at the disrespect to a fine weapon by using it as a cane.

The two hundred yards to the house seemed three miles or more. We took it slow and cautious. I kept a wary eye out for returning Windago.

King Scazzy awaited me. He perched on the slanted cellar doors. "Congratulations. You took the Windago out in pairs, including the one you know as Lilia David and the partner of the one Donovan killed earlier. The survivors will not seek revenge." He bowed graciously.

"Well, bully for me." I was so tired I didn't care about anything but a hot shower and bed. Not necessarily in that order.

"I will take my charge now," King Scazzy said imperiously.

"Back off, twerp. She's mine. I won her fair and square." I jabbed at him with the tines of the imp wood blade. Donovan had proved it to be nearly as lethal as the real one.

Scazzy hopped higher on the cellar doors, closer to the house's foundations. "This is not over, Tess Noncoiré." He popped out of view. "We will meet again," he warned from across the ether. His disembodied voice raised the hairs on the back of my neck and sent shudders through my exhausted body and spirit.

Chapter 40

*G*ollum appeared out of nowhere. "You take care of that one. I'll deal with Tess." He scooped me up into his arms and carried me through the back door into the apartment.

Donovan, still carrying WindScribe, proceeded to his car. I heard them drive off and thought nothing more of them.

I let Gollum cradle me, gaining tiny morsels of warmth wherever my body came in contact with his. It felt so very good and comforting to rest my head on his shoulder, to give him control.

Safe. He made me feel safe.

His big hands made gentle work of cleaning my wounds. He whistled through his teeth at the blood still oozing from the long gash on my arm.

"The frostbite will heal clean. But this . . ." He shook his head. "This is going to scar."

"One more to add to the collection." I just shrugged and let him soothe my hurts with a foul-smelling ointment and bandages.

"You should have some antibiotics. I'll take you to the emergency room."

"Scrap will take care of it when he recovers."

"You sure?" He looked almost scared.

I nodded, eyes closed. Too heavy to keep them open.

Another long moment of silence while I dredged up enough energy to ask the next question.

"The coven?"

"MoonFeather called in some favors and found places for them to go for the night. With other Wiccans I gathered. They seemed obligated to offer hospitality, and intellectually interested in their travels to and from Faery. They will do their best to keep their presence discreet. Allie thinks the FBI will arrive in the morning with tons of questions. We'll reassess the situation in the morning. MoonFeather is quite something. I'd like to spend more time picking her brain."

The rest of his statement drifted through the cobwebs in my mind. I'm not sure how much I heard and how much I dreamed.

I slept the sleep of the just. Or the dead. Ensconced in Gollum's sofa with him watching over me from the armchair.

I awoke alone. Monday morning. Gollum was probably at the college.

Scrap got me up at some ungodly hour with his demands for more beer and orange juice. I joined him in his favorite restorative. Not bad.

From the dirty glasses in the sink, I gathered that Gollum had given him the first dose last night.

The sun poked her bleary head above the horizon. Life was looking better. I peeked beneath Gollum's expert bandage on my arm. A long black scab marked the gash. No trace of red infection. The cooling ointment now smelled of mint and didn't burn the wound at all.

We survived your first battle against Midori, Scrap said quietly around a mouthful of beer. *How do you feel?*

"You should know. You've always said we are linked closer than spouses. I get drunk, you get drunk. I'm happy, you're happy. So how do *we* feel? I'm too numb to figure it out."

Exhausted. Brittle. Fragile.

"Yeah, that about covers it."

Also a bit exhilarated.

"Yeah. That, too."

He flashed his pointy teeth at me and wiggled his fat bottom so that his barbed tail coiled and circled his glass. *I got a couple of new warts.* He showed me the hideous bumps on his elbows.

"Very pretty," I admired his new beauty marks. "Mostly, I'm hungry. How about a high-fat, high-carb breakfast at the diner on the interstate?" I asked him as he slurped the last dregs of his juice through a straw.

The imp had an orange tinge beneath the gray. He'd revive soon.

Not dressed like that, dahling. Scrap surveyed my crumpled jeans and baggy sweatshirt with disdain.

I smelled of sweat and fear gone rancid.

I'd fallen asleep in my clothes again. On Gollum's sofa. Again.

This was becoming a habit I needed to break.

But did I truly want to?

"Okay, I'll shower while you pick out something for me to wear."

I was halfway up the stairs when someone knocked imperiously on the kitchen door. At the same moment, the phone rang shrilly.

"Will someone get the door?" I yelled at the top of my lungs as I grabbed the phone in my office.

No one stirred, so I carried the handset to the kitchen door.

"Hello," I responded to both parties at the same time.

"Tess," Donovan sighed over the phone.

"Tess," Dad demanded at the door.

I motioned Dad and Bill into the kitchen while I turned my attention to Donovan.

"I have to go to Florida. Today," he said without preamble.

"So?"

"I've been on the phone all night to various relatives. There's a power struggle looming within the ranks of Damiri. D's death left a terrible vacuum."

"So go. If the police will let you." I tried to pretend his absence didn't leave an aching void in my gut.

What was it with this guy? Why couldn't I cast him off and forget that he was the world's sexiest man and most incredible lover?

Not bad in a fight either. Twice now, he'd done more than his fair share of subduing a demon horde.

He was also a demon—or a demon sympathizer. Not a safe or comfortable man to love.

That thought stopped me cold. I wasn't in love with Donovan. I couldn't be. I wasn't that self-destructive.

Was I?

"I can't leave WindScribe in the motel alone. I've given her some money to buy clothes and shoes. But she's so scattered and emotionally strung out I'm uncomfortable leaving her totally alone. Can you take her back, just for a few days?"

No, I wanted to scream. The gash on my arm throbbed in mute reminder of what lengths I had gone to in order to rescue her. "If I have to. She's going to have to grow up and take responsibility for herself sooner or later, though."

"Agreed. Just not today. Fetch her please, Tess. For me. For us."

"There is no us."

"They're calling my flight. I have to go. Just go get her. Or send someone to do it. Allie or Gollum. Someone."

He rang off before I could tell him to do something anatomically impossible.

"Your mother is on her knees in the Lady Chapel at St. Mary's with her rosary," Dad blurted out.

"And that affects me how?" All I wanted was food. Lots and lots of food, but people kept dumping other problems on me.

Welcome to the world of the Warrior, Scrap chided. He blew a smoke ring at me from his high corner perch above the refrigerator. *Pour me some more OJ and beer, and you eat some crackers. We'll call it good until we can split this place,* he added in his gangster accent.

"She's been there all night. Father Sheridan is very worried. You didn't answer your phone earlier, so he called me. She won't talk to anyone, wouldn't even acknowledge I was there." I'd never seen Dad look so sad and . . . inadequate.

"And all I wanted was a week in Mexico soaking up some sun and drinking *piña coladas* before I start my next book."

"You've got to go get her, Tess. She's so vulnerable right now. You're the only one she'll listen to."

"What makes you think she'll listen to me? As usual, this whole debacle will become my fault in her mind."

"Just go to the church and talk to her. Please."

"Tess," MoonFeather said quietly as she clumped into the kitchen. "You may need an exorcist for your mother. She needs a lot of healing, from within as well as from without."

Bye, babe, Scrap squeaked. He popped out in a puff of black cherry cheroot.

I grabbed a granola bar, thought twice, and threw two more into my purse. Barely enough to sustain life, but they should get me through another hour or so until I could find the time for real food.

My tires only skidded twice on leftover ice during the half-mile drive to St. Mary's. If Father Sheridan wanted one of his parishioners to *leave* their prayers on a weekday, then something terrible was eating away at Mom.

I found her in the third pew from the front, on her knees. She rapidly ran the beads of her rosary through anxious fingers, hardly having time to say one prayer before beginning the next.

Old habits die hard, or maybe I did still have some respect for the sanctity of this old church. I genuflected toward the altar and then knelt beside my mother, bowing my head.

"Can you ever forgive me, Tess?" She kept her eyes on

the rosary—blue milk glass beads worn smooth on some of
the facets with a Madonna Medal anchoring the prayer
chain. She'd used the same one for as long as I could remember.

"He used you, Mom. He manipulated you to gain his
own selfish ends. He did the same thing to Donovan
and . . ." Did I dare mention Mike Gionelli? Not yet. That
connection wasn't necessary at the moment.

"He only married me to get your house."

"My house?"

"There's something special about it. That's why you attract so many ghosts. He never said what. Just that he
needed your house."

There was more. I could tell in the way she paused between sentences, as if having to think how *not* to say something.

"What made him think marrying you would gain him
the house, Mom?"

A long pause. Then she finally looked up at the crucifix
above the altar. (I tried to avoid looking at the gruesome
agony of the man hanging there.)

"I . . . I let him believe that the house was mine. Mine
and yours."

"Why?"

"Trying to impress him. He was so handsome, so sophis-
ticated, and so *rich*! I could hardly believe he was interested in me at first. I have so little. You are my greatest
treasure and one success in life, Tess. But I wanted him to
want me. Just me. Not the mother of a famous writer. Just
me."

A bunch of things clicked into place. Something special
about the house. Joint ownership of the house between
mother and daughter. Marry the mother, kill the daughter.
Then kill the mother, too, and inherit sole ownership of the
house.

I had to keep her focused, help her heal. Then I'd worry
about the house and demons and ghosts and such.

"You are an attractive woman, Mom. Any beauty I have
I inherited from you. There is no reason a normal man
wouldn't be interested in *you*."

"But I don't attract *normal* men. First your father and his . . . well, you know your father. Then Darren. No one else has even looked at me twice."

"Um, Mom, you're half blind when it comes to men. You don't see them when they are flirting. Chief Halohan had the hots for you when his wife left him." Remember I said something about his son being a bully? Well, his mother gave up trying to reform him and convincing his dad that there was a problem. "You pushed him aside so often he gave up." Probably a good thing.

"Then there was George LaBlanc, the first owner of the antique shop. I think he sold out and moved to Maine because you broke his heart."

"Really?" A spark of interest in her eyes. Then it winked out just as rapidly. "I didn't see it. I'm blind to good men. What's wrong with me, Tess?"

"I don't know how to answer that, Mom. But you need to come home now. There's leftover chicken soup. You have a bowl of that and some bread, then take a nap. You haven't slept much since . . . since it happened."

"If I sleep, I'll dream of D. Every time I close my eyes I see the horrible wounds, his blood. So much blood. I can't ever go back to the cottage."

"Then don't. Sleep in the room next to mine. You know I'll keep you safe."

"You can't protect me from my nightmares."

"I can keep those nightmares from becoming real." I hoped.

"I . . . I just want everything the way it was. Before I went to Florida."

"We can't go back, Mom. We can only move forward." The meaning of my words slammed into my chest like a shock wave. I had to move forward, too. I had to put Dill and his death behind me once and for all.

I had to know who killed him and if I truly could have saved him. I had to know who killed Darren. I had to know what was so special about my house. Until then, I was wandering in circles and not moving forward.

With my arm around Mom's waist, and her weary head on my shoulder, we made our slow way back down the aisle. At the door to the narthex, she turned and made a deep reverence to the altar. I did, too. We needed all the help we could get. I'd take the Divine kind as well as my own powers with the Celestial Blade.

Old habits die hard.

Chapter 41

*As the sun sets, the moon rises, and the little people
play on every moonbeam, sprinkling their sparkling
moon dust down onto humankind.*

"TAKE ME TO BREAKFAST, Tess. I haven't
been out of the house in days. I need to breathe
different air," MoonFeather commanded, the moment I got
Mom settled in bed with a bowl of soup. Dad sat beside her,
worry clouding his eyes.

"Mom . . ."

"Needs to talk to your father and then be alone with her
thoughts for a while."

"I'll keep an eye on her," Gollum said. "You and your
aunt need to talk in private."

So we did talk. With a lumberjack omelet, hash browns,
toast with a fruit cup, and more OJ for Scrap, I filled up on
fat and carbohydrates and coffee. MoonFeather settled for
a vegetarian omelet and herb tea. By the time we finished
eating, we had the restaurant pretty much to ourselves. This
was a working class neighborhood. Most of the patrons had
departed to their jobs.

"What do you need to talk to me about?" I asked, savoring the thick coffee that was strong enough to etch a spoon.

"WindScribe."

"We'll check on her on the way home."

"You need to know some things first."

"Like what really happened on Midsummer's night nearly thirty years ago?"

"Yes." My aunt gathered herself and then speared me with her gaze. "To understand what went wrong that night, and I can only give you speculation since I was not there, you have to look at who WindScribe is."

"She's more than a drug addict teenager with great passion and little focus? Isn't that enough against her?"

"Every human is much more complex than that." She breathed deeply and launched into her narrative before she lost her courage. "WindScribe did not run to Wicca so much as run away from her mother. The woman was vicious, alcoholic, with no sense of right and wrong, knowing only that what pleased her must be right."

"That explains a lot of her daughter's values. She said something about being locked in the closet beneath the stairs and being afraid of the dark."

MoonFeather glared at me, a warning not to interrupt her. "I found love and companionship and a sense of connection to the entire universe in Wicca. I found joy in my femininity as the core of my being rather than a limitation because I was not male. WindScribe rejected that and looked only for power—a power that would allow her to wreak revenge on her mother and the world at large for the pain she suffered at her mother's hands."

I'd run into a few similar cases in the science fiction convention community. Usually the kids outgrew that phase and took responsibility for themselves and their actions. Some even went back to the families and religions they sought to flee.

My morning in the church made me think of something else. "Did she have problems with her mother's religion?"

MoonFeather gasped and speared me with a glare that could have stripped paint.

"Well, did she?"

"Do you really need to rehash the church scandals that dominate the news of late?"

"That bad, huh?"

"Worse."

I gulped and made a guess. "She was sexually abused by the local priest, probably because she asked too many questions and wouldn't take 'Because I said so,' as an answer."

"I did not say so."

"You don't have to. Is there more? Like her mother blaming her for deserving the abuse because she was disobedient. Then she got more punishment at home."

"Her mother and the local priest performed an exorcism. More like torture, if you ask me."

"No wonder she stole drugs and jewelry and ran away to Faery. She was desperate to escape this world of horror."

"Only now, after years of reflection and meeting a woman who was my contemporary at the time and is now young enough to be my daughter, can I recognize how warped WindScribe had become," MoonFeather continued.

She took a long drink of her tea and stared at her empty cup, lost in her memories. Just before I thought I should break the silence, she looked up at me again.

"At the time, we of the coven were all rebellious and gloried in just how outrageous we could appear to the staid society at large. We experimented with sex and nudity. We experimented with pot and LSD and then rejected them. They do not open the mind to psychic vision. Drugs cloud true vision. We did not see WindScribe as any different from ourselves."

I'd discovered the same thing in my own brief experiment with pot in college.

"So what happened that night?" I asked.

"The coven as a whole planned a ritual that we hoped would allow us to meet beings from otherworlds, hopefully from Faery. We wanted to invite them here to us, to help make our world better, happier, more colorful . . . different. But I had a fight with my father, and he locked me in my room. By the time I managed to climb out the window and walk to the meeting place, it was too late."

"Something went horribly wrong then," I mused. "This isn't just a numbers thing. Going from thirteen to twelve participants wouldn't change the spell. It might make it fail, or only work partially, but not totally reverse the outcome." I'd read a lot about ceremonial magic to include in my books. MoonFeather had pointed me toward good texts, even invited me to observe and participate in her rituals.

"You are correct. WindScribe changed the words, reversed the order of the dance. We underestimated her need to run away from reality. We didn't know she'd stocked up on drugs and stolen jewelry."

"And she's still running. She does things that blow up in her face—like trying to free Midori demons—and then refuses to take responsibility for them." Maybe I should have let the Windago have her.

But she was human. She belonged here on Earth. She'd only begin to learn right from wrong, heal mentally from the abuse, if she stayed here and faced her shortcomings.

"Yes. And now we must decide what to do with her. Like it or not, she is our responsibility," MoonFeather sighed.

"We'd better check on her." I paid the bill and hurried my aunt back to the car. I had a bad feeling in the pit of my stomach.

Allie's cruiser and a second squad car sitting in front of the motel told me precisely which room Donovan had rented.

Mike Gionelli leaned casually on the second cruiser—a pose I associated with Dill—available to help if needed, but not truly involved.

Only Dill wasn't available to help. He made sarcastic, and now nasty, comments and then disappeared without explanation.

"What's wrong now?" I asked Allie. We hadn't spoken since I left the police station yesterday with Josh. Anger at her still burned, but not as badly as my worry for what trouble WindScribe might have gotten into this time.

"Where's Donovan Estevez?" Allie returned my question with one of her own.

"Um . . . did you tell him not to leave town?"

"I take it he did, then?"

"This morning. He flew to Florida to straighten out some kind of family problem. What do you need him for?" Uh-oh. Did that mean suspicion had fallen on Donovan?

How did I feel about that? As much as I tried to tell myself that I was over Donovan Estevez, I knew that if he'd just come clean about his past I might commit to him.

He'd been a big help last night fighting the Windago. His bloodthirsty glee every time he killed one of them seemed all too human. On the other hand, he had the best motive of anyone to eliminate his adoptive father. How much did he have to gain? I'd really like to look at Darren's will.

"Any idea when—or if—he's coming back?" Allie's eyes drooped, masking her emotions.

I couldn't tell what she was thinking or feeling. And I didn't like it. We'd always been open and honest with each other.

Well, except about Scrap and the Celestial Blade thing. But I had come clean as soon as she needed to know.

"He didn't say. If it's a problem, he might have had to leave his return open-ended. He might have given Wind-Scribe some better idea of what's going on."

"She won't talk to us." Allie hitched her utility belt and shifted her feet uneasily. "Apparently, the FBI called her and tried to interview her over the phone. She hung up on them. They called me to finish their job. Coincides with my need to talk to Mr. Estevez."

"Did you ask to talk to her nicely?"

"Of course I did," Allie sneered. "Don't I always?"

"No. Not always." I stepped up to the door and knocked briskly.

"Go away!" WindScribe cried. She sounded desperate. Or unhappy. Or both.

"WindScribe, it's me, Tess. Are you okay? Did you get some breakfast?"

"Are the police still there?" Her voice sounded closer to the door.

"Yes. Allie is still here. She just wants to talk to you about Donovan. Can we come in please?"

"I don't have to talk to the police. I know my rights."

"No, you don't have to talk to Allie. But it would help us find Darren's murderer if you did."

"I'm confused. I don't know what to do."

"Then let us come in and talk to you," MoonFeather called with the authority of a high priestess to a new convert. She'd hobbled out of the car on her own, limping but relying on the crutches a lot less. "We can't help you if you won't talk to us."

"I don't know . . ."

"WindScribe, you must be hungry. How about if Moon-Feather and I take you over to the coffee shop across the street. Allie could join us in a few minutes when you feel better." Food was always my solution to problems. Good thing I didn't seem capable of gaining weight since I had the imp flu and Scrap joined me.

"No Mike," I whispered to Allie. "Can't take a chance he'll scare her away."

"Why would he . . ."

"He's a man."

"I'll come with you only if your imp comes, too. I want him to protect me."

That was a new one. I still hadn't figured out how she could see Scrap. But she claimed she'd lost the ability to see him after she left Faery. Had her perceptions changed again? No one else around me could see him or my scar. No normal person, that is. Another Warrior of the Celestial Blade could.

Was my supposed help hanging around? Neither Scrap nor I had seen hide nor hair of another Warrior.

"Sure. Scrap needs some more beer and OJ after last night. He'll be happy to join us."

You sure about that, babe? He popped into view right in front of me. Allie and MoonFeather didn't seem to notice the slight air displacement of his arrival.

Maybe WindScribe's time in Faery had sensitized her nose to Mike's demon smell. Scrap didn't turn red around him. He hadn't reacted to Vern and Myrna Abrams either. I had to presume Mike was one of the good guys.

The door opened a crack, the security chain still on. I could see one of WindScribe's eyes peering out at us. It didn't look bloodshot or swollen. If she'd been crying, it was a long time ago.

"Just the three of us," I soothed her, waving Allie to stand behind MoonFeather and out of sight.

"Okay. I'll come." She closed the door enough to release the chain and stepped out.

"For heaven's sake, child, put some shoes on. I know Donovan bought you some," MoonFeather admonished.

"And get a coat. I'll not be responsible for you catching pneumonia.

Even after a huge helping of strawberry waffles with whipped cream and three hot chocolates, also with whipped cream, WindScribe told us nothing we didn't know. Donovan had mentioned that Darren's family wanted to contest the will.

"What's in the will?" I asked.

Allie shrugged. "The investigators found one among his papers, but they aren't telling me anything."

"Your mother might know something," MoonFeather suggested.

I refrained from snorting. Mom avoided knowing anything about official stuff like investments and insurance policies. She left it all to me and Dad. We made sure there was enough in her checking account to cover her expenditures—which weren't much—and that was all she cared about. Dad invested part of her alimony each month so that she'd have a cushion if anything happened to him. She claimed she didn't understand things like that.

"I'd really like to get a look at that will. It might point us toward Darren's murderer," I said.

"Even if it points toward your mother?" Allie asked.

"Mom couldn't . . ."

MoonFeather cocked an eyebrow at me. "Do you really know that your mother isn't capable of violence given what we know about Darren Estevez?"

Mom wasn't the same woman who had left for Florida three weeks ago. This morning's confrontation proved that. And Saturday morning, right after her wedding night, her relationship with Darren was very strained.

If she knew that Darren threatened me, her daughter, would she resort to violence to defend her "greatest treasure and one success?"

"If we follow the money, Mom stands to lose a lot more by Darren's death. He didn't have time to change his will after the marriage. Her alimony from Dad stopped when she remarried," I defended her.

"Do we know that Darren didn't change his will?" Allie asked. "They went to Maine to get married. A *lawyer* can perform marriages there. A savvy lawyer might draw up new wills for both of them at the same time and sock them for double fees."

Hey, babe, keep an eye on the witchlet. I think she's going to bolt! Scrap warned me. He'd downed yet another glass each of beer and OJ and had regained much of his color and perkiness.

While we talked money, WindScribe had grown more and more silent. She seemed to fade into the wallpaper.

"What's wrong?" I asked, grabbing hold of her sleeve. My sleeve, actually. She had on another one of my outfits, this one in amethyst.

"It's all just too confusing. Nothing is where it should be. I'm not where I should be. It's all so *different*." She sniffed and rubbed her eyes, making them red. But no tears leaked out. She just looked as if they had.

"A lot happens in the real world in twenty-eight years." MoonFeather shrugged.

"But I've only been gone like a month! I know because I only bled once while I was gone."

"Time runs different in Faery. Everyone knows that," I said.

"I . . . I just want everything to be the way it was the day I left," WindScribe sobbed.

And I knew in that instant that she lied. I didn't even have to wear the comb to figure that out.

She's got secrets upon secrets upon secrets, Scrap said.

She had to know that Scrap would see that. Deep down, she wanted to tell someone the truth about that night twenty-eight years ago—two months before I was born. One month after Allie entered the world.

But did she know the truth or only the bits and pieces of it as she saw reality through her very warped perspective?

"This isn't getting me any closer to Donovan or to his father's death," Allie sighed. "I've got to get back to the station. The boss will probably put out an APB and a warrant on him. Fleeing the state moves Estevez up to the top of the suspect list."

"I don't think he did it," I said when she had left.

"What makes you think that?" WindScribe asked. She sounded wary and uncertain again.

"Because Donovan Estevez has deep control over his actions. If he planned it, he'd make it look like suicide or an accident, and he'd cover it up so well no one would need to ask questions. We might never have found the body. If he acted in the heat of anger, it would have been on the spur of the moment—and he has a hot temper. Believe me, I know." I rubbed the almost completely healed gash on my forearm. "If Donovan allowed the heat of anger to drive him, when he had the fight with Darren, that would have been about three hours before Darren died. Stealing the short sword took planning."

"If he didn't do it, then who did?" WindScribe turned wide and innocent eyes on me.

There's only one way to find out. Scrap departed so fast the vacuum he created robbed me of breath.

Chapter 42

Though rare, moon images are found in feminine form. Usually she is lovely, graceful, with classic facial features and hair perfectly coiffed under a stunning hat.

"SCRAP, GET YOUR SORRY ass back here!"
No answer.

"He has to return to you, doesn't he?" MoonFeather asked, searching the air with nose and eyes for a trace of my imp. Could she "sense" his presence even if she couldn't see him? If she did, that might explain why she felt the need to cleanse my house with ritual and burning sage.

"Eventually," I grumbled. "He's never far away, in case I need him, but he can stay out of sight for days if he wants." I threw money on the table for my second breakfast and stomped back to my car.

"What about me?" WindScribe wailed.

"What about you?" I snarled.

"I mean you . . . you can't just desert me. What will I do?"

"You should have thought of that before you set the Midori demons free." I eyed her narrowly as she tripped lightly in my wake. "How many faeries died because of that little stunt?"

"I don't know what you mean." She opened her eyes wide again feigning innocence.

I didn't believe her act for a second.

"Enough to get you sent to the cosmic prison for life," I finished for her.

"It was only three faeries! And they'd been mean to me!"

"Somehow, I don't think that's the end of the story."

"You're just as mean as they were." She ran back to the motel, oblivious to the traffic on the 6A.

Horns honked and brakes screeched. She didn't even look at them before slamming the door to her room so hard the frame quivered.

"Not the entire story by a long shot," MoonFeather added. "Let's go home. Scrap will return there more readily, I think."

"I can't leave the b—witch running around loose. She comes with us, if I have to drag her by the hair."

After some more conversation and a few threats, as well as cajoling and promises to call Donovan, WindScribe joined us. She didn't even fight the seat belt.

I wondered how much she feared being alone.

Gollum raised his eyebrows and made copious notes on his laptop when I told him the story. I should expect something different from him?

I curled up in my office with a short story that was due while I waited for Scrap to return. I waited a long time.

Darkness fell. Dad stayed with Mom. They talked and cried a lot. The red glint of demon thrall left her eyes. Wind-Scribe hovered in the library where she could peek out to find me in the office, or dash over to MoonFeather's room at the smallest sound. Old houses creak and groan at the best of times. She spent a lot of time running back and forth, then returning to her corner with a humph and "I didn't really do that" attitude.

I fixed spaghetti for dinner. We each took a plate back to our respective corners.

I was on my third glass of wine—Gollum was on his fifth judging by the few drops left in the bottle—when I sensed a tiny draft and a miniscule weight on my shoulder.

"Ready to talk about it, Scrap?"

It's dangerous.

"What in life isn't?"

This is really, really dangerous. I'm just a scrap of an imp and I don't know if I can control the energies involved.

"We've got to find out who murdered Darren, Scrap."

Even if it was your mother?

That was the first time he didn't call her "Mom." My dinner and the wine turned to ice in my belly.

"Yeah, even if it was her. I *have* to know."

First thing in the morning. I need daylight. Bring Gollum. I can't let you do this alone.

"Meaning that, if you fuck up, we all die together."

Better than dying alone.

Much better than dying alone.

Scrap disappeared again. To think. To rest. To study the energies. I finally had time for my own agenda.

"What's so special about the house, Dill?" I whispered when I finally had the kitchen to myself. He seemed to hang out here more than anyplace else in the house. But then, everyone hung out here more than anywhere else.

I hadn't really been working on the short story. I'd been re-creating conversations, making lists, drawing lines and connecting dots.

Silence.

"Dill, I know you're here. I can tell because the other ghosts are all in the cellar."

Was that a faint shimmer in the air leaning against the center island?

I couldn't tell for sure under the fluorescent light. So I went about gathering the ingredients for chocolate chip cookies. His favorite, my favorite, and Scrap's favorite, for that matter.

"I liked oatmeal and raisin almost as well as chocolate chip," he said almost petulantly.

"Too bad you're dead and can't eat them anymore."

"If you'd just get rid of the imp . . ."

"I'm tired of that line, Dill. Now tell me about the house. You were the one who insisted we spend more than we'd budgeted on it. I said it was too big and would cost a fortune to heat. But you insisted and filled my head full of dreams of a dozen children." I looked longingly at the new table and chairs in the nook. I'd burned the symbol, the promise of those children along with the round table Thursday. Now it was Monday night. Only four days. It seemed a lifetime ago.

"I didn't really want those kids. I just knew they'd happen. My family always has lots of children. Can't seem to stop it from happening." Dill looked over at the nook, too. He frowned at the new decor. Not his choice. Not his table. Not much left of the real Dill in this house.

"What's so special about this house that you chose it over newer places that required less maintenance and cost less to heat, with just as much floor space and land? Why is it the ghosts are content to stay here and not move on? Why was Darren willing to kill again to get his hands on this house?" I stood facing Dill, hands on hips, feet *en garde*.

"Can't you feel it, Tess?" he asked, eyes wide in innocence. "You're pretty dumb and insensitive if you can't. Just an ordinary bitch when I thought you a Celestial Warrior."

"Typical. When you don't want to answer, you sidestep the issue and accuse someone else of being inadequate."

"Well, you are," he sneered. "If the Powers That Be hadn't promised me a new life, I'd be outta here in a flash rather than be tied to a sniveling wimp like you."

I raised my right hand, clutching a huge wooden spoon, ready to clobber him. Only I couldn't. He was dead. And I was alive.

And I didn't have to put up with him much longer.

"Tess? Who are you talking to?" Gollum asked. His glasses stayed firmly on the bridge of his nose as he looked around the kitchen. Jaw dropping in amazement, his gaze lingered on the shimmer in the center.

"Guilford Van der Hoyden-Smythe, meet my ex, Dillwyn Bailey Cooper." I turned my back on them both and started blending flour and baking soda in a measuring cup.

"Uh . . . Tess . . . that isn't the ghost of Dillwyn Bailey Cooper," Gollum stammered.

I sensed him moving closer to me, standing between me and Dill.

"What do you mean it's not Dill?" I whirled to face them both.

The equinoctial moon, only one night off of full, chose that moment to peek through some light clouds and flood through the big bay windows of the nook.

I could still see Dill as a small, semisolid core within layers and layers of wavering black energy.

I wasn't wearing the comb. This was more than aura. More like a pure essence of darkness.

As I watched, a taller, darker being coalesced out of that miasma. Long fangs dripped red blood; pasty white skin stood head and shoulders above my tall husband. It had a human shape, but a blur where the face should be. Except for those fangs. It wore an old-fashioned black suit and opera cape.

My mouth went dry and my eyes froze open.

At the moment of recognition, the demon snapped out of this dimension in a rancid puff of black smoke.

My knees trembled. Gollum wilted.

We held each other up for a long moment, clinging together in disbelief.

"Was that Dill's true form?" I whispered, afraid I'd call it back into being.

"I don't think so," Gollum said on a gulp. "You said several times it acted out of character for Dill. What if it was a shape-changer?"

"Some*thing* that wanted me to believe it was Dill."

"An envoy of the Powers That Be. Something sent to trap you, make you willingly give up your status as a Warrior of the Celestial Blade."

"Not Dill." I blinked back hot, stinging tears. "Now that I've recognized it for what it is, it can't come back. Were any of my ghostly visitations my Dill?" A vast emptiness opened in me. Now I truly would never see Dill again.

"I don't know. I believe you must renounce Scrap and your Sisterhood voluntarily before it could kill you."

"Someone is so desperate to get rid of me, they sent *that*? So desperate they conned Darren into marrying my mother just to get the house. So desperate they told Darren how to free WindScribe from cosmic prison. I think I'm scared, Gollum."

"I think we need more information."

"Before they try again."

Chapter 43

*W*e spent the night together again, drinking my scotch and eating chocolate chip cookies until we fell asleep, me on the sofa, him in the armchair. We kept the nasties at bay and drew comfort from not being alone should they come again.

Tuesday morning Dad and Bill took Mom and Wind-Scribe to do some necessary shopping right after breakfast. I think my parents had more meaningful conversation and did more healing yesterday than they had in twenty years. Though still fragile, Mom appeared to have found a bit of acceptance of the weekend's events.

Gollum, MoonFeather, and I gathered for a council of war in the kitchen.

"Time travel has often been theorized. I don't recall anyone successfully completing it," Gollum mused when Scrap had outlined his plan.

Time is just another dimension, Scrap said importantly.

I think he warmed to the notion as we progressed.

"We only have to go back about forty hours," I said. "That can't be too dangerous. And we don't have to shift locations. We can go stand in the cottage. The police removed the crime scene tape yesterday afternoon."

If I manage the timing right, we won't be gone more than

a few minutes, Scrap said solemnly. His tail twitched nervously.

"Let's do this before I lose my nerve." I dragged Gollum out of the house to the cottage.

"You need a watcher," MoonFeather called after us. "And a ritual circle." She tossed one crutch away and clumped forward. She carried a small cloth drawstring bag with a pentacle embossed on it.

"She's probably right," Gollum admitted. He slowed to allow my aunt to catch up to him.

As I unlocked the cottage door, the smell of death rushed out to greet and smother me. I stepped back too quickly. Gollum caught me as I teetered on the top step. I let him hold me a moment until I regained my balance. It felt good. Like we were a team.

After a moment we crept inside. MoonFeather swept open the curtains, letting sunlight flood the small living room that ran the width of the building.

"Shouldn't we wait until midnight or something?" I asked. Something felt wrong, but I couldn't put my finger on it.

"Midnight rituals are really only to hide from prejudiced outsiders," MoonFeather said self-righteously. "Or if we needed a particular moon configuration."

I want the bright light of day to lead me back, Scrap said. He sounded uncertain. Maybe I was picking up his mood.

The chalk outline of the body stared up at me from the nubby green carpet. The dark stain from Darren's blood spread out beyond it. He had fallen below the window to my right. I hugged the built-in glass-fronted bookcases to my left.

Gollum walked around the outline, examining the position. "Was he faceup or facedown?"

"Faceup, I think." I didn't want to look at the outline. Memory of the sight of his lifeless eyes staring into the distance and his blood pooling beneath him set my breakfast of pancakes and bacon with grilled tomatoes to churning.

They tasted vile the second time around. Especially the strawberry jam I'd put on the pancakes. Too sweet.

"Over here, I think," MoonFeather mused, standing next to me. "You'll be in the shadows, and even a demon shouldn't detect your ghostly presence." She dug into her little bag and withdrew chalk. "Help me to sit on the floor, Tess."

I offered her my arm to lean on as she levered her way to a kneeling position. She settled back on her heels with a sigh. "Much better."

Gollum stood beside me. Scrap perched on my shoulder, wrapping his tail around my neck in a near choke hold. Except he didn't have enough substance to affect my breathing.

Deftly, MoonFeather drew a circle around Gollum and me. She looked like she'd had a lot of practice. Then she set stubby red candles at the four cardinal points of the compass. With a few muttered prayers and scatters of herbs she lit each candle in sequence, north, east, south, and west.

"Blessed be," she breathed at last. "Do your work, Scrap. You are protected from outside interference." She sat back on her heels and closed her eyes.

No matter what happens, do not speak, do not step outside the circle. In no way may you change the events you watch.

The light twisted and tilted, coruscating across my vision. Sparkles drifted around us. My sense of balance wavered. I clung to Gollum's hand.

As abruptly as it had shifted, the world righted. The darkness of the hours between midnight and dawn crowded my sight. Movement by the window caught my attention. The lamp by the armchair was on. The one closer to the sofa still lay broken on the carpet where it had fallen when Donovan and his foster father fought earlier—while Wind-Scribe, Gollum, and I listened outside the window. Darren stood half turned toward me in the circle of light, fists clenched, jaw tight, shoulders hunched. When he turned his head, the light made his eyes look red.

At his feet stood King Scazzamurieddu, equally angry, equally menacing. Except that his cap was missing.

Darren held it crumpled in one of his fists.

I let my gaze wander around the room, drinking in details that I might have missed back in real time. The chalk circle blazed an otherworldly blue white. The red candles and their flames appeared ghostly, mere suggestions of their place. Scrap, however, looked solid and nearly a third larger than I remembered. His weight dragged at my shoulder, so I shoved him atop my head where he proceeded to anchor himself by pulling on my hair.

Gollum and I looked mostly solid, and yet there was a subtle difference, an aftershadow of light every time we shifted or moved a hand.

"If I thought the bitch had a snowball's chance in hell of succeeding with her demon rebellion against the Powers That Be, I'd give her the lock codes to three black market weapons warehouses," Darren nearly shouted.

"But then you'd have to kill her." King Scazzy smiled. He looked so much like a harmless garden gnome the hairs on my nape stood at attention in alarm. He was his most dangerous when he appeared most innocent. "Like you killed Dillwyn when he tried to reveal to the archivist your plans to build a homeland for the Kajiri."

What? I nearly shouted. When? How? I needed to know more.

Gollum held me back from leaving the circle. Scrap took on an ominous shade of red.

"Damn straight I will kill her if I have to. When my people finally get their homeland, they are going to look to me as their leader, not some flighty teenager spaced out on faery mushrooms. I cut her loose from your prison for a reason, and that wasn't it."

Scazzy chuckled. "Don't underestimate that vacant look in her eyes. She's cunning and smart."

"Idiots are cunning. And she's an idiot, and an addict, incapable of stringing two coherent thoughts together. She's fulfilled her purpose." Darren shifted so that his back was fully to me.

"What do you plan to do with the Sanctuary, Estevez?" Scazzy asked.

Sanctuary? He'd referred to my house as a sanctuary once before.

"Would you believe me if I said I merely want to stay out of sight of the Powers That Be for a while? This land is neutral, has been since time out of mind."

"Which is why it is dangerous in the hands of an active Warrior of the Celestial Blade. She is not neutral." Scazzy pasted a fake smile on his face.

"So neutral that it seems only natural a new portal will open here eventually."

"With a little help from you, the legal owner, once you maneuver your name onto the deed."

That wasn't about to happen, even if he murdered me. The house went to charity, along with my royalties if I died.

I desperately wanted Darren to turn around so I could see his eyes, know what he was really thinking. Face the murderer of my husband. The man who had used my mother so mercilessly.

"WindScribe gets an idea in her head and she can't think any further." Darren heaved a sigh. "Passionate and single-minded. She uses sex as a drug and as a weapon. Very dangerous combinations. I need her to start a rebellion when and where I dictate. Won't help me much if she does it in a place so far away from *my* portal we can't use it."

"Then you'll give her back to me for safekeeping when you are done with her." Scazzy's gaze peered into every shadow in the dark room. I got the feeling he saw in the dark as well as in the light. Maybe better, considering Gollum wanted me to fight him at noon.

"You can have the brat now as far as I'm concerned. You just have to convince my new stepdaughter to let her go."

"If I take WindScribe before the honorably scheduled battle, will you back me with the Powers That Be?"

Darren paused. His neck and jaw muscles tensed.

"If you are fully committed to me in this. We eliminate the Powers That Be, and you are free of your job as prison warden. I want WindScribe out of the way, so I can get on with my own plans for Tess. Killing her at the moment would raise too many questions and bring too much official attention to me and my plans."

"You don't think I can take Tess Noncoiré out?" Scazzy cocked one bushy eyebrow.

Darren snorted in derision. "I've heard what she did to an entire clan of Sasquatch. I'm placing my bets on Tess. But I'll hand over the girl after Tess has it out with you. You can still honor your promise," he snorted in derision.

"I'd watch my back if I were you," King Scazzy said quietly. His gaze fixed on the door to the kitchenette.

I swung my head in that direction, deathly afraid I'd see

my mother there. Afraid that she'd heard this entire bizarre conversation.

The doorway was empty. But I heard a scratching sound, like someone moving from the back door in the kitchenette through the narrow passage.

I needed to break free of the circle, go see who approached, and if it was my mother; stop her from murdering her husband.

"Don't pull that trick on me, Your Majesty," Darren sneered. "You won't slip away from me so easily. I wasn't born yesterday." Darren kept his gaze fixed on the Orculli troll rather than heed his warning.

"I mean it, D. Look behind you." King Scazzy looked oh so smug. He knew what was about to happen and wasn't going to do more than the minimum to prevent it.

He had his own agenda. From the half grin on his face, I surmised that he was on an information-gathering mission rather than agreeing with Darren Estevez and his grand schemes.

"Why should I look? So you can run away from my summons the moment I take my eyes off of you?"

King Scazzy heaved a sigh.

WindScribe, wearing one of my pink flannel nightgowns, slipped silently into the room on bare feet. She held the German short sword in front of her in a classic *en garde,* as if she knew exactly how to wield the weapon.

I think I squeaked.

King Scazzy peered directly at me with a puzzled frown. Then he turned back to Darren. "Honor compels me to warn you once more to turn around and watch your back, D."

Darren finally looked over his shoulder. His eyes narrowed in suspicion as he turned to fully face WindScribe. "Put that down, little girl. Before you hurt yourself."

Silent, determined, and lethal, WindScribe advanced upon Darren.

He batted at the blade with his hand. It had no edge, but a wicked point. She performed a perfect circular parry and riposted beneath his guard. She thrust the sword into his gut, pushed upward and twisted in an assassin's expert move.

I almost heard his heart burst as the sword tip penetrated.

A gush of bloody air escaped his mouth. Then he just . . . crumpled.

Scazzy grabbed his red cap from the dying hand and popped out.

WindScribe smiled. "That will teach you to cross me, Darren Estevez. I will be queen of the otherworlds. I will create and control the new portal. No one will ever hurt me again." She left by the front door, closing it quietly behind her, the sword still dripping.

I gasped. Hot bile climbed up my throat.

Gollum pulled me against his side, burying his face in my hair.

Before I could react, Scrap whisked us away.

The world tilted again. Air rushed around us. I felt a chill. I had a vague impression of a vast open space. And something large, blue, and menacing advancing toward us.

Just passing through, guys, Scrap called.

Then with a thump and a give in my knees I was back in my cottage staring at the chalk outline of where Darren had died the day before.

A death I had just witnessed.

Chapter 44

"*I*T DIDN'T WORK," MoonFeather sighed, opening her eyes.

Gollum expertly brushed an opening in the chalk circle with his toe. "Oh, but it did," he said, stepping free of the dubious magical protection.

"But . . ."

I knew I could do it! Scrap chortled and preened. He glowed bright green with satisfaction. An undertone of pink on his skin told me we'd come close to a demon in the chat room between now and then.

"You never left!" MoonFeather protested.

Between one eye blink and the next. Scrap sounded surprised at his expertise in a precise takeoff and landing. He flitted about the cottage living room, hesitating over the places where King Scazzy, Darren, and WindScribe had stood.

"Someone moved the body," I breathed. The outline was slightly to the left of where I'd watched Darren crumple. "He landed on his side. We found him on his back."

"Are you certain?" Gollum asked. He planted his big feet within the chalk outline. "King Scazzamurieddu stood just there." He pointed to the spot beneath the window. "So Darren must have been here."

"Turn on the chair lamp," I instructed. I couldn't bring myself to step outside the protection of MoonFeather's magic circle. Something menacing still lingered in the room. Maybe it was just my imagination, but I couldn't seem to banish the image of Darren's bleeding body on the floor; the wet slurp of the sword piercing his heart; WindScribe's cold smile.

Maybe it was knowing that I was now a target for the Powers That Be because of my house.

What had Gollum said last night? I needed to voluntarily renounce Scrap and the Sisterhood, become a neutral person again.

Maybe it was Scazzy's accusation that Darren had killed my husband.

Dill, my heart screamed. *You didn't have to die!*

I turned cold and trembled from deep in my gut.

Gollum leaned over and flicked on the lamp. The sunshine flooding through the window masked the effect I sought.

"If you look closely, you can see the circle of light cast by the lamp. Darren stood inside that circle," I said, not looking at Gollum. Not daring to see the pain in his eyes.

Gollum peered closely at the carpet and took one long step to his right. "Good observation. But who moved the body?"

I grew colder still. "Mom. When she discovered the body. She turned him over to see why he didn't move. Maybe to see if he was still breathing."

"Judging from the amount of blood, he stayed alive for quite a while. You stop bleeding when the heart stops pumping," Gollum said. He had on his professor face, delivering facts in a lecture. No emotion. No horror.

"How? She stabbed him in the heart. I heard it!" No wonder Mom had come unhinged. I had when Dill died in my arms.

You didn't have to die, my heart kept screaming.

"She who?" MoonFeather asked. She wore a resigned look, as if she knew, but didn't want to admit it.

"Darren was part demon. Maybe his heart had an extra chamber or something," Gollum posited, ignoring my aunt.

"Would the autopsy show that?" I asked.

"She who?" MoonFeather demanded.

"WindScribe," I said quietly. "She came in the back door through the kitchen and killed him in cold blood."

MoonFeather sighed in relief.

"You didn't think that Mom . . ."

"I'm afraid I did, my dear." She straightened her slumping spine and settled her shoulders. "So how do we prove it?"

"I'm not sure. But I've got to call Allie." I finally gathered my courage and stepped outside the circle. I looked briefly at the telephone on the lamp table. No, I wanted out of this charnel house and back into the comfort of my own home. I also needed some time alone to think about Wind-Scribe's final statement.

I will be queen of the otherworlds. Worlds. Plural. A new portal here at the house. And Darren had said something about providing her with the lock codes to black market weapons warehouses. I had to stop the bitch before she led an army of fully armed Midori demons across all the dimensions right through my parlor.

And then I needed a long talk with Scrap about Dill.

"Witnesses," I muttered as I prowled my office. The black screen of the powered-down computer stared at me accusingly. If I wasn't going to write, I should be on vacation in Mexico soaking up sun and color and inspiration, not obsessing about the murder of my mother's husband.

The marriage only lasted thirty-six hours. Or less, for Goddess' sake!

Since my brain wasn't working at the moment, I took care of a little bookkeeping. Paying the bill for the storage of the Kynthia brooch gave me pause. On a whim I called the jewelry store in Boston. I needed to know the thing was still there.

"Thank you for returning my call," the head honcho said when we finally connected.

"Huh?"

"I left a message with a young woman yesterday afternoon."

WindScribe. Just like the flakey brat to forget an important message.

"Is everything all right? No one has stolen my . . . er . . . jewelry?"

"Of course not, Ms. Noncoiré. We have never had a single misplaced item."

I breathed a sigh of relief.

"I called because a registered package arrived in yesterday's mail for you in care of us. We took the liberty of opening it. A small, exquisitely cut black diamond, exceedingly rare, beautifully cut, with only a small flaw, arrived by post in an unmarked jeweler's pouch. The note simply said, 'For the brooch.'"

"For the brooch?" I gulped. Who? What? My mind spun with endless questions.

"I checked, personally. The stone will fit precisely into one, and only one of the empty settings on the brooch. Would you like us to set it for you? The cost is quite modest since you provided the stone."

"I did? I mean, yes. Please do."

"I presume the stone carries a significant symbolism for you. Congratulations on the occasion."

I rang off. A black diamond. What significance?

Of course, Scrap gave me the brooch in honor of defeating the Sasquatch in pitched battle. Could the black diamond be for my battle against the Windago?

If so, what would happen when I'd completed twelve battles and the anonymous donor had filled all the empty spaces on the brooch?

I should live so long.

Back to my current problem. I'd let the metaphysical stuff sort itself out on its own. It seemed to do that with or without my interference.

What was the easiest way to bring reliable witnesses into the situation and not alert WindScribe what I was up to?

"Hello, Cecilia. Mom wants to resume game night tonight," I told my sister on the phone. "She wants life to get back to normal. And she needs to have the family gathered close around her." The *only* way to get the family together without starting a war among us was to put a Trivial Pursuit game on the dining room table between us.

"I'll call Uncle George and Grandma Maria," Cecilia volunteered. She didn't even protest that it was Tuesday night instead of Sunday.

Then I called Dad and insisted he bring Bill, too. With the family lined up, I decided to add a few outsiders. Gollum was a given. He'd be there whether I wanted him or not. And I wanted him. Outsiders who represented the law came next, Allie and her boss Joe Halohan. Mike Gionelli?

No. I didn't think so. I'd deal with him when I had to. Not before.

That left one more player in the drama. My new stepbrother, now ex-stepbrother. Donovan Estevez.

"What?" he growled into his cell phone.

"How fast can you get back here?" I didn't bother introducing myself. He'd either recognized my number on caller ID or he'd know my voice. I'd never forget his.

"I can't leave. The family is tearing itself apart over D's will." He sounded frustrated, and a little scared. No matter how much he, or I, disdained our families, they were . . . family. Important to our emotional well-being, an anchor to who we were and where we came from.

"What is in the will?"

"You sure you want to know?"

"Yes."

"The police didn't tell you?"

"They've told me squat. But I'm about to reveal to them the real murderer. It would look better if you were here, since you are currently their prime suspect."

"Shit!"

"What's in the will?"

"He and your mom signed mutual wills at the time of their marriage. You do know that in Maine, any officer of the court, including lawyer, can perform a marriage?"

"Yeah. A couple in my senior high school class eloped. Their folks tried to have it annulled using that as their argument. The marriage wasn't legal because it hadn't been performed by a judge. What's in the will?"

"The lawyer who performed the marriage drew up a simple but ironclad will for each of them. They left all of their worldly goods to each other. Your mom is now a very wealthy woman. But D's kids and extended family are all set to contest it."

A long whistling breath escaped me. "I'm surprised Halohan didn't zero in on Mom as suspect number one."

"You say I'm their prime suspect now?"

"As of this morning. Your leaving town didn't help."

"Who did it?"

"I don't want to say on an open line." I might be on my cell phone—free long distance, minutes didn't even count when I called Donovan or Gollum since we all had the same carrier—but I suspected eavesdroppers within the house.

"If I leave now, all hell will break loose."

"You can go back tomorrow. But I need you back here by nine tonight. Ten at the latest."

"I'll do my best," he grumbled and muttered something more. A loud crash and shouting in the background, and he disconnected without further explanation.

"Wow!" Gollum said when I related the conversation. "Does she know?"

"I don't think so. She hasn't said anything to me. Or asked any questions about handling the money." I settled back onto his sofa. It felt like an old familiar friend after sleeping on it so many nights running. A big yawn threatened to take me to la la land once more.

"That family of half-blood Damiri could be your next battle." He settled in the armchair across from me and planted his feet on the coffee table. We'd done this before, here and in a couple of hotel rooms as we plotted the next move.

"I'll let the lawyers handle it. Right now, I need your help." I got up and grabbed a couple of beers from his fridge. We each took a long gulp before he spoke again.

"Help with what?"

"Making some new question cards for family game night. Then you can teach me how to stack the deck. You do know how, don't you?"

"What makes you think that?"

"Because you know or can find out anything."

Chapter 45

Moon symbolism has been present in religion since the beginning of recorded history. The crescent moon and star closely identified with Islam probably came originally from Byzantium, and may have been borrowed from ancient Persia before that.

I SERVED COFFEE AND tea and some bakery cookies. Gollum and I had eaten all the homemade ones. Grandma Maria, my mother's mother, complained a bit about the disruption of her "schedule," meaning a series of sitcom repeats on TV on Tuesday nights. Uncle George, my father's brother, demanded a drink before he'd cleared the doorway. Dad and Bill sort of slid in unnoticed by anyone but me. I was the one counting bodies.

Cecilia blew in wearing her red PTA power suit. She glowed with triumph and eagerness. Then she blew out again, in her yellow power pickup, more interested in pushing her agenda on some new playground equipment at the school than her agenda in controlling the family. "By the way, James Frazier is outside with his camera and a man in a black suit and sunglasses," she said offhandedly at the doorway, and was gone before I could question her further.

Allie and Joe Halohan came last, uniforms made casual looking by removal of ties and tool belts. I didn't doubt that they each had guns hidden on their persons somewhere.

Mike Gionelli followed in their wake. I hadn't invited him, but Allie insisted.

"You okay with him, Scrap?" I whispered while alone in the kitchen.

For now. He's got a lot more human in his bloodstream than demon. I can't smell any evil in him. Scrap perched on the mantel blowing smoke rings at all who passed by him.

"FBI and a reporter outside," Mike whispered as he passed me, confirming Cecilia's observation.

"We'll have something for them later," I returned, equally quietly.

Donovan would come when he could get here. A message on my cell phone had informed me he was hoping to get on a flight that would land in Providence at seven. An hour's drive from here. At eight, I hadn't heard from him.

His presence wasn't essential to the proceedings, but I hoped he'd arrive in time to be fully exonerated. Why, I don't know. Donovan in prison as an accessory to murder would make my life a whole lot simpler.

Gollum escorted WindScribe over from the bottom of the new stairs.

Twelve people gathered around the massive table, filling all of the high-backed chairs. Any more and I'd have to drag in extras from the kitchen. I bumped Uncle George from the armchair at the head of the table nearest the fireplace. This was my house, after all. He mumbled and grumbled about preferring his poker night with his drinking buddies at McTs. But he settled his ample butt next to Grandma Maria. Gollum took the place to my right, Allie to my left. Mom sat next to Allie, looking small and frail. This couldn't be easy for her. But she needed to confront the murderer of her husband.

I needed to do the same.

Somehow we all maneuvered things so that WindScribe sat opposite me at the other end of the table. Bill and Dad flanked her. She couldn't avoid my direct gaze.

We began in the normal fashion working our way through the normal deck of question cards. MoonFeather and Dad took on the job of moving game pieces around the board for those of us who couldn't reach.

With this many people, it took a while to work around the table. Gollum made sure that WindScribe's first four questions came from her own time period, Vietnam era politics, Nixon, the Bicentennial celebration, even sports. Her confidence and relief at answering each one correctly showed clearly in her expression and posture.

The rest of us got normal questions about more current events and scientific breakthroughs.

I watched a puzzled frown deepen on WindScribe's face between her turns as each round progressed. She seemed to shrink in her chair, trying to hide from the probability of getting a question she couldn't answer because she'd been stuck in Faery for twenty-eight years. With each move on the board, she became more and more aware of just how much she had missed and how hard she'd find it to fit in to modern life.

The theme from *Star Wars* on my cell phone stopped the action just before WindScribe's fifth question. Donovan's number flashed on the screen.

"I'm turning into your driveway now," he barked. He sounded tired.

"Just in time," I answered smoothly and hung up. "Go ahead with the game."

Gollum drew a card from the top of the pile. I watched him palm it and produce a forgery. No one commented on his sleight of hand. Either they didn't see it, or my family accepted cheating as normal. I was betting on the latter. We get cutthroat sometimes on game night.

"Name the scientist responsible for mapping the human genome," Gollum read in his professorial voice. He speared WindScribe with a look that would have set students quaking in their leather sandals.

I heard the crunch of gravel and the banging of a car door.

"Oh, who could that be?" WindScribe sprang to her feet and made a mad dash for the kitchen. "Donovan, you're back!" she squealed.

We all waited in silence. Answering a question or admitting you didn't know the answer was a nearly sacred ritual among us.

WindScribe appeared a moment later with Donovan's arm wrapped around her waist. She clung to him like a lifeline.

Scrap popped out of the room. Not far, I sensed.

"I guess we have to end the game now," she said brightly.

"Answer the question," Uncle George growled.

"We don't end the game until someone wins," Grandma Maria added.

"I . . . um . . . we can't continue and leave Donovan out. It wouldn't be polite." Near panic crossed WindScribe's features. Then her eyes narrowed, and she settled into a fiercely defiant posture.

I could well imagine an automatic weapon in her hand. Or an eighteenth-century German short sword.

"Answer the question," Halohan added. He'd become as deeply involved as the rest of us.

"Or take the penalty," Allie said.

"You're all being mean to me," WindScribe pouted prettily.

"Not at all, my dear," MoonFeather admonished. "We are simply playing a game. "Now abide by the rules." Her face took on a look of sternness that had sent me running for a place to hide in the woods when I was a child. "Rules are important."

"Donovan, make them stop," she pleaded.

"Far be it from me to break the rules." He shrugged and disengaged himself from her embrace. He moved to my end of the table and placed his hand on my shoulder as he dropped a kiss on top of my hair.

I almost leaned into his warmth and strength. His hand felt quite natural in the place where Scrap usually sat, as if we belonged together.

Gollum's look of sad resignation kept me upright and determined to proceed. Donovan and I didn't belong together. At least not in this lifetime.

"Glad to see you came back voluntarily," Joe Halohan said.

"I need to go back to Florida tomorrow, Chief, but I wanted you to know that I'm available should you need me in the investigation. I'm not guilty. I just have a volatile family that needs attending to."

Halohan grunted his acceptance of the explanation.

"Still not an excuse to skip town without notice," Mike said. He kept his eyes on his hands rather than meet Donovan's gaze.

Tension there. Something to deal with later. WindScribe was looking anxious and ready to flee.

"Perhaps you'd accept a different question, Wind-Scribe?" Gollum said. He pretended to draw another card. "Who is the King of the Orculli trolls?" He read it as if it were just another normal question from the pile.

"That's not a real question!" WindScribe nearly screamed.

"Oh, but it is," Gollum said. He held up the forged card for inspection. Amazing what you can accomplish with a scanner and a good graphics program.

"Answer the question, girl," Grandma Maria demanded. "I know the answer. Surely you should."

My mouth fell open at that.

"Well, anyone who's read one of the field guides to wild folk knows that," my grandmother retorted. I had to get my omnivorous reading habits from somewhere. Why not from her?

"You're ganging up on me. I won't stand for it." Wind-Scribe stamped her foot. She tried for that innocent little girl look and failed miserably.

"We're trying to get you to take responsibility for your commitment to the game," I said sternly. "But you aren't good at taking responsibility. Your mother was right. You aren't good at anything. You'll never be pretty enough or smart enough to do anything but fail." I echoed some of the things MoonFeather had told me about Mrs. Milner's abuse of her daughter.

"Do you suppose we should just throw her out?" Moon-Feather asked. "She doesn't seem interested in following the rules."

"And the next question is where were you going to get the weapons to lead an armed rebellion?" I added.

My family looked more than a little bewildered, but good sports, one and all, they played along with our charade.

"She couldn't follow through with that either," Donovan said on a yawn.

"I will!" WindScribe said. "I will lead the demon tribes to victory. I'll be queen of the otherworlds. And this one, too!"

"The wild imaginings of a drug addict," I said.

"Stop it! It's real. And I am not an addict." WindScribe shouted. She looked ready to tear her hair.

"If she's not an addict, why did she try to steal my migraine medication?" Mom asked. No coaching there. Mom had really caught the girl up to no good.

"Shut up. You're nothing but a demented, shriveled-up old woman. I don't know what D saw in you. You couldn't help him. But I could. I'm the one who killed the king of Faery and got access to the demons. I'm the one who planned everything."

"Is that why the ATF sent me down here, to stop your little war before it got started?" Mike asked.

That surprised everyone, including WindScribe.

She pulled an automatic weapon from the back of her waistband, beneath her sloppy blouse. My blouse that fit her sloppily, that is. She aimed it between my eyes. At this distance she could hardly miss.

Chapter 46

My skin turns bright vermilion. I stretch and twist as far as I can. But no command comes from Tess to transform. I can't get any closer to her than the doorway to the butler's pantry, right behind WindScribe.

She is the source of evil that compels me to become a weapon of good. Her lack of demon blood keeps me from overcoming the force field that surrounds Donovan. Even Mike's traces of demonhood is not enough to overcome Donovan.

His mojo is so powerful I don't want to ever get in a fight *against* him.

If I can't get closer to Tess, then Tess must come to me. Without Donovan.

I need a distraction.

Hmmm.

"Boo!" I shout in WindScribe's ear.

She remains impassive, as if I'm not truly here.

Damn. Why is it she can see me sometimes but not now when I need her to?

"I think you want to put that away," Halohan said sternly. His hand shifted to his hip. He hadn't worn a holster when he came in.

Allie's hand went to her boot top. She must have a gun hidden there.

I couldn't relax. The gaping maw of the gun muzzle stared right at me, followed me when I shoved my chair back and to the left, closer to Donovan.

Was she desperate enough to risk shooting her lover?

Gollum slouched in his chair, almost disappearing beneath the table. Great. Now he turns coward.

"Really, now, it's only a game!" Grandma Maria snorted.

"No, it's not. It's a bunch of silly rules that no one can understand," WindScribe insisted. Her eyes looked wild and unfocused, bright hair tangled as she combed it with the fingers of her left hand.

Halohan eyed her suspiciously.

"Well, I've had it with other people's rules. I'm in charge now." Suddenly she lost the druggie scatterbrained demeanor. She assumed a new air of confidence and serious menace. Lines radiating from her eyes made her look considerably older. Hard experience gave her those lines, not accumulated years.

"As long as you've got the gun, lady. Didn't know we were playing 'Clue,'" Uncle George muttered. He fiddled with his game piece.

Why couldn't he be his usually clumsy self and spill his beer or something, anything to get WindScribe's attention away from me and the trigger of her big honking gun.

"Is that what you did in Faery?" MoonFeather asked. "Take control of the rules, make your own?"

"Of course. But that silly little king kept getting in the way. He should have thanked me for opening the door between our two worlds. But no. He insisted I was violating some long tradition. He talks of hospitality and fair treatment, but he keeps the Cthulu demons locked up in cages. He *attacked* me when I let the poor beasts free."

"Poor beasts?" Donovan quirked one eyebrow up. "Last I heard, the Cthlulu eat everything and anything in their path, growing larger with each meal until one of them will fill an entire ocean. The magic of Faery that keeps every being the same size is the only way to contain them. They aren't even allowed to guard the chat room." He spoke softly.

No one but me was listening anyway.

Again I wondered why those things were allowed to survive. Balance be damned. I didn't want Cthlulus or Damiri, or Sasquatch, or any of the monsters loose in my universe. In any universe.

Gollum seemed to have melted into the floor. So much for his help.

"All creatures deserve to be free!" WindScribe screamed. Then calm descended on her like a cold mask. "So I snapped the Faery king's neck with a twist of my hands, easier than killing a chicken."

A whistle escaped through my teeth. "You killed the king of Faery?"

WindScribe shrugged. "So what?"

"And then you armed a band of demons and tried to take over," MoonFeather finished.

"Get off your high horse, old lady. You'd have done the same. I marched beside you in peace demonstrations. The place was ripe for revolution," WindScribe sneered.

"No, I wouldn't," MoonFeather sighed. "There is a difference between protest marches or organizing voter registration to right a wrong and . . . and arming thugs."

"Thugs with a taste for human blood," Donovan added.

"What in the hell are they talking about?" Dad asked.

"The girl's crazy. Clinically insane, if you ask me," Halohan replied. "And the rest of you are walking a fine line between vivid imagination and downright delusion."

"You got that right," I said. WindScribe might be crazy, but she remained incredibly focused with that gun.

Suddenly Mom's eyes cleared. I could almost see a light switch turning on in her brain. "Why did you kill my husband, Joyce Milner?" she asked. She fixed a gaze on WindScribe that would have made me squirm.

"My name is WindScribe!" she shouted. "I'm not Joyce. I will never be Joyce again." She waved the gun in a wild arc taking in the entire room.

All of us slouched a little lower in our chairs. Gollum actually disappeared beneath the table. Coward or practical?

"So why did you stab my husband and frame my daughter, *WindScribe*?" Mom pressed her. "What did I ever do to you? I used to babysit you."

"Nothing against you, Genny. You just happened to be in the middle," WindScribe dismissed her.

"I'd be interested in the why of it," Halohan said. He edged his chair back a little, making room to lunge for WindScribe. Allie did the same.

"He threatened you, WindScribe," Donovan said. He hadn't budged an inch, not even to cower away from that wicked little gun. Would the bullets penetrate his demon skin? "And he imposed rules on you. Rules that didn't make sense to you."

"Of course. He was all about rules," WindScribe replied. "He couldn't do this or that because it might expose him for a demon. I couldn't say this or that because it might alert his enemies to what he was doing and he was cheating everyone he met. Including you, Genny."

Mom paled. "The wills," she whispered.

"Yeah, the wills," I muttered. "His was a blind, a way of easing your mind so you'd bequeath everything to him, bypassing your children and your ex. He'd wait to kill you until he killed me and you'd inherited everything I own, including this house. You wouldn't have lasted long enough to grieve."

"You, Tess?" Donovan asked. "You were the real target?"

"Of course." Take out a Warrior of the Celestial Blade and take over the house. A very special house on neutral ground where he could build and control a new portal.

One look at Mike squirming in his chair under my scrutiny and I knew I'd guessed right.

"Sacred ground," he whispered. "Neutral ground to all races and tribes. Blessed by seven shamans thousands of years ago."

I might have been the only one to hear him.

"Only Darren hadn't counted on my will, which leaves everything to charity," I continued the primary conversation.

A dozen pairs of eyes riveted on me. "Why you?" Dad asked the question on everyone's lips.

I couldn't tell him. He'd never understand that I was a Warrior of the Celestial Blade living outside a Citadel. That I was a free radical who threatened Darren's plans to set up a home world for Kajiri demons.

"He wanted the house. He also wanted the research I'd stumbled on that would expose his scams and cheats," I said instead. "He may have been wealthy, but a lot of his money came from confidence games and semiorganized crime." That was close enough to the truth.

"It's not nice to speak ill of the dead," Mom remonstrated.

"But it's true!" WindScribe chortled. "That and much, much more. I had to kill him before he killed me. It was all too easy, hardly a challenge at all. Now the king of Faery required some planning. I made it look like an accident, but it was really me. I'm not stupid. And he found me beautiful. So does Donovan. I'm not a failure."

I rolled my eyes in dismissal.

"I'm not a failure!" WindScribe insisted. "And it's my turn to make the rules. None of you will dare break them. Because I'll shoot you dead. Now everyone lay down on the floor with your hands behind your necks."

We looked at each other rather than at her. Who was willing to take a bullet while the rest of us rushed her. An automatic. How fast could she fire? Would the recoil destroy her aim?

What did I know about guns? A blade I could judge. Guns? I didn't want to take a chance on her taking out my entire family.

Allie nodded ever so slightly to Halohan.

"No." I grabbed her wrist. "I won't let you do it."

"You don't have a choice," she said quietly. "I owe you one, Tess. It's my job to protect and to serve."

"No. You don't owe me anything. This is my house. My responsibility." *My job.*

"Quit stalling. Get on the floor," WindScribe ordered.

"I don't think so," Grandma Maria huffed. "My arthritis." She turned a glare on WindScribe that made Mom's look weak.

"Me either. I need another drink," Uncle George leaned back and looked through the butler's pantry as if he could levitate a beer from the fridge.

"You're breaking the rules!" WindScribe looked near panic. "Hey, where's the tall guy?"

"New rule," Gollum said from right behind her. "Never,

ever point a gun at someone unless you intend to shoot. And you'd better shoot quick or the rule maker will take the gun away from you."

He reached over her shoulder and pressed a nerve in her wrist. Her hand opened and the gun fell to the floor.

Allie scrambled to retrieve it.

WindScribe collapsed in upon herself, falling over the arm Gollum thrust in front of her.

I heaved a sigh of relief. Gollum was no coward. He outsmarted us all by sneaking under the table to get behind WindScribe. My estimation of him rose several notches.

Halohan was on his cell phone in seconds. Sirens sounded in the distance a heartbeat later.

Donovan tried to gather me in his arms. I resisted his allure, giving my smile to Gollum instead.

"I guess she forfeited her turn. Can we continue with the game now?" Grandma Maria whined.

▽△▼△▼▽

"Half of D's wealth goes into a blind trust, administered by me, to continue the family enterprise," Donovan told my mother over a brandy and cookies in the kitchen some hours later.

Halohan had taken WindScribe off to the mental ward of the hospital in an ambulance, with James and the FBI hot on their heels. Allie had left instructions for everyone to stop by the station tomorrow to give depositions on the evening's happenings. Bill took Uncle George and Grandma Maria home. MoonFeather had retired to her room with her cell phone to call Josh.

The house felt empty, even though it was still full.

Maybe because Gollum had retired to his apartment to leave the family discussion to the family.

"The other half of the estate, D left to you, Genevieve, naming me executor of the will," Donovan continued. "I'll do my best to see you get as much of it as possible, but he has legitimate sons and daughters who will contest the will in court."

"I . . . I didn't expect much. I knew he had money, but I didn't think he was *wealthy*," Mom replied. She seemed fascinated with the amber swirl of brandy in her glass.

I watched her closely for signs of the grief-madness or demon thrall that had possessed her earlier. For the moment she seemed lucid. She'd recovered faster than I did when widowed dramatically by murder.

"Is there enough in the estate for a compromise?" Dad asked. He had his calculator and a legal pad in front of him. He piled up numbers on the pad at an alarming rate. "Give half to the Estevez children from Genevieve's portion?"

"More than enough. I was going to suggest such a compromise to keep the lawyers from eating up a huge chunk of it. Even giving away half, there's enough for you to live comfortably for the rest of your life, Genevieve." Donovan patted her hand possessively.

I guess he did have a claim on her now. But she was *my* mother. I should be the one taking care of her.

"I don't think I want to buy the Milner place now. It's too big for just me."

"You're welcome to continue here," I offered. Somehow I couldn't imagine living here without her. "Will you want to go back to the cottage?" I asked tentatively. Or would Darren's ghost haunt her there?

Mom shook her head, her short hair bouncing against her cheeks, mingling with her slow tears. "I couldn't."

"Then I'll ask Gollum if he'd be comfortable there and you can have the apartment."

Mom raised hopeful eyes to me. "Th . . . thank you, Tess. I'll pay rent once Donovan clears the estate."

"You just keep cooking for me and we'll call it even."

"Thank you," Dad mouthed on a deep sigh.

A couple of problems under control. But I still had the misplaced coven to deal with. And I had some big questions for Scrap about Dill's death.

Mexico seemed farther away than ever.

Chapter 47

Women who live together in close quarters will often find their monthly cycles coinciding, usually at the dark of the moon, becoming most fertile two weeks later at the full moon.

"WE'RE HOLDING A MEMORIAL for D here on Wednesday morning. Tomorrow," Donovan said when he sought me out in the library a few minutes later. "Just your mom and your family, probably. Then I'll ship his body home to Florida for a funeral and burial on Thursday."

"What's in it for you, Donovan?" I asked quietly.

"It's just a funeral," he replied. He didn't look as confused as he tried to make his voice sound. The flickering light from the fireplace brought out the copper tones in his skin and revealed depths to his eyes I hadn't noticed before. They looked as deep and forbidding as the lake at the base of Dry Falls in Washington State, near his home.

"I meant the will. Why are you working so hard to help my mom and deprive Darren's children of their inheritance?" I held his gaze steadily, doing my best not to succumb to his allure and let my concerns all slide away.

"You aren't going to trust me on this one, are you?" He had the grace to look chagrined.

I knew in that moment that he had something to hide. Something more than usual.

"I don't trust you at all."

"You trusted me to watch your back in battle the night before last."

Was it only two nights ago? It seemed a lifetime had passed since then.

"I thank you for that. But you had something to prove. Watching my back in battle against full-blooded Windago was secondary." We glared at each other for many long moments.

The fire popped, sending an ember onto the hearth. We both jumped and did not relax afterward. I sensed Scrap hovering in the other room, anxious that he could not get close to me.

We both knew that we were too emotionally drained to engage in a fight again even if he could summon the strength to transform.

"What do you have to gain?" I asked again when the silence between us had stretched too long.

"The trust."

Control of half a large estate. He'd been close to bankruptcy last autumn when we destroyed his half-built casino rather than let the Sasquatch use it as a rogue portal into this world. A portal that bypassed the chat room where most dimensional passages took place. Did he need the money that badly to recoup his own fortune?

What about the big gaming deal he closed last Friday?

"What do you intend to do with the trust? I figure it has to be in the millions."

"Maybe buy an island in Polynesia and turn it into a resort where my people can go on vacation and let themselves be who they truly are without prejudice or restrictions." He settled into a wooden rocker across from me.

"And who are your people?"

"You know I can't tell you that."

"These Powers That Be sound like a cop-out to me. Something gets uncomfortable to talk about, and you blame your silence on them."

"That's not fair, Tess. You've never had to face them." He looked at the floor, studying the broad wooden planks intently.

"I've faced Sasquatch, Windago, and Orculli trolls. I've witnessed the Goddess of the Celestial Warriors in the sky.

Maybe I should face these mysterious Powers That Be and get some questions answered."

"If you think getting me to answer a question is hard, the Powers That Be make me look like a tattletale with diarrhea of the mouth."

"Then spill some information."

He replied with another lengthy silence.

"Okay, back to something you will talk about. The will. Why you? I heard you and Darren fighting. You worked hard to keep him from marrying my mother. Why did he trust you with that kind of money and responsibility?"

"Because he knew I'd do something with the money and not fritter it away on cars and drugs and unsound investments."

"Why didn't he do something with the money? Seems like he was just sitting on it for a long time."

"His dreams were too large. He wasn't willing to start small and build. He wanted it all at once or not at all. His kids are too inbred to dream at all."

"But you aren't inbred." I wasn't satisfied with that explanation. Not by a long shot, but I'd take what I could get. And this was more information than I'd been able to pry out of him yet.

"I'm one of a kind." He flashed me one of his disarming grins.

I ignored it, fingering the magic comb in my pocket.

"You are human. King Scazzy said as much. Extremely long-lived but human. How long is extremely long-lived?" Scazzy had told me. I wanted to hear it from Donovan himself.

"You don't want to know."

"Try me."

"I came to life at the same time as the Citadel near Dry Falls was first built to guard the demon portal."

Came to life, not became human. Came to life as what?

He looked too smug for that to be the entire explanation.

Then something else he had said hit me between the eyes just as powerfully. "When you said that Darren's kids would waste their money on cars, drugs, and fly-by-night investments, what kind of drugs do demon spawn use?"

He stood and turned his back to me, peering out the high, small windows into darkness.

"Do they consider blood a drug?"

He nodded.

"Human blood?" I felt suddenly dizzy and nauseous.

"When they can get it."

"And you *sympathize* with these beings? You work to give them a homeland!" I stood in my rage, fists knotted. I wanted to slay him as I had slain the Windago and the Sasquatch before them. But something about this man kept my imp at bay.

What? What? What?

"I watched the Kajiri struggle against prejudice and poverty too long. I know their intelligence, the contributions they can make to both cultures, human and demon. Some injustices cannot be measured." He rounded on me, fists as knotted as my own. "They are akin to former slaves in this country for many, many generations. Think about the prejudice African Americans have overcome and how long it took them; how much prejudice they still face. Then multiply that by one hundred."

"Scrap said that demons are locked up in ghettos for a reason. Like they *eat* other sentient beings. African Americans are human with human sensibilities. If I had my way, I'd slay every last demon that crosses into this dimension."

"And upset the cosmic balance no end." He tried to lull me with another smile. "Ever wonder why you humans don't have a balancing demon? It's because you are your own demons. The only race that murders each other with glee. By the thousands in war and individually."

You humans. He'd said *you humans.* Like he wasn't one of us.

My anger boiled so close to the surface his charm had no effect upon me.

"You are no better than WindScribe. One way or another I'll find evidence to get you locked up for a long, long time. In prison or a mental ward. Any way I can get you off the streets. To save humanity from your depredations and those of your . . . *people.*"

"Ah, Tess. Don't be that way. We were good together." He reached to trace my cheek with a gentle finger.

I ducked away from his touch.

"Remember, L'akita. Remember the night you spent in my arms, loving me time and again, hour after hour, never tiring of me?" His voice grew soft and persuasive.

Goddess help me, I did remember and longed for his touch with every breath.

"Get out of my house and out of my life. Now." I pointed toward the door.

"L'akita."

"Don't." I closed my eyes lest the sight of his awesome beauty make me forget what he truly was. Black of heart and soul.

And, oh, so achingly beautiful.

"Our lives are already entwined, L'akita. You can't banish me so easily."

"I can try. You know the way to the door." I turned my back on him, hugging myself against the need to reach out and hold him close.

"Honor obligates me to warn you. If your mother has not already passed through menopause—completely—there is a good chance she is pregnant. The Damiri are incredibly fertile."

I heard the menace of warning in his voice. My eyes flew open in horror. I was lucky I'd made him use condoms the one night we had spent together.

"Thank you for the warning. I'll keep an eye on her." He had no way of knowing Mom had had a hysterectomy right after I was born. Something had gone terribly wrong. I was six weeks premature. But he didn't know that, and I wasn't about to enlighten him. Let him worry.

"L'akita . . ."

"Scrap says that WindScribe is pregnant," I threw at him. Jealousy screamed through my body. Unreasonable, unthinkable, miserable, aching jealousy. I had no right to the emotion but it was there, like a cancer inside me.

"How?" His mouth flapped open and closed like a fish drowning in air.

"You know how it happens."

"I mean . . ." he swallowed deeply and flushed a charming shade of mahogany. "I mean, how can Scrap tell? It's only been a couple of days."

"He says he can smell it on her. As long as the cat isn't around clogging his sinuses."

"I have some plans to make. I'll petition the courts for custody, of course. I wish the baby was ours. He can be. We can raise him together." He reached to brush a curl off my brow.

I ducked away from his touch, too fragile to risk breaking if we made contact.

"Go. Just go."

"You going to sleep in your own bed tonight?" Gollum asked as I wandered toward the stairs yawning. He had a goofy grin on his face I couldn't interpret.

"How many nights have I slept on your sofa?" I stopped short, one foot on the first step.

He shrugged. "It felt right every time it happened."

"Yeah." Part of me yearned for the safety and security he gave me. But I couldn't allow myself to depend upon him. "But not tonight."

I was too fragile after banishing Donovan. I needed to learn to be alone again.

"Whatever. Holler if you need me to hold your hand after a nightmare." He turned away toward his apartment.

I almost called him back to fill the cold emptiness that yawned inside me.

"I don't have nightmares."

Scrap snorted at that.

I ignored him and made my weary way up to bed.

Mom had already tucked herself in and lay softly weeping. A hard knot in my gut reminded me how I had felt when Dill died. How close to insanity I'd strayed. I'd loved him deeply. I still did. But I also had accepted his death—finally—and knew I couldn't go back; couldn't bring him back.

We all had to move forward somehow. I was still wandering in circles.

"I need to find out one way or another if Darren Estevez murdered you, Dill. And why," I whispered to my memories of my husband, not the apparition I'd seen in the kitchen.

Softly, I pulled up a chair beside Mom's single bed and sat. She lay on her side with one hand outside the covers. I took it in mine and just held it.

And prayed that this midnight vigil would end more happily than the last one I'd sat. With Sister Jenny at the Citadel.

A tiny smile flickered through Mom's tears. "He wasn't truly human," she whispered.

"I know, Mom. I know."

I wondered what he had done to her that had nearly broken her mind. The aura of tension between them Saturday morning had disappeared. Had he used his demon whammy to abate her fears? Had he used the same unnatural charm to win her in the first place?

Undoubtedly. Donovan was capable of the same kind of unnatural influence. I'd seen it in action. That didn't make me any less lonely for banishing him from my life.

I was cold and cramped when I awoke several hours later. Mom's hand still lay in mine, slack with sleep. Her tears had dried and she breathed evenly. I crept away on tiptoe, leaving the door between our rooms open.

▽▲▽▲▽

"Scrap," I called softly into the shadows of the cellar. "Where are you?"

No answer. I could sense him nearby, but he wasn't willing to show himself on demand. He must know what I was up to.

"I've got mold, Scrap." I held up a jar of peach jam half full of the spoiled remains. Nearly a half inch of fuzzy green and white crusted the top. I'd been saving it for emergencies. This seemed like an emergency.

Bribery will get you anything your sweet heart desires, dahling. Scrap popped into view right in front of me. He stuck his nose into the jar, wings beating overtime in his excitement over the culinary treat I held. He lifted his head on a deep inhale, as if savoring the scent of fine wine or perfume.

I pulled the jar back just enough to make it awkward for him to reach.

Faery giver! Scrap pouted.

"It's all yours, friend. If you do something special for me." I pushed the jar out just a little, just enough for him to get another whiff of the putrid stuff.

What? He backed off suspiciously, crossing his pudgy arms above his rotund tummy.

"I want to go back."

Back where? He didn't relax his guard at all.

"To the night Dill was murdered."

It was a fire. An accident.

"It was arson. That makes it murder. You heard Darren claim to have been behind it." I extended the jam a little further. "There's no dairy in this. It won't upset your tummy."

Scrap sniffed appreciatively. He turned pink, then purple. Then virulent yellow. His hunger warred with his conscience.

Don't make me do it, Tess.

I was in trouble if he called me by name. No softening to "babe" or a drawled "dahling."

"Please, Scrap. I have to know what happened." Another proffering of the treat. I waved it beneath his nose. He crept a little closer, salivating.

You were there. You should know what happened.

"I was asleep until Dill woke me and the room was full of smoke and heat. Everything was dark, misshapen by the flickering flames. You know I won't rest until I know for certain if Darren Estevez murdered my husband." And who helped him.

No. It's too dangerous.

"More dangerous than giving in to Dill's demands and replacing you with him?"

Scrap panicked. He flashed green, red, yellow, red, purple, red, blue, and back to red again in rapid succession.

You're dead either path. You die: I die, Scrap gibbered. *Sorry.* And he popped out, leaving me holding the smelly jar of mold and shattered hopes of closure.

No Fair! No Fair! No Fair!

I can't do it.

I won't do it. It's too dangerous. The time separation is three years. Three years, I tell you. And the distance. Three thousand miles back to Half Moon Lake. She doesn't know what she asks.

I can't do it. I'm not skilled enough with dimensional manipulation. The Barrister demons are guarding the chat room. They'll never let me through on such a mission. Never.

But Tess is my Warrior. How can I deny her what she truly needs?

I sense that she does need to do this. She'll never be able to truly move on and send Dillwyn Bailey Cooper back where he belongs unless she does this.

Oh, what to do? What to do?

Chapter 48

"**W**E WANT TO GO back," the plump woman from the coven announced shortly after dawn Wednesday morning. She and her companions descended upon us *en masse,* and the words came out before I'd fully opened the kitchen door to them.

I had a funeral to go to at noon, then plans for afterward.

"Dragonfly, you know we can't go back. The new rulers of Faery don't like us very much," FireHind reprimanded her. "None of the candidates voted to keep us there."

I noted that they were all clad in various forms of jeans and sweatshirts, and barefoot. What was it with these women that they disdained shoes? The temperatures had warmed to the low fifties, but the air and land were still soggy with melting snow.

"I should think the new rulers of Faery would fear you after what WindScribe did," I said as they trooped into my kitchen and settled around the table and on the counters. "Killing the king of Faery couldn't have been easy."

Scrap flitted about, tweaking curls and blowing smoke in their faces. Our previous argument was ignored but not forgotten by either of us. He punctuated his displeasure with me with an occasional fart that reeked of his lactose intolerance.

Some of the younger members of the coven kept fanning the air in front of their faces and looking about bewildered, the curious and outspoken Larch among them. The rest were oblivious to my imp's tricks.

"She snapped his neck like it was a twig she wanted to use for kindling," Dragonfly grumbled. "Then she threw him against an oak tree. No remorse, no second thoughts. He got in her way and she just did it."

"Hush," FireHind reprimanded. "We do not speak of it. We agreed."

"Under threat of death and dismemberment," Larch muttered. "But we aren't in Faery anymore. They can't touch us here in our home dimension."

Now that is something I need to find out. Can the faeries pursue these women like the Orculli pursued WindScribe?

I'm in luck. J'appel dragons are on duty. Tiny things, hardly bigger than I am. They can flame me, but they have to smell me first, and they are constant victims of sinus infections—from the sulfur fumes they burn. And their eyesight is notoriously weak until someone calls them by their true name and they grow and grow and grow to fill the chat room with angry, reptilian, winged-beasties.

So I use my small size and the stealth I learned in order to survive my siblings (not all of them survived me, however) and hop over to the leather curtain that covers the doorway I want. Beyond the curtain a clear force field in front of Faery is wavering like ripples on a smooth pond. The colors of grass and flowers are dim, the chuckling creek has become a raging muddy torrent. Uh-oh. Trouble in Paradise.

Changing air pressure makes my ears pop as I fly into Faery. No matter how big or small you are, when you come to Faery, you are the same size as the faeries. That's the magic this place holds. Sort of defines equal opportunity.

Don't know if I grew or shrank. That's also part of the magic. And how faeries defend themselves. With deception and mystery. No one knows much about them other than that they are incredibly beautiful. Even without warts.

"You have violated our fundamental laws of hospitality!" a feminine voice screeches.

I creep closer to the knot of winged creatures gathering about the sacred oak tree in the center of Faery. Half male, half female. All wearing flowing draperies in lovely jewel tones sprinkled tastefully with diamonds and emeralds and rubies and sapphires and freshwater pearls. They all sparkle in the watery sunlight without ostentation. It is too easy to go overboard with precious gems when they are plentiful, or you are incredibly rich. Not these guys. They know when to quit. Makes them even more elegant. Even their delicate wings glisten with just a hint of sparkly Faery dust.

"I had no choice. Those women violated every cosmic law of hospitality, good manners, and trust," a male in ruby trews and tunic replied. He wears a princely circlet.

"That is for others to judge. Now we are accused of criminal behavior," the female in white and diamonds says with her delicate, long-fingered hands bunched onto her slender hips. Her circlet is platinum and set with diamonds. She outranks him.

The bunches of lesser faeries shift and form up, taking sides.

"I stand by my ruling. The human women are exiled," Prince insists. His folks nod their heads in agreement. So do some of Queenie's faeries.

"You aren't king yet," Queenie says. Her eyes narrow as she calculates her next move. "You have done nothing about the predators kidnapping our citizens. You aren't a decent prince, how can you expect to be an adequate king?"

"Thinking about seizing the crown yourself?" Prince flits one pace forward.

Have I mentioned that faeries rarely let their feet touch the ground? Well, they don't. Like insects, their wings are in constant motion, wafting a gentle perfumed breeze throughout Faery. If you ever catch a whiff of flowers out of season or climate, a faery probably just flew by.

"I will make a better ruler than you," Queenie says. "I'm older, more experienced. More concerned about my people. Wiser than you by a long shot."

This time she commands the nodding heads.

I might also take the opportunity to let you know that most faeries don't have the longest attention span. Nor are they great at making decisions. That's why they rely so heavily on their king—or queen—to think for them.

"You carry not any royal blood. You only married it," Prince snarls.

"Considering how you have mucked up," Queenie points to the raging, muddy torrent behind her. "Royal blood doesn't guarantee a gift for ruling."

"The disruption is only temporary. As soon as I state my case to the Powers That Be . . ."

"We have never had to state our case to them." Queenie almost spat. She looked angry enough to strangle her opponent on the spot. "Now we are out of balance. Our doors are open to thieves, criminals, and predators."

Uh-oh. Faeries don't fight. They live in peace and plenty. They are truly the paradise of the universes.

"Hey!" I shout at them. "Time to step back and think."

They all turn their heads to me. Questions and haughty disdain shine in their eyes.

"This all goes back to WindScribe and her coven, doesn't it?"

They continue staring at me in silence.

"Well, doesn't it? Who else could violate enough cosmic rules to get thrown out of paradise and into an Orculli prison? Now, if you tell me what they did and how they did it, maybe I can help set things right. Before you resort to violence and upset the balance even further."

Things must be really out of whack if I'm advocating peace and compromise. I'm an imp. I am the Celestial Blade of Tess Noncoiré. I thrive on blood and battle. How else do you think I survived the wars with my siblings? They didn't all come through unscathed. Some didn't come through at all. But that's the nature of imps.

Sometimes.

Okay, maybe we don't all kill our own siblings in battles over Mum's love and her lovely home. But we do fight each other for supremacy and the right to be claimed by the next Warrior of the Celestial Blade.

I'm wondering if I should regret some of my actions.

Nah, that's just Faery. Peace and justice permeate the air and seep into you through your pores. Whether you want it or not.

WindScribe is really screwed up if she managed to violate that peace.

They turn on me en masse and blast me with negative psychic energy. I could have withstood it. Imps are pretty good at setting up mind blocks. But I decide to retreat. If they don't want my help, it's their loss. Let 'em live with chaos for a bit. Then they'll welcome my advice.

Time to check back with Tess. I should be able to return about one heartbeat after I left. She'll never know I was gone.

The coven really can't come back to Faery.

⧖⧗⧖⧗⧖

I called Gollum and MoonFeather in to help sort this out.

"Still running away from reality?" MoonFeather asked mildly. She had forsaken her crutches and leaned on one of my long staffs. This one had a brass dragon as a finial. One of my favorites. It suited her better than me.

"That isn't fair, MoonFeather," FireHind defended herself. "You have had decades to adjust to all these changes gradually. We have to face and accept them all at once. It's too much."

"What about WindScribe?" I asked. "She seemed to be adapting. She's criminally insane in my opinion, but she accepted that life does not stagnate, nor do people."

According to Allie's phone call this morning—at an even more ungodly hour than this invasion—the district attorney was willing to forgo the expense and trouble of a trial if the state would take the raving lunatic off his hands. WindScribe's story of being kidnapped into Faery for nearly thirty years, and then releasing demons into the world for an armed rebellion had convinced everyone, including the FBI, that she was not competent to stand trial, nor was she the woman who had disappeared twenty-eight years ago. She showed no remorse over killing Darren. In the eyes of the legal authorities that made her a sociopath.

No easy solution to that cold case.

Apparently, the FBI hadn't yet heard about the other eleven escapees.

"WindScribe is no longer one of us," Dragonfly said, almost proudly. "We banished her."

"Evicting a member from the coven is a serious matter," MoonFeather said. She assumed the captain's chair at the head of the table.

For once FireHind acceded the place of authority to her maturity, and (I hoped) wisdom.

"WindScribe acted in complete opposition to our goals, our ideals, our *faith*," FireHind said. Her voice was quiet, neutral, stating facts. Still, there was a crack in her posture, a shadow in her eyes that shouted how deeply WindScribe had wounded her personally and the coven as a whole by her violence and betrayal.

"Granted." MoonFeather nodded her head once.

"I want to go back," Dragonfly sobbed. "It's always warm there, the flowers bloom, the land never pricks our bare feet. We can be ourselves there."

That's what she thinks! Scrap chortled. *Lots of chaos and political power struggles in Faery. There's power leaking out into the chat room. Upsetting the balance.*

"Civilization does have rules of conformity to keep things running smoothly for the majority," I admitted. "Free spirits have trouble fitting in." I had experienced that as much as anyone. But I still tried to make my life look normal on the outside. I liked my life just the way it was.

Most of the time. In retrospect, now that I knew I had lived through it, I even liked the adrenaline rush of this never ending crisis-weekend-going-on-week.

"Can you send us back, MoonFeather?" FireHind asked, eyes open wide and trusting.

"What about the new king of Faery?" I asked. "Didn't I hear that he wasn't too pleased with you ladies?"

All eleven ladies shuddered.

"Didn't he kick you out as accomplices?"

"We didn't help her," Dragonfly protested. "We just didn't tell anyone what she was up to."

"Complicity in my book," I mumbled.

"Now that WindScribe has been locked up in a mental ward, we hope that the faeries will take us back. We made friends there quite easily until WindScribe . . . until she abused their hospitality in her misguided need to free all captive people," FireHind said. She, like MoonFeather, seemed deeply motivated to speak only positively about people. We were all having trouble finding positive things to say about WindScribe.

"I don't know," MoonFeather mused. She rubbed her chin with one hand and drummed the table with the fingers of the other hand. "The moon is in the wrong quarter. The season is wrong."

I could do it easily if it were All Hallows Eve, Scrap chimed in.

I ignored him for the moment. Halloween was still seven months away.

"What are we going to do?" FireHind asked, almost wailed.

"I need some time to think about this, do some research. Gollum, do you have any books that might help?" Moon-Feather looked brightly at the scholar in our midst.

"Most of them are in storage in Seattle," he admitted glumly. "I can ask around, see if some of my colleagues have copies or better texts. The trouble is we have no documented cases of anyone actually succeeding in this type of dimensional travel. Only hearsay. Our best chance would be to try to re-create the original ritual and adjust it to the season and the moon. Or wait for Halloween."

Eleven frowns met that statement.

Scrap hooted with laughter and whipped around the room. *Told you so!* he chortled. I noticed how far away from me he stayed. He wasn't willing to risk having to say no to me again.

"There is an alternative," King Scazzy popped into view on the counter that separated the breakfast nook from the kitchen proper.

As one, the coven ducked and made a curious warding gesture, crossed wrists and flapping hands. MoonFeather grabbed the staff and took a defensive position.

Scrap turned bright scarlet and landed on my hand; resident evil more powerful than a little tiff with me.

Gollum reached for his PDA and began taking notes.

Chapter 49

"*E*ASY, LADIES," the prison warden of the universe said. He held up both of his stubby hands, palms out. His nose and chin almost met as he frowned. "I come in peace, and I come alone."

Scrap and I relaxed a bit, though he remained red and stretched taller than normal. The coven all pressed themselves against walls, as far from the little man as possible.

Gollum kept taking notes.

"What do you want, King Scazzamurieddu?" I asked.

"I may be of service to your friends," he nodded his head a fraction toward me. "I can escort all eleven ladies with safe passage back to the land of Faery, with a letter of introduction to the new queen."

Oh-ho! Queenie prevailed over the young princeling. I knew she would. That lady has tougher balls than all the rest of Faery combined. If I liked women, I could go for her. Scrap bounced on my hand in his glee. *Did she get the stream running clear and soft again?*

"Partly. There are still disgruntled factions in Faery. Power leaking," Scazzy nodded at Scrap. "The portal gapes."

The coven all looked bewildered and uncertain, not being privy to the exchange.

Gollum kept taking notes.

"You'll take these women back to Faery in return for what?" The fine hairs on my nape rose straight up. I'd read enough folklore to know that fair trade across the dimensions was elusive. Bartering of favors was common, but getting the better end of the deal was tricky. Coming out of the bargain with your soul and your life intact were rare.

That's why Scrap had called me a Faery giver when I snatched the moldy jam away from him.

"I do this in exchange for your word as a Warrior of the Celestial Blade that WindScribe will never again leave the custody of your state mental hospital. And that someone honorable, like Madame MoonFeather will raise the baby she carries. We don't want the father to have full undivided influence over it."

"I can't promise that. She's not my responsibility anymore." I had an uneasy feeling in my gut. This was too easy.

"Security in that facility seems more rigorous than what I could provide in my own prison," King Scazzy chuckled. "The employees are less subject to bribes of shiny baubles. She has less chance of escape from there."

"So? Why my promise? I can't guarantee she'll stay there, or that the courts will give her baby to MoonFeather."

"You are the Warrior of the Celestial Blade. Should she ever leave her current prison, you must slay her. Should the child go to the Fallen One, you must get her back."

Oh-ho! The baby was a girl. Not the boy Donovan presumed.

"No. I don't kill humans. Even if they are homicidal maniacs. All I can promise is that if she is ever released, or escapes, I will notify you. Then she becomes your problem. If the authorities don't recapture her first. As for the baby? I can do my best to persuade Donovan to drop his custody suit. That's it."

"Granted." Scazzy bowed his head again. The gilded feather in his red cap bobbed with him, the only overt sign that he was a king and in absolute authority over his realm.

How far did his boundaries stretch into this dimension?

"And you will really take us back?" FireHind asked anxiously. She held her arms tight against her sides and her shoulders hunched, not quite daring to hope.

"You have my word."

"Give me your cap and repeat that," Gollum demanded, coming out of his intense record keeping.

I suspected he had his cell phone camera running and audio recording as well.

"I beg your pardon," King Scazzy replied, seriously affronted.

"Among the Orculli, an oath is not binding unless the opposite party holds your cap," Gollum returned. He fixed a fierce gaze upon Scazzy over the tops of his glasses.

A staring contest ensued.

The coven got restless, wiggling in their chairs or shifting from foot to foot where they stood. Their murmurs of discontent became an insistent hum.

"Enough!" MoonFeather finally broke the tension. "Do it, Your Majesty, or we'll be here all day. We have other obligations."

"A king does not remove his cap in the presence of lower life-forms." Scazzy levitated from the counter to the table to stand in front of her.

"Oh, yeah?" My aunt snatched the cap and held it above her head where he could not reach. "Now swear to safe passage for my friends, and Tess will swear to inform you if WindScribe ever escapes from the loony bin. And I swear that if I can legally gain custody of WindScribe's daughter, I will raise her with honor."

"Blood oath," Scazzy snarled. "Only way to make humans keep their word."

I shivered and looked to Gollum for confirmation.

"An oath signed in your blood will burst into flames if you break your oath. The flames will ignite the blood in your veins as well," he said as if reciting from a text.

I had a vision of Donovan signing numerous documents to refinance his casino in Half Moon Lake after it imploded. His bankers had dubious connections to the otherworlds and the ink looked thick and dark with reddish undertones like blood. No wonder he was so excited to make the big gaming software deal and take control of Darren's trust fund. If he paid off the note, then his blood no longer bound the deal.

An honest and aboveboard approach to business must have rankled his nerves no end.

And what about that other oath? The one not to reveal his origins.

I almost forgave him his silence. Almost. He was tricky enough to get around that oath if he really wanted my respect and trust. There are always ways around a bargain in Faery.

"The oath is simple enough. I agree," I sighed. "I'll sign a promise to contact you the moment I am informed if WindScribe escapes or is released."

"Or transferred to another facility," Scazzy added. "Someplace else might prove less secure."

"I agree to sign my portion of the bargain," Moon-Feather said with less hesitation. Honor was so ingrained in her, I doubted Scazzy even needed her oath.

"Okay." That came out on a long breath. Why did I feel like there was some trick here that I couldn't see? I checked with Gollum.

He shrugged and nodded.

Scazzy snapped his fingers and a piece of parchment appeared on the table in front of me, along with an ostentatious quill pen made from a peacock-blue ostrich feather—I wondered if it were dyed or came from some bird I'd never seen in another dimension. Beside the quill lay a small penknife. A wickedly sharp penknife for pricking my finger.

Or would he demand I slit my wrist and use arterial blood?

"But I don't want to go back," whispered a tiny voice from the corner behind me.

We all turned to stare at the young woman with reddish glints in her blonde hair. She had wide blue eyes that almost matched the quill in color.

"Larch, we all agreed," FireHind reprimanded her.

"I didn't. You all overrode my objection as if I didn't count. But I do count. I don't want to go back. I want to stay here and learn and grow like MoonFeather did."

"It's all of you or none of you, ladies," Scazzy said.

"Then it will be none, because I refuse to go," Larch insisted.

◣▽▲▽▲▽◢

OOooooh, this Larch person is someone to watch closely. She has brains and a truckload of steel in her spine. If she plays her cards right, she might become another Warrior of the Celestial Blade. We need more of them outside the Citadel.

Hmmmm, I wonder which of my siblings has a dose of imp flu to spare.

Later. Tess doesn't have time to nurse her through it or train her.

Not too much later. We need another warrior to guard this neutral sanctuary from demons like Darren or the Powers That Be.

Until then, my bets are on Larch either taking control of the coven or breaking it entirely.

"Brava, Larch," MoonFeather said. She beamed as if one of her own children had made the honor roll.

Plump and mousy-looking Larch returned the glow, suddenly becoming pretty in a quiet way.

"So now what?" I asked the obvious. I was really getting tired of having everyone else's problems dumped in my kitchen.

"You all go back to your hosts and ask hard questions. Like 'what am I going to do with the rest of my life.' And if the FBI asks, you are all your own daughters. The women who disappeared twenty-eight years ago are alive and well and living elsewhere," MoonFeather said. She held each woman's gaze a moment, like any good teacher allowing her students to form opinions and make decisions.

She'd raised two children, often alone, on a teacher's salary. She still substituted in her semiretirement. Josh supported her so that she could have the time and ease to pursue her other interests, like becoming a master recycler and a master gardener and passing on her knowledge to community groups.

"It's too hard," Dragonfly wailed. She appeared to be the youngest of the group. Probably only eighteen in physical years.

"Life is hard. Life isn't fair. We all have to learn to cope," I said, hoping my quiet words would insert themselves into a few receptive minds. "WindScribe refused to accept that, and look what happened to her."

The ladies remained silent, staring at each other and into the ether.

"I'm out of here, then," King Scazzy said. "May I have my cap back, since you don't need my oath or my services."

MoonFeather examined the cap a moment, then glared at him.

"Please," he gulped.

She extended the bit of red cloth and gilded feather on one finger. He snatched it along with the parchment and penknife and popped out before she could change her mind or make other demands.

"Larch, I would appreciate it if you would come home with me. I have need of assistance for a while. My injury is healing well, but my leg is still weak." MoonFeather rose gracefully, using the staff as a brace.

I thought she leaned a little too heavily on it, making a point rather than truly needing it.

"I . . . I'd like that, MoonFeather." Larch stood straight and as tall as her five-foot-nothing frame allowed. "Will you teach me about your herb garden? And how to use a computer?"

"I'll do better than that. I'll enroll you in the community college. Tuition, room, and board in exchange for housework and help in the garden until the end of summer. Then we will reevaluate. Now I have some packing to do, and Tess, we'd appreciate a ride back to my house."

"I'll take you in the van," Gollum offered. "And I can give Larch a preliminary lesson on your home computer. She won't get far at school if she doesn't know a few of the basics." He rose from his chair and pocketed his PDA and cell phone.

"What about us? Why aren't you helping us?" FireHind asked. A gloss of anger marred her classic features. I could see a harpy just beneath the surface of her personality. She wouldn't age gracefully.

"Larch showed some initiative and backbone. The rest of you were more interested in running away from reality than coping. In my mind, she has more potential than the entire lot of you." MoonFeather stalked back to her room without looking back. Larch joined her, a quirky bounce in her step.

"I'm going for a run." I stretched and yawned. "I expect to find my house empty and back to normal by the time I get back. Scrap, where are my running shoes?"

Chapter 50

 OW I'M IN FOR IT. Without the distraction of the coven and Donovan and Mom, my babe will be after me to go time traveling again. I know her. When she gets an idea in her head, she doesn't let go.

I wonder if I'd be safer taking a quick jaunt home to my own Mum? Maybe I can find a trinket in the Garbage Dump of the Universe to appease my babe for a while.

But that would make me little better than the coven, running away when life gets a bit sticky.

Scrap could run, but he couldn't hide. Not for long at least. He was tied to me with mystical bonds I didn't fully understand. He'd come back.

So while I waited, I stretched my muscles and let the adrenaline flow, eating up a few miles. I hadn't exercised since . . . well, since that fencing bout with Donovan a couple of days ago. And the fight against the Windago. Neither one of those sessions allowed my mind to go blank while my body drank in fresh air and worked stress toxins out in my sweat.

I didn't even mind stomping through puddles in the light

drizzle. The gray skies were brightening. Life was beginning to look good. I might even get a few days in sunny Mexico after all.

Except for the questions that nagged at my soul.

In the last year I'd learned that coincidences happen for a reason. Darren Estevez and WindScribe fell into my life to teach me something, or reveal something.

I knew how valuable my house was now.

I also knew my husband had been murdered. He didn't have to die. I couldn't prevent that from happening. But maybe I could put his soul, and my conscience, to rest if I found out what happened.

I veered down to the beach. My feet pounded the water-soaked sand until my thighs began to burn and ache. Still I ran. Wondering. Forming and tossing out plan after plan.

One way or another I had to go back to Half Moon Lake, Washington, Donovan's hometown. I had to find out what happened that awful night three years ago.

With Scrap or without him. I had to go.

You also need to find out if Dillwyn Bailey Cooper was a half-blood Damiri demon, Scrap whispered to me from afar. *Isn't that more important, babe, than witnessing a murder you know happened at the hands of Darren Estevez?*

"I'll do that later, Scrap. Darren had reasons to kill Dill that I can only discover by going back to that time and place."

The time and distance are too great, dahling. I don't know if I can keep you safe.

"I'm willing to risk it."

And if you die, who will take our place?

"Gollum will find someone to become the next Warrior of the Celestial Blade. Larch is looking like a good candidate."

Only your Goddess can select a Warrior of the Celestial Blade.

That didn't sound like the entire truth, but I'd accept it for now.

"Well, then, if I die, the Goddess will have to prod one of my Sisterhood to leave the Citadel and take my place. You're the one who keeps telling me there is a cosmic plan and to believe in some higher power."

The rain came down in earnest, soaking me more thoroughly. I ignored the chill, pushing myself to keep a steady pace as I turned back toward home.

Then a memory came to me. "Scrap, when we were in Half Moon Lake last autumn, the ghosts of the ancient guardians took us back twelve thousand years to witness the Sasquatch stealing the blanket of life. We survived that."

They are guardians. They have different skills and purposes in their existence. They didn't have the distance problem.

"Four years and three thousand miles doesn't add up to twelve thousand years in distance. I have faith in you, buddy. Why can't you have faith in yourself?"

Scrap didn't answer for almost a quarter mile.

It's the distance. It's more difficult than the time.

"How about if we get Mom through the memorial service at noon, then we fly to Half Moon Lake? I think there's a con in Seattle this weekend. We can go play there for a few days when we're done." Not as good as Mexico. More convenient. And cons had filk. I needed to sing again, blow out more mental toxins than running could accomplish.

So be it, Tess. But not alone. We need Gollum to watch our backs. We will go together. We live or die together.

I liked that idea. Gollum watching my back.

The path took me around Miller's Pond. I kept to the western edge of the water, away from the scene of my battle with the Windago. A familiar path. I knew every twist and imperfection on the trail.

Still I stumbled. I'll never know what tripped me up. But as I caught my balance against a conveniently placed oak (brimming with mistletoe in the upper branches), something square and regular in shape caught my eye.

This jarred me enough to stop me in my tracks. As far as I knew, Mother Nature didn't create much with right-angle corners.

I reached out and picked up the object at the base of the tree very gingerly with my fingernails.

Then I had to sit. Rapidly. With a thump of my butt on the squishy, waterlogged ground beside the beaten path.

I held the hand-carved frame set with agates and arrowheads that Dill had made for our wedding picture. The picture itself was an unrecognizable sodden mess. But the frame was intact, if a little dirty.

Gollum and I had stood ten yards south of where I sat now when I cast my votive offering into the pond. I'd seen it skid across the ice and plop into the water at the center.

A tear dripped down my cheek.

The Goddess had returned the precious gift to me. She approved of something I did. I hoped it was my proposed trip back in time. I hoped she smiled on the endeavor and would help bring me back alive.

"Before we go, I need to show you something," Gollum said quietly as I guided Mom through the ritual of dressing and eating before a memorial service. She looked and acted numb.

I'd put on a similar show for Dill's funeral; too filled with grief to know how to let it out. I hurt so much I was afraid, if I let one tear escape, I'd shatter into a million pieces and never be able to find them all again. I wasn't sure I wanted to at the time.

Gollum opened his laptop and awakened the thing. The scrambled symbols of a saved e-mail littered the screen.

"What am I looking at?" I asked scrolling down to find the body of the text.

A line caught my eye. An address that started db.cooper@ . . . My eyes blurred before I could read the rest.

"Dill?" Too shocked to ask the next question, I continued hitting the down button.

"He contacted me three years ago. Three days before the fire," Gollum said quietly.

I couldn't read Gollum's posture or gaze. Didn't care about that at the moment. I needed to read the message.

"You have a reputation as a demon hunter. I heard about you in Africa. We need to meet. I have information that will interest you. Use this e-mail. It's private and secure."

"That's it?" I breathed. I found my hand trembling where it hovered over the damn computer buttons. "Why?"

"I don't know. That's all I have. I e-mailed him back with questions and a suggested meeting time and place. He never showed. I know now that he couldn't come because he was dying in your arms at the time. I still have a lot of questions."

"Like how he knew what you were up to in Africa?" I had a few questions about that myself.

Easier to wonder about a living Gollum than dredge up old hurts and grief with questions about my husband.

"More than that. How he found a way to contact me on an address known to a very select few who also have reputations as demon hunters. But I'm not a hunter. I'm an archivist, duty bound to serve a Celestial Warrior who escapes a Citadel. There aren't many of you. Maybe one in each generation. Sometimes not that often."

"Gayla says there are more Warriors outside now. Too many new portals cropping up to park Citadels atop each." Speaking of which, where was the supposed help she promised me now that it was too late to help?

"I have already contacted my grandfather about that. He is searching for more archivists."

"So Dill knew about demons." My whole body shivered now. From the inside out.

"I think your husband knew about the 'Great Enterprise' of creating a homeland for half-blood demons. I think Dillwyn Bailey Cooper was going to betray Darren Estevez to me. And that's why Estevez killed him."

"How did he find out about it?"

Gollum answered me with a raised eyebrow.

"You think he was one of them?" I nearly gagged on my words. I suspected the same thing but was afraid to find out.

"I do believe that. I also know that as dangerous as your proposed time travel is, it will not bring you true closure. You have to go to Cooper's parents and find out for yourself if they are half-blood Damiri."

"Next lifetime. I can't deal with this now."

But you will have to deal with it eventually, babe.

Chapter 51

The word moon is probably connected with the Sanskrit root me-, to measure, because time was measured by the moon. It is common to all Teutonic languages and is almost always masculine.

MOM MADE A GOOD show of quiet dignity as I escorted her down the aisle of St. Mary's for the memorial of Darren Estevez. Watery sunshine brightened the interior of the old brick building. Tall stained-glass windows sent it sparkling onto the altar. Dust motes looked like Faery dust. The altar guild had recently replaced the egalitarian enclosed box pews with more accessible open benches. Mom had made two of the one hundred new needlepoint kneelers.

If she leaned a little heavily on my arm to steady her steps, I was the only one who knew. She wore a new wool black jersey dress with a crossover bodice and a skirt that draped on the bias. It made her look twenty pounds lighter and ten years younger. Her hat had a jaunty brim and a eyebrow-length veil that looked like Chantilly lace. The real thing, not some cheap machine-made imitation. The black set off her pale blondeness perfectly for the occasion.

I looked horrible in black and wore it rarely. It made my skin look sallow and my sandy-blonde hair more like dishwater than ever. Since I was not the widow at this occasion, I relieved my basic midnight-blue dress with a sapphire print scarf draped and pinned to the jewel neckline. Scrap had done the honors and made me look quite presentable.

Donovan showed up, of course. This was more his ritual than Mom's as the adopted son, executor, and custodian of the family trust. He looked magnificent in his black suit, blindingly white shirt, and a blood-red tie. I'd never seen him in formal clothes.

My knees nearly melted at the sight of him. I think I needed better knees.

A vast emptiness opened in my heart that I had to reject him, banish him from my life. With a deep breath and firm resolve I looked away.

Gollum flashed me a grim smile from the second pew, directly behind where I would sit. Watching my back as always. He looked quite distinguished in a charcoal suit with a pale blue shirt and subdued striped tie. I breathed a sigh of relief as Mom and I took our seats.

We recited the familiar prayers, sang the usual hymns, knelt and stood at the appropriate times. The service was mercifully short. After all, Donovan was the only person present who had known Darren for any length of time. No one had much to say on behalf of the deceased, including Donovan. Father Sheridan spoke briefly of the tragedy of cutting a life short and how those Darren left behind must move on and make the most of their lives. And that was it.

An hour later I put Mom and Donovan and Darren in his casket on board a plane to Florida. When we separated at security, I pulled Donovan aside.

"If anything happens to my mother, anything at all, I will come after you, with every weapon at my disposal," I whispered to him.

"Don't worry. I need her alive and well as much as you do," he replied with wounded dignity.

"Remember that!"

I turned and faced a shadowy figure beside a massive

support pillar. The moment Donovan and Mom stepped past into the secured concourse, I approached the figure with a humped stance and a shock of longish gray hair. He might be fifty or seventy, I couldn't tell. Only that he was of middling height and stood straight and strong.

A huge and ancient imp sat on the man's shoulder.

"You're a bit late, whoever you are."

"Am I?" He gave me a smile that made the few lines around his eyes deepen. But the smile never sent a twinkle in his deep brown eyes.

Scrap preened and flashed the warts on his bum at the new imp. Must be a male and Scrap was interested.

The dignified being tasted the air with a forked tongue, snorted, and turned his head away. He had a vast array of beauty spots along his spine. Much more senior than Scrap and not interested.

"I no longer have need of your assistance," I said, standing firm.

"Don't you?"

"You're as bad as Donovan at answering questions. Time to go back to whatever hidey-hole you crawled out of."

"Breven Sancroix, at your service, Tess Noncoiré." He bowed slightly. "I have a farm in western Pennsylvania and I've been watching you for a few days. You have more problems than you want to acknowledge." He jerked his chin in the direction of the security lines.

"I have banished Donovan Estevez from my life."

"If you want to believe that, and that he is your only problem, then you need more help than I can give." He bowed again and backed up. "We will meet later. If you need me, you have only to reach out through your meditation to find me." With that he faded into the crowd as if he'd never been there.

▽△▽△▽

MoonFeather, Larch, and Gollum had followed us to the airport in Providence along with our luggage. My aunt and her protégée weren't about to be left behind on the next phase of our adventure.

Gollum had performed miracles in getting us the right

connections to Seattle and then a shuttle to Moses Lake. We arrived late, cranky, and feeling grubby. But Larch rallied and took the wheel of our rental car, a nice sedan with lots of trunk space and leg room. She navigated us the hour north to Half Moon Lake and the Mowath Lodge.

The flat concrete slab that was all that remained of the run-down motel where Dill had died in the fire lay just across the parking lot from the new lodge.

Not for an instant did I forget that Donovan owned the hotel made up of fourplex log cabins, two suites up and two down. Each building was constructed of massive logs. Each interior was unique, decorated in more thick slabs of wood around a theme, location, or celebrity.

From the hotel office building Donovan ran Halfling Gaming Company, Inc. and the spa under construction.

We took over one large suite for one night—the John Wayne room with memorabilia from his life and movies and western-styled furniture. MoonFeather and Larch slept comfortably in the king-sized bed in the loft. I tossed and turned on the single bed tucked under the stairs. Gollum collapsed familiarly into the armchair with his feet on the coffee table and his computer in his lap. I could never tell if he slept or not. But I was comforted that he didn't change his habits from the last time we had stayed here.

MoonFeather roused us in the desert predawn for a light breakfast at the nearby café. I couldn't eat, so I took a run around the lake. My feet crunched through a crust of minerals that smelled of fish oil and salt.

I allowed my memory to drift to the time Dill and I had come here. I cherished the vision of him exclaiming excitedly over a special rock specimen. The warm glow of triumph I had felt when I found a fossilized leaf settled on me anew. Then the ecstasy of making love on that last night . . .

Good memories. A wonderful, if brief, time together.

Briefly, I considered trying to find the Citadel hidden in a deep ravine some twenty miles north of here. Would they acknowledge me if I pounded on their gates?

Doubtful.

I reminded myself that I didn't need them. They had never truly accepted me. Scrap and I were better off without them.

I'd welcome a little advice and support, though.

My stomach churned with trepidation. I could die in the next hour.

The Goddess had smiled on me.

As much as my mind rejected belief in a deity, my heart longed to believe in something. The picture frame could have been thrown back out of the ice by frost heave.

Yeah, right.

Eventually I had to return to the lodge. Best to get this journey over with. We had to check out by noon.

Once more, we gather around a magic circle, Tess, Gollum, MoonFeather, and myself. With Larch looking on as an apprentice.

MoonFeather draws a big circle on the floor with her colored chalk. Gollum sets out the colored candles, red at north, green at east, blue at south, and yellow at west. Larch sprinkles herbs in a circle around the candles.

Tess sits cross-legged in the center, palms resting upward on her knees. She closes her eyes and breathes deeply, evenly. She is open and receptive, going into a deep meditative trance.

I fear she will lose concentration. She's never been very good at meditation. Too restless, too eager to get on with the busyness of life, too curious to sit and let life come to her. She has to go and find trouble instead. That is why the Sisterhood rejected her and forced her out of the Citadel.

Life on the outside is not what I had planned when I attached myself to my Warrior. Life on the outside is not easy. Nor is it dull.

I like our life. I've killed more demons in the last six months than most imps do in a lifetime when locked up in a Citadel that guards a demon portal. And I've got the beautiful warts to prove it. Six new ones from the fight with the Windago. Midori count for more than Kajiri.

So I must be extra careful and bring my babe back home safe and sound.

MoonFeather is doing what she can to cast a circle of protection. But the onus of this journey is on me. I shiver in fear. And excitement. Not many can perform this feat.

I gather my energies.

MoonFeather lights the candles. She uses matches; no one carries a lighter anymore. She recites an invocation at each candle and drops a different herb into each flame.

I feel the energy building inside the circle. The scent of incense fills my head with new perceptions. Colors twist. The world tilts. Threads of life swirl through the air in impossible hues, blindingly bright. I grab hold of a promising tendril, the same color of pale blue as Tess' eyes, and whisk my Warrior away.

Through the chat room so fast no one notices us.

Back.

Back farther.

Back in time and space to a dimension I'd just as soon forget. Violence begets violence begets trauma and barriers in the mind. Those barriers have had three years to thicken and solidify. I'm not sure I have the cunning and intuition to break through them. But I do have a blackness in my soul and violence in my heart. They must serve me well for this journey.

◄▽▲▽▲▽►

Gravity shifted. The light became vertiginous. My balance adjusted. Wind swirled around me like a tiny tornado, tossing me here and there. I came to rest with a thump and opened my eyes.

I expected to view the shabby motel room from a distance, through a gray mist, like I did when I witnessed Darren's murder.

Instead, I found myself in my own body, the plump and unfit body of three years ago with my tight curls in a tangled mess reaching halfway down my back. Sleep crusted my eyes and left groggy cobwebs in my mind. I lay in bed next to Dill. Warm and gentle, beloved Dill. I wanted to reach out and touch him, hold him close once more, cherish his strength and his love.

Drowsiness left me enervated and incapable of moving.

Only your other self from the future is truly awake, Tess. Your body responds only as it did in this past time. You cannot change anything even if you try, Scrap whispered to me.

I couldn't see him or sense him. Only hear him.

A shadow passed across the curtained window of our ground-floor room. The shadow of a very large bat.

Panic closed my throat and choked my brain.

The sharp scent of smoke roused Dill.

Fear sent my heart to racing and my thoughts spinning in circles.

Chapter 52

A new moon teaches gradualness and deliberation and how one gives birth to oneself slowly. Patience with small details makes perfect a large work, like the universe.

— Rumi

"TESS, TESS, WAKE UP. We have to get out of here!" Dill shook me roughly.

Damn straight we did. That was *we,* not just me.

I threw my arms around him as he guided me into the bathroom. Somehow, I managed to kick the door shut behind us. I hadn't done that the last time I lived this scene.

Dill helped me climb into the shower tub. Together we pushed up the tiny window above the tile.

"You go first, lovey. I'm right behind you." He boosted me up until I lay half in and half out the window.

"No, Dill. You have to go first. You have to save yourself!" I cried.

He shoved me through the window with a sharp slap to my wide bottom.

I landed on the frosted grass with a jolt that nearly dislocated my shoulder. The cold kissed my skin but did not penetrate to the bone through my soft frilly nightie. I'd given up my favored less-than-sexy flannel when I married Dill. His body heat next to me in bed kept me warmer than cloth ever could.

Then I noticed the still healing gash on my arm from a Windago talon. It glowed and pulsed an ugly red.

I hadn't had the scar three years ago. Not everything was the same.

"Dill!" I screamed. Ignoring the pain that ran from the base of my skull all the way to my fingertips, I jumped up and grabbed the windowsill about a foot above my head. "Dill!"

Thick smoke roiled under the closed door to fill the bathroom.

"Dill!" Where was he?

Then I heard him coughing. With a supreme effort I pulled myself upward. The demon scar ached and drove sharp burns all the way through my arm and shoulder. The me of the future with the scar had the strength to climb back through the window. The me of three years ago wouldn't have dared try.

I looked down. Dill stood doubled over in the tub, trying desperately to clear his lungs of smoke. "Coming, lovey," he gasped. "I'm not going to leave you alone."

"Take my hand, Dill. You've got to get out. Now."

He reached upward. I clasped his hand firmly. My shoulders trembled with the strain of holding myself against the windowsill. As I prepared to yank and drop, dragging Dill through the window with me, the bathroom door banged inward. Two shadowy forms lunged and tackled Dill, dragging his hand from mine.

"We can't let you escape, Cooper. You've betrayed me for the last time," Darren Estevez croaked through the smoke.

He lifted his head and stared at me. Darren Estevez.

The other man kept his head down. I knew his figure was male, nothing more. He wore a dark watch cap and darker clothing. Broad shoulders. A heavy jacket masked weight and stature. No clues to identity.

"Dill!" I propped my knee on the little ledge, ready to dive back into the fray to free my husband.

Don't! Scrap yanked at my mind so hard I slid back down to the ground.

I scrambled back and jumped for the ledge.

No. Think, Tess. Think about who you are. Think about what you would become if Dill lived.

I tried to blot out the mental probe that pierced my mind like a migraine behind the eyes.

The demon scar throbbed, adding yet more pain to Scrap's admonitions.

You can only move forward, not back. You aren't really here. And you may not, cannot, change anything.

"Dill," I sobbed. "Don't die on me again."

Think, Tess. Would Dill have let you become the strong independent woman you are with a successful career? Would he? Or would he have pushed you to give up your writing to cater to his career and push out a new baby every other year? Would he have given you the freedom to grow? Would he have let you sing filk songs at conventions when you have a better voice than he?

I paused long enough to breathe.

Sirens wailed around the corner. Men shouted and dragged hoses. They smashed open doors with axes.

And I knew in my mind that Scrap was right.

But that didn't ease the pain in my heart.

I'm sorry, babe, Scrap whispered. *You loved him and he loved you. But you cannot change the past, only observe it.*

Two bats flew out the window over my head. Bats! The one creature I fear most. Bats of my nightmares. Big bats that sucked blood.

My phobia overcame my love of Dill.

I huddled on the ground in absolute panic, covering my head with my hands, gibbering nonsense. One of them grabbed a lock of my hair and yanked it out of my scalp with its vicious claws and a squeak of glee.

Once more, firemen found me cowering on the ground in a fetal position and took me out front to the ambulance where they tried to give me oxygen. Once more, men in heavy coats with fluorescent yellow bands dragged Dill's burned body free of the carnage of the flames. Once more, I held him in my arms.

I wept softly, smoothing his sizzled hair away from his face, not minding the way it crumbled to ash in my hands.

He opened pain-racked eyes in a ravaged face. Muscle, blood, and bone shone through the cracked and blackened skin.

"I love you, Tess."

And then he heaved one last rattling breath and released the pain and agony of living.

I collapsed over him, too filled with grief to cry. Too choked to object when gentle hands dragged me away from the love of my life.

Chapter 53

THE WORLD SWIRLED about me in pain and the reek of rancid, waterlogged smoke. I didn't care. Dill was dead. I had failed to save him.

Twice.

"Welcome back," Gollum said quietly.

He crouched beside me on the floor. The chalk circle around me looked smudged where he'd trod on the markings. Gently, he brushed a tangled curl off my forehead with a single finger.

I was back in the new Mowath Lodge with massive logs forming the walls. Bright woods and clean upholstery decorated the large and luxurious room. A far cry from the shabby, generic motel that had stood on these grounds three years ago.

The only trace of old smoke that lingered was in my memory.

Outside, I could hear MoonFeather and Larch arguing about packing the rental car with luggage for four for a long weekend in Seattle.

"Want to talk about it?" he asked me.

"Oh, Gollum." My throat closed upon my tears.

He wrapped his arms around me and lifted me onto his lap. There he held me for countless moments, my face pressed against his shoulders, his hands comforting, secure. Safe.

I cried. My shoulders heaved. My gut ached. And still I cried.

All the tears I had held back for three years came forth in a tangled river of grief and pain and loneliness.

And still I cried.

Not a word passed between us. He just held me. He let me have the time to cry and cry some more until there was nothing left inside me but a gaping hole where Dill had dwelled.

And still I cried.

And still he held me. Undemanding. Keeping me safe while I was vulnerable.

Eventually, the storm of grief and tears passed. I don't know how long we sat there with me in his lap like a small child. When there was nothing left but the shudders, he continued to hold me.

At last, as limp as a wet dish rag, I roused enough to feel the strength in his arms, to cherish the calm and quiet in his heart beating beneath my ear.

"Thank you," I said and kissed his cheek. "Let's go to a con and sing silly filk songs. Then I'm going back to work. Vacations are too trying."

"Good-bye, lovey," Dill whispered. His ghostly hand might have ruffled my curls.

Then he was gone. Nothing left of him but my memories.

Gollum gave me a quick squeeze of reassurance. We untangled ourselves and joined the rest of the world hand in hand.

Just then Larch started the car. The CD picked up where it had left off.

Heather Alexander singing quietly in a pain-racked alto.

> *"I looked across the battlefield*
> *Blood seeping from my wounds—*
> *My comrades they did never yield,*
> *For courage knows no bounds—*
> *And yet, I thought as I stood there,*
> *Of all that it had cost—*
> *For what we gained, it seemed not fair*
> *For all that we had lost—*

They spoke of honor, faith, and pride,
    Defending for our home—
Through honor all my friends have died,
    Their faith left me alone—
We fought for greed, we fought for fame,
    We killed too much to tell—
    The devil and God were both the same,
    We worshiped only hell—

We fought, it seemed, for a thousand years,
    A million nights and days—
Sharing one laugh with a hundred tears,
    Seeing clearly through a haze—
Then came that day I know not when,
    Beneath a blood-red sun,
    Atop a pile of dying men,
    They said that we had won—

Another tract of land is all
    The territory gained—
Will that ever pay for all
The lives here lost or maimed?
    Bodies lying all around,
    Blood bathing them in red,
Their white eyes staring at the sun,
    These the countless dead?

I looked across the battlefield
    Blood seeping from my wounds—
My comrades, they did never yield,
    For courage knows no bounds—

Tanya Huff

"The Gales are an amazing family, the aunts will strike fear into your heart, and the characters Allie meets are both charming and terrifying."
—#1 *New York Times* bestselling author
Charlaine Harris

"Thoughtful and leisurely, this fresh urban fantasy from Canadian author Huff features an ensemble cast of nuanced characters in Calgary, Alberta.... Fantasy buffs will find plenty of humor, thrills and original mythology to chew on, along with refreshingly three-dimensional women in an original, fully realized world." —*Publishers Weekly*

The Enchantment Emporium
978-0-7564-0605-9

The Wild Ways
978-0-7564-0763-6

and now...
The Future Falls
978-0-7564-0753-7

To Order Call: 1-800-788-6262
www.dawbooks.com